A TREASURY OF SWASHBUCKLING ADVENTURES

A TREASURY OF SWASHBUCKLING ADVENTURES

FALL RIVER PRESS

New York

FALL RIVER PRESS

New York

An Imprint of Sterling Publishing Co., Inc.
1166 Avenue of the Americas
New York, NY 10036

ISBN 978-1-4351-6283-9

Manufactured in the United States of America

2 4 6 8 10 9 7 5 3 1

www.sterlingpublishing.com

CONTENTS

INTRODUCTION

Pikes, cutlasses and pistols, the weapons of the pirate men, clashed and exploded as the crews came to grips. At the head of the boarding party was the massive form of Jolly Roger, while the Atlantean figure of Daniel Tucker led the defense. Lesser men were hurled aside, as the two giants strode through the melee toe to toe.

The quote above, excerpted from James Perley Hughes's "Scourge of the Main," captures the essence of the tale of swashbuckling adventure. The pikes, cutlasses, and pistols are the familiar hardware flashed by the swordsmen, soldiers, freebooters, and pirates who give swashbuckling fiction its flare and style. Equally familiar is the adversarial relationship between the pirate Jolly Roger, the titular "Scourge of the Main," and Daniel Tucker, second-in-command of an English warship. The "massive" Jolly Roger represents the brutish type of villain who exists primarily to be vanquished by "Atlantean" figures like Daniel Tucker—sophisticated men of character and intelligence whose strong code of personal honor compels them to risk death in mortal combat with their foes. There is rarely any doubt in stories of this type who of these two opponents will prevail—and who will live to make the most of the love interest common to them.

The tale of swashbuckling adventure came into vogue in the nineteenth century as a subgenre of historical fiction, which itself had become a popular form of literature in the wake of the gothic era and its tales steeped in antiquity and legacies from the medieval past. It drew not only on the type of colorful historic pageantry that had helped to make the historical novels of Sir Walter Scott runaway bestsellers at the turn of the century, but also on ideas of chivalry expressed in the Arthurian romances, then popular in the poetry of the day. The leading exponent of the swashbuckling saga was Alexandre Dumas, who early in his writing career had mastered the skill of shaping narratives from the outcome of historical events and dressing them with the most romantic accoutrements possible. His novels *The Three Musketeers* (1844) and *The Count of Monte Cristo* (1844–1845) forged the template for swashbuckling adventure fiction with their dazzling accounts of swordplay and duels, all fought for the sake of honor and to avenge injustices.

The extent to which swashbuckling adventure fiction could combine genuine history with colorful glosses on it is epitomized in one of this volume's selections, *The Story of Cyrano de Bergerac* (1898). De Bergerac was a real person, known in his time for his soldierly skill at dueling as much as for the plays and stories he left behind. Edmond Rostand's famous play about De Bergerac's skills as a swordsman and a lover, presented here in novelized form, have so overtaken the reality of the historical Cyrano, that the reader is left to conclude that if the exploits of the swashbuckling Cyrano are not true, they should be. The same could be said for the heroes of all the stories in this anthology.

By the end of the nineteenth century many writers of popular fiction had produced swashbuckling stories in which they tried to carve a special niche for their contributions. Anthony Hope conjured an imaginary kingdom based on a European model in *The Prisoner of Zenda* (1894), and with it launched the Ruritanian romance subgenre. Arthur Conan Doyle wrote a series of stories featuring Etienne Gerard, a swaggering swashbuckling anti-hero. Looking to the bloody aftermath of the French Revolution, the Baroness Orczy created the Scarlet Pimpernel, a noble aristocrat who travels incognito and risks life and limb to save the unfortunate victims of the Reign of Terror. Inspired by the tale of pirate adventure made enormously popular by Robert Louis Stevenson's *Treasure Island*, Rafael Sabatini wrote *Captain Blood* (1922), about a virtuous pirate hero.

Sabatini's fiction appeared often in the pulp fiction magazines of the first half of the twentieth century and the swashbuckling adventure found a welcome home in these Depression-era vehicles for escapist fiction. Magazines such as *Adventure*, *Pirate Stories*, *Mammoth Adventure*, *Argosy*, and *Golden Fleece* all published rip-roaring adventure stories that added to the larger-than-life luster of the swashbuckling hero. The same audience that read the pulp magazines flocked to movie theaters to see cinematic adaptations of stories featuring Robin Hood, the masked crusader Zorro, and even Captain Blood, frequently starring Douglas Fairbanks, Errol Flynn, and other leading men of their day.

Though the tale of swashbuckling adventure peaked in the late-nineteenth and early-twentieth century, its influence can still be seen in fiction and film today. This volume features stories culled from its golden age. They still have the power to transport readers back in time to ages even earlier than those in which they were written, when honor was proven at the end of a sword point, death was just a musket shot away, and heroes dispatched their sneering adversaries in dazzling displays of courage and then laughed with confidence at just another day of dauntless derring-do.

THE PRISONER OF ZENDA

ANTHONY HOPE

I. THE RASSENDYLLS—WITH A WORD ON THE ELPHBERGS

I wonder when in the world you're going to do anything, Rudolf?" said my brother's wife.

"My dear Rose," I answered, laying down my egg-spoon, "why in the world should I do anything? My position is a comfortable one. I have an income nearly sufficient for my wants (no one's income is ever quite sufficient, you know). I enjoy an enviable social position: I am brother to Lord Burlesdon, and brother-in-law to that charming lady his countess. Behold, it is enough!"

"You are nine-and-twenty," she observed, "and you've done nothing but—"

"Knock about? It is true. Our family doesn't need to do things."

This remark of mine rather annoyed Rose, for everybody knows (and therefore there can be no harm in referring to the fact) that, pretty and accomplished as she herself is, her family is hardly of the same standing as the Rassendylls. Besides her attractions, she possessed a large fortune, and my brother Robert was wise enough not to mind about her ancestry. Ancestry is, in fact, a matter concerning which the next observation of Rose's has some truth.

"Good families are generally worse than any others," she said.

Upon this I stroked my hair: I knew quite well what she meant.

"I'm so glad Robert's is black!" she cried.

At this moment Robert (who rises at seven and works before breakfast) came in. He glanced at his wife: her cheek was slightly flushed; he patted it caressingly.

"What's the matter, my dear?" he asked.

"She objects to my doing nothing and having red hair," said I in an injured tone.

"Oh! of course he can't help his hair," admitted Rose.

"It generally crops out once in a generation," said my brother. "So does the nose. Rudolf has got them both."

"I wish they didn't crop out," said Rose, still flushed.

"I rather like them myself," said I, and, rising, I bowed to the portrait of Countess Amelia.

My brother's wife uttered an exclamation of impatience.

"I wish you'd take that picture away, Robert," said she.

"My dear!" he cried.

"Good heavens!" I added.

"Then it might be forgotten," she continued.

"Hardly—with Rudolf about," said Robert, shaking his head.

"Why should it be forgotten?" I asked.

"Rudolf!" exclaimed my brother's wife, blushing very prettily.

I laughed, and went on with my egg. At least I had shelved the question of what (if anything) I ought to do. And by way of closing the discussion—and also, I must admit, of exasperating my strict little sister-in-law a trifle more—I observed:

"I rather like being an Elphberg myself."

When I read a story I skip the explanations; yet the moment I begin to write one I find that I must have an explanation. For it is manifest that I must explain why my sister-in-law was vexed with my nose and hair, and why I ventured to call myself an Elphberg. For, eminent as, I must protest, the Rassendylls have been for many generations, yet participation in their blood of course does not, at first sight, justify the boast of a connection with the grander stock of the Elphbergs or a claim to be one of that Royal House. For what relationship is there between Ruritania and Burlesdon, between the Palace at Strelsau or the Castle of Zenda and Number 305 Park Lane, W.?

Well, then—and I must premise that I am going, perforce, to rake up the very scandal which my dear Lady Burlesdon wishes forgotten—in the year 1733, George II. sitting then on the throne, peace reigning for the moment, and the King and the Prince of Wales being not yet at loggerheads, there came on a visit to the English court a certain prince, who was afterwards known to history as Rudolf the Third of Ruritania. The prince was a tall, handsome young fellow, marked (maybe marred, it is not for me to say) by a somewhat unusually long, sharp, and straight nose, and a mass of dark-red hair—in fact, the nose and the hair which have stamped the Elphbergs time out of mind. He stayed some months in England, where he was most courteously received; yet in the end he left rather under a cloud. For he fought a duel (it was considered highly well bred of him to waive all question of his rank) with a nobleman, well known in the society of the day, not only for his own merits, but as the husband of a very beautiful wife. In that duel Prince Rudolf received a severe wound, and recovering therefrom, was adroitly smuggled off by the Ruritanian ambassador, who had found him a pretty handful. The nobleman was not wounded in the duel; but the morning being raw and damp on the occasion of the meeting, he contracted a severe chill, and failing to throw it off, he died some six months after the departure of Prince Rudolf, without having found leisure to adjust his relations with his wife—who after another two months bore an heir to the title and estates of the family of Burlesdon. This lady was the Countess Amelia, whose picture my sister-in-law wished to remove from the drawing room in Park Lane; and her husband was James, fifth Earl of Burlesdon and twenty-second Baron Rassendyll, both in the peerages of England, and a Knight of the Garter. As for Rudolf, he went back to Ruritania, married a wife, and ascended the throne, whereon his progeny in the direct line have sat from then till this very hour—with one short interval. And, finally, if you walk through the picture galleries at Burlesdon, among the fifty portraits or so of the last century and a half, you will find five or six, including that of the sixth earl, distinguished by long, sharp, straight noses and a quantity of dark-red hair; these five or six have also blue eyes, whereas among the Rassendylls dark eyes are the commoner.

That is the explanation, and I am glad to have finished it: the blemishes on honourable lineage are a delicate subject, and certainly this heredity we hear so much about is the finest scandalmonger in the world; it laughs at discretion, and writes strange entries between the lines of the "Peerages."

It will be observed that my sister-in-law, with a want of logic that must have been peculiar to herself (since we are no longer allowed to lay it to the charge of her sex), treated my complexion almost as an offence for which I was responsible, hastening to assume from that external sign inward qualities of which I protest my entire innocence; and this unjust inference she sought to buttress by pointing to the uselessness of the life I had led. Well, be that as it may, I had picked up a good deal of pleasure and a good deal of knowledge. I had been to a German school and a German university, and spoke German as readily and perfectly as English; I was thoroughly at home in French; I had a smattering of Italian, and enough Spanish to swear by. I was, I believe, a strong, though hardly a fine, swordsman and a good shot. I could ride anything that had a back to sit on; and my head was as cool a one as you could find, for all its flaming cover. If you say that I ought to have spent my time in useful labour I am out of Court and have nothing to say, save that my parents had no business to leave me two thousand pounds a year and a roving disposition.

"The difference between you and Robert," said my sister-in-law, who often (bless her!) speaks on a platform, and oftener still as if she were on one, "is that he recognizes the duties of his position, and you only see the opportunities of yours."

"To a man of spirit, my dear Rose," I answered, "opportunities are duties."

"Nonsense!" said she, tossing her head; and after a moment she went on: "Now here's Sir Jacob Borrodaile offering you exactly what you might be equal to."

"A thousand thanks!" I murmured.

"He's to have an Embassy in six months, and Robert says he is sure that he'll take you as an *attaché*. Do take it, Rudolf—to please me."

Now, when my sister-in-law puts the matter in that way, wrinkling her pretty brows, twisting her little hands, and growing wistful in the eyes, all on account of an idle scamp like myself, for whom she has no natural responsibility, I am visited with compunction. Moreover, I thought it possible that I could pass the time in the position suggested with some tolerable amusement. Therefore I said:

"My dear sister, if in six months' time no unforeseen obstacle has arisen, and Sir Jacob invites me, hang me if I don't go with Sir Jacob!"

"O Rudolf, how good of you! I am glad!"

"Where's he going to?"

"He doesn't know yet; but it's sure to be a good Embassy."

"Madame," said I, "for your sake I'll go if it's no more than a beggarly Legation. When I do a thing I don't do it by halves."

My promise, then, was given; but six months are six months, and seem an eternity, and inasmuch as they stretched between me and my prospective industry (I suppose *attachés* are industrious; but I know not, for I never became *attaché* to Sir Jacob or anybody else) I cast about for some desirable mode of spending them. And it occurred to me suddenly that I would visit Ruritania. It may seem strange that I had never visited that country yet; but my father (in spite of a sneaking fondness for the Elphbergs, which led him to give me, his second son, the famous Elphberg name of Rudolf) had always been averse from my going, and since his death my brother, prompted by Rose, had accepted the family tradition which taught that a wide berth was to be given to that country. But the moment Ruritania had come into my head I was eaten up with a curiosity to see it. After all, red hair and long noses are not confined to the House of Elphberg, and the old story seemed a preposterously insufficient reason for debarring myself from acquaintance with a highly interesting and important kingdom, one which had played no small part in European history, and might do the like again under the sway of a young and vigorous ruler, such as the new King was rumoured to be. My determination was clinched by reading in *The Times* that Rudolf the Fifth was to be crowned at Strelsau in the course of the next three weeks, and that great magnificence was to mark the occasion. At once I made up my mind to be present, and began my preparations. But inasmuch as it has never been my practice to furnish my relatives with an itinerary of my journeys, and in this case I anticipated opposition to my wishes, I gave out that I was going for a ramble in the Tyrol—an old haunt of mine—and propitiated Rose's wrath by declaring that I intended to study the political and social problems of the interesting community which dwells in that neighbourhood.

"Perhaps," I hinted darkly, "there may be an outcome of the expedition."

"What do you mean?" she asked.

"Well," said I carelessly, "there seems a gap that might be filled by an exhaustive work on—"

"Oh! will you write a book?" she cried, clapping her hands. "That would be splendid, wouldn't it, Robert?"

"It's the best of introductions to political life nowadays," observed my brother, who has, by the way, introduced himself in this manner several times over. Burlesdon on "Ancient Theories and Modern Facts" and "The Ultimate Outcome," by a Political Student, are both works of recognized eminence.

"I believe you are right, Bob, my boy," said I.

"Now promise you'll do it," said Rose earnestly.

"No, I won't promise; but if I find enough material I will."

"That's fair enough," said Robert.

"Oh! material doesn't matter," she said, pouting.

But this time she could get no more than a qualified promise out of me. To tell the truth, I would have wagered a handsome sum that the story of my expedition that summer would stain no paper and spoil not a single pen. And that shows how little we know what the future holds; for here I am, fulfilling my qualified promise, and writing, as I never thought to write, a book—though it will hardly serve as an introduction to political life, and has not a jot to do with the Tyrol.

Neither would it, I fear, please Lady Burlesdon, if I were to submit it to her critical eye—a step which I have no intention of taking.

II. CONCERNING THE COLOUR OF MEN'S HAIR

It was a maxim of my Uncle William's that no man should pass through Paris without spending four-and-twenty hours there. My uncle spoke out of a ripe experience of the world, and I honoured his advice by putting up for a day and a night at The Continental on my way to—the Tyrol. I called on George Featherly at the

Embassy, and we had a bit of dinner together at Durand's, and afterwards dropped in to the Opera; and after that we had a little supper, and after that we called on Bertram Bertrand, a versifier of some repute and Paris correspondent to *The Critic*. He had a very comfortable little suite of rooms, and we found some pleasant fellows smoking and talking. It struck me, however, that Bertram himself was absent and in low spirits, and when everybody except ourselves had gone I rallied him on his moping preoccupation. He fenced with me for a while, but at last, flinging himself on a sofa, he exclaimed:

"Very well; have it your own way. I am in love—infernally in love!"

"Oh, you'll write the better poetry," said I by way of consolation.

He ruffled his hair with his hand and smoked furiously. George Featherly, standing with his back to the mantelpiece, smiled unkindly.

"If it's the old affair," said he, "you may as well throw it up, Bert. She's leaving Paris to-morrow."

"I know that," snapped Bertram.

"Not that it would make any difference if she stayed," pursued the relentless George. "She flies higher than the paper trade, my boy!"

"Hang her!" said Bertram.

"It would make it more interesting for me," I ventured to observe, "if I knew who you were talking about."

"Antoinette Mauban," said George.

"De Mauban," growled Bertram.

"Oho!" said I, passing by the question of the *de*. "You don't mean to say, Bert—"

"Can't you let me alone?"

"Where's she going to?" I asked, for the lady was something of a celebrity.

George jingled his money, smiled cruelly at poor Bertram, and answered pleasantly:

"Nobody knows. By the way, Bert, I met a great man at her house the other night— at least, about a month ago. Did you ever meet him—the Duke of Strelsau?"

"Yes, I did," growled Bertram.

"An extremely accomplished man, I thought him."

It was not hard to see that George's references to the duke were intended to aggravate poor Bertram's sufferings, so that I drew the inference that the duke had distinguished Madame. de Mauban by his attentions. She was a widow, rich, handsome, and, according to repute, ambitious. It was quite possible that she, as George put it, was flying as high as a personage who was everything he could be short of enjoying strictly royal rank: for the duke was the son of the late King of Ruritania by a second and morganatic marriage, and half brother to the new king. He had been his father's favourite, and it had occasioned some unfavourable comment when he had been created a duke, with a title derived from no less a city than the capital itself. His mother had been of good, but not exalted, birth.

"He's not in Paris now, is he?" I asked.

"Oh, no! He's gone back to be present at the King's coronation; a ceremony which, I should say, he'll not enjoy much. But, Bert, old man, don't despair! He won't marry the fair Antoinette—at least, not unless another plan comes to nothing. Still, perhaps, she—" He paused and added, with a laugh: "Royal attentions are hard to resist—you know that, don't you, Rudolf?"

"Confound you!" said I; and rising, I left the hapless Bertram in George's hands and went home to bed.

The next day George Featherly went with me to the station, where I took a ticket for Dresden.

"Going to see the pictures?" asked George, with a grin.

George is an inveterate gossip, and had I told him that I was off to Ruritania the news would have been in London in three days and in Park Lane in a week. I was therefore about to return an evasive answer when he saved my conscience by leaving me suddenly and darting across the platform. Following him with my eyes, I saw him lift his hat and accost a graceful, fashionably dressed woman who had just appeared from the booking office. She was perhaps a year or two over thirty, tall, dark, and of rather full figure. As George talked, I saw her glance at me, and my vanity was hurt by the thought that, muffled in a fur coat and a neck wrapper (for it was a chilly April day) and wearing a soft travelling hat pulled down to my ears, I must be looking very far from my best. A moment later George rejoined me.

"You've got a charming traveling companion," he said. "That's poor Bert Bertrand's goddess, Antoinette de Mauban, and, like you, she's going to Dresden—also, no doubt, to see the pictures. It's very queer, though, that she doesn't at present desire the honour of your acquaintance."

"I didn't ask to be introduced," I observed, a little annoyed.

"Well, I offered to bring you to her; but she said, 'Another time.' Never mind, old fellow, perhaps there'll be a smash, and you'll have a chance of rescuing her and cutting out the Duke of Strelsau!"

No smash, however, happened, either to me or to Madame de Mauban. I can speak for her as confidently as for myself; for when, after a night's rest in Dresden, I continued my journey she got into the same train. Understanding that she wished to be let alone,

I avoided her carefully, but I saw that she went the same way as I did to the very end of my journey, and I took opportunities of having a good look at her, when I could do so unobserved.

As soon as we reached the Ruritanian frontier (where the old officer who presided over the Custom House favoured me with such a stare that I felt surer than before of my Elphberg physiognomy) I bought the papers, and found in them news which affected my movements. For some reason, which was not clearly explained and seemed to be something of a mystery, the date of the coronation had been suddenly advanced, and the ceremony was to take place on the next day but one. The whole country seemed in a stir about it, and it was evident that Strelsau was thronged. Rooms were all let and hotels overflowing; there would be very little chance of my obtaining a lodging, and I should certainly have to pay an exorbitant charge for it. I made up my mind to stop at Zenda, a small town fifty miles short of the capital, and about ten from the frontier. My train reached there in the evening; I would spend the next day, Tuesday, in a wander over the hills, which were said to be very fine, and in taking a glance at the famous Castle, and go over by train to Strelsau on the Wednesday morning, returning at night to sleep at Zenda.

Accordingly at Zenda I got out, and as the train passed where I stood on the platform, I saw my friend Madame de Mauban in her place; clearly she was going through to Strelsau, having, with more providence than I could boast, secured apartments there. I smiled to think how surprised George Featherly would have been to know that she and I had been fellow travellers for so long.

I was very kindly received at the hotel—it was really no more than an inn—kept by a fat old lady and her two daughters. They were good, quiet people, and seemed very little interested in the great doings at Strelsau. The old lady's hero was the duke, for he was now, under the late king's will, master of the Zenda estates and of the Castle, which rose grandly on its steep hill at the end of the valley, a mile or so from the inn. The old lady, indeed, did not hesitate to express regret that the duke was not on the throne instead of his brother.

"We know Duke Michael," said she. "He has always lived among us; every Ruritanian knows Duke Michael. But the King is almost a stranger; he has been so much abroad not one in ten knows him even by sight."

"And now," chimed in one of the young women, "they say he has shaved off his beard, so that no one at all knows him."

"Shaved his beard!" exclaimed her mother. "Who says so?"

"Johann, the duke's keeper. He has seen the King."

"Ah, yes. The King, sir, is now at the duke's hunting lodge in the forest here; from here he goes to Strelsau to be crowned on Wednesday morning."

I was interested to hear this, and made up my mind to walk next day in the direction of the lodge on the chance of coming across the King. The old lady ran on garrulously:

"Ah! and I wish he would stay at his hunting—that and wine (and one thing more) are all he loves, they say—and suffer our duke to be crowned on Wednesday. That I wish, and I don't care who knows it."

"Hush, mother!" urged the daughters.

"Oh, there's many to think as I do!" cried the old woman stubbornly.

I threw myself back in my deep armchair and laughed at her zeal.

"For my part," said the younger and prettier of the two daughters, a fair, buxom, smiling wench, "I hate Black Michael! A red Elphberg for me, mother! The King, they say, is as red as a fox or as—"

And she laughed mischievously as she cast a glance at me, and tossed her head at her sister's reproving face.

"Many a man has cursed their red hair before now," muttered the old lady—and I remembered James, fifth Earl of Burlesdon.

"But never a woman!" cried the girl.

"Aye, and women, when it was too late," was the stern answer, reducing the girl to silence and blushes.

"How comes the King here?" I asked, to break an embarrassed silence. "It is the duke's land here, you say."

"The duke invited him, sir, to rest here till Wednesday. The duke is at Strelsau, preparing the King's reception."

"Then they're friends?"

"None better," said the old lady.

But my rosy damsel tossed her head again; she was not to be repressed for long, and she broke out again:

"Ay, they love one another as men do who want the same place and the same wife!"

The old woman glowered; but the last words pricked my curiosity, and I interposed before she could begin scolding:

"What, the same wife, too! How's that, young lady?"

"All the world knows that Black Michael—well, then, mother, the duke—would give his soul to marry his cousin, the Princess Flavia, and that she is to be the queen."

"Upon my word," said I, "I begin to be sorry for your duke. But if a man will be a younger son, why, he must take what the elder leaves, and be as thankful to God as he can"; and, thinking of myself, I shrugged my shoulders and laughed. And then I thought also of Antoinette de Mauban and her journey to Strelsau.

"It's little dealing Black Michael has with—" began the girl, braving her mother's anger; but as she spoke a heavy step sounded on the floor, and a gruff voice asked in a threatening tone:

"Who talks of 'Black Michael' in his Highness' own burgh?"

The girl gave a little shriek, half of fright—half, I think, of amusement.

"You'll not tell of me, Johann?" she said.

"See where your chatter leads," said the old lady.

The man who had spoken came forward.

"We have company, Johann," said my hostess, and the fellow plucked off his cap. A moment later he saw me, and to my amazement he started back a step, as though he had seen something wonderful.

"What ails you, Johann?" asked the elder girl. "This is a gentleman on his travels, come to see the coronation."

The man had recovered himself, but he was staring at me with an intense, searching, almost fierce glance.

"Good-evening to you," said I.

"Good-evening, sir," he muttered, still scrutinizing me, and the merry girl began to laugh as she called:

"See, Johann, it is the colour you love! He started to see your hair, sir. It's not the colour we see most of here in Zenda."

"I crave your pardon, sir," stammered the fellow, with puzzled eyes. "I expected to see no one."

"Give him a glass to drink my health in; and I'll bid you good-night, and thanks to you, ladies, for your courtesy and pleasant conversation."

So speaking, I rose to my feet, and with a slight bow turned to the door. The young girl ran to light me on the way, and the man fell back to let me pass, his eyes still fixed on me. The moment I was by, he started a step forward, asking:

"Pray, sir, do you know our King?"

"I never saw him," said I. "I hope to do so on Wednesday."

He said no more, but I felt his eyes following me till the door closed behind me. My saucy conductor, looking over her shoulder at me as she preceded me upstairs, said:

"There's no pleasing Master Johann for one of your colour, sir."

"He prefers yours, maybe?" I suggested.

"I meant, sir, in a man," she answered, with a coquettish glance.

"What," asked I, taking hold of the other side of the candlestick, "does colour matter in a man?"

"Nay, but I love yours—it's the Elphberg red."

"Colour in a man," said I, "is a matter of no more moment than that!"—and I gave her something of no value.

"God send the kitchen door be shut!" said she.

"Amen!" said I, and left her.

In fact, however, as I now know, colour is sometimes of considerable moment to a man.

III. A Merry Evening with a Distant Relative

I was not so unreasonable as to be prejudiced against the duke's keeper because he disliked my complexion; and if I had been his most civil and obliging conduct (as it seemed to me to be) next morning would have disarmed me. Hearing that I was bound for Strelsau, he came to see me while I was breakfasting, and told me that a sister of his, who had married a well-to-do tradesman and lived in the capital, had invited him to occupy a room in her house. He had gladly accepted, but now found that his duties would not permit of his absence. He begged, therefore, that if such humble (though, as he added, clean and comfortable) lodgings would satisfy me I would take his place. He pledged his sister's acquiescence, and urged the inconvenience and crowding to which I should be subject in my journeys to and from Strelsau the next day. I accepted his offer without a moment's hesitation, and he went off to telegraph to his sister, while I packed up and prepared to take the next train. But I still hankered after the forest and the hunting lodge, and when my little maid told me that I could, by walking ten miles or so through the forest, hit the railway at a roadside station, I decided to send my luggage direct to the address which Johann had given, take my walk, and follow to Strelsau myself. Johann had gone off and was not aware of the change in my plans; but, as its only effect was to delay my arrival at his sister's for a few hours, there was no reason for troubling to inform him of it. Doubtless the good lady would waste no anxiety on my account.

I took an early luncheon, and having bidden my kind entertainers farewell, promising to return to them on my way home, I set out to climb the hill that led to the Castle, and thence to the forest of Zenda. Half an hour's leisurely walking brought me to the Castle. It had been a fortress in old days, and the ancient keep was still in good preservation and very imposing. Behind it stood another portion of the original castle, and behind that again, and separated from it by a deep and broad moat, which ran all round the old buildings, was a handsome modern *château*, erected by the last King, and now forming the country residence of the Duke of Strelsau. The old and the new portions were connected by a drawbridge, and this indirect mode of access formed the only passage between the old building and the outer world; but leading to the modern *château* there was a broad and handsome avenue. It was an ideal residence: when "Black Michael" desired company, he could dwell in his *château*; if a fit of misanthropy seized him he had merely to cross the bridge and draw it up after him (it ran on rollers), and nothing short of a regiment and a train of artillery could fetch him out. I went on my way, glad that poor Black Michael, though he could not have the throne or the princess, had at least got as fine a residence as any prince in Europe.

Soon I entered the forest, and walked on for an hour or more in its cool, sombre shade. The great trees enlaced with one another over my head, and the sunshine stole through in patches as bright as diamonds, and hardly bigger. I was enchanted with the place, and finding a felled tree trunk, propped my back against it, and stretching my legs out, gave myself up to undisturbed contemplation of the solemn beauty of the woods and to the comfort of a good cigar. And when the cigar was finished, and I had (I suppose) inhaled as much beauty as I could, I went off into the most delightful sleep, regardless of my train to Strelsau and of the fast waning afternoon. To remember a train in such a spot would have been rank sacrilege. Instead of that, I fell to dreaming that I was married to the Princess Flavia and dwelt in the Castle of Zenda, and beguiled whole days with my love in the glades of the forest, which made a very pleasant dream. In fact, I was just impressing a fervent kiss on the charming lips of the princess when I heard (and the voice seemed at first a part of the dream) someone exclaim, in rough, strident tones:

"Why, the devil's in it! Shave him and he'd be the King!"

The idea seemed whimsical enough for a dream: by the sacrifice of my heavy moustache and carefully pointed imperial I was to be transformed into a monarch! I was about to kiss the princess again when I arrived (very reluctantly) at the conclusion that I was awake.

I opened my eyes, and found two men regarding me with much curiosity. Both wore shooting costumes and carried guns. One was rather short and very stoutly built, with a big bullet-shaped head, a bristly grey moustache, and small pale-blue eyes, a trifle bloodshot. The other was a slender young fellow, of middle height, dark in complexion, and bearing himself with grace and distinction. I set the one down as an old soldier; the other for a gentleman accustomed to move in good society, but not unused to military life either. It turned out afterwards that my guess was a good one.

The elder man approached me, beckoning the younger to follow. He did so, courteously raising his hat. I rose slowly to my feet.

"He's the height, too!" I heard the elder murmur as he surveyed my six feet two inches of stature. Then, with a cavalier touch of the cap, he addressed me:

"May I ask your name?"

"As you have taken the first step in the acquaintance, gentlemen," said I, with a smile, "suppose you give me a lead in the matter of names."

The young man stepped forward with a pleasant smile.

"This," said he, "is Colonel Sapt, and I am called Fritz von Tarlenheim; we are both in the service of the King of Ruritania."

I bowed and, baring my head, answered:

"I am Rudolf Rassendyll. I am a traveller from England; and once for a year or two I held a commission from her Majesty the Queen."

"Then we are all brethren of the sword," answered Tarlenheim, holding out his hand, which I took readily.

"Rassendyll, Rassendyll!" muttered Colonel Sapt; then a gleam of intelligence flitted across his face.

"By Heaven!" he cried, "you're of the Burlesdons?"

"My brother is now Lord Burlesdon," said I.

"Thy head betrayeth thee," he chuckled, pointing to my uncovered poll. "Why, Fritz, you know the story?"

The young man glanced apologetically at me. He felt a delicacy which my sister-in-law would have admired. To put him at his ease I remarked, with a smile:

"Ah! the story is known here as well as among us, it seems."

"Known!" cried Sapt. "If you stay here the deuce a man in all Ruritania will doubt of it—or a woman either."

I began to feel uncomfortable. Had I realized what a very plainly written pedigree I carried about with me I should have thought long before I visited Ruritania. However, I was in for it now.

At this moment a ringing voice sounded from the wood behind us:

"Fritz, Fritz! where are you, man?"

Tarlenheim started, and said hastily:

"It's the King!"

Old Sapt chuckled again.

Then a young man jumped out from behind the trunk of a tree and stood beside us. As I looked at him I uttered an astonished cry; and he, seeing me, drew back in sudden wonder. Saving the hair on my face and a manner of conscious dignity which his position gave him, saving also that he lacked perhaps half an inch—nay, less than that, but still something—of my height, the King of Ruritania might have been Rudolf Rassendyll, and I Rudolf the King.

For an instant we stood motionless, looking at one another. Then I bared my head again and bowed respectfully. The King found his voice, and asked in bewilderment:

"Colonel—Fritz—who is this gentleman?"

I was about to answer, when Colonel Sapt stepped between the King and me, and began to talk to his Majesty in a low growl. The King towered over Sapt, and as he listened his eyes now and again sought mine. I looked at him long and carefully. The likeness was certainly astonishing, though I saw the points of difference also. The King's face was slightly more fleshy than mine, the oval of its contour the least trifle more pronounced, and, as I fancied, his mouth lacking something of the firmness (or obstinacy) which was to be gathered from my close-shutting lips. But for all that, and above all minor distinctions, the likeness rose striking, salient, wonderful.

Sapt ceased speaking, and the King still frowned. Then, gradually, the corners of his mouth began to twitch, his nose came down (as mine does when I laugh), his eyes twinkled, and, behold! he burst into the merriest fit of irrepressible laughter, which rang through the woods and proclaimed him a jovial soul.

"Well met, cousin!" he cried, stepping up to me, clapping me on the back, and laughing still. "You must forgive me if I was taken aback. A man doesn't expect to see double at this time of day, eh, Fritz?"

"I must pray pardon, sire, for my presumption," said I. "I trust it will not forfeit your Majesty's favour."

"By Heaven! you'll always enjoy the King's countenance," he laughed, "whether I like it or not; and, sir, I shall very gladly add to it what services I can. Where are you travelling to?"

"To Strelsau, sire—to the coronation."

The King looked at his friends: he still smiled, though his expression hinted some uneasiness. But the humorous side of the matter caught him again.

"Fritz, Fritz!" he cried, "a thousand crowns for a sight of brother Michael's face when he sees a pair of us!" and the merry laugh rang out again.

"Seriously," observed Fritz von Tarlenheim, "I question Mr. Rassendyll's wisdom in visiting Strelsau just now."

The King lit a cigarette.

"Well, Sapt?" said he questioningly.

"He mustn't go," growled the old fellow.

"Come, colonel, you mean that I should be in Mr. Rassendyll's debt if—"

"Oh, ay! wrap it up in the right way," said Sapt, hauling a great pipe out of his pocket.

"Enough, sire," said I. "I'll leave Ruritania to-day."

"No, by thunder, you shan't—and that's *sans phrase*, as Sapt likes it. For you shall dine with me to-night, happen what will afterwards. Come, man, you don't meet a new relation every day!"

"We dine sparingly to-night," said Fritz von Tarlenheim.

"Not we—with our new cousin for a guest!" cried the King; and as Fritz shrugged his shoulders, he added: "Oh! I'll remember our early start, Fritz."

"So will I—to-morrow morning," said old Sapt, pulling at his pipe.

"Oh, wise old Sapt!" cried the King. "Come, Mr. Rassendyll—by the way, what name did they give you?"

"Your Majesty's," I answered, bowing.

"Well, that shows they weren't ashamed of us," he laughed. "Come, then, cousin Rudolf; I've got no house of my own here, but my dear brother Michael lends us a place of his, and we'll make shift to entertain you there"; and he put his arm through mine and, signing to the others to accompany us, walked me off, westerly, through the forest.

We walked for more than half an hour, and the King smoked cigarettes and chattered incessantly. He was full of interest in my family, laughed heartily when I told him of the portraits with Elphberg hair in our galleries, and yet more heartily when he heard that my expedition to Ruritania was a secret one.

"You have to visit your disreputable cousin on the sly, have you?" said he.

Suddenly emerging from the wood, we came on a small and rude hunting lodge. It was a one-storey building, a sort of bungalow, built entirely of wood. As we approached it a little man in a plain livery came out to meet us. The only other person I saw about the place was a fat elderly woman, whom I afterwards discovered to be the mother of Johann, the duke's keeper.

"Well, is dinner ready, Josef?" asked the King.

The little servant informed us that it was, and we soon sat down to a plentiful meal. The fare was plain enough: the King ate heartily, Fritz von Tarlenheim delicately, old Sapt voraciously. I played a good knife and fork, as my custom is; the King noticed my performance with approval.

"We're all good trenchermen, we Elphbergs," said he. "But what?—we're eating dry! Wine, Josef! wine, man! Are we beasts, to eat without drinking? Are we cattle, Josef?"

At this reproof Josef hastened to load the table with bottles.

"Remember to-morrow!" said Fritz.

"Ay—to-morrow!" said old Sapt.

The King drained a bumper to his "Cousin Rudolf," as he was gracious—or merry—enough to call me; and I drank its fellow to the "Elphberg red," whereat he laughed loudly.

Now, be the meat what it might, the wine we drank was beyond all price or praise, and we did it justice. Fritz ventured once to stay the King's hand.

"What?" cried the King. "Remember you start before I do, Master Fritz—you must be more sparing by two hours than I."

Fritz saw that I did not understand.

"The colonel and I," he explained, "leave here at six; we ride down to Zenda and return with the guard of honour to fetch the King at eight, and then we all ride together to the station."

"Hang that same guard!" growled Sapt.

"Oh! it's very civil of my brother to ask the honour for his regiment," said the King. "Come, cousin, you need not start early. Another bottle, man!"

I had another bottle—or, rather, a part of one, for the larger half travelled quickly down his Majesty's throat. Fritz gave up his attempts at persuasion: from persuading he fell to being persuaded, and soon we were all of us as full of wine as we had any right to be. The King began talking of what he would do in the future, old Sapt of what he had done in the past, Fritz of some beautiful girl or other, and I of the wonderful merits of the Elphberg dynasty. We all talked at once, and followed to the letter Sapt's exhortation to let the morrow take care of itself.

At last the King set down his glass and leant back in his chair.

"I have drunk enough," said he.

"Far be it from me to contradict the King," said I.

Indeed, his remark was most absolutely true—so far as it went.

While I yet spoke Josef came and set before the King a marvellous old wicker-covered flagon. It had lain so long in some darkened cellar that it seemed to blink in the candlelight.

"His Highness the Duke of Strelsau bade me set this wine before the King when the King was weary of all other wines, and pray the King to drink for the love that he bears his brother."

"Well done, Black Michael!" said the King. "Out with the cork, Josef. Hang him! Did he think I'd flinch from his bottle?"

The bottle was opened, and Josef filled the King's glass. The King tasted it. Then, with a solemnity born of the hour and his own condition, he looked round on us:

"Gentlemen, my friends—Rudolf, my cousin ('tis a scandalous story, Rudolf, on my honour!)—everything is yours to the half of Ruritania. But ask me not for a single drop of this divine bottle, which I will drink to the health of that—that sly knave, my brother, Black Michael."

And the King seized the bottle and turned it over his mouth, and drained it and flung it from him, and laid his head on his arms on the table.

And we drank pleasant dreams to his Majesty—and that is all I remember of the evening. Perhaps it is enough.

IV. THE KING KEEPS HIS APPOINTMENT

Whether I had slept a minute or a year I knew not. I awoke with a start and a shiver; my face, hair, and clothes dripped water, and opposite me stood old Sapt, a sneering smile on his face and an empty bucket in his hand. On the table by him sat Fritz von Tarlenheim, pale as a ghost and black as a crow under the eyes.

I leapt to my feet in anger.

"Your joke goes too far, sir!" I cried.

"Tut, man, we've no time for quarrelling. Nothing else would rouse you. It's five o'clock."

"I'll thank you, Colonel Sapt—" I began again, hot in spirit, though I was uncommonly cold in body.

"Rassendyll," interrupted Fritz, getting down from the table and taking my arm, "look here."

The King lay full length on the floor. His face was red as his hair, and he breathed heavily. Sapt, the disrespectful old dog, kicked him sharply. He did not stir, nor was there any break in his breathing. I saw that his face and head were wet with water, as were mine.

"We've spent half an hour on him," said Fritz.

"He drank three times what either of you did," growled Sapt.

I knelt down and felt his pulse. It was alarmingly languid and slow. We three looked at one another.

"Was it drugged—that last bottle?" I asked in a whisper.

"I don't know," said Sapt.

"We must get a doctor."

"There's none within ten miles, and a thousand doctors wouldn't take him to Strelsau to-day. I know the look of it. He'll not move for six or seven hours yet."

"But the coronation!" I cried in horror.

Fritz shrugged his shoulders, as I began to see was his habit on most occasions.

"We must send word that he's ill," he said.

"I suppose so," said I.

Old Sapt, who seemed as fresh as a daisy, had lit his pipe and was puffing hard at it.

"If he's not crowned to-day," said he, "I'll lay a crown he's never crowned."

"But, heavens, why?"

"The whole nation's there to meet him; half the army—ay, and Black Michael at the head. Shall we send word that the King's drunk?"

"That he's ill," said I, in correction.

"Ill!" echoed Sapt, with a scornful laugh. "They know his illnesses too well. He's been 'ill' before!"

"Well, we must chance what they think," said Fritz helplessly. "I'll carry the news and make the best of it."

Sapt raised his hand.

"Tell me," said he: "do you think the King was drugged?"

"I do," said I.

"And who drugged him?"

"That damned hound, Black Michael," said Fritz between his teeth.

"Ay," said Sapt, "that he might not come to be crowned. Rassendyll here doesn't know our pretty Michael. What think you, Fritz—has Michael no King ready? Has half Strelsau no other candidate? As God's alive, man, the throne's lost if the King show himself not in Strelsau to-day. I know Black Michael."

"We could carry him there," said I.

"And a very pretty picture he makes," sneered Sapt.

Fritz von Tarlenheim buried his face in his hands. The King breathed loudly and heavily. Sapt stirred him again with his foot.

"The drunken dog!" he said. "But he's an Elphberg and the son of his father, and may I rot in hell before Black Michael sits in his place!"

For a moment or two we were all silent; then Sapt, knitting his bushy grey brows, took his pipe from his mouth and said to me:

"As a man grows old he believes in Fate. Fate sent you here. Fate sends you now to Strelsau."

I staggered back, murmuring, "Good God!"

Fritz looked up with an eager, bewildered gaze.

"Impossible!" I muttered. "I should be known."

"It's a risk— against a certainty," said Sapt. "If you shave I'll wager you'll not be known. Are you afraid?"

"Sir!"

"Come, lad, there, there; but it's your life, you know, if you're known—and mine— and Fritz's here. But if you don't go I swear to you Black Michael will sit to-night on the throne, and the King lie in prison or his grave."

"The King would never forgive it," I stammered.

"Are we women? Who cares for his forgiveness?"

The clock ticked fifty times, and sixty and seventy times, as I stood in thought. Then I suppose a look came over my face, for old Sapt caught me by the hand, crying:

"You'll go?"

"Yes, I'll go," said I, and I turned my eyes on the prostrate figure of the King on the floor.

"To-night," Sapt went on in a hasty whisper, "we are to lodge in the Palace. The moment they leave us you and I will mount our horses—Fritz must stay there and guard the King's room—and ride here at a gallop. The King will be ready—Josef will tell him—and he must ride back with me to Strelsau, and you ride as if the devil were behind you to the frontier."

I took it all in in a second, and nodded my head.

"There's a chance," said Fritz, with his first sign of hopefulness.

"If I escape detection," said I.

"If we're detected," said Sapt. "I'll send Black Michael down below before I go myself, so help me heaven! Sit in that chair, man."

I obeyed him.

He darted from the room, calling "Josef! Josef!" In three minutes he was back, and Josef with him. The latter carried a jug of hot water, soap, and razors. He was trembling as Sapt told him how the land lay, and bade him shave me.

Suddenly Fritz smote on his thigh:

"But the guard! They'll know! they'll know!"

"Pooh! We shan't wait for the guard. We'll ride to Hofban and catch a train there. When they come the bird'll be flown."

"But the King?"

"The King will be in the wine cellar. I'm going to carry him there now."

"If they find him?"

"They won't. How should they? Josef will put them off."

"But—"

Sapt stamped his foot.

"We're not playing," he roared. "My God! don't I know the risk? If they do find him he's no worse off than if he isn't crowned to-day in Strelsau."

So speaking, he flung the door open and, stooping, put forth a strength I did not dream he had, and lifted the King in his hands. And as he did so the old woman, Johann the keeper's mother, stood in the doorway. For a moment she stood, then she turned on her heel, without a sign of surprise, and clattered down the passage.

"Has she heard?" cried Fritz.

"I'll shut her mouth!" said Sapt grimly, and he bore off the King in his arms.

For me, I sat down in an armchair, and as I sat there, half dazed, Josef clipped and scraped me till my moustache and imperial were things of the past and my face was as bare as the King's. And when Fritz saw me thus he drew a long breath and exclaimed:

"By Jove, we shall do it!"

It was six o'clock now, and we had no time to lose. Sapt hurried me into the King's room, and I dressed myself in the uniform of a colonel of the Guard, finding time as I slipped on the King's boots to ask Sapt what he had done with the old woman.

"She swore she'd heard nothing," said he; "but to make sure I tied her legs together and put a handkerchief in her mouth and bound her hands, and locked her up in the coal cellar, next door to the King. Josef'll look after them both later on."

Then I burst out laughing, and even old Sapt grimly smiled.

"I fancy," said he, "that when Josef tells them the King is gone they'll think it is because we smelt a rat. For you may swear Black Michael doesn't expect to see him in Strelsau to-day."

I put the King's helmet on my head. Old Sapt handed me the King's sword, looking at me long and carefully.

"Thank God, he shaved his beard!" he exclaimed.

"Why did he?" I asked.

"Because Princess Flavia said he grazed her cheek when he was graciously pleased to give her a cousinly kiss. Come, though, we must ride."

"Is all safe here?"

"Nothing's safe anywhere," said Sapt, "but we can make it no safer."

Fritz now rejoined us in the uniform of a captain in the same regiment as that to which my dress belonged. In four minutes Sapt had arrayed himself in his uniform. Josef called that the horses were ready. We jumped on their backs and started at a rapid trot. The game had begun. What would the issue of it be?

The cool morning air cleared my head, and I was able to take in all Sapt said to me. He was wonderful. Fritz hardly spoke, riding like a man asleep; but Sapt, without another word for the King, began at once to instruct me most minutely in the history of my past life, of my family, of my tastes, pursuits, weaknesses, friends, companions, and servants. He told me the etiquette of the Ruritanian court, promising to be constantly at my elbow to point out everybody whom I ought to know, and give me hints with what degree of favour to greet them.

"By the way," he said, "you are a Catholic, I suppose?"

"Not I," I answered.

"Lord, he's a heretic!" groaned Sapt, and forthwith he fell to a rudimentary lesson in the practices and observances of the Romish faith.

"Luckily," said he, "you won't be expected to know much, for the King's notoriously lax and careless about such matters. But you must be as civil as butter to the Cardinal. We hope to win him over, because he and Michael have a standing quarrel about their precedence."

We were by now at the station. Fritz had recovered nerve enough to explain to the astonished station master that the King had changed his plans. The train steamed up. We got into a first-class carriage, and Sapt, leaning back on the cushions, went on with his lesson. I looked at my watch—the King's watch it was, of course. It was just eight.

"I wonder if they've gone to look for us," I said.

"I hope they won't find the King," said Fritz nervously, and this time it was Sapt who shrugged his shoulders.

The train travelled well, and at half-past nine, looking out of the window, I saw the towers and spires of a great city.

"Your capital, my liege," grinned old Sapt, with a wave of his hand, and, leaning forward, he laid his finger on my pulse. "A little too quick," said he in his grumbling tone.

"I'm not made of stone!" I exclaimed.

"You'll do," said he, with a nod. "We must say Fritz here has caught the ague. Drain your flask, Fritz, for heaven's sake, boy!"

Fritz did as he was bid.

"We're an hour early," said Sapt. "We'll send word forward for your Majesty's arrival, for there'll be no one here to meet us yet. And meanwhile—"

"Meanwhile," said I, "the King'll be hanged if he doesn't have some breakfast."

Old Sapt chuckled, and held out his hand.

"You're an Elphberg, every inch of you," said he. Then he paused, and looking at us, said quietly, "God send we may be alive to-night!"

"Amen!" said Fritz von Tarlenheim.

The train stopped. Fritz and Sapt leapt out, uncovered, and held the door for me. I choked down a lump that rose in my throat, settled my helmet firmly on my head, and (I'm not ashamed to say it) breathed a short prayer to God. Then I stepped on the platform of the station at Strelsau.

A moment later all was bustle and confusion: men hurrying up, hats in hand, and hurrying off again; men conducting me to the *buffet*; men mounting and riding in hot haste to the quarters of the troops, to the Cathedral, to the residence of Duke Michael. Even as I swallowed the last drop of my cup of coffee the bells throughout all the city broke out into a joyful peal, and the sound of a military band and of men cheering smote upon my ear.

King Rudolf the Fifth was in his good city of Strelsau! And they shouted outside: "God save the King!"

Old Sapt's mouth wrinkled into a smile.

"God save 'em both!" he whispered. "Courage, lad!" and I felt his hand press my knee.

V. The Adventures of an Understudy

With Fritz von Tarlenheim and Colonel Sapt close behind me I stepped out of the buffet on to the platform. The last thing I did was to feel if my revolver were handy and my sword loose in the scabbard. A gay group of officers and high dignitaries stood waiting me, at their head a tall old man, covered with medals, and of military bearing. He wore the yellow and red ribbon of the Red Rose of Ruritania— which, by the way, decorated my unworthy breast also.

"Marshal Strakencz," whispered Sapt, and I knew that I was in the presence of the most famous veteran of the Ruritanian army.

Just behind the Marshal stood a short, spare man, in flowing robes of black and crimson.

"The Chancellor of the kingdom," whispered Sapt.

The Marshal greeted me in a few loyal words, and proceeded to deliver an apology from the Duke of Strelsau. The duke, it seemed, had been afflicted with a sudden indisposition which made it impossible for him to come to the station, but he craved leave to await his Majesty at the Cathedral. I expressed my concern, accepted the Marshal's excuses very suavely, and received the compliments of a large number of distinguished personages. No one betrayed the least suspicion, and I felt my nerve returning and the agitated beating of my heart subsiding. But Fritz was still pale, and his hand shook like a leaf as he extended it to the Marshal.

Presently we formed procession and took our way to the door of the station. Here I mounted my horse, the Marshal holding my stirrup. The civil dignitaries went off to their carriages, and I started to ride through the streets with the Marshal on my right and Sapt (who, as my chief aide-de-camp, was entitled to the place) on my left. The city of Strelsau is partly old and partly new. Spacious modern boulevards and residential quarters surround and embrace the narrow, tortuous, and picturesque streets of the original town. In the outer circles the upper classes live; in the inner the shops are situated; and, behind their prosperous fronts lie hidden populous but wretched lanes and alleys, filled with a poverty-stricken, turbulent, and (in large measure) criminal class. These social and local divisions corresponded, as I knew from Sapt's information, to another division more important to me. The New Town was for the King; but to the Old Town Michael of Strelsau was a hope, a hero, and a darling.

The scene was very brilliant as we passed along the Grand Boulevard and on to the great square where the Royal Palace stood. Here I was in the midst of my devoted adherents. Every house was hung with red and bedecked with flags and mottoes. The streets were lined with raised seats on each side, and I passed along, bowing this way and that, under a shower of cheers, blessings, and waving handkerchiefs. The balconies were full of gaily dressed ladies, who clapped their hands and courtesied and threw their brightest glances at me. A torrent of red roses fell on me; one bloom lodged in my horse's mane, and I took it and stuck it in my coat. The Marshal smiled grimly. I had stolen some glances at his face, but he was too impassive to show me whether his sympathies were with me or not.

"The red rose for the Elphbergs, marshal," said I gaily, and he nodded.

I have written "gaily," and a strange word it must seem. But the truth is that I was drunk with excitement. At that moment I believed—I almost believed—that I was in very truth the king; and, with a look of laughing triumph, I raised my eyes to the beauty-laden balconies again . . . and then I started. For looking down on me, with her handsome face and proud smile, was the lady who had been my fellow traveller— Antoinette de Mauban; and I saw her also start, and her lips moved, and she leant forward and gazed at me. And I, collecting myself, met her eyes full and square, while again I felt my revolver. Suppose she had cried aloud, "That's not the king!"

Well, we went by; and then the Marshal, turning round in his saddle, waved his hand, and the Cuirassiers closed round us, so that the crowd could not come near me. We were leaving my quarter and entering Duke Michael's, and this action of the Marshal's showed me more clearly than words what the state of feeling in the town must be. But if Fate made me a King the least I could do was to play the part handsomely.

"Why this change in our order, Marshal?" said I.

The Marshal bit his white moustache.

"It is more prudent, sire," he murmured.

I drew rein.

"Let those in front ride on," said I, "till they are fifty yards ahead. But do you, Marshal, and Colonel Sapt and my friends wait here till I have ridden fifty yards. And see that no one is nearer to me. I will have my people see that their King trusts them."

Sapt laid his hand on my arm. I shook him off. The Marshal hesitated.

"Am I not understood?" said I; and, biting his moustache again, he gave the orders. I saw old Sapt smiling into his beard, but he shook his head at me. If I had been killed in open day in the streets of Strelsau Sapt's position would have been a difficult one.

Perhaps I ought to say that I was dressed all in white, except my boots. I wore a silver helmet with gilt ornaments, and the broad ribbon of the Rose looked well across my chest. I should be paying a poor compliment to the King if I did not set modesty aside and admit that I made a very fine figure. So the people thought; for when I, riding alone, entered the dingy, sparsely decorated, sombre streets of the Old Town there was first a murmur, then a cheer, and a woman, from a window above a cookshop, cried the old local saying:

"If he's red he's right!" whereat I laughed and took off my helmet that she might see that I was of the right colour, and they cheered me again at that.

It was more interesting riding thus alone, for I heard the comments of the crowd.

"He looks paler than his wont," said one.

"You'd look pale if you lived as he did," was the highly disrespectful retort.

"He's a bigger man than I thought," said another.

"So he had a good jaw under that beard after all," commented a third.

"The pictures of him aren't handsome enough," declared a pretty girl, taking great care that I should hear. No doubt it was mere flattery.

But in spite of these signs of approval and interest the mass of the people received me in silence and with sullen looks, and my dear brother's portrait ornamented most of the windows—which was an ironical sort of greeting to the King. I was quite glad that he had been spared the unpleasant sight. He was a man of quick temper, and perhaps he would not have taken it so placidly as I did.

At last we were at the Cathedral. Its great grey front, embellished with hundreds of statues and boasting a pair of the finest oak doors in Europe, rose for the first time before me, and the sudden sense of my audacity almost overcame me. Everything was in a mist as I dismounted. I saw the Marshal and Sapt dimly, and dimly the throng of gorgeously robed priests who awaited me. And my eyes were still dim as I walked up the great nave, with the pealing of the organ in my ears. I saw nothing of the brilliant throng that filled it; I hardly distinguished the stately figure of the Cardinal as he rose from the archiepiscopal throne to greet me. Two faces only stood out side by side clearly before my eyes—the face of a girl, pale and lovely, surmounted by a crown of the glorious Elphberg hair (for in a woman it is glorious), and the face of a man, whose full-blooded red cheeks, black hair, and dark, deep eyes told me that at last I was in presence of my brother, Black Michael. And when he saw me his red cheeks went pale all in a moment, and his helmet fell with a clatter on the floor. Till that moment I believe that he had not realized that the King was in very truth come to Strelsau.

Of what followed next I remember nothing. I knelt before the altar and the Cardinal anointed my head. Then I rose to my feet, and stretched out my hand and took from him the crown of Ruritania and set it on my head, and I swore the old oath of the King;

and (if it were a sin may it be forgiven me) I received the Holy Sacrament there before them all. Then the great organ pealed out again, the Marshal bade the heralds proclaim me, and Rudolf the Fifth was crowned King; of which imposing ceremony an excellent picture hangs now in my dining room. The portrait of the King is very good.

Then the lady with the pale face and the glorious hair, her train held by two pages, stepped from her place and came to where I stood. And a herald cried:

"Her Royal Highness the Princess Flavia!"

She curtsied low, and put her hand under mine and raised my hand and kissed it. And for an instant I thought what I had best do. Then I drew her to me and kissed her twice on the cheek, and she blushed red, and—why, then his Eminence the Cardinal Archbishop slipped in front of Black Michael, and kissed my hand and presented me with a letter from the Pope—the first and last which I have received from that exalted quarter!

And then came the Duke of Strelsau. His step trembled, I swear, and he looked to the right and to the left, as a man looks who thinks on flight; and his face was patched with red and white, and his hand shook so that it jumped under mine, and I felt his lips dry and parched. And I glanced at Sapt, who was smiling again into his beard, and, resolutely doing my duty in that station of life to which I had been marvellously called, I took my dear Michael by both hands and kissed him on the cheek. I think we were both glad when that was over!

But neither in the face of the princess nor in that of any other did I see the least doubt or questioning. Yet had I and the King stood side by side they could have told us in an instant, or, at least, on a little consideration. But neither they nor anyone else dreamed or imagined that I could be other than the King. So the likeness served, and for an hour I stood there, feeling as weary and *blasé* as though I had been a King all my life; and everybody kissed my hand, and the ambassadors paid me their respects, among them old Lord Topham, at whose house in Grosvenor Square I had danced a score of times. Thank heaven, the old man was as blind as a bat, and did not claim my acquaintance.

Then back we went through the streets to the Palace, and I heard them cheering Black Michael; but he, Fritz told me, sat biting his nails like a man in a reverie, and even his own friends said that he should have made a braver show. I was in a carriage now, side by side with the Princess Flavia, and a rough fellow cried out:

"And when's the wedding?" and as he spoke another struck him in the face, crying, "Long live Duke Michael!" and the princess colored—it was an admirable tint—and looked straight in front of her.

Now I felt in a difficulty, because I had forgotten to ask Sapt the state of my affections, or how far matters had gone between the princess and myself. Frankly, had I been the King the further they had gone the better should I have been pleased. For I am not a slow-blooded man, and I had not kissed Princess Flavia's cheek for nothing. These thoughts passed through my head, but, not being sure of my ground, I said nothing; and in a moment or two the princess, recovering her equanimity, turned to me.

"Do you know, Rudolf," said she, "you look somehow different to-day?"

The fact was not surprising, but the remark was disquieting.

"You look," she went on, "more sober, more sedate; you're almost careworn, and I declare you're thinner. Surely it's not possible that you've begun to take anything seriously?"

The princess seemed to hold of the King much the same opinion that Lady Burlesdon held of me.

I braced myself up to the conversation.

"Would that please you?" I asked softly.

"Oh, you know my views," said she, turning her eyes away.

"Whatever pleases you I try to do," I said; and, as I saw her smile and blush I thought that I was playing the King's hand very well for him. So I continued, and what I said was perfectly true:

"I assure you, my dear cousin, that nothing in my life has affected me more than the reception I've been greeted with to-day."

She smiled brightly, but in an instant grew grave again, and whispered:

"Did you notice Michael?"

"Yes," said I; adding, "He wasn't enjoying himself."

"Do be careful!" she went on. "You don't—indeed you don't— keep enough watch on him. You know—"

"I know," said I, "that he wants what I've got."

"Yes. Hush!"

Then—and I can't justify it, for I committed the King far beyond what I had a right to do—I suppose she carried me off my feet—I went on:

"And, perhaps, also something which I haven't got yet, but hope to win some day."

This was my answer—had I been the King I should have thought it encouraging: "Haven't you enough responsibilities on you for one day, cousin?"

Bang, bang! Blare, blare! We were at the Palace. Guns were firing and trumpets blowing. Rows of lackeys stood waiting, and, handing the princess up the broad marble staircase, I took formal possession, as a crowned King, of the house of my ancestors, and sat down at my own table, with my cousin on my right hand, on her other side Black Michael, and on my left his Eminence the Cardinal. Behind my chair stood Sapt; and at the end of the table I saw Fritz von Tarlenheim drain to the bottom his glass of champagne rather sooner than he decently should.

I wondered what the King of Ruritania was doing.

VI. THE SECRET OF A CELLAR

We were in the King's dressing room—Fritz von Tarlenheim, Sapt, and I. I flung myself exhausted into an armchair. Sapt lit his pipe. He uttered no congratulations on the marvellous success of our wild risk, but his whole bearing was eloquent of satisfaction. The triumph, aided perhaps by good wine, had made a new man of Fritz.

"What a day for you to remember!" he cried. "Gad, I'd like to be King for twelve hours myself! But, Rassendyll, you mustn't throw your heart too much into the part. I don't wonder Black Michael looked blacker than ever—you and the princess had so much to say to one another."

"How beautiful she is!" I exclaimed.

"Never mind the woman," growled Sapt. "Are you ready to start?"

"Yes," said I, with a sigh.

It was five o'clock, and at twelve I should be no more than Rudolf Rassendyll. I remarked on it in a joking tone.

"You'll be lucky," observed Sapt grimly, "if you're not the late Rudolf Rassendyll. By Heaven! I feel my head wobbling on my shoulders every minute you're in the city. Do you know, friend, that Michael has had news from Zenda? He went into a room alone to read it—and he came out looking like a man dazed."

"I'm ready," said I, this news making me none the more eager to linger.

Sapt sat down.

"I must write us an order to leave the city. Michael's Governor, you know, and we must be prepared for hindrances. You must sign the order."

"My dear colonel, I've not been bred a forger!"

Out of his pocket Sapt produced a piece of paper.

"There's the King's signature," he said, "and here," he went on, after another search in his pocket, "is some tracing paper. If you can't manage a 'Rudolf' in ten minutes, why—I can."

"Your education has been more comprehensive than mine," said I. "You write it."

And a very tolerable forgery did this versatile hero produce.

"Now, Fritz," said he, "the King goes to bed. He is upset. No one is to see him till nine o'clock to-morrow. You understand—no one?"

"I understand," answered Fritz.

"Michael may come, and claim immediate audience. You'll answer that only princes of the blood are entitled to it."

"That'll annoy Michael," laughed Fritz.

"You quite understand?" asked Sapt again. "If the door of this room is opened while we're away you're not to be alive to tell us about it."

"I need no schooling, colonel," said Fritz, a trifle haughtily.

"Here, wrap yourself in this big cloak," Sapt continued to me, "and put on this flat cap. My orderly rides with me to the hunting lodge to-night."

"There's an obstacle," I observed. "The horse doesn't live that can carry me forty miles."

"Oh, yes, he does—two of him: one here—one at the lodge. Now, are you ready?"

"I'm ready," said I.

Fritz held out his hand.

"In case," said he; and we shook hands heartily.

"Damn your sentiment!" growled Sapt. "Come along."

He went, not to the door, but to a panel in the wall.

"In the old King's time," said he, "I knew this way well."

I followed him, and we walked, as I should estimate, near two hundred yards along a narrow passage. Then we came to a stout oak door. Sapt unlocked it. We passed through, and found ourselves in a quiet street that ran along the back of the Palace gardens. A man was waiting for us with two horses. One was a magnificent bay, up to any weight; the other a sturdy brown. Sapt signed to me to mount the bay. Without a word to the man we mounted and rode away. The town was full of noise and merriment, but we took secluded ways. My cloak was wrapped over half my face; the capacious flat cap hid every lock of my telltale hair. By Sapt's directions, I crouched on my saddle, and rode with such a round back as I hope never to exhibit on a horse again. Down a long, narrow lane we went, meeting some wanderers and some roisterers; and as we rode we heard the Cathedral bells still clanging out their welcome to the King. It was half-past six, and still light. At last we came to the city wall and to a gate.

"Have your weapon ready," whispered Sapt. "We must stop his mouth if he talks."

I put my hand on my revolver. Sapt hailed the doorkeeper. The stars fought for us! A little girl of fourteen tripped out.

"Please, sir, father's gone to see the King."

"He'd better have stayed here," said Sapt to me, grinning.

"But he said I wasn't to open the gate, sir."

"Did he, my dear?" said Sapt, dismounting. "Then give me the key."

The key was in the child's hand. Sapt gave her a crown.

"Here's an order from the King. Show it to your father. Orderly, open the gate!"

I leapt down. Between us we rolled back the great gate, led our horses out, and closed it again.

"I shall be sorry for the doorkeeper if Michael finds out that he wasn't there. Now then, lad, for a canter. We mustn't go too fast while we're near the town."

Once, however, outside the city we ran little danger, for everybody else was inside, merry-making; and as the evening fell we quickened our pace, my splendid horse bounding along under me as though I had been a feather. It was a fine night, and presently the moon appeared. We talked little on the way, and chiefly about the progress we were making.

"I wonder what the duke's despatches told him," said I, once.

"Ay, I wonder!" responded Sapt.

We stopped for a draught of wine and to bait our horses, losing half an hour thus. I dared not go into the inn, and stayed with the horses in the stable. Then we went ahead again, and had covered some five-and-twenty miles when Sapt abruptly stopped.

"Hark!" he cried.

I listened. Away, far behind us, in the still of the evening—it was just half-past nine—we heard the beat of horses' hoofs. The wind, blowing strong behind us, carried the sound. I glanced at Sapt.

"Come on!" he cried, and spurred his horse into a gallop. When we next paused to listen the hoof-beats were not audible, and we relaxed our pace. Then we heard them again. Sapt jumped down and laid his ear to the ground.

"There are two," he said. "They're only a mile behind. Thank God, the road curves in and out, and the wind's our way."

We galloped on. We seemed to be holding our own. We had entered the outskirts of the forest of Zenda, and the trees, closing in behind us as the track zigged and zagged, prevented us seeing our pursuers, and them from seeing us.

Another half hour brought us to a divide of the road. Sapt drew rein.

"To the right is our road," he said. "To the left, to the Castle. Each about eight miles. Get down."

"But they'll be on us!" I cried.

"Get down!" he repeated brusquely; and I obeyed.

The wood was dense up to the very edge of the road. We led our horses into the covert, bound handkerchiefs over their eyes, and stood beside them.

"You want to see who they are?" I whispered.

"Ay, and where they're going," he answered.

I saw that his revolver was in his hand.

Nearer and nearer came the hoofs. The moon shone out now clear and full, so that the road was white with it. The ground was hard, and we had left no traces.

"Here they come!" whispered Sapt.

"It's the duke!"

"I thought so!" he answered.

It was the duke; and with him a burly fellow whom I knew well, and who had cause to know me afterwards—Max Holf, brother to Johann the keeper, and body servant to his Highness. They were up to us; the duke reined up. I saw Sapt's finger curl lovingly towards the trigger. I believe he would have given ten years of his life for a shot; and he could have picked off Black Michael as easily as I could a barn-door fowl in a farmyard. I laid my hand on his arm. He nodded reassuringly: he was always ready to sacrifice inclination to duty.

"Which way?" asked Black Michael.

"To the Castle, your Highness," urged his companion. "There we shall learn the truth."

For an instant the duke hesitated.

"I thought I heard hoofs," said he.

"I think not, your Highness."

"Why shouldn't we go to the lodge?"

"I fear a trap. If all is well why go to the lodge? If not, it's a snare to trap us."

Suddenly the duke's horse neighed. In an instant we folded our cloaks close round our horses' heads, and, holding them thus, covered the duke and his attendant with our revolvers. If they had found us they had been dead men, or our prisoners.

Michael waited a moment longer. Then he cried:

"To Zenda, then!" and setting spurs to his horse, galloped on.

Sapt raised his weapon after him, and there was such an expression of wistful regret on his face that I had much ado not to burst out laughing.

For ten minutes we stayed where we were.

"You see," said Sapt, "they've sent him news that all is well."

"What does that mean?" I asked.

"God knows," said Sapt, frowning heavily. "But it's brought him from Strelsau in a rare puzzle."

Then we mounted, and rode fast as our weary horses could lay their feet to the ground. For those last eight miles we spoke no more. Our minds were full of apprehension. "All is well." What did it mean? Was all well with the King?

At last the lodge came in sight. Spurring our horses to a last gallop, we rode up to the gate. All was still and quiet. Not a soul came to meet us. We dismounted in haste. Suddenly Sapt caught me by the arm.

"Look there!" he said, pointing to the ground.

I looked down. At my feet lay five or six silk handkerchiefs, torn and slashed and rent. I turned to him questioningly.

"They're what I tied the old woman up with," said he. "Fasten the horses and come along."

The handle of the door turned without resistance. We passed into the room which had been the scene of last night's bout. It was still strewn with the remnants of our meal and with empty bottles.

"Come on," cried Sapt, whose marvellous composure had at last almost given way.

We rushed down the passage towards the cellars. The door of the coal cellar stood wide open.

"They found the old woman," said I.

"You might have known that from the handkerchiefs," he said.

Then we came opposite the door of the wine cellar. It was shut. It looked in all respects as it had looked when we left it that morning.

"Come, it's all right," said I.

A loud oath from Sapt rang out. His face turned pale, and he pointed again at the floor. From under the door a red stain had spread over the floor of the passage and dried there. Sapt sank against the opposite wall. I tried the door. It was locked.

"Where's Josef?" muttered Sapt.

"Where's the King?" I responded.

Sapt took out a flask and put it to his lips. I ran back to the dining room, and seized a heavy poker from the fireplace. In my terror and excitement I rained blows on the lock of the door, and I fired a cartridge into it. It gave way, and the door swung open.

"Give me a light," said I; but Sapt still leant against the wall.

He was, of course, more moved than I, for he loved his master. Afraid for himself he was not—no man ever saw him that; but to think what might lie in that dark cellar was enough to turn any man's face pale. I went myself, and took a silver candlestick from the dining table and struck a light, and as I returned I felt the hot wax drip on my naked hand as the candle swayed to and fro; so that I cannot afford to despise Colonel Sapt for his agitation.

I came to the door of the cellar. The red stain, turning more and more to a dull brown, stretched inside. I walked two yards into the cellar, and held the candle high above my head. I saw the full bins of wine; I saw spiders crawling on the walls; I saw, too, a couple of empty bottles lying on the floor; and then, away in the corner, I saw the body of a man, lying flat on his back, with his arms stretched wide, and a crimson gash across his throat. I walked to him and knelt down beside him, and commended to God the soul of a faithful man. For it was the body of Josef, the little servant, slain in guarding the King.

I felt a hand on my shoulder, and, turning, saw Sapt's eyes, glaring and terror-struck, beside me.

"The King! My God! the King!" he whispered hoarsely.

I threw the candle's gleam over every inch of the cellar.

"The King is not here," said I.

VII. His Majesty Sleeps in Strelsau

I put my arm round Sapt's waist and supported him out of the cellar, drawing the battered door close after me. For ten minutes or more we sat silent in the dining room. Then old Sapt rubbed his knuckles into his eyes, gave one great gasp, and was himself again. As the clock on the mantelpiece struck one he stamped his foot on the floor, saying:

"They've got the King!"

"Yes," said I, "'all's well!' as Black Michael's despatch said. What a moment it must have been for him when the royal salutes fired at Strelsau this morning! I wonder when he got the message?"

"It must have been sent in the morning," said Sapt. "They must have sent it before news of your arrival at Strelsau reached Zenda—I suppose it came from Zenda."

"And he's carried it about all day!" I exclaimed. "Upon my honor, I'm not the only man who's had a trying day! What did he think, Sapt?"

"What does that matter? What does he think, lad, now?"

I rose to my feet.

"We must get back," I said, "and rouse every soldier in Strelsau. We ought to be in pursuit of Michael before midday."

Old Sapt pulled out his pipe and carefully lit it from the candle which guttered on the table.

"The King may be murdered while we sit here!" I urged.

Sapt smoked on for a moment in silence.

"That cursed old woman!" he broke out. "She must have attracted their attention somehow. I see the game. They came up to kidnap the King, and—as I say—somehow they found him. If you hadn't gone to Strelsau, you and I and Fritz had been in heaven by now!"

"And the King?"

"Who knows where the King is now?" he asked.

"Come, let's be off!" said I; but he sat still. And suddenly he burst into one of his grating chuckles:

"By Jove, we've shaken up Black Michael!"

"Come, come!" I repeated impatiently.

"And we'll shake him up a bit more," he added, a cunning smile broadening on his wrinkled, weather-beaten face and his teeth working on an end of his grizzled moustache. "Ay, lad, we'll go back to Strelsau. The King shall be in his capital again to-morrow."

"The King?"

"The crowned King!"

"You're mad!" I cried.

"If we go back and tell the trick we played what would you give for our lives?"

"Just what they're worth," said I.

"And for the King's throne? Do you think that the nobles and the people will enjoy being fooled as you've fooled them? Do you think they'll love a King who was too drunk to be crowned, and sent a servant to personate him?"

"He was drugged—and I'm no servant."

"Mine will be Black Michael's version."

He rose, came to me, and laid his hand on my shoulder.

"Lad," he said, "if you play the man you may save the King yet. Go back and keep his throne warm for him."

"But the duke knows—the villains he has employed know—"

"Ay, but they can't speak!" roared Sapt in grim triumph. "We've got 'em! How can they denounce you without denouncing themselves? 'This is not the King, because we kidnapped the king and murdered his servant.' Can they say that?"

The position flashed on me. Whether Michael knew me or not, he could not speak. Unless he produced the King, what could he do? And if he produced the King where was he? For a moment I was carried away headlong; but in an instant the difficulties came strong upon me.

"I must be found out," I urged.

"Perhaps; but every hour's something. Above all, we must have a King in Strelsau, or the city will be Michael's in four-and-twenty hours, and what would the King's life be worth then—or his throne? Lad, you must do it!"

"Suppose they kill the King?"

"They'll kill him, if you don't."

"Sapt, suppose they have killed the King?"

"Then, by heaven, you're as good an Elphberg as Black Michael, and you shall reign in Ruritania! But I don't believe they have; nor will they kill him if you're on the throne. Will they kill him to put you in?"

It was a wild plan—wilder even and hopeless than the trick we had already carried through; but as I listened to Sapt I saw the strong points in our game. And then I was a young man and I loved action, and I was offered such a hand in such a game as perhaps never man played yet.

"I shall be found out," I said.

"Perhaps," said Sapt. "Come! to Strelsau! We shall be caught like rats in a trap if we stay here."

"Sapt," I cried, "I'll try it!"

"Well played!" said he. "I hope they've left us the horses. I'll go and see."

"We must bury that poor fellow," said I.

"No time," said Sapt.

"I'll do it."

"Hang you!" he grinned. "I make you a King, and— Well, do it. Go and fetch him, while I look to the horses. He can't lie very deep, but I doubt if he'll care about that. Poor little Josef! He was an honest bit of a man."

He went out and I went to the cellar. I raised poor Josef in my arms and bore him into the passage and thence towards the door of the house. Just inside I laid him down, remembering that I must find spades for our task. At this instant Sapt came up.

"The horses are all right; there's the own brother to the one that brought you here. But you may save yourself that job."

"I'll not go before he's buried."

"Yes, you will."

"Not I, Colonel Sapt; not for all Ruritania."

"You fool!" said he. "Come here."

He drew me to the door. The moon was sinking, but about three hundred yards away, coming along the road from Zenda, I made out a party of men. There were seven or eight of them; four were on horseback and the rest were walking, and I saw that they carried long implements, which I guessed to be spades and mattocks, on their shoulders.

"They'll save you the trouble," said Sapt. "Come along."

He was right. The approaching party must, beyond doubt, be Duke Michael's men, come to remove the traces of their evil work. I hesitated no longer, but an irresistible desire seized me. Pointing to the corpse of poor little Josef, I said to Sapt:

"Colonel, we ought to strike a blow for him!"

"You'd like to give him some company, eh? But it's too risky work, your Majesty."

"I must have a slap at 'em," said I.

Sapt wavered.

"Well," said he, "it's not business, you know; but you've been a good boy—and if we come to grief, why, hang me, it'll save us lot of thinking! I'll show you how to touch them."

He cautiously closed the open chink of the door. Then we retreated through the house and made our way to the back entrance. Here our horses were standing. A carriage drive swept all around the lodge.

"Revolver ready?" asked Sapt.

"No; steel for me," said I.

"Gad, you're thirsty to-night," chuckled Sapt. "So be it."

We mounted, drawing our swords, and waited silently for a minute or two. Then we heard the tramp of men on the drive the other side of the house. They came to a stand, and one cried:

"Now then, fetch him out!"

"Now!" whispered Sapt.

Driving the spurs into our horses, we rushed at a gallop round the house, and in a moment we were among the ruffians. Sapt told me afterwards that he killed a man, and I believe him; but I saw no more of him. With a cut I split the head of a fellow on a brown horse, and he fell to the ground. Then I found myself opposite a big man, and I was half conscious of another to my right. It was too warm to stay, and with a simultaneous action I drove my spurs into my horse again and my sword full into the big man's breast. His bullet whizzed past my ear—I could almost swear it touched it. I wrenched at the sword, but it would not come, and I dropped it and galloped after Sapt, whom I now saw about twenty yards ahead. I waved my hand in farewell and dropped it a second later with a yell, for a bullet had grazed my finger and I felt the blood. Old Sapt turned round in the saddle. Someone fired again, but they had no rifles, and we were out of range. Sapt fell to laughing.

"That's one to me and two to you, with decent luck," said he. "Little Josef will have company."

"Ay, they'll be a *partie carrée*," said I. My blood was up, and I rejoiced to have killed them.

"Well, a pleasant night's work to the rest!" said he. "I wonder if they noticed you?"

"The big fellow did; as I stuck him I heard him cry, 'The King!'"

"Good! good! Oh, we'll give Black Michael some work before we've done!"

Pausing an instant, we made a bandage for my wounded finger, which was bleeding freely and ached severely, the bone being much bruised. Then we rode on, asking of our good horses all that was in them. The excitement of the fight and of our great resolve died away, and we rode in gloomy silence. Day broke clear and cold. We found a farmer just up, and made him give us sustenance for ourselves and our horses. I, feigning a toothache, muffled my face closely. Then ahead again, till Strelsau lay before us. It was eight o'clock or nearing nine, and the gates were all open, as they always were save when the duke's caprice or intrigues shut them. We rode in by the same way as we had come out the evening before, all four of us—the men and the horses—wearied and jaded. The streets were even quieter than when we had gone; everyone was sleeping off last night's revelry, and we met hardly a soul till we reached the little gate of the Palace. There Sapt's old groom was waiting for us.

"Is all well, sir?" he asked.

"All's well," said Sapt, and the man, coming to see, took my hand to kiss.

"The King's hurt!" he cried.

"It's nothing," said I as I dismounted; "I caught my finger in the door."

"Remember—silence!" said Sapt. "Ah! but, my good Freyler, I do not need to tell you that!"

The old fellow shrugged his shoulders.

"All young men like to ride abroad now and again; why not the King?" said he; and Sapt's laugh left his opinion of my motives undisturbed.

"You should always trust a man," observed Sapt, fitting the key in the lock— "just as far as you must."

We went in and reached the dressing room. Flinging open the door, we saw Fritz von Tarlenheim stretched, fully dressed, on the sofa. He seemed to have been sleeping, but our entry woke him. He leapt to his feet, gave one glance at me, and with a joyful cry threw himself on his knees before me.

"Thank God, sire! thank God, you're safe!" he cried, stretching his hand up to catch hold of mine.

I confess that I was moved. This King, whatever his faults, made people love him. For a moment I could not bear to speak or break the poor fellow's illusion. But tough old Sapt had no such feeling. He slapped his hand on his thigh delightedly.

"Bravo, lad!" cried he. "We shall do!"

Fritz looked up in bewilderment. I held out my hand.

"You're wounded, sire!" he exclaimed.

"It's only a scratch," said I, "but—" I paused.

He rose to his feet with a bewildered air. Holding my hand, he looked me up and down, and down and up. Then suddenly he dropped my hand and reeled back.

"Where's the King? Where's the King?" he cried.

"Hush, you fool!" hissed Sapt. "Not so loud! Here's the King!"

A knock sounded on the door. Sapt seized me by the hand.

"Here, quick, to the bedroom! Off with your cap and boots. Get into bed. Cover everything up."

I did as I was bid. A moment later Sapt looked in, nodded, grinned, and introduced an extremely smart and deferential young gentleman, who came up to my bedside, bowing again and again, and informed me that he was of the household of the Princess Flavia, and that her Royal Highness had sent him especially to enquire how the King's health was after the fatigues which his Majesty had undergone yesterday.

"My best thanks, sir, to my cousin," said I; "and tell her Royal Highness that I was never better in my life."

"The King," added old Sapt (who, I began to find, loved a good lie for its own sake), "has slept without a break all night."

The young gentleman (he reminded me of *Osric* in "Hamlet") bowed himself out again. The farce was over, and Fritz von Tarlenheim's pale face recalled us to reality—though, in faith, the farce had to be reality for us now.

"Is the King dead?" he whispered.

"Please God, no," said I. "But he's in the hands of Black Michael!"

VIII. A Fair Cousin and a Dark Brother

A real King's life is perhaps a hard one; but a pretended King's is, I warrant, much harder. On the next day Sapt instructed me in my duties—what I ought to do and what I ought to know—for three hours; then I snatched breakfast, with Sapt still opposite me, telling me that the King always took white wine in the morning and was known to detest all highly seasoned dishes. Then came the Chancellor for another three hours; and to him I had to explain that the hurt to my finger (we turned that bullet to happy account) prevented me from writing—whence arose great to-do, hunting of precedents and so forth, ending in my "making my mark," and the Chancellor attesting it with a superfluity of solemn oaths. Then the French ambassador was introduced, to present his credentials; here my ignorance was of no importance, as the King would have been equally raw to the business (we worked through the whole *corps diplomatique* in the next few days, a demise of the Crown necessitating all this bother).

Then, at last, I was left alone. I called my new servant (we had chosen, to succeed poor Josef, a young man who had never known the King), had a brandy and soda brought to me, and observed to Sapt that I trusted that I might now have a rest.

Fritz von Tarlenheim was standing by.

"By heaven!" he cried, "we waste time. Aren't we going to throw Black Michael by the heels?"

"Gently, my son, gently," said Sapt, knitting his brows. "It would be a pleasure, but it might cost us dear. Would Michael fall and leave the King alive?"

"And," I suggested, "while the King is here in Strelsau, on his throne, what grievance has he against his dear brother Michael?"

"Are we to do nothing, then?"

"We're to do nothing stupid," growled Sapt.

"In fact, Fritz," said I, "I am reminded of a situation in one of our English plays—

'The Critic'—have you heard of it? Or, if you like, of two men, each covering the other with a revolver. For I can't expose Michael without exposing myself—"

"And the King," put in Sapt.

"And, hang me, if Michael won't expose himself if he tries to expose me!"

"It's very pretty," said old Sapt.

"If I'm found out," I pursued, "I will make a clean breast of it, and fight it out with the duke; but at present I'm waiting for a move from him."

"He'll kill the King," said Fritz.

"Not he," said Sapt.

"Half of the Six are in Strelsau," said Fritz.

"Only half? You're sure?" asked Sapt eagerly.

"Yes—only half."

"Then the King's alive, for the other three are guarding him!" cried Sapt.

"Yes—you're right!" exclaimed Fritz, his face brightening. "If the King were dead and buried they'd all be here with Michael. You know Michael's back, colonel?"

"I know, curse him!"

"Gentlemen, gentlemen," said I, "who are the Six?"

"I think you'll make their acquaintance soon," said Sapt. "They are six gentlemen whom Michael maintains in his household: they belong to him body and soul. There are three Ruritanians; then there's a Frenchman, a Belgian, and one of your countrymen."

"They'd all cut a throat if Michael told them," said Fritz.

"Perhaps they'll cut mine," I suggested.

"Nothing more likely," agreed Sapt. "Who are here, Fritz?"

"De Gautet, Bersonin, and Detchard."

"The foreigners! It's as plain as a pikestaff. He's brought them, and left the Ruritanians with the King: that's because he wants to commit the Ruritanians as deep as he can."

"They were none of them among our friends at the lodge, then?" I asked.

"I wish they had been," said Sapt wistfully. "They had been, not Six, but Four, by now."

I had already developed one attribute of royalty—a feeling that I need not reveal all my mind or my secret designs even to my intimate friends. I had fully resolved on my course of action. I meant to make myself as popular as I could, and at the same time to show no disfavour to Michael. By these means I hoped to allay the hostility of his adherents, and make it appear, if an open conflict came about, that he was ungrateful and not oppressed.

Yet an open conflict was not what I hoped for.

The King's interest demanded secrecy; and while secrecy lasted I had a fine game to play in Strelsau. Michael should not grow stronger for delay!

I ordered my horse, and, attended by Fritz von Tarlenheim, rode in the grand new avenue of the Royal Park, returning all the salutes which I received with punctilious politeness. Then I rode through a few of the streets, stopped and bought flowers of a pretty girl, paying her with a piece of gold; and then, having attracted the desired amount of attention (for I had a trail of half a thousand people after me), I rode to the residence of the Princess Flavia, and asked if she would receive me. This step created much interest, and was met with shouts of approval. The princess was very popular, and the Chancellor himself had not scrupled to hint to me that the more I pressed my suit, and the more rapidly I brought it to a prosperous conclusion, the stronger should I be in the affection of my subjects. The Chancellor, of course, did not understand the difficulties which lay in the way of following his loyal and excellent advice. However, I thought I could do no harm by calling; and in this view Fritz supported me with a cordiality that surprised me, until he confessed that he also had his motives for liking a visit to the princess' house, which motive was no other than a great desire to see the princess's lady in waiting and bosom friend, the Countess Helga von Strofzin.

Etiquette seconded Fritz's hopes. While I was ushered into the princess' room he remained with the countess in the antechamber: in spite of the people and servants who were hanging about I doubt not that they managed a *tête-à-tête*; but I had no leisure to think of them, for I was playing the most delicate move in all my difficult game. I had to keep the princess devoted to me—and yet indifferent to me; I had to show affection for her—and not feel it. I had to make love for another, and that to a girl who—princess or no princess—was the most beautiful I had ever seen. Well, I braced myself to the task, made no easier by the charming embarrassment with which I was received. How I succeeded in carrying out my programme will appear hereafter.

"You are gaining golden laurels," she said. "You are like the prince in Shakspere who was transformed by becoming King. But I'm forgetting you are King, sire."

"I ask you to speak nothing but what your heart tells you—and to call me nothing but my name."

She looked at me for a moment.

"Then I'm glad and proud, Rudolf," said she. "Why, as I told you, your very face is changed."

I acknowledged the compliment, but I disliked the topic; so I said:

"My brother is back, I hear. He made an excursion, didn't he?"

"Yes, he is here," she said, frowning a little.

"He can't stay long from Strelsau, it seems," I observed, smiling. "Well, we are all glad to see him. The nearer he is the better."

The princess glanced at me with a gleam of amusement in her eyes.

"Why, cousin? Is it that you can—"

"See better what he's doing? Perhaps," said I. "And why are you glad?"

"I didn't say I was glad," she answered.

"Some people say so for you."

"There are many insolent people," she said, with delightful haughtiness.

"Possibly you mean that I am one?"

"Your Majesty could not be," she said, courtesying in feigned deference, but adding, mischievously, after a pause: "Unless, that is—"

"Well, unless what?"

"Unless you tell me that I mind a snap of my fingers where the Duke of Strelsau is."

Really, I wished that I had been the King.

"You don't care where Cousin Michael—"

"Ah, Cousin Michael! I call him the Duke of Strelsau."

"You call him Michael when you meet him?"

"Yes—by the orders of your father."

"I see. And now by mine?"

"If those are your orders."

"Oh, decidedly! We must all be pleasant to our dear Michael."

"You order me to receive his friends, too, I suppose?"

"The Six?"

"You call them that, too?"

"To be in the fashion I do. But I order you to receive no one unless you like."

"Except yourself?"

"I pray for myself. I could not order."

As I spoke there came a cheer from the street. The princess ran to the window.

"It is he!" she cried. "It is—the Duke of Strelsau!"

I smiled, but said nothing. She returned to her seat. For a few moments we sat in silence. The noise outside subsided, but I heard the tread of feet in the anteroom. I began to talk on general subjects. This went on for some minutes. I wondered what had become of Michael, but it did not seem to be for me to interfere. All at once, to my great surprise, Flavia, clasping her hands, asked in an agitated voice:

"Are you wise to make him angry?"

"What? Who? How am I making him angry?"

"Why, by keeping him waiting."

"My dear cousin, I don't want to keep him—"

"Well, then, is he to come in?"

"Of course, if you wish it."

She looked at me curiously.

"How funny you are," she said. "Of course no one could be announced while I was with you."

Here was a charming attribute of royalty!

"An excellent etiquette!" I cried. "But I had clean forgotten it; and if I were alone with someone else couldn't you be announced?"

"You know as well as I do. I could be, because I am of the Blood"; and she still looked puzzled.

"I never could remember all these silly rules," said I rather feebly as I inwardly cursed Fritz for not posting me up. "But I'll repair my fault."

I jumped up, flung open the door, and advanced into the anteroom. Michael was sitting at a table, a heavy frown on his face. Everyone else was standing, save that impudent young dog Fritz, who was lounging easily in an armchair, and flirting with the Countess Helga. He leapt up as I entered, with a deferential alacrity that lent point to his former nonchalance. I had no difficulty in understanding that the duke might not like young Fritz.

I held out my hand, Michael took it, and I embraced him. Then I drew him with me into the inner room.

"Brother," I said, "if I had known you were here you should not have waited here a moment before I asked the princess to permit me to bring you to her."

He thanked me, but coldly. The man had many qualities, but he could not hide his feelings. A mere stranger could have seen that he hated me, and hated worse to see me with Princess Flavia; yet I am persuaded that he tried to conceal both feelings, and, further, that he tried to persuade me that he believed I was verily the King. I did not know, of course; but, unless the King were an impostor, at once cleverer and more audacious than I (and I began to think something of myself in that rôle), Michael could not believe that. And if he didn't how he must have loathed paying me deference, and hearing my "Michael" and my "Flavia"!

"Your hand is hurt, sire," he observed with concern.

"Yes; I was playing a game with a mongrel dog (I meant to stir him), and you know, brother, such have uncertain tempers."

He smiled sourly, and his dark eyes rested on me for a moment.

"But is there no danger from the bite?" cried Flavia anxiously.

"None from this," said I. "If I gave him a chance to bite deeper it would be different, cousin."

"But surely he has been destroyed?" said she.

"Not yet. We're waiting to see if his bite is harmful."

"And if it is?" asked Michael, with his sour smile.

"He'll be knocked on the head, brother," said I.

"You won't play with him any more?" urged Flavia.

"Perhaps I shall."

"He might bite again."

"Doubtless he'll try," said I, smiling.

Then, fearing Michael would say something which I must appear to resent (for, though I might show him my hate, I must seem to be full of favour), I began to compliment him on the magnificent condition of his regiment, and of their loyal greeting to me on the day of my coronation. Thence I passed to a rapturous description of the hunting lodge which he had lent me. But he rose suddenly to his feet. His temper was failing him, and as an excuse he said farewell. However, as he reached the door he stopped, saying:

"Three friends of mine are very anxious to have the honour of being presented to you, sire. They are here in the antechamber."

I joined him directly, passing my arm through his. The look on his face was honey to me. We entered the antechamber in fraternal fashion. Michael beckoned, and three men came forward.

"These gentlemen," said Michael, with a stately courtesy which, to do him justice, he could assume with perfect grace and ease, "are the loyalest and most devoted of your Majesty's servants, and are my very faithful and attached friends."

"On the last ground as much as the first," said I, "I am very pleased to see them."

They came one by one and kissed my hand—De Gautet, a tall, lean fellow, with hair standing straight up and waxed moustache; Bersonin, the Belgian, a portly man of middle height with a bald head (though he was not far past thirty); and last, the Englishman, Detchard, a narrow-faced fellow, with close-cut fair hair and a bronzed complexion. He was a finely made man, broad in the shoulder and slender in the hips. A good fighter, but a crooked customer, I put him down for. I spoke to him in English, with a slight foreign accent, and I swear the fellow smiled, though he hid the smile in an instant.

"So Mr. Detchard is in the secret," thought I.

Having got rid of my dear brother and his friends, I returned to make my adieu to my cousin. She was standing at the door. I bade her farewell, taking her hand in mine.

"Rudolf," she said, very low, "be careful, won't you?"

"Of what?"

"You know—I can't say. But think what your life is to—"

"Well, to—?"

"To Ruritania."

Was I right to play the part, or wrong to play the part? I know not; evil lay both ways, and I dared not tell her the truth.

"Only to Ruritania?" I asked softly.

A sudden flush spread over her incomparable face.

"To your friends, too," she said.

"Friends?"

"And to your cousin," she whispered, "and loving servant."

I could not speak. I kissed her hand, and went out cursing myself.

Outside I found Master Fritz, quite reckless of the footmen, playing at cat's-cradle with the Countess Helga.

"Hang it!" said he, "we can't always be plotting. Love claims his share."

"I'm inclined to think he does," said I; and Fritz, who had been by my side, dropped respectfully behind.

IX. A NEW USE FOR A TEA TABLE

If I were to detail the ordinary events of my daily life at this time they might prove instructive to people who are not familiar with the inside of palaces; if I revealed some of the secrets I learnt they might prove of interest to the statesmen of Europe. I intend to do neither of these things. I should be between the Scylla of dullness and the Charybdis of indiscretion, and I feel that I had far better confine myself strictly to the underground drama which was being played beneath the surface of Ruritanian politics. I need only say that the secret of my imposture defied detection. I made mistakes. I had bad minutes: it needed all the tact and graciousness whereof I was master to smooth over some apparent lapses of memory and unmindfulness of old acquaintances of which I was guilty. But I escaped, and I attributed my escape, as I have said before, most of all to the very audacity of the enterprise. It is my belief that, given the necessary physical likeness, it was far easier to pretend to be king of Ruritania than it would have been to personate my next-door neighbour.

One day Sapt came into my room. He threw me a letter, saying:

"That's for you—a woman's hand, I think. But I've some news for you first."

"What's that?"

"The King's at the Castle of Zenda," said he.

"How do you know?"

"Because the other half of Michael's Six are there. I had enquiries made, and they're all there—Lauengram, Krafstein, and young Rupert Hentzau: three rogues, too, on my honour, as fine as live in Ruritania."

"Well?"

"Well, Fritz wants you to march to the Castle with horse, foot, and artillery."

"And drag the moat?" I asked.

"That would be about it," grinned Sapt; "and we shouldn't find the King's body then."

"You think it's certain he's there?"

"Very probable. Besides the fact of those three being there, the drawbridge is kept up and no one goes in without an order from young Hentzau or Black Michael himself. We must tie Fritz up."

"I'll go to Zenda," said I.

"You're mad."

"Some day."

"Oh, perhaps. You'll very likely stay there, though, if you do."

"That may be, my friend," said I carelessly.

"His Majesty looks sulky," observed Sapt. "How's the love affair?"

"Damn you, hold your tongue!" I said.

He looked at me for a moment; then he lit his pipe. It was quite true that I was in a bad temper, and I went on perversely:

"Wherever I go I'm dodged by half a dozen fellows."

"I know you are; I send 'em," he replied composedly.

"What for?"

"Well," said Sapt, puffing away, "it wouldn't be exactly inconvenient for Black Michael if you disappeared. With you gone the old game that we stopped would be played—or he'd have a shot at it."

"I can take care of myself."

"De Gautet, Bersonin, and Detchard are in Strelsau; and any one of them, lad, would cut your throat as readily—as readily as I would Black Michael's and a deal more treacherously. What's the letter?"

I opened it and read it aloud:

"If the King desires to know what it deeply concerns the King to know let him do as this letter bids him. At the end of the New Avenue there stands a house in large grounds. The house has a portico, with a statue of a nymph on it. A wall encloses the garden; there is a gate in the wall at the back. At twelve o'clock to-night, if the King enters alone by that gate, turns to the right, and walks twenty yards, he will find a summerhouse, approached by a flight of six steps. If he mounts and enters, he will find someone who will tell him what touches most dearly his life and his throne. This is written by a faithful friend. He must be alone. If he neglects the invitation his life will be in danger. Let him show this to no one, or he will ruin a woman who loves him: Black Michael does not pardon."

"No," observed Sapt as I ended, "but he can dictate a very pretty letter."

I had arrived at the same conclusion, and was about to throw the letter away, when I saw there was more writing on the other side.

"Hallo! there's some more."

"If you hesitate" [the writer continued] "consult Colonel Sapt—"

"Eh!" exclaimed that gentleman, genuinely astonished. "Does she take me for a greater fool than you?"

I waved to him to be silent.

"Ask him what woman would do most to prevent the duke from marrying his cousin, and therefore most to prevent him becoming King? And ask if her name begins with—A."

I sprang to my feet. Sapt laid down his pipe.

"Antoinette de Mauban, by heaven!" I cried.

"How do you know?" asked Sapt.

I told him what I knew of the lady, and how I knew it. He nodded.

"It's so far true that she's had a great row with Michael," said he thoughtfully.

"If she would she could be useful," I said.

"I believe, though, that Michael wrote that letter."

"So do I, but I mean to know for certain. I shall go, Sapt."

"No, I shall go," said he.

"You may go as far as the gate."

"I shall go to the summerhouse."

"I'm hanged if you shall!"

I rose and leant my back against the mantelpiece.

"Sapt, I believe in that woman, and I shall go."

"I don't believe in any woman," said Sapt, "and you shan't go."

"I either go to the summerhouse or back to England," said I.

Sapt began to know exactly how far he could lead or drive, and when he must follow.

"We're playing against time," I added. "Every day we leave the King where he is there is fresh risk. Every day I masquerade like this there is fresh risk. Sapt, we must play high; we must force the game."

"So be it," he said, with a sigh.

To cut the story short, at half-past eleven that night Sapt and I mounted our horses. Fritz was again left on guard, our destination not being revealed to him. It was a very dark night. I wore no sword, but I carried a revolver, a long knife, and a bull's-eye lantern. We arrived outside the gate. I dismounted. Sapt held out his hand.

"I shall wait here," he said. "If I hear a shot I'll—"

"Stay where you are; it's the King's only chance. You mustn't come to grief too."

"You're right, lad. Good luck!"

I pressed the little gate. It yielded, and I found myself in a wild sort of shrubbery. There was a grass-grown path and, turning to the right as I had been bidden, I followed it cautiously. My lantern was closed, the revolver was in my hand. I heard not a sound. Presently a large dark object loomed out of the gloom ahead of me. It was the summerhouse. Reaching the steps, I mounted them and found myself confronted by a weak, rickety wooden door, which hung upon the latch. I pushed it open and walked in. A woman flew to me and seized my hand.

"Shut the door," she whispered.

I obeyed, and turned the light of my lantern on her. She was in evening dress, arrayed very sumptuously, and her dark striking beauty was marvellously displayed in the glare of the bull's-eye. The summerhouse was a bare little room, furnished only with a couple of chairs and a small iron table, such as one sees in a tea garden or an open-air café.

"Don't talk," she said. "We've no time. Listen! I know you, Mr. Rassendyll. I wrote that letter at the duke's orders."

"So I thought," said I.

"In twenty minutes three men will be here to kill you."

"Three—the three?"

"Yes. You must be gone by then. If not to-night you'll be killed—"

"Or they will."

"Listen, listen! When you're killed your body will be taken to a low quarter of the town. It will be found there. Michael will at once arrest all your friends—Colonel Sapt and Captain von Tarlenheim first—proclaim a state of siege in Strelsau, and send a messenger to Zenda. The other three will murder the King in the Castle, and the duke will proclaim either himself or the princess—himself if he is strong enough. Anyhow, he'll marry her, and become King in fact, and soon in name. Do you see?"

"It's a pretty plot. But why, madame, do you—?"

"Say I'm a Christian—or say I'm jealous. My God! shall I see him marry her? Now go; but remember—this is what I have to tell you—that never by night or by day are you safe. Three men follow you as a guard. Is it not so? Well, three follow them. Michael's three are never two hundred yards from you. Your life is not worth a moment if ever they find you alone. Now go. Stay, the gate will be guarded by now. Go down softly, go past the summerhouse, on for a hundred yards, and you'll find a ladder against the wall. Get over it and fly for your life."

"And you?" I asked.

"I have my game to play, too. If he finds out what I have done we shall not meet again. If not I may yet— But never mind. Go at once."

"But what will you tell him?"

"That you never came—that you saw through the trick."

I took her hand and kissed it.

"Madame," said I, "you have served the King well to-night. Where is he in the Castle?"

She sank her voice to a fearful whisper. I listened eagerly.

"Across the drawbridge you come to a heavy door; behind that lies— Hark! What's that?"

There were steps outside.

"They're coming! They're too soon! Heavens! they're too soon!" and she turned pale as death.

"They seem to me," said I, "to be in the nick of time."

"Close your lantern. See, there's a chink in the door. Can you see them?"

I put my eye to the chink. On the lowest step I saw three dim figures. I cocked my revolver. Antoinette hastily laid her hand on mine.

"You may kill one," said she. "But what then?"

A voice came from outside—a voice that spoke perfect English.

"Mr. Rassendyll," it said.

I made no answer.

"We want to talk to you. Will you promise not to shoot till we've done?"

"Have I the pleasure of addressing Mr. Detchard?" I said.

"Never mind names."

"Then let mine alone."

"All right, *sire*. I've an offer for you."

I still had my eye to the chink. The three had mounted two steps more; three revolvers pointed full at the door.

"Will you let us in? We pledge our honour to observe the truce."

"Don't trust them," whispered Antoinette.

"We can speak through the door," said I.

"But you might open it and fire," objected Detchard; "and though we should finish you, you might finish one of us. Will you give your honour not to fire while we talk?"

"Don't trust them," whispered Antoinette again.

A sudden idea struck me. I considered it for a moment. It seemed feasible.

"I give my honour not to fire before you do," said I; "but I won't let you in. Stand outside and talk."

"That's sensible," he said.

The three mounted the last step, and stood just outside the door. I laid my ear to the chink. I could hear no words, but Detchard's head was close to that of the taller of his companions (De Gautet, I guessed).

"H'm! Private communications," thought I. Then I said aloud:

"Well, gentlemen, what's the offer?"

"A safe conduct to the frontier, and fifty thousand pounds English."

"No, no," whispered Antoinette in the lowest of whispers. "They are treacherous."

"That seems handsome," said I, reconnoitring through the chink. They were all close together, just outside the door now.

I had probed the hearts of the ruffians, and I did not need Antoinette's warning. They meant to "rush" me as soon as I was engaged in talk.

"Give me a minute to consider," said I; and I thought I heard a laugh outside.

I turned to Antoinette.

"Stand up close to the wall, out of the line of fire from the door," I whispered.

"What are you going to do?" she asked in fright.

"You'll see," said I.

I took up the little iron table. It was not very heavy for a man of my strength, and I held it by the legs. The top, protruding in front of me, made a complete screen for my head and body. I fastened my closed lantern to my belt and put my revolver in a handy pocket. Suddenly I saw the door move ever so slightly—perhaps it was the wind, perhaps it was a hand trying it outside.

I drew back as far as I could from the door, holding the table in the position that I have described. Then I called out:

"Gentlemen, I accept your offer, relying on your honour. If you will open the door—"

"Open it yourself," said Detchard.

"It opens outwards," said I. "Stand back a little, gentlemen, or I shall hit you when I open it."

I went and fumbled with the latch. Then I stole back to my place on tiptoe.

"I can't open it!" I cried. "The latch has caught."

"Tut! I'll open it!" cried Detchard. "Nonsense, Bersonin, why not? Are you afraid of one man?"

I smiled to myself. An instant later the door was flung back. The gleam of a lantern showed me the three close together outside, their revolvers levelled. With a shout I charged at my utmost pace across the summerhouse and through the doorway. Three shots rang out and battered into my shield. Another moment, and I leapt out and the table caught them full and square, and in a tumbling, swearing, struggling mass they and I and that brave table rolled down the steps of the summerhouse to the ground below. Antoinette de Mauban shrieked, but I rose to my feet, laughing aloud.

De Gautet and Bersonin lay like men stunned. Detchard was under the table, but as I rose he pushed it from him and fired again. I raised my revolver and took a snap shot. I heard him curse, and then I ran like a hare, laughing as I went, past the summerhouse and along by the wall. I heard steps behind me, and, turning round, I fired again for luck. The steps ceased.

"Please God," said I, "she told me the truth about the ladder!" for the wall was high and topped with iron spikes.

Yes, there it was. I was up and over in a minute. Doubling back, I saw the horses. Then I heard a shot. It was Sapt. He had heard us and was battling and raging with the locked gate, hammering it and firing into the keyhole like a man possessed. He had quite forgotten that he was not to take part in the fight. Whereat I laughed again, and said as I clapped him on the shoulder:

"Come home to bed, old chap. I've got the finest tea-table story that ever you heard!"

He started and cried: "You're safe!" and wrung my hand. But a moment later he added:

"And what the devil are you laughing at?"

"Four gentlemen round a tea table," said I, laughing still, for it had been uncommonly ludicrous to see the formidable three altogether routed and scattered with no more deadly weapon than an ordinary tea table.

Moreover, you will observe that I had honourably kept my word and not fired till they did.

X. A GREAT CHANCE FOR A VILLAIN

It was the custom that the Prefect of Police should send every afternoon a report to me on the condition of the capital and the feeling of the people: the document included also an account of the movements of any persons whom the police had received instructions to watch. Since I had been in Strelsau Sapt had been in the habit of reading the report and telling me any items of interest which it might contain. On the day after my adventure in the summerhouse he came in as I was playing a hand of écarté with Fritz von Tarlenheim.

"The report is rather full of interest this afternoon," he observed, sitting down.

"Do you find," I asked, "any mention of a certain fracas?"

He shook his head with a smile.

"I find this first," he said: "'His Highness the Duke of Strelsau left the city (so far as it appears, suddenly), accompanied by several of his household. His destination is believed to be the Castle of Zenda, but the party travelled by road and not by train. MM. De Gautet, Bersonin, and Detchard followed an hour later, the last named carrying his arm in a sling. The cause of his wound is not known, but it is suspected that he has fought a duel, probably incidental to a love affair.'"

"That is remotely true," I observed, very well pleased to find that I had left my mark on the fellow.

"Then we come to this," pursued Sapt, "'Madame de Mauban, whose movements have been watched according to instructions, left by train at midday. She took a ticket for Dresden—'"

"It's an old habit of hers," said I.

"'The Dresden train stops at Zenda.' An acute fellow, this. And finally listen to this: 'The state of feeling in the city is not satisfactory. The King is much criticised' (you know he's told to be quite frank) 'for taking no steps about his marriage. From enquiries among the *entourage* of the Princess Flavia her Royal Highness is believed to be deeply offended by the remissness of his Majesty. The common people are coupling her name with that of the Duke of Strelsau, and the duke gains much popularity from the suggestion. I have caused the announcement that the King gives a ball to-night in honour of the princess to be widely diffused, and the effect is good.'"

"That is news to me," said I.

"Oh, the preparations are all made!" laughed Fritz. "I've seen to that."

Sapt turned to me and said, in a sharp, decisive voice:

"You must make love to her to-night, you know."

"I think it very likely I shall if I see her alone," said I. "Hang it, Sapt, you don't suppose I find it difficult?"

Fritz whistled a bar or two; then he said: "You'll find it only too easy. Look here, I hate telling you this, but I must. The Countess Helga told me that the princess had become most attached to the King. Since the coronation her feelings have undergone a marked development. It's quite true that she is deeply wounded by the King's apparent neglect."

"Here's a kettle of fish!" I groaned.

"Tut, tut!" said Sapt. "I suppose you've made pretty speeches to a girl before now? That's all she wants."

Fritz, himself a lover, understood better my distress. He laid his hand on my shoulder, but said nothing.

"I think, though," pursued that cold-blooded old Sapt, "that you'd better make your offer to-night."

"Good heavens!"

"Or, any rate, go near it; and I shall send a 'semi-official' to the papers."

"I'll do nothing of the sort—no more will you!" said I. "I utterly refuse to take part in making a fool of the princess."

Sapt looked at me with his small keen eyes. A slow, cunning smile passed over his face.

"All right, lad, all right," said he. "We mustn't press you too hard. Soothe her down a bit, if you can, you know. Now for Michael!"

"Oh, damn Michael!" said I. "He'll do to-morrow. Here, Fritz, come for a stroll in the garden."

Sapt at once yielded. His rough manner covered a wonderful tact—and as I came to recognize more and more, a remarkable knowledge of human nature. Why did he urge me so little about the princess? Because he knew that her beauty and my ardour would carry me further than all his arguments—and that the less I thought about the thing the more likely was I to do it. He must have seen the unhappiness he might bring on the princess; but that went for nothing with him. Can I say, confidently, that he was wrong? If the King were restored the princess must turn to him, either knowing or not knowing the change. And if the King were not restored to us? It was a subject that we had never yet spoken of. But I had an idea that, in such a case, Sapt meant to seat me on the throne of Ruritania for the term of my life. He would have set Satan himself there sooner than that pupil of his, Black Michael.

The ball was a sumptuous affair. I opened it by dancing a quadrille with Flavia; then I waltzed with her. Curious eyes and eager whispers attended us. We went in to supper; and halfway through, I, half mad by then, for her glance had answered mine, and her quick breathing met my stammered sentences—I rose in my place before all the brilliant crowd, and taking the Red Rose that I wore, flung the ribbon with its jewelled badge round her neck. In a tumult of applause I sat down; I saw Sapt smiling over his wine, and Fritz frowning. The rest of the meal passed in silence; neither Flavia nor I could speak. Fritz touched me on the shoulder, and I rose, gave her my arm, and walked down the hall into a little room, where coffee was served to us. The gentlemen and ladies in attendance withdrew, and we were alone.

The little room had French windows opening on the gardens. The night was fine, cool, and fragrant. Flavia sat down, and I stood opposite her. I was struggling with myself; if she had not looked at me I believe that even then I should have won my fight. But suddenly, involuntarily, she gave me one brief glance—a glance of question, hurriedly turned aside; a blush that the question had overcome spread over her cheek, and she caught her breath.

Ah, if you had seen her! I forgot the King in Zenda. I forgot the King in Strelsau. She was a princess—and I an impostor. Do you think I remembered that? I threw myself on my knee and seized her hands in mine. I said nothing. Why should I? The soft sounds of the night set my wooing to a wordless melody as I pressed my kisses on her lips.

She pushed me from her, crying suddenly:

"Ah! is it true? or is it only because you must?"

"It's true!" I said in low, smothered tones—"true that I love you more than life—or truth—or honour!"

She set no meaning to my words, treating them as one of love's sweet extravagances. She came close to me, and whispered:

"Oh, if you were not the King! Then I could show you how I love you! How is it that I love you now, Rudolf?"

"Now?"

"You just lately, I—I never did before."

Pure triumph filled me. It was I—Rudolf Rassendyll—who had won her! I caught her round the waist.

"You didn't love me before?" I asked.

She looked up into my face, smiling, as she whispered:

"It must have been your Crown. I felt it first on the Coronation Day."

"Never before?" I asked eagerly.

She laughed low.

"You speak as if you would be pleased to hear me say 'Yes' to that," she said.

"Would 'Yes' be true?"

"Yes," I just heard her breathe, and she went on in an instant: "Be careful, Rudolf; be careful, dear. He will be mad now."

"What, Michael? If Michael were the worst—"

"What worse is there?"

There was yet a chance for me. Controlling myself with a mighty effort, I took my hands off her and stood a yard or two away. I remember now the note of the wind in the elm trees outside.

"If I were not the King," I began, "if I were only a private gentleman—"

Before I could finish, her hand was in mine.

"If you were a convict in the prison of Strelsau you would be my King," she said.

And under my breath I groaned, "God forgive me!" and, holding her hand in mine, I said again:

"If I were not the King—"

"Hush, hush!" she whispered. "I don't deserve it—I don't deserve to be doubted. Ah, Rudolf! does a woman who marries without love look on the man as I look on you?"

And she hid her face from me.

For more than a minute we stood there together; and I, even with my arm about her, summoned up what honour and conscience her beauty and the toils that I was in had left me.

"Flavia," I said, in a strange, dry voice that seemed not my own, "I am not—"

As I spoke—as she raised her eyes to me—there was a heavy step on the gravel outside, and a man appeared at the window. A little cry burst from Flavia as she sprang back from me. My half-finished sentence died on my lips. Sapt stood there, bowing low, but with a stern frown on his face.

"A thousand pardons, sire," said he, "but his Eminence the Cardinal has waited this quarter of an hour to offer his respectful adieu to your Majesty."

I met his eye full and square; and I read in it an angry warning. How long he had been a listener I knew not, but he had come in upon us in the nick of time.

"We must not keep his Eminence waiting," said I.

But Flavia, in whose love there lay no shame, with radiant eyes and blushing face held out her hand to Sapt. She said nothing, but no man could have missed her meaning who had ever seen a woman in the exaltation of love. A sour, yet sad, smile passed over the old soldier's face, and there was tenderness in his voice as, bending to kiss her hand, he said:

"In joy and sorrow, in good times and bad, God save your Royal Highness!"

He paused and added, glancing at me and drawing himself up to military erectness:

"But before all comes the King—God save the King!"

And Flavia caught at my hand and kissed it, murmuring:

"Amen! Good God, Amen!"

We went into the ballroom again. Forced to receive adieus, I was separated from Flavia; everyone, when he left me, went to her. Sapt was out and in of the throng, and where he had been glances, smiles, and whispers were rife. I doubted not that, true to his relentless purpose, he was spreading the news that he had learnt. To uphold the Crown and beat Black Michael—that was his one resolve. Flavia, myself—ay, and the real King in Zenda, were pieces in his game; and pawns have no business with passions. Not even at the walls of the Palace did he stop; for when at last I handed Flavia down the broad marble steps and into her carriage there was a great crowd awaiting us, and we were welcomed with deafening cheers. What could I do? Had I spoken then they would have refused to believe that I was not the King; they might have believed that the King had run mad. By Sapt's devices and my own ungoverned passion I had been forced on, and the way back had closed behind me; and the passion still drove me in the same direction as the devices seduced me. I faced all Strelsau that night as the King and the accepted suitor of the Princess Flavia.

At last, at three in the morning, when the cold light of dawning day began to steal in, I was in my dressing room, and Sapt alone was with me. I sat like a man dazed, staring into the fire; he puffed at his pipe; Fritz was gone to bed, having almost refused to speak to me. On the table by me lay a rose; it had been in Flavia's dress, and as we parted she had kissed it and given it to me.

Sapt advanced his hand towards the rose, but, with a quick movement, I shut mine down upon it.

"That's mine," I said, "not yours—nor the King's either."

"We struck a good blow for the King to-night," said he.

I turned on him fiercely.

"What's to prevent me striking a blow for myself?" I said.

He nodded his head.

"I know what's in your mind," he said. "Yes, lad; but you're bound in honour."

"Have you left me any honour?"

"Oh, come, to play a little trick on a girl—"

"You can spare me that. Colonel Sapt, if you would not have me utterly a villain—if you would not have your King rot in Zenda, while Michael and I play for the great stake outside— You follow me?"

"Ay, I follow you."

"We must act, and quickly! You saw to-night—you heard to-night—"

"I did," said he.

"Your cursed acuteness told you what I should do. Well, leave me here a week—and there's another problem for you. Do you find the answer?"

"Yes, I find it," he answered, frowning heavily. "But if you did that you'd have to fight me first—and kill me."

"Well, and if I had—or a score of men? I tell you, I could raise all Strelsau on you in an hour, and choke you with your lies—yes, your mad lies—in your mouth."

"It's gospel truth," he said—"thanks to my advice, you could."

"I could marry the princess, and send Michael and his brother together to—"

"I'm not denying it, lad," said he.

"Then, in God's name," I cried, stretching out my hands to him, "let us go to Zenda and crush this Michael, and bring the King back to his own again."

The old fellow stood and looked at me for full a minute.

"And the princess?" he said.

I bowed my head to meet my hands, and crushed the rose between my fingers and my lips.

I felt his hand on my shoulder, and his voice sounded husky as he whispered low in my ear:

"Before God, you're the finest Elphberg of them all. But I have eaten of the King's bread, and I am the King's servant. Come, we will go to Zenda!"

And I looked up and caught him by the hand. And the eyes of both of us were wet.

XI. Hunting a Very Big Boar

The terrible temptation which was assailing me will now be understood. I could so force Michael's hand that he must kill the King. I was in a position to bid him defiance and tighten my grasp on the crown—not for its own sake, but because the King of Ruritania was to wed the Princess Flavia. What of Sapt and Fritz? Ah! but a man cannot be held to write down in cold blood the wild and black thoughts that storm his brain when an uncontrolled passion has battered a breach for them. Yet, unless he sets up as a saint, he need not hate himself for them. He is better employed, as it humbly seems to me, in giving thanks that power to resist was vouchsafed to him than in fretting over wicked impulses which come unsought and extort an unwilling hospitality from the weakness of our nature.

It was a fine bright morning when I walked, unattended, to the princess' house, carrying a nosegay in my hand. Policy made excuses for love, and every attention that I paid her, while it riveted my own chains, bound closer to me the people of the great city, who worshipped her. I found Fritz's *inamorata*, the Countess Helga, gathering blooms in the garden for her mistress' wear, and prevailed on her to take mine in their place. The girl was rosy with happiness, for Fritz, in his turn, had not wasted his evening, and no dark shadow hung over his wooing, save the hatred which the Duke of Strelsau was known to bear him.

"And that," she said, with a mischievous smile, "your Majesty has made of no moment. Yes, I will take the flowers; shall I tell you, sire, what is the first thing the princess does with them?"

We were talking on a broad terrace that ran along the back of the house, and a window above our heads stood open.

"Madame!" cried the countess merrily, and Flavia herself looked out. I bared my head and bowed. She wore a white gown, and her hair was loosely gathered in a knot. She kissed her hand to me, crying:

"Bring the King up, Helga; I'll give him some coffee."

The countess, with a gay glance, led the way, and took me into Flavia's morning room. And, left alone, we greeted one another as lovers are wont. Then the princess laid two letters before me. One was from Black Michael—a most courteous request that she would honour him by spending a day at his Castle of Zenda, as had been her custom once a year in the summer, when the place and its gardens were in the height of their great beauty. I threw the letter down in disgust, and Flavia laughed at me. Then, growing grave again, she pointed to the other sheet.

"I don't know who that comes from," she said. "Read it."

I knew in a moment. There was no signature at all this time, but the handwriting was the same as that which had told me of the snare in the summerhouse: it was Antoinette de Mauban's.

> I have no cause to love you [it ran], but God forbid that you should fall into the power of the duke. Accept no invitations of his. Go nowhere without a large guard—a regiment is not too much to make you safe. Show this, if you can, to him who reigns in Strelsau.

"Why doesn't it say 'the King'?" asked Flavia, leaning over my shoulder, so that the ripple of her hair played on my cheek. "Is it a hoax?"

"As you value life, and more than life, my queen," I said, "obey it to the very letter. A regiment shall camp round your house to-day. See that you do not go out unless well guarded."

"An order, sire?" she asked, a little rebellious.

"Yes, an order, madame—if you love me."

"Ah!" she cried; and I could not but kiss her.

"You know who sent it?" she asked.

"I guess," said I. "It is from a good friend—and I fear, an unhappy woman. You must be ill, Flavia, and unable to go to Zenda. Make your excuses as cold and formal as you like."

"So you feel strong enough to anger Michael?" she said, with a proud smile.

"I'm strong enough for anything while you are safe," said I.

Soon I tore myself away from her, and then, without consulting Sapt, I took my way to the house of Marshal Strakencz. I had seen something of the old general, and I liked and trusted him. Sapt was less enthusiastic, but I had learnt by now that Sapt was best pleased when he could do everything, and jealousy played some part in his views. As things were now, I had more work than Sapt and Fritz could manage, for they must come with me to Zenda, and I wanted a man to guard what I loved most in all the world, and suffer me to set about my task of releasing the King with a quiet mind.

The Marshal received me with most loyal kindness. To some extent I took him into my confidence. I charged him with the care of the princess, looking him full and significantly in the face as I bade him let no one from her cousin the duke approach her, unless he himself were there and a dozen of his men with him.

"You may be right, sire," said he, shaking his grey head sadly. "I have known better men than the duke do worse things than that for love."

I could quite appreciate the remark, but I said:

"There's something beside love, Marshal. Love's for the heart; is there nothing my brother might like for his head?"

"I pray that you wrong him, sire."

"Marshal, I'm leaving Strelsau for a few days. Every evening I will send a courier to you. If for three days none comes you will publish an order which I will give you, depriving Duke Michael of the governorship of Strelsau and appointing you in his place. You will declare a state of siege. Then you will send word to Michael that you demand an audience of the King— You follow me?"

"Ay, sire."

"In twenty-four hours. If he does not produce the King"—I laid my hand on his knee—"then the King is dead, and you will proclaim the next heir. You know who that is?"

"The Princess Flavia."

"And swear to me, on your faith and honour, and by the fear of the living God, that you will stand by her to the death, and kill that reptile, and seat her where I sit now."

"On my faith and honour, and by the fear of God, I swear it! And may Almighty God preserve your Majesty, for I think that you go on an errand of danger."

"I hope that no life more precious than mine may be demanded," said I, rising. Then I held out my hand to him.

"Marshal," I said, "in days to come, it may be—I know not—that you will hear strange things of the man who speaks to you now. Let him be what he may, and who he may, what say you of the manner in which he has borne himself as King in Strelsau?"

The old man, holding my hand, spoke to me, man to man.

"I have known many of the Elphbergs," said he, "and I have seen you. And, happen what may, you have borne yourself as a wise King and a brave man; ay, and you have proved as courteous a gentleman and as gallant a lover as any that have been of the House."

"Be that my epitaph," said I, "when the time come that another sits on the throne of Ruritania."

"God send a far day, and may I not see it!" said he.

I was much moved, and the Marshal's worn face twitched. I sat down and wrote my order.

"I can hardly yet write," said I; "my finger is stiff still."

It was, in fact, the first time that I had ventured to write more than a signature; and in spite of the pains I had taken to learn the King's hand I was not yet perfect in it.

"Indeed, sire," he said, "it differs a little from your ordinary handwriting. It is unfortunate, for it may lead to a suspicion of forgery."

"Marshal," said I, with a laugh, "what use are the guns of Strelsau if they can't assuage a little suspicion?"

He smiled grimly and took the paper.

"Colonel Sapt and Fritz von Tarlenheim go with me," I continued.

"You go to seek the duke?" he asked in a low tone.

"Yes, the duke, and someone else of whom I have need and who is at Zenda," I replied.

"I wish I could go with you," he cried, tugging at his white moustache. "I'd like to strike a blow for you and your crown."

"I leave you what is more than my life and more than my crown," said I, "because you are the man I trust more than all others in Ruritania."

"I will deliver her to you safe and sound," said he, "and, failing that, I will make her queen."

We parted, and I returned to the Palace and told Sapt and Fritz what I had done. Sapt had a few faults to find and a few grumbles to utter. This was merely what I expected, for Sapt liked to be consulted beforehand, not informed afterwards; on the whole, he approved of my plans, and his spirits rose high as the hour of action drew nearer and nearer. Fritz, too, was ready; though he, poor fellow, risked more than Sapt did, for he was a lover, and his happiness hung in the scale. Yet how I envied him! For the triumphant issue which would crown him with happiness and unite him to his mistress, the success for which we were bound to hope and strive and struggle, meant to me sorrow more certain and greater than if I were doomed to fail. He understood something of this, for when we were alone (save for old Sapt, who was smoking at the other end of the room) he passed his arm through mine, saying:

"It's hard for you. Don't think I don't trust you; I know you have nothing but true thoughts in your heart."

But I turned away from him, thankful that he could not see what my heart held, but only be witness to the deeds that my hands were to do.

Yet even he did not understand, for he had not dared to lift his eyes to the Princess Flavia, as I had lifted mine.

Our plans were now all made, even as we proceeded to carry them out, and as they will hereafter appear. The next morning we were to start on the hunting excursion. I had made all arrangements for being absent, and now there was only one thing left to do—the hardest, the most heart-breaking. As evening fell I drove through the busy streets to Flavia's residence. I was recognized as I went and heartily cheered. I played my part, and made shift to look the happy lover. In spite of my depression I was almost amused at the coolness and delicate *hauteur* with which my sweet lover received me. She had heard that the King was leaving Strelsau on a hunting expedition.

"I regret that we cannot amuse your Majesty here in Strelsau," she said, tapping her foot lightly on the floor. "I would have offered you more entertainment, but I was foolish enough to think—"

"Well, what?" I asked, leaning over her.

"That just for a day or two, after—after last night—you might be happy without much gaiety"; and she turned pettishly from me, as she added, "I hope the boars will be more engrossing."

"I'm going after a very big boar," said I; and, because I could not help it, I began to play with her hair, but she moved her head away.

"Are you offended with me?" I asked in feigned surprise, for I could not resist tormenting her a little. I had never seen her angry, and every fresh aspect of her was a delight to me.

"What right have I to be offended? True, you said last night that every hour away from me was wasted. But a very big boar! that's a different thing."

"Perhaps the boar will hunt me," I suggested. "Perhaps, Flavia, he'll catch me."

She made no answer.

"You are not touched even by that danger?"

Still she said nothing; and I, stealing round, found her eyes full of tears.

"You weep for my danger?"

Then she spoke very low:

"This is like what you used to be; but not like the King— the King I—I have come to love!"

With a sudden great groan I caught her to my heart.

"My darling!" I cried, forgetting everything but her, "did you dream that I left you to go hunting?"

"What then, Rudolf? Ah! you're not going—?"

"Well, it is hunting. I go to seek Michael in his lair."

She had turned very pale.

"So you see, sweet, I was not so poor a lover as you thought me. I shall not be long gone."

"You will write to me, Rudolf?"

I was weak, but I could not say a word to stir suspicion in her.

"I'll send you all my heart every day," said I.

"And you'll run no danger?"

"None that I need not."

"And when will you be back? Ah, how long will it be!"

"When shall I be back?" I repeated.

"Yes, yes! Don't be long, dear, don't be long. I shan't sleep while you're away."

"I don't know when I shall be back," said I.

"Soon, Rudolf, soon?"

"God knows, my darling. But if never—"

"Hush, hush!" and she pressed her lips to mine.

"If never," I whispered, "you must take my place; you'll be the only one of the House then. You must reign, and not weep for me."

For a moment she drew herself up like a very queen.

"Yes, I will!" she said. "I will reign. I will do my part; though all my life will be empty and my heart dead, yet I'll do it!"

She paused, and sinking against me again, wailed softly:

"Come soon! come soon!"

Carried away, I cried loudly:

"As God lives, I—yes, I myself—will see you once more before I die!"

"What do you mean?" she exclaimed with wondering eyes; but I had no answer for her, and she gazed at me with her wondering eyes.

I dared not ask her to forget; she would have found it an insult. I could not tell her then who and what I was. She was weeping and I had but to dry her tears.

"Shall a man not come back to the loveliest lady in all the wide world?" said I. "A thousand Michaels should not keep me from you!"

She clung to me a little comforted.

"You won't let Michael hurt you?"

"No, sweetheart."

"Or keep you from me?"

"No, sweetheart."

"Nor anyone else?"

And again I answered:

"No, sweetheart."

Yet there was one—not Michael—who, if he lived, must keep me from her; and for whose life I was going forth to stake my own. And his figure—the lithe, buoyant figure I had met in the woods of Zenda—the dull, inert mass I had left in the cellar of the hunting lodge—seemed to rise, double-shaped, before me, and to come between us, thrusting itself in even where she lay, pale, exhausted, fainting, in my arms, and yet looking up at me with those eyes that bore such love as I have never seen, and haunt me now, and will till the ground closes over me—and (who knows?) perhaps beyond.

XII. I RECEIVE A VISITOR AND BAIT A HOOK

About five miles from Zenda, on the opposite side from that on which the Castle was situated, there lies a large tract of wood. It is rising ground, and in the centre of the demesne, on the top of the hill, stands a fine modern *château*, the property of a distant kinsman of Fritz's, the Count Stanislas von Tarlenheim. Count Stanislas himself was a student and a recluse. He seldom visited the house, and had, on Fritz's request, very readily and courteously offered me its hospitality for myself and my party. This, then, was our destination; chosen ostensibly for the sake of the boar hunting (for the wood was carefully preserved, and boars, once common all over Ruritania, were still to be found there in considerable numbers), really because it brought us within striking distance of the Duke of Strelsau's more magnificent dwelling on the other side of the town. A large party of servants, with horses and luggage, started early in the morning; we followed at midday, travelling by train for thirty miles, and then mounting our horses to ride the remaining distance to the *château*.

We were a gallant party. Besides Sapt and Fritz, I was accompanied by ten gentlemen. Every one of them had been carefully chosen, and no less carefully sounded by my two friends, and all were devotedly attached to the person of the King. They were told a part of the truth. The attempt on my life in the summerhouse was revealed to them as a spur to their loyalty and an incitement against Michael. They were also informed that a friend of the King's was suspected to be forcibly confined within the Castle of Zenda. His rescue was one of the objects of the expedition; but, it was added, the King's main desire was to carry into effect certain steps against his treacherous brother, as to the precise nature of which they could not at present be further enlightened. Enough that the King commanded their services and would rely on their devotion when occasion arose to call for it. Young, well bred, brave, and loyal, they asked no more. They were ready to prove their dutiful obedience, and prayed for a fight as the best and most exhilarating mode of showing it.

Thus the scene was shifted from Strelsau to the *château* of Tarlenheim and Castle of Zenda which frowned at us across the valley. I tried to shift my thoughts also, to forget my love, and to bend all my energies to the task before me. It was to get the King out of the Castle alive. Force was useless: in some trick lay the chance; and I had already an inkling of what we must do. But I was terribly hampered by the publicity which attended my movements. Michael must know by now of my expedition; and I knew Michael too well to suppose that his eyes would be blinded by the feint of the boar hunt. He would understand very well what the real quarry was. That, however, must be risked—that and all it might mean; for Sapt, no less than myself, recognized that the present state of things had become unendurable. And there was one thing that I dared to calculate on—not, as I now know, without warrant. It was this—that Black Michael would not believe that I meant well by the King. He could not appreciate—I will not say an honest man, for the thoughts of my own heart have been revealed—but a man acting honestly. He saw my opportunity as I had seen it, as Sapt had seen it; he knew the princess—nay (and I declare that a sneaking sort of pity for him invaded me), in his way he loved her; he would think that Sapt and Fritz could be bribed, so the bribe was large enough. Thinking thus, would he kill the King, my rival and my danger? Ay, verily, that he would, with as little compunction as he would kill a rat. But he would kill Rudolf Rassendyll first, if he could; and nothing but the certainty of being utterly damned by the release of the King alive and his restoration to the throne would drive him to throw away the trump card which he held in reserve to baulk the supposed game of the impudent impostor Rassendyll. Musing on all this as I rode along, I took courage.

Michael knew of my coming, sure enough. I had not been in the house an hour when an imposing Embassy arrived from him. He did not quite reach the impudence of sending my would-be assassins, but he sent the other three of his famous Six—the three Ruritanian gentlemen—Lauengram, Krafstein, and Rupert Hentzau. A fine, strapping trio they were, splendidly horsed and admirably equipped. Young Rupert, who looked a dare-devil, and could not have been more than twenty-two or twenty-three, took the lead, and made us the neatest speech, wherein my devoted subject and loving brother Michael of Strelsau, prayed me to pardon him for not paying his addresses in person, and, further, for not putting his Castle at my disposal; the reason for both of these apparent derelictions being that he and several of his servants lay sick of scarlet fever, and were in a very sad, and also a very infectious, state. So declared young Rupert with an insolent smile on his curling upper lip and a toss of his thick hair—he was a handsome villain, and the gossip ran that many a lady had troubled her heart for him already.

"If my brother has scarlet fever," said I, "he is nearer my complexion than he is wont to be, my lord. I trust he does not suffer?"

"He is able to attend to his affairs, sire."

"I hope all beneath your roof are not sick. What of my good friends De Gautet, Bersonin, and Detchard? I heard the last had suffered a hurt."

Lauengram and Krafstein looked glum and uneasy, but young Rupert's smile grew broader.

"He hopes soon to find a medicine for it, sire," he answered.

And I burst out laughing, for I knew what medicine Detchard longed for—it is called Revenge.

"You will dine with us, gentlemen?" I asked.

Young Rupert was profuse in apologies. They had urgent duties at the Castle.

"Then," said I, with a wave of my hand, "to our next meeting, gentlemen. May it make us better acquainted!"

"We will pray your Majesty for an early opportunity," quoth Rupert airily; and he strode past Sapt with such jeering scorn on his face that I saw the old fellow clench his fist and scowl black as night.

For my part, if a man must needs be a knave I would have him a debonair knave, and I liked Rupert Hentzau better than his long-faced, close-eyed companions. It makes your sin no worse, as I conceive, to do it à la mode and stylishly.

Now it was a curious thing that on this first night, instead of eating the excellent dinner my cooks had prepared for me, I must needs leave my gentlemen to eat it alone, under Sapt's presiding care, and ride myself with Fritz to the town of Zenda and a certain little inn that I knew of. There was little danger in the excursion; the evenings were long and light, and the road this side of Zenda well frequented. So off we rode, with a groom behind us. I muffled myself up in a big cloak.

"Fritz," said I as we entered the town, "there's an uncommonly pretty girl at this inn."

"How do you know?" he asked.

"Because I've been there," said I.

"Since—" he began.

"No. Before," said I.

"But they'll recognize you?"

"Well, of course they will. Now don't argue, my good fellow, but listen to me. We're two gentlemen of the King's household, and one of us has a toothache. The other will order a private room and dinner, and further, a bottle of the best wine for the sufferer. And if he be as clever a fellow as I take him for the pretty girl and no other will wait on us."

"What if she won't?" objected Fritz.

"My dear Fritz," said I, "if she won't for you she will for me."

We were at the inn. Nothing of me but my eyes was visible as I walked in. The landlady received us; two minutes later my little friend (ever, I fear me, on the lookout for such guests as might prove amusing) made her appearance. Dinner and the wine were ordered. I sat down in the private room. A minute later Fritz came in.

"She's coming," he said.

"If she were not, I should have to doubt the Countess Helga's taste."

She came in. I gave her time to set the wine down—I didn't want it dropped. Fritz poured out a glass and gave it to me.

"Is the gentleman in great pain?" the girl asked sympathetically.

"The gentleman is no worse than when he saw you last," said I, throwing away my cloak.

She started with a little shriek. Then she cried:

"It was the King, then! I told mother so the moment I saw his picture. Oh, sir, forgive me!"

"Faith, you gave me nothing that hurt much," said I.

"But the things we said!"

"I forgive them for the thing you did."

"I must go and tell mother."

"Stop," said I, assuming a graver air. "We are not here for sport to-night. Go and bring dinner, and not a word of the King being here."

She came back in a few minutes, looking grave, yet very curious.

"Well, how is Johann?" I asked, beginning my dinner.

"Oh, that fellow, sir—my lord King, I mean!"

"'Sir' will do, please. How is he?"

"We hardly see him now, sir."

"And why not?"

"I told him he came too often, sir," said she, tossing her head.

"So he sulks and stays away?"

"Yes, sir."

"But you could bring him back?" I suggested, with a smile.

"Perhaps I could," said she.

"I know your powers, you see," said I, and she blushed with pleasure.

"It's not only that, sir, that keeps him away. He's very busy at the Castle now."

"But there's no shooting on now."

"No, sir; but he's in charge of the house."

"Johann turned housemaid?"

The little girl was brimming over with gossip.

"Well, there are no others," said she. "There's not a woman there—not as a servant, I mean. They do say—but perhaps it's false, sir."

"Let's have it for what it's worth," said I.

"Indeed, I'm ashamed to tell you, sir."

"Oh, see, I'm looking at the ceiling."

"They do say there is a lady there, sir; but, except for her, there's not a woman in the place. And Johann has to wait on the gentlemen."

"Poor Johann! He must be overworked. Yet I'm sure he could find half an hour to come and see you."

"It would depend on the time, sir, perhaps."

"Do you love him?" I asked.

"Not I, sir."

"And you wish to serve the King?"

"Yes, sir."

"Then tell him to meet you at the second milestone out of Zenda to-morrow evening at ten o'clock. Say you'll be there and will walk home with him."

"Do you mean him harm, sir?"

"Not if he will do as I bid him. But I think I've told you enough, my pretty maid. See that you do as I bid you. And, mind, no one is to know that the King has been here."

I spoke a little sternly, for there is seldom harm in infusing a little fear into a woman's liking for you, and I softened the effect by giving her a handsome present. Then we dined, and wrapping my cloak about my face, with Fritz leading the way, we went downstairs to our horses again.

It was but half-past eight, and hardly yet dark; the streets were full for such a quiet little place, and I could see that gossip was all agog. With the King on one side and the duke on the other, Zenda felt itself the centre of all Ruritania. We jogged gently through the town, but set our horses to a sharper pace when we reached the open country.

"You want to catch this fellow Johann?" asked Fritz.

"Ay, and I fancy I've baited the hook right. Our little Delilah will bring our Samson. It is not enough, Fritz, to have no women in a house, though brother Michael shows some wisdom there. If you want safety you must have none within fifty miles."

"None nearer than Strelsau, for instance," said poor Fritz, with a lovelorn sigh.

We reached the avenue of the *château*, and were soon at the house. As the hoofs of our horses sounded on the gravel Sapt rushed out to meet us.

"Thank God, you're safe!" he cried. "Have you seen anything of them?"

"Of whom?" I asked, dismounting.

He drew us aside, that the grooms might not hear.

"Lad," he said to me, "you must not ride about here, unless with half a dozen of us. You know among our men a tall young fellow, Bernenstein by name?"

I knew him. He was a fine, strapping young man, almost of my height, and of light complexion.

"He lies in his room upstairs, with a bullet through his arm."

"The deuce he does!"

"After dinner he strolled out alone, and went a mile or so into the wood; and as he walked he thought he saw three men among the trees; and one levelled a gun at him. He had no weapon, and he started at a run back towards the house. But one of them fired, and he was hit, and had much ado to reach here before he fainted. By good luck, they feared to pursue him nearer the house."

He paused and added:

"Lad, the bullet was meant for you."

"It is very likely," said I, "and it's first blood to brother Michael."

"I wonder which three it was," said Fritz.

"Well, Sapt," I said, "I went out to-night for no idle purpose, as you shall hear. But there's one thing in my mind."

"What's that?" he asked.

"Why this," I answered. "That I shall ill requite the very great honours Ruritania has done me if I depart from it leaving one of those Six alive—neither, with the help of God, will I."

And Sapt shook my hand on that.

XIII. An Improvement on Jacob's Ladder

In the morning of the day after that on which I swore my oath against the Six I gave certain orders and then rested in greater contentment than I had known for some time. I was at work; and work, though it cannot cure love, is yet a narcotic to it. So that Sapt, who grew feverish, marvelled to see me sprawling in an armchair in the sunshine, listening to one of my friends who sang me amorous songs in a mellow voice and induced in me a pleasing melancholy. Thus was I engaged when young Rupert Hentzau, who feared neither man nor devil, and rode through the demesne—where every tree might hide a marksman, for all he knew—as though it had been the park at Strelsau, cantered up to where I lay, bowing with burlesque deference, and craving private speech with me in order to deliver a message from the Duke of Strelsau. I made all withdraw, and then he said, seating himself by me:

"The King is in love, it seems?"

"Not with life, my lord," said I, smiling.

"It is well," he rejoined. "Come, we are alone. Rassendyll—"

I rose to a sitting posture.

"What's the matter?" he asked.

"I was about to call one of my gentlemen to bring your horse, my lord. If you do not know how to address the King my brother must find another messenger."

"Why keep up the farce?" he asked, negligently dusting his boot with his glove.

"Because it is not finished yet; and meanwhile I'll choose my own name."

"Oh, so be it! Yet I spoke in love for you; for indeed you are a man after my own heart."

"Saving my poor honesty," said I, "maybe I am. But that I keep faith with men, and honour with women, maybe I am, my lord."

He darted a glance at me—a glance of anger.

"Is your mother dead?" said I.

"Aye, she's dead."

"She may thank God," said I, and I heard him curse me softly. "Well, what's the message?" I continued.

I had touched him in the raw, for all the world knew he had broken his mother's heart and flaunted his mistresses in her house; and his airy manner was gone for the moment.

"The duke offers you more than I would," he growled. "A halter for you, *sire*, was my suggestion. But he offers you safe conduct across the frontier and a million crowns."

"I prefer your offer, my lord, if I am bound to one."

"You refuse?"

"Of course."

"I told Michael you would"; and the villain, his temper restored, gave me the sunniest of smiles. "The fact is, between ourselves," he continued, "Michael doesn't understand a gentleman."

I began to laugh.

"And you?" I asked.

"I do," he said. "Well, well, the halter be it."

"I'm sorry you won't live to see it," I observed.

"Has his Majesty done me the honour to fasten a particular quarrel on me?"

"I would you were a few years older, though."

"Oh, God gives years, but the devil gives increase," laughed he. "I can hold my own."

"How is your prisoner?" I asked.

"The k—"

"Your prisoner."

"I forgot your wishes, sire. Well, he is alive."

He rose to his feet; I imitated him. Then, with a smile, he said:

"And the pretty princess? Faith, I'll wager the next Elphberg will be red enough, for all that Black Michael will be called his father."

I sprang a step towards him, clenching my hand. He did not move an inch, and his lip curled in insolent amusement.

"Go, while your skin's whole!" I muttered. He had repaid me with interest my hit about his mother.

Then came the most audacious thing I have known in my life. My friends were some thirty yards away. Rupert called to a groom to bring him his horse, and dismissed the fellow with a crown. The horse stood near. I stood still, suspecting nothing. Rupert made as though to mount; then he suddenly turned to me: his left hand resting in his belt, his right outstretched:

"Shake hands," he said.

I bowed, and did as he had foreseen—I put my hands behind me. Quicker than thought his left hand darted out at me, and a small dagger flashed in the air; he struck me in the left shoulder—had I not swerved it had been my heart. With a cry I staggered back. Without touching the stirrup, he leapt upon his horse and was off like an arrow, pursued by cries and revolver shots,—the last as useless as the first,—and I sank into my chair, bleeding profusely, as I watched the devil's brat disappear down the long avenue. My friends surrounded me, and then I fainted.

I suppose that I was put to bed, and there lay unconscious or half conscious for many hours; for it was night when I awoke to my full mind, and found Fritz beside me. I was weak and weary, but he bade me be of good cheer, saying that my wound would soon heal, and that meanwhile all had gone well, for Johann, the keeper, had fallen into the snare we had laid for him, and was even now in the house.

"And the queer thing is," pursued Fritz, "that I fancy he's not altogether sorry to find himself here. He seems to think that when Black Michael has brought off his *coup*, witnesses of how it was effected—saving, of course, the Six themselves—will not be at a premium."

This idea argued a shrewdness in our captive which led me to build hopes on his assistance. I ordered him to be brought in at once. Sapt conducted him, and set him in a chair by my bedside. He was sullen and afraid; but, to say truth, after young Rupert's exploit we also had our fears, and if he got as far as possible from Sapt's formidable six-shooter, Sapt kept him as far as he could from me. Moreover, when he came in his hands were bound, but that I would not suffer.

I need not stay to recount the safeguards and rewards we promised the fellow—all of which were honourably observed and paid, so that he lives now in prosperity (though where I may not mention); and we were the more free inasmuch as we soon learnt that he was rather a weak man than a wicked, and had acted throughout this matter more from fear of the duke and of his own brother Max than for any love of what was done. But he had persuaded all of his loyalty; and though not in their secret counsels, was yet, by his knowledge of their dispositions within the Castle, able to lay bare before us the very heart of their devices. And here, in brief is his story:

Below the level of the ground in the Castle, approached by a flight of stone steps which abutted on the end of the drawbridge, were situated two small rooms, cut out of the rock itself. The outer of the two had no windows, but was always lighted with candles; the inner had one square window, which gave upon the moat. In the outer room there lay always, day and night, three of the Six; and the instructions of Duke Michael were that on any attack being made on the outer room the three were to defend the door of it so long as they could without risk to themselves. But so soon as the door should be in danger of being forced, then Rupert Hentzau or Detchard (for one of these two was always there) should leave the others to hold it as long as they could, and himself pass into the inner room, and without more ado kill the King, who lay there, well treated indeed, but without weapons, and with his arms confined in fine steel chains, which did not allow him to move his elbow more than three inches from his shoulder. Thus before the outer door were stormed the King would be dead. And his body? For his body would be evidence as damning as himself.

"Nay, sir," said Johann, "his Highness has thought of that. While the two hold the outer room the one who has killed the King unlocks the bars in the square window (they turn on a hinge). The window now gives no light, for its mouth is choked by a great pipe of earthenware; and this pipe, which is large enough to let pass through it the body of a man, passes into the moat, coming to an end immediately above the surface of the water, so that there is no perceptible interval between water and pipe. The King being dead, his murderer swiftly ties a weight to the body, and dragging it to the window, raises it by a pulley (for, lest the weight should prove too great, Detchard has provided one) till it is level with the mouth of the pipe. He inserts the feet in the pipe, and pushes the body down. Silently, without splash or sound, it falls into the water and thence to the bottom of the moat, which is twenty feet deep thereabouts. This done, the murderer cries loudly, 'All's well!' and himself slides down the pipe; and the others, if they can and the attack is not too hot, run to the inner room and, seeking a moment's delay, bar the door, and in their turn slide down. And though the King rises not from the bottom, they rise and swim round to the other side, where the orders are for men to wait them with ropes, to haul them out, and horses. And here, if things go ill, the duke will join them and seek safety by riding; but if all goes well they will return to the Castle, and have their enemies in a trap. That, sir, is the plan of his Highness for the disposal of the King in case of need. But it is not to be used till the last; for, as we all know, he is not minded to kill the King unless he can, before or soon after, kill you also, sir. Now, sir, I have spoken the truth, as God is my witness, and I pray you to shield me from the vengeance of Duke Michael; for if, after he knows what I have done, I fall into his hands, I shall pray for one thing out of all the world—a speedy death, and that I shall not obtain from him!"

The fellow's story was rudely told, but our questions supplemented his narrative. What he had told us applied to an armed attack; but if suspicions were aroused and there came overwhelming force—such, for instance, as I, the King, could bring—the idea of resistance would be abandoned. The King would be quietly murdered and slid down the pipe. And—here comes an ingenious touch—one of the Six would take his place in the cell, and, on the entrance of the searchers loudly demand release and redress; and Michael, being summoned, would confess to hasty action, but he would say the man had angered him by seeking the favour of a lady in the Castle (this was Antoinette de Mauban) and he had confined him there, as he conceived he, as Lord of Zenda, had right to do. But he was now, on receiving his apology, content to let him go, and so end the gossip which, to his Highness' annoyance, had arisen concerning a prisoner in Zenda, and had given his visitors the trouble of this enquiry. The visitors, baffled, would retire, and Michael could, at his leisure, dispose of the body of the King.

Sapt, Fritz, and I in my bed looked round on one another in horror and bewilderment at the cruelty and cunning of the plan. Whether I went in peace or in war, openly at the head of a *corps*, or secretly by a stealthy assault, the King would be dead before I could come near him. If Michael were stronger and overcame my party there would be an end. But if I were stronger I should have no way to punish him, no means of proving any guilt in him without proving my own guilt also. On the other hand, I should be left as King (ah! for a moment my pulse quickened), and it would be for the future to witness the final struggle between him and me. He seemed to have made triumph possible and ruin impossible. At the worst he would stand where he had stood before I crossed his path—with but one man between him and the throne, and that man an impostor; at best there would be none left to stand against him. I had begun to think that Black Michael was overfond of leaving the fighting to his friends; but now I acknowledged that the brains, if not the arms, of the conspiracy were his.

"Does the King know this?" I asked.

"I and my brother," answered Johann, "put up the pipe, under the orders of my Lord of Hentzau. He was on guard that day, and the King asked my lord what it meant. 'Faith,' he answered, with his airy laugh, 'it's a new improvement on the ladder of Jacob, whereby, as you have read, sire, men pass from the earth to heaven. We thought it not meet that your Majesty should go, in case, sire, you must go, by the common route. So we have made you a pretty private passage, where the vulgar cannot stare at you or incommode your passage. That, sire, is the meaning of that pipe.' And he laughed and bowed, and prayed the King's leave to replenish the King's glass—for the King was at supper. And the King, though he is a brave man, as are all of his House, grew red and then white as he looked on the pipe and at the merry devil who mocked him. Ah, sir,"— and the fellow shuddered,—"it is not easy to sleep quiet in the Castle of Zenda, for all of them would as soon cut a man's throat as play a game at cards; and my Lord Rupert would choose it sooner for a pastime than any other—ay, sooner than he would ruin a woman, though that he loves also."

The man ceased, and I bade Fritz take him away and have him carefully guarded; and, turning to him, I added:

"If anyone asks you if there is a prisoner in Zenda, you may answer 'Yes.' But if any asks who the prisoner is, do not answer. For all my promises will not save you if any man here learns from you the truth as to the prisoner in Zenda. I'll kill you like a dog if the thing be so much as breathed within the house!"

Then when he was gone I looked at Sapt.

"It's a hard nut!" said I.

"So hard," said he, shaking his grizzled head, "that, as I think, this time next year is like to find you still King of Ruritania!" and he broke out into curses on Michael's cunning.

I lay back on my pillows.

"There seems to me," I observed, "to be two ways by which the King can come out of Zenda alive. One is by treachery in the duke's followers."

"You can leave that out," said Sapt.

"I hope not," I rejoined, "because the other I was about to mention is—by a miracle from heaven!"

XIV. A NIGHT OUTSIDE THE CASTLE

I t would have surprised the good people of Ruritania to know of the foregoing talk; for according to the official reports I had suffered a grievous and dangerous hurt from an accidental spear thrust, received in the course of my sport. I caused the bulletins to be of a very serious character, and created great public excitement, whereby three things occurred: first, I gravely offended the medical faculty of Strelsau by refusing to summon to my bedside any of them, save a young man, a friend of Fritz's, whom we could trust; secondly, I received word from Marshal Strakencz that my orders seemed to have no more weight than his, and that the Princess Flavia was leaving for Tarlenheim under his unwilling escort (news whereat I strove not to be glad and proud); and thirdly, my brother, the Duke of Strelsau, although too well informed to believe the account of the origin of my sickness, was yet persuaded by the reports and by my seeming inactivity that I was in truth incapable of action, and that my life was in some danger. This I learnt from the man Johann, whom I was compelled to trust and send back to Zenda, where, by the way, Rupert Hentzau had him soundly flogged for daring to smirch the morals of Zenda by staying out all night in the pursuits of love. This, from Rupert, Johann deeply resented, and the duke's approval of it did more to bind the keeper to my side than all my promises.

On Flavia's arrival I cannot dwell. Her joy at finding me up and well, instead of on my back and fighting with death, makes a picture that even now dances before my eyes till they grow too dim to see it; and her reproaches that I had not trusted even her must excuse the means I took to quiet them. In truth, to have her with me once more was like a taste of heaven to a damned soul, the sweeter for the inevitable doom that was to follow; and I rejoiced in being able to waste two whole days with her. And when I had wasted two days the Duke of Strelsau arranged a hunting party.

The stroke was near now. For Sapt and I, after anxious consultations, had resolved that we must risk a blow, our resolution being clinched by Johann's news that the King grew peaked, pale, and ill, and that his health was breaking down under his rigorous confinement. Now a man—be he King or no King—may as well die swiftly, and as becomes a gentleman, from bullet or thrust, as rot his life out in a cellar! That thought made prompt action advisable in the interests of the King; from my own point of view it grew more and more necessary. For Strakencz urged on me the need of a speedy marriage, and my own inclinations seconded him with such terrible insistence that I feared for my resolution. I do not believe that I should have done the deed I dreamt of; but I might have come to flight, and my flight would have ruined the cause. And—yes, I am no saint (*ask* my little sister-in-law), and worse still might have happened.

It is perhaps as strange a thing as has ever been in the history of a country that the King's brother and the King's personator, in a time of profound outward peace, near a placid, undisturbed country town, under semblance of amity, should wage a desperate war for the person and life of the King. Yet such was the struggle that began now between Zenda and Tarlenheim. When I look back on the time I seem to myself to have been half mad. Sapt has told me that I suffered no interference and listened to no remonstrances; and if ever a King of Ruritania ruled like a despot I was, in those days, the man. Look where I would I saw nothing that made life sweet to me, and I took my life in my hand and carried it carelessly as a man dangles an old glove. At first they strove to guard me, to keep me safe, to persuade me not to expose myself; but when they saw how I was set there grew up among them—whether they knew the truth or not—a feeling that Fate ruled the issue, and that I must be left to play my game with Michael my own way.

Late next night I rose from table, where Flavia had sat by me, and conducted her to the door of her apartments. There I kissed her hand, and bade her sleep sound and wake to happy days. Then I changed my clothes and went out. Sapt and Fritz were waiting for me with three men and the horses. Over his saddle Sapt carried a long coil of rope, and both were heavily armed. I had with me a short stout cudgel and a long knife. Making a circuit, we avoided the town, and in an hour found ourselves slowly mounting the hill that led to the Castle of Zenda. The night was dark and very stormy; gusts of wind and spits of rain caught us as we breasted the incline, and the great trees moaned and sighed. When we came to a thick clump, about a quarter of a mile from the Castle, we bade our three friends hide there with the horses. Sapt had a whistle, and they could rejoin us in a few moments if danger came: but up till now we had met no one. I hoped that Michael was still off his guard, believing me to be safe in bed. However that might be, we gained the top of the hill without accident, and found ourselves on the edge of the moat where it sweeps under the road, separating the old Castle from it. A tree stood on the edge of the bank, and Sapt silently and diligently set to make fast the rope. I stripped off my boots, took a pull at a flask of brandy, loosened the knife in its sheath, and took the cudgel between my teeth. Then I shook hands with my friends, not heeding a last look of entreaty from Fritz, and laid hold of the rope. I was going to have a look at Jacob's Ladder.

Gently I lowered myself into the water. Though the night was wild, the day had been warm and bright and the water was not cold. I struck out and began to swim round the great walls which frowned above me. I could see only three yards ahead. I had then good hopes of not being seen, as I crept along close under the damp, moss-grown masonry. There were lights from the new part of the Castle on the other side, and now and again I heard laughter and merry shouts. I fancied I recognized young Rupert Hentzau's ringing tones, and pictured him flushed with wine. Recalling my thoughts to the business in hand, I rested a moment. If Johann's description were right I must be near the window now. Very slowly I moved; and out of the darkness ahead loomed a shape. It was the pipe, curving from the window to the water. About two feet of its surface were displayed; it was as big round as two men. I was about to approach it when I saw something else, and my heart stood still. The nose of a boat protruded beyond the pipe on the other side; and listening intently, I heard a slight shuffle—as of a man shifting his position. Who was the man who guarded Michael's invention? Was he awake or was he asleep? I felt if my knife were ready, and trod water. As I did so I found bottom under my feet. The foundations of the Castle extended some fifteen inches, making a ledge; and I stood on it, out of water from my armpits upwards. Then I crouched and peered through the darkness under the pipe, where, curving, it left a space.

There was a man in the boat. A rifle lay by him—I saw the gleam of the barrel. Here was the sentinel! He sat very still. I listened: he breathed heavily, regularly, monotonously. By heaven, he slept! Kneeling on the shelf, I drew forward under the pipe till my face was within two feet of his. He was a big man, I saw. It was Max Holf, the brother of Johann. My hand stole to my belt, and I drew out my knife. Of all the deeds of my life I love the least to think of this, and whether it were the act of a man or a traitor I will not ask. I said to myself: "It is war—and the King's life is the stake." And I raised myself from beneath the pipe and stood up by the boat, which lay moored by the ledge. Holding my breath, I marked the spot and raised my arm. The great fellow stirred. He opened his eyes—wide, wider. He grasped in terror at my face and clutched at his rifle. I struck home. And I heard the chorus of a love-song from the opposite bank.

Leaving him where he lay, a huddled mass, I turned to "Jacob's Ladder." My time was short. This fellow's turn of watching might be over directly, and relief would come. Leaning over the pipe, I examined it, from the point it left the water to the topmost extremity where it passed, or seemed to pass, through the masonry of the wall. There was no break in it, no chink. Dropping on my knees, I tested the under side. And my breath went quick and fast, for on this lower side, where the pipe should have clung close to the masonry, there was a gleam of light! That light must come from the cell of the King! I set my shoulder against the pipe and exerted my strength. The chink widened a very, very little, and hastily I desisted; I had done enough to show that the pipe was not fixed in the masonry at the lower side.

Then I heard a voice—a harsh, grating voice:

"Well, sire, if you have had enough of my society I will leave you to repose; but I must fasten the little ornaments first."

It was Detchard! I caught the English accent in a moment.

"Have you anything to ask, sire, before we part?"

The King's voice followed. It was his, though it was faint and hollow—different from the merry tones I had heard in the glades of the forest.

"Pray my brother," said the King, "to kill me. I am dying by inches here."

"The duke does not desire your death, sire—yet," sneered Detchard; "when he does behold your path to heaven!"

The King answered:

"So be it! And now, if your orders allow it, pray leave me."

"May you dream of paradise!" said the ruffian.

The light disappeared. I heard the bolts of the door run home. And then I heard the sobs of the King. He was alone, as he thought. Who dares mock at him?

I did not venture to speak to him. The risk of some exclamation escaping him in surprise was too great. I dared do nothing that night; and my task now was to get myself away in safety, and to carry off the carcass of the dead man. To leave him there would tell too much. Casting loose the boat, I got in. The wind was blowing a gale now, and there was little danger of oars being heard. I rowed swiftly round to where my friends waited. I had just reached the spot when a loud whistle sounded over the moat behind me.

"Hullo, Max!" I heard shouted.

I hailed Sapt in a low tone. The rope came down. I tied it round the corpse, and then went up it myself.

"Whistle you too," I whispered, "for our men, and haul in the line. No talk now."

They hauled up the body. Just as it reached the road three men on horseback swept round from the front of the Castle. We saw them; but, being on foot ourselves, we escaped their notice. But we heard our men coming up with a shout.

"The devil, but it's dark!" cried a ringing voice.

It was young Rupert. A moment later shots rang out. Our people had met them. I started forward at a run, Sapt and Fritz following me.

"Thrust, thrust!" cried Rupert again, and a loud groan following told that he himself was not behindhand.

"I'm done, Rupert!" cried a voice. "They're three to one. Save yourself!"

I ran on, holding my cudgel in my hand. Suddenly a horse came towards me. A man was on it, leaning over his shoulder.

"Are you cooked too, Krafstein?" he cried.

There was no answer.

I sprang to the horse's head. It was Rupert Hentzau.

"At last!" I cried.

For we seemed to have him. He had only his sword in his hand. My men were hot upon him; Sapt and Fritz were running up. I had outstripped them; but if they got close enough to fire, he must die or surrender.

"At last!" I cried.

"It's the play-actor!" cried he, slashing at my cudgel. He cut it clean in two; and, judging discretion better than death, I ducked my head and (I blush to tell it) scampered for my life. The devil was in Rupert Hentzau; for he put spurs to his horse, and I, turning to look, saw him ride, full gallop, to the edge of the moat and leap in, while the shots of our party fell thick round him like hail. With one gleam of moonlight we should have riddled him with balls; but in the darkness he won to the corner of the Castle, and vanished from our sight.

"The deuce take him!" grinned Sapt.

"It's a pity," said I, "that he's a villain. Whom have we got?"

We had Lauengram and Krafstein: they lay stiff and dead; and, concealment being no longer possible, we flung them, with Max, into the moat; and, drawing together in a compact body, rode off down the hill. And in our midst went the bodies of three gallant gentlemen. Thus we travelled home, heavy at heart for the death of our friends, sore uneasy concerning the King, and cut to the quick that young Rupert had played yet another winning hand with us.

For my own part, I was vexed and angry that I had killed no man in open fight, but only stabbed a knave in his sleep. And I did not love to hear Rupert call me a play-actor.

XV. I TALK WITH A TEMPTER

Ruritania is not England, or the quarrel between Duke Michael and myself could not have gone on, with the remarkable incidents which marked it, without more public notice being directed to it. Duels were frequent among all the upper classes, and private quarrels between great men kept the old habit of spreading to their friends and dependents. Nevertheless, after the affray which I have just related, such reports began to circulate that I felt it necessary to be on my guard. The death of the gentlemen involved could not be hidden from their relatives. I issued a stern order, declaring that duelling had attained unprecedented licence (the Chancellor drew up the document for me, and very well he did it), and forbidding it save in the gravest cases. I sent a public and stately apology to Michael, and he returned a deferential and courteous reply to me; for our one point of union was—and it underlay all our differences and induced an unwilling harmony between our actions—that we could neither of us afford to throw our cards on the table. He, as well as I, was a "play-actor," and, hating one another, we combined to dupe public opinion. Unfortunately, however, the necessity for concealment involved the necessity of delay: the King might die in his prison, or even be spirited off somewhere else; it could not be helped. For a little while I was compelled to observe a truce, and my only consolation was that Flavia most warmly approved of my edict against duelling; and when I expressed delight at having won her favour, prayed me, if her favour were any motive to me, to prohibit the practice altogether.

"Wait till we are married," said I, smiling.

Not the least peculiar result of the truce and of the secrecy which dictated it was that the town of Zenda became in the daytime—I would not have trusted far to its protection by night—a sort of neutral zone, where both parties could safely go; and I, riding down one day with Flavia and Sapt, had an encounter with an acquaintance, which presented a ludicrous side, but was at the same time embarrassing. As I rode along I met a dignified-looking person driving in a two-horsed carriage. He stopped his horses, got out, and approached me, bowing low. I recognized the Head of the Strelsau Police.

"Your Majesty's ordinance as to duelling is receiving our best attention," he assured me.

If the best attention involved his presence in Zenda I determined at once to dispense with it.

"Is that what brings you to Zenda, Prefect?" I asked.

"Why, no, sire; I am here because I desired to oblige the British Ambassador."

"What's the British Ambassador doing *dans cette galère*?" said I carelessly.

"A young countryman of his, sire—a man of some position—is missing. His friends have not heard from him for two months, and there is reason to believe that he was last seen in Zenda."

Flavia was paying little attention. I dared not look at Sapt.

"What reason?"

"A friend of his in Paris—a certain M. Featherly—has given us information which makes it possible that he came here, and the officials of the railway recollect his name on some luggage."

"What was his name?"

"Rassendyll, sire," he answered; and I saw that the name meant nothing to him. But, glancing at Flavia, he lowered his voice, as he went on: "It is thought that he may have followed a lady here. Has your Majesty heard of a certain Madame de Mauban?"

"Why, yes," said I, my eye involuntarily travelling towards the Castle. "She arrived in Ruritania about the same time as this Rassendyll."

I caught the Prefect's glance; he was regarding me with enquiry writ large on his face.

"Sapt," said I, "I must speak a word to the Prefect. Will you ride on a few paces with the princess?" And I added to the Prefect: "Come, sir, what do you mean?"

He drew close to me, and I bent in the saddle.

"If he were in love with the lady?" he whispered. "Nothing has been heard of him for two months"; and this time it was the eye of the Prefect which travelled towards the Castle.

"Yes, the lady is there," I said quietly. "But I don't suppose Mr. Rassendyll—is that the name?—is."

"The duke," he whispered, "does not like rivals, sire."

"You're right there," said I, with all sincerity. "But surely you hint at a very grave charge?"

He spread his hands out in apology. I whispered in his ear:

"This is a grave matter. Go back to Strelsau—"

"But, sire, if I have a clew here?"

"Go back to Strelsau," I repeated. "Tell the Ambassador that you have a clew, but that you must be left alone for a week or two. Meanwhile I'll charge myself with looking into the matter."

"The Ambassador is very pressing, sire."

"You must quiet him. Come, sir; you see that if your suspicions are correct it is an affair in which we must move with caution. We can have no scandal. Mind you return to-night."

He promised to obey me, and I rode on to rejoin my companions, a little easier in my mind. Enquiries after me must be stopped at all hazards for a week or two; and this clever official had come surprisingly near the truth. His impression might be useful some day, but if he acted on it now it might mean the worse to the King. Heartily did I curse George Featherly for not holding his tongue.

"Well," asked Flavia, "have you finished your business?"

"Most satisfactorily," said I. "Come, shall we turn round? We are almost trenching on my brother's territory."

We were, in fact, at the extreme end of the town, just where the hill begins to mount towards the Castle. We cast our eyes up, admiring the massive beauty of the old walls, and we saw a *cortège* winding slowly down the hill. On it came.

"Let us go back," said Sapt.

"I should like to stay," said Flavia; and I reined my horse beside hers.

We could distinguish the approaching party now. There came first two mounted servants in black uniforms, relieved only by a silver badge. These were followed by a car drawn by four horses: on it, under a heavy pall, lay a coffin; behind it rode a man in plain black clothes, carrying his hat in his hand. Sapt uncovered, and we stood waiting, Flavia keeping by me and laying her hand on my arm.

"It is one of the gentlemen killed in the quarrel, I expect," she said.

I beckoned to a groom.

"Ride and ask whom they escort," I ordered.

He rode up to the servants, and I saw him pass on to the gentleman who rode behind.

"It's Rupert of Hentzau," whispered Sapt.

Rupert it was, and directly afterwards, waving to the procession to stand still, Rupert trotted up to me. He was in a frock coat, tightly buttoned, and trousers. He wore an aspect of sadness, and he bowed with profound respect. Yet suddenly he smiled, and I smiled too, for old Sapt's hand lay in his left breast pocket, and Rupert and I both guessed what lay in the hand inside the pocket.

"Your Majesty asks whom we escort," said Rupert. "It is my dear friend Albert of Lauengram."

"Sir," said I, "no one regrets the unfortunate affair more than I. My ordinance, which I mean to have obeyed, is witness to it."

"Poor fellow!" said Flavia softly, and I saw Rupert's eyes flash at her. Whereat I grew red; for if I had my way Rupert Hentzau should not have defiled her by so much as a glance. Yet he did it, and dared to let admiration be seen in his look.

"Your Majesty's words are gracious," he said. "I grieve for my friend. Yet, sire, others must soon lie as he lies now."

"It is a thing we all do well to remember, my lord," I rejoined.

"Even Kings, sire," said Rupert in a moralizing tone; and old Sapt swore softly by my side.

"It is true," said I. "How fares my brother, my lord?"

"He is better, sire."

"I am rejoiced."

"He hopes soon to leave for Strelsau, when his health is secured."

"He is only convalescent, then?"

"There remain one or two small troubles," answered the insolent fellow in the mildest tone in the world.

"Express my earnest hope," said Flavia, "that they may soon cease to trouble him."

"Your Royal Highness' wish is, humbly, my own," said Rupert with a bold glance that brought a blush to Flavia's cheek.

I bowed; and Rupert, bowing lower, backed his horse and signed to his party to proceed. With a sudden impulse I rode after him. He turned swiftly, fearing that even in the presence of the dead and before a lady's eyes I meant him mischief.

"You fought as a brave man the other night," I said. "Come, you are young, sir. If you will deliver your prisoner alive to me you shall come to no hurt."

He looked at me with a mocking smile; but suddenly he rode nearer to me.

"I'm unarmed," he said; "and our old Sapt there could pick me off in a minute."

"I'm not afraid," said I.

"No, curse you!" he answered. "Look here, I made you a proposal from the duke once."

"I'll hear nothing from Black Michael," said I.

"Then hear one from me." He lowered his voice to a whisper. "Attack the Castle boldly. Let Sapt and Tarlenheim lead."

"Go on," said I.

"Arrange the time with me."

"I have such confidence in you, my lord!"

"Tut! I'm talking business now. Sapt there and Fritz will fall; Black Michael will fall—"

"What!"

"Black Michael will fall, like the dog he is; the prisoner, as you call him, will go by Jacob's Ladder—ah, you know that!—to hell! Two men will be left—I, Rupert Hentzau, and you, the King of Ruritania."

He paused, and then, in a voice that quivered with eagerness, added:

"Isn't that a hand to play?—a throne and yon princess! And for me, say a competence and your Majesty's gratitude."

"Surely," I exclaimed, "while you're above ground hell wants its master!"

"Well, think it over," he said. "And, look you, it would take more than a scruple or two to keep me from yonder girl," and his evil eye flashed again at her I loved.

"Get out of my reach!" said I; and yet in a moment I began to laugh for the very audacity of it.

"Would you turn against your master?" I asked.

He swore at Michael for being what the offspring of a legal, though morganatic, union should not be called, and said to me in an almost confidential and apparently friendly tone:

"He gets in my way, you know. He's a jealous brute! Faith, I nearly stuck a knife into him last night; he came most cursedly *mal àpropos*!"

My temper was well under control now: I was learning something.

"A lady?" I asked negligently.

"Ay, and a beauty," he nodded. "But you've seen her."

"Ah! was it at a tea party, when some of your friends got on the wrong side of the table?"

"What can you expect of fools like Detchard and De Gautet? I wish I'd been there."

"And the duke interferes?"

"Well," said Rupert meditatively, "that's hardly a fair way of putting it, perhaps. I want to interfere."

"And she prefers the duke?"

"Ay, the silly creature! Ah, well, you think about my plan"; and, with a bow, he pricked his horse and trotted after the body of his friend.

I went back to Flavia and Sapt, pondering on the strangeness of the man. Wicked men I have known in plenty, but Rupert Hentzau remains unique in my experience. And if there be another anywhere let him be caught and hanged out of hand. So say I!

"He's very handsome, isn't he?" said Flavia.

Well, of course she didn't know him as I did; yet I was put out, for I thought his bold glances would have made her angry. But my dear Flavia was a woman, and so—she was not put out. On the contrary, she thought young Rupert was very handsome—as, beyond question, the ruffian was.

"And how sad he looked at his friend's death!" said she.

"He'll have better reason to be sad at his own," observed Sapt, with a grim smile.

As for me, I grew sulky; unreasonable it was, perhaps, for what better business had I to look at her with love than had even Rupert's lustful eyes? And sulky I remained till, as evening fell and we rode up to Tarlenheim, Sapt having fallen behind in case anyone should be following us, Flavia, riding close beside me, said softly, with a little half-ashamed laugh:

"Unless you smile, Rudolf, I cry. Why are you angry?"

"It was something that fellow said to me," said I; but I was smiling as we reached the door and dismounted.

There a servant handed me a note; it was unaddressed.

"Is it for me?" I asked.

"Yes, sire; a boy brought it."

I tore it open:

> Johann carries this for me. I warned you once. In the name of God, and if you are a man, rescue me from this den of murderers!
>
> A. de M.

I handed it to Sapt; but all that the tough old soul said in reply to this piteous appeal was: "Whose fault brought her there?"

Nevertheless, not being faultless myself, I took leave to pity Antoinette de Mauban.

XVI. A DESPERATE PLAN

As I had ridden publicly in Zenda, and had talked there with Rupert Hentzau, of course all pretence of illness was at an end. I marked the effect on the garrison of Zenda: they ceased to be seen abroad; and any of my men who went near the castle reported that the utmost vigilance prevailed there. Touched as I was by Madame de Mauban's appeal, I seemed as powerless to befriend her as I had proved to help the King. Michael bade me defiance; and—although he too had been seen outside the walls—with more disregard for appearances than he had hitherto shown, he did not take the trouble to send any excuse for his failure to wait on the King. Time ran on in inactivity, when every moment was pressing; for not only was I faced with the new danger which the stir about my disappearance brought on me, but great murmurs had arisen in Strelsau at my continued absence from the city. They had been greater but for the knowledge that Flavia was with me; and for this reason I suffered her to stay, though I hated to have her where danger was, and though every day of our present sweet intercourse strained my endurance almost to breaking. As a final blow nothing would content my advisers, Strakencz and the Chancellor (who came out from Strelsau to make an urgent representation to me), save that I should appoint a day for the public solemnization of my betrothal, a ceremony which in Ruritania is well nigh as binding and great a thing as the marriage itself. And this—with Flavia sitting by me—I was forced to do, setting a date a fortnight ahead, and appointing the Cathedral in Strelsau as the place. And this formal act being published far and wide, caused great joy throughout the kingdom, and was the talk of all tongues; so that I reckoned there were but two men who chafed at it—I mean Black Michael and myself; and but one who did not know of it—that one the man whose name I bore, the King of Ruritania.

In truth, I heard something of the way the news was received in the Castle; for after an interval of three days, the man Johann, greedy for more money, though fearful for his life, again found means to visit us. He had been waiting on the duke when the tidings came. Black Michael's face had grown blacker still, and he had sworn savagely; nor was he better pleased when young Rupert took oath that I meant to do as I said, and turning to Madame de Mauban, wished her joy on a rival gone. Michael's hand stole towards his sword (said Johann), but not a bit did Rupert care; for he rallied the duke on having made a better King than had reigned for years past in Ruritania. "And," said he, with a meaning bow to his exasperated master, "the devil sends the princess a finer man than heaven had marked out for her; by my soul, it does!" Then Michael harshly bade him hold his tongue and leave them; but Rupert must needs first kiss madame's hand, which he did as though he loved her, while Michael glared at him.

This was the lighter side of the fellow's news; but more serious came behind, and it was plain that if time pressed at Tarlenheim it pressed none the less fiercely at Zenda. For the King was very sick; Johann had seen him, and he was wasted and hardly able to move. "There could be no thought of taking another for him now." So alarmed were they that they had sent for a physician from Strelsau; and the physician having been introduced into the King's cell, had come forth pale and trembling, and urgently prayed the duke to let him go back and meddle no more in the affair; but the duke would not, and held him there a prisoner, telling him his life was safe if the King lived while the duke desired and died when the duke desired—not otherwise. And, persuaded by the physician, they had allowed Madame de Mauban to visit the King and give him such attendance as his state needed, and as only a woman can give. Yet his life hung in the balance; and I was still strong and whole and free. Wherefore great gloom reigned at

Zenda; and save when they quarrelled, to which they were very prone, they hardly spoke. But the deeper the depression of the rest, young Rupert went about Satan's work with a smile in his eye and a song on his lip; and laughed "fit to burst" (said Johann) because the duke always set Detchard to guard the King when Madame de Mauban was in the cell—which precaution was, indeed, not unwise in my careful brother. Thus Johann told his tale and seized his crowns. Yet he besought us to allow him to stay with us in Tarlenheim, and not venture his head again in the lion's den; but we had need of him there, and although I refused to constrain him, I prevailed on him by increased rewards to go back and carry tidings to Madame de Mauban that I was working for her, and that, if she could, she should speak one word of comfort to the King. For while suspense is bad for the sick, yet despair is worse still, and it might be that the King lay dying of mere hopelessness, for I could learn of no definite disease that afflicted him.

"And how do they guard the King now?" I asked, remembering that two of the Six were dead, and Max Holf also.

"Detchard and Bersonin watch by night, Rupert Hentzau and De Gautet by day, sir," he answered.

"Only two at a time?"

"Ay, sir; but the others rest in a room just above, and are within sound of a cry or a whistle."

"A room just above? I didn't know of that. Is there any communication between it and the room where they watch?"

"No, sir. You must go down a few stairs and through the door by the drawbridge, and so to where the King is lodged."

"And that door is locked?"

"Only the four lords have keys, sir."

I drew nearer to him.

"And have they keys of the grating?" I asked in a low whisper.

"I think, sir, only Detchard and Rupert."

"Where does the duke lodge?"

"In the *château*, on the first floor. His apartments are on the right as you go toward the drawbridge."

"And Madame de Mauban?"

"Just opposite, on the left. But her door is locked after she has entered."

"To keep her in?"

"Doubtless, sir."

"Perhaps for another reason?"

"It is possible."

"And the duke, I suppose, has the key?"

"Yes. And the drawbridge is drawn back at night, and of that too the duke holds the key, so that it cannot be run across the moat without application to him.".

"And where do you sleep?"

"In the entrance hall of the *château*, with five servants."

"Armed?"

"They have pikes, sir, but no firearms. The duke will not trust them with firearms."

Then at last I took the matter boldly in my hands. I had failed once at Jacob's Ladder; I should fail again there. I must make the attack from the other side.

"I have promised you twenty thousand crowns," said I. "You shall have fifty thousand if you will do what I ask of you to-morrow night. But, first, do those servants know who your prisoner is?"

"No, sir. They believe him to be some private enemy of the duke's."

"And they would not doubt that I am the King?"

"How should they?" he asked.

"Look to this, then. To-morrow, at two in the morning exactly, fling open the front door of the *château*. Don't fail by an instant."

"Shall you be there, sir?"

"Ask no questions. Do what I tell you. Say the hall is close, or what you will. That is all I ask of you."

"And may I escape by the door, sir, when I have opened it?"

"Yes, as quick as your legs will carry you. One thing more. Carry this note to madame,—oh, it's in French, you can't read it,—and charge her, for the sake of all our lives, not to fail in what it orders."

The man was trembling, but I had to trust to what he had of courage and to what he had of honesty. I dared not wait, for I feared that the King would die.

When the fellow was gone I called Sapt and Fritz to me, and unfolded the plan that I had formed. Sapt shook his head over it.

"Why can't you wait?" he asked.

"The King may die."

"Michael will be forced to act before that."

"Then," said I, "the King may live."

"Well, and if he does?"

"For a fortnight?" I asked simply.

And Sapt bit his moustache.

Suddenly Fritz von Tarlenheim laid his hand on my shoulder.

"Let us go and make the attempt," said he.

"I mean you to go—don't be afraid," said I.

"Ay, but do you stay here, and take care of the princess."

A gleam came into old Sapt's eye.

"We should have Michael one way or the other then," he chuckled; "whereas if you go and are killed with the King what will become of those of us who are left?"

"They will serve Queen Flavia," said I, "and I would to God I could be one of them."

A pause followed. Old Sapt broke it by saying sadly, yet with an unmeant drollery that set Fritz and me laughing:

"Why didn't old Rudolf the Third marry your—great-grandmother, was it?"

"Come," said I, "it is the King we are thinking about."

"It is true," said Fritz.

"Moreover," I went on, "I have been an impostor for the profit of another, but I will not be one for my own; and if the King is not alive and on his throne before the day of betrothal comes I will tell the truth, come what may."

"You shall go, lad," said Sapt.

Here is the plan I had made: A strong party under Sapt's command was to steal up to the door of the *château*. If discovered prematurely they were to kill anyone who found them—with their swords, for I wanted no noise of firing. If all went well they would be at the door when Johann opened it. They were to rush in and secure the servants if their mere presence and the use of the King's name were not enough. At the same moment—and on this hinged the plan—a woman's cry was to ring out loud and shrill from Antoinette de Mauban's chamber. Again and again she was to cry: "Help, help! Michael, help!" and then to utter the name of young Rupert Hentzau. Then, as we hoped, Michael, in fury, would rush out of his apartments opposite, and fall alive into the hands of Sapt. Still the cries would go on; my men would let down the drawbridge; and it would be strange if Rupert, hearing his name thus taken in vain, did not descend from where he slept and seek to cross. De Gautet might or might not come with him: that must be left to chance.

And when Rupert set his foot on the drawbridge? There was my part: for I was minded for another swim in the moat; and, lest I should grow weary, I had resolved to take with me a small wooden ladder, on which I could rest my arms in the water—and my feet when I left it. I would rear it against the wall just by the bridge; and when the bridge was across, I would stealthily creep on to it—and then if Rupert or De Gautet crossed in safety it would be my misfortune, not my fault. They dead, two men only would remain; and for them we must trust to the confusion we had created and to a sudden rush. We should have the keys of the door that led to the all-important rooms. Perhaps they would rush out. If they stood by their orders, then the King's life hung on the swiftness with which we could force the outer door; and I thanked God that not Rupert Hentzau watched, but Detchard. For though Detchard was a cool man, relentless, and no coward, he had neither the dash nor the recklessness of Rupert. Moreover, he, if any one of them, really loved Black Michael, and it might be that he would leave Bersonin to guard the King and rush across the bridge to take part in the affray on the other side.

So I planned—desperately. And, that our enemy might be the better lulled to security, I gave orders that our residence should be brilliantly lighted from top to bottom, as though we were engaged in revelry; and should so be kept all night, with music playing and people moving to and fro. Strakencz would be there, and he was to conceal our departure, if he could, from Flavia. And if we came not again by the morning he was to march, openly and in force, to the Castle, and demand the person of the King: if Black Michael were not there, as I did not think he would be, the Marshal would take Flavia with him, as swiftly as he could, to Strelsau, and there proclaim Black Michael's treachery and the probable death of the King, and rally all that there was honest and true round the banner of the princess. And, to say truth, this was what I thought most likely to happen.

For I had great doubts whether either the King or Black Michael or I had more than a day to live. Well, if Black Michael died, and if I, the play-actor, slew Rupert Hentzau with my own hand, and then died myself, it might be that Fate would deal as lightly with Ruritania as could be hoped, notwithstanding that it demanded the life of the King—and to her dealing thus with me I was in no temper to make objection.

It was late when we rose from conference, and I betook me to the princess' apartments. She was pensive that evening; yet when I left her she flung her arms about me and grew, for an instant, bashfully radiant as she slipped a ring on my finger. I was wearing the King's ring; but I had also on my little finger a plain band of gold engraved with the motto of our family: "*Nil Quae Feci*." This I took off and put on her finger and signed to her to let me go. And she, understanding, stood away and watched me with dimmed eyes.

"Wear that ring, even though you wear another when you are queen," I said.

"Whatever else I wear this I will wear till I die, and after," said she as she kissed the ring.

XVII. Young Rupert's Midnight Diversions

The night came fine and clear. I had prayed for dirty weather, such as had favoured my previous voyage in the moat, but Fortune was this time against me. Still I reckoned that by keeping close under the wall and in the shadow I could escape detection from the windows of the *château* that looked out on the scene of my efforts. If they searched the moat, indeed my scheme must fail; but I did not think they would. They had made Jacob's Ladder secure against attack. Johann had himself helped to fix it closely to the masonry on the under side, so that it could not now be moved from below any more than from above. An assault with explosives or a long battering with picks alone could displace it, and the noise involved in either of these operations put them out of the question. What harm, then, could a man do in the moat? I trusted that Black Michael, putting this query to himself, would answer confidently, "None"; while even if Johann meant treachery he did not know my scheme, and would doubtless expect to see me, at the head of my friends, before the front entrance to the *château*. There, I said to Sapt, was the real danger.

"And there," I added, "you shall be. Doesn't that content you?"

But it did not. Dearly would he have liked to come with me had I not utterly refused to take him. One man might escape notice; to double the party more than doubled the risk: and when he ventured to hint once again that my life was too valuable, I, knowing the secret thought he clung to, sternly bade him be silent, assuring him that unless the King lived through the night I would not live through it either.

At twelve o'clock Sapt's command left the *château* of Tarlenheim and struck off to the right, riding by unfrequented roads, and avoiding the town of Zenda. If all went well they would be in front of the Castle by about a quarter to two. Leaving their horses half a mile off, they were to steal up to the entrance and hold themselves in readiness for the opening of the door. If the door were not opened by two they were to send Fritz von Tarlenheim round to the other side of the Castle. I would meet him there if I were alive, and we would consult whether to storm the Castle or not. If I were not there they were to return with all speed to Tarlenheim, rouse the Marshal, and march in force on Zenda. For if not there I should be dead; and I knew that the King would not be alive five minutes after I ceased to breathe.

I must now leave Sapt and his friends, and relate how I myself proceeded on this eventful night. I went out on the good horse which had carried me, on the night of the coronation, back from the hunting lodge to Strelsau. I carried a revolver in the saddle and my sword. I was covered with a large cloak, and under this I wore a warm, tight-fitting woollen jersey, a pair of knickerbockers, thick stockings, and light canvas shoes. I had rubbed myself thoroughly with oil, and I carried a large flask of whisky. The night was warm, but I might probably be immersed a long while, and it was necessary to take every precaution against cold: for cold not only saps a man's courage if he has to die, but impairs his energy if others have to die, and, finally, gives him rheumatics, if it be God's will that he lives. Also I tied round my body a length of thin but stout cord, and I did not forget my ladder. I, starting after Sapt, took a shorter route, skirting the town to the left, and found myself in the outskirts of the forest at about half-past twelve. I tied my horse up in a thick clump of trees, leaving the revolver in its pocket in the saddle,—it would be no use to me,—and, ladder in hand, made my way to the edge of the moat. Here I unwound my rope from about my waist, bound it securely round the trunk of a tree on the bank, and let myself down. The Castle clock struck a quarter to one as I felt the water under me and began to swim round the keep, pushing the ladder before me, and hugging the Castle wall. Thus voyaging, I came to my old friend "Jacob's Ladder," and felt the ledge of the masonry under me. I crouched down in the shadow of the great pipe,—I tried to stir it, but it was quite immovable,—and waited. I remember that my predominant feeling was neither anxiety for the King nor longing for Flavia, but an intense desire to smoke; and this craving, of course, I could not gratify.

The drawbridge was still in its place. I saw its airy, light framework above me, some ten yards to my right, as I crouched with my back against the wall of the King's cell. I made out a window two yards my side of it and nearly on the same level. That, if Johann spoke true, must belong to the duke's apartments; and on the other side, in about the same relative position, must be Madame de Mauban's window. Women are careless, forgetful creatures. I prayed that she might not forget that she was to be the victim of a brutal attempt at two o'clock precisely. I was rather amused at the part I had assigned to my young friend Rupert Hentzau; but I owed him a stroke—for, even as I sat, my shoulder ached where he had, with an audacity that seemed half to hide his treachery, struck at me, in the sight of all my friends, on the terrace at Tarlenheim.

Suddenly the duke's window grew bright. The shutters were not closed, and the interior became partially visible to me as I cautiously raised myself till I stood on tiptoe. Thus placed, my range of sight embraced a yard or more inside the window, while the radius of light did not reach me. The window was flung open and someone looked out. I marked Antoinette de Mauban's graceful figure, and though her face was in shadow, the fine outline of her head was revealed against the light behind. I longed to cry softly "Remember!" but I dared not—and happily, for a moment later a man came up and stood by her. He tried to put his arm round her waist, but with a swift motion she sprang away and leant against the shutter, her profile towards me. I made out who the newcomer was: it was young Rupert. A low laugh from him made me sure, as he leant forward, stretching out his hand towards her.

"Gently, gently!" I murmured. "You're too soon, my boy!"

His head was close to hers. I suppose he whispered to her, for I saw her point to the moat, and I heard her say, in slow and distinct tones:

"I had rather throw myself out of this window!"

He came close up to the window and looked out.

"It looks cold," said he. "Come, Antoinette, are you serious?"

She made no answer, so far as I heard; and he, smiting his hand petulantly on the window sill, went on, in the voice of some spoilt child:

"Hang Black Michael! Isn't the princess enough for him? Is he to have everything? What the devil do you see in Black Michael?"

"If I told him what you say—" she began.

"Well, tell him," said Rupert carelessly; and, catching her off her guard, he sprang forward and kissed her, laughing, and crying, "There's something to tell him!"

If I had kept my revolver with me I should have been very sorely tempted. Being spared the temptation, I merely added this new score to his account.

"Though, faith," said Rupert, "it's little he cares. He's mad about the princess, you know. He talks of nothing but cutting the play-actor's throat."

Didn't he, indeed?

"And if I do it for him what do you think he's promised me?"

The unhappy woman raised her hands above her head, in prayer or in despair.

"But I detest waiting," said Rupert; and I saw that he was about to lay his hand on her again when there was a noise of a door in the room opening, and a harsh voice cried:

"What are you doing here, sir?"

Rupert turned his back to the window, bowed low, and said, in his loud, merry tones:

"Apologizing for your absence, sir. Could I leave the lady alone?"

The newcomer must be Black Michael. I saw him directly, as he advanced towards the window. He caught young Rupert by the arm.

"The moat would hold more than the King!" said he, with a significant gesture.

"Does your Highness threaten me?" asked Rupert.

"A threat is more warning than most men get from me."

"Yet," observed Rupert, "Rudolf Rassendyll has been much threatened, and yet lives!"

"Am I in fault because my servants bungle?" asked Michael scornfully.

"Your Highness has run no risk of bungling!" sneered Rupert.

It was telling the duke that he shirked danger as plain as ever I have heard a man told. Black Michael had self-control. I dare say he scowled,—it was a great regret to me that I could not see their faces better,—but his voice was even and calm as he answered:

"Enough, enough! We mustn't quarrel, Rupert. Are Detchard and Bersonin at their posts?"

"They are, sir."

"I need you no more."

"Nay, I'm not oppressed with fatigue," said Rupert.

"Pray, sir, leave us," said Michael more impatiently. "In ten minutes the drawbridge will be drawn back, and I presume you have no wish to swim to your bed."

Rupert's figure disappeared. I heard the door open and shut again. Michael and Antoinette de Mauban were left together. To my chagrin, the duke laid his hand on the window and closed it. He stood talking to Antoinette for a moment or two. She shook her head, and he turned impatiently away. She left the window. The door sounded again, and Black Michael closed the shutters.

"De Gautet, De Gautet, man!" sounded from the drawbridge. "Unless you want a bath before your bed, come along!"

It was Rupert's voice, coming from the end of the drawbridge. A moment later he and De Gautet stepped out on the bridge. Rupert's arm was through De Gautet's, and in the middle of the bridge he detained his companion and leant over. I dropped behind the shelter of "Jacob's Ladder."

Then Master Rupert had a little sport. He took from De Gautet a bottle which he carried, and put it to his lips.

"Hardly a drop!" he cried discontentedly, and flung it in the moat.

It fell, as I judged from the sound and the circles on the water, within a yard of the pipe. And Rupert, taking out his revolver, began to shoot at it. The first two shots missed the bottle, but hit the pipe. The third shattered the bottle. I hoped that the young ruffian would be content; but he emptied the other barrels at the pipe, and one, skimming over the pipe, whistled through my hair as I crouched on the other side.

"Ware bridge!" a voice cried, to my relief.

Rupert and De Gautet cried, "A moment!" and ran across. The bridge was drawn back, and all became still. The clock struck a quarter past one. I rose and stretched myself and yawned.

I think some ten minutes had passed when I heard a slight noise to my right. I peered over the pipe, and saw a dark figure standing in the gateway that led to the bridge. It was a man. By the careless, graceful poise I guessed it to be Rupert again. He held a sword in his hand, and he stood motionless for a minute or two. Wild thoughts ran through me. On what mischief was the young fiend bent now? Then he laughed low to himself; then he turned his face to the wall, took a step in my direction, and to my surprise began to climb down the wall. In an instant I saw that there must be steps in the wall; it was plain. They were cut into or affixed to the wall at intervals of about eighteen inches. Rupert set his foot on the lower one. Then he placed his sword between his teeth, turned round, and noiselessly let himself down into the water. Had it been a matter of my life only I would have swum to meet him. Dearly would I have loved to fight it out with him then and there—with steel, on a fine night and none to come between us. But there was the King! I restrained myself, but I could not bridle my swift breathing, and I watched him with the intensest eagerness.

He swam leisurely and quietly across. There were more footsteps up on the other side, and he climbed them. When he set foot in the gateway, standing on the drawn-back bridge, he felt in his pocket and took something out. I heard him unlock the door. I could hear no noise of its closing behind him. He vanished from my sight.

Abandoning my ladder,—I saw I did not need it now,—I swam to the side of the bridge, and climbed halfway up the steps. There I hung, with my sword in my hand, listening eagerly. The duke's room was shuttered and dark. There was a light in the window on the opposite side of the bridge. Not a sound broke the silence, till half-past one chimed from the great clock in the tower of the *château*.

There were other plots than mine afoot in the Castle that night.

XVIII. The Forcing of the Trap

The position wherein I stood does not appear very favourable to thought; yet for the next moment or two I thought profoundly. I had, I told myself, scored one point. Be Rupert Hentzau's errand what it might, and the villainy he was engaged on what it would, I had scored one point. He was on the other side of the moat from the King, and it would be by no fault of mine if ever he set foot on the same side again. I had three left to deal with: two on guard and De Gautet in his bed. Ah, if I had the keys! I would have risked everything and attacked Detchard and Bersonin before their friends could join them. But I was powerless. I must wait till the coming of my friends enticed someone to cross the bridge—someone with the keys. And I waited, as it seemed, for half an hour, really for about five minutes, before the next act in the rapid drama began.

All was still on the other side. The duke's room remained inscrutable behind its shutters. The light burnt steadily in Madame de Mauban's window. Then I heard the faintest, faintest sound; it came from behind the door which led to the drawbridge on the other side of the moat. It but just reached my ear, yet I could not be mistaken as to what it was. It was made by a key being turned very carefully and slowly. Who was turning it? And of what room was it the key? There leapt before my eyes the picture of young Rupert, with the key in one hand, his sword in the other, and an evil smile on his face. But I did not know what door it was, nor on which of his favourite pursuits young Rupert was spending the hours of that night.

I was soon to be enlightened, for the next moment—before my friends could be near the château door—before Johann, the keeper, would have thought to nerve himself for his task—there was a sudden crash from the room with the lighted window. It sounded as though someone had flung down a lamp, and the window went dark and black. At the same instant a cry rang out, shrill in the night: "Help, help! Michael, help!" and was followed by a shriek of utter terror.

I was tingling in every nerve. I stood on the topmost step, clinging to the threshold of the gate with my right hand and holding my sword in my left. Suddenly I perceived that the gateway was broader than the bridge; there was a dark corner on the opposite side where a man could stand. I darted across and stood there. Thus placed, I commanded the path, and no man could pass between the château and the old Castle till he had tried conclusions with me.

There was another shriek. Then a door was flung open and clanged against the wall, and I heard the handle of a door savagely twisted.

"Open the door! In God's name, what's the matter?" cried a voice—the voice of Black Michael himself.

He was answered by the very words I had written in my letter.

"Help, Michael—Hentzau!"

A fierce oath rang out from the duke, and with a loud thud he threw himself against the door. At the same moment I heard a window above my head open, and a voice cried: "What's the matter?" and I heard a man's hasty footsteps. I grasped my sword. If De Gautet came my way the Six would be less by one more.

Then I heard the clash of crossed swords and a tramp of feet, and—I cannot tell the thing so quickly as it happened, for all seemed to come at once. There was an angry cry from madame's room, the cry of a wounded man; the window was flung open; young Rupert stood there sword in hand. He turned his back, and I saw his body go forward to the lunge.

"Ah, Johann, there's one for you! Come on, Michael!"

Johann was there, then—come to the rescue of the duke! How would he open the door for me? For I feared that Rupert had slain him.

"Help!" cried the duke's voice, faint and husky.

I heard a step on the stairs above me; and I heard a stir down to my right, in the direction of the King's cell. But, before anything happened on my side of the moat I saw five or six men round young Rupert in the embrasure of madame's window. Three or four times he lunged with incomparable dash and dexterity. For an instant they fell back, leaving a ring round him. He leapt on the parapet of the window, laughing as he leapt, and waving his sword in his hand. He was drunk with blood, and he laughed again wildly as he flung himself headlong into the moat.

What became of him then? I did not see: for as he leapt, De Gautet's lean face looked out through the door by me, and without a second's hesitation I struck at him with all the strength God had given me, and he fell dead in the doorway without a word or a groan. I dropped on my knees by him. Where were the keys? I found myself muttering: "The keys, man, the keys?" as though he had been yet alive and could listen; and when I could not find them I—God forgive me!—I believe I struck a dead man's face.

At last I had them. There were but three. Seizing the largest, I felt the lock of the door that led to the cell. I fitted in the key. It was right! The lock turned. I drew the door close behind me and locked it as noiselessly as I could, putting the key in my pocket.

I found myself at the top of a flight of steep stone stairs. An oil lamp burnt dimly in the bracket. I took it down and held it in my hand; and I stood and listened.

"What in the devil can it be?" I heard a voice say.

It came from behind a door that faced me at the bottom of the stairs.

And another answered:

"Shall we kill him?"

I strained to hear the answer, and could have sobbed with relief when Detchard's voice came grating and cold:

"Wait a bit. There'll be trouble if we strike too soon."

There was a moment's silence. Then I heard the bolt of the door cautiously drawn back. Instantly I put out the light I held, replacing the lamp in the bracket.

"It's dark—the lamp's out. Have you a light?" said the other voice—Bersonin's.

No doubt they had a light, but they should not use it. It was come to the crisis now, and I rushed down the steps and flung myself against the door. Bersonin had unbolted it and it gave way before me. The Belgian stood there, sword in hand, and Detchard was sitting on a couch at the side of the room. In astonishment at seeing me, Bersonin recoiled; Detchard jumped to his sword. I rushed madly at the Belgian: he gave way before me, and I drove him up against the wall. He was no swordsman, though he fought bravely, and in a moment he lay on the floor before me. I turned—Detchard was not there. Faithful to his orders, he had not risked a fight with me, but had rushed straight to the door of the King's room, opened it and slammed it behind him. Even now he was at his work inside.

And surely he would have killed the King, and perhaps me also, had it not been for one devoted man who gave his life for the King. For when I forced the door, the sight I saw was this: the King stood in the corner of the room: broken by his sickness, he could do nothing; his fettered hands moved uselessly up and down, and he was laughing horribly in half-mad delirium. Detchard and the doctor were together in the middle of the room; and the doctor had flung himself on the murderer, pinning his hands to his sides for an instant. Then Detchard wrenched himself free from the feeble grip, and as I entered drove his sword through the hapless man.

Then he turned on me, crying:

"At last!"

We were sword to sword. By blessed chance neither he nor Bersonin had been wearing their revolvers. I found them afterwards, ready loaded, on the mantelpiece of the outer room; it was hard by the door, ready to their hands, but my sudden rush in had cut off access to them. Yes, we were man to man: and we began to fight, silently, sternly, and hard. Yet I remember little of it, save that the man was my match with the sword—nay, and more, for he knew more tricks than I; and that he forced me back against the bars that guarded the entrance to "Jacob's Ladder." And I saw a smile on his face, and he wounded me in the left arm.

No glory do I take for that contest. I believe that the man would have mastered me and slain me, and then done his butcher's work, for he was the most skilful swordsman

I have ever met; but even as he pressed me hard the half-mad, wasted, wan creature in the corner leaped high in lunatic mirth, shrieking:

"It's Cousin Rudolf! Cousin Rudolf! I'll help you, Cousin Rudolf!" and catching up a chair in his hands (he could but just lift it from the ground and hold it uselessly before him), he came towards us. Hope came to me.

"Come on!" I cried. "Come on! Drive it against his legs."

Detchard replied with a savage thrust. He all but had me.

"Come on! Come on, man!" I cried. "Come and share the fun!"

And the King laughed gleefully, and came on, pushing his chair before him.

With an oath Detchard skipped back, and before I knew what he was doing had turned his sword against the King. He made one fierce cut at the King, and the King, with a piteous cry, dropped where he stood. The stout ruffian turned to face me again. But his own hand had prepared his destruction; for in turning he trod in the pool of blood that flowed from the dead physician. He slipped; he fell. Like a dart I was upon him. I caught him by the throat, and before he could recover himself I drove my blade through his neck, and with a stifled curse he fell across the body of his victim.

Was the King dead? It was my first thought. I rushed to where he lay. Ay, it seemed as if he were dead, for he had a great gash across his forehead, and he lay still in a huddled mass on the floor. I dropped on my knees beside him, and leant my ear down to hear if he breathed. But before I could there was a loud rattle from the outside. I knew the sound: the drawbridge was being pushed out. A moment later it rang home against the wall on my side of the moat. I should be caught in a trap and the King with me, if he yet lived. He must take his chance, to live or to die. I took my sword, and passed into the outer room. Who were pushing the drawbridge out—my men? If so, all was well. My eye fell on the revolvers, and I seized one; and paused to listen in the doorway of the outer room. To listen, say I? Yes, and to get my breath: and I tore my shirt and twisted a strip of it round my bleeding arm; and stood listening again. I would have given the world to hear Sapt's voice. For I was faint, spent, and weary. And that wildcat Rupert Hentzau was yet at large in the Castle. Yet, because I could better defend the narrow door at the top of the stairs than the wider entrance to the room, I dragged myself up the steps, and stood behind it, listening.

What was the sound? Again a strange one for the place and time. An easy, scornful, merry laugh—the laugh of young Rupert Hentzau! I could scarcely believe that a sane man would laugh. Yet the laugh told me that my men had not come; for they must have shot Rupert ere now if they had come. And the clock struck half-past two! My God! The door had not been opened! They had gone to the bank! They had not found me! They had gone by now back to Tarlenheim, with the news of the King's death—and mine. Well, it would be true before they got there. Was not Rupert laughing in triumph?

For a moment I sank, unnerved, against the door. Then I started up alert again, for Rupert cried scornfully:

"Well, the bridge is there! Come over it! And in God's name, let's see Black Michael keep back you curs! Michael, come and fight for her!"

If it were a three-cornered fight I might yet bear my part. I turned the key in the door and looked out.

XIX. FACE TO FACE IN THE FOREST

For a moment I could see nothing, for the glare of lanterns and torches caught me full in the eyes from the other side of the bridge. But soon the scene grew clear; and it was a strange scene. The bridge was in its place. At the far end of it stood a group of the duke's servants; two or three carried the lights which had dazzled me, three or four held pikes in rest. They were huddled together; their weapons were protruded before them; their faces were pale and agitated. To put it plainly, they looked in as arrant a fright as I have seen men look, and they gazed apprehensively at a man who stood in the middle of the bridge, sword in hand. Rupert Hentzau was in his trousers and shirt; the white linen was stained with blood; but his easy, buoyant pose told me that he was himself either not touched at all or merely scratched. There he stood, holding the bridge against them, and daring them to come on; or, rather, bidding them and Black Michael to him; and they, having no firearms, cowered before the desperate man and dared not attack him. They whispered to one another; and in the backmost rank, I saw my friend Johann, leaning against the portal of the door and stanching with a handkerchief the blood which flowed from a wound in his cheek.

By marvellous chance, I was master. The cravens would oppose me no more than they dared attack Rupert. I had but to raise my revolver, and I sent him to his account with his sins on his head. He did not so much as know that I was there. I did nothing—why, I hardly know to this day. I had killed one man stealthily that night, and another by luck rather than skill—perhaps it was that. Again, villain as the man was, I did not relish being one of a crowd against him—perhaps it was that. But stronger than either of these restraining feelings came a curiosity and a fascination which held me spellbound, watching for the outcome of the scene.

"Michael, you dog! Michael! If you can stand, come on!" cried Rupert; and he advanced a step, the group shrinking back a little before him. "Michael, you bastard! come on!"

The answer to his taunts came in the wild cry of a woman:

"He's dead! My God, he's dead!"

"Dead!" shouted Rupert. "I struck better than I knew!" and he laughed triumphantly. Then he went on: "Down with your weapons there! I'm your master now! Down with them, I say!"

I believe they would have obeyed, but as he spoke came new things. First, there arose a distant sound, as of shouts and knockings from the other side of the *château*. My heart leapt. It must be my men, come by a happy disobedience to seek me. The noise continued, but none of the rest seemed to heed it. Their attention was chained by what now happened before their eyes. The group of servants parted and a woman staggered on to the bridge. Antoinette de Mauban was in a loose white robe, her dark hair streamed over her shoulders, her face was ghastly pale, and her eyes gleamed wildly in the light of the torches. In her shaking hand she held a revolver, and as she tottered forward she fired it at Rupert Hentzau. The ball missed him and struck the woodwork over my head.

"Faith, madame," laughed Rupert, "had your eyes been no more deadly than your shooting I had not been in this scrape—nor Black Michael in hell—to-night!"

She took no notice of his words. With a wonderful effort she calmed herself till she stood still and rigid. Then very slowly and deliberately she began to raise her arm again, taking most careful aim.

He would be mad to risk it. He must rush on her, chancing the bullet, or retreat towards me. I covered him with my weapon.

He did neither. Before she had got her aim, he bowed in his most graceful fashion, cried, "I can't kill where I've kissed," and before she or I could stop him laid his hand on the parapet of the bridge, and lightly leapt into the moat.

At that very moment I heard a rush of feet, and a voice I knew—Sapt's—cry: "God! it's the duke—dead!" Then I knew that the King needed me no more, and, throwing down my revolver, I sprang out on the bridge. There was a cry of wild wonder, "The King!" and then I, like Rupert Hentzau, sword in hand, vaulted over the parapet, intent on finishing my quarrel with him where I saw his curly head fifteen yards off in the water of the moat.

He swam swiftly and easily. I was weary and half crippled with my wounded arm. I could not gain on him. For a time I made no sound, but as we rounded the corner of the old keep I cried:

"Stop, Rupert, stop!"

I saw him look over his shoulder, but he swam on. He was under the bank now, searching, as I guessed, for a spot that he could climb. I knew there to be none—but there was my rope, which would still be hanging where I had left it. He would come to where it was before I could. Perhaps he would miss it—perhaps he would find it; and if he drew it up after him, he would get a good start of me. I put forth all my remaining strength and pressed on. At last I began to gain on him; for he, occupied with his search, unconsciously slackened his pace.

Ah, he had found it! A low shout of triumph came from him. He laid hold of it and began to haul himself up. I was near enough to hear him mutter: "How the devil comes this here?" I was at the rope, and he, hanging in mid air, saw me, but I could not reach him.

"Hullo! who's here?" he cried in startled tones.

For a moment I believe he took me for the King—I dare say I was pale enough to lend colour to the thought; but an instant later he cried:

"Why it's the play-actor! How come you here, man?"

And so saying he gained the bank.

I laid hold of the rope, but I paused. He stood on the bank, sword in hand, and he could cut my head open or spit me through the heart as I came up. I let go the rope.

"Never mind," said I; "but as I am here I think I'll stay."

He smiled down on me.

"These women are the deuce—" he began, when suddenly the great bell of the Castle started to ring furiously, and a loud shout reached us from the moat.

Rupert smiled again and waved his hand to me.

"I should like a turn with you, but it's a little too hot!" said he, and he disappeared from above me.

In an instant, without thinking of danger, I laid my hand to the rope. I was up. I saw him thirty yards off, running like a deer towards the shelter of the forest. For once Rupert Hentzau had chosen discretion for his part. I laid my feet to the ground and rushed after him, calling to him to stand. He would not. Unwounded and vigorous, he gained on me at every step; but, forgetting everything in the world except him and my thirst for his blood, I pressed on, and soon the deep shades of the forest of Zenda engulfed us both, pursued and pursuer.

It was three o'clock now, and day was dawning. I was on a long, straight grass avenue, and a hundred yards ahead ran young Rupert, his curls waving in the fresh breeze. I was weary and panting; he looked over his shoulder and waved his hand again to me. He was mocking me, for he saw he had the pace of me. I was forced to pause for breath. A moment later, Rupert turned sharply to the right and was lost from my sight.

I thought all was over, and in deep vexation sank on the ground. But I was up again directly, for a scream rang through the forest—a woman's scream. Putting forth the last of my strength, I ran on to the place where he had turned out of my sight, and turning also, I saw him again. But alas! I could not touch him. He was in the act of lifting a girl down from her horse; doubtless it was her scream that I heard. She looked like a small farmer's or a peasant's daughter, and she carried a basket on her arm. Probably she was on her way to the early market at Zenda. Her horse was a stout, well-shaped animal. Master Rupert lifted her down amid her shrieks—the sight of him frightened her; but he treated her gently, laughed, kissed her, and gave her money. Then he jumped on the horse, sitting sideways like a woman; and then he waited for me. I, on my part, waited for him.

Presently he rode towards me, keeping his distance however. He lifted up his hand, saying:

"What did you in the Castle?"

"I killed three of your friends," said I.

"What! You got to the cells?"

"Yes."

"And the King?"

"He was hurt by Detchard before I killed Detchard, but I pray that he lives."

"You fool!" said Rupert pleasantly.

"One thing more I did."

"And what's that?"

"I spared your life. I was behind you on the bridge, with a revolver in my hand."

"No? Faith, I was between two fires!"

"Get off your horse," I cried, "and fight like a man."

"Before a lady!" said he, pointing to the girl. "Fie, your Majesty!"

Then in my rage, hardly knowing what I did, I rushed at him. For a moment he seemed to waver. Then he reined his horse in and stood waiting for me. On I went in my folly. I seized the bridle and I struck at him. He parried and thrust at me. I fell back a pace and rushed in at him again; and this time I reached his face and laid his cheek open, and darted back before he could strike me. He seemed almost dazed at the fierceness of my attack; otherwise I think he must have killed me. I sank on my knee, panting, expecting him to ride at me. And so he would have done, and then and there, I doubt not, one or both of us would have died; but at the moment there came a shout from behind us, and, looking round, I saw just at the turn of the avenue a man on a horse. He was riding hard, and he carried a revolver in his hand. It was Fritz von Tarlenheim, my faithful friend. Rupert saw him, and knew that the game was up. He checked his rush at me and flung his leg over the saddle, but yet for just a moment he waited. Leaning forward, he tossed his hair off his forehead and smiled, and said:

"*Au revoir*, Rudolf Rassendyll!"

Then, with his cheek streaming blood, but his lips laughing and his body swaying with ease and grace, he bowed to me; and he bowed to the farm-girl, who had drawn near in trembling fascination; and he waved his hand to Fritz, who was just within range and let fly a shot at him. The ball came nigh doing its work, for it struck the sword he held, and he dropped the sword with an oath, wringing his fingers, and clapped his heels hard on his horse's belly, and rode away at a gallop.

And I watched him go down the long avenue, riding as though he rode for his pleasure and singing as he went, for all there was that gash in his cheek.

Once again he turned to wave his hand, and then the gloom of thickets swallowed him and he was lost from our sight. Thus he vanished—reckless and wary, graceful and graceless, handsome, debonair, vile, and unconquered. And I flung my sword passionately on the ground and cried to Fritz to ride after him. But Fritz stopped his horse, and leapt down and ran to me, and knelt, putting his arm about me. And indeed it was time, for the wound that Detchard had given me was broken forth afresh, and my blood was staining the ground.

"Then give me the horse!" I cried, staggering to my feet and throwing his arms off me. And the strength of my rage carried me so far as where the horse stood, and then I fell prone beside it. And Fritz knelt by me again.

"Fritz!" I said.

"Ay, friend—dear friend!" he said, tender as a woman.

"Is the King alive?"

He took his handkerchief and wiped my lips, and bent and kissed me on the forehead.

"Thanks to the most gallant gentleman that lives," said he softly, "the King is alive!"

The little farm-girl stood by us, weeping for fright and wide-eyed for wonder; for she had seen me at Zenda; and was not I, pallid, dripping, foul, and bloody as I was— yet was not I the King?

And when I heard that the King was alive I strove to cry "Hurrah!" But I could not speak, and I laid my head back in Fritz's arms and closed my eyes, and I groaned; and then, lest Fritz should do me wrong in his thoughts, I opened my eyes and tried to say "Hurrah!" again. But I could not. And being very tired, and now very cold, I huddled myself close up to Fritz, to get the warmth of him, and shut my eyes again and went to sleep.

XX. THE PRISONER AND THE KING

In order to a full understanding of what had occurred in the Castle of Zenda it is necessary to supplement my account of what I myself saw and did on that night by relating briefly what I afterwards learnt from Fritz and Madame de Mauban. The story told by the latter explained clearly how it happened that the cry which I had arranged as a stratagem and a sham had come, in dreadful reality, before its time, and had thus, as it seemed at the moment, ruined our hopes, while in the end it had favoured them. The unhappy woman, fired, I believe by a genuine attachment to the Duke of Strelsau, no less than by the dazzling prospects which a dominion over him opened before her eyes, had followed him at his request from Paris to Ruritania. He was a man of strong passions, but of stronger will, and his cool head ruled both. He was content to take all and give nothing. When she arrived she was not long in finding that she had a rival in the Princess Flavia; rendered desperate, she stood at nothing which might give or keep for her her power over the duke. As I say, he took and gave not. Simultaneously Antoinette found herself entangled in his audacious schemes. Unwilling to abandon him, bound to him by the chains of shame and hope, she yet would not be a decoy, nor at his bidding lure me to death. Hence the letters of warning she had written. Whether the lines she sent to Flavia were inspired by good or bad feeling, by jealousy or by pity, I do not know; but here also she served us well. When the duke went to Zenda she accompanied him; and here for the first time she learnt the full measure of his cruelty, and was touched with compassion for the unfortunate King. From this time she was with us; yet, from what she told me, I know that she still (as women will) loved Michael, and trusted to gain his life, if not his pardon, from the King as the reward for her assistance. His triumph she did not desire, for she loathed his crime, and loathed yet more fiercely what would be the prize of it—his marriage with his cousin, Princess Flavia.

At Zenda new forces came into play—the lust and daring of young Rupert. He was caught by her beauty, perhaps; perhaps it was enough for him that she belonged to another man, and that she hated him. For many days there had been quarrels and ill will between him and the duke, and the scene which I had witnessed in the duke's room was but one of many. Rupert's proposals to me, of which she had of course been ignorant, in no way surprised her when I related them; she had herself warned Michael against Rupert, even when she was calling on me to deliver her from both of them. On this night, then, Rupert had determined to have his will. When she had gone to her room he, having furnished himself with a key to it, had made his entrance. Her cries had brought the duke, and there in the dark room while she screamed, the men had fought; and Rupert, having wounded his master with a mortal blow, had, on the servants rushing in, escaped through the window as I have described. The duke's blood, spurting out, had stained his opponent's shirt; but Rupert, not knowing that he had dealt Michael his death, was eager to finish the encounter. How he meant to deal with the other three of the band I know not. I dare say he did not think, for the killing of Michael was not premeditated. Antoinette, left alone with the duke, had tried to stanch his wound, and thus was she busied till he died; and then, hearing Rupert's taunts, she had come forth to avenge him. Me she had not seen, nor did she till I darted out of my ambush and leapt after Rupert into the moat.

The same moment found my friends on the scene. They had reached the *château* in due time, and waited ready by the door. But Johann, swept with the rest to the rescue of the duke, did not open it; nay, he took a part against Rupert, putting himself forward more bravely than any in his anxiety to avert suspicion; and he had received a wound, in the embrasure of the window. Till nearly half-past two Sapt waited; then, following my orders, he had sent Fritz to search the banks of the moat. I was not there. Hastening back, Fritz told Sapt; and Sapt was for following orders still, and riding at full speed back to Tarlenheim; while Fritz would not hear of abandoning me, let me have ordered what I would. On this they disputed some few minutes; then Sapt, persuaded by Fritz, detached a party under Bernenstein to gallop back to Tarlenheim and bring up the marshal, while the rest fell to on the great door of the *château*. For near fifteen minutes it resisted them; then, just as Antoinette de Mauban fired at Rupert of Hentzau on the bridge, they broke in, eight of them in all: and the first door they came to was the door of Michael's room; and Michael lay dead across the threshold, with a sword thrust through his breast. Sapt cried out at his death, as I had heard, and they rushed on the servants; but these, in fear, dropped their weapons, and Antoinette flung herself weeping at Sapt's feet. And all she cried was that I had been at the end of the bridge and leapt off. "What of the prisoner?" asked Sapt; but she shook her head. Then Sapt and Fritz, with the gentlemen behind them, crossed the bridge, slowly, warily, and without noise; and Fritz stumbled over the body of De Gautet in the way of the door. They felt him and found him dead.

Then they consulted, listening eagerly for any sound from the cells below; but there came none, and they were greatly afraid that the King's guards had killed him, and having pushed his body through the great pipe, had escaped the same way themselves. Yet, because I had been seen here, they had still some hope (thus indeed Fritz, in his friendship, told me); and going back to Michael's body, pushing aside Antoinette, who prayed by it, they found a key to the door which I had locked, and opened the door. The staircase was dark, and they would not use a torch at first, lest they should be the more exposed to fire. But soon Fritz cried: "The door down there is open! See, there is light!" So they went on boldly, and found none to oppose them. And when they came to the outer room and saw the Belgian, Bersonin, lying dead, they thanked God, Sapt saying: "Ay, he has been here." Then rushing into the King's cell, they found Detchard lying dead across the dead physician, and the King on his back with his chair by him. And Fritz cried: "He's dead!" and Sapt drove all out of the room except Fritz, and knelt down by the King; and, having learnt more of wounds and the sign of death than I, he soon knew that the King was not dead, nor, if properly attended, would die. And they covered his face and carried him to Duke Michael's room, and laid him there; and Antoinette rose from praying by the body of the duke and went to bathe the King's head and dress his wounds, till a doctor came. And Sapt, seeing I had been there, and having heard Antoinette's story, sent Fritz to search the moat and then the forest. He dared send no one else. And Fritz found my horse, and feared the worst. Then, as I have told, he found me, guided by the shout with which I had called on Rupert to stop and face me. And I think a man has never been more glad to find his own brother alive than was Fritz to come on me; so that, in love and anxiety for me, he thought nothing of a thing so great as would have been the death of Rupert Hentzau. Yet had Fritz killed him I should have grudged it.

The enterprise of the King's rescue being thus prosperously concluded, it lay on Colonel Sapt to secure secrecy as to the King ever having been in need of rescue. Antoinette de Mauban and Johann, the keeper (who, indeed, was too much hurt to be wagging his tongue just now), were sworn to reveal nothing; and Fritz went forth to find—not the King, but the unnamed friend of the King, who had lain in Zenda and flashed for a moment before the dazed eyes of Duke Michael's servants on the drawbridge. The metamorphosis had happened; and the King, wounded almost to death by the attacks of the gaolers who guarded his friend, had at last overcome them, and rested now, wounded, but alive, in Black Michael's own room in the Castle. There he had been carried, his face covered with a cloak, from the cell; and thence orders issued that if his friend were found he should be brought directly and privately to the King, and that meanwhile messengers should ride at full speed to Tarlenheim to tell Marshall Strakencz to assure the princess of the King's safety, and to come himself with all speed to greet the King. The princess was enjoined to remain at Tarlenheim, and there await her cousin's coming or his further injunctions. Thus the King would come to his own again, having wrought brave deeds, and escaped, almost by a miracle, the treacherous assault of his unnatural brother.

This ingenious arrangement of my long-headed old friend prospered in every way, save where it encountered a force that often defeats the most cunning schemes. I mean nothing else than the pleasure of a woman. For, let her cousin and sovereign send what command he chose (or Colonel Sapt chose for him), and let Marshal Strakencz insist as he would, the Princess Flavia was in no way minded to rest at Tarlenheim while her lover lay wounded at Zenda; and when the Marshal, with a small suite, rode forth from Tarlenheim on the way to Zenda the princess' carriage followed immediately behind, and in this order they passed through the town, where the report was already rife that the King, going the night before to remonstrate with his brother, in all friendliness, for that he held one of the King's friends in confinement in the Castle, had been most traitorously set upon; that there had been a desperate conflict; that the duke was slain with several of his gentlemen; and that the King, wounded as he was, had seized and held the Castle of Zenda. All of which talk made, as may be supposed, a mighty excitement: and the wires were set in motion, and the tidings came to Strelsau only just after orders had been sent thither to parade the troops and overawe the dissatisfied quarters of the town with a display of force.

Thus the Princess Flavia came to Zenda. And as she drove up the hill, with the Marshal riding by the wheel and still imploring her to return in obedience to the King's orders, Fritz von Tarlenheim, with the prisoner of Zenda, came to the edge of the forest. I had revived from my swoon, and walked, resting on Fritz's arm; and looking out from the cover of the trees, I saw the princess. Suddenly understanding from a glance at my companion's face that we must not meet her, I sank on my knees behind a clump of bushes. But there was one whom we had forgotten, but who followed us, and was not disposed to let slip the chance of earning a smile and maybe a crown or two; and while we lay hidden the little farm-girl came by us and ran to the princess, courtesying and crying:

"Madame, the King is here—in the bushes! May I guide you to him, madame?"

"Nonsense, child!" said old Strakencz; "the King lies wounded in the Castle."

"Yes, sir, he's wounded, I know; but he's there—with Count Fritz—and not at the Castle," she persisted.

"Is he in two places, or are there two Kings?" asked Flavia, bewildered. "And how should he be here?"

"He pursued a gentleman, madame, and they fought till Count Fritz came; and the other gentleman took my father's horse from me and rode away; but the King is here with Count Fritz. Why, madame, is there another man in Ruritania like the King?"

"No, my child," said Flavia softly (I was told it afterward), and she smiled and gave the girl money. "I will go and see this gentleman," and she rose to alight from the carriage.

But at this moment Sapt came riding from the Castle, and, seeing the princess, made the best of a bad job, and cried to her that the King was well tended and in no danger.

"In the Castle?" she asked.

"Where else, madame?" said he, bowing.

"But this girl says he is yonder—with Count Fritz."

Sapt turned his eyes on the child with an incredulous smile.

"Every fine gentleman is a King to such," said he.

"Why, he's as like the King as one pea to another, madame!" cried the girl, a little shaken, but still obstinate.

Sapt started round. The old Marshal's face asked unspoken questions. Flavia's glance was no less eloquent. Suspicion spreads quick.

"I'll ride myself and see this man," said Sapt hastily.

"Nay, I'll come myself," said the princess.

"Then come alone," he whispered.

And she, obedient to the strange hinting in his face, prayed the Marshal and the rest to wait; and she and Sapt came on foot towards where we lay, Sapt waving to the farm-girl to keep at a distance. And when I saw them coming I sat in a sad heap on the ground, and buried my face in my hands. I could not look at her. Fritz knelt by me, laying his hand on my shoulder.

"Speak low, whatever you say," I heard Sapt whisper as they came up, and the next thing I heard was a low cry—half of joy, half of fear—from the princess:

"It is he! Are you hurt?"

And she fell on the ground by me and gently pulled my hands away; but I kept my eyes to the ground.

"It is the King!" she said. "Pray, Colonel Sapt, tell me where lay the wit of the joke you played on me?"

We answered none of us; we three were silent before her. Regardless of them, she threw her arms round my neck and kissed me. Then Sapt spoke in a low, hoarse whisper:

"It is not the King. Don't kiss him; he's not the King."

She drew back for a moment; then, with an arm still round my neck, she asked in superb indignation:

"Do I not know my love? Rudolf, my love!"

"It is not the King," said old Sapt again; and a sudden sob broke from tender-hearted Fritz.

It was the sob that told her no comedy was afoot.

"He is the King!" she cried. "It is the King's face—the King's ring—my ring! It is my love!"

"Your love, madame," said old Sapt, "but not the King. The King is there in the Castle. This gentleman—"

"Look at me, Rudolf! look at me!" she cried, taking my face between her hands. "Why do you let them torment me? Tell me what it means!"

Then I spoke, gazing into her eyes.

"God forgive me, madame!" I said. "I am not the King!"

I felt her hands clutch my cheeks. She gazed at me as never man's face was scanned yet. And I, silent again, saw wonder born, and doubt grow, and terror spring to life as she looked. And very gradually the grasp of her hands slackened; she turned to Sapt, to Fritz, and back to me; then suddenly she reeled forward and fell in my arms; and with a great cry of pain I gathered her to me and kissed her lips. Sapt laid his hand on my arm. I looked up in his face. And I laid her softly on the ground, and stood up, looking on her, cursing heaven that young Rupert's sword had spared me for this sharper pang.

XXI. If Love Were All!

It was night, and I was in the cell wherein the King had lain in the Castle of Zenda. The great pipe that Rupert of Hentzau had nicknamed "Jacob's Ladder" was gone, and the lights in the room across the moat twinkled in the darkness. All was still; the din and clash of strife were gone. I had spent the day hidden in the forest from the time when Fritz had led me off, leaving Sapt with the princess. Under cover of dusk, muffled up, I had been brought to the Castle and lodged where I now lay. Though three men had died there—two of them by my hand—I was not troubled by ghosts. I had thrown myself on a pallet by the window, and was looking out on the black water; Johann, the keeper, still pale from his wound, but not much hurt besides, had brought me supper. He told me that the King was doing well, that he had seen the princess; that she and he, Sapt and Fritz had been long together. Marshal Strakencz was gone to Strelsau; Black Michael lay in his coffin, and Antoinette de Mauban watched by him. Had I not heard from the chapel priests singing mass for him?

Outside there were strange rumours afloat. Some said that the prisoner of Zenda was dead; some, that he had vanished yet alive; some, that he was a friend who had served the King well in some adventure in England; others, that he had discovered the Duke's plots, and had therefore been kidnapped by him. One or two shrewd fellows shook their heads and said only that they would say nothing, but they had suspicions that more was to be known than was known if Colonel Sapt would tell all he knew.

Thus Johann chattered till I sent him away and lay there alone, thinking, not of the future, but—as a man is wont to do when stirring things have happened to him—rehearsing the events of the past weeks, and wondering how strangely they had fallen out. And above me in the stillness of the night I heard the standards flapping against their poles, for Black Michael's banner hung there half-mast high, and above it the royal flag of Ruritania, floating for one night more over my head. Habit grows so quick that only by an effort did I recollect that it floated no longer for me.

Presently Fritz von Tarlenheim came into the room. I was standing then by the window; the glass was opened, and I was idly fingering the cement which clung to the masonry where "Jacob's Ladder" had been. He told me briefly that the King wanted me, and together we crossed the drawbridge and entered the room that had been Black Michael's.

The King was lying there in bed; our doctor from Tarlenheim was in attendance on him, and whispered to me that my visit must be brief. The King held out his hand and shook mine. Fritz and the doctor withdrew to the window.

I took the King's ring from my finger and placed it on his.

"I have tried not to dishonour it, sire," said I.

"I can't talk much to you," he said in a weak voice. "I have had a great fight with Sapt and the Marshal—for we have told the Marshal everything. I wanted to take you to Strelsau and keep you with me, and tell everyone of what you had done; and you would have been my best and nearest friend, Cousin Rudolf. But they tell me I must not, and that the secret must be kept—if kept it can be."

"They are right, sire. Let me go. My work here is done."

"Yes, it is done, as no man but you could have done it. When they see me again, I shall have my beard on; I shall—yes, faith, I shall be wasted with sickness. They will not wonder that the King looks changed in face. Cousin, I shall try to let them find him changed in nothing else. You have shown me how to play the King."

"Sire," said I, "I can take no praise from you. It is by the narrowest grace of God that I was not a worse traitor than your brother."

He turned inquiring eyes on me; but a sick man shrinks from puzzles, and he had no strength to question me. His glance fell on Flavia's ring, which I wore. I thought he would question me about it; but after fingering it idly he let his head fall on his pillow.

"I don't know when I shall see you again," he said faintly, almost listlessly.

"If I can ever serve you again, sire," I answered.

His eyelids closed. Fritz came with the doctor. I kissed the King's hand, and let Fritz lead me away. I have never seen the King since.

Outside, Fritz turned, not to the right, back towards the drawbridge, but to the left, and, without speaking, led me upstairs, through a handsome corridor in the *château*.

"Where are we going?" I asked.

Looking away from me, Fritz answered:

"She has sent for you. When it is over come back to the bridge. I'll wait for you there."

"What does she want?" said I, breathing quickly.

He shook his head.

"Does she know everything?"

"Yes, everything."

He opened a door, and gently pushing me in, closed it behind me. I found myself in a drawing room, small and richly furnished. At first I thought that I was alone, for the light that came from a pair of shaded candles on the mantelpiece was very dim. But presently I discerned a woman's figure standing by the window. I knew it was the princess, and I walked up to her, fell on one knee, and carried the hand that hung by her side to my lips. She neither moved nor spoke. I rose to my feet, and, piercing the gloom with my eager eyes, saw her pale face and the gleam of her hair, and before I knew I spoke softly:

"Flavia!"

She trembled a little, and looked round. Then she darted to me, taking hold of me.

"Don't stand, don't stand! No, you mustn't! You're hurt! Sit down—here, here!"
She made me sit on a sofa, and put her hand on my forehead.

"How hot your head is!" she said, sinking on her knees by me. Then she laid her head against me, and I heard her murmur: "My darling, how hot your head is!"

Somehow love gives even to a dull man the knowledge of his lover's heart. I had come to humble myself and pray pardon for my presumption; but what I said now was:

"I love you with all my heart and soul!"

For what troubled and shamed her? Not her love for me, but the fear that I had counterfeited the lover as I had acted the King, and taken her kisses with a smothered smile.

"With all my life and heart!" said I, as she clung to me. "Always, from the first moment I saw you in the Cathedral! There has been but one woman in the world to me—and there will be no other. But God forgive me the wrong I've done you!"

"They made you do it!" she said quickly; and she added, raising her head and looking in my eyes: "It might have made no difference if I'd known it. It was always you, never the King!" and she raised herself and kissed me.

"I meant to tell you," said I. "I was going to on the night of the ball in Strelsau, when Sapt interrupted me. After that, I couldn't—I couldn't risk losing you before—before—I must! My darling, for you I nearly left the King to die!"

"I know, I know! What are we to do now, Rudolf?"

I put my arm round her and held her up while I said:

"I am going away to-night."

"Ah, no, no!" she cried. "Not to-night!"

"I must go to-night, before more people have seen me. And how would you have me stay, sweetheart, except—"

"If I could come with you!" she whispered very low.

"My God!" said I roughly, "don't talk about that!" and I thrust her a little back from me.

"Why not? I love you. You are as good a gentleman as the King!"

Then I was false to all that I should have held by. For I caught her in my arms and prayed her, in words that I will not write, to come with me, daring all Ruritania to take her from me. And for a while she listened, with wondering, dazzled eyes. But as her eyes looked on me I grew ashamed, and my voice died away in broken murmurs and stammerings, and at last I was silent.

She drew herself away from me and stood against the wall, while I sat on the edge of the sofa, trembling in every limb, knowing what I had done—loathing it, obstinate not to undo it. So we rested a long time.

"I am mad!" I said sullenly.

"I love your madness, dear," she answered.

Her face was away from me, but I caught the sparkle of a tear on her cheek. I clutched the sofa with my hand and held myself there.

"Is love the only thing?" she asked, in low, sweet tones that seemed to bring a calm even to my wrung heart. "If love were the only thing I would follow you—in rags, if need be—to the world's end; for you hold my heart in the hollow of your hand! But is love the only thing?"

I made no answer. It gives me shame now to think that I would not help her.

She came near me and laid her hand on my shoulder. I put my hand up and held hers.

"I know people write and talk as if it were. Perhaps, for some, Fate lets it be. Ah, if I were one of them! But if love had been the only thing you would have let the King die in his cell."

I kissed her hand.

"Honour binds a woman too, Rudolf. My honour lies in being true to my country and my House. I don't know why God has let me love you; but I know that I must stay!"

Still I said nothing; and she, pausing a while, then went on:

"Your ring will always be on my finger, your heart in my heart, the touch of your lips on mine. But you must go and I must stay. Perhaps I must do what it kills me to think of doing."

I knew what she meant, and a shiver ran through me. But I could not utterly fail her. I rose and took her hand.

"Do what you will or what you must," I said. "I think God shows His purposes to such as you. My part is lighter; for your ring shall be on my finger and your heart in mine, and no touch save of your lips will ever be on mine. So, may God comfort you, my darling!"

There struck on our ears the sound of singing. The priests in the chapel were singing masses for the souls of those who lay dead. They seemed to chant a requiem over our buried joy, to pray forgiveness for our love that would not die. The soft, sweet, pitiful music rose and fell as we stood opposite one another, her hands in mine.

"My queen and my beauty!" said I.

"My lover and true knight!" she said. "Perhaps we shall never see one another again. Kiss me, my dear, and go!"

I kissed her as she bade me; but at the last she clung to me, whispering nothing but my name, and that over and over again—and again—and again; and then I left her.

Rapidly I walked down to the bridge. Sapt and Fritz were waiting for me. Under their directions I changed my dress, and muffling my face, as I had done more than once before, I mounted with them at the door of the Castle, and we three rode through the night and on to the breaking of day, and found ourselves at a little roadside station just over the border of Ruritania. The train was not quite due, and I walked with them in a meadow by a little brook while we waited for it. They promised to send me all news; they overwhelmed me with kindness—even old Sapt was touched to gentleness, while Fritz was half unmanned. I listened in a kind of dream to all they said. "Rudolf! Rudolf! Rudolf!" still rang in my ears—a burden of sorrow and of love. At last they saw that I could not heed them, and we walked up and down in silence, till Fritz touched me on the arm, and I saw, a mile or more away, the blue smoke of the train. Then I held out a hand to each of them.

"We are all but half men this morning," said I, smiling. "But we have been men, eh, Sapt and Fritz, old friends? We have run a good course between us."

"We have defeated traitors and set the King firm on his throne," said Sapt.

Then Fritz von Tarlenheim suddenly, before I could discern his purpose or stay him, uncovered his head and bent as he used to do, and kissed my hand; and as I snatched it away he said, trying to laugh:

"Heaven doesn't always make the right men Kings!"

Old Sapt twisted his mouth as he wrung my hand.

"The devil has his share in most things," said he.

The people at the station looked curiously at the tall man with the muffled face, but we took no notice of their glances. I stood with my two friends, and waited till the train came up to us. Then we shook hands again, saying nothing; and both this time—and, indeed, from old Sapt it seemed strange—bared their heads, and so stood still till the train bore me away from their sight. So that it was thought some great man travelled privately for his pleasure from the little station that morning; whereas, in truth, it was only I, Rudolf Rassendyll, an English gentleman, a cadet of a good house, but a man of no wealth nor position, nor of much rank. They would have been disappointed to know that. Yet had they known all they would have looked more curiously still. For, be I what I might now, I had been for three months a King, which, if not a thing to be proud of, is, at least, an experience to have undergone. Doubtless I should have thought more of it had there not echoed through the air, from the towers of Zenda that we were leaving far away, into my ears and into my heart the cry of a woman's love—"Rudolf! Rudolf! Rudolf!"

Hark! I hear it now!

XXII. Present, Past—and Future?

The details of my return home can have but little interest. I went straight to the Tyrol and spent a quiet fortnight—mostly on my back, for a severe chill developed itself; and I was also the victim of a nervous reaction, which made me weak as a baby. As soon as I had reached my quarters I sent an apparently careless postcard to my brother, announcing my good health and prospective return. That would serve to satisfy the inquiries as to my whereabouts, which were probably still vexing the Prefect of the Police of Strelsau. I let my moustache and imperial grow again; and as hair comes quickly on my face, they were respectable, though not luxuriant, by the time that I landed myself in Paris and called on my friend George Featherly. My interview with him was chiefly remarkable for the number of unwilling but necessary falsehoods that I told; and I rallied him unmercifully when he told me that he had made up his mind that I had gone in the track of Madame de Mauban to Strelsau. The lady, it appeared, was back in Paris, but was living in great seclusion—a fact for which gossip found no difficulty in accounting. Did not all the world know of the treachery and death of Duke Michael? Nevertheless, George bade Bertram Bertrand be of good cheer, "for," said he flippantly, "a live poet is better than a dead duke." Then he turned on me and asked:

"What have you been doing to your moustache?"

"To tell the truth," I answered, assuming a sly air, "a man now and then has reasons for wishing to alter his appearance. But it's coming on very well again."

"What? Then I wasn't so far out! If not the fair Antoinette, there was a charmer."

"There is always a charmer," said I sententiously.

But George would not be satisfied till he had wormed out of me (he took much pride in his ingenuity) an absolutely imaginary love affair, attended with the proper *soupçon* of scandal, which had kept me all this time in the peaceful regions of the Tyrol. In return for this narrative George regaled me with a great deal of what he called "inside information" (known only to diplomatists) as to the true course of events in Ruritania, the plots and counterplots. In his opinion, he told me, with a significant nod, there was more to be said for Black Michael than the public supposed; and he hinted at a well-founded suspicion that the mysterious prisoner of Zenda, concerning whom a good many paragraphs had appeared, was not a man at all, but (here I had much ado not to smile) a woman disguised as a man; and that strife between the King and his brother for this imaginary lady's favour was at the bottom of their quarrel.

"Perhaps it was Madame de Mauban herself," I suggested.

"No!" said George decisively. "Antoinette de Mauban was jealous of her, and betrayed the duke to the King for that reason. And, to confirm what I say, it's well known that the Princess Flavia is now extremely cold to the King, after having been most affectionate."

At this point I changed the subject, and escaped from George's "inspired" delusions. But if diplomatists never know anything more than they had succeeded in finding out in this instance, they appear to me to be somewhat expensive luxuries.

While in Paris I wrote to Antoinette, though I did not venture to call upon her. I received in return a very affecting letter, in which she assured me that the King's generosity and kindness, no less than her regard for me, bound her conscience to absolute secrecy. She expressed the intention of settling in the country, and withdrawing herself entirely from society. Whether she carried out her designs I have never heard; but as I have not met her, or heard news of her up to this time, it is probable that she did. There is no doubt that she was deeply attached to the Duke of Strelsau; and her conduct at the time of his death proved that no knowledge of the man's real character was enough to root her regard for him out of her heart.

I had one more battle left to fight—a battle that would, I knew, be severe, and was bound to end in my complete defeat. Was I not back from the Tyrol, without having made any study of its inhabitants, institutions, scenery, fauna, flora, or other features? Had I not simply wasted my time in my usual frivolous, good-for-nothing way? That was the aspect of the matter which, I was obliged to admit, would present itself to my sister-in-law; and against a verdict based on such evidence, I had really no defence to offer. It may be supposed, then, that I presented myself in Park Lane in a shamefaced, sheepish fashion. On the whole, my reception was not so alarming as I had feared. It turned out that I had done, not what Rose wished, but—the next best thing—what she prophesied. She had declared that I should make no notes, record no observations, gather no materials. My brother, on the other hand, had been weak enough to maintain that a serious resolve had at length animated me.

When I returned empty-handed, Rose was so occupied in triumphing over Burlesdon that she let me down quite easily, devoting the greater part of her reproaches to my failure to advertise my friends of my whereabouts.

"We've wasted a lot of time trying to find you," she said.

"I know you have," said I. "Half our ambassadors have led weary lives on my account. George Featherly told me so. But why should you have been anxious? I can take care of myself."

"Oh, it wasn't that," she cried scornfully; "but I wanted to tell you about Sir Jacob Borrodaile. You know he's got an Embassy—at least, he will have in a month—and he wrote to say he hoped you would go with him."

"Where's he going to?"

"He's going to succeed Lord Topham at Strelsau," said she. "You couldn't have a nicer place, short of Paris."

"Strelsau! H'm!" said I, glancing at my brother.

"Oh, *that* doesn't matter!" exclaimed Rose impatiently. "Now you will go, won't you?"

"I don't know that I care about it!"

"Oh, you're too exasperating!"

"And I don't think I can go to Strelsau. My dear Rose, would it be—suitable?"

"Oh, nobody remembers that horrid old story now."

Upon this, I took out of my pocket a portrait of the King of Ruritania. It had been taken a month or two before he ascended the throne, and he wore a full beard. Nevertheless she could not miss my point when I said, putting it into her hands:

"In case you've not seen or not noticed a picture of Rudolf V., there he is. Don't you think they might recall the story if I appeared at the Court of Ruritania?"

My sister-in-law looked at the portrait, and then at me.

"Good gracious!" she said, and flung the photograph down on the table.

"What do you say, Bob?" I asked.

Burlesdon got up, went to a corner of the room, and searched in a heap of newspapers. Presently he came back with a copy of the *Illustrated London News*. Opening the paper, he displayed a double-page engraving of the Coronation of Rudolf V. at Strelsau. The photograph and the picture he laid side by side. I sat at the table fronting them; and as I looked I grew absorbed. My eye travelled from my own portrait to Sapt, to Strakencz, to the rich robes of the Cardinal, to Black Michael's face, to the stately figure of the princess by his side. Long I looked and eagerly. I was roused by my brother's hand on my shoulder. He was gazing down at me with a puzzled expression.

"It's a remarkable likeness, you see," said I. "I really think I had better not go to Ruritania."

Rose, though half convinced, would not abandon her position.

"It's just an excuse," she said pettishly. "You don't want to do anything. Why, you might become an ambassador!"

"I don't think I want to be an ambassador," said I.

"It's more than you ever will be," she retorted.

That is very likely true, but it is not more than I have been. The idea of being an ambassador could scarcely dazzle me. I had been a King!

So pretty Rose left us in dudgeon; and Burlesdon, lighting a cigarette, looked at me still with that curious gaze.

"That picture in the paper——" he said.

"Well, what of it? It shows that the King of Ruritania and your humble servant are as like as two peas."

My brother shook his head.

"I suppose so," he said. "But I should know you from the man in the photograph."

"And not from the picture in the paper?"

"I should know the photograph from the picture: the picture's very like the photograph, but——"

"Well?"

"It's more like you," said my brother.

My brother is a good man and true—so that, for all that he is a married man and mighty fond of his wife, he should know any secret of mine. But this secret was not mine, and I could not tell it to him.

"I don't think it's so much like me as the photograph," said I boldly. "But anyhow, Bob, I won't go to Strelsau."

"No, don't go to Strelsau, Rudolf," said he.

And whether he suspects anything, or has a glimmer of the truth, I do not know. If he has, he keeps it to himself, and he and I never refer to it. And we let Sir Jacob Borrodaile find another *attaché*.

Since all these events whose history I have set down happened I have lived a very quiet life at a small house which I have taken in the country. The ordinary ambitions and aims of men in my position seem to me dull and unattractive. I have little fancy for the whirl of society, and none for the jostle of politics. Lady Burlesdon utterly despairs of me; my neighbours think me an indolent, dreamy, unsociable fellow. Yet I am a young man; and sometimes I have a fancy—the superstitious would call it a presentiment—that my part in life is not yet altogether played; that, somehow and some day, I shall mix again in great affairs, I shall again spin policies in a busy brain, match my wits against my enemies', brace my muscle to fight a good fight and strike stout blows. Such is the tissue of my thoughts as, with gun or rod in hand, I wander through the woods or by the side of the stream. Whether the fancy will be fulfilled, I cannot tell—still less whether the scene that, led by memory, I lay for my new exploits will be the true one—for I love to see myself once again in the crowded streets of Strelsau, or beneath the frowning keep of the Castle of Zenda.

Thus led, my broodings leave the future, and turn back on the past. Shapes rise before me in long array—the wild first revel with the King, the rush with my brave tea table, the night in the moat, the pursuit in the forest: my friends and my foes, the people who learnt to love and honour me, the desperate men who tried to kill me. And, from amidst these last, comes one who alone of all of them yet moves on earth, though where I know not, yet plans (as I do not doubt) wickedness, yet turns women's hearts to softness and men's to fear and hate. Where is young Rupert of Hentzau—the boy who came so nigh to beating me? When his name comes into my head I feel my hand grip and the blood move quicker through my veins: and the hint of Fate—the presentiment—seems to grow stronger and more definite, and to whisper insistently in my ear that I have yet a hand to play with young Rupert; therefore I exercise myself in arms, and seek to put off the day when the vigour of youth must leave me.

One break comes every year in my quiet life. Then I go to Dresden, and there I am met by my dear friend and companion Fritz von Tarlenheim. Last time his pretty wife Helga came, and a lusty crowing baby with her. And for a week Fritz and I are together, and I hear all of what falls out in Strelsau; and in the evenings, as we walk and smoke together, we talk of Sapt, and of the King, and often of young Rupert; and, as the hours grow small, at last we speak of Flavia. For every year Fritz carries with him to Dresden a little box; in it lies a red rose, and round the stalk of the rose is a slip of paper with the words written: "Rudolf—Flavia—always." And the like I send back by him. That message, and the wearing of the rings, are all that now bind me and the Queen of Ruritania. Far—nobler, as I told her, for the act—she has followed where her duty to her country and her House led her, and is the wife of the King, uniting his subjects to him by the love they bear to her, giving peace and quiet days to thousands by her self-sacrifice. There are moments when I dare not think of it, but there are others when I rise in spirit to where she ever dwells; then I can thank God that I love the noblest lady in the world, the most gracious and beautiful, and that there was nothing in my love that made her fall short in her high duty.

Shall I see her face again—the pale face and the glorious hair? Of that I know nothing; Fate has no hint, my heart no presentiment. I do not know. In this world, perhaps—nay, it is likely—never. And can it be that somewhere, in a manner whereof our flesh-bound minds have no apprehension, she and I will be together again, with nothing to come between us, nothing to forbid our love? That I know not, nor wiser heads than mine. But if it be never—if I can never hold sweet converse again with her, or look upon her face, or know from her her love, why, then, this side the grave, I will live as becomes the man whom she loves; and for the other side I must pray a dreamless sleep.

How the Brigadier Bore Himself at Waterloo

Arthur Conan Doyle

I. The Story of the Forest Inn

Of all the great battles in which I had the honour of drawing my sword for the Emperor and for France there was not one which was lost. At Waterloo, although, in a sense, I was present, I was unable to fight, and the enemy was victorious. It is not for me to say that there is a connection between these two things. You know me too well, my friends, to imagine that I would make such a claim. But it gives matter for thought, and some have drawn flattering conclusions from it. After all, it was only a matter of breaking a few English squares and the day would have been our own. If the Hussars of Conflans, with Étienne Gerard to lead them, could not do this, then the best judges are mistaken. But let that pass. The Fates had ordained that I should hold my hand and that the Empire should fall. But they had also ordained that this day of gloom and sorrow should bring such honour to me as had never come when I swept on the wings of victory from Boulogne to Vienna. Never had I burned so brilliantly as at that supreme moment when the darkness fell upon all around me. You are aware that I was faithful to the Emperor in his adversity, and that I refused to sell my sword and my honour to the Bourbons. Never again was I to feel my war horse between my knees, never again to hear the kettledrums and silver trumpets behind me as I rode in front of my little rascals. But it comforts my heart, my friends, and it brings the tears to my eyes, to think how great I was upon that last day of my soldier life, and to remember that of all the remarkable exploits which have won me the love of so many beautiful women, and the respect of so many noble men, there was none which, in splendour, in audacity, and in the great end which was attained, could compare with my famous ride upon the night of June 18th, 1815. I am aware that the story is often told at mess-tables and in barrack-rooms, so that there are few in the army who have not heard it, but modesty has sealed my lips, until now, my friends, in the privacy of these intimate gatherings, I am inclined to lay the true facts before you.

In the first place, there is one thing which I can assure you. In all his career Napoleon never had so splendid an army as that with which he took the field for that campaign. In 1813 France was exhausted. For every veteran there were five children—Marie Louises, as we called them, for the Empress had busied herself in raising levies while the Emperor took the field. But it was very different in 1815. The prisoners had all come back—the men from the snows of Russia, the men from the dungeons of Spain, the men from the hulks in England. These were the dangerous men, veterans of twenty battles, longing for their old trade, and with hearts filled with hatred and revenge. The ranks were full of soldiers who wore two and three chevrons, every chevron meaning five years' service. And the spirit of these men was terrible. They were raging, furious, fanatical, adoring the Emperor as a Mameluke does his prophet, ready to fall upon their own bayonets if their blood could serve him. If you had seen these fierce old veterans going into battle, with their flushed faces, their savage eyes, their furious yells, you would wonder that anything could stand against them. So high was the spirit of France at that time that every other spirit would have quailed before it; but these people, these English, had neither spirit nor soul, but only solid, immovable beef, against which we broke ourselves in vain. That was it, my friends! On the one side, poetry, gallantry, self-sacrifice—all that is beautiful and heroic. On the other side, beef. Our hopes, our ideals, our dreams—all were shattered on that terrible beef of Old England.

You have read how the Emperor gathered his forces, and then how he and I, with a hundred and thirty thousand veterans, hurried to the northern frontier and fell upon the Prussians and the English. On the 16th of June, Ney held the English in play at Quatre-Bras while we beat the Prussians at Ligny. It is not for me to say how far I contributed to that victory, but it is well known that the Hussars of Conflans covered themselves with glory. They fought well, these Prussians, and eight thousand of them were left upon the field. The Emperor thought that he had done with them, as he sent Marshal Grouchy with thirty-two thousand men to follow them up and to prevent their interfering with his plans. Then with nearly eighty thousand men, he turned upon these "Goddam" Englishmen. How much we had to avenge upon them, we Frenchmen—the guineas of Pitt, the hulks of Portsmouth, the invasion of Wellington, the perfidious victories of Nelson! At last the day of punishment seemed to have arisen.

Wellington had with him sixty-seven thousand men, but many of them were known to be Dutch and Belgian, who had no great desire to fight against us. Of good troops he had not fifty thousand. Finding himself in the presence of the Emperor in person with eighty thousand men, this Englishman was so paralysed with fear that he could neither move himself nor his army. You have seen the rabbit when the snake approaches. So stood the English upon the ridge of Waterloo. The night before, the Emperor, who had lost an aide-de-camp at Ligny, ordered me to join his staff, and I had left my Hussars to the charge of Major Victor. I know not which of us was the most grieved, they or I, that I should be called away upon the eve of battle, but an order is an order, and a good soldier can but shrug his shoulders and obey. With the Emperor I rode across the front of the enemy's position on the morning of the 18th, he looking at them through his glass and planning which was the shortest way to destroy them. Soult was at his elbow, and Ney and Foy and others who had fought the English in Portugal and Spain. "Have a care, Sire," said Soult. "The English infantry is very solid."

"You think them good soldiers because they have beaten you," said the Emperor, and we younger men turned away our faces and smiled. But Ney and Foy were grave and serious. All the time the English line, chequered with red and blue and dotted with batteries, was drawn up silent and watchful within a long musket-shot of us. On the other side of the shallow valley our own people, having finished their soup, were assembling for the battle. It had rained very heavily, but at this moment the sun shone out and beat upon the French army, turning our brigades of cavalry into so many dazzling rivers of steel, and twinkling and sparkling on the innumerable bayonets of the infantry. At the sight of that splendid army, and the beauty and majesty of its appearance, I could contain myself no longer, but, rising in my stirrups, I waved my busby and cried, "*Vive l'Empereur!*" a shout which growled and roared and clattered from one end of the line to the other, while the horsemen waved their swords and the footmen held up their shakos upon their bayonets. The English remained petrified upon their ridge. They knew that their hour had come.

And so it would have come if at that moment the word had been given and the whole army had been permitted to advance. We had but to fall upon them and to sweep them from the face of the earth. To put aside all question of courage, we were the more numerous, the older soldiers, and the better led. But the Emperor desired to do all things in order, and he waited until the ground should be drier and harder, so that his artillery could manœuvre. So three hours were wasted, and it was eleven o'clock before we saw Jerome Buonaparte's columns advance upon our left and heard the crash of the guns which told that the battle had begun. The loss of those three hours was our destruction. The attack upon the left was directed upon a farm-house which was held by the English Guards, and we heard the three loud shouts of apprehension which the defenders were compelled to utter. They were still holding out, and D'Erlon's corps was advancing upon the right to engage another portion of the English line, when our attention was called away from the battle beneath our noses to a distant portion of the field of action.

The Emperor had been looking through his glass to the extreme left of the English line, and now he turned suddenly to the Duke of Dalmatia, or Soult, as we soldiers preferred to call him.

"What is it, Marshal?" said he.

We all followed the direction of his gaze, some raising our glasses, some shading our eyes. There was a thick wood over yonder, then a long, bare slope, and another wood beyond. Over this bare strip between the two woods there lay something dark, like the shadow of a moving cloud.

"I think that they are cattle, Sire," said Soult.

At that instant there came a quick twinkle from amid the dark shadow.

"It is Grouchy," said the Emperor, and he lowered his glass. "They are doubly lost, these English. I hold them in the hollow of my hand. They cannot escape me."

He looked round, and his eyes fell upon me.

"Ah! here is the prince of messengers," said he. "Are you well mounted, Colonel Gerard?"

I was riding my little Violette, the pride of the brigade. I said so.

"Then ride hard to Marshal Grouchy, whose troops you see over yonder. Tell him that he is to fall upon the left flank and rear of the English while I attack them in front. Together we should crush them and not a man escape."

I saluted and rode off without a word, my heart dancing with joy that such a mission should be mine. I looked at that long, solid line of red and blue looming through the smoke of the guns, and I shook my fist at it as I went. "We shall crush them and not a man escape." They were the Emperor's words, and it was I, Etienne Gerard, who was to turn them into deeds. I burned to reach the Marshal, and for an instant I thought of riding through the English left wing, as being the shortest cut. I have done bolder deeds and come out safely, but I reflected that if things went badly with me and I was taken or shot the message would be lost and the plans of the Emperor miscarry. I passed in front of the cavalry, therefore, past the Chasseurs, the Lancers of the Guard, the Carabineers, the Horse Grenadiers, and, lastly, my own little rascals, who followed me wistfully with their eyes. Beyond the cavalry the Old Guard was standing, twelve regiments of them, all veterans of many battles, sombre and severe, in long blue overcoats and high bearskins from which the plumes had been removed. Each bore within the goatskin knapsack upon his back the blue and white parade uniform which they would use for their entry into Brussels next day. As I rode past them I reflected that these men had never been beaten, and as I looked at their weather-beaten faces and their stern and silent bearing, I said to myself that they never would be beaten. Great heavens, how little could I foresee what a few more hours would bring!

On the right of the Old Guard were the Young Guard and the 6th Corps of Lobau, and then I passed Jacquinot's Lancers and Marbot's Hussars, who held the extreme flank of the line. All these troops knew nothing of the corps which was coming toward them through the wood, and their attention was taken up in watching the battle which raged upon their left. More than a hundred guns were thundering from each side, and the din was so great that of all the battles which I have fought I cannot recall more than half-a-dozen which were as noisy. I looked back over my shoulder, and there were two brigades of Cuirassiers, English and French, pouring down the hill together, with the sword-blades playing over them like summer lightning. How I longed to turn Violette, and to lead my Hussars into the thick of it! What a picture! Etienne Gerard with his back to the battle, and a fine cavalry action raging behind him. But duty is duty, so I rode past Marbot's vedettes and on in the direction of the wood, passing the village of Frishermont upon my left.

In front of me lay the great wood, called the Wood of Paris, consisting mostly of oak trees, with a few narrow paths leading through it. I halted and listened when I reached it, but out of its gloomy depths there came no blare of trumpet, no murmur of wheels, no tramp of horses to mark the advance of that great column which, with my own eyes, I had seen streaming toward it. The battle roared behind me, but in front all was as silent as that grave in which so many brave men would shortly sleep. The sunlight was cut off by the arches of leaves above my head, and a heavy damp smell rose from the sodden ground. For several miles I galloped at such a pace as few riders would care to go with roots below and branches above. Then, at last, for the first time I caught a glimpse of Grouchy's advance guard. Scattered parties of Hussars passed me on either side, but some distance off, among the trees. I heard the beating of a drum far away, and the low, dull murmur which an army makes upon the march. Any moment I might come upon the staff and deliver my message to Grouchy in person, for I knew well that on such a march a Marshal of France would certainly ride with the van of his army.

Suddenly the trees thinned in front of me, and I understood with delight that I was coming to the end of the wood, whence I could see the army and find the Marshal. Where the track comes out from amid the trees there is a small cabaret, where wood-cutters and waggoners drink their wine. Outside the door of this I reined up my horse for an instant while I took in the scene which was before me. Some few miles away I saw a second great forest, that of St. Lambert, out of which the Emperor had seen the troops advancing. It was easy to see, however, why there had been so long a delay in their leaving one wood and reaching the other, because between the two ran the deep defile of the Lasnes, which had to be crossed. Sure enough, a long column of troops—horse, foot, and guns—was streaming down one side of it and swarming up the other, while the advance guard was already among the trees on either side of me. A battery of Horse Artillery was coming along the road, and I was about to gallop up to it and ask the officer in command if he could tell me where I should find the Marshal, when suddenly I observed that, though the gunners were dressed in blue, they had not the dolman trimmed with red brandenburgs as our own horse-gunners wear it. Amazed at the sight, I was looking at these soldiers to left and right when a hand touched my thigh, and there was the landlord, who had rushed from his inn.

"Madman!" he cried, "why are you here? What are you doing?"

"I am seeking Marshal Grouchy."

"You are in the heart of the Prussian army. Turn and fly!"

"Impossible; this is Grouchy's corps."

"How do you know?"

"Because the Emperor has said it."

"Then the Emperor has made a terrible mistake! I tell you that a patrol of Silesian Hussars has this instant left me. Did you not see them in the wood?"

"I saw Hussars."

"They are the enemy."

"Where is Grouchy?"

"He is behind. They have passed him."

"Then how can I go back? If I go forward I may see him yet. I must obey my orders and find him whereever he is."

The man reflected for an instant.

"Quick! quick!" he cried, seizing my bridle. "Do what I say and you may yet escape. They have not observed you yet. Come with me and I will hide you until they pass."

Behind his house there was a low stable, and into this he thrust Violette. Then he half led and half dragged me into the kitchen of the inn. It was a bare, brick-floored room. A stout, red-faced woman was cooking cutlets at the fire.

"What's the matter now?" she asked, looking with a frown from me to the innkeeper. "Who is this you have brought in?"

"It is a French officer, Marie. We cannot let the Prussians take him."

"Why not?"

"Why not? Sacred name of a dog, was I not myself a soldier of Napoleon? Did I not win a musket of honour among the Vélites of the Guard? Shall I see a comrade taken before my eyes? Marie, we must save him." But the lady looked at me with most unfriendly eyes.

"Pierre Charras," she said, "you will not rest until you have your house burned over your head. Do you not understand, you blockhead, that if you fought for Napoleon it was because Napoleon ruled Belgium? He does so no longer. The Prussians are our allies and this is our enemy. I will have no Frenchman in this house. Give him up!"

The innkeeper scratched his head and looked at me in despair, but it was very evident to me that it was neither for France nor for Belgium that this woman cared, but that it was the safety of her own house that was nearest her heart.

"Madame," said I, with all the dignity and assurance I could command, "the Emperor is defeating the English, and the French army will be here before evening. If you have used me well you will be rewarded, and if you have denounced me you will be punished and your house will certainly be burned by the provost-martial."

She was shaken by this, and I hastened to complete my victory by other methods.

"Surely," said I, "it is impossible that anyone so beautiful can also be hard-hearted? You will not refuse me the refuge which I need."

She looked at my whiskers and I saw that she was softened. I took her hand, and in two minutes we were on such terms that her husband swore roundly that he would give me up himself if I pressed the matter farther.

"Besides, the road is full of Prussians," he cried. "Quick! quick! into the loft!"

"Quick! quick! into the loft!" echoed his wife, and together they hurried me toward a ladder which led to a trap-door in the ceiling. There was loud knocking at the door, so you can think that it was not long before my spurs went twinkling through the hole and the board was dropped behind me. An instant later I heard the voices of the Germans in the rooms below me.

The place in which I found myself was a single long attic, the ceiling of which was formed by the roof of the house. It ran over the whole of one side of the inn, and through the cracks in the flooring I could look down either upon the kitchen, the sitting-room, or the bar at my pleasure. There were no windows, but the place was in the last stage of disrepair, and several missing slates upon the roof gave me light and the means of observation. The place was heaped with lumber—fodder at one end and a huge pile of empty bottles at the other. There was no door or window save the hole through which I had come up.

I sat upon the heap of hay for a few minutes to steady myself and to think out my plans. It was very serious that the Prussians should arrive upon the field of battle earlier than our reserves, but there appeared to be only one corps of them, and a corps more or less makes little difference to such a man as the Emperor. He could afford to give the English all this and beat them still. The best way in which I could serve him, since Grouchy was behind, was to wait here until they were past, and then to resume my journey, to see the Marshal, and to give him his orders. If he advanced upon the rear of the English instead of following the Prussians all would be well. The fate of France depended upon my judgment and my nerve. It was not the first time, my friends, as you are well aware, and you know the reasons that I had to trust that neither nerve nor judgment would ever fail me. Certainly, the Emperor had chosen the right man for his mission. "The prince of messengers" he had called me. I would earn my title.

It was clear that I could do nothing until the Prussians had passed, so I spent my time in observing them. I have no love for these people, but I am compelled to say that they kept excellent discipline, for not a man of them entered the inn, though their lips were caked with dust and they were ready to drop with fatigue. Those who had knocked at the door were bearing an insensible comrade, and having left him they returned at once to the ranks. Several others were carried in in the same fashion and laid in the kitchen, while a young surgeon, little more than a boy, remained behind in charge of them. Having observed them through the cracks in the floor, I next turned my attention to the holes in the roof, from which I had an excellent view of all that was passing outside. The Prussian corps was still streaming past. It was easy to see that they had made a terrible march and had little food, for the faces of the men were ghastly, and they were plastered from head to foot with mud from their falls upon the foul and slippery roads. Yet, spent as they were, their spirit was excellent, and they pushed and hauled at the gun-carriages when the wheels sank up to the axles in the mire, and the weary horses were floundering knee-deep unable to draw them through. The officers rode up and down the column encouraging the more active with words of praise, and the laggards with blows from the flat of their swords. All the time from over the wood in front of them there came the tremendous roar of the battle, as if all the rivers on earth had united in one gigantic cataract, booming and crashing in a mighty fall. Like the spray of the cataract was the long veil of smoke which rose high over the trees. The officers pointed to it with their swords, and with hoarse cries from their parched lips the mud-stained men pushed onward to the battle. For an hour I watched them pass, and I reflected that their vanguard must have come into touch with Marbot's vedettes and that the Emperor knew already of their coming. "You are going very fast up the road, my friends, but you will come down it a great deal faster," said I to myself, and I consoled myself with the thought.

But an adventure came to break the monotony of this long wait. I was seated beside my loophole and congratulating myself that the corps was nearly past, and that the road would soon be clear for my journey, when suddenly I heard a loud altercation break out in French in the kitchen.

"You shall not go!" cried a woman's voice.

"I tell you that I will!" said a man's, and there was a sound of scuffling.

In an instant I had my eye to the crack in the floor. There was my stout lady, like a faithful watch-dog, at the bottom of the ladder, while the young German surgeon, white with anger, was endeavouring to come up it. Several of the German soldiers who had recovered from their prostration were sitting about on the kitchen floor and watching the quarrel with stolid, but attentive, faces. The landlord was nowhere to be seen.

"There is no liquor there," said the woman.

"I do not want liquor; I want hay or straw for these men to lie upon. Why should they lie on the bricks when there is straw overhead?"

"There is no straw."

"What is up there?"

"Empty bottles."

"Nothing else?"

"No."

For a moment it looked as if the surgeon would abandon his intention, but one of the soldiers pointed up to the ceiling. I gathered from what I could understand of his words that he could see the straw sticking out between the planks. In vain the woman protested. Two of the soldiers were able to get upon their feet and to drag her aside, while the young surgeon ran up the ladder, pushed open the trap-door, and climbed into the loft. As he swung the door back I slipped behind it, but as luck would have it he shut it again behind him, and there we were left standing face to face.

Never have I seen a more astonished young man.

"A French officer!" he gasped.

"Hush!" said I, "hush! Not a word above a whisper." I had drawn my sword.

"I am not a combatant," he said; "I am a doctor. Why do you threaten me with your sword? I am not armed."

"I do not wish to hurt you, but I must protect myself. I am in hiding here."

"A spy!"

"A spy does not wear such a uniform as this, nor do you find spies on the staff of an army. I rode by mistake into the heart of this Prussian corps, and I concealed myself here in the hope of escaping when they are past. I will not hurt you if you do not hurt me, but if you do not swear that you will be silent as to my presence you will never go down alive from this attic."

"You can put up your sword, sir," said the surgeon, and I saw a friendly twinkle in his eyes. "I am a Pole by birth, and I have no ill-feeling to you or your people. I will do my best for my patients, but I will do no more. Capturing Hussars is not one of the duties of a surgeon. With your permission I will now descend with this truss of hay to make a couch for these poor fellows below."

I had intended to exact an oath from him, but it is my experience that if a man will not speak the truth he will not swear the truth, so I said no more. The surgeon opened the trap-door, threw out enough hay for his purpose, and then descended the ladder, letting down the door behind him. I watched him anxiously when he rejoined his patients, and so did my good friend the landlady, but he said nothing and busied himself with the needs of his soldiers.

By this time I was sure that the last of the army corps was past, and I went to my loophole confident that I should find the coast clear, save, perhaps, for a few stragglers, whom I could disregard. The first corps was indeed past, and I could see the last files of the infantry disappearing into the wood; but you can imagine my disappointment when out of the Forest of St. Lambert I saw a second corps emerging, as numerous as the first. There could be no doubt that the whole Prussian army, which we thought we had destroyed at Ligny, was about to throw itself upon our right wing while Marshal Grouchy had been coaxed away upon some fool's errand. The roar of guns, much nearer than before, told me that the Prussian batteries which had passed me were already in action. Imagine my terrible position! Hour after hour was passing; the sun was sinking toward the west. And yet this cursed inn, in which I lay hid, was like a little island amid a rushing stream of furious Prussians. It was all important that I should reach Marshal Grouchy, and yet I could not show my nose without being made prisoner. You can think how I cursed and tore my hair. How little do we know what is in store for us! Even while I raged against my ill-fortune, that same fortune was reserving me for a far higher task than to carry a message to Grouchy—a task which could not have been mine had I not been held tight in that little inn on the edge of the Forest of Paris.

Two Prussian corps had passed and a third was coming up, when I heard a great fuss and the sound of several voices in the sitting-room. By altering my position I was able to look down and see what was going on.

Two Prussian generals were beneath me, their heads bent over a map which lay upon the table. Several aides-de-camp and staff officers stood round in silence. Of the two generals, one was a fierce old man, white-haired and wrinkled, with a ragged, grizzled moustache and a voice like the bark of a hound. The other was younger, but long-faced and solemn. He measured distances upon the map with the air of a student, while his companion stamped and fumed and cursed like a corporal of Hussars. It was strange to see the old man so fiery and the young one so reserved. I could not understand all that they said, but I was very sure about their general meaning.

"I tell you we must push on and ever on!" cried the old fellow, with a furious German oath. "I promised Wellington that I would be there with the whole army even if I had to be strapped to my horse. Bülow's corps is in action, and Ziethen's shall support it with every man and gun. Forward, Gneisenau, forward!"

The other shook his head.

"You must remember, your Excellency, that if the English are beaten they will make for the coast. What will your position be then, with Grouchy between you and the Rhine?"

"We shall beat them, Gneisenau; the Duke and I will grind them to powder between us. Push on, I say! The whole war will be ended in one blow. Bring Pirsch up, and we can throw sixty thousand men into the scale while Thielmann holds Grouchy beyond Wavre."

Gneisenau shrugged his shoulders, but at that instant an orderly appeared at the door.

"An aide-de-camp from the Duke of Wellington," said he.

"Ha, ha!" cried the old man; "let us hear what he has to say!"

An English officer, with mud and blood all over his scarlet jacket, staggered into the room. A crimson-stained handkerchief was knotted round his arm, and he held the table to keep himself from falling.

"My message is to Marshal Blucher," said he.

"I am Marshal Blucher. Go on! go on!" cried the impatient old man.

"The Duke bade me to tell you, sir, that the British Army can hold its own and that he has no fears for the result. The French cavalry has been destroyed, two of their divisions of infantry have ceased to exist, and only the Guard is in reserve. If you give us a vigorous support the defeat will be changed to absolute rout and—" His knees gave way under him and he fell in a heap upon the floor.

"Enough! enough!" cried Blucher. "Gneisenau, send an aide-de-camp to Wellington and tell him to rely upon me to the full. Come on, gentlemen, we have our work to do!" He bustled eagerly out of the room with all his staff clanking behind him, while two orderlies carried the English messenger to the care of the surgeon.

Gneisenau, the Chief of the Staff, had lingered behind for an instant, and he laid his hand upon one of the aides-de-camp. The fellow had attracted my attention, for I have always a quick eye for a fine man. He was tall and slender, the very model of a horseman; indeed, there was something in his appearance which made it not unlike my own. His face was dark and as keen as that of a hawk, with fierce black eyes under thick, shaggy brows, and a moustache which would have put him in the crack squadron of my Hussars. He wore a green coat with white facings, and a horse-hair helmet—a Dragoon, as I conjectured, and as dashing a cavalier as one would wish to have at the end of one's sword-point.

"A word with you, Count Stein," said Gneisenau. "If the enemy are routed, but if the Emperor escapes, he will rally another army, and all will have to be done again. But if we can get the Emperor, then the war is indeed ended. It is worth a great effort and a great risk for such an object as that."

The young Dragoon said nothing, but he listened attentively.

"Suppose the Duke of Wellington's words should prove to be correct, and the French army should be driven in utter rout from the field, the Emperor will certainly take the road back through Genappe and Charleroi as being the shortest to the frontier. We can imagine that his horses will be fleet, and that the fugitives will make way for him. Our cavalry will follow the rear of the beaten army, but the Emperor will be far away at the front of the throng."

The young Dragoon inclined his head.

"To you, Count Stein, I commit the Emperor. If you take him your name will live in history. You have the reputation of being the hardest rider in our army. Do you choose such comrades as you may select—ten or a dozen should be enough. You are not to engage in the battle, nor are you to follow the general pursuit, but you are to ride clear of the crowd, reserving your energies for a nobler end. Do you understand me?"

Again the Dragoon inclined his head. This silence impressed me. I felt that he was indeed a dangerous man.

"Then I leave the details in your own hands. Strike at no one except the highest. You cannot mistake the Imperial carriage, nor can you fail to recognise the figure of the Emperor. Now I must follow the Marshal. Adieu! If ever I see you again I trust that it will be to congratulate you upon a deed which will ring through Europe."

The Dragoon saluted and Gneisenau hurried from the room. The young officer stood in deep thought for a few moments. Then he followed the Chief of the Staff. I looked with curiosity from my loophole to see what his next proceeding would be. His horse, a fine, strong chestnut with two white stockings, was fastened to the rail of the inn. He sprang into the saddle, and, riding to intercept a column of cavalry which was passing, he spoke to an officer at the head of the leading regiment. Presently after some talk I saw two Hussars—it was a Hussar regiment—drop out of the ranks and take up their position beside Count Stein. The next regiment was also stopped, and two Lancers were added to his escort. The next furnished him with two Dragoons and the next with two Cuirassiers. Then he drew his little group of horsemen aside and he gathered them round him, explaining to them what they had to do. Finally the nine soldiers rode off together and disappeared into the Wood of Paris.

I need not tell you, my friends, what all this portended. Indeed, he had acted exactly as I should have done in his place. From each colonel he had demanded the two best horsemen in the regiment, and so he had assembled a band who might expect to catch whatever they should follow. Heaven help the Emperor if, without an escort, he should find them on his track!

And I, dear friends—imagine the fever, the ferment, the madness of my mind! All thought of Grouchy had passed away. No guns were to be heard to the east. He could not be near. If he should come up he would not now be in time to alter the event of the day. The sun was already low in the sky and there could not be more than two or three hours of daylight. My mission might be dismissed as useless. But here was another mission, more pressing, more immediate, a mission which meant the safety, and perhaps the life, of the Emperor. At all costs, through every danger, I must get back to his side. But how was I to do it? The whole Prussian army was now between me and the French lines. They blocked every road, but they could not block the path of duty when Etienne Gerard sees it lie before him. I could not wait longer. I must be gone.

There was but the one opening to the loft, and so it was only down the ladder that I could descend. I looked into the kitchen and I found that the young surgeon was still there. In a chair sat the wounded English aide-de-camp, and on the straw lay two Prussian soldiers in the last stage of exhaustion. The others had all recovered and been sent on. These were my enemies, and I must pass through them in order to gain my horse. From the surgeon I had nothing to fear; the Englishman was wounded, and his sword stood with his cloak in a corner; the two Germans were half insensible, and their muskets were not beside them. What could be simpler? I opened the trap-door, slipped down the ladder, and appeared in the midst of them, my sword drawn in my hand.

What a picture of surprise! The surgeon, of course, knew all, but to the Englishman and the two Germans it must have seemed that the god of war in person had descended from the skies. With my appearance, with my figure, with my silver and grey uniform, and with that gleaming sword in my hand, I must indeed have been a sight worth seeing. The two Germans lay petrified with staring eyes. The English officer half rose, but sat down again from weakness, his mouth open and his hand on the back of his chair.

"What the deuce!" he kept on repeating, "what the deuce!"

"Pray do not move," said I; "I will hurt no one, but woe to the man who lays hands upon me to stop me. You have nothing to fear if you leave me alone, and nothing to hope if you try to hinder me. I am Colonel Etienne Gerard, of the Hussars of Conflans."

"The deuce!" said the Englishman. "You are the man that killed the fox." A terrible scowl had darkened his face. The jealousy of sportsmen is a base passion. He hated me, this Englishman, because I had been before him in transfixing the animal. How different are our natures! Had I seen him do such a deed I would have embraced him with cries of joy. But there was no time for argument.

"I regret it, sir," said I; "but you have a cloak here and I must take it."

He tried to rise from his chair and reach his sword, but I got between him and the corner where it lay.

"If there is anything in the pockets—"

"A case," said he.

"I would not rob you," said I; and raising the cloak I took from the pockets a silver flask, a square wooden case and a field-glass. All these I handed to him. The wretch opened the case, took out a pistol, and pointed it straight at my head.

"Now, my fine fellow," said he, "put down your sword and give yourself up."

I was so astounded at this infamous action that I stood petrified before him. I tried to speak to him of honour and gratitude, but I saw his eyes fix and harden over the pistol.

"Enough talk!" said he. "Drop it!"

Could I endure such a humiliation? Death were better than to be disarmed in such a fashion. The word "Fire!" was on my lips when in an instant the English man vanished from before my face, and in his place was a great pile of hay, with a red-coated arm and two Hessian boots waving and kicking in the heart of it. Oh, the gallant landlady! It was my whiskers that had saved me.

"Fly, soldier, fly!" she cried, and she heaped fresh trusses of hay from the floor on to the struggling Englishman. In an instant I was out in the courtyard, had led Violette from her stable, and was on her back. A pistol bullet whizzed past my shoulder from the window, and I saw a furious face looking out at me. I smiled my contempt and spurred out into the road. The last of the Prussians had passed, and both my road and my duty lay clear before me. If France won, all well. If France lost, then on me and my little mare depended that which was more than victory or defeat—the safety and the life of the Emperor. "On, Etienne, on!" I cried. "Of all your noble exploits, the greatest, even if it be the last, lies now before you!"

II. The Story of the Nine Prussian Horsemen

I told you when last we met, my friends, of the important mission from the Emperor to Marshal Grouchy, which failed through no fault of my own, and I described to you how during a long afternoon I was shut up in the attic of a country inn, and was prevented from coming out because the Prussians were all around me. You will remember also how I overheard the Chief of the Prussian Staff give his instructions to Count Stein, and so learned the dangerous plan which was on foot to kill or capture the Emperor in the event of a French defeat. At first I could not have believed in such a thing, but since the guns had thundered all day, and since the sound had made no advance in my direction, it was evident that the English had at least held their own and beaten off all our attacks.

I have said that it was a fight that day between the soul of France and the beef of England, but it must be confessed that we found the beef was very tough. It was clear that if the Emperor could not defeat the English when alone, then it might, indeed, go hard with him now that sixty thousand of these cursed Prussians were swarming on his flank. In any case, with this secret in my possession, my place was by his side.

I had made my way out of the inn in the dashing manner which I have described to you when last we met, and I left the English aide-de-camp shaking his foolish fist out of the window. I could not but laugh as I looked back at him, for his angry red face was framed and frilled with hay. Once out on the road I stood erect in my stirrups, and I put on the handsome black riding-coat, lined with red, which had belonged to him. It fell to the top of my high boots, and covered my tell-tale uniform completely. As to my busby, there are many such in the German service, and there was no reason why it should attract attention. So long as no one spoke to me there was no reason why I should not ride through the whole of the Prussian army; but though I understood German, for I had many friends among the German ladies during the pleasant years that I fought all over that country, still I spoke it with a pretty Parisian accent which could not be confounded with their rough, unmusical speech. I knew that this quality of my accent would attract attention, but I could only hope and pray that I would be permitted to go my way in silence.

The Forest of Paris was so large that it was useless to think of going round it, and so I took my courage in both hands and galloped on down the road in the track of the Prussian army. It was not hard to trace it, for it was rutted two feet deep by the gun-wheels and the caissons. Soon I found a fringe of wounded men, Prussians and French, on each side of it, where Bülow's advance had come into touch with Marbot's Hussars. One old man with a long white beard, a surgeon, I suppose, shouted at me, and ran after me still shouting, but I never turned my head and took no notice of him save to spur on faster. I heard his shouts long after I had lost sight of him among the trees.

Presently I came up with the Prussian reserves. The infantry were leaning on their muskets or lying exhausted on the wet ground, and the officers stood in groups listening to the mighty roar of the battle and discussing the reports which came from the front. I hurried past at the top of my speed, but one of them rushed out and stood in my path with his hand up as a signal to me to stop. Five thousand Prussian eyes were turned upon me. There was a moment! You turn pale, my friends, at the thought of it. Think how every hair upon me stood on end. But never for one instant did my wits or my courage desert me. "General Blucher!" I cried. Was it not my guardian angel who whispered the words in my ear? The Prussian sprang from my path, saluted, and pointed forward. They are well disciplined, these Prussians, and who was he that he should dare to stop the officer who bore a message to the general? It was a talisman that would pass me out of every danger, and my heart sang within me at the thought. So elated was I that I no longer waited to be asked, but as I rode through the army I shouted to right and left, "General Blucher! General Blucher!" and every man pointed me onward and cleared a path to let me pass. There are times when the most supreme impudence is the highest wisdom. But discretion must also be used, and I must admit that I became indiscreet. For as I rode upon my way, ever nearer to the fighting line, a Prussian officer of Uhlans gripped my bridle and pointed to a group of men who stood near a burning farm. "There is Marshal Blucher. Deliver your message!" said he, and sure enough, my terrible old grey-whiskered veteran was there within a pistol-shot, his eyes turned in my direction.

But the good guardian angel did not desert me. Quick as a flash there came into my memory the name of the general who commanded the advance of the Prussians. "General Bülow!" I cried. The Uhlan let go my bridle. "General Bülow! General Bülow!" I shouted, as every stride of the dear little mare took me nearer my own people. Through the burning village of Planchenoit I galloped, spurred my way between two columns of Prussian infantry, sprang over a hedge, cut down a Silesian Hussar who flung himself before me, and an instant afterward, with my coat flying open to show the uniform below, I passed through the open files of the tenth of the line, and was back in the heart of Lobau's corps once more. Outnumbered and outflanked, they were being slowly driven in by the pressure of the Prussian advance. I galloped onward, anxious only to find myself by the Emperor's side.

But a sight lay before me which held me fast as though I had been turned into some noble equestrian statue. I could not move, I could scarce breathe, as I gazed upon it. There was a mound over which my path lay, and as I came out on the top of it I looked down the long, shallow valley of Waterloo. I had left it with two great armies on either side and a clear field between them. Now there were but long, ragged fringes of broken and exhausted regiments upon the two ridges, but a real army of dead and wounded lay between. For two miles in length and half a mile across the ground was strewed and heaped with them. But slaughter was no new sight to me, and it was not that which held me spellbound. It was that up the long slope of the British position was moving a walking forest—black, tossing, waving, unbroken. Did I not know the bearskins of the Guard? And did I not also know, did not my soldier's instinct tell me, that it was the last reserve of France; that the Emperor, like a desperate gamester, was staking all upon his last card? Up they went and up—grand, solid, unbreakable, scourged with musketry, riddled with grape, flowing onward in a black, heavy tide, which lapped over the British batteries. With my glass I could see the English gunners throw themselves under their pieces or run to the rear. On rolled the crest of the bearskins, and then, with a crash which was swept across to my ears, they met the British infantry. A minute passed, and another, and another. My heart was in my mouth. They swayed back and forward; they no longer advanced; they were held. Great Heaven! was it possible that they were breaking? One black dot ran down the hill, then two, then four, then ten, then a great, scattered, struggling mass, halting, breaking, halting, and at last shredding out and rushing madly downward. "The Guard is beaten! The Guard is beaten!" From all around me I heard the cry. Along the whole line the infantry turned their faces and the gunners flinched from their guns.

"The Old Guard is beaten! The Guard retreats!" An officer with a livid face passed me yelling out these words of woe. "Save yourselves! Save yourselves! You are betrayed!" cried another. "Save yourselves! Save yourselves!" Men were rushing madly to the rear, blundering and jumping like frightened sheep. Cries and screams rose from all around me. And at that moment, as I looked at the British position, I saw what I can never forget. A single horseman stood out black and clear upon the ridge against the last red angry glow of the setting sun. So dark, so motionless, against that grim light, he might have been the very spirit of Battle brooding over that terrible valley. As I gazed, he raised his hat high in the air, and at the signal, with a low, deep roar like a breaking wave, the whole British army flooded over their ridge and came rolling down into the valley. Long steel-fringed lines of red and blue, sweeping waves of cavalry, horse batteries rattling and bounding—down they came on to our crumbling ranks. It was over. A yell of agony, the agony of brave men who see no hope, rose from one flank to the other, and in an instant the whole of that noble army was swept in a wild, terror-stricken crowd from the field. Even now, dear friends, I cannot, as you see, speak of that dreadful moment with a dry eye or with a steady voice.

At first I was carried away in that wild rush, whirled off like a straw in a flooded gutter. But, suddenly, what should I see amongst the mixed regiments in front of me but a group of stern horsemen, in silver and grey, with a broken and tattered standard held aloft in the heart of them! Not all the might of England and of Prussia could break the Hussars of Conflans. But when I joined them it made my heart bleed to see them. The major, seven captains, and five hundred men were left upon the field. Young Captain Sabbatier was in command, and when I asked him where were the five missing squadrons he pointed back and answered: "You will find them round one of those British squares." Men and horses were at their last gasp, caked with sweat and dirt, their black tongues hanging out from their lips; but it made me thrill with pride to see how that shattered remnant still rode knee to knee, with every man, from the boy trumpeter to the farrier-sergeant, in his own proper place. Would that I could have brought them on with me as an escort for the Emperor! In the heart of the Hussars of Conflans he would be safe indeed. But the horses were too spent to trot. I left them behind me with orders to rally upon the farm-house of St. Aunay, where we had camped two nights before. For my own part, I forced my horse through the throng in search of the Emperor.

There were things which I saw then, as I pressed through that dreadful crowd, which can never be banished from my mind. In evil dreams there comes back to me the memory of that flowing stream of livid, staring, screaming faces upon which I looked down. It was a nightmare. In victory one does not understand the horror of war. It is only in the cold chill of defeat that it is brought home to you. I remember an old Grenadier of the Guard lying at the side of the road with his broken leg doubled at a right angle. "Comrades, comrades, keep off my leg!" he cried, but they tripped and stumbled over him all the same. In front of me rode a Lancer officer without his coat. His arm had just been taken off in the ambulance. The bandages had fallen. It was horrible. Two gunners tried to drive through with their gun. A Chasseur raised his musket and shot one of them through the head. I saw a major of Cuirassiers draw his two holster pistols and shoot first his horse and then himself. Beside the road a man in a blue coat was raging and raving like a madman. His face was black with powder, his clothes were torn, one epaulette was gone, the other hung dangling over his breast. Only when I came close to him did I recognise that it was Marshal Ney. He howled at the flying troops and his voice was hardly human. Then he raised the stump of his sword—it was broken three inches from the hilt. "Come and see how a Marshal of France can die!" he cried. Gladly would I have gone with him, but my duty lay elsewhere. He did not, as you know, find the death he sought, but he met it a few weeks later in cold blood at the hands of his enemies.

There is an old proverb that in attack the French are more than men, in defeat they are less than women. I knew that it was true that day. But even in that rout I saw things which I can tell with pride. Through the fields which skirt the road moved Cambronne's three reserve battalions of the Guard, the cream of our army. They walked slowly in square, their colours waving over the sombre line of the bearskins. All round them raged the English cavalry and the black Lancers of Brunswick, wave after wave thundering up, breaking with a crash, and recoiling in ruin. When last I saw them, the English guns, six at a time, were smashing grape-shot through their ranks and the English infantry were closing in upon three sides and pouring volleys into them; but still, like a noble lion with fierce hounds clinging to its flanks, the glorious remnant of the Guard, marching slowly, halting, closing up, dressing, moved majestically from their last battle. Behind them the Guard's battery of twelve-pounders was drawn up upon the ridge. Every gunner was in his place, but no gun fired. "Why do you not fire?" I asked the colonel as I passed. "Our powder is finished." "Then why not retire?" "Our appearance may hold them back for a little. We must give the Emperor time to escape." Such were the soldiers of France.

Behind this screen of brave men the others took their breath, and then went on in less desperate fashion. They had broken away from the road, and all over the countryside in the twilight I could see the timid, scattered, frightened crowd who ten hours before had formed the finest army that ever went down to battle. I with my splendid mare was soon able to get clear of the throng, and just after I passed Genappe I overtook the Emperor with the remains of his Staff. Soult was with him still, and so were Drouot, Lobau, and Bertrand, with five Chasseurs of the Guard, their horses hardly able to move. The night was falling, and the Emperor's haggard face gleamed white through the gloom as he turned it toward me.

"Who is that?" he asked.

"It is Colonel Gerard," said Soult.

"Have you seen Marshal Grouchy?"

"No, Sire. The Prussians were between."

"It does not matter. Nothing matters now. Soult, I will go back."

He tried to turn his horse, but Bertrand seized his bridle. "Ah, Sire," said Soult, "the enemy has had good fortune enough already." They forced him on among them. He rode in silence with his chin upon his breast, the greatest and the saddest of men. Far away behind us those remorseless guns were still roaring. Sometimes out of the darkness would come shrieks and screams and the low thunder of galloping hoofs. At the sound we would spur our horses and hasten onward through the scattered troops. At last, after riding all night in the clear moonlight, we found that we had left both pursued and pursuers behind. By the time we passed over the bridge at Charleroi the dawn was breaking. What a company of spectres we looked in that cold, clear, searching light, the Emperor with his face of wax, Soult blotched with powder, Lobau dabbled with blood! But we rode more easily now, and had ceased to glance over our shoulders, for Waterloo was more than thirty miles behind us. One of the Emperor's carriages had been picked up at Charleroi, and we halted now on the other side of the Sambre, and dismounted from our horses.

You will ask me why it was that during all this time I had said nothing of that which was nearest my heart, the need for guarding the Emperor. As a fact, I had tried to speak of it both to Soult and to Lobau, but their minds were so overwhelmed with the disaster and so distracted by the pressing needs of the moment that it was impossible to make them understand how urgent was my message. Besides, during this long flight we had always had numbers of French fugitives beside us on the road, and, however demoralised they might be, we had nothing to fear from the attack of nine men. But now, as we stood round the Emperor's carriage in the early morning, I observed with anxiety that not a single French soldier was to be seen upon the long, white road behind us. We had outstripped the army. I looked round to see what means of defence were left to us. The horses of the Chasseurs of the Guard had broken down, and only one of them, a grey-whiskered sergeant, remained. There were Soult, Lobau, and Bertrand; but, for all their talents, I had rather, when it came to hard knocks, have a single quartermaster-sergeant of Hussars at my side than the three of them put together. There remained the Emperor himself, the coachman, and a valet of the household who had joined us at Charleroi—eight all told; but of the eight only two, the Chasseur and I, were fighting soldiers who could be depended upon at a pinch. A chill came over me as I reflected how utterly helpless we were. At that moment I raised my eyes, and there were the nine Prussian horsemen coming over the hill.

On either side of the road at this point are long stretches of rolling plain, part of it yellow with corn and part of it rich grass land watered by the Sambre. To the south of us was a low ridge, over which was the road to France. Along this road the little group of cavalry was riding. So well had Count Stein obeyed his instructions that he had struck far to the south of us in his determination to get ahead of the Emperor. Now he was riding from the direction in which we were going the last in which we could expect an enemy. When I caught that first glimpse of them they were still half a mile away.

"Sire!" I cried, "the Prussians!"

They all started and stared. It was the Emperor who broke the silence.

"Who says they are Prussians?"

"I do, Sire—I, Etienne Gerard!"

Unpleasant news always made the Emperor furious against the man who broke it. He railed at me now in the rasping, croaking, Corsican voice which only made itself heard when he had lost his self-control.

"You were always a buffoon," he cried. "What do you mean, you numskull, by saying that they are Prussians? How could Prussians be coming from the direction of France? You have lost any wits that you ever possessed."

His words cut me like a whip, and yet we all felt toward the Emperor as an old dog does to its master. His kick is soon forgotten and forgiven. I would not argue or justify myself. At the first glance I had seen the two white stockings on the forelegs of the leading horse, and I knew well that Count Stein was on its back. For an instant the nine horsemen had halted and surveyed us. Now they put spurs to their horses, and with a yell of triumph they galloped down the road. They had recognised that their prey was in their power.

At that swift advance all doubt had vanished. "By heavens, Sire, it is indeed the Prussians!" cried Soult. Lobau and Bertrand ran about the road like two frightened hens. The sergeant of Chasseurs drew his sabre with a volley of curses. The coachman and the valet cried and wrung their hands. Napoleon stood with a frozen face, one foot on the step of the carriage. And I—ah, my friends, I was magnificent! What words can I use to do justice to my own bearing at that supreme instant of my life? So coldly alert, so deadly cool, so clear in brain and ready in hand. He had called me a numskull and a buffoon. How quick and how noble was my revenge! When his own wits failed him, it was Etienne Gerard who supplied the want.

To fight was absurd; to fly was ridiculous. The Emperor was stout, and weary to death. At the best he was never a good rider. How could he fly from these, the picked men of an army? The best horseman in Prussia was among them. But I was the best horseman in France. I, and only I, could hold my own with them. If they were on *my* track instead of the Emperor's, all might still be well. These were the thoughts which flashed so swiftly through my mind that in an instant I had sprung from the first idea to the final conclusion. Another instant carried me from the final conclusion to prompt and vigorous action. I rushed to the side of the Emperor, who stood petrified, with the carriage between him and our enemies. "Your coat, Sire! your hat!" I cried. I dragged them off him. Never had he been so hustled in his life. In an instant I had them on and had thrust him into the carriage. The next I had sprung on to his famous white Arab and had ridden clear of the group upon the road.

You have already divined my plan; but you may well ask how could I hope to pass myself off as the Emperor. My figure is as you still see it, and his was never beautiful, for he was both short and stout. But a man's height is not remarked when he is in the saddle, and for the rest one had but to sit forward on the horse and round one's back and carry oneself like a sack of flour. I wore the little cocked hat and the loose grey coat with the silver star which was known to every child from one end of Europe to the other. Beneath me was the Emperor's own famous white charger. It was complete.

Already as I rode clear the Prussians were within two hundred yards of us. I made a gesture of terror and despair with my hands, and I sprang my horse over the bank which lined the road. It was enough. A yell of exultation and of furious hatred broke from the Prussians. It was the howl of starving wolves who scent their prey. I spurred my horse over the meadow-land and looked back under my arm as I rode. Oh, the glorious moment when one after the other I saw eight horsemen come over the bank at my heels! Only one had stayed behind, and I heard shouting and the sounds of a struggle. I remembered my old sergeant of Chasseurs, and I was sure that number nine would trouble us no more. The road was clear and the Emperor free to continue his journey.

But now I had to think of myself. If I were overtaken the Prussians would certainly make short work of me in their disappointment. If it were so—if I lost my life—I should still have sold it at a glorious price. But I had hopes that I might shake them off. With ordinary horsemen upon ordinary horses I should have had no difficulty in doing so, but here both steeds and riders were of the best. It was a grand creature that I rode, but it was weary with its long night's work, and the Emperor was one of those riders who do not know how to manage a horse. He had little thought for them and a heavy hand upon their mouths. On the other hand, Stein and his men had come both far and fast. The race was a fair one.

So quick had been my impulse, and so rapidly had I acted upon it, that I had not thought enough of my own safety. Had I done so in the first instance I should, of course, have ridden straight back the way we had come, for so I should have met our own people. But I was off the road and had galloped a mile over the plain before this occurred to me. Then when I looked back I saw that the Prussians had spread out into a long line, so as to head me off from the Charleroi road. I could not turn back, but at least I could edge toward the north. I knew that the whole face of the country was covered with our flying troops, and that sooner or later I must come upon some of them.

But one thing I had forgotten—the Sambre. In my excitement I never gave it a thought until I saw it, deep and broad, gleaming in the morning sunlight. It barred my path, and the Prussians howled behind me. I galloped to the brink, but the horse refused the plunge. I spurred him, but the bank was high and the stream deep. He shrank back trembling and snorting. The yells of triumph were louder every instant. I turned and rode for my life down the river bank. It formed a loop at this part, and I must get across somehow, for my retreat was blocked. Suddenly a thrill of hope ran through me, for I saw a house on my side of the stream and another on the farther bank. Where there are two such houses it usually means that there is a ford between them. A sloping path led to the brink and I urged my horse down it. On he went, the water up to the saddle, the foam flying right and left. He blundered once and I thought we were lost, but he recovered and an instant later was clattering up the farther slope. As we came out I heard the splash behind me as the first Prussian took the water. There was just the breadth of the Sambre between us.

I rode with my head sunk between my shoulders in Napoleon's fashion, and I did not dare to look back for fear they should see my moustache. I had turned up the collar of the grey coat so as partly to hide it. Even now if they found out their mistake they might turn and overtake the carriage. But when once we were on the road I could tell by the drumming of their hoofs how far distant they were, and it seemed to me that the sound grew perceptibly louder, as if they were slowly gaining upon me. We were riding now up the stony and rutted lane which led from the ford. I peeped back very cautiously from under my arm and I perceived that my danger came from a single rider, who was far ahead of his comrades. He was a Hussar, a very tiny fellow, upon a big black horse, and it was his light weight which had brought him into the foremost place. It is a place of honour; but it is also a place of danger, as he was soon to learn. I felt the holsters, but, to my horror, there were no pistols. There was a field-glass in one and the other was stuffed with papers. My sword had been left behind with Violette. Had I only my own weapons and my own little mare I could have played with these rascals. But I was not entirely unarmed. The Emperor's own sword hung to the saddle. It was curved and short, the hilt all crusted with gold—a thing more fitted to glitter at a review than to serve a soldier in his deadly need. I drew it, such as it was, and I waited my chance. Every instant the clink and clatter of the hoofs grew nearer. I heard the panting of the horse, and the fellow shouted some threat at me. There was a turn in the lane, and as I rounded it I drew up my white Arab on his haunches. As we spun round I met the Prussian Hussar face to face. He was going too fast to stop, and his only chance was to ride me down. Had he done so he might have met his own death, but he would have injured me or my horse past all hope of escape. But the fool flinched as he saw me waiting and flew past me on my right. I lunged over my Arab's neck and buried my toy sword in his side. It must have been the finest steel and as sharp as a razor, for I hardly felt it enter, and yet his blood was within three inches of the hilt. His horse galloped on and he kept his saddle for a hundred yards before he sank down with his face on the mane and then dived over the side of the neck on to the road. For my own part I was already at his horse's heels. A few seconds had sufficed for all that I have told.

I heard the cry of rage and vengeance which rose from the Prussians as they passed their dead comrade, and I could not but smile as I wondered what they could think of the Emperor as a horseman and a swordsman. I glanced back cautiously as before, and I saw that none of the seven men stopped. The fate of their comrade was nothing compared to the carrying out of their mission. They were as untiring and as remorseless as bloodhounds. But I had a good lead and the brave Arab was still going well. I thought that I was safe. And yet it was at that very instant that the most terrible danger befell me. The lane divided, and I took the smaller of the two divisions because it was the more grassy and the easier for the horse's hoofs. Imagine my horror when, riding through a gate, I found myself in a square of stables and farm-buildings, with no way out save that by which I had come! Ah, my friends, if my hair is snowy white, have I not had enough to make it so?

To retreat was impossible. I could hear the thunder of the Prussians' hoofs in the lane. I looked round me, and Nature has blessed me with that quick eye which is the first of gifts to any soldier, but most of all to a leader of cavalry. Between a long, low line of stables and the farm-house there was a pig-sty. Its front was made of bars of wood four feet high; the back was of stone, higher than the front. What was beyond I could not tell. The space between the front and the back was not more than a few yards. It was a desperate venture, and yet I must take it. Every instant the beating of those hurrying hoofs was louder and louder. I put my Arab at the pig-sty. She cleared the front beautifully and came down with her forefeet upon the sleeping pig within, slipping forward upon her knees. I was thrown over the wall beyond, and fell upon my hands and face in a soft flower-bed. My horse was upon one side of the wall, I upon the other, and the Prussians were pouring into the yard. But I was up in an instant and had seized the bridle of the plunging horse over the top of the wall. It was built of loose stones, and I dragged down a few of them to make a gap. As I tugged at the bridle and shouted the gallant creature rose to the leap, and an instant afterward she was by my side and I with my foot on the stirrup.

An heroic idea had entered my mind as I mounted into the saddle. These Prussians, if they came over the pig-sty, could only come one at once, and their attack would not be formidable when they had not had time to recover from such a leap. Why should I not wait and kill them one by one as they came over? It was a glorious thought. They would learn that Etienne Gerard was not a safe man to hunt. My hand felt for my sword, but you can imagine my feelings, my friends, when I came upon an empty scabbard. It had been shaken out when the horse had tripped over that infernal pig. On what absurd trifles do our destinies hang—a pig on one side, Etienne Gerard on the other! Could I spring over the wall and get the sword? Impossible! The Prussians were already in the yard. I turned my Arab and resumed my flight.

But for a moment it seemed to me that I was in a far worse trap than before. I found myself in the garden of the farm-house, an orchard in the centre and flower-beds all round. A high wall surrounded the whole place. I reflected, however, that there must be some point of entrance, since every visitor could not be expected to spring over the pig-sty. I rode round the wall. As I expected, I came upon a door with a key upon the inner side. I dismounted, unlocked it, opened it, and there was a Prussian Lancer sitting his horse within six feet of me.

For a moment we each stared at the other. Then I shut the door and locked it again. A crash and a cry came from the other end of the garden. I understood that one of my enemies had come to grief in trying to get over the pig-sty. How could I ever get out of this *cul-de-sac*? It was evident that some of the party had galloped round, while some had followed straight upon my tracks. Had I my sword I might have beaten off the Lancer at the door, but to come out now was to be butchered. And yet if I waited some of them would certainly follow me on foot over the pig-sty, and what could I do then? I must act at once or I was lost. But it is at such moments that my wits are most active and my actions most prompt. Still leading my horse, I ran for a hundred yards by the side of the wall away from the spot where the Lancer was watching. There I stopped, and with an effort I tumbled down several of the loose stones from the top of the wall. The instant I had done so I hurried back to the door. As I had expected, he thought I was making a gap for my escape at that point, and I heard the thud of his horse's hoofs as he galloped to cut me off. As I reached the gate I looked back, and I saw a green-coated horseman, whom I knew to be Count Stein, clear the pig-sty and gallop furiously with a shout of triumph across the garden. "Surrender, your Majesty, surrender!" he yelled; "we will give you quarter!" I slipped through the gate, but had no time to lock it on the other side. Stein was at my very heels, and the Lancer had already turned his horse. Springing upon my Arab's back, I was off once more with a clear stretch of grass land before me. Stein had to dismount to open the gate, to lead his horse through, and to mount again before he could follow. It was he that I feared rather than the Lancer, whose horse was coarse-bred and weary. I galloped hard for a mile before I ventured to look back, and then Stein was a musket-shot from me, and the Lancer as much again, while only three of the others were in sight. My nine Prussians were coming down to more manageable numbers, and yet one was too much for an unarmed man.

It had surprised me that during this long chase I had seen no fugitives from the army, but I reflected that I was considerably to the west of their line of flight, and that I must edge more toward the east if I wished to join them. Unless I did so it was probable that my pursuers, even if they could not overtake me themselves, would keep me in view until I was headed off by some of their comrades coming from the north. As I looked to the eastward I saw afar off a line of dust which stretched for miles across the country. This was certainly the main road along which our unhappy army was flying. But I soon had proof that some of our stragglers had wandered into these side tracks, for I came suddenly upon a horse grazing at the corner of a field, and beside him, with his back against the bank, his master, a French Cuirassier, terribly wounded and evidently on the point of death. I sprang down, seized his long, heavy sword, and rode on with it. Never shall I forget the poor man's face as he looked at me with his failing sight. He was an old, grey-moustached soldier, one of the real fanatics, and to him this last vision of his Emperor was like a revelation from on high. Astonishment, love, pride—all shone in his pallid face. He said something—I fear they were his last words—but I had no time to listen, and I galloped on my way.

All this time I had been on the meadow-land, which was intersected in this part by broad ditches. Some of them could not have been less than from fourteen to fifteen feet, and my heart was in my mouth as I went at each of them, for a slip would have been my ruin. But whoever selected the Emperor's horses had done his work well. The creature, save when it balked on the bank of the Sambre, never failed me for an instant. We cleared everything in one stride. And yet we could not shake off those infernal Prussians. As I left each water-course behind me I looked back with renewed hope; but it was only to see Stein on his white-legged chestnut flying over it as lightly as I had done myself. He was my enemy, but I honoured him for the way in which he carried himself that day.

Again and again I measured the distance which separated him from the next horseman. I had the idea that I might turn and cut him down, as I had the Hussar, before his comrade could come to his help. But the others had closed up and were not far behind. I reflected that this Stein was probably as fine a swordsman as he was a rider, and that it might take me some little time to get the better of him. In that case the others would come to his aid and I should be lost. On the whole, it was wiser to continue my flight.

A road with poplars on either side ran across the plain from east to west. It would lead me toward that long line of dust which marked the French retreat. I wheeled my horse, therefore, and galloped down it. As I rode I saw a single house in front of me upon the right, with a great bush hung over the door to mark it as an inn. Outside there were several peasants, but for them I cared nothing. What frightened me was to see the gleam of a red coat, which showed that there were British in the place. However, I could not turn and I could not stop, so there was nothing for it but to gallop on and to take my chance. There were no troops in sight, so these men must be stragglers or marauders, from whom I had little to fear. As I approached I saw that there were two of them sitting drinking on a bench outside the inn door. I saw them stagger to their feet, and it was evident that they were both very drunk. One stood swaying in the middle of the road. "It's Boney! So help me, it's Boney!" he yelled. He ran with his hands out to catch me, but luckily for himself his drunken feet stumbled and he fell on his face on the road. The other was more dangerous. He had rushed into the inn, and just as I passed I saw him run out with his musket in his hand. He dropped upon one knee, and I stooped forward over my horse's neck. A single shot from a Prussian or an Austrian is a small matter, but the British were at that time the best shots in Europe, and my drunkard seemed steady enough when he had a gun at his shoulder. I heard the crack, and my horse gave a convulsive spring which would have unseated many a rider. For an instant I thought he was killed, but when I turned in my saddle I saw a stream of blood running down the off hind-quarter. I looked back at the Englishman, and the brute had bitten the end off another cartridge and was ramming it into his musket, but before he had it primed we were beyond his range. These men were foot-soldiers and could not join in the chase, but I heard them whooping and tally-hoing behind me as if I had been a fox. The peasants also shouted and ran through the fields flourishing their sticks. From all sides I heard cries, and everywhere were the rushing, waving figures of my pursuers. To think of the great Emperor being chivvied over the country-side in this fashion! It made me long to have these rascals within the sweep of my sword.

But now I felt that I was nearing the end of my course. I had done all that a man could be expected to do—some would say more—but at last I had come to a point from which I could see no escape. The horses of my pursuers were exhausted, but mine was exhausted and wounded also. It was losing blood fast, and we left a red trail upon the white, dusty road. Already his pace was slackening, and sooner or later he must drop under me. I looked back, and there were the five inevitable Prussians—Stein a hundred yards in front, then a Lancer, and then three others riding together. Stein had drawn his sword, and he waved it at me. For my own part I was determined not to give myself up. I would try how many of these Prussians I could take with me into the other world. At this supreme moment all the great deeds of my life rose in a vision before me, and I felt that this, my last exploit, was indeed a worthy close to such a career. My death would be a fatal blow to those who loved me, to my dear mother, to my Hussars, to others who shall be nameless. But all of them had my honour and my fame at heart, and I felt that their grief would be tinged with pride when they learned how I had ridden and how I had fought upon this last day. Therefore I hardened my heart and, as my Arab limped more and more upon his wounded leg, I drew the great sword which I had taken from the Cuirassier, and I set my teeth for my supreme struggle. My hand was in the very act of tightening the bridle, for I feared that if I delayed longer I might find myself on foot fighting against five mounted men. At that instant my eye fell upon something which brought hope to my heart and a shout of joy to my lips.

From a grove of trees in front of me there projected the steeple of a village church. But there could not be two steeples like that, for the corner of it had crumbled away or been struck by lightning, so that it was of a most fantastic shape. I had seen it only two days before, and it was the church of the village of Gosselies. It was not the hope of reaching the village which set my heart singing with joy, but it was that I knew my ground now, and that farm-house not half a mile ahead, with its gable end sticking out from amid the trees, must be that very farm of St. Aunay where we had bivouacked, and which I had named to Captain Sabbatier as the rendezvous of the Hussars of Conflans. There they were, my little rascals, if I could but reach them. With every bound my horse grew weaker. Each instant the sound of the pursuit grew louder. I heard a gust of crackling German oaths at my very heels. A pistol bullet sighed in my ears. Spurring frantically and beating my poor Arab with the flat of my sword I kept him at the top of his speed. The open gate of the farm-yard lay before me. I saw the twinkle of steel within. Stein's horse's head was within ten yards of me as I thundered through. "To me, comrades! To me!" I yelled. I heard a buzz as when the angry bees swarm from their nest. Then my splendid white Arab fell dead under me and I was hurled on to the cobble-stones of the yard, where I can remember no more.

Such was my last and most famous exploit, my dear friends, a story which rang through Europe and has made the name of Etienne Gerard famous in history. Alas! that all my efforts could only give the Emperor a few weeks more liberty, since he surrendered upon the 15th of July to the English. But it was not my fault that he was not able to collect the forces still waiting for him in France, and to fight another Waterloo with a happier ending. Had others been as loyal as I was the history of the world might have been changed, the Emperor would have preserved his throne, and such a soldier as I would not have been left to spend his life in planting cabbages or to while away his old age telling stories in a café. You ask me about the fate of Stein and the Prussian horsemen! Of the three who dropped upon the way I know nothing. One you will remember that I killed. There remained five, three of whom were cut down by my Hussars, who, for the instant, were under the impression that it was indeed the Emperor whom they were defending. Stein was taken, slightly wounded, and so was one of the Uhlans. The truth was not told to them, for we thought it best that no news, or false news, should get about as to where the Emperor was, so that Count Stein still believed that he was within a few yards of making that tremendous capture. "You may well love and honour your Emperor," said he, "for such a horseman and such a swordsman I have never seen." He could not understand why the young colonel of Hussars laughed so heartily at his words—but he has learned since.

THE CAPTAIN MORATTI'S LAST AFFAIR

SIDNEY LEVETT-YEATS

I. "ARCADES AMBO"

H alt!" The word, which seemed to come from nowhere, rang out into the crisp winter moonlight so sharply, so suddenly, so absolutely without warning, that the Cavaliere Michele di Lippo, who was ambling comfortably along, reined in his horse with a jerk; and with a start, looked into the night. He had not to fret his curiosity above a moment, for a figure gliding out from the black shadows of the pines, fencing in each side of the lonely road, stepped full into the white band of light, stretching between the darkness on either hand and stood in front of the horse. As the two faced each other, it was not the fact that there was a man in his path that made the rider keep a restraining hand on his bridle. It was the persuasive force, the voiceless command, in the round muzzle of an arquebuse pointed at his heart, and along the barrel of which di Lippo could see the glint of the moonlight, a thin bright streak ending in the wicked blinking star of the lighted fuse. The cavaliere took in the position at a glance, and being a man of resolution, hurriedly cast up his chances of escape by spurring his horse, and suddenly riding down the thief. In a flash the thought came and was dismissed. It was impossible; for the night-hawk had taken his stand at a distance of about six feet off, space enough to enable him to blow his quarry's heart out, well before the end of any sudden rush to disarm him. The mind moves like lightning in matters of this kind, and di Lippo surrendered without condition. Though his heart was burning within him, he was outwardly cool and collected. He had yielded to force he could not resist. Could he have seen ever so small a chance, the positions might have been reversed. As it was, Messer the bandit might still have to look to himself, and his voice was icy as the night as he said: "Well! I have halted. What more? It is chill, and I care not to be kept waiting."

The robber was not without humour, and a line of teeth showed, for an instant, behind the burning match of the weapon he held steadily before him. He did not, however, waste words. "Throw down your purse."

The cavaliere hesitated. Ducats were scarce with him, but the bandit had a short patience. "*Diavolo!* Don't you hear, signore?"

It was useless to resist. The fingers of the cavaliere fumbled under his cloak, and a fat purse fell squab into the snow, where it lay, a dark spot in the whiteness around, for all the world like a sleeping toad. The bandit chuckled as he heard the plump thud of the purse, and di Lippo's muttered curse was lost in the sharp order: "Get off the horse."

"But—"

"I am in a hurry, signore." The robber blew on the match of his arquebuse, and the match in its glow cast a momentary light on his face, showing the outlines of high aquiline features, and the black curve of a pair of long moustaches.

"*Maledetto!*" and the disgusted cavaliere dismounted, the scabbard of his useless sword striking with a clink against the stirrup iron, and he unwillingly swung from the saddle and stood in the snow—a tall figure, lean and gaunt.

As he did this, the bandit stepped back a pace, so as to give him the road. "Your excellency," he said mockingly, "is now free to pass—on foot. A walk will doubtless remove the chill your excellency finds so unpleasant."

But di Lippo made no advance. In fact, as his feet touched the snow, he recovered the composure he had so nearly lost, and saw his way to gain some advantage from defeat. It struck him that here was the very man he wanted for an affair of the utmost importance. Indeed, it was for just such an instrument that he had been racking his brains, as he rode on that winter night through the Gonfolina defile, which separates the middle and the lower valleys of the Arno. And now—a hand turn—and he had found his man. True, an expensive find; but cheap if all turned out well—that is, well from di Lippo's point of view. This thing the cavaliere wanted done he could not take into his own hands. Not from fear—it was no question of that; but because it was not convenient; and Michele di Lippo never gave himself any inconvenience, although it was sometimes thrust upon him in an unpleasant manner by others. If he could but induce the man before him to undertake the task, what might not be? But the knight of the road was evidently very impatient.

"Blood of a king!" he swore, "are you going, signore? Think you I am to stand here all night?"

"Certainly not," answered di Lippo in his even voice, "nor am I. But to come to the point. I want a little business managed, and will pay for it. You appear to be a man of courage—will you undertake the matter?"

"*Cospetto!* But you are a cool hand! Who are you?"

"Is it necessary to know? I offer a hundred crowns, fifty to be paid to you if you agree, and fifty on the completion of the affair."

"A matter of the dagger?"

"That is for you to decide."

The bandit almost saw the snarl on di Lippo's lips as he dropped out slowly: "You are too cautious, my friend—you think to the skin. The rack will come whether you do my business or not." The words were not exactly calculated to soothe, and called up an unpleasant vision before the robber's eyes. A sudden access of wrath shook him. "Begone, signore!" he burst out, "lest my patience exhausts itself, and I give you a bed in the snow. Why I have spared your life, I know not. Begone; warm yourself with a walk—"

"I will pay a hundred crowns," interrupted di Lippo.

"A hundred devils—begone!"

"As you please. Remember, it is a hundred crowns, and, on the faith of a noble, I say nothing about to-night. Where can I find you, in case you change your mind? A hundred crowns is a comfortable sum of money, mind you."

There was no excitement about di Lippo. He spoke slowly and distinctly. His cool voice neither rose nor dropped, but he spoke in a steady, chill monotone. A hundred crowns *was* a comfortable sum of money. It was a sum not to be despised. For a tithe of that—nay, for two pistoles—the Captain Guido Moratti would have risked his life twice over, things had come to such a pass with him. Highway robbery was not exactly his line, although sometimes, as on this occasion, he had been driven to it by the straits of the times. But suppose this offer was a blind? Suppose the man before him merely wanted to know where to get at him, to hand him over to the tender mercies of the thumbscrew and the rack? On the other hand, the man might be in earnest—and a hundred crowns! He hesitated.

"A—hun—dred—crowns." The cavaliere repeated these words, and there was a silence. Finally the bandit spoke:

"I frankly confess, signore, that stealing purses, even as I have done to-day, is not my way; but a man must live. If you mean what you say, there must be no half-confidences. Tell me who you are, and I will tell you where to find me."

"I am the Cavaliere Michele di Lippo of Castel Lippo on the Greve."

"Where is Castel Lippo?"

"At the junction of the Arno and the Greve—on the left bank."

"Very well. In a week you will hear from me again."

"It is enough. You will allow me to ransom the horse. I will send you the sum. On my word of honour, I have nothing to pay it at once."

"The signore's word of honour is doubtless very white. But a can in the hand is a can in the hand, and I need a horse—Good-night!"

"Good-night! But a can in the hand is not always wine to the lips, though a hundred crowns is ever a hundred crowns"; and saying this, di Lippo drew his cloak over the lower part of his face, and turned sharply to the right into the darkness, without so much as giving a look behind him. His horse would have followed; but quick as thought, Moratti's hand was on the trailing reins, and holding them firmly, he stooped and picked up the purse, poising it at arm's-length in front of him.

"Silver," he muttered, as his fingers felt the coins through the soft leather—"thirty crowns at the most, perhaps an odd gold piece or so—and now to be off. *Hola!* Steady!" and mounting the horse, he turned his head round, still talking to himself: "I am in luck. Cheese falls on my macaroni—thirty broad pieces and a horse, and a hundred crowns more in prospect. Captain Guido Moratti, the devil smiles on you— you will end a Count. *Animo!*" He touched the horse with his heels, and went forward at a smart gallop; and as he galloped, he threw his head back and laughed loudly and mirthlessly into the night.

In the meantime it was with a sore heart that the cavaliere made his way through the forest to the banks of the Arno, and then plodded along the river-side, through the wood, by a track scarcely discernible to any but one who had seen it many times. On his right hand the river hummed drearily; on his left, the trees sighed in the night-wind; and before him the narrow track wound, now up, then down, now twisting amongst the pines in darkness, then stretching in front, straight as a plumb-line. It was gall to di Lippo to think of the loss of the crowns and the good horse; it was bitterness to trudge it in the cold along the weary path that led to the ferry across the Arno, which he would have to cross before reaching his own home; and he swore deeply, under the muffling of his cloak, as he pressed on at his roundest pace. He soon covered the two miles that lay between him and the ferry; but it was past midnight ere he did this, and reaching the ferryman's hut, battered at the door with the hilt of his sword. Eventually he aroused the ferryman, who came forth grumbling. Had it been any one else, honest Giuseppe would have told him to go hang before he would have risen from his warm bed; but the Cavaliere Michele was a noble, and, although poor, had a lance or two, and Castel Lippo, which bore an ill name, was only a mangonel shot from the opposite bank. So Giuseppe punted his excellency across; and his excellency vented his spleen with a curse at everything in general, and the bandit in particular, as he stepped ashore and hurried to his dwelling. It was a steep climb that led up by a bridle-path to his half-ruined tower, and di Lippo stood at the postern, and whistled on his silver whistle, and knocked for many a time, before he heard the chains clanking, and the bar put back. At last the door opened, and a figure stood before him, a lantern in one hand.

"St. John! But it is your worship! We did not expect you until sunrise. And the horse, excellency?"

"Stand aside, fool. I have been robbed, that is all. Yes—let the matter drop; and light me up quick. Will you gape all night there?"

The porter, shutting the gate hastily, turned, and walking before his master, led him across the courtyard. Even by the moonlight, it could be seen that the flagstones were old and worn with age. In many places they had come apart, and with the spring, sprouts of green grass and white serpyllum would shoot up from the cracks. At present, these fissures were choked with snow. Entering the tower by an arched door at the end of the courtyard, they ascended a winding stair, which led into a large but only partially furnished room. Here the man lit two candles, and di Lippo, dropping his cloak, sank down into a chair, saying: "Make up a fire, will you—and bring me some wine; after that, you may go."

The man threw a log or two into the fireplace, where there was already the remains of a fire, and the pinewood soon blazed up cheerfully. Then he placed a flask of Orvieto and a glass at his master's elbow, and wishing him good-night, left him.

Michele di Lippo poured himself out a full measure and drained it at a draught. Drawing his chair close to the blazing wood, he stretched out his feet, cased in long boots of Spanish leather, and stared into the flames. He sat thus for an hour or so without motion. The candles burned out, and the fire alone lit the room, casting strange shadows on the moth-eaten tapestry of the hangings, alternately lighting and leaving in darkness the corners of the room, and throwing its fitful glow on the pallid features of the brooding man, who sat as if cut out of stone. At last the cavaliere moved, but it was only to fling another log on the flames. Then he resumed his former attitude, and watched the fire. As he looked, he saw a picture. He saw wide lands, lands rich with olive and vine, that climbed the green hills between which the Aulella babbles. He saw the grey towers of the castle of Pieve. Above the donjon, a broad flag flapped lazily in the air, and the blazon on it—three wasps on a green field—was his own. He was no longer the ruined noble, confined to his few acres, living like a goat amongst the rocks of the Greve; but my lord count, ruffling it again in Rome, and calling the mains with

Riario, as in the good old times ten years ago. *Diavolo!* But those were times when the Borgia was Pope! What nights those were in the Torre Borgia! He had one of Giulia Bella's gloves still, and there were dark stains on its whiteness—stains that were red once with the blood of Monreale, who wore it over his heart the day he ran him through on the Ripetta. *Basta!* That was twelve years ago! Twelve years! Twelve hundred years it seemed. And he was forty now. Still young enough to run another man through, however. *Cospetto!* If the bravo would only undertake the job, everything might be his! He would live again—or perhaps! And another picture came before the dreamer. It had much to do with death—a bell was tolling dismally, and a chained man was walking to his end, with a priest muttering prayers into his ears. In the background was a gallows, and a sea of heads, an endless swaying crowd of heads, with faces that looked on the man with hate, and tongues that jeered and shouted curses at him. And the voices of the crowd seemed to merge into one tremendous roar of hatred as the condemned wretch ascended the steps of the platform on which he was to find a disgraceful death.

Michele di Lippo rose suddenly with a shiver and an oath: "*Maledetto!* I must sleep. It touches the morning, and I have been dreaming too long."

II. At "The Devil on Two Sticks"

It was mid-day, and the Captain Guido Moratti was at home in his lodging in "The Devil on Two Sticks." Not an attractive address; but then this particular hostel was not frequented by persons who were squeamish about names, or—any other thing. The house itself lay in the Santo Spirito ward of Florence, filling up the end of a *chiassolino* or blind alley in a back street behind the church of Santa Felicita, and was well known to all who had "business" to transact. It had also drawn towards it the attention of the *Magnifici Signori*, and the long arm of the law would have reached it ere this but for the remark made by the Secretary Machiavelli, "One does not purify a city by stopping the sewers," he said; and added with a grim sarcasm, "and any one of us might have an urgent affair to-morrow, and need an agent—let the devil rest on his two sticks." And it was so.

Occasionally, the talons of Messer the Gonfaloniere would close on some unfortunate gentleman who had at the time no "friends," and then he was never seen again. But arrests were never made in the house, and it was consequently looked upon as a secure place by its customers. The room occupied by Moratti was on the second floor, and was lighted by a small window which faced a high dead wall, affording no view beyond that of the blackened stonework. The captain, being a single man, could afford to live at his ease, and though it was mid-day, and past the dinner hour, had only just risen, and was fortifying himself with a measure of Chianti. He was seated in a solid-looking chair, his goblet in his hand, and his long legs clothed in black and white trunks, the Siena colours, resting on the table. The upper part of his dress consisted of a closely fitting pied surcoat, of the same hues as his trunks; and round his waist he wore a webbed chain belt, to which was attached a plain, but useful-looking poniard. The black hair on his head was allowed to grow long, and fell in natural curls to his broad shoulders. He had no beard; but under the severe arch of his nose was a pair of long dark moustaches that completely hid the mouth, and these he wore in a twist that almost reached his ears. On the table where his feet rested was his cap, from which a frayed feather stuck out stiffly; likewise his cloak, and a very long sword in a velvet and wood scabbard. The other articles on the table were a half-empty flask of wine, a few dice, a pack of cards, a mask, a wisp of lace, and a broken fan. The walls were bare of all ornament, except over the entrance door, whence a crucified Christ looked down in His agony over the musty room. A spare chair or two, a couple of valises and a saddle, together with a bed, hidden behind some old and shabby curtains, completed the furniture of the chamber; but such as it was, it was better accommodation than the captain had enjoyed for many a day. For be it known that "The Devil on Two Sticks" was meant for the aristocrats of the "profession." The charges were accordingly high, and there was no credit allowed. No! No! The *padrone* knew better than to trust his longest-sworded clients for even so small a matter as a brown *paolo*. But at present Moratti was in funds, for thirty broad crowns in one's pocket, and a horse worth full thirty more, went a long way in those days, and besides, he had not a little luck at the cards last night. He thrust a sinewy hand into his pocket, and jingled the coins there, with a comfortable sense of proprietorship, and for the moment his face was actually pleasant to look upon. The face was an eminently handsome one. It was difficult to conceive that those clear, bold features were those of a thief. They were rather those of a soldier, brave, resolute, and hasty perhaps, though hardened, and marked by excess. There was that in them which seemed to point to a past very different from the present. And it had been so. But that story is a secret, and we must take the captain as we find him, nothing more or less than a bravo. Let it be remembered, however, that this hideous profession, although looked upon with fear by all, was not in those days deemed so dishonourable as to utterly cast a man out of the pale of his fellows. Troches, the bravo of Alexander VI., was very nearly made a cardinal; Don Michele, the strangler of Cesare Borgia, became commander-in-chief of the Florentine army, and had the honour of a conspiracy being formed against him—he was killed whilst leaving the house of Chaumont. Finally, there was that romantic scoundrel "Il Medighino," who advanced from valet to bravo, from bravo to be a pirate chief and the brother of a pontiff, ending his days as Marquis of Marignano and Viceroy of Bohemia. So that, roundly speaking, if the profession of the dagger did lead to the galleys or the scaffold, it as often led to wealth, and sometimes, as in the case of Giangiacomo Medici, to a coronet. Perhaps some such thoughts as these flitted in the captain's mind as he jingled his crowns and slowly sipped his wine. His fellow-men had made him a wolf, and a wolf he was now to the end of his spurs, as pitiless to his victims as they had been to him. He was no longer young; but a man between two ages, with all the strength and vitality of youth and the experience of five-and-thirty, so that with a stroke of luck he might any day do what the son of Bernardino had done. He had failed in everything up to now, although he had had his chances. His long sword had helped to stir the times when the Duke of Bari upset all Italy, and the people used to sing:

Cristo in cielo é il Moro in terra, Solo sa il fine di questa guerra.

He had fought at Fornovo and at Mertara; and in the breach at Santa Croce had even crossed swords with the Count di Savelli, the most redoubted knight, with the exception of Bayard, of the age. He had been run through the ribs for his temerity; but it was an honour he never forgot. Then other things had happened, and he had sunk, sunk to be what he was, as many a better man had done before him. A knock at the door disturbed his meditations. He set down his empty glass and called out, "Enter!"

The door opened, and the Cavaliere Michele di Lippo entered the room. Moratti showed no surprise, although the visit was a little unexpected; but beyond pointing to a chair, gave di Lippo no other greeting, saying simply: "Take a seat, signore—and shut the door behind you. I did not expect you until to-morrow."

"True, captain; But you see I was impatient. I got your letter yesterday, and, the matter being pressing, came here at once."

"Well—what is the business?"

The cavaliere's steel-grey eyes contracted like those of a cat when a sudden light is cast upon them, and he glanced cautiously around him. "This place is safe—no eavesdroppers?" he asked.

"None," answered Moratti; and slowly putting his feet down from the table, pushed the wine towards di Lippo. "Help yourself, signore—No! Well, as you wish. And now, your business?"

There was a silence in the room, and each man watched the other narrowly. Moratti looked at the cavaliere's long hatchet face, at the cruel close-set eyes, at the thin red hair showing under his velvet cap, and at the straight line of the mouth, partly hidden by a moustache, and short peaked beard of a slightly darker red than the hair on di Lippo's head. Michele di Lippo, in his turn, keenly scanned the seamed and haughty features of the bravo, and each man recognised in the other the qualities he respected, if such a word may be used. At last the cavaliere spoke: "As I mentioned, captain, my business is one of the highest importance, and—"

"You are prepared to pay in proportion—eh?" and Moratti twirled his moustache between his fingers.

"Exactly. I have made you my offer."

"But have not told me what you want done."

"I am coming to that. Permit me; I think I will change my mind"; and as Moratti nodded assent, di Lippo poured himself out a glass of wine and drained it slowly. When he had done this, he set the glass down with extreme care, and continued: "I am, as you see, captain, no longer a young man, and it is inconvenient to have to wait for an inheritance"—and he grinned horribly.

"I see, cavaliere—you want me to anticipate matters a little— Well, I am willing to help you if I can."

"It is a hundred crowns, captain, and the case lies thus. There is but one life between me and the County of Pieve in the Val di Magra, and you know how uncertain life is."

He paused; but as Guido Moratti said nothing, continued with his even voice: "Should the old Count of Pieve die—and he is on the edge of the grave—the estate will pass to his daughter. In the event of *her* death—"

"*Whew!*" Moratti emitted a low whistle, and sat bolt upright. "So it is the lady," he cried. "That is not my line, cavaliere. It is more a matter of the poison-cup, and I don't deal in such things. Carry your offer elsewhere."

"It will be a new experience, captain—and a hundred crowns."

"Blood of a king, man! do you think I hesitate over a paltry hundred crowns? Had it been a man, it would have been different—but a woman! No! No! It is not my way"; and he rose and paced the room.

"Tush, man! It is but a touch of your dagger, and you have done much the same before."

Moratti faced di Lippo. "As you say, I have executed commissions before, but never on a woman, and never on a man without giving him a chance."

"You are too tender-hearted for your profession, captain. Have you never been wronged by a woman? They can be more pitiless than men, I assure you."

The bronze on Moratti's cheek paled to ashes, and his face hardened with a sudden memory. He turned his back upon di Lippo, and stared out of the window at the dead wall which was the only view. It was a chance shot, but it had told. The cavaliere rose slowly and flung a purse on the table. "Better give him the whole at once," he muttered. "Come, captain," he added, raising his voice. "It will be over in a moment; and after all, neither you nor I will ever see heaven. We might as well burn for something; and if I mistake not, both you and I are like those Eastern tigers, who once having tasted blood must go on forever—see!" and he laid his lean hand on the bravo's shoulder, "why not revenge on the whole sex the wrong done you by one—"

The captain swung round suddenly and shook off di Lippo's hand. "Don't touch me," he cried; "at times like this I am dangerous. What demon put into your mouth the words you have just used? They have served your purpose—and she shall die. Count me out the money, the full hundred—and go."

"It is there"; and di Lippo pointed with his finger to the purse. "You will find the tale complete—a hundred crowns—count them at your leisure. *Addio!* captain. I shall hear good news soon, I trust." Rubbing the palms of his hands together, he stepped softly from the room.

Guido Moratti did not hear or answer him. His mind had gone back with a rush for ten years, when the work of a woman had made him sink lower than a beast. Such things happen to men sometimes. He had sunk like a stone thrown into a lake; he had been destroyed utterly, and it was sufficient to say that he lived now to prey on his fellow-creatures. But he had never thought of the revenge that di Lippo had suggested. Now that he did think of it, he remembered a story told in the old days round the camp fires, when they were hanging on the rear of Charles's retreating army, just before he turned and rent the League at Fornovo. Rodrigo Gonzaga, the Spaniard, had told it of a countryman of his, a native of Toledo, who for a wrong done to him by a girl had devoted himself to the doing to death of women. It was horrible; and at the time he had refused to believe it. Now he was face to face with the same horror—nay, he had even embraced it. He had lost his soul; but the price of it was not yet paid in revenge or gold, and, by Heaven! he would have it. He laughed out as loudly and cheerlessly as on that winter's night when he rode off through the snow; and laying hands on the purse, tore it open, and the contents rolled out upon the table. "The price of my soul!" he sneered as he held up a handful of the coins, and let them drop again with a clash on the heap on the table. "It is more than Judas got for his—ha! ha!"

III. FELICITÀ

Some few days after his interview with di Lippo, the Captain Guido Moratti rode his horse across the old Roman bridge which at that time spanned the Aulella, and directed his way towards the castle of Pieve, whose outlines rose before him, cresting an eminence about a league from the bridge. The captain was travelling as a person of some quality, the better to carry out a plan he had formed for gaining admission to Pieve, and a lackey rode behind him holding his valise. He had hired horse and man in Florence, and the servant was an honest fellow enough, in complete ignorance of his master's character and profession. Both the captain and his man bore the appearance of long travel, and in truth they had journeyed with a free rein; and now that a stormy night was setting in, they were not a little anxious to reach their point. The snow was falling in soft flakes, and the landscape was grey with the driving mist, through which the outlines of the castle loomed large and shadowy, more like a fantastic creation in cloudland than the work of human hands. As the captain pulled down the lapels of his cap to ward off the drift which was coming straight in his face, the bright flare of a beacon fire shone from a tower of the castle, and the rays from it stretched in broad orange bands athwart the rolling mist, which threatened, together with the increasing darkness, to extinguish all the view that was left, and make the league to Pieve a road of suffering. With the flash of the fire a weird, sustained howl came to the travellers in an eerie cadence; and as the fearsome call died away, it was picked up by an answering cry from behind, then another and yet another. There could be no mistaking these signals; they meant pressing and immediate danger.

"Wolves!" shouted Moratti; and turning to his knave: "Gallop, Tito!—else our bones will be picked clean by morning. Gallop!"

They struck their spurs into the horses; and the jaded animals, as if realizing their peril, made a brave effort, and dashed off at their utmost speed. It was none too soon, for the wolves, hitherto following in silence, had given tongue at the sight of the fire; and as if knowing that the beacon meant safety for their prey, and that they were like to lose a dinner unless they hurried, laid themselves on the track of the flying horses with a hideous chorus of yells. They could not be seen for the mist; but they were not far behind. They were going at too great a pace to howl now; but an occasional angry "yap" reached the riders, and reached the horses too, whose instinct told them what it meant; and they needed no further spurring, to make them strain every muscle to put a distance between themselves and their pursuers. Moratti thoroughly grasped the situation. He had experienced a similar adventure in the Pennine Alps, when carrying despatches for Paolo Orsini, with this difference, that then he had a fresh horse, and could see where he was going; whereas now, although the distance to Pieve was short, and in ten minutes he might be safe and with a whole skin, yet a false step, a stumble, and nothing short of a miracle could prevent him becoming a living meal to the beasts behind.

He carried, slung by a strap over his shoulder, a light bugle, which he had often found useful before, but never so useful as now. Thrusting his hand under his cloak, he drew it out, and blew a long clear blast; and, to his joy, there came an answer through the storm from the castle. Rescue was near at hand, and faster and faster they flew; but as surely the wolves gained on them, and they could hear the snarling of the leaders as they jostled against and snapped at each other in their haste. Moratti looked over his shoulder. He could see close behind a dark crescent moving towards them with fearful rapidity. He almost gave a groan. It was too horrible to die thus! And he dug his spurs again and again into the heaving flanks of his horse, with the vain hope of increasing its speed. They had now reached the ascent to Pieve. They could see the lights at the windows. In two hundred yards there was safety; when Moratti's horse staggered under him, and he had barely time to free his feet from the stirrups and lean well back in the saddle ere the animal came down with a plunge. Tito went by like a flash, as the captain picked himself up and faced the wolves, sword in hand. There was a steep bank on the side of the road. He made a dash to gain the summit of this; but had hardly reached half-way up when the foremost wolf was upon him, and had rolled down again with a yell, run through the heart. His fellows tore him to shreds, and in a moment began to worry at the struggling horse, whose fore-leg was broken. In a hand-turn the matter was ended, and the wretched beast was no longer visible, all that could be seen being a black swaying mass of bodies, as the pack hustled and fought over the dead animal.

Nevertheless, there were three or four of the wolves who devoted their attention to Moratti, and he met them with the courage of despair. But the odds were too many, and he began to feel that he could not hold out much longer. One huge monster, his shaggy coat icy with the sleet, had pulled him to his knees, and it was only a lucky thrust of the dagger, he held in his left hand, that saved him. He regained his feet only to be dragged down again, and to rise yet once more. He was bleeding and weak, wounded in many places, and the end could not be far off. It was not thus that he had hoped to die; and he was dying like a worried lynx.

The thought drove him to madness. He was of Siena, and somewhere in his veins, though he did not know it, ran the blood of the Senonian Gauls, and it came out now— he went Berserker, as the old northern pirates were wont to do. Sliding down the bank, he jumped full into the pack, striking at them in a dumb fury. He was hardly human himself now, and he plunged his sword again and again into the heaving mass around him, and felt no pain from the teeth of the wolves as they rent his flesh. A fierce mad joy came upon him. It was a glorious fight after all, and he was dying game. It was a glorious fight, and, when he felt a grisly head at his throat, and the weight of his assailant brought him down once more, he flung aside his sword, and grappling his enemy with his hands, tore asunder the huge jaws, and flung the body from him with a yell. Almost at that very instant there was the sharp report of firearms, the rush of hurrying feet, and the blaze of torches. Moratti, half on his knees, was suddenly pulled to his feet by a strong hand, and supported by it he stood, dizzy and faint, bleeding almost everywhere, but safe. The wolves had fled in silence, vanishing like phantoms across the snow; and shot after shot was fired in their direction by the rescue party.

"*Per Bacco!*" said the man who was holding Moratti up; "but it was an affair between the skin and the flesh, signore—steady!" and his arm tightened round the captain. As he did this, a long defiant howl floated back to them through the night, and Guido Moratti knew no more. He seemed to have dropped suddenly into an endless night. He seemed to be flying through space, past countless millions of stars, which, bright themselves, were unable to illumine the abysmal darkness around, and then— there was nothing.

When Moratti came to himself again, he was lying in a bed, in a large room, dimly lighted by a shaded lamp, set on a tall Corinthian pillar of marble. After the first indistinct glance around him, he shut his eyes, and was lost in a dreamy stupor. In a little, he looked again, and saw that the chamber was luxuriously fitted, and that he was not alone, for, kneeling at a *prie-dieu*, under a large picture of a Madonna and Child, was the figure of a woman. Her face was from him; but ill as he was, Moratti saw that the tight-fitting dress showed a youthful and perfect figure, and that her head was covered with an abundance of red-gold hair. The man was still in the shadowland caused by utter weakness, and for a moment he thought that this was nothing but a vision of fancy; but he rallied half unconsciously, and looked again; and then, curiosity overcoming him, attempted to turn so as to obtain a better view, and was checked by a twinge of pain, which, coming suddenly, brought an exclamation to his lips. In an instant the lady rose, and moving towards him, bent over the bed. As she did this, their eyes met, and the fierce though dulled gaze of the bravo saw before him a face of ideal innocence, of such saintlike purity, that it might have been a dream of Raffaelle. She placed a cool hand on his hot forehead, and whispered softly: "Be still—and drink this—you will sleep." Turning to a side table, she lifted a silver goblet therefrom, and gave him to drink. The draught was cool and refreshing, and he gathered strength from it.

"Where am I?" he asked; and then, with a sudden courtesy, "Madonna—pardon me—I thank you."

"Hush!" she answered, lifting a small hand. "You are in Pieve, and you have been very ill. But I must not talk—sleep now, signore."

"I remember now," he said dreamily—"the wolves; but it seems so long ago."

She made no reply, but stepped softly out of the room, and was gone. Moratti would have called out after her; but a drowsiness came on him, and closing his eyes, he slept.

It takes a strong man some time to recover from wounds inflicted by a wild animal; and when a man has, like Guido Moratti, lived at both ends, it takes longer still, and it was weeks before the captain was out of danger. He never saw his fair visitor again. Her place was taken by a staid and middle-aged nurse, and he was visited two or three times daily by a solemn-looking physician. But although he did not see her whom he longed to see, there was a message both morning and evening from the Count of Pieve and his daughter, hoping the invalid was better—the former regretting that his infirmities prevented his paying a personal visit, and the inquiries of the latter being always accompanied by a bouquet of winter flowers. But strange as it may seem, when he was under the influence of the opiate they gave him nightly, he was certain of the presence of the slight graceful figure of the lady of the *prie-dieu*, as he called her to himself. He saw again the golden-red hair and the sweet eyes, and felt again the touch of the cool hand. He began to think that this bright presence which lit his dreams was but a vision after all, and used to long for the night and the opiate.

At last one fine morning Tito appeared, and began to set out and brush the captain's apparel as if nothing had ever happened. Moratti watched him for a space, and then rising up against his pillows, spoke: "Tito!"

"Signore!"

"How is it that you have not been here before?"

"I was not allowed, Excellency, until to-day—your worship was too ill."

"Then I am better."

"Excellency!"

There was a silence of some minutes, and the captain spoke again: "Tito!"

"Signore!"

"Have you seen the Count and his daughter?"

"Excellency!"

"What are they like?"

"The Count old, and a cripple. Madonna Felicità, small, thin, red-haired like my wife Sancia."

Moratti sank down again upon the bed, a satisfied smile upon his lips. So there was truth in his dreams. The vision of the night was a reality. He would see her soon, as soon as he could rise, and he was fast getting well, very fast. He had gone back many years in his illness. He had thoughts stirred within him that he had imagined dead long ago. He was the last man to day-dream, to build castles in the air; but as he lay idly watching Tito, who was evidently very busy cleaning something—for he was sitting on a low chair with his back towards the captain, and his elbow moving backwards and forwards rapidly—the bravo pictured himself Guido Moratti as he might have been, a man able to look all men in the face, making an honourable way for himself, and worthy the love of a good woman. The last thought brought before him a fair face and sweet eyes, and a dainty head crowned with red-gold hair, and the strong man let his fancy run on with an uprising of infinite tenderness in his heart. He was lost in a cloudland of dreams.

"Signore!"

Tito's harsh voice had pulled down the castle in Spain, and Tito himself was standing at the bedside holding a bright and glittering dagger in his hand. But he had done more than upset his master's dreams. He had, all unwittingly, brought him back in a flash to the hideous reality, for, as a consequence of his long illness, of the weeks of fever and delirium, Moratti had clean forgotten the dreadful object of his coming to Pieve. It all came back to him with a blinding suddenness, and he closed his eyes with a shudder of horror as Tito laid the poniard upon the bed, asking: "Will the signore see if the blade is keen enough? A touch of the finger will suffice."

IV. Conclusion—The Torre Dolorosa

Days were yet to pass before Guido Moratti was able to leave his chamber; but at last the leech who attended him said he might do so with safety; and later on, the steward of the household brought a courteous invitation from the Count of Pieve to dine with him. As already explained, Moratti had not as yet seen his host; and since he was well enough to sit up, there were no more dreamy visions of the personal presence of Felicità. He had made many resolutions whilst left to himself, and had determined that as soon as he was able to move he would leave the castle, quit Italy, and make a new name for himself, or die in the German wars. He was old enough to build no great hopes on the future; but fortune might smile on him, and then—many things might happen. At any rate, he would wipe the slate clean, and there should be no more ugly scores on it.

Not that he was a reformed man; he was only groping his way back to light. Men do not cast off the past as a snake sheds his skin. He knew that well enough, but he knew, too, that he had seen a faint track back to honour; and difficult as it was, he had formed a determination to travel by it. He had been so vile, he had sunk so low, that there were moments when a despair came on him; but with a new country and new scenes, and the little flame of hope that was warming his dead soul back to life, there might yet be a chance. He knew perfectly that he was in love, and when a man of his age loves, it is for the remainder of his life. He was aware—none better—that his love was madness, all but an insult, and that it was worse than presumption to even entertain the thought that he had inspired any other feeling beyond that of pity in the heart of Felicità. It is enough to say that he did not dare to hope in this way; but he meant to so order his future life, as to feel that any such sentiment as love in his heart towards her would not be sacrilege.

He sent back a civil answer to the invitation; and a little after eleven, descended the stairway which led from his chamber to the Count's apartments, looking very pale and worn, but very handsome. For he was, in truth, a man whose personal appearance took all eyes. The apartments of the Count were immediately below Moratti's own chamber, and on entering, he saw the old knight himself reclining in a large chair. He was alone, except for a hound which lay stretched out on the hearth, its muzzle between its forepaws, and a dining-table set for three was close to his elbow. Bernabo of Pieve received his guest with a stately courtesy, asking pardon for being unable to rise, as he was crippled. "They clipped my wings at Arx Sismundea, captain—before your time; but of a truth I am a glad man to see you strong again. It was a narrow affair."

"I cannot thank you in words, Count; you and your house have placed a debt on me I can never repay."

"Tush, man! There must be no talk of thanks. If there are to be any, they are due to the leech, and to Felicità, my daughter. She is all I have left, for my son was killed at Santa Croce."

"I was there, Count."

"And knew him?"

"Alas, no. I was on the side of Spain."

"With the besieged, and he with the League. He was killed on the breach—poor lad."

At this moment a curtain at the side of the room was lifted, and Felicità entered. She greeted Moratti warmly, and with a faint flush on her cheeks, inquired after his health, hoping he was quite strong again.

"So well, Madonna, that I must hurry on my journey to-morrow."

"To-morrow!" Her large eyes opened wide in astonishment, and there was a pain in her look. "Why," she continued, "it will be a fortnight ere you can sit in the saddle again."

"It might have been never, but for you," he answered gravely, and her eyes met his, and fell. At this moment the steward announced that the table was ready; and by the time the repast was ended, Moratti had forgotten his good resolutions for instant departure, and had promised to stay for at least a week, at the urgent intercession of both the Count and his daughter. He knew he was wrong in doing so, and that, whatever happened, it was his duty to go at once; but he hesitated with himself. He would give himself one week of happiness, for it was happiness to be near her, and then—he would go away forever. And she would never know, in her innocence and purity, that Guido Moratti, bravo—he shuddered at the infamous word—loved her better than all the world beside, and that for her sake he had become a new man.

After dinner the Count slept, and, the day being bright, they stepped out into a large balcony and gazed at the view. The balcony, which stretched out from a low window of the dining chamber, terminated on the edge of a precipice which dropped down a clear two hundred feet; and leaning over the moss-grown battlements, they looked at the white winter landscape before them. Behind rose the tower they had just quitted, and Felicità, turning, pointed to it, saying: "We call this the Torre Dolorosa."

"A sad name, Madonna. May I ask why?"

"Because all of our house who die in their beds die here."

"And yet you occupy this part of the castle."

"Oh, I do not. My chamber is there—in Count Ligo's Tower"; and she pointed to the right, where another grey tower rose from the keep. "But my father likes to occupy the Torre Dolorosa himself. He says he is living with his ancestors—to whom he will soon go, as he always adds."

"May the day be far distant."

And she answered "Amen."

After this, they went in, and the talk turned on other matters. The week passed and then another, but at last the day came for Moratti's departure. He had procured another horse. It was indeed a gift which the old Count pressed upon him, and he had accepted it with much reluctance, but much gratitude. In truth, the kindness of these people towards him was unceasing, and Moratti made great strides towards his new self in that week. He was to have started after the mid-day dinner; but with the afternoon he was not gone, and sunset found him on the balcony of the Torre Dolorosa with Felicità by his side.

"You cannot possibly go to-night," she said.

"I will go to-morrow, then," replied Moratti, and she looked away from him.

It was a moment of temptation. Almost did a rush of words come to the captain's lips. He felt as if he must take her in his arms and tell her that he loved her as man never loved woman. It was an effort; but he was getting stronger in will daily, and he crushed down the feeling.

"It is getting chill for you," he said; "we had better go in."

"Tell me," she answered, not heeding his remark, "tell me exactly where you are going?"

"I do not know—perhaps to join Piccolomini in Bohemia—perhaps to join Alva in the Low Countries—wherever a soldier's sword has work to do."

"And you will come back?"

"Perhaps."

"A great man, with a *condotta* of a thousand lances—and forget Pieve."

"As God is my witness—never—but it is chill, Madonna—come in."

When they came in, Bernabo of Pieve was not alone, for standing close to the old man, his back to the fire, and rubbing his hands softly together, was the tall, gaunt figure of the Cavaliere Michele di Lippo.

"A sudden visit, dear cousin," he said, greeting Felicità, and turning his steel-grey eyes, with a look of cold inquiry in them, on Moratti.

"The Captain Guido Moratti—my cousin, the Cavaliere di Lippo."

"Of Castel Lippo, on the Greve," put in di Lippo. "I am charmed to make the acquaintance of the Captain Moratti. Do you stay long in Pieve, captain?"

"I leave to-morrow." Moratti spoke shortly. His blood was boiling, as he looked on the gloomy figure of the cavaliere, who watched him furtively from under his eyelids, the shadow of a sneer on his face. He was almost sick with shame when he thought how he was in di Lippo's hands, how a word from him could brand him with ignominy beyond repair. Some courage, however, came back to him with the thought that, after all, he held cards as well, as for his own sake, di Lippo would probably remain quiet.

"So soon!" said di Lippo with a curious stress on the word soon, and then added, "That is bad news."

"I have far to go, signore," replied Moratti coldly, and the conversation then changed. It was late when they retired; and as the captain bent over Felicità's hand, he held it for a moment in his own broad palm, and said: "It is good-bye, lady, for I go before the dawn to-morrow."

She made no answer; but, with a sudden movement, detached a bunch of winter violets she wore at her neck, and thrusting them in Moratti's hand, turned and fled. The Count was half asleep, and did not notice the passage; but di Lippo said with his icy sneer: "Excellent—you work like an artist, Moratti."

"I do not understand you"; and turning on his heel, the captain strode off to his room.

An hour or so later, he was seated in a low chair, thinking. His valise lay packed, and all was ready for his early start. He still held the violets in his hand, but his face was dark with boding thoughts. He dreaded going and leaving Felicità to the designs of di Lippo. There would be other means found by di Lippo to carry out his design; and with a groan, the captain rose and began to pace the room. He was on the cross with anxiety. If he went without giving warning of di Lippo's plans, he would still be a sharer in the murder—and the murder of Felicità, for a hair of whose head he was prepared to risk his soul. If, on the other hand, he spoke, he would be lost forever in her eyes. Although it was winter, the room seemed to choke him, and he suddenly flung open the door and, descending the dim stairway, went out into the balcony. It was bright with moonlight, and the night was clear as crystal. He leaned over the battlements and racked his mind as to his course of action. At last he resolved. He would take the risk, and speak out, warn Bernabo of Pieve at all hazards, and would do so at once. He turned hastily, and then stopped, for before him in the moonlight stood the Cavaliere Michele di Lippo.

"I sought you in your chamber, captain," he said in his biting voice, "and not finding you, came here—"

"And how did you know I would be here?"

"Lovers like the moonlight, and you can see the light from her window in Ligo's Tower," said di Lippo, and added sharply: "So you are playing false, Moratti."

The captain made no answer; there was a singing in his ears, and a sudden and terrible thought was working. His hand was on the hilt of his dagger, a spring, a blow, and di Lippo would be gone. And no one would know. But the cavaliere went on, unheeding his silence.

"You are playing false, Moratti. You are playing for your own hand with my hundred crowns. You think your ship has come home. Fool! Did you imagine I would allow this? But I still give you a chance. Either do my business to-night—the way is open—or to-morrow you are laid by the heels as a thief and a bravo. What will your Felicità—"

"Dog—speak her name again, and you die!" Moratti struck him across the face with his open palm, and Michele di Lippo reeled back a pace, his face as white as snow. It was only a pace, however, for he recovered himself at once, and sprung at Moratti like a wild-cat. The two closed. They spoke no word, and nothing could be heard but their laboured breath as they gripped together. Their daggers were in their hands; but each man knew this, and had grasped the wrist of the other. Moratti was more powerful; but his illness had weakened him, and the long lean figure of Michele di Lippo was as strong as a wire rope. Under the quiet moon and the winter stars, they fought, until at last di Lippo was driven to the edge of the parapet, and in the moonlight he saw the meaning in Moratti's set face. With a superhuman effort, he wrenched his hand free, and the next moment his dagger had sunk to the hilt in the captain's side, and Moratti's grasp loosened, but only for an instant. He was mortally wounded, he knew. He was going to die; but it would not be alone. He pressed di Lippo to his breast. He lifted him from his feet, and forced him through an embrasure which yawned behind. Here, on its brink, the two figures swayed for an instant, and then the balcony was empty, and from the deep of the precipice two hundred feet below, there travelled upwards the sullen echo of a dull crash, and all was quiet again.

When the stars were paling, the long howl of a wolf rang out into the stillness. It reached Felicità in Count Ligo's Tower, and filled her with a nameless terror. "Guard him, dear saints," she prayed; "shield him from peril, and hold him safe."

How Jean-Pierre Met
the Scarlet Pimpernel

Baroness Orczy

I

A h, monsieur! the pity of it, the pity! Surely there are sins which *le bon Dieu* Himself will condone. And if not—well, I had to risk His displeasure anyhow. Could I see them both starve, monsieur? I ask you! and M. le Vicomte had become so thin, so thin, his tiny, delicate bones were almost through his skin. And Mme. la Marquise! an angel, monsieur! Why, in the happy olden days, before all these traitors and assassins ruled in France, M. and Mme. la Marquise lived only for the child, and then to see him dying—yes, dying, there was no shutting one's eyes to that awful fact—M. le Vicomte de Mortaine was dying of starvation and of disease.

There we were all herded together in a couple of attics—one of which little more than a cupboard—at the top of a dilapidated, half-ruined house in the Rue des Pipots—Mme. la Marquise, M. le Vicomte and I—just think of that, monsieur! M. le Marquis had his château, as no doubt you know, on the outskirts of Lyons. A loyal high-born gentleman; was it likely, I ask you, that he would submit passively to the rule of those execrable revolutionaries who had murdered their King, outraged their Queen and Royal family, and, God help them! had already perpetrated every crime and every abomination for which of a truth there could be no pardon either on earth or in Heaven? He joined that plucky but, alas! small and ill-equipped army of royalists who, unable to save their King, were at least determined to avenge him.

Well, you know well enough what happened. The counter-revolution failed; the revolutionary army brought Lyons down to her knees after a siege of two months. She was then marked down as a rebel city, and after the abominable decree of October 9th had deprived her of her very name, and Couthon had exacted bloody reprisals from the entire population for its loyalty to the King, the infamous Laporte was sent down in order finally to stamp out the lingering remnants of the rebellion. By that time, monsieur, half the city had been burned down, and one-tenth and more of the inhabitants—men, women and children—had been massacred in cold blood, whilst most of the others had fled in terror from the appalling scene of ruin and desolation. Laporte completed the execrable work so ably begun by Couthon. He was a very celebrated and skilful doctor at the Faculty of Medicine, now turned into a human hyena in the name of Liberty and Fraternity.

M. le Marquis contrived to escape with the scattered remnant of the Royalist army into Switzerland. But Mme. la Marquise throughout all these strenuous times had stuck to her post at the château like the valiant creature that she was. When Couthon entered Lyons at the head of the revolutionary army, the whole of her household fled, and I was left alone to look after her and M. le Vicomte.

Then one day when I had gone into Lyons for provisions, I suddenly chanced to hear outside an eating-house that which nearly froze the marrow in my old bones. A captain belonging to the Revolutionary Guard was transmitting to his sergeant certain orders, which he had apparently just received.

The orders were to make a perquisition at ten o'clock this same evening in the château of Mortaine as the Marquis was supposed to be in hiding there, and in any event to arrest every man, woman and child who was found within its walls.

"Citizen Laporte," the captain concluded, "knows for a certainty that the *ci-devant* Marquise and her brat are still there, even if the Marquis has fled like the traitor that he is. Those accursed English spies who call themselves the League of the Scarlet Pimpernel have been very active in Lyons of late, and citizen Laporte is afraid that they might cheat the guillotine of the carcases of those aristos, as they have already succeeded in doing in the case of a large number of traitors."

I did not, of course, wait to hear any more of that abominable talk. I sped home as fast as my old legs would carry me. That self-same evening, as soon as it was dark, Mme. la Marquise, carrying M. le Vicomte in her arms and I carrying a pack with a few necessaries on my back, left the ancestral home of the Mortaines never to return to it again: for within an hour of our flight a detachment of the revolutionary army made a descent upon the château; they ransacked it from attic to cellar, and finding nothing there to satisfy their lust of hate, they burned the stately mansion down to the ground.

We were obliged to take refuge in Lyons, at any rate for a time. Great as was the danger inside the city, it was infinitely greater on the high roads, unless we could arrange for some vehicle to take us a considerable part of the way to the frontier, and above all for some sort of passports—forged or otherwise—to enable us to pass the various toll-gates on the road, where vigilance was very strict. So we wandered through the ruined and deserted streets of the city in search of shelter, but found every charred and derelict house full of miserable tramps and destitutes like ourselves. Half dead with fatigue, Mme. la Marquise was at last obliged to take refuge in one of these houses which was situated in the Rue des Pipots. Every room was full to overflowing with a miserable wreckage of humanity thrown hither by the tide of anarchy and of bloodshed. But at the top of the house we found an attic. It was empty save for a couple of chairs, a table and a broken-down bedstead on which were a ragged mattress and pillow.

Here, monsieur, we spent over three weeks, at the end of which time M. le Vicomte fell ill, and then there followed days, monsieur, through which I would not like my worst enemy to pass.

Mme. la Marquise had only been able to carry away in her flight what ready money she happened to have in the house at the time. Securities, property, money belonging to aristocrats had been ruthlessly confiscated by the revolutionary government in Lyons. Our scanty resources rapidly became exhausted, and what was left had to be kept for milk and delicacies for M. le Vicomte. I tramped through the streets in search of a doctor, but most of them had been arrested on some paltry charge or other of rebellion, whilst others had fled from the city. There was only that infamous Laporte—a vastly clever doctor, I knew—but as soon take a lamb to a hungry lion as the Vicomte de Mortaine to that bloodthirsty cut-throat.

Then one day our last franc went, and we had nothing left. Mme. la Marquise had not touched food for two days. I had stood at the corner of the street, begging all the day until I was driven off by the *gendarmes*. I had only obtained three sous from the passers-by. I bought some milk and took it home for M. le Vicomte. The following morning when I entered the larger attic I found that Mme. la Marquise had fainted from inanition.

I spent the whole of the day begging in the streets and dodging the guard, and even so I only collected four sous. I could have got more perhaps, only that at about midday the smell of food from an eating-house turned me sick and faint, and when I regained consciousness I found myself huddled up under a doorway and evening gathering in fast around me. If Mme. la Marquise could go two days without food I ought to go four. I struggled to my feet; fortunately I had retained possession of my four sous, else of a truth I would not have had the courage to go back to the miserable attic which was the only home I knew.

I was wending my way along as fast as I could—for I knew that Mme. la Marquise would be getting terribly anxious—when, just as I turned into the Rue Blanche, I spied two gentlemen—obviously strangers, for they were dressed with a luxury and care with which we had long ceased to be familiar in Lyons—walking rapidly towards me. A moment or two later they came to a halt, not far from where I was standing, and I heard the taller one of the two say to the other in English—a language with which I am vaguely conversant: "All right again this time, what, Tony?"

Both laughed merrily like a couple of schoolboys playing truant, and then they disappeared under the doorway of a dilapidated house, whilst I was left wondering how two such elegant gentlemen dared be abroad in Lyons these days, seeing that every man, woman and child who was dressed in anything but threadbare clothes was sure to be insulted in the streets for an aristocrat, and as often as not summarily arrested as a traitor.

However, I had other things to think about, and had already dismissed the little incident from my mind, when at the bottom of the Rue Blanche I came upon a knot of gaffers, men and women, who were talking and gesticulating very excitedly outside the door of a cook-shop. At first I did not take much notice of what was said: my eyes were glued to the front of the shop, on which were displayed sundry delicacies of the kind which makes a wretched, starved beggar's mouth water as he goes by; a roast capon especially attracted my attention, together with a bottle of red wine; these looked just the sort of luscious food which Mme. la Marquise would relish.

Well, sir, the law of God says: "Thou shalt not covet," and no doubt I committed a grievous sin when my hungry eyes fastened upon that roast capon and that bottle of Burgundy. We also know the stories of Judas Iscariot and of Jacob's children who sold their own brother Joseph into slavery—such a crime, monsieur, I took upon my conscience then; for just as the vision of Mme. la Marquise eating that roast capon and drinking that Burgundy rose before my eyes, my ears caught some fragments of the excited conversation which was going on all around me.

"He went this way!" someone said.

"No; that!" protested another.

"There's no sign of him now, anyway."

The owner of the shop was standing on his own doorstep, his legs wide apart, one arm on his wide hip, the other still brandishing the knife wherewith he had been carving for his customers.

"He can't have gone far," he said, as he smacked his thick lips.

"The impudent rascal, flaunting such fine clothes—like the aristo that he is."

"Bah! these cursed English! They are aristos all of them! And this one with his followers is no better than a spy!"

"Paid by that damned English Government to murder all our patriots and to rob the guillotine of her just dues."

"They say he had a hand in the escape of the *ci-devant* Due de Sermeuse and all his brats from the very tumbril which was taking them to execution."

A cry of loathing and execration followed this statement. There was vigorous shaking of clenched fists and then a groan of baffled rage.

"We almost had him this time. If it had not been for these confounded, ill-lighted streets—"

"I would give something," concluded the shopkeeper, "if we could lay him by the heels."

"What would you give, citizen Dompierre?" queried a woman in the crowd, with a ribald laugh, "one of your roast capons?"

"Aye, little mother," he replied jovially, "and a bottle of my best Burgundy to boot, to drink confusion to that meddlesome Englishman and his crowd and a speedy promenade up the steps of the guillotine."

Monsieur, I assure you that at that moment my heart absolutely stood still. The tempter stood at my elbow and whispered, and I deliberately smothered the call of my conscience. I did what Joseph's brethren did, what brought Judas Iscariot to hopeless remorse. There was no doubt that the hue and cry was after the two elegantly dressed gentlemen whom I had seen enter the dilapidated house in the Rue Blanche. For a second or two I closed my eyes and deliberately conjured up the vision of Mme. la Marquise fainting for lack of food, and of M. le Vicomte dying for want of sustenance; then I worked my way to the door of the shop and accosted the burly proprietor with as much boldness as I could muster.

"The two Englishmen passed by me at the top of the Rue Blanche," I said to him. "They went into a house . . . I can show you which it is—"

In a moment I was surrounded by a screeching, gesticulating crowd. I told my story as best I could; there was no turning back now from the path of cowardice and of crime. I saw that brute Dompierre pick up the largest roast capon from the front of his shop, together with a bottle of that wine which I had coveted; then he thrust both these treasures into my trembling hands and said:

"*En avant!*"

And we all started to run up the street, shouting: "Death to the English spies!" I was the hero of the expedition. Dompierre and another man carried me, for I was too weak to go as fast as they wished. I was hugging the capon and the bottle of wine to my heart; I had need to do that, so as to still the insistent call of my conscience, for I felt a coward—a mean, treacherous, abominable coward!

When we reached the house and I pointed it out to Dompierre, the crowd behind us gave a cry of triumph. In the topmost storey a window was thrown open, two heads appeared silhouetted against the light within, and the cry of triumph below was answered by a merry, prolonged laugh from above.

I was too dazed to realise very clearly what happened after that. Dompierre, I know, kicked open the door of the house, and the crowd rushed in in his wake. I managed to keep my feet and to work my way gradually out of the crowd. I must have gone on mechanically, almost unconsciously, for the next thing that I remember with any distinctness was that I found myself once more speeding down the Rue Blanche, with all the yelling and shouting some little way behind me.

With blind instinct, too, I had clung to the capon and the wine, the price of my infamy. I was terribly weak and felt sick and faint, but I struggled on for a while, until my knees refused me service, and I came down on my two hands, whilst the capon rolled away into the gutter, and the bottle of Burgundy fell with a crash against the pavement, scattering its precious contents in every direction.

There I lay, wretched, despairing, hardly able to move, when suddenly I heard rapid and firm footsteps immediately behind me, and the next moment two firm hands had me under the arms, and I heard a voice saying:

"Steady, old friend. Can you get up? There! Is that better?"

The same firm hands raised me to my feet. At first I was too dazed to see anything, but after a moment or two I was able to look around me, and, by the light of a street lanthorn immediately overhead, I recognised the tall, elegantly dressed Englishman and his friend, whom I had just betrayed to the fury of Dompierre and a savage mob.

I thought that I was dreaming, and I suppose that my eyes betrayed the horror which I felt, for the stranger looked at me scrutinisingly for a moment or two, then he gave the quaintest laugh I had ever heard in all my life, and said something to his friend in English, which this time I failed to understand.

Then he turned to me:

"By my faith," he said in perfect French—so that I began to doubt if he was an English spy after all—"I verily believe that you are the clever rogue, eh? who obtained a roast capon and a bottle of wine from that fool Dompierre. He and his boon companions are venting their wrath on you, old compeer; they are calling you liar and traitor and cheat, in the intervals of wrecking what is left of the house, out of which my friend and I have long since escaped by climbing up the neighbouring gutter-pipes and scrambling over the adjoining roofs."

Monsieur, will you believe me when I say that he was actually saying all this in order to comfort me? I could have sworn to that because of the wonderful kindliness which shone out of his eyes, even through the good-humoured mockery wherewith he obviously regarded me. Do you know what I did then, monsieur? I just fell on my knees and loudly thanked God that he was safe; at which both he and his friend once again began to laugh, for all the world like two schoolboys who had escaped a whipping rather than two men who were still threatened with death.

"Then it *was* you!" said the taller stranger, who was still laughing so heartily that he had to wipe his eyes with his exquisite lace handkerchief.

"May God forgive me," I replied.

The next moment his arm was again round me. I clung to him as to a rock, for of a truth I had never felt a grasp so steady and withal so gentle and kindly, as was his around my shoulders. I tried to murmur words of thanks, but again that wretched feeling of sickness and faintness overcame me, and for a second or two it seemed to me as if I were slipping into another world. The stranger's voice came to my ear, as it were through cotton-wool.

"The man is starving," he said. "Shall we take him over to your lodgings, Tony? They are safer than mine. He may be able to walk in a minute or two, if not I can carry him."

My senses at this partly returned to me, and I was able to protest feebly:

"No, no! I must go back—I must—kind sirs," I murmured. "Mme. la Marquise will be getting so anxious."

No sooner were these foolish words out of my mouth than I could have bitten my tongue out for having uttered them; and yet, somehow, it seemed as if it was the stranger's magnetic personality, his magic voice and kindly act towards me, who had so basely sold him to his enemies, which had drawn them out of me. He gave a low, prolonged whistle.

"Mme. la Marquise?" he queried, dropping his voice to a whisper.

Now to have uttered Mme. la Marquise de Mortaine's name here in Lyons, where every aristocrat was termed a traitor and sent without trial to the guillotine, was in itself an act of criminal folly, and yet—you may believe me, monsieur, or not—there was something within me just at that moment that literally compelled me to open my heart out to this stranger, whom I had so basely betrayed, and who requited my abominable crime with such gentleness and mercy. Before I fully realised what I was doing, monsieur, I had blurted out the whole history of Mme. la Marquise's flight and of M. le Vicomte's sickness to him. He drew me under the cover of an open doorway, and he and his friend listened to me without speaking a word until I had told them my pitiable tale to the end.

When I had finished he said quietly:

"Take me to see Mme. la Marquise, old friend. Who knows? perhaps I may be able to help."

Then he turned to his friend.

"Will you wait for me at my lodgings, Tony," he said, "and let Ffoulkes and Hastings know that I may wish to speak with them on my return?"

He spoke like one who had been accustomed all his life to give command, and I marvelled how his friend immediately obeyed him. Then when the latter had disappeared down the dark street, the stranger once more turned to me.

"Lean on my arm, good old friend," he said, "and we must try and walk as quickly as we can. The sooner we allay the anxieties of Mme. la Marquise the better."

I was still hugging the roast capon with one arm, with the other I clung to him as together we walked in the direction of the Rue des Pipots. On the way we halted at a respectable eating-house, where my protector gave me some money wherewith to buy a bottle of good wine and sundry provisions and delicacies which we carried home with us.

II

Never shall I forget the look of horror which came in Mme. la Marquise's eyes when she saw me entering our miserable attic in the company of a stranger. The last of the little bit of tallow candle flickered in its socket. Madame threw her emaciated arms over her child, just like some poor hunted animal defending its young. I could almost hear the cry of terror which died down in her throat ere it reached her lips. But then, monsieur, to see the light of hope gradually illuminating her pale, wan face as the stranger took her hand and spoke to her—oh! so gently and so kindly—was a sight which filled my poor half-broken heart with joy.

"The little invalid must be seen by a doctor at once," he said, "after that only can we think of your ultimate safety."

Mme. la Marquise, who herself was terribly weak and ill, burst out crying. "Would I not have taken him to a doctor ere now?" she murmured through her tears. "But there is no doctor in Lyons. Those who have not been arrested as traitors have fled from this stricken city. And my little José is dying for want of medical care."

"Your pardon, madame," he rejoined gently, "one of the ablest doctors in France is at present in Lyons—"

"That infamous Laporte," she broke in, horrified. "He would snatch my sick child from my arms and throw him to the guillotine."

"He would save your boy from disease," said the stranger earnestly, "his own professional pride or professional honour, whatever he might choose to call it, would compel him to do that. But the moment the doctor's work was done that of the executioner would commence."

"You see, milor," moaned Madame in pitiable agony, "that there is no hope for us."

"Indeed there is," he replied. "We must get M. le Vicomte well first—after that we shall see."

"But you are not proposing to bring that infamous Laporte to my child's bedside!" she cried in horror.

"Would you have your child die here before your eyes," retorted the stranger, "as he undoubtedly will this night?"

This sounded horribly cruel, and the tone in which it was said was commanding. There was no denying its truth. M. le Vicomte was dying. I could see that. For a moment or two madame remained quite still, with her great eyes, circled with pain and sorrow, fixed upon the stranger. He returned her gaze steadily and kindly, and gradually that frozen look of horror in her pale face gave place to one of deep puzzlement, and through her bloodless lips there came the words, faintly murmured: "Who are you?"

He gave no direct reply, but from his little finger he detached a ring and held it out for her to see. I saw it too, for I was standing close by Mme. la Marquise, and the flickering light of the tallow candle fell full upon the ring. It was of gold, and upon it there was an exquisitely modelled, five-petalled little flower in vivid red enamel.

Madame la Marquise looked at the ring, then once again up into his face. He nodded assent, and my heart seemed even to stop its beating as I gazed upon his face. Had we not—all of us—heard of the gallant Scarlet Pimpernel? And did I not know—far better than Mme. la Marquise herself—the full extent of his gallantry and his self-sacrifice? The hue and cry was after him. Human bloodhounds were even now on his track, and he spoke calmly of walking out again in the streets of Lyons and of affronting that infamous Laporte, who would find glory in sending him to death. I think he guessed what was passing in my mind, for he put a finger up to his lip and pointed significantly to M. le Vicomte.

But it was beautiful to see how completely Mme. la Marquise now trusted him. At his bidding she even ate a little of the food and drank some wine—and I was forced to do likewise. And even when anon he declared his intention of fetching Laporte immediately, she did not flinch. She kissed M. le Vicomte with passionate fervour, and then gave the stranger her solemn promise that the moment he returned she would take refuge in the next room and never move out of it until Laporte had departed.

When he went I followed him to the top of the stairs. I was speechless with gratitude and also with fears for him. But he took my hand and said, with that same quaint, somewhat inane laugh which was so characteristic of him:

"Be of good cheer, old fellow! Those confounded murderers will not get me this time."

III

Less than half an hour later, monsieur, citizen Laporte, one of the most skillful doctors in France and one of the most bloodthirsty tyrants this execrable Revolution has known, was sitting at the bedside of M. le Vicomte de Mortaine, using all the skill, all the knowledge he possessed in order to combat the dread disease of which the child was dying, ere he came to save him—as he cynically remarked in my hearing—for the guillotine.

I heard afterwards how it all came about.

Laporte, it seems was in the habit of seeing patients in his own house every evening after he had settled all his business for the day. What a strange contradiction in the human heart, eh, monsieur? The tiger turned lamb for the space of one hour in every twenty-four—the butcher turned healer. How well the English milor had gauged the strange personality of that redoubtable man! Professional pride— interest in intricate cases—call it what you will—was the only redeeming feature in Laporte's abominable character. Everything else in him, every thought, every action was ignoble, cruel and vengeful.

Milor that night mingled with the crowd who waited on the human hyena to be cured of their hurts. It was a motley crowd that filled the dreaded pro-consul's ante-chamber—men, women and children—all of them too much preoccupied with their own troubles to bestow more than a cursory glance on the stranger who, wrapped in a dark mantle quietly awaited his turn. One or two muttered curses were flung at the aristo, one or two spat in his direction to express hatred and contempt, then the door which gave on the inner chamber would be flung open—a number called—one patient would walk out, another walk in—and in the ever-recurring incident the stranger for the nonce was forgotten.

His turn came—his number being called—it was the last on the list, and the ante-chamber was now quite empty save for him. He walked into the presence of the pro-consul. Claude Lemoine, who was on guard in the room at the time, told me that just for the space of two seconds the two men looked at one another. Then the stranger threw back his head and said quietly:

"There's a child dying of pleurisy, or worse, in an attic in the Rue des Pipots. There's not a doctor left in Lyons to attend on him, and the child will die for want of medical skill. Will you come to him, citizen doctor?"

It seems that for a moment or two Laporte hesitated.

"You look to me uncommonly like an aristo, and therefore a traitor," he said, "and I've half a mind—"

"To call your guard and order my immediate arrest," broke in milor with a whimsical smile, "but in that case a citizen of France will die for want of a doctor's care. Let me take you to the child's bedside, citizen doctor, you can always have me arrested afterwards."

But Laporte still hesitated

"How do I know that you are not one of those English spies?" he began.

"Take it that I am," rejoined milor imperturbably, "and come and see the patient."

Never had a situation been carried off with so bold a hand. Claude Lemoine declared that Laporte's mouth literally opened for the call which would have summoned the sergeant of the guard into the room and ordered the summary arrest of this impudent stranger. During the veriest fraction of a second life and death hung in the balance for the gallant English milor. In the heart of Laporte every evil passion fought the one noble fibre within him. But the instinct of the skilful healer won the battle, and the next moment he had hastily collected what medicaments and appliances he might require, and the two men were soon speeding along the streets in the direction of the Rue des Pipots.

During the whole of that night milor and Laporte sat together by the bedside of M. le Vicomte. Laporte only went out once in order to fetch what further medicaments he required. Mme. la Marquise took the opportunity of running out of her hiding-place in order to catch a glimpse of her child. I saw her take milor's hand and press it against her heart in silent gratitude. On her knees she begged him to go away and leave her and the boy to their fate. Was it likely that he would go? But she was so insistent that at last he said:

"Madame, let me assure you that even if I were prepared to play the coward's part which you would assign to me, it is not in my power to do so at this moment. Citizen Laporte came to this house under the escort of six picked men of his guard. He has left these men stationed on the landing outside this door."

Madame la Marquise gave a cry of terror, and once more that pathetic look of horror came into her face. Milor took her hand and then pointed to the sick child.

"Madame," he said, "M. le Vicomte is already slightly better. Thanks to medical skill and a child's vigorous hold on life, he will live. The rest is in the hands of God."

Already the heavy footsteps of Laporte were heard upon the creaking stairs. Mme. la Marquise was forced to return to her hiding-place.

Soon after dawn he went. M. le Vicomte was then visibly easier. Laporte had all along paid no heed to me, but I noticed that once or twice during his long vigil by the sick-bed his dark eyes beneath their overhanging brows shot a quick suspicious look at the door behind which cowered Mme. la Marquise. I had absolutely no doubt in my mind then that he knew quite well who his patient was.

He gave certain directions to milor—there were certain fresh medicaments to be got during the day. While he spoke there was a sinister glint in his eyes—half cynical, wholly menacing—as he looked up into the calm, impassive face of milor.

"It is essential for the welfare of the patient that these medicaments be got for him during the day," he said dryly, "and the guard have orders to allow you to pass in and out. But you need have no fear," he added significantly, "I will leave an escort outside the house to accompany you on your way."

He gave a mocking, cruel laugh, the meaning of which was unmistakable. His well-drilled human bloodhounds would be on the track of the English spy, whenever the latter dared to venture out into the streets.

Mme. la Marquise and I were prisoners for the day. We spent it in watching alternately beside M. le Vicomte. But milor came and went as freely as if he had not been carrying his precious life in his hands every time that he ventured outside the house.

In the evening Laporte returned to see his patient, and again the following morning, and the next evening. M. le Vicomte was making rapid progress towards recovery.

The third day in the morning Laporte pronounced his patient to be out of danger, but said that he would nevertheless come again to see him at the usual hour in the evening.

Directly he had gone, milor went out in order to bring in certain delicacies of which the invalid was now allowed to partake. I persuaded Madame to lie down and have a couple of hours' good sleep in the inner attic while I stayed to watch over the child.

To my horror, hardly had I taken up my stand at the foot of the bed when Laporte returned; he muttered something as he entered about having left some important appliance behind, but I was quite convinced that he had been on the watch until milor was out of sight, and then slipped back in order to find me and Madame here alone.

He gave a glance at the child and another at the door of the inner attic, then he said in a loud voice:

"Yes, another twenty-four hours and my duties as doctor will cease and those of patriot will recommence. But Mme. la Marquise de Mortaine need no longer be in any anxiety about her son's health, nor will Mme. la Guillotine be cheated of a pack of rebels."

He laughed, and was on the point of turning on his heel when the door which gave on the smaller attic was opened and Mme. la Marquise appeared upon the threshold.

Monsieur, I had never seen her look more beautiful than she did now in her overwhelming grief. Her face was as pale as death, her eyes, large and dilated, were fixed upon the human monster who had found it in his heart to speak such cruel words. Clad in a miserable, threadbare gown, her rich brown hair brought to the top of her head like a crown, she looked more regal than any queen.

But proud as she was, monsieur, she yet knelt at the feet of that wretch. Yes, knelt, and embraced his knees and pleaded in such pitiable accents as would have melted the heart of a stone. She pleaded, monsieur—ah, not for herself. She pleaded for her child and for me, her faithful servant, and she pleaded for the gallant gentleman who had risked his life for the sake of the child, who was nothing to him.

"Take me!" she said. "I come of a race that have always known how to die! But what harm has that innocent child done in this world? What harm has poor old Jean-Pierre done, and, oh . . . is the world so full of brave and noble men that the bravest of them all be so unjustly sent to death?"

Ah, monsieur, any man, save one of those abject products of that hideous Revolution, would have listened to such heartrending accents. But this man only laughed and turned on his heel without a word.

Shall I ever forget the day that went by? Mme. la Marquise was well-nigh prostrate with terror, and it was heartrending to watch the noble efforts which she made to amuse M. le Vicomte. The only gleams of sunshine which came to us out of our darkness were the brief appearances of milor. Outside we could hear the measured tramp of the guard that had been set there to keep us close prisoners. They were relieved every six hours, and, in fact, we were as much under arrest as if we were already incarcerated in one of the prisons of Lyons.

At about four o'clock in the afternoon milor came back to us after a brief absence. He stayed for a little while playing with M. le Vicomte. Just before leaving he took Madame's hand in his and said very earnestly, and sinking his voice to the merest whisper:

"To-night! Fear nothing! Be ready for anything! Remember that the League of the Scarlet Pimpernel have never failed to succour, and that I hereby pledge you mine honour that you and those you care for will be out of Lyons this night."

He was gone, leaving us to marvel at his strange words. Mme. la Marquise after that was just like a person in a dream. She hardly spoke to me, and the only sound that passed her lips was a quaint little lullaby which she sang to M. le Vicomte ere he dropped off to sleep.

The hours went by leaden-footed. At every sound on the stairs Madame started like a frightened bird. That infamous Laporte usually paid his visits at about eight o'clock in the evening, and after it became quite dark, Madame sat at the tiny window, and I felt that she was counting the minutes which still lay between her and the dreaded presence of that awful man.

At a quarter before eight o'clock we heard the usual heavy footfall on the stairs. Madame started up as if she had been struck. She ran to the bed—almost like one demented, and wrapping the one poor blanket round M. le Vicomte, she seized him in her arms. Outside we could hear Laporte's raucous voice speaking to the guard. His usual query: "Is all well?" was answered by the brief: "All well, citizen." Then he asked if the English spy were within, and the sentinel replied: "No, citizen, he went out at about five o'clock and has not come back since."

"Not come back since five o'clock?" said Laporte with a loud curse. "*Pardi!* I trust that that fool Caudy has not allowed him to escape."

"I saw Caudy about an hour ago, citizen," said the man.

"Did he say anything about the Englishman then?"

It seemed to us, who were listening to this conversation with bated breath, that the man hesitated a moment ere he replied; then he spoke with obvious nervousness.

"As a matter of fact, citizen," he said, "Caudy thought then that the Englishman was inside the house, whilst I was equally sure that I had seen him go downstairs an hour before."

"A thousand devils!" cried Laporte with a savage oath, "if I find that you, citizen sergeant, or Caudy have blundered there will be trouble for you."

To the accompaniment of a great deal more swearing he suddenly kicked open the door of our attic with his boot, and then came to a standstill on the threshold with his hands in the pockets of his breeches and his legs planted wide apart, face to face with Mme. la Marquise, who confronted him now, herself like a veritable tigress who is defending her young.

He gave a loud, mocking laugh.

"Ah, the aristos!" he cried, "waiting for that cursed Englishman, what? to drag you and your brat out of the claws of the human tiger. . . . Not so, my fine *ci-devant* Marquise. The brat is no longer sick—he is well enough, anyhow, to breathe the air of the prisons of Lyons for a few days pending a final rest in the arms of Mme. la Guillotine. Citizen sergeant," he called over his shoulder, "escort these aristos to my carriage downstairs. When the Englishman returns, tell him he will find his friends under the tender care of Doctor Laporte. *En avant*, little mother," he added, as he gripped Mme. la Marquise tightly by the arm, "and you, old scarecrow," he concluded, speaking to me over his shoulder, "follow the citizen sergeant, or—"

Mme. la Marquise made no resistance. As I told you, she had been, since dusk, like a person in a dream; so what could I do but follow her noble example? Indeed, I was too dazed to do otherwise.

We all went stumbling down the dark, rickety staircase, Laporte leading the way with Mme. la Marquise, who had M. le Vicomte tightly clasped in her arms. I followed with the sergeant, whose hand was on my shoulder; I believe that two soldiers walked behind, but of that I cannot be sure.

At the bottom of the stairs through the open door of the house I caught sight of the vague outline of a large barouche, the lanthorns of which threw a feeble light upon the cruppers of two horses and of a couple of men sitting on the box.

Mme. la Marquise stepped quietly into the carriage. Laporte followed her, and I was bundled in in his wake by the rough hands of the soldiery. Just before the order was given to start, Laporte put his head out of the window and shouted to the sergeant:

"When you see Caudy tell him to report himself to me at once. I will be back here in half an hour; keep strict guard as before until then, citizen sergeant."

The next moment the coachman cracked his whip, Laporte called loudly, "*En avant!*" and the heavy barouche went rattling along the ill-paved streets.

Inside the carriage all was silence. I could hear Mme. la Marquise softly whispering to M. le Vicomte, and I marvelled how wondrously calm—nay, cheerful, she could be. Then suddenly I heard a sound which of a truth did make my heart stop its beating. It was a quaint and prolonged laugh which I once thought I would never hear again on this earth. It came from the corner of the barouche next to where Mme. la Marquise was so tenderly and gaily crooning to her child. And a kindly voice said merrily:

"In half an hour we shall be outside Lyons. To-morrow we'll be across the Swiss frontier. We've cheated that old tiger after all. What say you, Mme. la Marquise?"

It was milor's voice, and he was as merry as a schoolboy.

"I told you, old Jean-Pierre," he added, as he placed that firm hand which I loved so well upon my knee, "I told you that those confounded murderers would not get me this time."

And to think that I did not know him, as he stood less than a quarter of an hour ago upon the threshold of our attic in the hideous guise of that abominable Laporte. He had spent two days in collecting old clothes that resembled those of that infamous wretch, and in taking possession of one of the derelict rooms in the house in the Rue des Pipots. Then while we were expecting every moment that Laporte would order our arrest, milor assumed the personality of the monster, hoodwinked the sergeant on the dark staircase, and by that wonderfully audacious coup saved Mme. la Marquise, M. le Vicomte and my humble self from the guillotine.

Money, of which he had plenty, secured us immunity on the way, and we were in safety over the Swiss frontier, leaving Laporte to eat out his tigerish heart with baffled rage.

THE ADVENTURES OF A NIGHT

JOHN BLOUNDELLE-BURTON

I. AN OLD ACQUAINTANCE

I, Adrian Trent, now known as Lord Trent, and a captain of *Les Mousquetaires Gris*, sat in my little salon in the Lion d'Or, in the Rue Louis le Grand in Paris, on Midsummer Day, in the year of our Lord 1726. And in my hand I held a little perfumed billet, which I had turned over in my fingers a dozen times, and had, perhaps, read twice as often. For it recalled to me a strange meeting, and some strange scenes in which I had been concerned when I was but a *porte-drapeau*. Also it recalled to me some other things far sweeter, which, to a young man, must needs be pleasant recollections—to wit, things such as a lovely face flushed now and again with the colour that adorns the blushing rose of Provence; dark eyes, sometimes as soft as velvet, and sometimes sparkling like ice beneath the winter sun; black hair that once— in an awful moment of fear and extremity—I had seen adown the owner's back, almost to her feet; a supple girlish form, and other charms. A girl whom, although I had not seen her for five years, I had never forgotten, but whom I always strove to forget, because she was wealthy and I was poor; because, although I was a man of good rank in my own country, she was almost of the very highest in hers; because she was, in truth, as far above me as the sun is above the earth. Yet once, for a little while, that girl and I had been the best of friends; once, too, it seemed as if that friendship had been very near to a softer and more tender emotion, and as if Adrian Trent and Ana, Princesa de Carbajal, were falling in love with each other—if they had not already done so.

Whereupon, thinking over all these things, I again turned the letter in my hands, and again I read it.

So you are back in Paris, I hear, (it ran); and would you not like to see a girl called Damaris whom once you knew? I think you would—perhaps in memory of having saved that girl's life on one occasion; of also having once called her by the prettiest epithet a man can bestow on any woman, and of having been much teased and pestered by that girl. If so, then come

to the Marais, to the Rue des Vraies Femmes, and to the house which bears
the name of my family, and if you come at the proper time I will give you
some chocolate and a bonbon. I wonder if you are much changed, and if
you will find me so!

Damaris.

The prettiest epithet a man can bestow on any woman! So she remembered it!
remembered that I had called her "sweetheart" in all the impudence of boyhood and
the possession of my guidon in the *mousquetaires*, and when I did not know that she
was a princess of one of the most ancient and powerful families in Catalonia, and in
possession of enormous estates and great wealth.

But did she remember another thing also—namely, that after being highly indignant
with me for my presumption, she had laughed and whispered that pretty word to me in
return? Did she remember that? If not, I did. And now I would see for it.

An hour later I was outside the great door of the Hôtel de Carbajal, and a lackey
answering my summons, I learned that the Princess was within. Whereon I bade him
say that Lord Trent waited below to pay his devoirs to her, if it might be that she would
receive him.

"Her Highness expects milor," the man said. "Will milor give himself the trouble
to follow me?"

Whereon "milor," attired in his best black satin suit—for, alas! he had but recently
returned from England, and the funeral of his father—and silver lace, did follow the
man through the great gloomy house, and along corridor after corridor, he thinking
all the time of what the fellow had said—that "her Highness expected him." "So,"
"milor" said to himself, "she knew I would come."

Then the door opened, and the footman announced "Milor Trent," and for some
reason the midsummer sun seemed to dazzle my eyes, and I saw a figure spring—
that is the word, "spring"—from a deep fauteuil, and I felt two slim hands in mine,
and I heard a well-remembered voice say, "So you have come, my lord."

"Yes, I have come, your Highness. You knew very well that I should come. Yet,
yet," for, somehow, I at once began to grow bold, "there was no word of 'Highness'
nor of 'lord' in the old days. Then you were 'a girl called Damaris,' and—"

"And," she interrupted, with a soft laugh, "you were an impudent young soldier
called Blue Eyes. But now we are old, staid people. I am twenty-four."

"And I am twenty-five," I interrupted in my turn.

"Wherefore we have grown sober and steady. Still, notwithstanding that, you may tell me if you choose whether you think I have aged very much."

Aged very much! Yes, she had aged, if being more beautiful than ever meant having aged. For now the sun dazzled me no longer, and I could see all her loveliness, I could observe that the tall, slim form had grown a little, just a little, more womanly; that the soft dark eyes had just a little more of calmness in their gaze; that the scarlet lips were as full, and the small white teeth, which I had always admired so much, as brilliant.

"But all the same," she said, while I surveyed her, "you need not hold my hand so long. One does not look at another with their fingers."

Then, when I had released that hand, which, I protest, I did not know I was holding, she bade me sit down by her side, she herself taking a seat upon a great Segovian ottoman close by, and drawing up to her a little ebony table upon which was a little gilt coach, with the doors and windows of glass, and with four little silver horses to it, and a coachman and footman in gold. And she opened one of the doors of this little coach and popped her long slim fingers in and drew out a bonbon, and, I thought, was going to pop it in my mouth too. But, if that had been her intention, she considered better of it, perhaps because she was now "sober and steady," and so, instead, laid it gravely down on the ebony table, and pointed to it, and said, "Eat it"; which I did.

"Now," she said, "we will drink something, *à la bonne chance*. I drink chocolate; but since you are a great big *mousquetaire* you may have some wine if you choose. Let me see; there is Florence wine, and Lunel and Muscadine, and—"

"I shall drink the chocolate or nothing," I said firmly, since I was not going to sit toping like a rude *mousquetaire* before my Princess while she drank the other. Whereon she told me to ring the bell and order the chocolate, and in ten minutes we were discussing that beverage, and the footman had left us alone.

"Oh!" she exclaimed volatilely, "do you remember, Blue Eyes—I mean, my lord—when I sat on the table in the inn at Toulouse and drank wine out of your cup, surrounded by you and your huge troopers, and when I was supposed to be a wandering vagrant girl called Damaris?"

"You will always be Damaris to me. *I* shan't call you 'Princess' nor 'Highness,' and I wish you would not call me by that silly title of 'lord.' And I've only been one a month, and have not grown used to it."

"But what am I to call you? I mustn't call you Blue Eyes any more, because we are now grave and staid; and Adrian is too familiar. I should poniard you if you were to call me Ana."

"There was another name exchanged between us once," I said—"one alluded to in your letter received by me to-day."

"Ah!" she said, with a little shriek, "don't recall that. How dare you! I only wrote it to bring myself back to your memory."

"Oh!" I said, "did you? Well, now, what did your high—I mean you, Damaris—send for me for at all, if it was only to be so haughty and distant? There are no more burning houses to save you from; and as for—for—old Alberoni—"

"Monseigneur the Cardinal Alberoni, if you please."

"As for Monseigneur the Cardinal Alberoni—well! what has become of him? He has finished his sch—politics—I suppose?"

"He lives the life of a saint at Piacenza. But—but I did not send for you to talk about his Eminence."

"What then, Da—I mean—well!—you understand?"

"You remember," she said, "that you did save my life once? Of course you do; you have but just referred to it."

"Is it in danger now? And am I to save it again?"

"My happiness is. I want you to save me from a man—a man who, though perhaps it may surprise you, wants to marry me."

"Ah! bah!" I said, forgetting my manners and jumping out of my chair, and beginning to walk about the room. "Bah! A man wants to marry you, indeed!" and I felt quite angry at the very idea of such a thing.

"It is strange that he should desire to do so, is it not?" she said, with a queer little, but very pretty, grimace. "All the same, it's the truth. It is indeed, Blue—I mean, my lord."

"Who is the fellow?"

"Oh!" she said, with another of her little shrieks. "The fellow! Why—er—Lord Trent—he is one of the scions of our royal house—of Austria and Spain."

"Shall I run him through? I will if he wants to marry you—and—and—you bid me do so."

"You might have to run more than one through, at that rate, Blue Eyes," and this time she forgot to correct herself, which, if I remember rightly, seemed to please me; "I think you might, indeed. But, no! I imagine you can do better than that."

"How? I'll do it."

"Will you, my lord?" ("Vengeance confound that title!" thought I.) "I wonder if you will?"

"What shall I do? Tell me and it shall be done, Damaris," forgetting myself also in my agitation.

"I suppose," she said, speaking slowly, and with a wondrous look in those witching eyes, "you would not condescend to play at being my lover, would you?—only for a little while—say for a week or so."

"Wouldn't I! Try me! But—but—am I to have all the privileges of a lover during that week or so? Eh, Damaris?"

"Don't call me Damaris; it is not respectful. Yes, you may have all the privileges of a lover—in public."

"Oh! in *public*. But—in private! Then—"

"Then I am the Princesa de Carbajal and you are Lord Trent."

"What are a lover's privileges in public—I mean with princesses and scions of ancient houses? He has to be a kind of slave, a worshipper, does he not?"

"He does as a rule; but then, you see, Blu—my lord," and while she spoke she held a bonbon out tantalisingly before my eyes, "you have got to play a different part from the ordinary one of a lover to a princess. You will play it, won't you—Adrian?"

"I'll play anything," I said, much agitated by the last word she uttered.

"*Bueno!* Well, now, see. You must be a humble lover—one beneath me, with whom I have fallen in love in a manner discreditable to my rank. And, thereby, you will make my suitor jealous—oh! so jealous—because we will play such tricks upon him that he will renounce me. Oh! I have invented such schemes to make him do so. Neither Quevedo nor Vega ever thought of such tricks."

"It will be a dangerous game," I said meditatively.

"Dangerous! Dangerous!" she exclaimed. "Why, Blue Eyes, you are not afraid of a Spanish don although he is of the royal house, are you? Fie! and you a soldier."

"That isn't the danger I meant," I replied quietly, so quietly that she guessed my meaning in a moment, as I saw by the rich crimson which mantled her cheek instantly, and the increased brilliancy of her lovely, starlike eyes.

"Dangerous to whom, pray?" she demanded.

"To me!" I answered boldly; "because I shall lo—"

"Hsh! hsh! hsh!" she said, putting her hand up quickly. "None of that! none of that! Yet, nevertheless, there will be danger—to—"

"Whom?" I asked now.

"To you, of course. Oh! not to me, Blue Eyes. Oh no! no!" she continued somewhat nervously, I thought. "Not to me. Oh no. Think not that, my lord."

"I can think what I like," I said. "Even a *slave's* thoughts are his own. But where's the danger, if you mean ordinary danger?"

"He is great," she almost whispered now, "and powerful, even in Paris. He is, too, enormously rich, richer than I am, and can hire people to do whatsoever he wishes. He *might* hire vagabonds to assault you—to—to—oh! Adrian!—throw you into the Seine with your throat cut, or stab you under the shoulder in a dark alley, and—and— all because you do this out of friendship for me, and with no hope of reward."

"I shall get my reward," I said quietly.

For a moment she regarded me calmly; then she said, "You are very confident, very masterful."

"Yes," I replied, "very confident, and—well! very masterful."

II. DANGER AHEAD

In looking back upon the events of those days—as I now do from the calm autumn of my life—I am always struck by the extraordinary fact that I am still alive. For, from the moment that it began to be whispered about in the fashionable parts of Paris that the Princesa Ana de Carbajal was tricking his Highness the Prince of Csaba (in Hungary) and Miranda Vitoria (in Spain), who, although of the Royal House of Austria, intended to espouse her morganatically if he possibly could, my life began to be in danger. That is to say, it would begin to be in danger directly the Prince of Csaba learned, as he very soon must learn, that the Princess was being gallanted about by an Englishman, who was considered to be so far her inferior as to cause it to be said that she had contracted a love affair with a person beneath her.

For these haughty, arrogant Spanish-Austrians living in Paris had the impertinence to state that I, Adrian Trent, an English gentleman (to say nothing of my being also an English nobleman and an officer of French *mousquetaires*), was beneath the Princess, or—or Damaris, as I always thought of her. It made my blood boil, I can tell you, when I learned such was the case (and I hope it makes yours boil, too, who read, if you are a countryman of mine), and if there had ever been on my part any idea of drawing back from the part I had agreed to play with Damaris—which, in solemn truth, there was not—it only confirmed me all the more in the determination to play that part out to the very end.

I would, I swore to myself, so enact the part of the girl's lover that Csaba should have nothing left to do but to retire from his position of *prétendu* and *aspirant* and resign all claims to her hand; and also, which I hoped would be the case, I would so irritate his absurd hidalgo pride as to draw him into an embroglio with me; and then—even though he were forty times the hidalgo and don he was, and had forty times the blood of *Charles qui triche* and of that murderer, Philip II. in his veins—I would so humiliate him and all his following that they would never dare to be insolent to any English gentleman again.

Only—I forgot one thing. Or, perhaps, I did not know one thing which I should have known. I should not have forgotten that no descendant of Philip, nor any one who was related to him, was likely to meet me in a fair and open way. Not they! Be sure of that. And it was from this lack of knowledge, or this forgetfulness, that I nearly got caught in a trap, that I was nearly done barbarously to death, and that I nearly lost the great happiness of my life. However, this you shall read.

But Damaris knew, and, knowing, she did not mean to have me fall into the trap. And all this you are to read as well.

"Now, my lord," she said to me one fine night, when I had waited on her, "this is the very occasion when we are to begin to arouse the demon of jealousy in Csaba's manly bosom. To-night we are going to sow the poison seed. Therefore prepare yourself."

"I am prepared. What is to be done?"

"I am going to the ball at the Hôtel d'Aragon, his house. But you are not—yet you will be there. See, here is his invitation to Monsieur—blank. That blank is left because I forced him to give me an invitation for a friend of mine, whose name I would fill up. Observe, *mon ami*, I fill it up with yours." Whereon, stooping over a scrutoire, she wrote in the name of Lord Trent.

"It will be pleasant to go to the ball," I said. "I presume I shall have one dance with you?"

"You will not go to the ball, and you will not dance with me."

"What am I to do then? Go to bed, perhaps!"

"Nor that either. In a manner of speaking, indeed, you will go to the ball, but only to pass through the great apartments, making your obeisance to Csaba as you do so; then—well, then—you will go out into the garden and wait until I come to you. Wait by a fountain in the middle of the garden—within it, in the centre, a representation of Hercules destroying the Hydra. Wait, and do exactly what I tell you."

"Shall you be alone?"

"Nay, nay," she replied, with one of her usual smiles. "Ah no, he will be with me. But of that take no notice. Do exactly what I tell you—when we meet—and when he *overhears* what I say."

"When he overhears!"

"'Tis so. Now, for last instructions, take these. Come not to the Hôtel d'Aragon till midnight strikes. I shall be there earlier, but come not yourself till then."

"And—?"

"Take your cue from me."

At midnight I *was* there, outside the great doors of the Hôtel d'Aragon, descending from my *chaise-roulante* and seeing a few late arrivals like myself pass in, as well as perceiving through those wide open doors a mighty great assembly within. Whereon I, too, went in, the Prince's menials bawling out my name, though, as not one of them pronounced it aright, simple though it was, they might as well not have done so at all.

Through a vast crowd of ladies and of gentlemen in wigs and scarlet coats, with, for the former, flowered dresses and hoops and panniers and Heaven knows what, I passed, looking right and left for where the Prince might be. Then, suddenly, on a little daïs I saw him seated with, for companion by his side, Damaris, or rather Ana, Princess of Carbajal; and he was bending over her, talking with what our beloved friends call *empressement*, and it seemed to me as though he were utterly oblivious of every other person there.

But, since I stood at the foot of the daïs waiting to attract his attention and then pay my respects to him, I observed that she—my confederate—or rather she whose confederate I was—gave a slight start, and into her face there came a lovely, heavenly tinge of red, while from between her parted lips I heard the whispered word "Adrian." Also I saw her left hand, which lay along her dress, clutch a fold or so of that dress as though in agitation extreme.

And the Prince heard the word too, since, after a momentary glance at her, he cast his eyes in my direction and then again bent them on the girl.

"Monseigneur," she said, "it is the gentleman for whom I demanded an invitation."

"Ha!" he said, rising and bowing somewhat stiffly to me I thought. "Ha! a gentleman named Adrian."

"Nay," she replied; "a gentleman, an English nobleman, called Lord Trent."

"I ask a thousand pardons," he said, bending low before her. "I thought you uttered the name Adrian." Then he turned to me, saying coldly, "My lord, you are welcome," after which he turned away and began talking to his companion again, whereon I sought the garden as she had bid me do.

"Was she acting?" I asked myself, as I passed through the windows to the gardens beyond, to find and take up my station by the fountain in which was the statue of

Hercules killing the Hydra; "was she acting when she whispered my name and when she made that slight but perceptible clutch at her dress?" As for the tinge of red, I doubted if she could act that, since, so far as I knew, it was not to be accomplished—no! not even by La Gautier, whom I had seen often enough in the past at the Odéon. Still, I remembered she was a good actress—had she not impersonated a wandering singing-girl from Provence when I first knew her; and had she not deceived even so astute a beast as Marcieu, the spy who tried to arrest her! So I could not answer the question, but went on down the *allées*, and past stone fauns and satyrs, and gentlemen in togas and ladies in—well! not in gowns made by court furnishers—and, at last, in the centre of a great *rond*, covered with crushed shells and tiny pebbles that hurt the feet, I came upon the fountain and the figure of Hercules. Then, being there, I sat me down on the high stone rim of the basin, into which the water was falling from the hydra heads with a vastly cool and pleasing splash, and waited, beneath the moon, which sailed clear and cloudless in the skies, for the dénouement. That, however, was a little while in coming, and though more than one couple passed me, the vizard-masked face of the cavalier being almost invariably bent down over the upturned vizard-masked face of the accompanying dame (so that one might well guess it was the eternal romance being whispered in willing ears), she for whom I waited did not herself appear.

Not for a little while, as I have said—yet, at last.

Down one of the little pleached alleys I heard the rustle of a woman's robe, and saw the long, lithe figure that I knew so well—that I had never forgotten since I first saw it in the spangled dress of the mountebank she pretended to be. I saw, too, the moonbeams glint upon the lovely face, and recognised it instantly, though she, too, wore her vizard-mask. Then she was close to me, close to where I had stepped out on to the shell-strewn path, and calling "Adrian"—somewhat loudly, as I thought—while she drew near.

"I am here," I said, joining her.

Then, speaking in a lower tone now, she said, "He is close behind—behind a bosquet in the alley. He is watching us, I know. Kiss my hand—do something lover-like—call me by some lover's name of endearment. And speak in French; he knows no English."

"Kiss my hand—do something lover-like."

"*A la fin! ma mie*," I said, falling in with her cue at once, and going on in the tongue she bade me speak. "I thought you would never come"; after which, remembering her injunction, I stooped and kissed her hand, holding it to my lips for some seconds, while all the time the great jewels on her fingers sparkled in the moonlight.

"Farewell," she said, "I may not stay. To-night—to-night," and now she spoke loudly again, clearly, so that none within fifty paces of us could fail to hear her words— "to-night at two o'clock come to supper with me at my house. I await you. Till then, adieu. And come to the side-door, that opening on to the Rue des Fleurs. Till then, adieu."

"Do you mean it?" I whispered now, wondering if this was play-acting too. "Do you mean it, Damaris?"

"Ay, I mean it. We must play the comedy out. But," and now she spoke in English, and her voice sunk to its deepest whisper, "forget not your rapier. You may need it."

"I shall not forget." Then, while again she had given me her hand, which, at this moment, she was making great pretence of withdrawing from my grasp, I whispered, also in English, "But this has got to be paid for, Damaris; and the reward I shall demand will be enormous."

But she only laughed, showing her little white teeth, and went swiftly back up the alley she had come down, turning once and saying in a fairly clear voice, "Remember."

Whereon, when she had gone and joined her companion, as I could tell very well by overhearing them talking as they withdrew, I sat me down on the stone edge of the fountain and fell a-musing.

"Bring my rapier, she said," I muttered to myself. "Ay, and so I will. But not this plaything by my side, fit only to match a court suit. Instead, my good Flamberg. 'Ware that, my illustrious rival, if you come near me! Ay, I will in truth bring it. And so— so—so—I shall win her. For though Damaris were forty thousand times a Spanish and Austrian Princess, this thing has gone too far to stop here. She has got to sink her title now in a lowlier one, namely, that of the Viscountess Trent, or—or—"

I paused. Adown another path than that along which she had come to me there was advancing a tall and stately gentleman, alone. A man with a peaked beard, and dressed all in black satin—like myself; a man who walked with gravity extreme. Then, as he drew close to me, he removed the hat he wore, and standing stock-still before me, said in French—

"Have I the honour to address the Milord Trent?"

"That, sir, is my name," I said, rising from my seat and removing also my hat, since I could not allow myself to be outdone in politeness by a foreigner, by which I mean a man who was not an Englishman.

"I have a little message," he proceeded, "from my master, the Prince of Csaba and Miranda Vitoria—from your host of the moment."

"I shall be honoured to receive it, sir."

"It is," the grave and courteous gentleman said, "a warning, a hint. The Prince, my master, desires me to tell you that it will not be for your good to go out to supper to-night—not for the good of your health."

"The Prince, your master, being aware, sir," I demanded, "that it is to an Englishman he sends this message?"

"I imagine his Highness may be aware that such is the case."

"Will you, sir, then, in your courtesy, constitute yourself the bearer of my reply?"

"I am your servant, sir; I shall deem it an honour to do so."

"Sir, you place me in your debt. And, such being the case, will you please to tell the Prince, your master, that I look forward with eagerness to my supper to-night, to which I shall proceed without fail; also that my health is most excellent, as are both my appetite and digestion; and, likewise, that when I require a doctor's advice I shall not insult so illustrious a person as the Prince by asking him to take so humble a function as that on himself? Sir, I salute you."

Whereon, with the exchange of most polite bows between us, I strode away, leaving him alone.

III. DANGER CLOSE AT HAND

By now it was half after one o'clock, and I, leaning out of my salon window in the Lion d'Or, knew that it was time for me to be away; to reach Damaris— "my Damaris" I called her now, since I had resolved that mine she had got to be—and see what sort of a supper she proposed to offer me. For my part, I thought the dishes were as like as not to consist of some unwholesome cold steel, or a leaden bullet out of a Spanish *trabuco* or musquetoon—that is to say, offered but not accepted, if I was to have any word in the matter.

Dallying idly over the window-sill, I thought, I say, of all this, while at the same time there rose ever before me the beauteous features and the laughing eyes of the Princess. And I wondered if she would laugh if she heard the clash of arms outside her side-door in the Rue des Fleurs. Likewise, I wondered if she would laugh, too, when she learnt, after this pleasing little entertainment of the small hours was over, of how masterful an individual I could be—it was her own term, you will please to remember; her very own!—and how I was the sort of man who would know how to turn this "playing" at being her lover into being her lover in true and actual fact. Poor Damaris! Poor, stately, yet roguish Damaris, what a come-down it would seem to her!—to give up her great position to become my wife.

But would it? Would it? Well! I did not quite know. She was a Spaniard, and the Spaniards had the reputation of being very firm in their affections when once they were set in a certain direction. And I thought, only thought—though, perhaps, I hoped too—that those affections were set more or less in my direction. And now, to-night, I was going to see.

I had brought back to Paris from England with me a servant: a rough, queer creature, with an enormous appetite and a desire for sleep which I had never seen equalled; yet one who had served my dear father for many years, and had followed him about over Europe in those pilgrimages which I once told you he had been in the habit of making, in the footsteps of *our* King, James III. At Rome this man had been, also in Spain, and in these places he had picked up a smattering of tongues other than his own, as well as having the French very well; while, as he had earlier ridden trooper in the regiment of Blues, and, still earlier, had been a sailor for a time, he was a brave and valiant fellow. A rough kind of spaniel thing he was, which would cling close to its master's heels, yet yap and snap and sniff at every one a-nigh that master until sure that such person boded no ill to him. Now, I went to wake him—for, as always, he slept when he had no work to do—from his slumbers in a cupboard on the landing.

"Get up, Giles" (for Giles Bates was his name, and a good honest English one, too, though it had no spot of Norman in it), I cried, stamping on the floor at the same time to wake him. "Get up at once."

"Is the house afire?" he asked, yawning and rubbing his eyes all the time. "I would not be surprised if 'twere so in this silly land. Or is the breakfast ready? I am mortal hungry. Oh!" he exclaimed, seeing me, his master, "it is you, my lord. What is to do now, my lord?"

"I am going to supper at a lady's house, or, at least, I am going to a lady's house. Don't roll your eyes up like that, you fool! the lady will be my wife ere long, I hope. Meanwhile, I have enemies, rivals, and may be attacked, and I want your company."

In a minute he was up off his pallet and had seized his sword and was buckling it on to him, his gooseberry-looking eyes gleaming with delight; for Giles Bates loved a fight as well as any of our island breed, and was ever ready for one.

For myself, I needed no buckling on of my blade. I had, since I returned from the Hôtel d'Aragon, changed my clothes, putting off my fashionable suit of black, and assuming a plainer one in which I travelled. My Flamberg was also already on my thigh, wherefore I felt equal to meeting any of the Prince of Csaba's Spanish *asesinos* whom he might see fit to send out to attack me in the neighbourhood of my sweetheart's house.

That they would be Spanish I felt sure, for more reasons than one; the first of many such reasons being that the Prince was surrounded by a train of Spaniards; and the second, that he would have had no time to procure Frenchmen, even if Frenchmen would have served him, which, since the French are not midnight cut-throats, whatever their other failings may be, I did not think very likely.

A little later and we drew near to where the Paris mansion of the Carbajals stood in the Marais, it being by this time hard on two o'clock of the morning, and all the streets around very still beneath the light of the moon as she sailed above. The revellers and wassailers seemed to have gone to their beds, and we scarce passed any one as we approached nearer and nearer to the spot we were making for, and all was very calm except for the barking of a dog once and again. Yet, notwithstanding the peacefulness of the night and the desolation of the streets, I observed my mastiff keeping his eyes ever open warily, and glinting first one and then the other into dark corners and up alleys and *ruelles*.

"A sweet fine night," he muttered to himself, "for a fight. Oh! 'twould make a shark sob" (he had been a sailor, amongst other things, as I have said) "to think we should not come to loggerheads with some one on such a night as this."

"Be still," I said; "we draw near to the house, to—"

"My lady's bower!" he murmured, regarding me with his fish-like eyes, so that I knew not whether he meant to be impertinent—which I did not think he did—or was quoting from some of the sheets of love-ballads I had more than once caught him poring over. "Oh, love! love! love!"

"Peace, fool!" I said, "and hold your silly tongue. We are there."

And so we were; we being now outside a small oak door let into the side of the Carbajal mansion, which stood up grey and solemn in the moonlight.

"Now," I continued, "to get in."

"Ay, my lord," said Giles; "and to get out again afterwards. Do I enter with you?"

"You shall know later. Meanwhile, stand back in the shadow. And take my cloak; 'twill but encumber me if there should be any sword-play inside."

"And serve as guard for my arm if twisted round it," said Giles, as he took the cloak, "if there should be any outside. 'Tis four years since I fleshed a Spaniard. 'Twas by the Puerta del Sol, and he was attacking a Northumbrian Jacobite gentleman, who, alas! was lurching about like the *Royal Sovereign* in a gale—"

"Silence," I said. "See, the wicket opens"; as in truth it did, and through the bars I saw a moment or so later a pair of soft roguish eyes glistening in the moonlight—eyes that

I knew well and loved to see, they making then, as always they have made, a summer in my heart by their glances.

"Are you alone, Adrian?" a gentle voice, equally dear to me as the eyes, whispered.

"Alone," I whispered back, "except for a fool mastiff creature, who is, however, faithful, and can fight as well as be trusted."

"Ay, he can," I heard my follower mutter to himself, "and will not be contented if he fight not to-night."

"Come in," Damaris said, opening now the door (in which the wicket was) about half a foot, so that I might squeeze in, "and leave your watch-dog there. He may be attacked—"

"So much the better," growled Giles, he hearing all.

"You understand?" I said to him; "you understand? You may be attacked."

"Ay, my lord, I understand. I am not afeard. Yet I wish I had the wherewithal for supper. I am parlous hungry—"

"Bah! Keep watch well." Whereon I entered by the half-open door, and joined Damaris.

It was quite dark in the passage when I got there—except for the rays of the moon, which glinted and glistened from windows on high—there being no lights in the house so far as I could see. Then, while I was noting this, my girl whispered to me, "There are two in the garden now. I have seen them! have been close to them! Do you know what they are here for, in their long cloaks and vizard-masks?"

"I can guess well enough. Who are they?"

"Menials, I take it. Menials come to—to—O Adrian!"

"I understand. Damaris, you have got to pay me for this service."

"I thought," she whispered, "that English gentlemen, English noblemen, did not ask payment from ladies for services rendered."

"One payment it is always permissible to ask. I mean to have it too."

"It is impossible," she said—"impossible."

"I intend to make it possible. You told me I was very masterful, and I shall be— if I live through this night."

Whereon she only whispered again, "O Adrian!" and then said, "Come and see these men; and—and—loosen your sword in its sheath."

"Never fear," said I. "That's ready."

After which I followed her along the dark corridor or passage, and through a hall, large and lofty—they had built good houses in the old days in that portion of Paris known as the Marais—from out of which there opened the reception saloons, as well as a great *salle* or banqueting-room. Now, into that hall there shone, from two great windows high up on either side of it, the full moon, so that I could perceive the form of my young princess almost as clearly as I might have done in daylight, and to my intense astonishment I observed that she was very little like a princess now, if such personages are to be judged by the garb they wear. For, now, she was arrayed in the dark Nîmes serge of a waiting-maid; upon her head was the provincial cap worn by so many of those women, hers being the head-dress of Brittany, which, as all the travelled world knows, hides every hair upon a woman's head and quite destroys any good looks that a serving-girl may happen to possess. And I noticed, too, that her hands were no longer adorned with flashing gems; nor were they either the little white snowflakes I had always gazed upon with such rapture—since now they were of a discoloured yellow-brown hue, and the nails discoloured also.

"More play-acting," I said to her, "more play-acting. 'Tis like the night in Toulouse when you played a part."

"Ay, 'tis," she answered; "and, I protest, as necessary now as then that I should play it well. And," she went on, "I am going to play one, and you shall see me do it. Now," she continued, "I must leave you, as I am about to go into the garden."

"Then I go too," I said. "Why! suppose one is Csaba—the Prince."

"Well! he would not hurt me. He pretends to love me—*does* love me."

"He might carry you off."

"Might he! What! with my faithful Adrian looking at him out of the darkness of this room, and ready to spring forth like a great fierce English lion—that great lion that is so dominating and contemptuous over all the other beasts and fowls of Europe. Might he? Not he. Nor will he while I have this," and, in the moonbeams, I saw her draw a little stiletto from out the pocket of her serving-woman's gown. "Now," she said, "you stay here till I come back. Be a good boy, Blue Eyes, and do what I tell you."

"You do love me, don't you, Damaris? That's understood."

"It is understood that you do as I tell you. Now I go."

Whereon she went through the door from the hall and into the great *salle*, and then down the huge steps leading from the verandah on to the broad walk, on which there stood large tubs, having in them oleanders and orange and lemon trees. And be sure that, creeping after her, I followed as far as I might without exposing myself to the view of any who might be in the garden; and then, from behind the heavy window-hangings, I gazed out, while listening with all my ears.

Now, no sooner had my girl gotten down some yards upon the broad walk—she having, as she went, thrown a common kind of hood, such as Spanish peasant women wear in the streets over her head—than she commenced, gently, but still audibly, to say, "Hst! hst! Isidore. I am here. Isidore, where are you? Have you kept tryst? Isidore, I say!" and then gave a little kind of muffled shriek as a figure, enshrouded in a cloak and wearing a mask (and followed by another attired in a similar manner), stepped out from behind a lemon-tree tub and seized her by the arm.

IV. A Finale

That figure stepped forth and seized her by the arm while saying, in tones quite loud enough for me to hear, "What are you making that noise for here? and who are you? and who, in the fiend's name, is Isidore?"

"O kind sir! O monsieur!" I heard the girl answer. "Oh! please, sir, don't kill me, and don't wake the Princess. Oh! what are you doing in her garden at this hour?"

"Who is Isidore?" the masked one asked sternly.

"O kind sir, he is the coachman. We are to be married soon, and we make a little tryst at night when it is fine above. O sir, if the Princess should wake?"

"Wake! How should she be asleep? Is she not entertaining some Englishman to supper to-night?"

"Ah, monsieur! Ah, *mon Dieu!* You believe that! 'Tis a cold supper then! Look, monsieur, at the *salle-a-manger.*"

"Bah! She has a boudoir, I suppose?"

"Ah! monsieur, would you believe that of the Princess! And all because she played a little jest upon a foolish Englishman who pesters her with his attentions, a poor half-witted thing, who even now, at this moment, is dilly-dallying at the side-door, thinking he will be let in. *Peste!* he will wait a long while," and she began to sing a song out of Regnard's new comedy about a man waiting for a lady under an elm, and waiting a mighty long time too—

"Attendez-moi sous l'orme," she sang, "vous m'attendrez longtemps."

"A little jest," the cloaked and masked man said, turning round to his companion; "a little jest. And the animal is by the side-door. Is this the truth?" re-turning his face towards the girl.

"Ah! monsieur. The truth! How can it be aught else—when—when the Prince of Csaba and Miranda Vitoria honours her with his admiration."

"Come," the man said to his companion now. "Come. We, too, will go round to the side-door and see this ardent lover—and, perhaps, punish his insolence. These English are insupportable. As for you—go to your Isidore, your coachman."

"Oh! *non, monsieur, non!* He will not come now. There will be no Isidore to-night. He is timorous. If he has seen monsieur, he will have shrunk away."

"Go then to your bed, and stay in it; and, above all, say nothing to the Princess of our being in this garden to-night."

"For certain, monsieur, otherwise I should have to say I was here too. Good-night, monsieur." Then, as the man turned to move away, she suddenly stopped him by catching the end of his cloak, and, thereby, forcing him to turn; he saying somewhat haughtily, "What is it, good woman? What?"

"Only that monsieur will not laugh at the poor Englishman, will not deride him. They cannot bear that!"

"No," the other said, "I will not laugh at him. Rely on me. There will be no laughing," and again he turned and went upon his way, accompanied by the other.

"You have done a fine thing for poor Giles," I said to the Princess, as now she rejoined me in the great *salle*. "A fine thing. I must get back to him at once and lend a hand if I would not find him hacked to pieces by those two cut-throats sent out by your precious Prince."

"Why," she said calmly, "I thought you said he was a fighter. Is he not so?" she went on, while all the time she was unwrapping the hood from her head and—next—taking off the horrible Brittany cap which hid her beautiful hair that, now it was no longer obscured, gleamed a superb dark chestnut in the rays of the moon.

"He is that," I replied, "and a good one, as most men who have been soldier and sailor both, to say nothing of wandering about Europe as an adherent of an unhappy cause, are like to be. But the man is a good tilter who can hold his own against two."

"Perhaps he will not have to fight two of them," she said, still very calmly. "One has, I imagine, no fighting in him."

"What makes you think that?"

"Oh! Oh! Well, let us wait and see. Perhaps—well! I can't say."

"You observed that fellow well, anyhow. And heard his voice."

"Yes, yes!" she said; "yes, but it was no— Come," she said, "let us go and look after the watchdog."

Whereon we now retraced our steps, passing out of the great hall and down the corridor towards where the side-door with the little wicket in it was.

And then, as we drew near that door, we heard (and more especially we did so because Damaris had forgotten to close the little wicket after she had looked through it at me, so that noises outside, if any, might plainly be distinguished) the clash of arms, a sound sweet enough to a soldier's ears.

"Hark!" I said, redoubling my pace as I did so, and catching hold of the girl's hand, whereby she was compelled also to move more swiftly, though, in sober truth, I think she was as anxious to reach the door and get it open as I was myself. "Hark! they have set upon him. And there *were* two. Oh! this is cowardly, murderous! I must take my share."

"Pray Heaven he, your man, kills not two of them. That would cause a terrible stir, and—and—and would part us for ever, Adrian."

"Nothing shall do that," I muttered determinately, perhaps grimly, through my lips. "Nothing!"

Then, we being by this time close to the door, I seized the latch and opened it, running out into the little open *place* in front of it, which was flooded by the glorious splendour of the full moon.

What a strange scene it was upon which my eyes lit, even as I heard my sweetheart murmur, "God be praised! he, at least, is not slain—yet."

A strange scene indeed, though with a ludicrous side to it; one that might have made me laugh, maybe, at any other time, and if I had not myself been concerned deeply in all that was a-doing. For there was my brave, courageous servitor, this man who had been a wandering sailor as well as soldier, and also a faithful follower of a hardly-treated race, standing up manfully against another swordsman who was making swift passes at him, they fighting across the body of a third who lay prone and prostrate with Giles's foot upon his body.

And that last was the fact which would have made me laugh in any other circumstance, for, swiftly, I recalled how in the days of my childhood this very Giles had taken me to see Barton Booth in one of Mr. Sotherne's beautiful tragedies at the theatre in Lincoln's Inn Fields, and how, when the actor struck the villain down— exactly in the middle of the stage!—he had placed his foot upon his chest, and waved his triumphant sword over the fallen one. I recalled, too, how Giles had applauded, and had said, "O Master Adrian, Master Adrian, that is the way to conquer, to subdue a villain!"

And now the poor faithful, honest fool had himself struck a villain down, and with his foot upon that villain's chest—in a splendid, tragic, and theatrical manner—was as like to strike another one down ere long; for, even as I tore open the little door, and rushed out followed by Damaris, he disarmed the other fighter, lunged at him, and, missing his heart, yet brought him to his knee, while he drew back his sword once more to plunge it through the other's body.

"Stop!" rang out the Princess's voice, clear and imperious; "stop, man, I command you. Adrian, forbid him. It is the Prince," she whispered in my ear; "I recognised his voice easily in the garden."

"Why?" I asked, hot and excited myself now, "why stop? Why should he, this midnight assassin, be spared?"

"'Tis Csaba, I tell you," she said. "'Tis the Prince. If he is slain there can never be," and she lowered her voice more deeply still, "any union betwixt *England* and *Spain*."

"Hold your weapon, Giles," I cried, understanding in a moment what she would convey, and, in honest truth, not deeming this contemptible Prince's life worth the cost of a broken union 'twixt an Englishman and a Spanish girl who loved each other. "Hold up. Be still, I say."

And, obedient to my command, perhaps obedient also to those earlier, haughtier commands uttered in the girl's clear tones, Giles did hold, yet muttering while doing so that he would have been through the other's lungs in a moment.

"So, monseigneur," my sweetheart said, addressing the masked Prince, who now rose from off the knee on to which he had been beaten, "you are content to play the part of murderer, are you? And on a serving-man! For shame!"

"He wore his master's cloak," a deep, muffled voice said. "Until that master appeared just now at your side I thought I was fighting with him."

"Therefore you and your confederate," and I glanced at the dead man at our feet, "sought to murder me. Wherefore?"

"Ay, wherefore?" repeated Damaris.

"Because you loved him, and—and I loved you."

"Nay," she said softly, "I did not love him then; I—I do not think I did, though, in honesty, I will say I deemed him the brightest, most worthy, pleasant man I have ever known. But now—"

"Now!" came from both our pairs of lips, from Csaba's and from mine.

"Now I love him, and no other man shall ever have my heart."

For a moment there was silence amongst us all, though I stole my hand towards that of Damaris, and, finding it, held it fast; yet but a little later Csaba muttered—

"It is impossible. He is beneath you."

Now, though I had heard those sweet words of the girl's only a moment before, these latter ones angered me, drove me beside myself, for I was weary of hearing so often that I, an Englishman, was unworthy to be the mate of any one, no matter how high that one might be placed. Wherefore, furious, and stepping up to this man, this prince who skulked about in the night with secret murder in his heart, I said, bending my face forward so that it was very near to his, and doing so with a desire to give weight to my words—

"Hark you, I have heard these words before. But now, unless you are an arrant cur—such as assassins always are—you shall retract them, or I will cram them down your throat. For if you say that not only I, but also any Englishman, high or low, gentle or simple, is not the equal of any foreigner, even though he be a prince of Austria or of Spain, then you lie. I say, you lie. Do you hear—you lie."

While, even as he started and staggered back, clutching his cloak convulsively with the hand that held its folds together, I continued—

"Now, if there is any fight left in you after the defeat you have received at the hands of this simple, honest English peasant, take your sword in hand and let us see whether you will justify your words or swallow mine." Then, turning to Giles, I said, "Pick up this fellow's weapon and give it to him."

"No," exclaimed Damaris; while, looking round as Giles did as I bade him, I saw her standing by me, pale, and like a statue, yet with her beautiful eyes ablaze. "No, you shall not fight with him, Adrian. Prince as he is, and, alas! of my land, he is unworthy to cross swords with you.—As for you," she said, addressing Csaba, "begone. Begone from off this *place*, which belongs to my hotel and is mine, and let me never see your face again. Go," she said, stamping her foot on the rough cobblestones; "go, I say."

Yet still he did not move, but, instead, stood there looking like some great black statue in his long cloak and mask, and with his head bent towards the ground, so that I concluded he knew not what to do, but, in his pride and rage, was determined not to quit the ground at her orders.

And she, seeing this, and, as she told me afterwards, understanding very well the tempest that must be raging in his heart, said, "Come, Adrian. Since he will not go, we must."

Wherefore we went back to her house followed by Giles, and leaving the Prince of Csaba and Miranda Vitoria still standing in the open space before the little door.

Now the story is done—done, that is, unless you would desire me to tell you what you doubtless can very well imagine; namely, that it was not long before the Princess and I became man and wife. Yet hard enough that marriage was in making, I can assure you, and one which I thought would never be completed. For, although my girl, having once acknowledged that she loved me, was as willing to be my wife as I was eager to have her, the forms and ceremonies we had to go through to get what Giles called "triced up" were enough to irritate one of Damaris's own saints; for there was the Consul of Spain—the Consul of the, by her, hated Philip V.—to be invoked, and the English ambassador to be consulted, who, since he represented King George, was not agreeable to me; and the permission of the Archbishop of Lyons, Primate of France, to be obtained, and a permission sent over from England from the Archbishop of Canterbury, the head of my church. And we went through all kinds of ceremonies, and were half-married a week before we were finally allowed to consider ourselves man and wife, while I became very irritable through it all, and Damaris muttered all kinds of strange little expletives in Spanish through her pretty teeth and scarlet lips, which, she told me afterwards, would not have sounded so nicely in English. Also, I should not forget to say that Giles signed countless papers and parchments as a witness, and looked very important over it all, and whispered lines of love-ballads to me at intervals to cheer me up, and ate enormously at every opportunity which offered.

However, done it was at last, and we were wedded. And, although my wife could not take me to any of her great possessions because she would not set foot in Spain while Philip ruled, and I could not take her to my home in Staffordshire (where the Trent rises) because of my political principles, we were very well content—since we were both young and hopeful!—and so we settled down in the old Paris house of the Carbajals in the Marais, and have, up to now, lived happy ever after, as the chapbooks say; a happiness which, you may be very sure, was not ruffled when we heard that the Prince of Csaba and Miranda Vitoria had married a princess of the ancient house of Ponte-Casoria (which is allied to the greater house of Bourbon), who was extremely rich, but as wizened as a monkey (as my wife told me), and who, report declared, led Csaba a terrible life.

The Story of Cyrano de Bergerac

Edmond Rostand and Anne O'Hagan

I

Pit and stage alike were dusky that afternoon in 1640 when all Paris gathered in the Hotel de Bourgogne to see produced the play to which Master Balthazar Baro looked for fame—his comedy "Clorise."

The candles were not yet lighted, but the house hummed with sounds. Now an imprecation smote through the buzzing when one of the troopers of the Household of His Majesty Louis XIII. knocked insolently against one of the guard of the great Cardinal Armand de Richelieu. Now there was the clash of foils where two gentlemen passed the tedious time of waiting at fencing. Pages played pranks, and pickpockets likewise.

Now a swagger seized a kiss from a pretty shop girl, and now the foaming of wine bespoke a man about to quench his thirst.

Honest burghers made their sober way among the roysterers of the aristocracy and those of the gutters. Sometimes a ripple of laughter floated musically from the galleries where the ladies' boxes were—the ladies whose slumbrous eyes roused love their scornful lips pretended to disdain.

Now a band of young marquises burst through the doors, swords clattering at their sides. They came bent on their favorite sport—the baiting of the burghers. In the semi-darkness they could not make out the crowd.

"Ah, Cuigy," cried one, when his eyes had swept the dim theater, "what sport is here? Where are the good people we were to rush? Pshaw! Not a toe have we trodden upon. We come in like a band of woollen drapers. Is this your fun?"

"You should have waited at least till the candles were lighted," said Cuigy. "Ah! Here come the lighters now."

The crowd gathered around the candle-bearers. By their light the little group of nobles made one another out. The theater where the king's own players were to perform was plain in the light. Above the tapestried curtains that hid the stage the royal arms were crossed. The hall was a sort of tennis court, arranged and decorated for a theatrical performance.

On both sides of the stage were benches, and steps led from it down to the floor. On either side of these were places for the violinists. In the pit where the men of the audience gathered there were no seats, and in the rear of it, beneath the steps that led to the ladies' gallery, was the buffet where a girl sold cakes, tarts and sweet drinks.

The lights showed two men, both striking and strikingly alike. Ligniere, already half-drunk, though the day was young, piloted his friend Christian, the Baron de Nervilette, about the pit, presenting him to one group of nobles after another.

Christian's "delighteds" were perfunctory. His eyes ceaselessly sought the gallery. He was indifferent to the scarcely whispered comments of his new acquaintances. He heard, as from a distance, Ligniere explaining that his friend was but new come to Paris from Touraine, and that the next day he was to join the guards as a cadet. He bent his head in acknowledgment of the congratulations, but his eyes were still upturned toward the boxes where the grand dames of Paris gathered to pass their pretty judgment upon Master Baro's work. Ligniere marked his abstraction.

"The lady comes not," he said. "Release me from my guidance. I will betake me to my favorite tavern."

"Stay," begged Christian. "You who know the town can tell me who she is for love of whom I die. You must stay and tell me who she is. Yet what will it boot?" he added gloomily. "I come from Touraine, and the ways of the court sit not easily upon me. I do not know its language. That they speak here to-day—ay, and write, too—confounds me. I am but an honest soldier—a lubberly one, if you will. What could she see in me?"

He turned gloomily toward the buffet, and when next he looked the empty box toward which his eyes had been directed was no longer empty.

"Look!" cried Christian, seizing Ligniere's arm. "Look! 'Tis she!"

Ligniere glanced toward the box. He did not even cease to sip his *rivesalte* as he answered:

"Ah! She is Magdeleine Robin—'Roxane,' they call her. She is a wit—a *precieuse*. Cyrano de Bergerac is her cousin. She is orphaned. There is the Count de Guiche speaking to her now, the blue-ribboned nobleman there. He is enamored of her, though he has wed the Cardinal's niece himself. He would marry her to Monsieur de Valvert—a most complaisant viscount. But Roxane will none of that bargain, though De Guiche may persecute her for her obstinacy. See, she looks at you!"

It was true. The *precieuse* had bent her eyes upon him. He stood transfixed, the gentleman from Touraine. Ligniere, delayed beyond his wont from his favorite tavern, made his escape from the love-lorn youth's side.

The audience was growing impatient.

It had been promised a rare treat—rarer than good Master Baro's "Clorise" afforded. Ragueneau, king of pastry cooks, patron of poets and playwrights, had circulated among them, telling them of the bargain of Cyrano de Bergerac.

"He has got a hate of Montfleury," said Ragueneau. "He has forbid the actor to set foot upon the stage again for a month. And to-day Montfleury is billed to play! Surely there will be rare sport when our Cyrano sees him!"

"Who is this Cyrano," asked Christian, "that he should dictate to the king's players?"

"Know you not?" cried Ragueneau. "He is a poet, a philosopher, a musician, a soldier. You should see him fence! He is a cadet in the guards, the maddest fighter of them all. You should see him with his triple-plumed beaver, and his six-pointed doublet—his sword point out beneath his coat like a pert cock's tail! He is ruffed, and ah! you should see his nose above his ruff. The nose of a false face, it is. One must believe thiat he plays a joke and that it will come off. But 'tis his own, and off it will not come. And woe to you, my master, if you dare but stare at it!"

"Ah, well! He will not come to-day to clear the stage of Montfleury! You'll see," said one.

The young Christian, half divided between the tale of the great Cyrano and watching Roxane, felt suddenly a hand in his pocket. Clasping it he swung around and faced a pickpocket. But the rogue was clever.

"You sought?" he hazarded.

"A glove," said Christian. He did not add that it was his intention to throw the glove into the face of the complaisant Valvert, designed by De Guiche for Roxane's husband, and fighting him, perhaps, to rid the world of him.

"You find a hand," said the ready scoundrel. "I am here to warn you of a plot against your friend Ligniere, who left you but a while ago. A hundred men lie in wait for him. He has offended the great nobleman De Guiche, who married the Cardinal's niece. I am one of the hundred, but I have no stomach for the job. Go you and warn him!"

So Christian, easily put off, hastened from the theater and missed, not Master Balthazar Baro's Comedy of Clorise, but the play between Cyrano de Bergerac and Montfleury.

Montfleury had come upon the stage and had mouthed his opening lines. The nobles whispered one to another: "De Bergerac not here?" Ragueneau, the pastry cook, breathlessly loyal, had wagered a fowl, à la Ragueneau, upon his coming. Suddenly from the center of the pit there came a voice:

"Villain! And did I not forbid you to set foot upon this stage for a month?"

Montfleury broke off in his mouthings. The crowd stood dazed for a second. Then came a shout. The nobles recognized de Bergerac. Montfleury, interrupted, stammered wildly:

"Dare you defy me?" cried the voice.

"On, Montfleury, on!" cried the nobles.

Montfleury stammered another line.

"So you itch for a taste of my cane?" said the voice, and in the pit a hand lifted above the heads of the spectators waved a cane.

"Hap-Happy he," began Montfleury, for the third time.

Then Cyrano sprang upon a chair, a terrible figure to see, with his crossed arms, his cocked beaver, his bristling mustache and his great nose.

"Go!" he cried fiercely. "Go!"

"Help, help!" begged the actor.

"Go on, Montfleury," advised the nobles indifferently. "We will protect you."

"Another moment!" cried Cyrano, "and I must even slit his ears off. My anger rises." He left his chair and stood in the middle of a circle.

"Your protectors," he said politely, "I will meet first—one after the other. Gentlemen, come on! What, none? Ah, then, to you alone I will devote myself. Thrice will I clap my hands, thus. At the third clap get you gone. One!"

Montfleury wavered. "He'll stay!" shouted the crowd.

"Two!"

"Gentlemen," begged Montfleury, "'twere discreet, methinks—"

"Three!"

And the stage was rid of Montfleury. Cyrano, center of a circle, bandied jests. Jodelet, the manager, mourned over entrance fees to be returned.

"Here, you take that," called Cyrano, and tossed him a bag of gold.

And all the while the eyes of his cousin, the dainty wit Roxane, were bent upon him from her box.

II

Jodelet weighed in his hand the purse that Cyrano had just thrown to him on the stage, and told him that at this price he was welcome to stop a play every night.

The audience rose and prepared to leave the theater. The ladies in the galleries stopped in adjusting their mantles and scarfs to listen to Cyrano, who again had the floor.

"It's shameful. Montfleury is protected by the Duke of Candal. Have you a patron?" demanded a bore of Cyrano.

"No patron, nor protector," answers Cyrano, grasping his sword, "but I have a protectress here."

"You'll have to leave town. The Duke has a long arm."

"Not so long as mine when it's lengthened out," retorted Cyrano, holding out his sword. "Show your heels now, or tell me why you stare so at my nose."

"Your grace mistakes," apologized the bore, drawing back.

"Come, now," said Cyrano; "what amuses you? Is it that it's dangling like an elephant's trunk, or crooked like an owl's beak? Or is it the fly that takes the air on the tip?"

"I—I did not look. I was careful—I knew better."

"Then why did you look at my nose, sir? Does it disgust you? Is its hue unwholesome to you, or its proportions too large?"

"No, no!" gasped the bore. "It is small, quite minute, in fact. Heaven help me!"

"It's enormous," said Cyrano, "and I am proud to possess it. Every meddler knows that a big nose is indicative of an affable soul." And to illustrate his point he soundly cuffed the bore, and, having taken him by the shoulders, turned him round, that he might administer a parting kick.

The bore ran away, calling to the guard for help, and Cyrano having convinced the audience that he was a man of his word, warned them that the next who finds amusement in his nose shall have a taste of his sword and not his boot.

Down from the stage came De Guiche, with his friend, the Viscount De Valvert, their swords clattering at their sides, and both annoyed at the turn events had taken and disappointed at not having seen the play, and jealous, perhaps, a bit, of Cyrano, hero of the evening.

"This fellow becomes a nuisance," said De Guiche, shrugging his shoulders.

"A swaggerer," said De Valvert. "Will no one put him down?"

"I," answered the Viscount, "will treat him to one of my quips. See here, sir, your nose is—h'm—very big!"

"Very," answered Cyrano gravely. "Is that all you can say, young blade? Your repartee is a trifle short. You might have said at least a hundred things. Aggressively, you might have said, sir, if I had such a nose I'd amputate it; or, it must fill your cup when you drink, you ought to have a drinking trough of special shape; or, when you smoke your pipe do not the neighbors cry, 'The chimney's afire?' or, pray have an umbrella made that the sun may not destroy its color; or, this useful crook is the latest thing to hang your hat on, friend; or, as a rustic, 'tis a dwarf pumpkin or a prize turnip; or, behold the nose that wears the harmony of its master's phiz! blushing its treachery.

"Such, my dear sir, is what you might have said if you had wit or letters, but the only letters that you have are three, and they spell ASS! Had you the wit to serve me these pleasantries I quote—you would not have been let to quote one—I take them from myself in good part, but not from any other man that breathes."

De Guiche, alarmed at the turn of affairs, tried to draw away the Viscount, who, choking with rage, cried out: "A country lout who has no gloves and goes without sleeve-knots, ribbons or lace."

"True," said Cyrano, "I wear no gloves, but what of that? I had one once, and not knowing what to do with it, threw it in the face of a young fool."

"Base scoundrel! Rascally, flat-footed lout!"

Cyrano took off his hat and bowed low, as if the Viscount bad introduced himself.

"My name is Cyrano Savinen Hercule de Bergerac."

The audience, delighted with Cyrano's wit, roared with laughter, and the Viscount turned his back and started to leave.

Cyrano doubled up as if seized sudden cramps and called out, "Aie! Aie!"

"What is he saying?" said the Viscount, turning back.

"The cramp in my sword," said Cyrano; "it comes of leaving it in idleness; it is getting stiff, I vow."

"Good!" and the Viscount, drew his sword for answer, exclaiming contemptuously, "Poet!"

"In proof of which I'll compose a ballad while we fence," said Cyrano, and then he went on in a sing-song voice as if he had been reciting a lesson, that a ballad should contain three eight-verse couplets and an *envoi* of four lines. "I'll make one while we fight, and touch you at the final line."

"No!" exclaimed the Viscount.

"No?" said Cyrano, and he began to declaim:

"The duel in Hotel of Burgundy—fought by de Bergerac and a good-for-nought."

Marquises and officers mingled in the pit with the common people. Pages climbed on one another's shoulders, the ladies leaned over from the galleries to see the better. "Give room! Great sport!" called out the audience as a space was hastily cleared in the center.

Roxane, pale as a lily, leaned forward to watch her cousin and her suitor fight. Cyrano, as he fought, composed, suiting every act to the word. And this was his ballad of the duel:

THE BALLAD OF THE DUEL

"I cast my soft hat on the ground—
I slowly unwind, without aid,
The cloak which about me is wound;
With a jerk my big blade
Is, like Celadon, played,
And, like Scaramouche, light;
This boast is now made:
At the finish of 'l'Envoi' I bite.

"You should have been neutral, or older;
Well, turkey, where will you be larded?
In the flank, or under the shoulder?
Or the heart, by its blue ribbon guarded?
My ear by strange bells is bombarded—
The point of my blade, how it lights—
(Decidedly he'll have to be larded.)
At the finish of 'l'Envoi' it bites.

"I'm seeking a word for my rhyme—
You look broken—as white as your shirt.
The word 'coward' will serve us this time.
Ah! so! Parry the hurt—
You aimed at me curt,
I open a line—I make light—
Hold tighter to thy skewer, thou swine,
At the finish of 'l'Envoi' I bite.

envoi.

"Prince, ask for thy pardon on high!

I skirmish so near I can hit.

I cut and I thrust. Ah! you sigh!

At the finish of 'l'Envoi' I bite."

And with the word he pierced the Viscount.

All was confusion in an instant. Ragueneau danced about the hero of the hour. Cyrano's bosom friend, Le Bret, hovered near him, anxious in his happiness. Valvert's friends bore him away. Women applauded; noblemen congratulated the fighter. Roxane's eyes looked down upon him. The buffet-girl pressed the great man to eat.

"Ah!" cried he, "I have no money."

Blushing, she put all the contents of the buffet at his service.

"I could not take them from you, child," he said, "so keen is our Gascon pride. But fear of hurting you outweighs the pride. There—these few grapes, this water, a half a macaroon—and leave to kiss your hand for dessert."

Deeper grew the little maid's blushes.

"I thank you, sir," she said, and courtesied out of sight.

"She admired you," said Le Bret.

"She? Ah! Admired me—but another does not. How could I hope it? Look you on my nose. Where'er I go it is still a quarter of a mile ahead of me—ridiculous, hideous. And I—of course I love the fairest, the most brilliant, most refined, most golden haired—a sweet perfumed rose, full of unconscious charms. Ah, me!"

"Your cousin, Madeline?" cried Le Bret.

"My cousin Madeline, Roxane—the beauty and the wit—Roxane."

"She was death-white the duel through."

"Pale at my danger? She?" cried Cyrano. And he himself grew pale at the thought. He trembled now.

And while he trembled and whitened the *duenna* of fair Roxane came gliding to his side.

"My lady goes to mass at St. Roch to-morrow," she whispered. "We will be at the pastry cook's—Ragueneau's—at seven. There craves she speech with her most valiant cousin."

"My God! with me?" cried Cyrano, faint with rapture.

"Will you be there?"

"Will I be there? Oh, madam, without fail. Le Bret, Le Bret! You heard what yon retreating lady said? My cousin knows I live. Roxane has seen me!"

III

Had Cyrano had time to dream, that night would have passed in ecstasy of hope. But there was other work cut out for him. He might not spend the hours of darkness tormenting himself with whimsical imaginings about deformity and with golden anticipations roused by the beloved Roxane's message. His sword had work to do, and though that work might lay him low and close his eyes forever before they rested on the face of his beloved, he must do it. A hundred men threatened Ligniere, the drunkard, the balladist, the man whose verse had stung the great De Gruiche, the man whom Cyrano de Bergerac named friend.

"But, prithee, why embroil yourself for him?" demanded Le Bret when Cyrano, forgetful of the roseate Roxane, had gripped his sword to use upon the hundred cutthroat hirelings of De Guiche. "He's but a wine cask at the best."

"He is my friend. And for this reason is he dear to me. His love was a lady of devout ways—and Ligniere, whom water poisons, saw her white fingers touch a font of holy water—little lilies ruffling a clear pond. Swiftly he seized the stoup and drained to the last drop the water her fingertips had sanctified. Was it not a pretty thing? Shall I not be proud to name him friend? And shall I not lead the charge upon those who seek to do him harm? Bear me no aid, I pray you, gentlemen, when I fall fierce upon them. Come you, if you will. But watchers be, not actors. Ahead of you at twenty paces, I, all alone shall dare them. Come on!"

They followed him to see the sport—those gay Parisians, to whom all things were but a spectacle. And the sight they witnessed drove them mad with delight. Cyrano bore down upon the thugs like an avalanche. Before his fury they fled away. Those who would have withstood him fell beneath his sword. There was no resisting him. The joy of battle against fearful odds was upon him. The message from Roxane sang itself in his heart. No man could hold his own against the strong son of Gascony.

How he escaped the crowd that pressed upon him, eager to touch his hand, eager to felicitate him it is hard telling. But somehow he managed it. When the last flying form of his foes had sped through the nebulous moonlight, before the nobles and the officers who had witnessed the affair could seize Cyrano to bear him to his lodgings in triumph, he was gone. Hurrying to his house they did not find him.

He walked deserted streets and quays while the moon traveled mistily down the sky and the sun rose up through a ruddy smoke in the east. A thousand times he addressed Roxane in fancy. The blood that rushed swiftly through his veins after the fight throbbed to her name now that battle was done. In lines that wove themselves together like the tendrils of a vine he addressed her. The lilt of birds' songs, the sobbing of the sea, colors like gems, perfumes as of flowers, all mingled in his senses as he framed the speech in which he would address her. Then, silhouetted on a gray wall, he would catch sight of his reflection. Grotesque, ungainly, monstrous, his nose was cut in the black shadow and his words took wing.

Long before St. Roch's worshipers had left the chapel, he was at the pastry cook's. He paced up and down. His eyes took in the burnished brightness of the copper pans, the sputtering flames where from a fowl revolving on a spit a drop of grease would fall. He looked upon the plates high heaped with tarts and cakes. He saw a swaggering musketeer pay compliments to Lise, the buxom wife of Ragueneau. He saw Ragueneau, connoisseur of cakes and couplets, composer of tarts and triolets, adept at poetry and at pies, bustling about his shop, blind to the musketeer, keenly alive to the hungry poets whom he fed—at so many verses a meal.

But though Cyrano's eyes saw all the scene, but one thought filled his mind— Roxane. Would she never come?

Would the slow minutes never drag themselves by? He whiled away the tedious time by writing her a love letter.

Words ran like liquid fire from his pen—and, looking up, he saw that she had come. He bowed low to her duenna.

"Love you sweets, madam?" he asked. "Yes? Take then these cream cakes—see, I put them in a sonnet of Monsieur Beuserade; and here are little puffs—six of them, done up in a poem by Saint Armant—and here are hot cakes. Go, I beg, and eat them and come not back until the last crumb is eaten."

Laden with her sweet spoils the duenna withdrew.

"And now," said he, turning to Roxane, "I bless the hour when you remembered that I lived. You come to tell me—"

"That I thank you first of all. Your brave blade yesterday at the play smote down the man a great lord seeks to make my husband."

"Ay—husband à la mode," said Cyrano. "I thank my destiny that I fought not for my ugliness alone, but for your beauty also."

"And—more than that have I to say. But be again my cousin of old days. Play we were once again two children frolicking at Bergerac. So shall I speak with better grace and surer courage. Your sword was then of reeds—and all I bade you do, you did."

"Ay, for my cousin Madeleine that's now Roxane the beauty."

"Was I fair then?"

"Not altogether ill to see!"

"Remember you how all your scratches I would bind, but scold you, motherwise, at first? Give me your hand so, now. What, cousin! Here's a scratch, indeed! When got you that?"

Cyrano tugged his hand away.

"A game, last night," he answered.

"Now I will bind your wounds again, as in the old days there at Bergerac. With my own kerchief, see, I wipe away the blood. How many fought you?"

"Oh, a hundred."

"Tell me true. You jest with me."

"Nay, what of that? Tell you what is the other thing you came to speak to me."

"Draw not your hand away, dear cousin. Be but the Cyrano I knew long since in Bergerac, and I am bold to speak. Bend low and listen. I—I love."

"Ah," breathed Cyrano.

"And he—knows not—guesses not."

The room swam before Cyrano's eyes. He held his breath.

"He knows not yet, but soon he shall learn it. Bend lower. Listen. He—has loved me from afar. I saw. He dares not speak."

There was a cloud of rose and amethyst before Cyrano's dazzled eyes. He scarce could bear his happiness—his hand in hers, her words in his ear, her whisper on his cheek.

"Draw not your hand away, dear cousin. Hear me still. He—a chance—he is of your regiment—cadet of your own company!"

It was as though she rained spirit kisses on his lips. He half fainted with ecstasy.

"His brow," she went on—"his brow bears genius' stamp. He is noble, proud, valorous—and fair."

"Fair!" cried Cyrano, springing to his feet.

In a copper pan his face was reflected—misshapen.

"Why, cousin, what is it? What ails you?" begged Roxane.

"The—scratch—your hands had dressed, my gentle cousin. It stung again," he smiled. "But—tell me now his name. How can I serve you?"

"He is Baron Christian de Neuvillette. This day he joins the guards. I know he loves me. Eyes are eloquent—ay, and gossips, too."

"But you, my cousin, how know you that you love him? You delight in wit. Suppose his wit were slow? You love fancy. What were his fancy dull?"

"It is not. I know it is not!" cried Roxane, stamping her foot. Cyrano paused.

"How may I serve you?" he then asked.

"Cousin, he joins your Gascon regiment, and I hear that you provoke all but pure Gascons who are admitted there. I trembled for him—till I saw you—invincible, all-conquering. Then said I: 'If my cousin would—'"

"I will befriend your little baron," said Cyrano.

"You promise you'll do this for me? You'll be his friend? You'll let him fight no duels? They'll put no affront upon your *protégé*?"

"I swear," said Cyrano.

Roxane paused. She took her veil, her mask.

"I've always held my cousin tenderly," she said. "How good you are!"

She blew him a kiss airily from her finger tips.

"Tell me of last night's fray," she pressed him politely. "A hundred men you said. You'll bid my Christian write? What odds against you, bravest coz? Another time you'll tell me all. How well you fought, how well."

"I have fought better since," he answered and bowed low to let her pass.

IV

When Roxane, veiled and masked again, had glided from the pastry cook's, Cyrano stood erect and stiff. Sorrow's shaft had transfixed him where he stood. Blind and deaf to all about him for a few seconds. Then a door flung open. Pellmell a crowd rushed in.

"Cyrano!" cried voices.

"Hero!"

"Cyrano! Cyrano!"

Ragueneau, upset by the excitement, dashed hither and thither. Half of Cyrano's regiment crowded about him. Nobles and actors, poets and artists pushed and shoved to get nearer the hero of the last night's fray. The captain of the Gascon company, Carbon de Castel-Jaloux, was at the head of his men.

"They seek you, Cyrano, to call you brother, to embrace you, to hear—"

"I would not see—I am not—I desire not—" began Cyrano.

"The hero has the sulks, my Gascons," cried Carbon. But, regardless of the feelings of the hero, the men crowded around saluting and embracing their comrade. Nobles who the day before had not known the Gascon fighter, begged to present him to fair and haughty dames who waited but to know him. Rich men tried to patronize him.

The great De Guiche himself entered the pastry shop to congratulate the man who had overcome his own hirelings. Versifiers begged permission to make rhymes upon his exploit. Interviewers sought the privilege of writing of his exploit for the *Court Gazette*, and Cyrano to all was curt and spurned the flatteries.

De Cxuiche, whose manners were a little too fine to be good, expressed his admiration rather boldly:

"So marvelous a feat I could not credit had I not heard these gentlemen swear they saw it. You are brave, sir. And you serve in that company of hotheads, the Gascons?"

"With the cadets," said Cyrano.

"My company is here assembled," said Carbon de Castel-Jaloux. "Cyrano, present them to the Count, if you please."

The band of famous dare-devils looked insolently at De Guiche as they ranged themselves beside Cyrano. He had overcome his sadness and had thrown himself into the task of showing a cheerful Gascon face to the rabble of flatterers. Now at his captain's command he stepped forward toward De Guiche and waving his hand toward his comrades in arms, broke into a ready rhythmic introduction:

> "My Lord, Gascon cadets are they,
> Of Carbon of Castel-Jaloux;
> Boasters, swaggers, bold and gay,
> Cadets of Gascony are they.
>
> "Their pride, their daring race, alway,
> Their blood, than oldest blood more blue,
> Cadets of Gascony are they,
> Of Carbon of Castel-Jaloux.
>
> "Thin, stork legs and eagle eyes—
> Bristling beard and wolfish teeth!
> They charge the rabble; the rabble flies,
> See, their plumes! Guess what lies
>
> "Hidden under? Holes are beneath.
> Thin, stork legs and eagle eyes—
> Bristling beard and wolfish teeth."

"A poet, too, as well as warrior," half-sneered De Guiche. "Ah, well. It is the fashion. Will you be mine?"

"Not yours or any man's."

"My uncle Richelieu, a word from me would do you service there. Shall I not say it? He is a patron of letters, and you, I'll wager have written five acts or so in rhyme? Ah! I see you have. Take your play to him. I'll speak to him."

Cyrano wavered.

There was a play he longed to see upon the stage.

"I would gladly," he began.

"My uncle is a critic skilled. A line or two he may change, but no more," said De Guiche.

"He will not change so much," retorted Cyrano. "He shall not see the play."

"You're proud."

"Ah, have you noticed that?"

The cadets came laughing to Cyrano. They bore a pile of hats.

"See what your enemies left as they fled," they cried—"their hats."

"Sooth, it must be a sore day for him who laid that snare for Ligniere," said one.

"Who was it, think you?"

"'Twas I, myself, gentlemen," broke in De Guiche. "It was not work for my sword to punish a drunken rhymster. I hired those your comrade routed."

A silence fell. The cadet who had piled the hats into Cyrano's arms stood ill at ease.

"What shall I do with them?" he asked.

"My lord will render them unto his friends again," said Cyrano, dropping them at De Guiche's feet.

The nobleman looked furiously at the Gascon.

"My chair!" he cried. "And you, good sir, I counsel you to read your 'Don Quixote.' He battled with a windmill. Who battles thus 'gainst one—"

"Who shifts with every wind," said Cyrano, bowing low.

"May find himself swept low into the mire."

"Or upward to the stars," said Cyrano, as the great man stepped into the chair.

"So," cried his friend Le Bret, in a passion of disappointment. "So! Each chance that fate has offered you this morning you have flung away. What fool's idea is this, to raise an enemy at every step?"

"Ah, friend, I step more surely when eyes send forth upon me shot of hostile looks. I embrace hatred and she gives me the ruff that holds my head up high; each enemy's another fold to bind the more, and add a ray of glory. For hatred, like the ruff of Spanish pattern, grips like a vice, but is an aureole."

"So say aloud. Be proud and bitter," said Le Bret. "But whisper me just this, she does not love you."

V

Scarcely had Le Bret's shrewd guess hit its mark than the door swung open and in came Cyrano's successful rival, the young Baron de Neuvillette. He made his way quietly to a table, but the Gascons, inflamed by the victory of their brother-in-arms, were not minded to let him be quiet. They taunted him with being a northern greenhorn, a sickly apprentice at the art of war. They dared him to try Cyrano.

"There's one among us," boasted a cadet, "to whom you no more dare say 'Somewhat' than cry 'Rope' at him, whose father died dangling at a noose's end."

Then he proceeded to elucidate.

"Scoff—nay—suggest a comment of Cyrano's nose and your life is done," said he.

"Ah, so?" queried Christian.

Whereupon there was enacted the strangest drama the bold cadets of Gascony had ever seen. Cyrano began to tell the story of his fight. At every second he was interrupted by the new recruit from Touraine with courteously insolent queries about his nose, and with surmises as to the part it had taken in the fray. The Gascons looked for the stranger's annihilation, but Cyrano, though the veins in his face were whipcords with suppressed rage, still let young Christian live, and even forced himself on with his tale. Finally the stranger's insolence could no longer be brooked.

"Leave me! Leave me with him!" cried Cyrano to his friends, and they passed out, believing that the end had come for Christian.

But the promise to Roxane was all that dwelt in Cyrano's memory.

"Embrace me!" he said to Christian, when the room was cleared. "Embrace me! I am her brother—her cousin-brother—and she loves you."

They talked together, the two men who loved Roxane. They planned for her. Christian admitted all his dullness. Cyrano would tutor him in wit.

"I'll daily teach your tongue," said he. "Only remember and repeat to her the things I bid. So shall she never have a disillusion. Alone you fear to chill her heart. Take, then, my words—and so you shall win her. Wed them to your lips. It will amuse me. It is a good experience for a poet. Will you not do it?"

And Christian, half-dazed, sealed the bargain, and the wooing of Roxane began. Daily the lover, who could think and feel and mold his thoughts to beauty, taught the lover who was dumb. Daily Roxane, hearing Cyrano's impassioned speeches through Christian's chiselled lips, was borne deeper and deeper into the ecstasy of love. Daily Roxane told her cousin of her lover's wit and fancy. She read Cyrano verses he had written, and when he seemed scarce enthusiastic over them she taunted him with being jealous of a better poet than himself. Then Cyrano's eyes would flash with merriment, and over his mismated face a smile would run. He was not altogether sad in those days.

But Roxane's love for Christian was confessed more freely to Cyrano than to Christian himself. And as for the rest of the world, she hid it completely, fearing the vengeance of the disappointed De Guiche, who still pursued her with attentions. He had been made commander of the army. He had it in his power to send her lover to death. She beguiled him a little now and then, and when finally the orders came that the French forces should proceed to Arras, she arranged with him that the company of Cyrano should be left behind—and in that company was Christian, of whom the lord commander had not heard.

"So you will be revenged upon my cousin for his mockery of your patronage and his insolence to you," she said. "He is a very fire-eater! How he will gnash his teeth to be with all his cadets left at home when there is fighting afield."

"Who but a woman would be subtle enough to plan such a revenge!" cried the admiring De Guiche.

It was at this time that Christian was pleased to indulge in a fit of the sulks. He would have none of Cyrano's aid. He would be loved for himself, and not for Cyrano's fine speeches. He would woo Roxane in his own fashion. And he did—to such effect that Roxane, bored, dismissed him till such time as he should have his wits again.

Christian, properly repentant, overtook his tutor in the art of love beneath Roxane's balcony.

The wall that ran about the sweet green garden had benches set against it. The balcony of Roxane's window overhung the quiet little street. Dew-heavy vines fell from it, veiling all the wall in beauty.

"Oh, I shall die, Cyrano! Help me! Teach me! She has sent me away!" wailed Christian.

In the latticed window above the greenery a light flitted.

"Ssh!" cautioned Cyrano, drawing Christian back beneath the screen of vines and into the black shadow of the wall. "Ssh! She's there, and all may be repaired. Call to her, then speak as I shall bid you speak."

Then in the darkness, in the shadow of the wall beneath the lady's balcony, one lover, in low whispers, taught the other how to speak. And, that no passer-by should spoil the plan, he bade his pages play, at the entrance to the street, a tune if any one should come—"gay if a woman, sad if a man," said Cyrano.

"Roxane," called Christian's voice.

Roxane glimmered in white upon the balcony.

"Who's there?" she asked.

"'Tis I—Christian. I would speak with you."

"No! You speak too ill. Begone!"

"I pray—"

"No! You do not love me!"

"You accuse me—kind heaven, hear her!—of loving no more, when I love more and more."

"Ah!" cried Roxane. "That is a little better."

"Love grew great rocked in my restless heart, which he—the cruel—took for a cradle. And for that he was cruel. I have tried to stifle him—but vain the effort. New-born, he is still a young Hercules. And as if they were naught, he strangled the two serpents—Pride and Doubt."

"Ah! That is very good," cried Roxane. She left the shuttered window where she had been standing, as though to re-enter her room, and leaned over the balcony, peering into the darkness.

"But why do you speak so slowly?" she asked. "Have you some palsy of imagination?"

Cyrano pushed Christian further into the background, and schooling his voice to be like the youth's, answered her.

"It is that night is come," he said, "and in the dark my words must creep to find your ear."

"My words encounter no such difficulty."

"The winged words from you, madame, come down. They travel quickly. But mine must climb, and that needs longer time."

"But now they mount with speed, methinks."

"They've had practice. They have caught the art."

"I speak to you, in truth, from a great height," sighed Roxane. "I think I will come down."

"No, no!"

"Stand, then, upon the bench beneath my balcony."

"No!"

"And pray why not?"

"To speak thus, without seeing—'tis sweet. We scarce divine each other. You see a darkness, cloaked and tall, and I—the whiteness of a robe of spring. I am but a shadow, and you are light. You do not know what these minutes are to me. If sometimes I am eloquent—"

"You are?"

"Never until this hour have my words sprung straight from my heart. A blindness falls upon me when your eyes look into mine. To-night—to-night, for the first time, it seems to me that I am speaking straight to you."

"A new tone's in your voice."

"A new tone, true; for in the night that hides me I dare at last to be myself. I dare—I know not what. Forgive me that I'm moved. This—this is so sweet—so strange—"

"So strange?"

"Yes—strange to be sincere. The fear of being mocked has always locked my heart."

"Mocked? But why?"

"Ah—for my heart's wild beating! I sought to clothe my love with witty words, to hide it from the curious gaze. I longed to reach up starward, and am afraid of ridicule. I stooped and picked a wild flower. This wit of ours! To catch your fancy at the first—'twas good. But now 'twould be a profanation of the calm night to speak the words that garnish fine love letters. Come, let us look upon the stars. Let the wide sky take from us all our make-believes. I dread that, in the alchemy we're skilled in, the very essence of our love may dissolve—escape us. Ah, it is sin in love to play at fencing. The moment comes—and blessed that moment!—when every polished phrase and rounded word is sad and vain."

"And if that moment's come for us?" floated the whisper down from the balcony.

"All, all that came to me I'd toss to you in one wild cluster, not set in a bouquet. I love you! I stifle—I love! I'm mad! Do you not begin to understand, my sweet? Do you not feel my soul mount up to you? Ah, this is too beautiful, too dear—that I should tell you all and you should listen. It is too much. I never hoped for this. Could I but die now! Have words of mine the power to make you tremble there among the branches? For you do tremble like a leaf among the leaves! I feel it!

Whether you will it or not, the blessed trembling of your hand thrills through the tendrils of your jasmine."

He caught the vine and kissed it passionately.

"Oh!" cried Roxane, in a voice faint with excess of happiness, "I tremble! I weep! I love thee! I am thine! Ah, thou hast conquered me!"

And then, though Cyrano's were the words that won her, Christian's were the feet to mount to her balcony, Christian's the arms to enfold her, his the face for her kisses.

"Ah, well!" mused Cyrano, in the gloom, all sweet with white stars of flowers. "Ah, me! Some crumbs of joy still fall to me. For though you kiss his lips, the words you kiss are mine!"

VI

Now it was no part of my Lord de Guiche's plan to betake himself to Arras without pursuing the advantage he thought he had won with Roxane. She had pretended an interest in his movements. She had suggested to him a subtle scheme of revenge upon her insolent cousin. She had called him "Antoine." Surely when she had yielded so far to his love-making, surely he had but to make love a little longer to win more favor. What if she had besought him, by his love for her, to go where glory waited? Glory should wait on love.

Therefore it happened that on the night when Cyrano's love-making, mounting to Roxane's balcony, through the jasmined darkness, had broken down her coldness and had won her—for Christian—there came a friar through the still street where the ugly eloquent waited. The pages guarding the corner had played two times—gay and sad.

"Gay?" said Cyrano. "A woman passes. No. Sad? Ah, gay and sad. It is a monk."

And through the street there glided a cowled and vestured figure.

"I seek Mme. Robin—Mme. Madeleine Robin," announced the friar. "Lives she not here?"

Some subtle sense of danger to his lady made Cyrano delay the priest an instant, and while they talked Roxane and Christian came to the door with her duenna to learn the cause of the chatter.

"I have a message for your fairness," exclaimed the friar, "from a great noble."

"Ah—De Guiche!" breathed Roxane softly.

"'Tis here," and the friar drew forth the note and gave it to Roxane.

Behind Roxane stood Ragueneau, whom hungry poets had eaten out of stock and shop and whom a gay news-dealer had bereft of his wife also. At Cyrano's prayer

Roxane had made the ex-pastry cook one of her retainers, and his was the hand that held the lantern by which she read De Guiche's note. It ran:

> "Mademoiselle: The drums beat; my regiment girds its armor on; it starts. And I—they believe me gone already, but I wait. I disobey you. I am here— hidden in the convent. To-night I come to you. I send you this, to let you know, by a poor monk, as simple as a child, who has no understanding of the thing he bears. Your lips have smiled on me too sweetly, and I must see them once again. Send every one away. Receive me all alone—the bold one you forgive already—I hope it. For he is yours—"

Roxane had read the letter swiftly and softly. She turned her eyes upon its bearer and said:

"Father, this is what the letter bids me. Listen:

> "Mademoiselle: All must bow to the cardinal's will, no matter how hard it seems. Therefore I send these lines to your fair hands by this devout, this wise and cautious friar. It is our will that he pronounce upon you, in your own dwelling, within the hour, the nuptial benediction. Christian becomes your husband, secretly. We send him to you. He does not please you, but resign yourself. Think well how Heaven will reward your zeal, and be always assured, mademoiselle, of the respect of him who is and who will always be your very humble servant."

The simple friar looked up with delight.

"The noble gentleman!" he said. "I knew there was no wrong planned."

Roxane's smile for a second was inscrutable. Then she threw herself into her part.

"This—this is unbearable!" she cried. "Marry him!"

The friar looked at Cyrano.

"Is this the choice made for mademoiselle?" he asked with sympathy.

"No. I am!" cried Christian.

The good friar's lantern swung slowly around. He was puzzled. Why should Roxane object to wed this highly favored youth? Roxane saw the dawning suspicion in his eyes.

"Ah, stay!" she exclaimed. "A postscript!—'Give to the convent twenty pistoles.'"

"The noble lord!" said the reassured friar. "Come, mademoiselle, resign yourself to the cardinal's will."

"I am resigned," said Roxane, with the air of a martyr. Then she said in a quick undertone to Cyrano:

"De Guiche comes. Keep him out till I am wed."

"Father," said Cyrano, "how long will this marrying take?"

"A quarter of an hour will suffice."

"No one shall enter for that time," whispered Cyrano to Roxane; and as the wedding party filed into the house he began his lonely guarding beneath the balcony.

At the corner of the street the flutes played a sad air. The pages thus announced the coming of a man.

"It's he," said Cyrano. "How shall I keep him? How detain him? I have it! Now, Cyrano, forget the Paris accent. Assume again the twang of Bergerac."

He climbed lithe as a cat into the branches by Roxane's balcony. He clung to them, ready to fall at the proper instant. De Guiche came along, grumbling softly to himself in the darkness.

"Which is the house?" he growled. "This mask half blinds me. Ah! That's it. I think that's it. What can that idiot friar be about? What's this? What's this? Where did that man fall from?"

For Cyrano had fallen straight before his path heavily, as though from some great height.

"From the moon," he answered gruffly.

"What!" cried De Guiche, retreating a step from the madman.

"Where am I? What's the hour? What country is this? What day of the week? What time of the year? I am stunned. I fell like a bomb straight from the moon."

De Guiche made fruitless efforts to stay the apparent maniac's flow of words or to pass him. But Cyrano rushed on.

"It may have been a hundred years. It may have been a second only. I do not know. I only know that there—up in that ball of yellow saffron—"

"Let me pass, sir!" cried De Guiche.

"Oh, where am I? Tell me the truth, keep nothing back. Where is it that I am? Where have I fallen like a shooting star? I had no time to choose the place where I should land. Oh, tell me? Where am I? But great heavens. Let me look on you! You're black! Have I, then, fallen into Africa? Are you a native?"

De Guiche, puzzled for an instant by the reference to his complexion, suddenly recalled his mask.

"Oh, my mask!" he exclaimed.

"Ah! am I, then, in Venice? Or in Rome?"

"I go—a lady waits me!"

"Now I am sure!" cried Cyrano. "I am in Paris!"

In spite of himself the impatient lord laughed. At once the maniac from the moon, with an air of complete good comradeship, began to apologize for his appearance.

"So 'tis to Paris that I've fallen! You'll pardon me my looks? I've journeyed far, you see. My eyes are full of star dust. And my spurs are tangled with the planets' filaments. See, I must brush me! A comet's hair is on my doublet. In my leg, if you'll believe me—nay, do not hurry—there's a tooth of the Great Bear who bit me as I passed. And if you'd press my nose, monsieur, between your fingers, milk would run forth. You are astonished? 'Twas from the Milky Way. A most amazing journey. I mean to write it for a book, and the small gold stars I carry will serve for asterisks."

Again and again De Guiche essayed to pass. Again and again Cyrano frustrated him. He did it all with such whimsical grace that, despite his annoyance, the noble lord found himself amused and interested. A rendezvous with a lady, no matter how fair—that might befall one any night, but a talk with a man who, crazy though he certainly was, had all astronomy and all mythology at his tongue's tip—that was of less frequent possibility.

Cyrano was in the midst of a description of his method of mounting to the moon.

"At the hour when the moon woos the sea," he said, "I lay me on the shore fresh from the sea bath. And keeping the head first— for the hair holds sea water—I mounted in the air, straight, straight as an angel! Then—"

"Then?" queried the half-hypnotized De Guiche.

"Then—but the quarter of an hour is passed. Sir, you are free; the marriage is made!"

De Guiche sprang forward.

"What!" he cried. "Am I mad? That voice! That nose! Cyrano?"

Cyrano bowed low.

"Cyrano, at your service," he replied. "While we have chatted they have plighted vows."

VII

One thing Roxane had overlooked in making her hasty plans for a wedding to thwart De Guiche's hopes. She had forgotten that, while the commander of the forces remained in Paris, the soldiers left there were under his direction. Her husband and her cousin must do the bidding of their chief. And the chief's bidding that night, when he found himself fooled by the woman he had believed half-won to his dishonorable love, and by her insolent cousin, to whom he owed a long-due grudge, was not a light one. The Gascon cadets were ordered straight to Arras.

No time was given the young bride to weep farewells. Her husband, before the marriage vows had ceased to vibrate in the air, was hurried forth. Scarce had she time to beg her valiant cousin to keep her lord safe in battle, prudent in danger, faithful to her, and a dozen other easy things, when both were gone, and De Guiche, vanquished in love, felt himself victor at any rate in cruelty.

At Arras life was not a pleasant affair. Though the French troops were the besiegers, they suffered for provisions almost as keenly as if they had been in the fortified town they attacked. For, while they bombarded the town, the troops of Spain gathered about them, and thus there was a siege within a siege, and the forces of France were as hungry as the men in the town.

Things had reached a crisis one morning. Even the Gascons vowed that they had not come out to fight the gray wolf hunger. They grumbled fiercely at their lot. They picked the commander to pieces; they found fault with his wide lace collar and his manners of the court. Hunger gnawed at them until they were ready to mutiny against even their beloved captain, Carbon de Castel-Jaloux.

Cyrano, returning from a mad dash he made each morning through the Spanish lines, that he might send to Roxane in Paris love letters all signed Christian, for the bargain made in Ragueneau's bakeshop still held force, found all the camp in turmoil. The men had vowed they would no longer stand their lot.

Cyrano himself was scarcely ruddy, scarcely strong. But it took more than the want of food to kill his courage. At his captain's command he began to rally the men. First it was with jests.

"If you be so hungry, eat your patience, then," he counseled one grumbler.

"Always your pointed word!" cried the man whom he rebuked.

"So would I die," said Cyrano, "like this, making a pointed word for a good cause, felled by a thrust from some brave adversary's sword. Thus would I die—upon the blood-stained earth—a point within my heart, a point upon my lips."

They did not care for that, the Gascons. Their answer was:

"We're hungry!"

Then Cyrano bade the fifer play and do the work his wit had failed in doing.

"Play not the calls to battle," he commanded, "but simple things they heard of old in Gascony—each piping note like the call of a little sister. Let them rise slow, like the slow rising smoke that curls from out our chimneys there. Play the tunes the goatherds play—now heard, now lost down in the valley. Hear you it not? See you not your country the evening purpling on the river, the woods, the hills, with huddling sheep the shepherd drives? See you not Gascony?"

The men sat staring—not at the camp, not the arms, the sentinels, the trappings of war, but far past all these into far Gascony. The higher love had killed the lower. Homesickness drove out hunger.

It was thus that De Guiche found them—Gascons again, who could laugh at starvation as they would laugh at whistling bullets. They were ready to bear themselves before him with their customary air of insolent high spirit.

He did not like their manner. He, too, was hungry. Their eyes seemed always to challenge his courage. Today he even went as far as to boast of his stratagem of the day before, when, dropping the white scarf that showed his rank, he had escaped from a detachment of the enemy, only to return later and rout it.

"Ah!" said Cyrano. "The white plume of Henry of Navarre had not been dropped thus. Some would not so lightly abdicate the honor of serving for a target. Had I been there, I would have picked it up and put it on."

"A Gascon boast," sneered De Guiche.

"Nay, give it me and I will wear it."

"Another boast. It's gone—dropped in the Spanish lines where none may venture—as you knew."

From his pocket Cyrano drew forth the scarf.

"I found it there this morning," said he, bowing. "Permit that I return it."

The rage on the commander's face gave place to an uglier look.

"I thank you," he said. "I'll use it for a signal. See, here upon the ramparts I wave it. A man below there runs—a false Spanish spy. He came to warn me that the Spanish will this day attack us, for our force is weakened. Perhaps you did not know it, but the marshal secretly has gone with a strong escort to Dourleus, where the king's provisions are. Our camp being thus made vulnerable, the Spanish will attack it. And with the scarf you very kindly gave to me I have just signaled to the false spy to tell his general that this is the weakest spot to fall upon. Here the attack will begin. You'll have a chance to prove your boasted courage, sirs. The marshal shall return in time to save the day for us, but not to save the men who are first assaulted. Brave Gascons, who complain of paltry odds, be good enough to let yourselves be killed."

He finished with his sneer. Carbon was already forming his men in line of resistance. Cyrano bowed low to De Guiche in thanks, and to the cadets he cried:

"So we shall win for the Gascon coat-of-arms, with its six bars of blue and gold, the blood-red one it lacked."

And to Christian he said:

"My heart misgave me this would be to-day. Here is the letter that I wrote for you to send Roxane. A farewell letter. It is sad. Death matters not, but not to look upon her face again—for you, I mean—oh, that is terrible!"

On the rampart a sentinel called. There was a rumble of wheels. Men rushed to the wall. A cry came from a carriage.

"In the king's service!" was the reply to the challenge.

"The kings?" exclaimed De Guiche.

The carriage rolled in, dusty and mud-bespattered. It pulled up suddenly. The drums beat a salute. The carriage steps were lowered—and Roxane jumped out.

"Good-day, sirs," she called cheerfully, as they all fell back and gazed at her.

No one spoke until De Guiche forced his question.

"On the king's service?"

"To be sure!" cried she merrily. "King love's! What other king!"

VIII

They gazed at her, stupefied with surprise, the men of Gascony. Christian stared dumfounded like the rest. Through Cyrano's lips a cry had come—a cry of pain and joy and loneliness and adoration for her daring. The others merely gaped like rustics.

"The siege," said Roxane airily, as though she spoke of a play. "The siege is too long."

De Guiche aroused himself. He remembered the fluttering white scarf that had bade his foes attack this spot.

"Madame," he cried, "you cannot stay here!"

"Oh, but I can!" retorted Roxane, still roseate, dimpled, daring mistress of the situation, queen of the men. "Will not some one roll a drum here? I would sit upon it. Ah! thank you. They fired at my carriage. Think of that. Good-morrow, Christian. Catch this salute I waft you from my finger tips. Yes, fired at it. How came I through? The Spanish lines, of course. A difficult matter, do you think? Nay, not at all. I told the truth—used no diplomacy. Whenever some fierce don would stop and demand my passport of me, I smiled upon him through the window; and when he asked whither I journeyed, I answered truly, 'I go to see my lover.' And then not one tried to stay me!"

She finished proudly, simply, with a look at Christian. Cyrano, watching her, went wild. But De Guiche, with the thought of his order in his mind, had no time to rage at lovers' glances. "You must leave this place at once," he said. "There is no time to lose. It is not safe."

"You are going to fight!" she cried. "I shall stay here."

"It is a post of deadly danger," said De Guiche.

"Of danger? So, sir, you would make a widow of me? You protest? No matter. I will not stir a step from here. A fight? I never saw one. It will be amusing! And my hat! You will observe it could not have been chosen better to accord with a battle scene. And you, my Lord de Guiche, were it not wise that you retire to headquarters? The attack may soon begin."

"This is unbearable!" cried his lordship. "I go—but for a few minutes only. I will return."

His departure was the signal for the wildest outbreak on the part of the Gascons. Hair was curled, doublets laced, ruffles smoothed, presentations made to the beauty and the wit of Paris, whom love for one of them had brought so far afield.

"Had I but a nut to eat," cried one youth, "I could die happy, having looked upon her face."

"Hungry?" called Roxane. "Ah, Ragueneau, Ragueneau!"

And forthwith out from the carriage sprang the ex-cook. He carried food; he bore bottles. The Gascons shouted with joy to see the viands. And there, with death hastening to them, the cadets picnicked, banqueted, and made merry in the presence of Roxane.

Cyrano had sought out Christian early in her visit.

"Be not surprised," he whispered, "to learn that you have written oftener than you knew. I have—I have sent her more than you knew of. . . . I've written—frequently. Before dawn I've slipped through the lines to send them—a mere trifle."

"How often have you written?" demanded Christian. "Twice a week?"

"Oh, oftener!"

"Daily?"

"Yes; twice a day."

"And the author's joy was so mad a one to you that you dared death—"

"Hush!" whispered Cyrano. "Here she comes."

Christian went to meet his wife.

"Now tell me all," he said, "why you have come this perilous way, why you have braved these dangers—roughnesses."

"You drew me here," she answered, "your letters, love. The last one—reading it, I could not bear to stay from you. Oh, love! Do not speak. Let me tell you all the tale—how from the night when, underneath my window, you sent your soul to mine, I have adored you. Before—I blush to own it—I crave your pardon for it— I loved you only for your look. But then, your soul, your soul it was! And all your letters since. Ah! I have grown altogether yours; this month as I have read, my soul was faint for love. Ah, Christian, you have triumphed over yourself: you've won me anew. I love you only for your soul who loved you once but for your beauty."

"Do not say it," he appealed.

"But I must! Were you ugly—hideous—I still should love you utterly!"

"My God!" cried Christian chokingly, seeing the whole miserable web he had spun for himself. But before Roxane could even ask the cause of his dismay the cadets were crowding about their queen. Their captain had fastened her little lace handkerchief on a pole for a flag. They pressed about her, glad to look on her before they died. Apart from them, Christian, half-mad with bitterness, had sought Cyrano.

"It's you she loves," he said. "She told me so. My soul, she called it, would have loved me had my face been ugly. I will no longer bear this. I'll be loved for myself alone, for myself as I am. I'll tell her all. She shall choose between us. Nay, do not try to stay me. Shall I, because by chance my face is fair, destroy your happiness? I'll tell her. Our marriage, secret, unwitnessed, can easily be set aside. You'll have your chance. She'll have her choice."

"She will choose you," said Cyrano.

"Roxane, Roxane!" called Christian.

She came toward them, smiling, sweet, her face effulgent with the love that glowed within her heart. Cyrano grew dizzy at the sight and the wild hope of happiness that had leaped to life.

"Cyrano has something to tell you," said Christian, and was gone.

"He doubts my love!" said she, looking half-puzzled after him. "He did not quite believe that I would love him were he—"

"Ugly?" said Cyrano.

"Ugly," said she, blushing to say the word before him.

"Were he hideous—disfigured, grotesque."

"He could not be grotesque to me! I'd love him all the more."

The blood rushed through Cyrano's veins like fire. He trembled, lost himself.

"Roxane," he cried. "Roxane! I have something to tell you."

"Listen! I—"

Beyond them was a sound of firing.

He ceased to speak. He listened. Roxane, cold with a sudden sense of danger, looked up. A messenger hurried toward them. Behind him came cadets bearing something shapeless covered over.

"Now I can tell her," muttered Cyrano.

Roxane pushed forward. The cadets lay their burden down. Some sought to hold her back, but she flew toward the cloaked, still figure lying there. She screamed and pushed the cloak aside.

"Christian!" she screamed. "Christian! Christian!"

But Christian could not hear.

IX

So, ironically, fate had sped the bullets there at Arras. The young husband, adored and adoring, died. The man who prayed but for a soldier's death, the man whose hopeless ugliness forbade him hope of love, and whose high honor would not let him tell the story of the wooing—he lived on.

Roxane, widowed thus, went back to Paris. But she was no more the *precieuse* Roxane. She sought the peace of the convent—not as a nun, for she would not so falsify the human love her heart held for the lover killed at Arras, but as a boarder merely. There she could brood upon her sorrow, there live again the brief hours she had lived with Christian. She had no duties save to his memory. She cherished in her heart all the words of fire and honey dew that once thrilled through her veins. Upon her bosom always lay the letter they found upon him there at Arras—the letter he had meant to send Roxane, a blood-stained, tear-stained missive.

She was not unhappy in the still convent and in the great park that surrounded it. At first De Guiche came often to her, but the great nobleman grew busier as years went by, and his calls upon her were less frequent. But Cyrano never failed her. Week after week, year after year, the same hour of the same day brought him to her—still the poet, the philosopher—still the warrior, fighting shams and wrongs with naked blade, and knowing not the uses of diplomacy, always at heart the lover of Roxane, always in manner her faithful friend.

The good sisters liked him more than passing well. They liked the gossip of the court with which he brightened Roxane's days. They liked—sweet souls—his teasing of their piety.

One Saturday, fifteen years after the day when the white scarf of De Guiche had bade the Spanish attack at Arras, Roxane sat waiting for her friend. She had been receiving somewhat that afternoon. De Guiche had called upon her—changed, bent with weight of many honors. Le Bret had been there, telling her of Cyrano's impudences.

"True," she said, "he has never taught his tongue to wait upon his interests. He makes fresh enemies, I know. But still his sword is long. He holds his foes in check."

Le Bret had shaken his head dubiously. Then he had said:

"I fear for him not simply an attack, but loneliness and hunger, and the cold within his dreary chamber. He is poor, madame. He has but one shabby suit of serge."

"Yet," the duke had interrupted, "he is not to be pitied."

"The Lord Marshal of France may well make little of the trifling discomforts of my friend," Le Bret answered somewhat bitterly.

"I know that I have all and he has nothing," said De Guiche, "but I'd be proud to take his hand—I envy him. When life seems most successful, though one has won success by no foul means, even then there is a vague unrest. It's not remorse. It's disillusion. Ah, the ermined mantle of the duke rustles as it moves with sound of lost hopes and vain regrets, as a woman's gown sweeps dead leaves in its folds. . . . Cyrano's happier."

Then he turned toward Le Bret as Roxane walked toward a sister in the garden.

"Monsieur Le Bret," he said, "it is true that none dare openly attack your friend. But he has many foes. It was but yesterday at the queen's card-table that I heard them say: 'Cyrano may die yet—by accident.' Bid him be prudent; stay at home."

"Cyrano prudent!" said Le Bret. "Ah, well, I'll warn him."

Then Roxane's callers had gone, and she waited in the mellow afternoon for the coming of the one her heart named friend.

X

When her callers had left her alone Roxane played with her embroidery silk and waited for the coming of her friend. Beyond the garden wall Le Bret, advancing on his way to give Cyrano the warning from the duke, was suddenly stopped by Ragueneau.

Ragueneau was white to the very lips. His eyes stuck out with mortal horror.

"Listen, listen!" he cried breathlessly. "Your friend—our friend—Cyrano—"

"What is it? What is it?" pressed Le Bret, in terror, shaking the unnerved newsbearer's arm. "Speak quick, man! Speak!"

"He came from out his house just now—a little while ago. He turned the corner— he was coming here. I saw him. I hurried toward him, and I saw—from out a window, a lackey throw a block of wood. Perhaps an accident—"

"But Cyrano? Oh, the cowards!"

"I ran. I saw him, sir. Our friend, our poet, struck straight to the ground, bleeding from a great wound in his head!"

"Not dead? Not dead?" cried Le Bret in an agony of fear.

"Not yet. I bore him to his room—his garret."

"Does he suffer much?"

"Not at all. He is unconscious," replied Ragueneau.

"You called a doctor?"

"One came—he was charitable."

"My poor Cyrano! Roxane must not learn this too suddenly. What did the doctor say?"

"Oh, I don't know," said Ragueneau impatiently. "He spoke of fever—meningitis. But, pray you, come. He's all alone. Ah! Could you see him—all his head bound up, his poor white face, unseeing eyes! Come. Should he come to himself and move upon his bed with no one by, he'd die."

Le Bret nodded, and the two men ran toward Cyrano's lodging. In the garden Roxane still waited for her friend. She bent over her embroidery frame and watched the sisters bring the armchair where he was wont to sit beside her.

"He's late!" she said. "What can it be? My faithful *Court Gazette* behind his time after so many years? The portress keeps him—preaching how to save his soul. Ah, yes! That must be it."

She played with her needle, scanned the sky, mused, smiling, on his goodness to her, fumbled in her workbag for her thimble, frowned at her pattern, tapped her foot impatiently, then resolved to work, and began her stitching.

"Monsieur de Bergerac," announced a little sister, coming up behind her.

"At last," said Roxane. She did not turn or raise her eyes. Some faint coquetry even in that she called her friendship bade her play thus with him. Besides, his coming was the punctual coming of the sun, and she took it with the same calm habit. She searched among her silks as she spoke to him.

"You're late! The first time in all these years."

Cyrano's face was very white. He had walked toward her stiffly, as one holds himself who fears to fall. Each step was taken with a pulling at the legs. His hat, jammed low upon his face, concealed a bandage round his head.

"I was stayed," he apologized, "by a most unwelcome visitor." He seemed to wrench the words out from his chest by jerks as he had pulled himself along to where she sat.

"Some creditor, I suppose?" said Roxane.

"The last creditor who has a debt to collect from me!"

"Ah, fortunate man, so nearly clear of debt! And is it paid?"

"Not yet, I bade him wait. I said I had a rendezvous which nothing should defer. I told him to call again in just an hour."

"A creditor can always wait," said Roxaue airily. "You shall not leave me until twilight time. But what's the matter? You have not teased Sister Martha?"

Sister Martha was walking by. Cyrano called to her. But his teasing lacked its old ring, and suddenly he said:

"Listen, sister! I give you leave to pray for me to-night at chapel time."

"I have not waited your permission to pray for you," said she, smiling, and walked on. Cyrano watched Roxane's fingers over her embroidery.

"I'll never see it finished," he said.

"Ah! I knew that time-worn jest would come," laughed Roxane. Then a silence fell between them, broken only by the swirling of the golden autumn leaves.

"My *Court Gazette* seems dull to-day," she ventured finally.

Then, whiter and whiter, he forced the story of a week's gossip to his lips and weakened at the end of it, fell back, Roxane looked toward him in alarm.

"It's nothing," he said, recovering himself. "My old wound—got at Arras—it still troubles me."

"Ah, both of us were wounded there, and both still bear the marks of our hurt," said Roxane. "I have his letter still resting just above my heart."

"You said that some day I should read it."

"And so you shall, to-day. See, here it is, hung in this bag. Open it and read."

"I have your leave to read it now?" he asked, holding it tenderly with a queer smile about the corners of his ashy lips.

"I fain would hear you read it," she said softly.

The smile deepened, but it was not all a smile; it was a long regret, a memory and an adoration blent in one look. He opened it and looked on Christian's last words to his wife.

XI

Cyrano's face the tender light deepened. Roxane watched him with a curious eagerness. From the chapel came the full notes of the organ. The purple twilight began to gloom among the golden-tinted leaves.

"Roxane, farewell," read he, in a voice that pulsed with feeling. Then he repeated it:

> "Roxane, farewell! Death waits for me—
> This very night he claims me, dear.
> And all my soul bowed with the weight
> Of love untold, feels him draw near."

"How you read it!" cried Roxane. But Cyrano did not hear. He was reading with his heart, full of the stored love of years.

> "I die. I never more shall feast
> With hungry eyes upon the grace
> With which you move your hand to brush
> Your little curls or touch your face."

The purple deepened into black about them. Roxane waited. Still he read on:

> "I cry to you, my dear, my sweet!
> Not once has my heart swerved, my own.
> And I am he who now—and then—
> Beyond the stars—is yours alone."

His voice rang out, triumphant, glorious. The letter rested in his hand. Roxane touched him.

"You read the letter you had never seen—and look, it is too dark to see!"

"Roxane!" he cried with a great start.

"For fourteen years you've played this part. Ah, blind that I was! I should have known, I should have felt your voice each time be spoke my name!"

"Roxane!" cried Cyrano again, past all other speech.

"Those words of fire and honey dew—all yours, all yours! The voice that thrilled my jasmine vine to me—yours, yours. Your soul, your soul, in everything!"

"Indeed, indeed, it is not so," protested he. "It was your husband."

"You loved me," cried Roxane.

"Not I."

"See how you falter."

"No, no, my dear. I swear I never loved you."

"Your letter and your tears I've worn above my heart—the letter every word of which was yours."

"But all the bloodstains his."

"Why did you keep such silence? Why?" begged Roxane.

Cyrano hesitated, and while she looked to him for answer through the gates there broke Ragueneau and Le Bret.

"Madman!" cried Le Bret. "Ah, madame, pardon me, but he has courted death by coming here."

"True!" laughed Cyrano. "I forgot. The chronicle was never finished. Here is an item: 'On Saturday, at dinner time, the assassination of De Bergerac.' Mark you my bandages!"

He took his hat off, and for the first time Roxane saw the bandaged head. Half wild, she begged for enlightenment.

"All that I asked or hoped," said Cyrano, "was but to die a hero's death—'a point upon my lip, a point within my heart.' And see! I am struck down by a footman from the rear. Mocked even in death! There, Ragueneau, why weep you so? Come! Come! What is it you do now?"

"I trimmed the lights for Molière's stage," sobbed Ragueneau. "But I'll do so no more. But yesterday he brought on 'Scapin'—and a whole scene was yours—the one beginning *'Que Diabk allait—il faire.'* Ah! How they laughed."

"That was life," said Cyrano; "to be the one who prompted them and whom they all forget. Roxane, do you recall the night when Christian talked to you beneath your balcony? Ah, well! That was the story of my whole life there. While I stood low, deep in the shadow, the others climbed to snatch the kiss of glory. 'Tis justice. And here upon my grave's dim sill I approve it. Molière's genius, Christian's beauty."

Down the chapel alleyway the sisters, darkly seen through the sunlight, walked. The chapel bell rang.

"Sisters!" cried Roxane, starting toward them.

"Nay!" pleaded Cyrano. "Do not go for any one. When you came back I should be gone. Listen, the organ plays."

"I love you," cried Roxane. "Live, live for me."

"Nay," smiled Cyrano sadly. "In fairy tales alone do the ill-starred grow beautiful, when at the end the lady says 'I love you.' I, you see—I am the same up to the last."

"I made your misery. I—I."

"You made my happiness. I never knew the sweetness of a woman's love. My mother could not find me fair. I never had a sister. Later I feared a mistress would but mock at me. But I have had a friend; grace to you a woman's robe has fluttered in my life!"

The moon came up through the branches. He looked at it, but Roxane looked on him.

"To-night," he smiled with whimsical remembrance. "I'll make my lunar trip with no projectile's aid. There they will send me for my paradise. More than one soul I have loved is there in exile. I shall find again— Galileo, Socrates—. Come, come, you weep! Le Bret, you used to scold me. What? Ah, yes! Cadets of Gascony are there! Copernicus has said—"

"Oh!" wailed Roxane, "I cannot bear it."

"*Mais que diable allait—il faire en cette galire?*" he raved on.

"Philosopher, physician, versifier and musician. Made an aerial expedition and many famous duels fought. Lover, too—after a fashion. Here lies Hercule Savinien de Cyrano de Birgerac—a bit of everything, yet naught!"

He fell unhausted in his chair. He raised his eyes to Roxane and seemed again himself.

"Be not less faithful to his memory," he said, "but wear your weeds for two."

"I swear it."

His glazing eyes were fixed upon the trees. He started to his feet. They rushed to hold him, but he waved them back.

"It comes," he said, "I feel my feet shod with marble, my hands gloved heavily with lead. But since death treads the path, I'll wait him standing—and sword in hand."

"Cyrano!" cried Roxane, half-fainting. But he never heard her. His eyes were still fixed straight ahead.

"He looks upon my nose! The impudent! What's that you say? It's useless? Ah, I know it. But no one fights for mere success. No, no! It is more beautiful because it's fruitless. Who are you, there, you thousands? I know you every one. All my old enemies. Ah, Fakehood, there! Have at you! Have at you!"—his sword was aimed at the shadows. "And you old Compromise? And Prejudice and Treachery! See how I strike you! Treat with you? Never! And you there, too, Folly, you?—I always knew that at the end you'd throw me to the earth. What matters it? I fight, I fight, I fight you still!"

They watched him strike at his old foes, the few who loved him. He stopped, breathless. Then, after a pause, he went on:

"Yes, you have snatched from me the laurel and the rose. Take all! In spite of you there is one thing I bear, and when to-night I enter into heaven and widely make obeisance at the threshold blue, one thing without a crease—without a stain—I bear with me in spite of you."

In the moonlight they strained their eyes to see him. They listened, holding their breath, for the last word.

"And that—and that?" whispered Roxane.

He fell back into Le Bret's outstretched arms. But through the blue and silver of the night she saw his smile. She bent over him. She kissed his forehead. She whispered once again:

"And that?"

"And that?" he answered, smiling into her eyes, "is my soldier's plume unstained."

CRILLON'S STAKE

STANLEY J. WEYMAN

O N A CERTAIN WET NIGHT, IN THE SPRING OF THE YEAR 1587, THE RAIN WAS
doing its utmost to sweeten the streets of old Paris: the kennels were aflood
with it, and the March wind, which caused the crowded sign-boards to
creak and groan on their bearings, and ever and anon closed a shutter with the sound of
a pistol-shot, blew the downpour in sheets into exposed doorways, and drenched to the
skin the few wayfarers who were abroad. Here and there a stray dog, bent over a bone,
slunk away at the approach of a roisterer's footstep; more rarely a passenger, whose
sober or stealthy gait whispered of business rather than pleasure, moved cowering from
street to street, under such shelter as came in his way.

About two hours before midnight, a man issued somewhat suddenly from the
darkness about the head of the Pont du Change and turned the corner into the Rue
de St. Jacques la Boucherie, a street which ran parallel with the Quays, about half a
mile east of the Louvre. His heavy cloak concealed his figure, but he made his way in
the teeth of the wind with the spring and vigour of youth; and arriving presently at a
doorway, which had the air of retiring modestly under a couple of steep dark gables, and
yet was rendered conspicuous by the light which shone through the unglazed grating
above it, he knocked sharply on the oak. After a short delay the door slid open of itself
and the man entered. He showed none of a stranger's surprise at the invisibility of the
porter, but after staying to shut the door, he advanced along a short passage, which was
only partially closed at the further end by a high wooden screen. Coasting round this
he entered a large low-roofed room, lighted in part by a dozen candles, in part by a fire
which burned on a raised iron plate in the corner.

The air was thick with wood smoke, but the occupants of the room, a dozen men,
seated, some at a long table, and some here and there in pairs, seemed able to recognise
the newcomer through it, and hailed his appearance with a cry of welcome—a cry
that had in it a ring of derision. One man who stood near the fire, impatiently kicking
the logs with his spurred boots, turned, and seeing who it was moved towards him.
"Welcome, M. de Bazan," he said briskly; "so you have come to resume our duel! I had
given up hope of you."

"I am here," the newcomer answered. He spoke curtly, and as he did so he took off his horseman's cloak and laid it aside. The action disclosed a man scarcely twenty, moderately well dressed, and of slight though supple figure. His face wore an air of determination singular in one so young, and at variance with the quick suspicious glances with which he took in the scene. He did not waste time in staring, however, but quickly and with a businesslike air he seated himself at a small wooden table which stood in a warm corner of the hearth, and directly under a brace of candles. Calling for a bottle of wine, he threw a bag of coin on the table; at the same time he hitched forward his sword until the pommel of the weapon lay across his left thigh; a sinister movement which the debauched and reckless looks of some of his companions seemed to justify. The man who had addressed him took his seat opposite, and the two, making choice of a pair of dice-boxes, began to play.

They did not use the modern game of hazard, but simply cast the dice, each taking it in turn to throw, and a nick counting as a drawn battle. The two staked sums higher than were usual in the company about them, and one by one, the other gamblers forsook their tables, and came and stood round. As the game proceeded, the young stranger's face grew more and more pale, his eyes more feverish. But he played in silence. Not so his backers. A volley of oaths and exclamations almost as thick as the wood smoke that in part shrouded the game, began to follow each cast of the dice. The air, one moment still and broken only by the hollow rattle of the dice in the box, rang the next instant with the fierce outburst of a score of voices.

The place, known as Simon's, was a gaming-house of the second class: frequented, as the shabby finery of some and the tarnished arms of others seemed to prove, by the poorer courtiers and the dubious adventurers who live upon the great. It was used in particular by the Guise faction, at this time in power; for though Henry of Valois was legal and nominal King of France, Henry of Guise, the head of the League, and the darling of Paris, imposed his will alike upon the King and the favourites. He enjoyed the substance of power; the King had no choice but to submit to his policy. In secret Henry the Third resented the position, and between his immediate servants and the arrogant followers of the Guises there was bitter enmity.

As the game proceeded, a trifle showed that the young player was either ignorant of politics, or belonged to a party rarely represented at Simon's. For some time he and his opponent had enjoyed equal luck. Then they doubled the stakes, and fortune immediately declared herself against him; with wondrous quickness his bag grew lank and thin, the pile at the other's elbow a swollen sliding heap. The perspiration began to stand on the young man's face. His hand trembled as he shook out the last coins left in the bag and shoved them forward amid a murmur half of derision half of sympathy; for if he was a stranger from the country—that was plain, and they had recognised it at his first appearance among them three days before—at least he played bravely. His opponent, whose sallow face betrayed neither joy nor triumph, counted out an equal sum, and pushed it forward without a word. The young man took up the box, and for the first time seemed to hesitate; it could be seen that he had bitten his lip until it bled. "After you," he muttered at last, withdrawing his hand. He shrank from throwing his last throw.

"It is your turn," the other replied impassively, "but as you will." He shook the box, brought it down sharply on the table and raised it. "The Duke!" he said with an oath—he had thrown the highest possible. "Twelve is the game."

With a shiver the lad—he was little more than a lad, though in his heart, perhaps, the greatest gambler present—dashed down his box. He raised it. "The King!" he cried; "long life to him!" He had also thrown twelve. His cheek flushed a rosy red, and with a player's superstitious belief in his luck he regarded the check given to his opponent in the light of a presage of victory. They threw again, and he won by two points—nine to seven. Hurrah!

"King or Duke," the tall man answered, restraining by a look the interruption which more than one of the bystanders seemed about to offer, "the money is yours; take it."

"Let it lie," the young man answered joyously. His eyes sparkled. When the other had pushed an equal amount into the middle of the table, he threw again, and with confidence.

Alas! his throw was a deuce and an ace. The elder player threw four and two. He swept up the pile. "Better late than never," he said. And leaning back he looked about him with a grin of satisfaction.

The young man rose. The words which had betrayed that he was not of the Duke's faction, had cost him the sympathy the spectators had before felt for him; and no one spoke. It was something that they kept silence, that they did not interfere with him. His face, pale in the light of the candles which burned beside him, was a picture of despair. Suddenly, as if he bethought him of something, he sat down again, and with a shaking hand took from his neck a slender gold chain with a pendant ornament. "Will you stake against this?" he murmured with dry lips.

"Against that, or your sword, or your body, or anything but your soul!" the other answered, with a reckless laugh. He took up the chain and examined it. "I will set you thirty crowns against it!" he said.

They threw and the young man lost.

"I will stake ten crowns against your sword if you like," the victor continued, eyeing the curiously chased pommel.

"No," the young man replied, stung by something in the elder's tone. "That I may want. But I will set my life against yours!"

A chuckle went round. "Bravo!" cried half a dozen voices. One man in the rear, whose business it was to enlist men in the Duke's guard, pressed forward, scenting a recruit.

"Your life against mine! With these?" the winner answered, holding up the dice.

"Yes, or as you please." He had not indeed meant with those: he had spoken in the soreness of defeat, intending a challenge.

The other shook his head. "No," he said, "no. No man can say that Michel Berthaud ever balked his player, but it is not a fair offer. You have lost all, my friend, and I have won all. I am rich, you are poor. 'Tis no fair stake. But I will tell you what I will do. I will set you your gold chain and seventy crowns—against your life if you like."

A roar of laughter hailed the proposal. "A hundred!" cried several, "a hundred!"

"Very well. The gold chain and a hundred. Be it so!"

"But my life?" the young man muttered, gazing at him in bewilderment. "Of what use will it be to you, M. Berthaud?"

"That is my business," was the dry answer. "If you lose, it is forfeit to me. That is all, and the long and the short of it. To be frank, I have a service which I wish you to perform for me."

"And if I will not perform it?"

"Then I will take your word as a gentleman that you will kill yourself. Observe, however, that if I win I shall allow you a choice, my friend."

He leaned back with that, meeting with a faint smile and half-lowered eyelids, the various looks bent on him. Some stared, some nodded secret comprehension, some laughed outright, or nudged one another and whispered. For four evenings they, the *habitués* of the place, had watched this play duel go on, but they had not looked for an end so abnormal as this. They had known men stake wives and mistresses, love and honour, ay, their very clothes, and go home naked through the streets; for the streets of Paris saw strange things in those days. But life? Well, even that they had seen men stake in effect, once, twice, a hundred times; but never in so many words, never on a wager as novel as this. So with an amazement which no duel, fought as was the custom in that day, three to three, or six to six, would have evoked, they gathered round the little table under the candles and waited for the issue.

The young man shivered. Then, "I accept," he said slowly. In effect he was desperate, driven to his last straits. He had lost his all, the all of a young man sent up to Paris to make his fortune, with a horse, his sword, and a bag of crowns—the latter saved for him by a father's stern frugality, a mother's tender self-denial. A week ago he had never seen a game of chance. Then he had seen; the dice had fallen in his way, the devil of play, cursed legacy of some long-forgotten ancestor, had awoke within him, and this was the end. "I accept," he said slowly.

His opponent, still with his secretive smile, took up the caster. But a short, sturdy man, who was standing at his elbow, and who wore the colours of the Duke of Guise, intervened. "No, Michel," he said, with a good-natured glance at the young player. "Let the lad choose his bones, and throw first or last as he pleases."

"Right," said Berthaud, yawning. "It is no matter. My star is in the ascendant to-night. He will not win."

The young man took up the box, shook it, hesitated, swallowed, and threw seven!

Berthaud threw carelessly—seven!

Some shouted, some drew a deep breath, or whispered an oath. These wild spirits, who had faced death often in one form or another, were still children, and still in a new thing found a new pleasure.

"Your star may be in the ascendant," the man muttered who had intervened before, "but it—well, it twinkles, Michel."

Berthaud did not answer. The young man made him a sign to throw. He threw again—eight.

The young man threw with a hand that scarcely dared to let the dice go. Seven! He had lost.

An outburst might have been expected, some cry of violence, of despair. It did not come. And a murmur passed round the circle. "Berthaud will recruit him," growled one. "A queer game," muttered another, and thought hard. Nor did the men go back to their tables. They waited to see what would follow, what would come of it. For the young man who had lost sat staring at the table like one in a dream; until presently his opponent reaching out a hand touched his sleeve. "Courage!" Berthaud said, a flicker of triumph in his eye, "a word with you aside. No need of despair, man. You have but to do what I ask, and you will see sixty yet."

Obedient to his gesture the young man rose, and the other drawing him aside began to talk to him in a low voice. The remaining players loitering about the deserted table could not hear what was said; but one or two, by feigning to strike a sudden blow, seemed to pass on their surmises to those round them. One thing was clear. The lad objected to the proposal made, objected fiercely and with vehemence; and at last submitted only with reluctance. Submit in the end, however, he did; for after some minutes of this private talk he went to his cloak, and avoiding, as it seemed, his fellows' eyes, put it on. Berthaud accompanied him to the door, and the winner's last words were audible. "That is all," he said; "succeed, in what I impose, M. de Bazan, and I cry quits, and you shall have fifty crowns for your pains. Fail, and you will but be paying your debt. But you will not fail. Remember, half an hour after midnight. And courage!"

The young man nodded sullenly, and drawing his cloak about his throat, went through the passage to the street. The night was a little older than when he had entered, otherwise it was unchanged. The rain was still falling; the wind still buffeted the creaking shutters and the swinging sign-boards. But the man? He had entered, thinking nothing of rain or wind, thinking little even of the horse, and furniture, and the good clothes made under his mother's eye, which he had sacrificed to refill his purse. The warmth of the play fever coursing through his veins had clad him in proof against cold and damp and the depression of the gloomy streets, even against the thought of home. And for the good horse, and the laced shirts and the gold braid, the luck could not run against him again! He would win all back, and the crowns to boot.

So he had thought as he went in. And now? He stood a moment in the dark, narrow chasm of a street, and looked up, letting the rain cool his brow; looked up, and, seeing a wrack of clouds moving swiftly across the slit of stormy sky visible between the overhanging roofs, faced in a dull amazement the fact that he who now stood in the darkness, bankrupt even in life, was the same man who had entered Paris so rich in hope and youth and life a week—only a week—before. He remembered— it was an odd thing to occur to him when his thoughts should have been full of the events of the last hour—a fault of which he had been guilty down there in the country; and of which, taking advantage of a wrathful father's offer to start him in Paris, he had left the weaker sinner to bear the brunt. And it seemed to him that here was his punishment. The old grey house at home, quaint and weather-beaten, rose before him. He saw his mother's herb-garden, the great stackyard, and the dry moat, half filled with blackberry bushes, in which he had played as a boy. And on him fell a strange calm, between apathy and resignation. This, then, was his punishment. He would bear it like a man. There should be no flinching a second time, no putting the burden on others' shoulders, no self-sparing at another's cost.

He started to walk briskly in the direction of the Louvre. But when he had gained the corner of the open space in front of the palace, whence he had a view of the main gate between the two tennis-courts, he halted and looked up and down as if he hesitated. A watch-fire smouldering and sputtering in the rain was burning dully before the drawbridge; the forms of one or two men, apparently sentinels, were dimly visible about it. After standing in doubt more then a minute, Bazan glided quickly to the porch of the church of St. Germain l'Auxerrois, and disappeared in the angle between it and the cloisters.

He had been stationary in this position for some half-hour—in what bitterness of spirit, combating what regrets and painful thoughts it is possible only to imagine— when a slight commotion took place at the gate which faced him. Two men came out in close converse, and stood a moment looking up as if speaking of the weather. They separated then, and one who even by that uncertain light could be seen to be a man of tall, spare presence, came across the open space towards the end of the Rue des Fosses, which passed beside the cloisters. He had just entered the street, when Bazan, who had been closely watching his movements, stepped from the shadow of the houses and touched his sleeve.

The tall man recoiled sharply as he turned. He laid his hand on his sword and partly drew it. "Who are you?" he said, trying in the darkness to make out the other's features.

"M. de Crillon, is it not?" the young man asked.

"Yes. And you, young sir?"

"My name is Claude de Bazan, but you do not know me. I have a word to say to you."

"You have chosen an odd time, my friend."

"Some things are always timely," the young fellow answered, the excitement under which he laboured and the occasion imparting a spice of flippancy to his tone. "I come to warn you that your life is in danger. Do not go alone, M. de Crillon, or pass this way at night! And whatever you do, walk for the future in the middle of the street!"

"For the warning I am obliged to you," the tall man answered, his voice cool and satirical, while his eyes continued to scan the other's features. "But, I say again, you have chosen a strange time to give it, young sir. Moreover, your name is new to me, and I do not know your face."

"Nor need you," said Bazan.

"Aye, but I think I need, craving your pardon," replied the tall, spare man with some sternness. "I am not wont to be scared by little things, nor will I give any man the right to say that he has frightened me with a lighted turnip."

"Will it convince you if I tell you that I came hither to kill you?" the young man cried impetuously.

"Yes, if you will say also why you did not—at least try?" Crillon answered drily.

Bazan had not meant to explain himself; he had proposed to give his warning, and to go. But on the impulse of the moment, carried away by his excitement, he spoke, and told the story, and Crillon, after leading him aside, so that a building sheltered them from the rain, listened. He listened, who knew all the dark plans, all the scandals, all the jealousies, all the vile or frantic schemings of a court, that, half French, half Italian, mingled so grimly force and fraud. Nay, when all was told, when Bazan, passing lightly over the resolution he had formed to warn the victim instead of attacking him, came suddenly and lamely to a stop, he still for a time stood silent. At last, "And what will you do now, my friend?" he asked.

"Go back," the young man answered.

"And then?"

"Pay my debt."

The courtier swore a great oath—it was his failing—and with sudden violence he seized his companion by the arm, and hurried him into the roadway, and along the street. "To Simon's!" he muttered. "To Simon's, my friend. I know the place. I will cut that villain Berthaud's throat."

"But what shall I be the better of that?" the young man answered, somewhat bitterly. "I have none the less lost, and must pay."

Crillon stopped short, the darkness hiding alike his face and his feelings. "So!" he said slowly, "I did not think of that! No, I did not think of that. But do you mean it? What if I kill him?"

"I have played for my life, and lost," Bazan answered proudly. "I promised, and I am a gentleman."

"Pheugh!" Crillon whistled. He swore again, and stood. He was a great man, and full of expedients, but the position was novel. Yet, after a minute's thought, he had an idea. He started off again, taking Bazan's arm, and impelling him onwards, with the same haste and violence. "To Simon's! to Simon's!" he cried as before. "Courage, my friend, I will play him for you and win you: I will redeem you. After all, it is simple, absolutely simple."

"He will not play for me," the young man answered despondently. Nevertheless he suffered himself to be borne onwards. "What will you set against me?"

"Anything, everything!" his new friend cried recklessly. "Myself, if necessary. Courage, M. de Bazan, courage! What Crillon wills, Crillon does. You do not know me yet, but I have taken a fancy to you, I have!"——He swore a grisly oath. "And I will make you mine."

He gave the young man no time for further objection, but, holding him firmly by the arm, he hurried him through the streets to the door below the two gables. On this he knocked with the air of one who had been there before, and to whom all doors opened. In the momentary pause before it yielded Bazan spoke. "Will you not be in danger here?" he asked, wondering much. "It is a Guise house? True, it is. But there is danger everywhere. No man dies more than once or before God wills it! And I am Crillon!"

The superb air with which he said this last prepared Bazan for what followed. The moment the door was opened, Crillon pushed through the doorway, and with an assured step strode down the passage. He turned the corner of the screen and stood in the room; and, calmly smiling at the group of startled, astonished faces which were turned on him, he drew off his cloak and flung it over his left arm. His height at all times made him a conspicuous figure; this night he was fresh from court. He wore black and silver, the hilt of his long sword was jewelled, the Order of the Holy Ghost glittered on his breast; and this fine array seemed to render more shabby the pretentious finery of the third-rate adventurers before him. He saluted them coolly. "It is a wet night, gentlemen," he said.

Some of those who sat farthest off had risen, and all had drawn together as sheep club at sight of the wolf. One of them answered sullenly that it was.

"You think I intrude, gentlemen?" he returned, smiling pleasantly, drinking in as homage the stir his entrance had caused. For he was vain. "I want only an old friend, M. Michel Berthaud, who is here, I think?"

"And for what do you want him?" the tall dark player answered defiantly; he alone of those present seemed in a degree a match for the newcomer, though even his gloomy eyes fell before Crillon's easy stare. "For what do you want me?"

"To propose a little game to you," Crillon answered: and he moved down the room, apparently at his ease. "My friend here has told me of his ill-luck. He is resolved to perform his bargain. But first, M. Berthaud, I have a proposal to make to you. His life is yours. You have won it. Well, I will set you five hundred crowns against it."

The scowl on Berthaud's face did not relax. "No," he said contemptuously. "I will not play with you, M. de Crillon. Let the fool die. What is he to you?"

"Nothing, and yet I have a fancy to win him," Crillon replied lightly. "Come, I will stake a thousand crowns against him! A thousand crowns for a life! *Mon Dieu*," he added, with a whimsical glance at Bazan, "but you are dear, my friend!"

Indeed, half a score of faces shone with cupidity, and twice as many bearded lips watered. A thousand crowns! A whole thousand crowns! But to the surprise of most—a few knew their man—Berthaud shook his head.

"No," he said, "I will not play! I won his life, and I will have it."

"Fifteen hundred crowns. I will set that! Fifteen—"

"No!"

"Two thousand, then! Two thousand, man! And I will throw in my chain. It is worth five hundred more."

"No! No! No!"

"Then, say what you will play for!" the great man roared, his face swelling with rage. "Thousand devils and all tonsured! I have a mind to win his life. What will you have against it?"

"Against it?"

"Aye!"

"Yours!" said M. Berthaud, very softly.

Bazan drew in his breath—sharply: otherwise the silence was so intense that the fall of the wood-ashes from the dying fire could be heard. The immense, the boundless audacity of the proposal made some smile and some start. But none smiled so grimly as M. Michel Berthaud, the challenger, and none started so little as M. de Crillon, the challenged.

"A high bid!" he said, lifting his chin with something almost of humour; and then glancing round him, as a wolf might glance, if the sheep turned on him. "You ask much, M. Berthaud."

"I will ask less then," replied Berthaud, with irony. "If I win, I will give you his life. He shall go free whether you win or lose, M. de Crillon."

"That is much!" with answering irony.

"Much or little—"

"It is understood?"

"It is," Berthaud rejoined with a sarcastic bow.

"Then I accept!" Crillon cried: and with a movement so brisk that some recoiled, he sat down at the table. "I accept. Silence!" he continued, turning sharply upon Bazan, whose cry of remonstrance rang above the astonished murmur of the bystanders. "Silence, fool!" He struck the table. "It is my will. Fear nothing! I am Crillon, and I do not lose."

There was a superb self-confidence in the man, an arrogance, a courage, which more than anything else persuaded his hearers that he was in earnest, that he was not jesting with them.

"The terms are quite understood," he proceeded, grimly. "If I win, we go free, M. Berthaud. If I lose, M. de Bazan goes free, and I undertake on the honour of a nobleman to kill myself before daylight. Shall I say within six hours? I have affairs to settle!"

Probably no one in the room felt astonishment equal to that of Berthaud. A faint colour tinged his sallow cheeks; a fierce gleam of joy flashed in his eyes. But all he said was, "Yes, I am satisfied."

"Then throw!" said Crillon, and leaning forward he took a candle from a neighbouring table, and placed it beside him. "My friend," he added, speaking to Bazan with earnest gravity, "I advise you to be quiet. If you do not we shall quarrel."

His smile was as easy, his manner as unembarrassed, his voice as steady, as when he had entered the room. The old gamesters who stood round the table, and had seen, with interest indeed and some pity, but with no great emotion, a man play his last stake, saw this, saw a man stake his life for a whim, with very different feelings; with astonishment, with admiration, with a sense of inferiority that did not so much gall their pride as awaken their interest. For the moment, the man who was above death, who risked it for a fancy, a trifle, a momentary gratification, was a demigod. "Throw!" repeated Crillon, heedless and apparently unconscious of the stir round him: "Throw! but beware of that candle! Your sleeve is in it."

It was; it was singeing. Berthaud moved the candle, and as if his enemy's *sang froid* wounded him, he threw savagely, dashing down the dice on the table, and lifting the box with a gesture of defiance. He swore a frightful oath: his face was livid. He had thrown aces only.

"So!" murmured his opponent quietly. "Is that all? A thousand crowns to a hundred that I better that! Five hundred to a hundred that I double it! Will no one take me? Then I throw. Courage, my friend. I am Crillon!"

He threw; an ace and a deuce.

"I waste nothing," he said.

But few heard the words—his opponent perhaps and one or two others; for from end to end the room rang and the oaken rafters shook with a great cry of "Long live Crillon! the brave Crillon!"—a cry which rose from a score of throats. Then and onwards till the day of his death, many years later, he was known throughout France by no other name. The great king's letter to him, "Hang yourself, brave Crillon. We have fought to-day, and you were not there!" is not yet forgotten— nay, never will be forgotten—in a land where, more than in other, the memories of the past have been swept away.

He rose from the table, bowing grandly, superbly, arrogantly. "Adieu, M. Berthaud—for the present," he said; and had he not seemed too proud to threaten, a threat might have underlain his words. "Adieu, gentlemen," he continued, throwing on his cloak. "A good night to you, and equal fortune. M. de Bazan, I will trouble you to accompany me? You have exchanged, let me tell you, one taskmaster for another."

The young man's heart was too full for words, and making no attempt to speak, or to thank his benefactor, before those who had seen the deed, he followed him from the room. Crillon did not speak or halt until they stood in the Rue des Fosses; nor even there, for after a momentary hesitation he passed through it, and led the way to the middle of the open space before the Louvre. Here he stopped, and touched his companion on the breast. "Now," he said, "we can speak with freedom, my friend. You wish to thank me? Do not. Listen to me instead. I have saved your life, ay, that have I; but I hold it at my will! Say, is it not so? Well, I, too, in my turn wish you to do something for me."

"Anything!" said the young man, passionately. The sight of the other's strange daring had stirred his untried nature to its depths. "You have but to ask and have."

"Very well," Crillon answered, gravely, "be it so. I take you at your word. Though, mind you, M. de Bazan, 'tis no light thing I ask. It is something," pausing, "from which I shrink myself."

"Then it is nothing you ask me to do?" Bazan answered.

"Not so," the courtier replied, though he looked far from ill-pleased by the compliment. "Listen. To-morrow the King sups at the house of Madame de Sauves. I shall be with him. Her house is in the Rue de l'Arbre Sec, two doors from the convent. Here are a hundred crowns. Dress yourself so that you may appear as one of my gentlemen, and wait near the gates till I come. Then follow me in, and at supper stand behind my chair, as the others of my suite will stand."

"And is that all?" Bazan asked in astonishment.

"No, not quite," Crillon answered dryly. "The rest I will whisper in your ear as I pass. Only do what I bid you boldly and faithfully, my friend, and afterwards, if all be well, I will not forget you."

"I am yours! Do with me as you will!" Bazan protested.

But to mortals the unknown is ever terrible; and for twenty-four hours Bazan had the unknown before him. What could that be from which Crillon himself said that he shrank—a man so brave? It could not be death, for that he had risked on the lightest, the flimsiest, the most fantastic provocation. Then what could it be? Bazan turned the question in his mind, turned it a hundred times that night, turned it a hundred times as he went about his preparations next day. Turned it and turned it, but instinctively, though no injunctions to that effect had been given him, took care to show himself as little as possible in public, and especially to shun all places where he might meet those who had been present at that strange game at Simon's.

A quarter before nine on the next evening, saw him waiting with a beating heart outside the house in the Rue de l'Arbre Sec. He formed one of a crowd of lackeys, and linkboys, citizens, apprentices, and chance passers who had been attracted to the spot by the lights and by the guards in the royal livery, who already, though the King was not come, kept the entrance to the courtyard. Bazan pushed himself with some difficulty into the front rank, and there waited, scanning with feverish eagerness everyone who entered.

Time passed, and no Crillon appeared, though presently a great shouting along the street proclaimed the approach of the Duke of Guise, and that nobleman passed slowly in, noting with a falcon's eye the faces of the bowing throng. He was a man of grand height and imperial front—a great scar seeming to make the latter more formidable—his smile a trifle supercilious, his eyes somewhat near one another; and under his glance Bazan felt for the moment small and mean. A little later, from the talk of those about him, the young man learned that the King was drawing near, and Henry's coach, surrounded by a dozen of the Forty-five, lumbered along the street. It was greeted with comparative coldness, only those who stood under the guards' eyes performing a careless salute.

Bazan was no Parisian, though for the present in Paris, and no Leaguer, though a Roman Catholic; and he forgot his present errand in the excitement of his rustic loyalty. Raising his bonnet, he cried loudly *Vive le Roi!*—cried it more than once. There were six in the coach, but Henry, whose pale meagre face with its almond eyes and scanty beard permitted no mistake, remarked the salutation and the giver, and his look cast the young man into a confusion which nearly cost him dearly; for it was only as the guards closed round the coach that he perceived Crillon sitting in the nearer boot. The moment he did see him he pushed forward among the running footmen who followed the coach, and succeeded in entering with it.

The courtyard, crowded with gentlemen, lackeys and torch-bearers, was a scene of great confusion, and Bazan had no difficulty in approaching Crillon and exchanging a sentence with him. That effected, so completely was he confounded by the order whispered in his ear, that he observed nothing more until he found himself in a long gallery, waiting with many others attached to the great men's suites, while the magnificoes themselves talked together at the upper end. By listening to the gossip round him, he learned that one dark handsome man among the latter was Alphonso d'Ornano, often called the Corsican Captain. A second was M. d'O, the Governor of Paris; a third, the Count of Soissons. But he had scarcely time to note these, or the novel and splendid scene in which he stood, before the double doors at the end of the gallery were thrown widely open, and amid a sudden hush the great courtiers passed into the supper-room in which the King, the Duke of Guise, and several ladies, already stood or sat in their places, having entered by another door. Bazan pressed in with the flock of attendant gentlemen, and seeing Crillon preparing to sit down not far from the daïs and canopy which marked the King's chair, he took his stand against the wall behind him.

If the words which Crillon had dropped into his ear had not occupied three-fourths of his thoughts, Bazan would have felt a keener admiration of the scene before him; which, as was natural, surpassed in luxury anything the country lad had ever imagined. The room, panelled and ceiled with cedar, was hung with blue velvet and lighted by a hundred tapers. The table gleamed with fine napery and gold plate, with Palissy ware and Cellini vases; and these, with the rich dresses and jewels and fair shoulders of the ladies, combined to form a beautiful interior which resounded with the babble of talk and laughter. It was hard to detect danger lurking under these things, under the silk, within the flashing gleaming cups, behind smiling eyes; still harder to discern below these fair appearances a peril from which a Crillon shrank.

But to Bazan, as he waited with tortured nerves, these things were nothing. They were no more than fair flowers to the man who espies the coils of a snake among the blossoms. Crillon's whisper had revealed all to him—all, in one brief sentence; so that when he presently recognised Michel Berthaud standing near the upper end of the table and on the farther side of it, in attendance upon the Duke of Guise, he felt no astonishment, but only a shrewd suspicion of the quarter from which the danger might be expected.

The King, a man of thirty-seven, so effeminate in appearance that it was hard to believe he had seen famous fields and once bidden fair to be a great Captain, was nursing a dog on his lap, the while he listened with a weary air to the whispers of the beautiful woman who sat next him. Apparently he had a niggard ear even for her witcheries, and little appetite save for the wine-flask. Lassitude lived in his eyes, his long thin fingers trembled. Bazan watched him drain his goblet of wine, almost as soon as he sat down, and watched him, too, hold out the gold cup to be filled again. The task was performed by an assiduous hand, and for a moment the King poised the cup in his fingers, speaking to his neighbour the while. Then he laid it down, but his hand did not quit its neighbourhood.

The next moment the room rang with a cry of alarm and indignation, and every face was turned one way. Bazan with unparalleled audacity had stepped forward, had seized the sacred cup almost from the royal hand, and drained it!

While some sprang from their seats, two or three seized the culprit and held him fast. One more enthusiastic than the others or more keenly sensitive to the outrage of which he had been guilty, aimed a fierce blow at his breast with a poniard. The stroke was well meant, nay was well directed; but it was adroitly intercepted by M. de Crillon, who had been among the first to rise. With a blow of his sheathed sword he sent the dagger spinning towards the ceiling.

"Back!" he cried, in a voice of thunder, placing himself before the culprit. "Stand back, I say! I will answer to the King for all!"

He cleared a space before him with his scabbard, and a quick signal brought to his side the two guards at the nearest door, who were men of his command. These, crossing their pikes before the prisoner, secured him from immediate attack. By this time all in the room had risen save the King, who appeared less moved than any by the incident. At this point he raised his hand to procure silence.

"Is he mad?" he asked calmly. "What is it, Crillon?"

"I will satisfy your Grace," the courtier answered. But the next moment, with a sudden change of tone, he cried loudly and rapidly, "Stop that man, I beg you, d'Ornano! Stop him!"

The warning came too late. The Corsican sprang indeed to the door, but the crowd impeded him; and the man to whom Crillon referred—the same who had struck at Bazan, and who was no other than Berthaud—got to it first, slipped out and was gone from sight, before those near the entrance had recovered from their surprise.

"Follow him," Crillon cried loudly. "Seize him at all hazards! *Mort de Dieu!* He has outwitted us at last."

"His Majesty has asked, M. de Crillon," said one at the table, speaking in the haughty, imperious tone of a man who never spoke unheeded, "what is the meaning of all this? Perhaps you will kindly satisfy him."

"I will satisfy him," Crillon answered, grimly fixing his eyes on the other's handsome face. "And you, too, M. de Guise. An attempt has been made to poison my master. This young man, observing that a strange hand poured the King's wine, has saved his Majesty's life by taking the poison himself!"

Henry of Guise laughed scornfully. "A likely story!" he said.

"And in my house!" Madame de Sauves cried in the same tone. "His Majesty will not believe that I—"

"I said nothing against Madame de Sauves," Crillon answered, with firmness. "For the rest, let the King be judge. The issue is simple. If the lad go scatheless, there was no poison in that cup and I am a liar. If he suffer, then let the King say who lies!"

A close observer might have seen an uneasy expression flit across more than one face, darken more than one pair of eyes. Crillon remained on his guard facing the table, his eyes keenly vigilant. The Count of Soissons, one of the younger Bourbons, had already stepped to the King's side and taken place by his chair, his hand on his hilt. D'Ornano, who had despatched two guards after Berthaud, openly drew his long sword and placed himself on the other side of the daïs. Nor was suspicion confined to their party. Half a dozen gentlemen had risen to their feet about the Duke of Guise, who continued to sit with folded arms, content to smile. He was aware that at the worst here in Paris he was safe; perhaps he was innocent of harm or intent.

The main effect, however, of Crillon's last words was to draw many eyes, and amongst them the King's, to the prisoner's face. Bazan was leaning against the wall, the cup still in his grasp. As they turned with a single movement towards him, his face began to grow a shade paler, a spasm moved his lips, and after the interval of a moment the cup fell from his hand to the ground. Thrusting himself with a convulsive movement from the wall, he put out his hands and groped with them as if he could no longer see; until, one of them meeting the pike of the nearest guard, he tried to support himself by this. At the same time he muttered hoarsely, "M. de Crillon, you saw it! We are—we are quits!"

He would have fallen on that, but the men caught him in their arms and held him up, amid a murmur of horror; to many brave men death in this special form is appalling. Here and there a woman shrieked; one fainted. Meanwhile, the young man's face was becoming livid; his neck seemed to stiffen, his eyes to protrude. The King looked at him and shuddered. "Saint Denis!" he muttered, the perspiration standing on his brow, "what an escape! What an escape! Can nothing be done for him?"

"I will try, Sire," Crillon answered, abandoning for the first time his attitude of watchfulness. Drawing a small phial from his pocket, he directed one of the guards to force open the lad's teeth, and then himself poured the contents of the bottle between them.

"Good lad," he muttered to himself, "he has drained the cup. I bade him drink only half. It would have been enough. But he is young and strong. He may surmount it."

The rest looked on, some in curiosity, some in pity, some in secret apprehension. It was the Duke of Guise who put into words the thoughts of many. "Those," he said scornfully, "who find the antidote, may know the poison, M. de Crillon."

"What do you mean, Duke?" Crillon replied passionately, as he sprang to his feet. "That I was in this? That I know more than I have told of it? If so, you lie, sir; and you know it!"

"I know it?" the Duke cried, his eyes aflame, his cheeks reddening. Never had he heard such words. "Do you dare to insinuate—that I know more of this plot than yourself—if plot there be?"

"Enough!" said the King, rising in great haste, and with a face which betrayed his emotion. "Silence, gentlemen! silence! And you, my cousin, not another word, I command you! Who poured out the wine?"

"A villain called Berthaud," Crillon answered promptly and fiercely, "who was in attendance upon the Duke of Guise."

"He was not in attendance on me!" the Duke answered, with spirit.

"Then on Madame de Sauves."

"I know nothing of him!" cried that lady, hysterically. "I never spoke to the man in my life. I do not know him!"

"Enough!" the King said with decision; but the gloom on his brow grew darker. "Enough. Until Berthaud is found, let no more be said. Cousin," he continued to the Count of Soissons, "you will see us home. D'Ornano, we return at once, and you will accompany us. For M. de Crillon, we commit to him the care of this young man, to whom we appear to be indebted, and whose thought for us we shall not forget. Madame, I kiss your hand."

Guise's salutation he acknowledged only by a grave bow. The last of the Valois could at times exert himself, could at times play again the hero of Jarnac and Montcontour, could even assume a dignity no whit less than that of Guise. As he retired all bowed low to him, and the greater part of the assemblage—even those who had not attended him to the house—left in his train. In three minutes Crillon, a couple of inferior officers, and a handful of guards alone remained round the young man.

"He will recover," Crillon said, speaking to the officer next him. "He is young, and they did not dare to make the dose too strong. We shall not, however, convict anyone now, unless Berthaud speaks."

"Berthaud is dead."

"What?"

"As dead as Clovis," the lieutenant repeated calmly. "He is lying in the passage, M. de Crillon."

"Who killed him?" cried Crillon, leaping up in a rage. "Who dared to kill him? Not those fools of guards when they knew it was his evidence we wanted."

"No, no," said the other coolly. "They found him dead not twenty paces from the house. He was a doomed man when he passed through the door. You understand, M. de Crillon? He knew too much to live."

"*Mort de Dieu?*" cried Crillon, raising his hands in admiration. "How clever they are! Not a thing forgotten! Well, I will to the King and tell him. It will put him on his guard. If I had not contrived to try the draught there and then, I could not have convinced him; and if I had not by a lucky hazard won this young man last night, I might have whistled for one to try it! But I must go."

Yet he lingered a minute to see how the lad progressed. The convulsions which had for a time racked Bazan's vigorous frame had ceased, and a profuse perspiration was breaking out on his brow.

"Yes, he will recover," said Crillon again, and with greater confidence.

As if the words had reached Bazan's brain, he opened his eyes.

"I did it!" he muttered. "I did it. We are quits, M. de Crillon!"

"Not so!" cried the other, stooping impetuously and embracing him. "Not quits! The balance is against me now, but I will redress it. Be easy; your fortune is made, M. de Bazan. While James Berthon de Crillon lives you shall not lack a friend!"

He kept his word. There can be little doubt that the Laurence de Bazan who held high office under the Minister Sully, and in particular rose to be Deputy Superintendent of the Finances in Guienne, was our young Bazan. This being so, it is clear that he outlived by many years his patron: for Crillon, "le brave Crillon," whose whim it was to dare greatly, and on small occasion, died early in the seventeenth century—in his bed—and lies under a famous stone in the Cathedral of Avignon. Whereas we find Bazan still flourishing, and a person of consequence at Court, when Richelieu came to the height of his power. Nevertheless on him there remains no stone; only some sketch of the above, and a crabbed note at the foot of a dusty page in a dark library.

THE CORSICAN BROTHERS

ALEXANDRE DUMAS

I

In the beginning of March, 1841, I was travelling in Corsica.

Nothing is more picturesque and more easy to accomplish than a journey in Corsica. You can embark at Toulon, in twenty hours you will be in Ajaccio, and then in twenty-four hours more you are at Bastia.

Once there you can hire or purchase a horse. If you wish to hire a horse you can do so for five francs a-day; if you purchase one you can have a good animal for one hundred and fifty francs. And don't sneer at the moderate price, for the horse hired or purchased will perform as great feats as the famous Gascon horse which leaped over the Pont Neuf, which neither Prospero nor Nautilus, the heroes of Chantilly and the Champ de Mars could do. He will traverse roads which Balmat himself could not cross without *crampons*, and will go over bridges upon which Auriol would need a balancing pole.

As for the traveller, all he has to do is to give the horse his head and let him go as he pleases; he does not mind the danger. We may add that with this horse, which can go anywhere, the traveller can accomplish his fifteen leagues a day without stopping to bait.

From time to time, while the tourist may be halting to examine some ancient castle, built by some old baron or legendary hero, or to sketch a tower built ages ago by the Genoese, the horse will be contented to graze by the road side, or to pluck the mosses from the rocks in the vicinity.

As to lodging for the night, it is still more simple in Corsica. The traveller having arrived at a village, passes down through the principal street, and making his own choice of the house wherein he will rest, he knocks at the door. An instant after, the master or mistress will appear upon the threshold, invite the traveller to dismount; offer him a share of the family supper and the whole of his own bed, and next morning, when seeing him safely resume his journey, will thank him for the preference he has accorded to his house.

As for remuneration, such a thing is never hinted at. The master would regard it as an insult if the subject were broached. If, however, the servant happen to be a young girl, one may fitly offer her a coloured handkerchief, with which she can make up a picturesque coiffure for a fête day. If the domestic be a male he will gladly accept a poignard, with which he can kill his enemy, should he meet him.

There is one thing more to remark, and that is, as sometimes happens, the servants of the house are relatives of the owner, and the former being in reduced circumstances, offer their services to the latter in consideration of board and lodging and a few piastres per month.

And it must not be supposed that the masters are not well served by their cousins to the fifteenth and sixteenth degree, because the contrary is the case, and the custom is not thought anything of. Corsica is a French Department certainly, but Corsica is very far from being France.

As for robbers, one never hears of them, yet there are bandits in abundance; but these gentlemen must in no wise be confounded one with another.

So go without fear to Ajaccio, to Bastia, with a purse full of money hanging to your saddle-bow, and you may traverse the whole island without a shadow of danger, but do not go from Oceana to Levaco, if you happen to have an enemy who has declared the Vendetta against you, for I would not answer for your safety during that short journey of six miles.

Well, then, I was in Corsica, as I have said, at the beginning of the month of March, and I was alone; Jadin having remained at Rome.

I had come across from Elba, had disembarked at Bastia, and there had purchased a horse at the above-mentioned price.

I had visited Corte and Ajaccio, and just then I was traversing the province of Sartène.

On the particular day of which I am about to speak I was riding from Sartène to Sullacaro.

The day's journey was short, perhaps a dozen leagues, in consequence of detours, and on account of my being obliged to climb the slopes of the mountain chain, which, like a backbone, runs through the island. I had a guide with me, for fear I should lose my way in the maquis.

It was about five o'clock in the afternoon when we arrived at the summit of the hill, which at the same time overlooks Olmeto and Sullacaro. There we stopped a moment to look about us.

"Where would your Excellency wish to stay the night?" asked the guide.

I looked down upon the village, the streets of which appeared almost deserted. Only a few women were visible, and they walked quickly along, and frequently looked cautiously around them.

As in virtue of the rules of Corsican hospitality, to which I have already referred, it was open to me to choose for my resting place any one of the hundred or hundred and twenty houses of which the village was composed, I therefore carried my eyes from house to house till they lighted upon one which promised comfortable quarters. It was a square mansion, built in a fortified sort of style and machicolated in front of the windows and above the door.

This was the first time I had seen these domestic fortifications; but I may mention that the province of Sartène is the classic ground of the Vendetta.

"Ah, good!" said my guide, as he followed the direction of my hand—"that is the house of Madame Savilia de Franchi. Go on, go on, Signor, you have not made a bad choice, and I can see you do not want for experience in these matters."

I should note here that in this 86th department of France Italian is universally spoken.

"But," I said, "may it not be inconvenient if I demand hospitality from a lady, for if I understand you rightly, this house belongs to a lady."

"No doubt," he replied, with an air of astonishment; "but what inconvenience does your lordship think you will cause?"

"If the lady be young," I replied, moved by a feeling of propriety—or, perhaps, let us say, of Parisian self-respect—"a night passed under her roof might compromise her."

"Compromise her!" repeated the guide, endeavouring to probe the meaning of the word I had rendered in Italian with all the emphasis which one would hazard a word in a strange tongue.

"Yes, of course," I replied, beginning to feel impatient; "the lady is a widow, I suppose?"

"Yes, Excellency."

"Well, then, will she receive a young man into her house?"

In 1841 I was thirty-six years old, or thereabouts, and was entitled to call myself young.

"Will she receive a young man!" exclaimed the guide; "why, what difference can it make whether you are young or old?"

I saw that I should get no information out of him by this mode of interrogation, so I resumed—

"How old is Madame Savilia?"

"Forty, or nearly so."

"Ah," I said, replying more to my thoughts than to my guide, "all the better. She has children, no doubt?"

"Yes, two sons—fine young men both."

"Shall I see them?"

"You will see one of them—he lives at home."

"Where is the other, then?"

"He lives in Paris."

"How old are these sons?"

"Twenty-one."

"What, both?"

"Yes, they are twins."

"What professions do they follow?"

"The one in Paris is studying law."

"And the other?"

"The other is a Corsican."

"Indeed!" was my reply to this characteristic answer, made in the most matter-of-fact tone. "Well, now, let us push on for the house of Madame Savilia de Franchi."

We accordingly resumed our journey, and entered the village about ten minutes afterwards.

I now remarked what I had not noticed from the hill, namely, that every house was fortified similarly to Madame Savilia's. Not so completely, perhaps, for that the poverty of the inhabitants could not attain to, but purely and simply with oaken planks, by which the windows were protected, loop-holes only being left for rifle barrels; some apertures were simply bricked up.

I asked my guide what he called these loop-holes, and he said they were known as *archères*—a reply which convinced me that they were used anterior to the invention of firearms.

As we advanced through the streets we were able the more fully to comprehend the profound character of the solitude and sadness of the place.

Many houses appeared to have sustained a siege, and the marks of the bullets dotted the walls.

From time to time as we proceeded we caught sight of a curious eye flashing upon us from an embrasure; but it was impossible to distinguish whether the spectator were a man or a woman.

We at length reached the house which I had indicated to my guide, and which was evidently the most considerable in the village.

As we approached it more nearly, one thing struck me, and that was, fortified to all outward appearance as it was, it was not so in reality, for there were neither oaken planks, bricks, nor loop-holes, but simple squares of glass, protected at night by wooden shutters.

It is true that the shutters showed holes which could only have been made by the passage of a bullet; but they were of old date, and could not have been made within the previous ten years.

Scarcely had my guide knocked, when the door was opened, not hesitatingly, nor in a timid manner, but widely, and a valet, or rather I should say a man appeared.

It is the livery that makes the valet, and the individual who then opened the door to us wore a velvet waistcoat, trowsers of the same material, and leather gaiters. The breeches were fastened at the waist by a parti-coloured silk sash, from the folds of which protruded the handle of a Spanish knife.

"My friend," I said, "is it indiscreet of me, who knows nobody in Sullacaro, to ask hospitality of your mistress?"

"Certainly not, your Excellency," he replied; "the stranger does honour to the house before which he stops. Maria," he continued, turning to a servant, who was standing behind him, "will you inform Madame Savilia that a French traveller seeks hospitality?"

As he finished speaking he came down the eight rough ladder-like steps which led to the entrance door, and took the bridle of my horse.

I dismounted.

"Your Excellency need have no further concern," he said; "all your luggage will be taken to your room."

I profited by this gracious invitation to idleness—one of the most agreeable which can be extended to a traveller.

II

I slowly ascended the steps and entered the house, and at a corner of the corridor I found myself face to face with a tall lady dressed in black.

I understood at once that this lady of thirty-eight or forty years of age, and still beautiful, was the mistress of the house.

"Madame," said I, bowing deeply, "I am afraid you will think me intrusive, but the custom of the country may be my excuse, and your servant's invitation my authority to enter."

"You are welcome to the mother," replied Madame de Franchi, "and you will almost immediately be welcomed by the son. From this moment, sir, the house belongs to you; use it as if it were your own."

"I come but to beg hospitality for one night, madame," I answered; "to-morrow morning, at daybreak, I will take my departure."

"You are free to do as you please, sir; but I hope that you will change your mind, and that we shall have the honour of your company for a longer period."

I bowed again, and Madame continued—

"Maria, show this gentleman to my son Louis' chamber; light the fire at once, and carry up some hot water. You will excuse me," she said, turning again to me as the servant departed, "but I always fancy that the first wants of a tired traveller are warm water and a fire. Will you please to follow my maid, sir; and you need have no hesitation in asking her for anything you may require. We shall sup in an hour, and my son, who will be home by that time, will have the honour to wait upon you."

"I trust you will excuse my travelling dress, madame."

"Yes, sir," she replied smiling; "but on condition that you, on your part, will excuse the rusticity of your reception."

I bowed my thanks, and followed the servant upstairs.

The room was situated on the first floor, and looked out towards the rear of the house, upon a pretty and extensive garden, well planted with various trees, and watered by a charming little stream, which fell into the Tavaro.

At the further end the prospect was bounded by a hedge, so thick as to appear like a wall. As is the case in almost all Italian houses, the walls of the rooms were white-washed and frescoed.

I understood immediately that Madame de Franchi had given me this, her absent son's chamber, because it was the most comfortable one in the house.

While Maria was lighting the fire and fetching the hot water, I took it into my head to make an inventory of the room, and try to arrive at an estimation of the character of its usual occupant by those means.

I immediately put this idea into execution, and beginning with the left hand, I took mental notes of the various objects by which I was surrounded.

The furniture all appeared to be modern, a circumstance which in that part of the island, where civilization had not then taken deep root, appeared to indicate no inconsiderable degree of luxury. It was composed of an iron bedstead and bedding, a sofa, four arm-chairs, six other occasional chairs, a wardrobe, half book case and half bureau, all of mahogany, from the first cabinet maker in Ajaccio.

The sofas and chairs were covered with chintz, and curtains of similar material fell before the windows, and hung round the bed.

I had got so far with my inventory when Maria left the room, and I was enabled to push my investigation a little closer.

I opened the book-case, and found within a collection of the works of our greatest poets. I noticed Corneille, Racine, Molière, La Fontaine, Ronsard, Victor Hugo, and Lamartine.

Our moralists—Montaigne, Pascal, Labruyère.

Our historians—Mezeray, Chateaubriand, Augustin Thierry.

Our philosophers—Cuvier, Beudant, Elie de Beaumont.

Besides these there were several volumes of romances and other books, amongst which I recognized, with a certain pride, my own "Impression of Travel."

The keys were in the drawer of the bureau. I opened one of them.

Here I found fragments of a history of Corsica, a work upon the best means of abolishing the Vendetta, some French verses, and some Italian sonnets, all in manuscript. This was more than I expected, and I had the presumption to conclude that I need not seek much farther to form my opinion of the character of Monsieur Louis de Franchi.

He appeared to be a quiet, studious young man, a partizan of the French reformers, and then I understood why he had gone to Paris to become an advocate.

There was, without doubt, a great future for him in this course. I made all these reflections as I was dressing. My toilette, as I had hinted to Madame de Franchi, although not wanting in a certain picturesqueness, demanded that some allowance should be made for it.

It was composed of a vest of black velvet, open at seams of the sleeves, so as to keep me cooler during the heat of the day, and slashed *à l'Espagnole*, permitting a silken chemise to appear underneath. My legs were encased in velvet breeches to the knee, and thence protected by Spanish gaiters, embroidered in Spanish silk. A felt hat, warranted to take any shape, but particularly that of a sombrero, completed my costume.

I recommend this dress to all travellers as being the most convenient I am acquainted with, and I was in the act of dressing, when the same man who had introduced me appeared at the door.

He came to announce that his young master, Monsieur Lucien de Franchi, had that instant arrived, and who desired to pay his respects to me if I were ready to receive him.

I replied that I was at the disposal of Monsieur Lucien de Franchi if he would do me the honour to come up.

An instant afterwards I heard a rapid step approaching my room, and almost immediately afterwards I was face to face with my host.

III

He was, as my guide had told me, a young man of about twenty-one years of age, with black hair and eyes, his face browned by the sun, rather under than over the average height, but remarkably well-proportioned.

In his haste to welcome me he had come up, just as he was, in his riding-costume, which was composed of a redingote of green cloth, to which a cartridge-pouch gave a somewhat military air, grey pantaloons with leather let in on the inner side, of the legs, boots and spurs. His head-dress was a cap similar to those worn by our Chasseurs d'Afrique.

From either side of his pouch there hung a gourd and a pistol, and he carried an English carbine in addition.

Notwithstanding the youthful appearance of my host, whose upper lip was as yet scarcely shaded by a moustache, he wore an air of independence and resolution, which struck me very forcibly.

Here was a man fitted for strife, and accustomed to live in the midst of danger, but without despising it, grave because he was solitary, calm because he was strong.

With a single glance he took me all in, my luggage, my arms, the dress I had just taken off, and that which I had just donned.

His glance was as rapid and as sure as that of a man whose very life may depend upon a hasty survey of his surroundings.

"I trust you will excuse me if I disturb you," he said; "but I come with good intentions. I wish to see if you require anything. I am always somewhat uneasy when any of you gentlemen from the continent pay us a visit, for we are still so uncivilized, we Corsicans, that it is really with fear and trembling that we exercise, particularly to Frenchmen, our own hospitality, which will, I fear, soon be the only thing that will remain to us."

"You have no reason to fear," I replied; "it would be difficult to say what more a traveller can require beyond what Madame de Franchi has supplied. Besides," I continued, glancing round the apartment, "I must confess I do not perceive any of the want of civilization you speak of so frankly, and were it not for the charming prospect from those windows, I should fancy myself in an apartment in the Chaussée d'Antin."

"Yes," returned the young man, "it is rather a mania with my poor brother Louis; he is so fond of living *à la Française*; but I very much doubt whether, when he leaves Paris, the poor attempt at civilization here will appear to him sufficient on his return home as it formerly did."

"Has your brother been long away from Corsica?" I inquired.

"For the last ten months."

"You expect him back soon?"

"Oh, not for three or four years."

"That is a very long separation for two brothers, who probably were never parted before."

"Yes, and particularly if they love each other as we do."

"No doubt he will come to see you before he finishes his studies?"

"Probably; he has promised us so much, at least."

"In any case, nothing need prevent you from paying him a visit?"

"No, I never leave Corsica."

There was in his tone, as he made this reply, that love of country which astonishes the rest of the universe.

I smiled.

"It appears strange to you," he said, smiling in his turn, "when I tell you that I do not wish to leave a miserable country like ours; but you must know that I am as much a growth of the island as the oak or the laurel; the air I breathe must be impregnated with the odours of the sea and of the mountains. I must have torrents to cross, rocks to scale, forests to explore. I must have space; liberty is necessary to me, and if you were to take me to live in a town I believe I should die."

"But how is it there is such a great difference between you and your brother in this respect?"

"And you would add with so great a physical resemblance, if you knew him."

"Are you, then, so very much alike?"

"So much so, that when we were children our parents were obliged to sew a distinguishing mark upon our clothes."

"And as you grew up?" I suggested.

"As we grew up our habits caused a very slight change in our appearance, that is all. Always in a study, poring over books and drawings, my brother grew somewhat pale, while I, being always in the open air, became bronzed, as you see."

"I hope," I said, "that you will permit me to judge of this resemblance, and if you have any commission for Monsieur Louis, you will charge me with it."

"Yes, certainly, with great pleasure, if you will be so kind. Now, will you excuse me? I see you are more advanced in your toilet than I, and supper will be ready in a quarter of an hour."

"You surely need not trouble to change on my account."

"You must not reproach me with this, for you have yourself set me the example; but, in any case, I am now in a riding dress, and must change it for a mountaineer's costume, as, after supper, I have to make an excursion in which boots and spurs would only serve to hinder me."

"You are going out after supper, then?" I asked.

"Yes," he repled, "to a rendezvous."

I smiled.

"Ah, not in the sense you understand it—this is a matter of business."

"Do you think me so presumptuous as to believe I have a right to your conscience?"

"Why not? One should live so as to be able to proclaim what one has done. I never had a mistress, and I never shall have one. If my brother should marry, and have children, it is probable that I shall never take a wife. If, on the contrary, he does not marry, perhaps I shall, so as to prevent our race from becoming extinct. Did I not tell you," he added, laughing, "that I am a regular savage, and had come into the world a hundred years too late? But I continue to chatter here like a crow, and I shall not be ready by the time supper is on the table."

"But cannot we continue the conversation?" I said. "Your chamber, I believe, is opposite, and we can talk through the open doors."

"We can do better than that; you can come into my room while I dress. You are a judge of arms, I fancy. Well, then, you shall look at mine. There are some there which are valuable—from an historical point of view, I mean."

IV

The suggestion quite accorded with my inclination to compare the chambers of the brothers, and I did not hesitate to adopt it. I followed my host, who, opening the door, paused in front of me to show me the way.

This time I found myself in a regular arsenal. All the furniture was of the fifteenth or sixteenth century—the carved and canopied bedstead, supported by great posts, was draped with green damask *à fleur d'or*; the window curtains were of the same material. The walls were covered with Spanish leather, and in the open spaces were sustained trophies of Gothic and modern arms.

There was no mistaking the tastes of the occupant of this room: they were as warlike as those of his brother were peaceable.

"Look here," he said, passing into an inner room, "here you are in three centuries at once—see! I will dress while you amuse yourself, for I must make haste or supper will be announced."

"Which are the historic arms of which you spoke amongst all these swords, arquebuses, and poignards?" I asked.

"There are three. Let us take them in order. If you look by the head of my bed you will find a poignard with a very large hilt—the pommel forms a seal."

"Yes, I have it."

"That is the dagger of Sampietro."

"The famous Sampietro, the assassin of Vanina?"

"The assassin! No, the avenger."

"It is the same thing, I fancy."

"To the rest of the world, perhaps—not in Corsica."

"And is the dagger authentic?"

"Look for yourself. It carries the arms of Sampietro—only the fleur-de-lis of France is missing. You know that Sampietro was not authorized to wear the lily until after the siege of Perpignan."

"No, I was not aware of that. And how did you become possessed of this poignard?"

"Oh! it has been in our family for three hundred years. It was given to a Napoleon de Franchi by Sampietro himself."

"Do you remember on what occasion?"

"Yes. Sampietro and my ancestor fell into an ambuscade of Genoese, and defended themselves like lions. Sampietro's helmet was knocked off, and a Genoese on horseback was about to kill Sampietro with his mace when my ancestor plunged his dagger into a joint in his enemy's armour. The rider feeling himself wounded spurred his horse, carrying away in his flight the dagger so firmly embedded in his armour that he was unable to withdraw it, and as my ancestor very much regretted the loss of his favourite weapon Sampietro gave him his own. Napoleon took great care of it, for it is of Spanish workmanship, as you see, and will penetrate two five-franc pieces one on top of another."

"May I make the attempt?"

"Certainly."

Placing the coins upon the floor, I struck a sharp blow with the dagger. Lucien had not deceived me.

When I withdrew the poignard I found both pieces pierced through and through, fixed upon the point of the dagger.

"This is indeed the dagger of Sampietro," I said. "But what astonishes me is that being possessed of such a weapon he should have employed the cord to kill his wife."

"He did not possess it at that time," replied Lucien; "he had given it to my ancestor."

"Ah! true!"

"Sampietro was more than sixty years old when he hastened from Constantinople to Aix to teach that lesson to the world, viz., that women should not meddle in state affairs."

I bowed in assent, and replaced the poignard.

"Now," said I to Lucien, who all this time had been dressing, "let us pass on from Sampietro to some one else."

"You see those two portraits close together?"

"Yes, Paoli and Napoleon."

"Well, near the portrait of Paoli is a sword."

"Precisely so."

"That is his sword."

"Paoli's sword? And is it as authentic as the poignard of Sampietro?"

"Yes, at least as authentic; though he did not give it to one of my male ancestors, but to one of the ladies."

"To one of your female ancestors?"

"Yes. Perhaps you have heard people speak of this woman, who in the war of independence presented herself at the Tower of Sullacaro, accompanied by a young man?"

"No, tell me the story."

"Oh, it is a very short one."

"So much the worse."

"Well, you see, we have not much time to talk now."

"I am all attention."

"Well, this woman and this young man presented themselves before the Tower of Sullacaro and requested to speak with Paoli; but as he was engaged writing, he declined to admit them; and then, as the woman insisted, the two sentinels repulsed her, when Paoli, who had heard the noise, opened the door and inquired the cause."

"'It is I,' said the woman; 'I wish to speak to you.'

"'What have you to say to me?'

"'I have come to tell you that I have two sons. I heard yesterday that one had been killed for defending his country, and I have come twenty leagues to bring you the other!!!'"

"You are relating an incident of Sparta," I said.

"Yes, it does appear very like it."

"And who was this woman?"

"She was my ancestress."

"Paoli took off his sword and gave it to her.

"'Take it,' he said, 'I like time to make my excuses to woman.'"

"She was worthy of both—is it not so?"

"And now this sabre?"

"That is the one Buonaparte carried at the battle of the Pyramids."

"No doubt it came into your family in the same manner as the poignard and the sword."

"Entirely. After the battle Buonaparte gave the order to my grandfather, who was an officer in the Guides, to charge with fifty men a number of Mamelukes who were at bay around a wounded chieftain. My grandfather dispersed the Mamelukes and took the chief back a prisoner to the First Consul. But when he wished to sheath his sword he found the blade had been so bent in his encounter with the Mamelukes that it would not go into the scabbard. My grandfather therefore threw sabre and sheath away as useless, and, seeing this, Buonaparte gave him his own."

"But," I said, "in your place I would rather have had my grandfather's sabre, all bent as it was, instead of that of the general's, which was in good condition."

"Look before you and you will find it. The First Consul had it recovered, and caused that large diamond to be inserted in the hilt. He then sent it to my family with the inscription which you can read on the blade."

I advanced between the windows, where, hanging half-drawn from its scabbard, which it could not fully enter, I perceived the sabre bent and hacked, bearing the simple inscription—

Battle of the Pyramids, 21st of July, 1798.

At that moment the servant came to announce that supper was served.

"Very well, Griffo," replied the young man; "tell my mother that we are coming down."

As he spoke he came forth from the inner room, dressed, as he said, like a mountaineer; that is to say, with a round velvet coat, trowsers, and gaiters; of his other costume he had only retained his pouch.

He found me occupied in examing two carbines hanging opposite each other, and both inscribed—

21st September, 1819: 11 A.M.

"Are these carbines also historical?" I asked.

"Yes," he answered. "For us, at least, they bear a historical significance. One was my father's—"

He hesitated.

"And the other," I suggested.

"And the other," he said, laughing, "is my mother's. But let us go downstairs; my mother will be awaiting us."

Then passing in front of me to show me the way he courteously signed to me to follow him.

V

I must confess that as I descended to the supper-room I could not help thinking of Lucien's last remark, "The other is my mother's carbine"; and this circumstance compelled me to regard Madame de Franchi more closely than I had hitherto done.

When her son entered the *salle à manger*, he respectfully kissed her hand, and she received this homage with queenly dignity.

"I am afraid that we have kept you waiting, mother," said Lucien; "I must ask your pardon."

"In any case, that would be my fault, madame," I said, bowing to her. "Monsieur Lucien has been telling me and pointing out many curious things, and by my reiterated questions I have delayed him."

"Rest assured," she said, "I have not been kept waiting; I have but this moment come downstairs. But," she continued, addressing Lucien, "I was rather anxious to ask you what news there was of Louis."

"Your son has been ill, madame?" I asked.

"Lucien is afraid so," she said.

"Have you received a letter from your brother?" I inquired.

"No," he replied, "and that is the very thing that makes me uneasy."

"But, then, how can you possibly tell that he is out of sorts?"

"Because during the last few days I have been suffering myself."

"I hope you will excuse my continual questions; but, really, your answer does not make matters any clearer."

"Well, you know that we are twins, don't you?"

"Yes, my guide told me as much."

"Were you also informed that when we came into the world we were joined together?"

"No; I was ignorant of that circumstance."

"Well, then, it was a fact, and we were obliged to be cut asunder. So that, you see, however distant we may be, we have ever the same body, so that any impression, physical or moral, which one may receive is immediately reflected in the other. During the last few days I felt *triste*, morose, dull, and without any predisposing cause, so far as I am aware. I have experienced terrible pains in the region of the heart, and palpitations, so it is evident to me that my brother is suffering some great grief."

I looked with astonishment at this young man, who affirmed such a strange thing without the slightest fear of contradiction, and his mother also appeared to entertain the same conviction as he did.

Madame de Franchi smiled sadly, and said, "The absent are in the hands of God, the great point is that you are certain that he is alive."

"Yes," replied Lucien, calmly, "for if he were dead I should have seen him."

"And you would have told me, would you not, my son?"

"Oh, of course, mother, at once."

"I am satisfied. Excuse me, monsieur," she continued, turning to me, "I trust you will pardon my maternal anxiety. Not only are Louis and Lucien my sons, but they are the last of their race. Will you please take the chair at my right hand? Lucien, sit here."

She indicated to the young man the vacant place at her left hand.

We seated ourselves at the extremity of a long table, at the opposite end of which were laid six other covers, destined for those who in Corsica are called the family; that is to say, the people who in large establishments occupy a position between the master and the servants.

The table was abundantly supplied with good cheer. But I confess that although at the moment blessed with a very good appetite, I contented myself with eating and drinking as it were mechanically, for my senses were not in any way attracted by the pleasures of the table. For, indeed, it appeared to me that I had entered into a strange world when I came into that house, and that I was now living in a dream.

Who could this woman be who was accustomed to carry a carbine like a soldier?

What sort of person could this brother be, who felt the same grief that his brother experienced at a distance of three hundred leagues?

What sort of mother could this be who made her son declare that if he saw the spirit of his dead brother he would tell her at once?

These were the questions that perplexed me, and it will be readily understood they gave me ample food for thought.

However, feeling that continual silence was not polite, I made an effort to collect my ideas. I looked up.

The mother and son at the same instant perceived that I wished to enter into conversation.

"So," said Lucien to me, as if he were continuing his remarks, "so you made up your mind to come to Corsica?"

"Yes, as you see, I had for a long time had a desire to do so, and at last I have accomplished it."

"*Ma foi!* you have done well not to delay your visit; for with the successive encroachments of French tastes and manners those who come to look for Corsica in a few years will not find it."

"However," I replied, "if the ancient national spirit retires before civilization and takes refuge in any corner of the island, it certainly will be in the province of Sartène, and in the valley of the Tavaro."

"Do you think so, really?" said the young man, smiling.

"Yes, and it appears to me that here at the present moment there is a beautiful and noble tablet of ancient Corsican manners."

"Yes, and nevertheless, even here, between my mother and myself, in the face of four hundred years of reminiscences of this old fortified mansion, the French spirit has come to seek out my brother—has carried him away to Paris, when he will return to us a lawyer. He will live in Ajaccio instead of dwelling in his ancestral home. He will plead—if he possess the talent—he may be nominated *procureur du roi* perhaps; then he will pursue the poor devils who have 'taken a skin,' as they say here. He will confound the assassin with the avenger—as you yourself have done already. He will demand, in the name of the law, the heads of those who had done what their fathers would have considered themselves dishonoured *not* to have done. He will substitute the judgment of men for the justice of God; and in the evening, when he shall have claimed a head for the scaffold, he will believe that he has performed his duty, and has brought his stone as a tribute to the temple of Civilization, as our préfect says. Oh! mon Dieu! mon Dieu!"

The young man raised his eyes to heaven, as Hannibal is reported to have done after the battle of Zama.

"But," I replied, "you must confess that it is the will of God to equalize these things, since in making your brother a proselyte of the new order He has kept you here as a representative of the old manners and customs."

"Yes; but what is there to prove that my brother will not follow the example of his uncle instead of following mine? And even I myself may be about to do something unworthy of a de Franchi."

"You!" I exclaimed, with astonishment.

"Yes, I."

"Do you wish me to tell you why you have come into this province of Sartène?"

"Yes, tell me."

"You have come here to satisfy your curiosity as a man of the world, an artist, or a poet. I do not know what you are, nor do I ask; you can tell us when you leave, if you wish, if not, you need not inform us; you are perfectly free to do as you like. Well, you have come in the hope of seeing some village Vendetta, of being introduced to some original bandit, such as Mr. Merimée has described in 'Columba.'"

"Well, it appears to me that I have not made such a bad choice, for if my eyes do not deceive me, your house is the only one in the village that is not fortified."

"That only proves I have degenerated, as I have said. My father, my grandfather, and my ancestors for many generations have always taken one side or the other in the disputes which in the last ten years have divided the village. And do you know what I have become in the midst of musket shots and stabs? Well, I am the arbitrator. You have come into the province of Sartène to see bandits; is not that the fact? So come with me this evening and I will show you one."

"What! will you really allow me to go with you this evening?"

"Certainly, if it will amuse you. It entirely depends upon yourself."

"I accept, then, with much pleasure."

"Our guest is fatigued," said Madame de Franchi, looking meaningly at her son, as if she felt ashamed Corsica had so far degenerated.

"No, mother, no, he had better come; and when in some Parisian *salon* people talk of the terrible Vendettas, of the implacable Corsican bandits who strike terror into the hearts of children in Bastia and Ajaccio, he will be able to tell them how things actually are."

"But what is the great motive for this feud, which, as I understand, is now by your intercession to be for ever extinguished?"

"Oh," replied Lucien, "in a quarrel it is not the motive that matters, it is the result. If a fly causes a man's death the man is none the less dead because a fly caused it."

I saw that he hesitated to tell me the cause of this terrible war, which for the last ten years had desolated the village of Sullacaro.

But, as may be imagined, the more he attempted to conceal it the more anxious I was to discover it.

"But," said I, "this quarrel must have a motive; is that motive a secret?"

"Good gracious, no! The mischief arose between the Orlandi and the Colona."

"On what occasion?"

"Well, a fowl escaped from the farm yard of the Orlandi and flew into that of the Colona."

"The Orlandi attempted to get back the hen, the Colona declared it belonged to them. The Orlandi then threatened to bring the Colona before the judge and make them declare on oath it was theirs. And then the old woman in whose house the hen had taken refuge wrung its neck, and threw the dead fowl into her neighbour's face, saying—

"'Well, then, if it belongs to you, eat it.'

"Then one of the Orlandi picked up the fowl by the feet, and attempted to beat the person who had thrown it in his sister's face; but just as he was about to do so, one of the Colona appeared, who, unfortunately, carried a loaded gun, and he immediately sent a bullet through the Orlandi's heart."

"And how many lives have been sacrificed since?"

"Nine people have been killed altogether."

"And all for a miserable hen not worth twelve sous?"

"Yes, but as I said just now, it is not the cause, but the effect that we have to look at."

"Since there were nine people killed, then, there might easily be a dozen."

"Yes, very likely there would be if they had not appointed me as arbitrator."

"At the intercession of one of the two families no doubt?"

"Oh! dear no, at my brother's request, who heard of the matter at the Chancellor's house. I asked him what on earth they had to do in Paris with the affairs of an out-of-the-way little village in Corsica; but it seems the préfect mentioned it when he wrote to Paris, and said that if I were to say a word the whole thing would finish like a farce, by a marriage and a public recitation; so my brother took the hint, and replied he would answer for me. What could I do?" added the young man, throwing back his head proudly; "it shall never be said that a de Franchi passed his word for his brother, and that his brother did not fulfil the engagement."

"And so you have arranged everything?"

"I am afraid so."

"And we shall see the chief of one of these two parties this evening, no doubt?"

"Just so; last night I saw the other."

"Are we going to see an Orlandi or a Colona?"

"An Orlandi."

"Is it far from here?"

"In the ruins of the Castle of Vicentello d'Istria."

"Ah! yes—they told me those ruins were close by."

"Yes, they are about a league from here."

"So in three-quarters of an hour we shall be there?"

"Yes, in about that time."

"Lucien," said Madame de Franchi, "remember you speak for yourself. For a mountaineer as you are it is scarcely three-quarters of an hour distance, but recollect that our guest may not be able to proceed so quickly."

"That is true; we had better allow ourselves an hour and a half at least."

"In that case you have no time to lose," said Madame de Franchi, as she glanced at the clock.

"Mother," said Lucien as he rose, "you will excuse our leaving you, will you not?"

She extended her hand to him, and the young man kissed it with the same respect as he had previously done.

Then turning to me, Lucien said—

"If you prefer to finish your supper quietly, and to smoke your cigar afterwards—"

"No, no!" I cried; "hang it, you have promised me a bandit, and I must have one."

"Well, then, let us take our guns and be off."

I bowed respectfully to Madame de Franchi, and we left the room, preceded by Griffo, who carried a light.

Our preparations did not occupy us very long.

I clasped a travelling belt round my waist, from which was suspended a sort of hunting-knife, and in the folds of which I carried powder and ball.

Lucien soon re-appeared with his cartridge case, and carrying a double-barrelled Manton, and a sort of peaked cap, woven for him by some Penelope of Sullacaro.

"Shall I go with your Excellency?" asked Griffo.

"No, it will be useless," replied Lucien; "but you may as well loose Diamond, as we might put up a pheasant, and the moon is so clear we should be able to shoot as well as in daylight."

An instant afterwards a great spaniel bounded out, and jumped joyously around its master.

We had not gone many paces from the house when Lucien turned round and said—

"By-the-by, Griffo, tell them if they hear any shots on the mountain that it is we who have fired them."

"Very well, your Excellency."

"If we did not take some such precautions," said Lucien, "they would think that hostilities had recommenced, and we should soon hear our shots echoing in the streets of Sullacaro. A little farther on you will see a footpath to the right that will lead us directly up the mountain."

VI

Although it was only the beginning of the month of March the weather was beautiful, and we should have said that it was hot, had it not been for a refreshing breeze which carried with it a savour of the sea.

The moon was rising brilliantly behind Mount Cagna, and the cascades of light were falling upon the southern slope which separates Corsica into two parts, and in a measure forms two different nations, which are always at war, or at least, detest one another heartily.

As we mounted we could see the gorge in which the Tavaro was buried in profound darkness, impossible to penetrate, but we could view the calm Mediterranean, like a vast steel mirror extending into the horizon.

There are certain noises one hears only at night, for during the day they are overcome by other sounds, or it may be they awake only with the darkness, and these produced not upon Lucien, who was familiar with them, but upon me, who was a stranger to them, curious sensations of surprise, and awoke in me a powerful interest in all that I saw.

When we reached the place where the path united with another—one going up the mountain direct, and the other to the right, Lucien turned to me and said—

"Are you anything of a mountaineer?"

"Yes, a little, as far as walking goes."

"You are likely to get giddy, then."

"I am afraid so. The precipice has an irresistible attraction for me."

"Then we had better take this foot-path where there are no precipices, but merely rough walking."

"I am quite equal to that."

"Very well, then, we have three-quarters of an hour's walk before us."

"Let us take the path."

Lucien then went first, and crossed through a little oak wood, into which I followed him.

Diamond trotted fifty or sixty paces away, beating right and left, and occasionally coming back to us, wagging his tail as much as to inform us that we might trust to him and continue our route in safety.

I saw that as some people like to possess a horse, equally for riding or driving, so Diamond had apparently been trained to hunt the biped or the quadruped, the bandit or the boar. I did not wish to appear altogether strange to Corsican manners, so I said as much to Lucien.

"You are mistaken," he replied; "Diamond is very useful in hunting men or animals, but he never chases bandits. It is the triple red of the gendarmes, the voltigeur, and the volunteer that he hunts."

"Then I suppose Diamond is a bandit's dog?"

"He is. He belongs to an Orlandi, to whom I sometimes used to send him into the country with bread, powder, bullets, or whatever he required. He was shot by a Colona, and the next day the dog came to me, for being accustomed to come to the house, he looked upon me as a friend."

"But," I said, "I fancied I saw another dog at your house."

"Yes, that is Brucso, he possesses the same qualities as Diamond, only he came to me from a Colona who was killed by an Orlandi, and so when I pay a visit to a Colona I take Brucso, but when I have business with an Orlandi I take Diamond. If I were to make a mistake and loose them both together they would kill each other. So," continued Lucien, with a bitter smile, "men can make it up, and will receive the sacrament together; the dogs will never eat from the same platter."

"Well," I said, laughing; "here are two regular Corsican dogs, but it seems to me that Diamond, like all other modest creatures, has gone out of earshot while we are speaking of him. I am afraid he has missed us."

"Oh, do not be alarmed," said Lucien, "I know where he is."

"May I inquire where?"

"He is at the Mucchio."

I was about to hazard another question, even at the risk of tiring my companion, when a long howl was heard, so lamentable, so sad, and so prolonged, that I shivered and stopped.

"What can that be?" I said.

"Nothing, it is only Diamond crying."

"What is he crying for?"

"His master. Do you not know that dogs do not forget those they have loved?"

"Ah, I understand," I said, as another prolonged howl rose through the night.

"Yes," I continued, "his master was shot, you say, and I suppose we are approaching the place where he was killed?"

"Just so, and Diamond has left us to go to Mucchio."

"That is where the man's tomb is?"

"Yes, that is to say, the monument which passers-by have raised to his memory, in the form of a cairn; so it follows that the tomb of the victim gradually grows larger, a symbol of the increasing vengeance of his relations."

Another long howl from Diamond's throat made me shudder again, though I was perfectly well aware of the cause of the noise.

At the next turn of the path we came upon the wayside tomb or cairn. A heap of stones formed a pyramid of four or five feet in height.

At the foot of this strange monument Diamond was lying with extended neck and open mouth. Lucien picked up a stone, and taking off his cap approached the mucchio.

I did the same, following his example closely.

When he had come close to the pyramid he broke a branch from a young oak and threw, first, the stone and then the branch upon the heap. He rapidly made the sign of the cross.

I imitated him exactly, and we resumed our route in silence, but Diamond remained behind.

About ten minutes afterwards we heard another dismal howling, and then almost immediately Diamond passed us, head and tail drooping, to a point about a hundred paces in front, when he suddenly resumed his hunting.

VII

We still kept advancing steadily, but, as Lucien had warned me, the path became rougher and more difficult.

I slung my gun over my shoulder, for I perceived that I should soon need both hands to assist me. As for my friend, he continued to press forward with the same easy gait, and did not appear to be at all inconvenienced by the difficult nature of the ground.

After some minutes' climbing over rocks, aided by bushes and roots, we reached a species of platform surmounted by some ruined walls. These ruins were those of the Castle of Vicentello d'Istria, our destination.

In about five minutes we had climbed up to the last terrace, Lucien in advance, and as he extended his hand to assist me he said:—

"Well done, well done; you have not climbed badly for a Parisian."

"Supposing that the Parisian you have assisted has already had some little experience in mountain scrambling?"

"Ah, true!" said Lucien, laughing. "Have you not a mountain near Paris called Montmartre?"

"Yes, but there are others beside Montmartre which I have ascended. For instance, the Rigi, the Faulhorn, the Gemmi, Vesuvius, Stromboli and Etna."

"Indeed! Now I suppose you will despise me because I have never done more than surmount Monte Rotundo! Well, here we are! Four centuries ago my ancestors would have opened the portal to you and bade you welcome to the castle. Now their descendants can only show you the place where the door used to be, and say to you, 'Welcome to the ruins!'"

"I suppose the chateau has been in possession of your family since the death of Vicentello d'Istria?" I said, taking up the conversation at the point at which we had dropped it previously.

"No, but before his birth. It was the last dwelling-place of our famous ancestress Savilia, the widow of Lucien de Franchi."

"Is there not some terrible history connected with this woman?"

"Yes; were it daylight I could now show you from this spot the ruins of the Castle of Valle. There lived the lord of Guidice, who was as much hated as she (Savilia) was beloved, as ugly as she was beautiful. He became enamoured of her, and as she did not quickly respond to his desires, he gave her to understand that if she did not accept him in a given time he would come and carry her off by force. Savilia made pretence of consenting, and invited Guidice to come to dinner at the castle. Guidice was overcome with joy at this, and forgetting that the invitation had only been extorted by menace, accepted it, and came attended only by a few body servants. The gate was closed behind them, and in a few minutes Guidice was a prisoner, and cast into a dungeon, yonder."

I passed on in the direction indicated, and found myself in a species of square court.

The moonlight streamed through the apertures time had made in the once solid walls, and threw dark and well-defined shadows upon the ground. All other portions of the ruins remained in the deep shade of the overhanging walls round about.

Lucien looked at his watch.

"Ah! we are twenty minutes too soon," he exclaimed. "Let us sit down; you are very likely tired."

We sat down; indeed, we extended ourselves at full length upon the grassy sward, in a position facing the great breach in the wall.

"But," said I to my companion, "it seems to me that you have not finished the story you began just now."

"No," replied Lucien. "Every morning and every evening Savilia came down to the dungeon in which Guidice was confined, and then separated from him only by a grating, she would undress herself, and expose herself naked to him, a captive.

"'Giudice,' she would say, 'how do you expect that such an ugly man as you are can ever hope to possess all this?'

"This trial lasted for three months, and was repeated twice a day. But at the end of that period, thanks to a waiting woman whom he had bribed, Guidice was enabled to escape. He soon returned with all his men, who were much more numerous than those Savilia could assemble, and took the castle by assault, and having first possessed himself of Savilia, he subsequently exposed her naked in an iron cage at the cross roads in the Bocca di Cilaccia, offering, himself, the key to any passer by who might be tempted to enter. After three days of this public prostitution Savilia died."

"Well," I said, "it seems to me that your ancestors had a very pretty idea of revenging themselves, and that in finishing off their enemies with dagger or gunshot their descendants have in a manner degenerated!"

"Without mentioning that the day may come when we shall not kill them at all!" replied Lucien. "But it has not come to that yet. The two sons of Savilia," he continued, "who were at Ajaccio with their uncle, were true Corsicans, and continued to make war against the sons of Guidice. This war lasted for four hundred years, and only finished, as you saw, by the dates upon the carbines of my parents, on the 21st September, 1819, at eleven o'clock A.M."

"Oh, yes, I remember the inscription; but I had not time to inquire its meaning, as just then we were summoned to supper."

"Well, this is the explanation: Of the family of Guidice there remained, in 1819, only two brothers. Of the de Franchi family there remained only my father, who had married his cousin. Three months after that the Guidice determined to exterminate us with one stroke. One of the brothers concealed himself on the road to Olmedo to await my father's coming home to Sartène—while the other, taking advantage of his absence, determined to attack our house. This plan was carried out, but with a different result to what had been anticipated. My father, being warned of the plot, was on his guard; my mother, who had also got a hint of the affair, assembled the shepherds, &c., so that when the attack was made the intended victims were prepared for it—my father on the mountains, my mother in the mansion. The consequence was that the two Guidici fell, one shot by my father, the other by my mother. On seeing his foe fall, my father drew out his watch and saw it was eleven o'clock. When my mother shot her assailant she turned to the timepiece and noticed that it was also eleven o'clock. The whole thing had taken place exactly at the same moment. There were no more Guidici left, the family was extinct, and our victorious family is now left in peace; and considering we carried on a war for four hundred years, we didn't want to meddle with it any more. My father had the dates engraved upon the carbines, and hung the pieces up on each side of the clock, as you saw. Seven months later my mother gave birth to twins, of whom one is your very humble servant, the Corsican Lucien; the other, the philanthropist, Louis, his brother."

As he ceased speaking, I noticed a shadow of a man accompanied by a dog projected in the doorway.

The shadows were those of the bandit Orlandi and his friend Diamond.

At that moment the village clock of Sullacaro was heard striking nine with measured strokes.

Evidently the Orlandi was of Louis XV.'s opinion, that punctuality is the politeness of kings!

It would have been impossible to have been more exact than was that king of the mountain, with whom Lucien had appointed a meeting at nine o'clock.

We both rose from our reclining posture when we saw the bandit approaching.

VIII

You are not alone, Monsieur Lucien," said the bandit.

"Do not let that disturb you, Orlandi. This gentleman is a friend of mine, who has heard me speak of you, and wished to pay you a visit. I could not think of refusing him that pleasure."

"Monsieur is welcome to the country," said the bandit, bowing as he advanced towards us.

I returned his salute with the most punctilious politeness.

"You must have been waiting here some time," continued Orlandi.

"Yes, about twenty minutes."

"Quite so. I heard Diamond howling at Mucchio, and he has been with me quite a quarter of an hour since then; he is a good and faithful dog, is he not, Monsieur Lucien?"

"Yes, indeed he is, Orlandi," replied Lucien, as he patted the animal.

"But," said I, "since you knew that Monsieur Lucien was here, why did you not come sooner?"

"Because our appointment was for nine o'clock," said the bandit, "and it is just as unpunctnal to be a quarter of an hour too soon as to arrive a quarter of an hour too late."

"That is meant for a hit at me, Orlandi," said Lucien, laughing.

"No, sir; you no doubt have your reasons; besides you have a companion, and it is likely on his account you may have started earlier, for I know your punctual habits, Monsieur Lucien, and I know also that you have been good enough to put yourself to inconvenience on my account frequently."

"Oh, do not say anything about that, Orlandi; this will probably be the last time."

"Have we not some few words to exchange upon that subject, Monsieur Lucien," said the bandit.

"Yes, if you will have the goodness to follow me."

"I am at your orders."

Lucien turned towards me, and said:

"Will you excuse me a moment?"

"Of course"; I replied.

The men then went away together, and ascending the breach through which Orlandi had appeared halted at the top of it, their figures standing out in strong relief in the moonlight.

Then I was able to take more particular note of this Orlandi. He was a tall man, who had fashioned his beard in exactly the same manner as young de Franchi, and was clothed like him; but his dress showed traces of more frequent contact with the bushes through which he was obliged to fly, and of the earth upon which he was obliged to lie, than did those of Lucien.

I could not hear what the men were talking about, and had I heard it I could not have understood it, as they spoke in the Corsican dialect.

But I was enabled to perceive by their gestures that the bandit was refuting with some heat a series of arguments which the young man was setting forth with an impartiality that did him honour.

At length the gestures of the Orlandi became less frequent and more energetic. His voice became subdued, and he at last bowed his head and held out his hand to the young man.

I concluded the conference was now over, and the men descended together towards me.

"My dear, sir," said Lucien, "Orlandi wishes to shake you by the hand, and to thank you."

"And for what?" I said.

"For being so good as to be one of his sponsors. I have answered for you!"

"If you have answered for me I will readily accept, without even asking what is in question."

I extended my hand to the bandit, who did me the honour to touch it with the tips of his fingers.

"You will now be able to tell my brother that all has been arranged according to his wishes," said Lucien, "and that you have signed the contract."

"Is there, then, a marriage about to take place?"

"No, not yet; but perhaps there may be shortly."

A disdainful smile passed over the bandit's face as he replied,

"We have made peace, Monsieur Lucien, because you wished it; but marriage is not included in the compact."

"No," replied Lucien, "it is only written in the future amongst the probabilities; but let us talk of something else. Did you not hear anything while I was talking with Orlandi?" he said, turning to me.

"Of what you were saying, do you mean?"

"No, but what you might have thought was a pheasant close by?"

"Well, I fancied I did hear a bird crow, but I thought I must have been mistaken!"

"No, you were not mistaken, there is a cock perched in the great chestnut tree you saw about a hundred paces from here. I heard him just now as I was passing."

"Well, then," said Lucien, "we must eat him tomorrow."

"He would have already been laid low," said Orlandi, "if I had not thought that in the village they would believe I was shooting at something besides a pheasant."

"I have provided against that," said Lucien. "By-the-by," he added, turning to me and throwing on his shoulder the gun he had already unslung, "the shot by courtesy belongs to you."

"One moment," I said. "I am not so sure of my aim as you, and I will be quite content to do my part in eating the bird. So do you fire."

"I suppose you are not so used to shooting at night as we are," replied Lucien, "and you would probably fire too low. But if you have nothing particular to do to-morrow you can come and take your revenge."

IX

We left the ruins on the side opposite to that on which we had entered, Lucien going first.

As soon as we had got into the brushwood a pheasant once more loudly announced his presence.

He was about eighty paces from us, roosting in the branches of the chestnut tree, the approach to which was prevented on all sides by the undergrowth.

"I do not quite see how you are going to get him," I said to Lucien; "it does not appear a very easy shot."

"No," he replied; "but if I could just see him, I would fire from here."

"You do not mean to say that your gun will kill a pheasant at eighty yards?"

"Not with shot," he replied; "it will with a bullet."

"Ah! that is a different thing altogether. I did not know you were loaded with ball. You were right to undertake the shot."

"Would you like to see the pheasant?" asked Orlandi.

"Yes," said Lucien, "I confess that I should."

"Wait a moment, then"; and Orlandi began to imitate the clucking of the hen pheasant.

Then, without our being able to see the bird, we perceived a movement in the leaves of the chestnut-tree. The pheasant was evidently mounting branch by branch as he replied to the call of the hen imitated by Orlandi.

At length he arrived at the end of a branch, and was quite visible in the moonlight.

Orlandi ceased, and the pheasant remained motionless.

At the same moment Lucien levelled his gun, and, with a quick aim, fired.

The pheasant fell like a stone.

"Fetch it!" said Lucien to Diamond.

The dog rushed into the brushwood, and soon returned with the bird, pierced by the bullet, in his mouth.

"That is a good shot," I said. "I congratulate you upon it, particularly with a fowling-piece."

"Oh," said Lucien, "I do not deserve your praise, for one barrel is rifled, and carries a ball like a carbine."

"Never mind, such a shot with a carbine deserves honourable mention."

"Bah!" said Orlandi; "why, with a carbine, Monsieur Lucien could hit a five-franc piece at three hundred paces."

"And can you shoot with a pistol as well as with a gun?"

"Yes," said Lucien, "very nearly. At twenty-five paces I can always divide six balls out of twelve on the blade of a knife."

I took off my hat and saluted the speaker, saying,

"Is your brother an equally good shot?"

"My brother?" he replied. "Poor Louis! he has never handled gun nor pistol in his life. My great fear is that he will get mixed up in some affair in Paris, and, brave as he undoubtedly is, he will be killed to sustain the honour of the country."

Lucien, as he spoke, thrust the pheasant into the great pocket of his velveteen coat.

"Now," he said, "my dear Orlandi, till to-morrow farewell."

"Till to-morrow, Monsieur Lucien?"

"I count upon your punctuality. At ten o'clock your friends and relatives will be at the end of the street. On the opposite side Colona, with his friends, will be likewise present, and we shall be on the steps of the church."

"That is agreed, Monsieur Lucien. Many thanks for your trouble; and to you, monsieur," he added, turning to me, "I am obliged for the honour you have done me."

After this exchange of compliments we separated, Orlandi disappearing in the brushwood, while we took our way back to the village.

As for Diamond, he was puzzled which to follow, and he stood looking right and left at the Orlandi and ourselves alternately. After hesitating for about five minutes, he did us the honour to accompany Lucien and me.

I must confess that while I had been scaling the ruined walls I had had my misgivings as to how I should descend, for the descent is usually more difficult, under such circumstances, than the ascent.

But I was glad to see that Lucien, apparently divining my thoughts, took another route home. This road, also, was advantageous in another respect, for it was not so rough, and conversation was easier.

At length, finding the path quite smooth, I continued my questions to my companion, in accordance with my usual custom, and said—

"Now peace is made, I suppose?"

"Yes, and as you see, it has not been concluded without some trouble. I have been obliged to represent all the advances as having been made by the Colona; for, you see, they have had five men killed, while the Orlandi have lost but four. The former consented to the arrangement yesterday, and the latter to-day. The upshot of it all is that the Colona have agreed to hand over a live hen to the Orlandi, a concession which will prove them in the wrong. This last consideration has settled the matter."

"And to-morrow this touching reconciliation will be effected?"

"Yes, to-morrow, at ten o'clock. You are still unfortunate; you hoped to see a Vendetta?"

The young man smiled bitterly as he continued—"But this is a finer thing than a Vendetta! isn't it? For four hundred years, in Corsica, they have been talking of nothing else. Now you will see a reconciliation. I assure you it is a much rarer sight than a Vendetta!"

I could not help laughing.

"There, you see, you are laughing at us," he said. "And you are right, after all. We are really a very droll people."

"No," I replied, "I was laughing at another strange thing, and that is, to see that you are annoyed with yourself because you have succeeded so well in bringing about a reconciliation."

"Ah!" he replied. "If you had understood what we said you would have admired my eloquence. But come back in ten years' time, and you will find us all speaking French."

"You would make a first-rate pleader."

"No, no—I am a referee—an arbitrator. What the deuce do you expect? Must not an arbitrator reconcile opposing factions? They might nominate me the arbiter between Heaven and Hell, that I might teach them to be reconciled, although, in my own heart, I should feel that I was a fool for my pains."

I perceived that this conversation was only irritating to my new acquaintance, so I let it drop, and as he did not attempt to resume it, we proceeded in silence, and did not speak again until we had reached his house.

X

Griffo was in attendance when we arrived, and before his master said a word the servant had taken the pheasant from Lucien's pocket. The valet had heard and had understood the object of the shot.

Madame de Franchi had not yet retired to rest, although she had gone upstairs, and she had left a message with Griffo to request her son to go into her room before she went to bed.

The young man first inquiring whether I was in want of anything, and on my reply in the negative, begged to be excused, to wait upon his mother.

Of course I acknowledged the politeness, and leaving him, went up to my own room.

I entered it with a certain feeling of self congratulation. I was pleased that I had divined the character of Louis, as I had found out Lucien's.

I undressed deliberately, and having taken down a volume of Victor Hugo's works, I lay down and enjoyed myself thoroughly with *Les Orientates*.

For the hundredth time I came upon *Le Feu du ciel*, and re-read it once more. I was fully occupied thus, when I fancied I heard a step upon the staircase, which stopped at my door. I suspected that my host had paused outside, wishing to bid me good-night, but scarcely liking to venture in for fear I should be asleep; so I cried out "Come in," and put my book upon the table.

In fact, as I spoke the door opened, and Lucien appeared.

"I trust you will excuse me," he said; "but it seems to me that I have been somewhat rude this evening, and I did not like to retire without making my excuses to you. So I have come to make the *amende honorable*—and as I daresay you have a number of questions to ask I am quite at your disposal."

"A thousand thanks," I replied; "but, thanks to your good nature, I am already well informed upon most topics concerning which I desired information, and there only remains one question, which I have made up my mind *not* to ask."

"Why?"

"Because it would appear too impertinent. However, if you remain here I confess I cannot answer for myself. I give you fair warning!"

"Well, then, go on. Curiosity unsatisfied is an uncomfortable companion, and awakens all kinds of suppositions; and two, at least, out of every three guesses concerning a fact are sure to be quite wide of the mark, and more likely to prejudice the object than to arrive at the truth concerning it."

"Well, you may rest easy. My worst suspicions concerning you lead me to regard you as a sorcerer!"

The young man laughed loudly.

"The devil! You have inoculated me with some of your curiosity: tell me why, I entreat you—speak out!"

"Well, then, you have had the kindness to clear up many things which were before obscure to me; but one thing you did not touch upon. You have shown me your beautiful weapons, which I should like to examine again before my departure."

"Granted. That's one reason."

"You have explained to me the inscriptions upon the carbines."

"That's another reason."

"You have made it clear to me that, thanks to the phenomenon of your birth, you always experience—although far away from him, the same sensations that agitate your brother, and no doubt he feels equally your troubles."

"That is a third reason for your belief in my sorcery!"

"Yes, but Madame de Franchi, when referring to the sadness you lately have experienced, and which leads you to think that some misfortune threatens your brother, asked you if you were sure he were not dead, and you replied 'No, for then I should have seen him.'"

"Yes, I remember I did say so."

"Well, then, if such an explanation may be entrusted to a stranger, will you explain to me how this could happen?"

The young man's face had assumed a very grave expression as I was speaking, and I hesitated to pronounce the last words.

He was silent for a moment after I ceased to speak, and I said—

"I am afraid that I have been too indiscreet; pray forget that I spoke on the subject at all."

"No," he replied, quietly; "no, but you are a man of the world, and as such inclined to be somewhat incredulous. So, you see, I am rather afraid you will treat as a superstition an old family tradition which has been handed down for centuries."

"Listen," I said. "I can declare one thing, and that is that no one is more easily convinced than I am on all questions of legendary or traditionary lore—and I am always ready to give credence to things regarded as impossible!"

"So you believe in ghosts?"

"Do you wish to hear me tell how I saw one?"

"Yes, that will encourage me."

"My father died in 1807, when I was three and a-half years old. When the doctor announced his speedy death I was sent away to the house of an old cousin in the country.

"She had made up a bed for me opposite her own, to which I was sent at the usual time, and, notwithstanding the trouble hanging over me, I fell fast asleep.

"I was suddenly awakened by three violent blows upon the door of the chamber; I got out of bed and walked across the floor to open it.

"'Where are you going?' asked my cousin.

"She had herself been awakened by the noise, but could not overcome her terror, knowing very well that as the front door was fastened no one would be likely to come to the room in which we were sleeping.

"'I am going to open the door to my father, who has come to bid me adieu,' I replied.

"It was then she jumped out of bed and insisted upon my lying down again. I cried for a long time and very bitterly, saying, 'Papa is at the door, and I want to see papa again before he goes away for ever.'"

"And has the apparition ever returned since?" asked Lucien.

"No, although I have often called upon it; but, perhaps, Providence permitted to the innocence and purity of the child what it declines to accord to the sinfulness of the man."

"Well, then," said Lucien smiling, "in our family we are more fortunate than you."

"Then you are enabled to see your deceased parents?"

"Yes, always when any great event is about to happen or has been accomplished."

"And to what do you attribute this privilege?"

"I will tell you the tradition that has been handed down. You remember that I told you that Savilia died leaving two sons."

"Yes, I recollect."

"Well, these children grew up concentrating on each other the affection they would have bestowed on other relatives had any been alive. They swore nothing should separate them, not even death, and after some incantation or other they wrote with their blood on two pieces of parchment, which they exchanged, the reciprocal oath that whichever died first should appear to the other at the moment of his own death, and, subsequently, at every important epoch of his brother's life. Three months afterwards one of the two brothers was killed in an ambuscade at the moment when the survivor was sealing a letter addressed to him. Just as he was pressing the signet upon the burning wax he heard a sigh behind him, and, turning round, perceived his brother standing behind him, and touching his shoulder, although he felt no pressure from the hand. Then, by a mechanical movement, he held out the letter that was destined for his brother, the spirit took the letter and disappeared. On the night before the survivor's death, the ghost appeared again.

"There is no doubt that the brothers not only made this engagement for themselves, but it applies also to their descendants, for spirits have appeared not only at the moment of the death of those who had passed away, but also on the eve of any great event in their lives."

"And have you never seen any apparition?"

"No; but like my father, who, during the night preceding his death, was warned by his father that he was about to die, so I presume my brother and I inherit the privilege of our ancestors, not having done anything to forfeit it."

"And is this privilege accorded to the males of the family only?"

"Yes."

"That is strange."

"It is as I say."

I looked at the young man as he was speaking to me. He was cool, calm, and grave, and I could not help repeating with Hamlet—

> "There are more things in heaven and earth, Horatio,
>   Than are dreamt of in your philosophy."

In Paris I should have thought that this young man was hoaxing me; but here in Corsica, in a little unknown village, one must look upon him either as a foolish person endeavouring to deceive one for his own purposes, or as a privileged being amongst other men.

"And now," he said, after a long silence, "are you satisfied?"

"Yes, thank you," I answered. "I appreciate your confidence, and will promise to keep your secret."

"Oh, goodness," he said, laughing, "there is no secret in the matter—the first peasant you meet would tell you all I have told you; I only hope that in Paris my brother has not boasted of this privilege, which would only cause men to laugh, and would frighten the ladies."

So saying, he bade me good-night, and retired to his room.

Although fatigued, I was not able to sleep for some time, and when I did at last sleep I was restless.

I appeared to see in a confused manner in my dreams all the people with whom I had come in contact that day. It was only when day broke that I fell into a sound sleep, and was awakened by the striking of a clock, close to my bed, apparently.

I rang the bell, without rising, for my lazy predecessor had provided a bell-rope close at hand, the only one probably in the village.

Griffo immediately appeared, carrying some warm water; I saw that this valet had been well drilled.

Lucien, he said, had twice inquired whether I was awake, and had told him that if I did not ring before half-past nine he would call me.

It was now twenty-five minutes past nine, so it would not be long before he came.

He soon made his appearance, dressed very elegantly in French style, with a black frock coat and white trowsers.

He noticed that I looked at him with some surprise.

"I hope you are admiring my dress," he said; "another proof that I am becoming civilized."

"Yes, indeed," I replied, "and I confess I am considerably astonished to find that you possess such a tailor in Ajaccio. I shall look quite the country bumpkin beside you."

"I assure you my dress is quite Parisian, my dear friend. You see my brother and I being exactly the same height, he for a joke sent me a regular outfit, which I only wear on grand occasions, to receive the préfect, for instance, or when the commandant makes his departmental inspection; or, better still, when I receive a guest like yourself, and when that pleasure is combined with such important business as we are about to accomplish to-day."

There was in this young man's manner of speaking a polished irony, and good-nature withal, which at once set people at their ease, and never passed the bounds of perfect politeness.

I simply bowed in reply, while he carefully inducted his hands into a pair of kid gloves of Paris manufacture.

As now attired, he looked a thorough Parisian.

All this time I was dressing rapidly.

A quarter to ten struck.

"Come along," said Lucien, "if you wish to see the play. I think it is time we took our seats, unless, indeed, you would rather have breakfast first, which appears to me only reasonable."

"Thank you, I seldom eat before eleven or twelve, so I am ready to face both operations."

"Come along, then."

I took up my hat and followed him upstairs.

XI

From the top of the steps by which one reached the door of the chateau usually inhabited by Madame de Franchi and her son, one could look over the square.

This square, so silent the night before, was now full of people, but curiously enough there was not a man to be seen, the crowd was composed of women and children under twelve.

On the lowest step of the church door we could perceive a man girdled with a tri-coloured sash. This was the mayor.

Under the portico, another man clothed in black was seated at a table. This was the notary, and the written paper under his hand was the act of reconciliation.

I took my place beside the tablet with the sponsors of the Orlandi. On the other side were the sponsors of the Colona faction. Lucien stood behind the notary so as to show that he acted for both.

In the choir of the church one could perceive the priests ready to solemnize the mass.

The clock struck ten.

At that moment a shiver pervaded the crowd and all eyes were turned towards the end of the street, if one could so call the unequal interval between the houses.

Immediately on the mountain side appeared the Orlandi, and in the direction of the river was the Colona, each followed by his partisans, but as had been arranged neither party carried arms.

The two chiefs presented a very vivid contrast.

Orlandi, as I said, was tall, brown, agile and thin.

Colona, on the other hand, was short, stoutish, and vigorous; he had red hair and beard, both of which wore short and curly.

Both men carried olive branches, the symbol of peace, which was the idea of the worthy mayor.

But besides this olive branch, the Colona held a white fowl by the feet; this bird was destined to replace that which had given rise to the quarrel, and the fowl was alive.

This last was a point that had long been discussed, and had very nearly upset the whole arrangement. The Colona looked upon it as a double humiliation to have to render back a living fowl for the one which his aunt had thrown dead in the face of the cousin of the Orlandi.

However, by force of reasoning, Lucien had persuaded the Colona to provide the fowl, as he had managed to induce the Orlandi to accept it.

When the two rivals appeared, the bells, which until now had been silent, broke forth into a merry peal.

When they caught sight of each other both Orlandi and his brother made a similar movement of repulsion, but, nevertheless, they both continued their way.

Just opposite the church door they stopped, a few paces only dividing them.

If three days previously these men had caught sight of each other within a hundred paces, one of the two certainly would have remained on the field.

For about five minutes there was a profound silence, a silence which, notwithstanding the peaceful nature of the ceremony, was anything but pacific.

Then at length the mayor spoke.

"Well, Colona," he said, "do you not know that you have to speak first?"

Colona made an effort and muttered some words in the Corsican patois.

I fancied I understood him to say that he regretted having been in Vendetta with his good neighbour Orlandi, and that he offered in reparation the white hen which he held in his hand.

Orlandi waited until his adversary had finished speaking, and replied in some words which I took to be a promise that he would forget everything but the solemn reconciliation that had that day taken place in the presence of Monsieur Lucien and the notary.

After that the rivals preserved a dogged silence.

"Now, gentlemen," said the mayor, "you have only got to shake hands."

By a simultaneous movement the rivals clasped their hands behind their backs.

The mayor descended from his elevated seat, and seizing the hand of Colona sought for the hand of the Orlandi, and having possessed himself of both he, with some effort, which he endeavoured to conceal with a smile, succeeded in joining the two hands.

The notary seized the moment, while the mayor held the two hands together, to stand up and read the deed declaring the feud to be at an end. The document was as follows:—

"In the presence of us, Giuseppe Antonia Sarrola, Notary Royal of Sullacaro in the Province of Sartène.

"In the grand place of the village opposite the church, in the presence of the mayor, the sponsors, and all the population.

"Between Gaetano Orso Orlandi, called Orlandini.

"And Marco Vincenzio Colona, called Schioppone.

"It is solemnly ratified as follows:—

"From this day, 4th of March, 1841, the Vendetta declared between the families shall cease.

"From the same period they shall live together as good neighbours and friends, as their relatives did before the unhappy disunion which has so long alienated their families.

"In witness whereof they have signed these presents under the portico of the village church, with Monsieur Polo Arbori, mayor of the commune, Monsieur Lucien de Franchi, arbitrator, the sponsors of the two contracting parties, and ourselves the Notary.

"Sullacaro, 4th of March, 1841."

I note with admiration that the mayor had very prudently omitted all mention of the hen which had put the Colona in such a bad position with the Orlandi.

So the face of the Colona got brighter in proportion as the figure of the Orlandi clouded; the latter looked at the hen which he was holding in his hand as if he had a great idea to throw it in the face of the Colona. But a glance from Lucien de Franchi checked this intention in the bud.

The mayor saw that he had no time to lose; he stepped back, holding the hands of the rivals, and without loosing them for a moment.

Then, in order to anticipate any discussion at the moment of signature, in view of each considering it a concession to sign before the other, he took the pen and wrote his own name first, and thus converting the shame into an honour, passed the pen to Orlandi, who took it, signed, and passed it to Lucien, who in his turn handed it to Colona, who made a cross.

At that moment the Te Deum was chanted as if for a victory.

We all signed afterwards, without distinction of rank or title, as the nobility of France a hundred years before had signed the protestation against Monsieur le Duc du Maine.

Then the heroes of the day entered the church, and knelt in the places appointed for them.

I saw that from this moment Lucien appeared perfectly at ease. All had been finished satisfactorily: the reconciliation had taken place not only before man but before Heaven.

The service terminated without any incident worth recording; and when it was over, Orlandi and Colona passed out with the same ceremony as before.

At the church door, at the instance of the mayor, they once again shook hands; and then each one, attended by his friends and relatives, made his way to his house, which for three years he had not entered.

Lucien and myself went back to Madame de Franchi's house, where dinner awaited us.

It is not difficult to perceive by the attentions I received that Lucien had read my name over my shoulder when I was signing the paper, and the name was not altogether unknown to him.

In the morning I had announced to Lucien my intention to depart after dinner. I was urgently recalled to Paris by the rehearsals of "Un Mariage sous Louis XV.," and notwithstanding the importunities of mother and son, I persisted in adhering to my first determination.

Lucien then asked permission to take advantage of my offer, and to take a letter to his brother; and Madame Franchi made me promise that I would hand this letter myself to her son.

There was really no trouble in the matter, for Louis de Franchi, like a true Parisian as he was, lived at No. 7, Rue du Helder.

I asked permission to see Lucien's room once again, and he himself conducted me thither, explaining everything to me.

"You know," he said, "if anything strikes you I hope you will take it, it is yours."

I unhooked a small poignard hanging in an obscure corner, as if to show that it had no value attached to it; and as I had seen Lucien notice with some curiosity my hunting-belt and its appurtenances, I begged him to accept it, and he had the good taste to take it without being pressed.

At that moment Griffo appeared to tell me that the horse was saddled and the guide waiting.

I put aside the little present I had intended to give to Griffo, which consisted of a hunting-knife and two pistols attached to it, the barrels of which were hidden in the hilt.

I never saw anybody so delighted as he was at this present.

I descended, and found Madame de Franchi at the bottom of the staircase, where she was waiting to bid me good-bye, in the same place where she had bade me welcome. I kissed her hand, feeling great respect for such a simple-minded and yet so dignified a woman.

Lucien accompanied me to the door.

"On any other day," he said, "I would saddle my horse, and ride with you beyond the mountain, but to-day I dare not quit Sullacaro for fear that one or other of the newly-made friends might commit some folly."

"You are quite right," I said; "and for my own part, I am very glad to have assisted at a ceremony so new to Corsica."

"Yes," he said, "you may well congratulate yourself, for you have to-day witnessed a thing which is enough to make our ancestors turn in their graves."

"I understand—their word was sufficient; they did not need a notary to reconcile them, I suppose?"

"They were never reconciled at all."

He then shook me by the hand.

"Have you no message for your brother?" I said.

"Yes, certainly, if it will not incommode you to deliver it."

"Well, then," said he, "let us embrace. I can only deliver that which I am able to receive."

So we embraced each other.

"We shall see you again some day?" I said.

"Yes, if you come to Corsica."

"No, but won't you come to Paris?"

"I shall never go there," replied Lucien.

"In any case, you will find my card on the mantelpiece in your brother's room—do not forget the address."

"I will promise you that should any event call me to the Continent you shall have my first visit."

"Very well, that is agreed."

We shook hands once again and parted; but I noticed, so long as he could see me, he followed me with his eyes.

All was quiet in the village, although, of course, there was the usual agitation which follows the completion of a great public act; and as I went along the street I sought my friend Orlandi, who had never addressed a word to me, nor even thanked me; and so I passed the last house in the village, and entered the open country without having seen any one like him.

I thought he had entirely forgotten me, and under the circumstances I quite excused him, but before I got very far out of the village I perceived a man stride from the underwood, and place himself in the middle of the road. I recognized him at once as the man who in my great regard for appearances, and in my impatience, I had accused of ingratitude.

He was dressed in the same costume as he had appeared in the previous evening in the ruins of Vicentello.

When I was about twenty paces distant from him he took off his hat; while I spurred my horse so as not to keep Orlandi waiting.

"Monsieur," he said, "I did not wish you to quit Sullacaro without accepting my thanks for the kindness you have shown to a poor peasant like myself, and as in the village I had not the heart, and could not command the language, to thank you, I waited for you here."

"I am obliged to you," I said; "but it was not necessary to take any trouble about it, and all the honour has been mine."

"And after all, monsieur," continued the bandit, "the habit of four years is not easily overcome. The mountain air is strong at first, almost suffocating—but now when I go to sleep in a house I should be afraid the roof would fall upon me."

"But surely," I said, "you will now resume your former habits. I understand you have a house, a field, and a vineyard."

"Yes, but my sister looks after the house; but the Lucquois are there to work in the field, and to raise the grapes. We Corsicans do not work."

"What do you do, then?"

"We overlook the labourers. We walk about with a gun upon our shoulders."

"Well, my dear Monsieur Orlandi," I said, extending my hand, "I wish you good luck; but recollect that my honour as well as your own will be compromised if you fire at anything but game or wild animals. You must never on any account draw a trigger on the Colona family."

"Ah! your Excellency," he replied, with an expression of countenance which I never remarked except amongst the natives of Normandy, "that hen they gave us was a very thin one."

And without another word he disappeared in the brushwood.

I continued my journey thinking that it was very likely that the meagre fowl would be the cause of another rupture between the Orlandi and the Colona.

That evening I slept at Albitucia, next day I reached Ajaccio.

Eight days afterwards I was in Paris.

XII

The day I arrived in Paris I called upon M. Louis de Franchi. He was not at home.

I left my card, with an intimation that I had just returned from Sullacaro, and that I was the bearer of a letter from M. Lucien, his brother. I inquired when he would be at home, as I had undertaken to deliver the letter with my own hand.

To conduct me to his master's study, where I wished to write a note, the valet led me through the dining-room and the *salon*.

I looked around me as I proceeded with a curiosity which will be understood, and I recognized the influence of the same taste which I had already perceived at Sullacaro; only the taste was here set off by true Parisian elegance. M. Louis de Franchi certainly appeared to have a very charming lodging for a bachelor.

Next morning, about eleven o'clock, my servant announced M. Louis de Franchi. I told the man to offer my visitor the papers and to say that I would wait on him as soon as I was dressed.

In five minutes I presented myself.

M. Louis do Franchi who was, no doubt from a sense of courtesy, reading a tale I had contributed to *La Presse*, raised his head as the door opened, and I entered.

I stood perfectly astounded at the resemblance between the two brothers. He rose.

"Monsieur," he said, "I could scarcely credit my good fortune when I read your note yesterday on my return home. I have pictured you twenty times so as to assure myself that it was in accord with your portraits, and at last I, this morning, determined to present myself at your house without considering the hour, and I fear I have been too early."

"I hope you will excuse me if I do not at once acknowledge your kindness in suitable terms, but may I inquire whether I have the honour to address M. Louis or M. Lucien de Franchi?"

"Are you serious? Yes, the resemblance is certainly wonderful, and when I was last at Sullacaro nearly every one mistook one of us for the other, yet, if he has not abjured the Corsican dress, you have seen him in a costume, which would make a considerable difference in our appearance."

"And justly so," I replied; "but as chance would have it, he was, when I left, dressed exactly as you are now, except that he wore white trowsers, so that I was not able to separate your presence from his memory with the difference in dress of which you speak, but," I continued, taking the letter from my pocket-book, "I can quite understand you are anxious to have news from home, so pray read this which I would have left at your house yesterday had I not promised Madame de Franchi to give it to you myself."

"They were all quite well when you left, I hope?"

"Yes, but somewhat anxious."

"On my account?"

"Yes; but read that letter, I beg of you."

"If you will excuse me."

So Monsieur Franchi read the letter while I made some cigarettes. I watched him as his eyes travelled rapidly over the paper, and I heard him murmur, "Dear Lucien, Darling Mother—yes—yes—I understand."

I had not yet recovered from the surprise the strange resemblance between the brothers had caused me, but now I noticed what Lucien had told me, that Louis was paler, and spoke French better than he did.

"Well," I said when he had finished reading the letter, and had lighted the cigarette, "You see, as I told you, that they are anxious about you, and I am glad that their fears are unfounded."

"Well, no," he said gravely, "not altogether; I have not been ill, it is true, but I have been out of sorts, and my indisposition has been augmented by this feeling that my brother is suffering with me."

"Monsieur Lucien has already told me as much, and had I been sceptical I should now have been quite sure that what he said was a fact. I should require no further proof than I now have. So you, yourself, are convinced, monsieur, that your brother's health depends to a certain extent on your own."

"Yes, perfectly so."

"Then," I continued, "as your answer will doubly interest me, may I ask, not from mere curiosity, if this indisposition of which you speak is likely soon to pass away?"

"Oh, you know, monsieur, that the greatest griefs give way to time, and that my heart, even if seared, will heal. Meantime, however, pray accept my thanks once more, and permit me to call on you occasionally to have a chat about Sullacaro."

"With the greatest pleasure," I replied; "but why not now continue our conversation, which is equally agreeable to both of us. My servant is about to announce breakfast. Will you do me the honour to join me, and we can talk at our ease?"

"I regret that it is impossible; I have an appointment with the Chancellor at twelve o'clock, and you will understand that such a young advocate as I am cannot afford to stay away."

"Ah, it is probably only about that Orlandi and Colona affair, as you, no doubt, are aware, and I can re-assure you on that point, for I myself signed the contract as sponsor for this Orlandi."

"Yes, my brother said as much."

"But," he added, looking at his watch, "it is nearly twelve o'clock; I must go and inform the Chancellor that my brother has redeemed my word."

"Ah, yes, most religiously, I can answer for that."

"Dear Lucien, I knew quite well, though our sentiments do not agree on this point, that he would do it for me."

"Yes, and I assure you it cost him something to comply."

"We will speak of all this later, for you can well understand how pleasant it is for me to re-visit with your assistance my mother, my brother, and our home surroundings, so if you will tell me when you are disengaged—"

"That will be somewhat difficult; for this next few days I shall be very busy, but will you tell me where I am likely to find you."

"Listen," he said, "to-morrow is Mi-Careme, is it not?"

"To-morrow?"

"Yes."

"Well."

"Are you going to the Opera Ball?"

"Yes and No. Yes, if you will meet me there. No, if I have no object in going."

"I must go, I am obliged to be there."

"Ah, yes," I said laughing, "I understand, as you said just now, time heals up the greatest griefs, and your seared heart must be healed."

"You are under a misapprehension, for I shall probably sustain new tortures by going."

"Then do not go."

"But what is one to do in this world? We cannot always do what we want; I am dragged thither by fate in spite of myself. I know I had better not go, and nevertheless I shall go."

"Well, then, to-morrow, at the Opera."

"Yes, agreed."

"At what time."

"Half-past twelve midnight, if that will suit you."

"And whereabouts?"

"In the *foyer*—at one, I will be in front of the clock."

"That is understood."

We then shook hands and he left the house quickly.

It was on the stroke of twelve.

As for me, I occupied myself all the afternoon and all the next day in those employments as a man is obliged to undertake on his return from a lengthened tour.

At half-past twelve o'clock at night I was at the rendezvous.

Louis had been waiting some time—he had been following a mask which he thought he recognized, but the lady had been lost in the crowd, and he had not been able to rejoin her.

I wished to speak of Corsica, but Louis was too absent to follow out such a grave subject of conversation. His eyes were constantly fixed on the clock, and suddenly he rushed away from my side, exclaiming:

"Ah, there is my bouquet of violets."

He pushed through the crowd to join a woman who, evidently with a purpose, was holding a large bouquet of violets in her hand.

There were bouquets of every species in the foyer, and I myself was soon accosted by a bouquet of camellias, which congratulated me upon my safe return to Paris.

To the camellias succeeded a bouquet of rose-pompons.

To these succeeded a bouquet of heliotrope.

In fact I was engaged with my fifteenth bouquet when I encountered D——.

"Ah, is it you, *mon cher?*" he cried. "Welcome back; you have returned just in time. I have a little supper party this evening—so-and-so and so-and-so—and we shall count upon you."

"A thousand thanks, my dear fellow; but though I am strongly tempted to accept your invitation, I can't. I am engaged to somebody."

"Yes; but everyone else will bring somebody also," said D——. "It is quite understood that there are to be six water-bottles, whose destiny it is to refresh bouquets."

"Ah, you are mistaken. I shall have no bouquet to put in a water-bottle; I am with a friend."

"Well, you know the proverb, 'Friends of our friends.'"

"It is a young gentleman whom you do not know."

"Well, then, we will make his acquaintance."

"I will tell him of his good fortune."

"Yes, and if he decline, bring him by force."

"I will do what I can, I promise you. At what time?"

"Three o'clock; but as supper will remain on table till six you have ample margin."

"Very well."

A bouquet of myosotis, which perhaps had heard the latter portion of our conversation, then took D——'s arm and walked on with him.

Shortly afterwards I met Louis, who had by this time got rid of his violets.

As the lady who honoured me with her attention just then was a trifle dull, I despatched her to one of my friends, and took Louis' arm.

"Well," I said, "have you learnt what you wanted to know?"

"Oh, yes! You know that at a masked ball people talk of the very things they ought to leave you in ignorance of."

"My poor friend," I said, "pardon me for thus addressing you; but it appears to me that I know you since I have known your brother. Look here—you are unhappy, are not you? Now what is it?"

"Oh, my goodness! Nothing worth talking about."

I saw that he did not wish to speak on the subject, so I said no more.

We took two or three turns in silence.—I was quite indifferent, for I expected nobody, but he was anxiously examining every domino that passed.

At length I said, "Do you know what you might do to-night?"

He started like a man suddenly aroused.

"I! No. I beg your pardon; what did you say?"

"I was about to propose a distraction which it seems to me you need."

"What is it?"

"Come to supper with a friend of mine, with me."

"Oh, no—I am not in a festive humour."

"Bah! They will talk nothing but nonsense, and that will amuse you."

"Well—but I am not invited!"

"You mistake—for you are."

"It is very kind on your part—but 'pon my word I am not worthy of—"

Just then we crossed D——. He seemed very much engaged with his bouquet of myosotis. Nevertheless he saw me.

"Well," he said, "is it settled? Three o'clock."

"Less settled than ever," I replied—"I cannot join you."

"Go to the Devil, then!"

And with this pious ejaculation he continued his course.

"Who is that gentleman?" inquired Louis.

"That is D——, one of my friends; a very cheerful youth, though he is the manager of one of our most respectable papers."

"Monsieur D——!" exclaimed Louis. "Do you know him?"

"Certainly. I have known him for some years."

"And is he the person with whom you are invited to sup this evening?"

"Yes, the same."

"Then it was to his house you intended to take me?"

"Yes."

"Then that alters the case. I accept, and with very great pleasure."

"All right. That settles the question."

"Perhaps, after all, I ought not to go," muttered Louis, smiling sadly. "But you remember what I said yesterday about my destiny. Here is the proof. I should have done better not to have come here this evening."

At this moment we again encountered D——. "My dear fellow," I said, "I have changed my mind!"

"And you will join us?"

"Yes."

"Bravo! But I ought to mention one thing."

"That is?"

"That whoever sups with us to-night, sups with us again to-morrow evening."

"By what law of society is that?"

"By the laws of the wager made with Chateau Renaud."

I felt Louis' arm quiver as it rested on mine—I turned round; but though his face was deadly pale, it was impassable.

"What is the wager?" I inquired.

"Oh, it would occupy too much time to repeat here, and, besides, some one interested might overhear, and it might thus be lost."

"What wonderful discretion you possess! At three, then."

"At three!"

Once more we separated, and as I glanced at the clock I saw it then was thirty-five minutes past two.

"Do you know this M. de Chateau Renaud?" asked Louis, who vainly attempted to command his voice, and to conceal his emotion.

"Only by sight. I have met him occasionally in society."

"Then he is not a friend of yours?"

"Not even an acquaintance."

"Ah, so much the better," replied Louis.

"Why so?"

"For no particular reason."

"But do you know him?"

"Indirectly."

Notwithstanding this evasive answer, it was easy to perceive that between Louis and Chateau Renaud there existed one of those mysterious bonds which could only be forged by a woman. An instinctive feeling assured me that it would be best for all if he and I returned home quietly.

"Will you take my advice, Monsieur de Franchi," I said.

"About what? tell me!"

"Do not go to supper at D——'s house."

"Why not? Does he not expect us? Have you not told him that you will bring a friend?"

"Yes, but that is not the point."

"What is the point then."

"I am sure you had better not go, that is all!"

"But surely you have some reason to give for your change of opinion? just now you were insisting on my presence at D——'s against my will."

"I did not then know that we should meet Chateau Renaud."

"But that is all the better. I believe he is a very pleasant companion, and I shall be glad to make his acquaintance."

"Very well," I replied—"so be it. Shall we go now?"

We accordingly went downstairs for our paletots.

D—— lived within a short distance of the opera house, the morning was very fine, and I hoped that the open air would enliven my companion. So I proposed that we should walk, and this he agreed to.

XIII

We found many of my friends assembled—habitués of the opera lobbies and of the greenroom, and, as I had expected, a few unmasked "bouquets" anxious for the time to come when the water-bottles would be used—supper time!

I introduced Louis to several friends, and it is needless to say that he was politely received and welcomed.

Ten minutes after our arrival D—— entered, accompanied by his bouquet of myosotis, who unmasked herself with a freedom and precision which argued a long acquaintance with these sort of parties.

I introduced Louis to D——.

"Now," said B——, "if all the presentations have been made, I suggest that we present ourselves at table."

"All the presentations are made, but all the guests have not arrived," replied D——.

"Who is expected then?"

"Chateau Renaud is still wanting to complete the party."

"Ah, just so. By-the-by, was there not some bet?"

"Yes. We laid a wager of a supper for twelve, that he would not bring a certain lady here to-night."

"And who is the lady," asked the bouquet of myosotis, "who is so very shy as to be made the subject of a bet?"

I looked at Louis de Franchi. He was outwardly composed, but pale as a corpse.

"Faith, I don't know that there is any great harm in telling you her name, especially as none of you know her I think. She is Madame——"

Louis placed his hand upon D——'s arm.

"Monsieur," he said; "will you grant me a favour? As a new acquaintance I venture to ask it!"

"What is it, monsieur?"

"Do not name the lady who is expected with M. de Chateau Renaud, you know she is a married woman!"

"Oh yes, but her husband is at Smyrna, in the East Indies, in Mexico, or some such place. When a husband lives so far away it is nearly the same as having no husband at all."

"Her husband will return in a few days. I know him. He is a gallant fellow. I would wish, if possible, to spare him the chagrin of learning on his return that his wife had made one at this supper-party."

"Excuse me, monsieur," said D——, "I was not aware that you are acquainted with the lady, and I did not think she was married. But since you know her and her husband——"

"I do know them."

"Then we must exercise greater discretion. Ladies and gentlemen, whether Chateau Renaud comes or not—whether he wins or loses his bet, I must beg of you all to keep this adventure secret."

We all promised, not because our moral senses were offended, but because we were hungry and wished to begin our supper.

"Thank you, monsieur," said Louis to D——, holding out his hand to him. "I assure you you are acting like a thorough gentleman in this matter."

We then passed into the supper-room, and each one took his allotted place. Two chairs were vacant, those reserved for Chateau Renaud and his expected companion.

The servant was about to remove them.

"No," said the master, "let them remain; Chateau Renaud has got until four o'clock to decide his wager. At four o'clock if he is not here he will have lost."

I could not keep my eyes from Louis de Franchi; I saw him watching the timepiece anxiously. It was then 3:40 A.M.

"Is that clock right?" asked Louis.

"That is not my concern," said D——, laughing. "I set it by Chateau Renaud's watch, so that there may be no mistake."

"Well, gentlemen," said the bouquet of myosotis, "it seems we cannot talk of anything but Chateau Renaud and his unknown fair one. We are getting horribly 'slow,' I think."

"You are quite right, my dear," replied V——. "There are so many women of whom we can speak, and who are only waiting to be spoken to——"

"Let us drink their health," cried D——.

So we did, and then the champagne went round briskly; every guest had a bottle at his or her elbow.

I noticed that Louis scarcely tasted his wine; "Drink, man!" I whispered: "don't you see that she will not come?"

"It still wants a quarter to four," said he; "at four o'clock, even though I shall be late in commencing, I promise you I will overtake some of you."

"Oh, very well!" I replied.

While we had been exchanging these few words in a low tone, the conversation had become general around the table. Occasionally D—— and Louis glanced at the clock, which ticked regularly on without any care for the impatience of the two men who were so intent upon its movements.

At five minutes to four I looked at Louis.

"To your health," I said.

He took his glass, smiled, and raised it to his lips. He had drunk about half its contents when a ring was heard at the front door.

I did not think it possible that Louis could become any paler than he was, but I saw my mistake then.

"'Tis he," he muttered.

"Yes, but perhaps he may have come alone," I replied.

"We shall see in a moment."

The sound of the bell had attracted everybody's attention, and the most profound silence suddenly succeeded the buzz of conversation which had till then prevailed.

Then the sound of talking was heard in the anteroom.

D—— rose and opened the door.

"I can recognize her voice," said Louis, as he grasped my arm with a vice-like grip.

"We shall see! wait! be a man!" I answered. "It must be evident that if she has thus come to supper with a man, of her own will, to the house of a stranger, she is not worthy your sympathy."

"I beg, madam, that you will enter," said D——'s voice in the outer room. "We are all friends here I assure you."

"Yes, come in, my dear Emily," said M. de Chateau Renaud, "you need not take off your mask if you do not wish to do so."

"The wretch," muttered Louis.

At that moment a lady entered, dragged in rather than assisted by D——, who fancied he was doing the honours, and by Chateau Renaud.

"Three minutes to four," said Chateau Renaud to D——, in a low voice.

"Quite right, my dear fellow, you have won."

"Not yet, monsieur," said the young unknown addressing Chateau Renaud, and drawing herself up to her full height. "I can now understand your persistence. You laid a wager that I would sup here. Is that so?"

Chateau Renaud was silent. Then addressing D——, she continued.

"Since this man cannot answer, will you, monsieur, reply. Did not M. de Chateau Renaud wager that he would bring me here to supper to-night?"

"I will not hide from you, madame, that he flattered us with that hope," replied D——.

"Well, then, M. de Chateau Renaud has lost, for I was quite unaware he was bringing me here. I believed we were to sup at the house of a friend of my own. So it appears to me that M. de Chateau Renaud has not won his wager."

"But now you are here, my dear Emily, you may as well remain; won't you? See, we have a good company and some pleasant young ladies too!"

"Now that I am here," replied the unknown, "I will thank the gentleman who appears to be the master of the house for the courtesy with which he has treated me. But as, unfortunately, I cannot accept his polite invitation I will beg M. Louis de Franchi to see me home."

Louis with a bound placed himself between the speaker and Chateau Renaud.

"I beg to observe, madam," said the latter between his shut teeth, "that I brought you hither and consequently I am the proper person to conduct you home."

"Gentlemen," said the unknown, "you are five, I put myself into your honourable care. I trust you will defend me from the violence of M. de Chateau Renaud!"

Chateau Renaud made a movement. We all rose at once.

"Very good, madame," he said. "You are at liberty. I know with whom I have to reckon."

"If you refer to me, sir," replied Louis de Franchi with an air of hauteur impossible to describe, "you will find me all day to-morrow at the Rue du Helder, No. 7."

"Very well, monsieur. Perhaps I shall not have the pleasure to call upon you myself, but I hope that two friends of mine may be as cordially received in my place."

"That was all that was necessary," said Louis, shrugging his shoulders disdainfully. "A challenge before a lady! Come, madame," he continued, offering his arm. "Believe me, I thank you from the bottom of my heart for the honour you do me."

And then they left the room, amidst the most profound silence.

"Well, gentlemen, so it seems I have lost," said Chateau Renaud, when the door closed. "That's all settled! To-morrow evening all of you sup with me at the Frères Provençaux."

XIV

The next day, or rather the same day, at ten o'clock, I called upon M. Louis de Franchi.

As I was ascending the staircase, I met two young men coming down. One was evidently a civilian, the other wore the Legion of Honour, and though in *mufti* I could see he was an officer.

I had no doubt that these gentlemen had just been with M. de Franchi, and I watched them downstairs. Then I continued my way to Louis' apartments and rang the bell.

The servant opened the door. His master was in his study.

When the man announced me, Louis, who was writing, looked up and exclaimed—

"Ah, welcome! I was just writing to you. I am very glad to see you. Joseph, I am not at home to any one."

The servant went out and left us alone.

"Didn't you meet two gentlemen upon the stairs?" asked Louis, as he placed a chair.

"Yes, one of them was decorated."

"The same."

"I fancied they had called upon you."

"You are quite right."

"Did they come on behalf of M. de Chateau Renaud?"

"They are his seconds."

"Ah! so he has taken this matter seriously it seems."

"He could scarcely do otherwise," replied Louis.

"So they came to—"

"To request me to name two friends who would confer with them; I thought of you."

"I am really honoured by your kindness. But I cannot go alone."

"I have also written to ask an old friend, the Baron Giordano Martelli, to breakfast here. He will come at eleven. We will breakfast together, and at twelve, perhaps, you will be kind enough to go and see these gentlemen who have promised to remain at home until three o'clock. Here are their names and addresses."

Louis handed me two cards as he spoke.

One card represented the Baron René de Chateaugrand, the other M. Adrien de Boissy.

The former lived in the Rue de la Paix, No. 12.

The latter, who I now saw, belonged to the army, was a lieutenant of Chasseurs d'Afrique, and lived in the Rue de Lille, No. 29.

I turned the cards over and over in my fingers.

"Well, what embarrasses you?" asked Louis.

"I should like to be told frankly if you look upon this as a serious matter. You know we must mould our conduct upon that."

"Indeed, I do consider it a very serious matter. You heard me place myself at M. de Chateau Renaud's disposal, he has sent to me. I must now go with the current."

"Yes, of course, but after all—"

"Go on," said Louis, smilingly.

"After all," I continued, "we must know what you are going to fight for. We cannot put two men up to cut and slash each other without having some ground for the encounter."

"Very well, let me tell you in as few words as possible, the head and front of the offending.

"When I first arrived in Paris I was introduced by a friend of mine, a captain in the navy, to his wife. She was young and beautiful. She made a deep impression upon me, and as I was really afraid I might end by falling in love with her, I very rarely went to my friend's house, although frequently pressed to do so.

"My friend was rather piqued at my absence, and at last I frankly told him the truth, that his wife being so charming I was rather afraid to go to his house. He laughed, shook hands with me, and asked me, even pressed me, to dine with him that same evening.

"'My dear Louis,' said he, after dinner. 'In a few weeks I shall sail for Mexico. I may be absent three months, perhaps six—or longer. We sailors sometimes know when we shall sail, but never when we may return. To you, I commend Emily during my absence. Emily, I beg of you to look upon M. Louis de Franchi as a brother.'

"The lady gave me her hand in token of agreement. I was stupefied! I did not know what to say, and I daresay I appeared very stupid to my future sister.

"Three weeks after this my friend sailed.

"During those three weeks he insisted that I should dine at least once a week with them *en famille*.

"Emily's mother then came to live with her. I need scarcely say that her husband's confidence was not abused, and though I loved her dearly I regarded her simply as a sister.

"Six months elapsed.

"Emily's mother still remained with her, but when he went away, her husband had entreated her to receive as usual. There was nothing my poor friend had a greater horror of than to appear as a jealous husband. He adored Emily and had every confidence in her.

"So Emily continued to receive, and they were very friendly receptions. But her mother's presence silenced all scandal or cause for it, and no one could say a word against her reputation.

"At the end of three months or so M. de Chateau Renaud appeared.

"You believe in presentiments, I daresay. When I first saw that man I disliked him and would not speak to him. I hated him.

"But why I disliked him I cannot tell you. I did!

"Most likely because I saw that even at his first appearance Emily seemed inclined to like him, and he evidently admired her. Perhaps I am mistaken, but, as at the bottom of my heart I had never ceased to love Emily, I suspect I was jealous.

"So on the next occasion I did not lose sight of M. de Chateau Renaud. Perhaps he noticed my looks and it seemed to me that he was chatting in undertones to Emily and holding me up to ridicule.

"Had I yielded to my feelings I would have challenged him that evening, but I reflected that such conduct would be absurd, and restrained myself.

"Every Wednesday thenceforth was a greater trial than the last.

"M. de Chateau Renaud is quite a man of the world, a dandy—a lion—I know how superior he is to me in many respects. But it seems to me that Emily values him more highly than he deserves.

"Soon I found out that I was not the only one who remarked her preference for M. de Chateau Renaud, and this preference increased to such an extent and became so obvious that one day Giordano, who like me was an habitué of the house, spoke to me about it.

"From that moment my resolution was taken. I determined to speak to Emily on the subject, convinced that she was only acting thoughtlessly and I had but to call her attention to the matter to have it remedied.

"But to my great astonishment she took my remonstrances in joke, pretended that I was mad, and that those who agreed with me were as stupid as I was.

"However, I insisted.

"Emily only replied, that she would leave to my own decision as to whether a man in love was not necessarily a prejudiced judge.

"I remained perfectly stupefied; her husband must have told her everything.

"Now you will understand that under these circumstances, and being an unhappy and jealous lover, and only making myself objectionable to the lady, I ceased to visit at the house.

"But although I did not go to her parties I did not the less hear the gossip that was afloat, nor was I the less unhappy, for these reports were assuming a tangible shape.

"I resolved therefore to write to her, and beg her in the strongest language of which I was capable, for her own and her husband's sake, to be careful. She never answered my letter.

"Some time afterwards I heard it publicly stated that Emily was actually the mistress of Chateau Renaud. What I suffered I cannot express.

"It was then my poor brother became conscious of my grief.

"Then, after about a fortnight, you came back to Paris. The very day you called upon me I received an anonymous letter from a lady unknown appointing a meeting at the Opera Ball.

"This woman said that she had certain information to convey to me respecting a lady friend of mine, whose Christian name only she would mention.

"The name was Emily.

"My correspondent said I should recognize her by her carrying a bouquet of violets.

"I told you at the time that I did not wish to go to the ball, but I repeat I was hurried thither by fate.

"I went as you know. I found my domino at the place at the hour indicated. She confirmed what I had already heard respecting Chateau Renaud and Emily, and if

I wished proof, she would give it me, for Chateau Renaud had made a bet that he would take his new mistress to supper at M. D——'s house that evening.

"Chance revealed to me that you knew M. D——, you suggested that I should accompany you. I accepted, you know the rest."

"Now, what more could I do but await and accept the proposals that were made to me?"

"But," I said, at length, as a sensation of fear crossed my mind, "I am afraid I heard your brother say that you had never handled a sword or a pistol."

"That is quite true!"

"Then you are absolutely at the mercy of your adversary!"

"I cannot help it. I am in the hands of Providence."

XV

As Louis was speaking, the servant announced the Baron Giordano Martelli. He was a young Corsican from Sartène. He had served in the 11th Regiment, in which his gallantry had secured him promotion at the age of twenty-three.

"Well," he said, after having bowed to me, "so things have come to a crisis, and no doubt you will soon have a visit from the seconds of Monsieur de Chateau Renaud."

"They have been here already."

"I suppose they have left their names and addresses?"

"Here are their cards."

"Good."

"Well, your servant has just told me that breakfast is waiting. Suppose we sit down, and after breakfast we can return their visit."

We entered the *Salle à manger*, and put aside all business for the present.

During the meal Louis questioned me closely concerning my journey in Corsica, and I told him all the incidents with which the reader is acquainted. He made me repeat, over and over again, all that his mother and brother had said. He was quite touched, knowing the true Corsican instincts of Lucien, with the care he had to taken to reconcile the Orlandi and the Colona.

The clock struck twelve.

"I do not wish to hurry you, gentlemen," said Louis, "but I think you should return the visit of those gentlemen. It will not do to put ourselves in the wrong."

"Oh, you may be quite easy on that point," I said, "we have plenty of time before us."

"No matter," said the Baron Giordano, "Louis is right."

"Now," said I, "we must know whether you prefer to fight with sword or pistol?"

"Ah," he replied, "it is all the same to me; I know as little about one as the other. Besides, Monsieur de Chateau Renaud will save me all trouble in choosing; he looks upon himself, no doubt, as the offended party, and as such will retain the choice of weapons."

"However, the offence is doubtful, you only offered your arm, as you were asked to do."

"My opinion is," said Louis, "that all discussion should tend towards a peaceable arrangement of this matter. My tastes are not warlike, as you know. Far from being a duellist, this is the first affair of the kind I have had, and just for this very reason I wish to come well out of it."

"That is very easy to say, my friend, but you have to play for your life, and you leave to us and before your family the responsibility of the result."

"Ah, as to that you may make your mind quite easy, I know my mother and brother well enough; they would only ask whether I had conducted myself as a brave man, and if you replied in the affirmative they would be satisfied."

"But, hang it, we must know which arm you prefer."

"Well, if they propose pistols, accept them at once."

"That is my advice, also," said the Baron.

"Very well, then, the pistol be it," I replied, "since that is the advice of both of you, but the pistol is a horrible weapon."

"Have I time to learn to fence between this and to-morrow?"

"No, unless, perhaps, you studied Grissier, and then you might learn enough to defend yourself."

Louis smiled.

"Believe me," said he, "that what will happen to-morrow is already written on high, and whatever we may do we cannot alter that."

We then shook hands with him and went downstairs.

Our first visit was naturally to the nearer of the two gentlemen who had called on behalf of our adversary.

We, therefore, visited Monsieur René de Chateaugrand, who lived, as we have said, at 12, Rue de la Paix.

Any other visitors were forbidden while we were calling, and we were at once introduced to his presence.

We found Monsieur de Chateaugrand a perfect man of the world—he would not for one moment give us the trouble of calling upon Monsieur de Boissy—he sent his own servant for him.

While we were waiting his appearance, we spoke of everything but the subject which had brought us thither, and in about ten minutes Monsieur de Boissy arrived.

The two gentlemen did not advance any pretensions to the choice of arms, the sword or pistol was equally familiar to M. de Chateau Renaud. They were quite willing to leave the selection to M. de Franchi, or to toss up. A louis was thrown into the air, face for sword, reverse for pistols. The coin came down reverse.

So it was decided. The combat was arranged to take place next morning at nine o'clock, in the wood of Vincennes, where the adversaries would be placed at twenty paces, and after the third signal given by clapping the hands they were to fire.

We returned to convey this decision to Louis de Franchi.

On my return home the same evening, I found the cards of MM. de Chateaugrand and de Boissy.

XVI

At eight o'clock that evening I called upon M. Louis de Franchi, to inquire whether he had anything to confide to me. But he begged me to wait till next morning, saying:

"The night will bring counsel with it."

Next morning, therefore, instead of calling at eight, which would have given us plenty of time to go to the meeting, I called at half-past seven.

Louis was already writing in his study.

He looked up as I entered, and I noticed how very pale he was.

"Excuse me," he said, "I am writing to my mother. You will find the morning papers there; if you can amuse yourself with them you will see a charming feuilleton by M. Mèry in the *Presse*."

I took the paper thus indicated, and contrasted the livid pallor of the speaker with his calm and sweet voice.

I endeavoured to read, but I could not fix my attention, the letters brought no meaning with them.

In about five minutes Louis said,

"There, I have finished." And he rang for his valet.

"Joseph," said he, "I am at home to no one, not even to the Baron Giordano. If he calls, ask him to wait in the *salon*. I wish to be alone with this gentlemen for ten minutes."

The valet shut the door and disappeared.

"Now, my dear Alexander, listen. Giordano is a Corsican, and has Corsican ideas. I cannot, therefore, confide all I desire to him. I will ask him to keep the secret, that's all. But as regards yourself, I wish you, if you will permit me, to request that you will promise to observe my instructions."

"Certainly. Is not that the duty of a second?"

"A duty more real than you imagine, for you can save our family a second misfortune if you will."

"A second misfortune!" I exclaimed.

"Wait. Read this letter."

I took the letter addressed to Madame de Franchi, and read as follows, with growing astonishment:—

My dearest Mother,—

If I did not know that you possessed Spartan fortitude allied with Christian submission, I would have used means to prepare you for the blow in store for you—for when you receive this letter you will have but one son!

Lucien, my dear brother, love our mother for both in future.

For some time I have been suffering from brain fever. I paid no attention to the premonitory symptoms—the doctor came too late. Darling mother, there is no hope for me now. I cannot be saved but by a miracle, and what right have I to suppose that Providence will work a miracle on my behalf?

I am writing to you in a lucid interval. If I die, this letter will be posted immediately after my death; for in the selfishness of my love for you I wish that you should know that I am dead without regretting anything in the world except your tenderness and my brother's.

Adieu, mother!

Do not weep for me. It is the soul that lives, not the body, and when the latter perishes the former will still live and love you.

Adieu, Lucien! Never leave our mother; and remember that she has you only to look to now.

Your Son,

Your Brother,

Louis De Franchi.

When I had finished the letter I turned to the writer and said—

"Well, and what does this mean?"

"Do you not understand?" he said.

"No!"

"I am going to be shot at ten minutes past nine."

"You are going to be shot?"

"Yes."

"You are mad! Why, what has put such an idea into your head?"

"I am not mad, my dear friend. I have been warned—that's all."

"Warned! By whom?"

"My brother has already told you, I think, that the male members of our family enjoy a singular privilege?"

"True," I replied, shuddering, in spite of myself. "He spoke to me about apparitions."

"Quite so. Well, then, my father appeared to me last night. That is why you find me so pallid. The sight of the dead pales the living!"

I gazed at him with astonishment, not unmixed with terror.

"You saw your father last night, you say?"

"Yes."

"And he spoke to you?"

"He announced my death!"

"Oh, it was some terrible dream!"

"It was a terrible *reality*."

"You were asleep, my friend."

"I was wide awake. Do you not believe that a father can appear to his son?"

I hung my head, for at the bottom of my heart I *did* believe in the possibility.

"What passed between you?" I asked.

"It is a very simple and very natural story. I was reading, expecting my father—for I knew if any danger threatened that he would appear to me—and at midnight the lamp burnt low, the door opened slowly, and my father appeared."

"In what form?" I asked.

"Just as if he were alive—dressed in his usual manner—only he was very pale, and his eyes were without expression."

"Good heavens!" I ejaculated.

"He slowly approached my bed. I raised myself with my elbow, and said, 'You are welcome, father.'"

"He came close, and regarded me fixedly, and it then appeared to me as if some sort of paternal solicitude was expressed in his face."

"Go on," I said; "this is terrible!"

"Then his lips moved, and, though I could hear no sound, I seemed to hear his words distinctly, though distant as an echo."

"What did he say?"

"'Think of God, my son!'

"'I shall be killed in this duel, then?' I asked.

"I saw the tears roll down the pallid visage of the spectre.

"'And at what hour?'

"He pointed towards the timepiece. I followed the direction of his finger. The clock showed ten minutes past nine.

"'So be it, my father,' I said; 'God's will be done. I leave my mother, but I rejoin you.'

"Then a faint smile passed over his face, he waved me a sign of farewell and glided away.

"The door opened as he advanced towards it, and when he had disappeared it shut of its own accord."

This recital was so simply and so naturally told, that it was evident to me the event had occurred just as de Franchi had related it, or he was the victim of an illusion, which he had believed to be real in consequence of the pre-occupation of his mind, and was therefore all the more terrible.

I wiped the perspiration from my forehead.

"Now," continued Louis; "you know my brother, don't you?"

"Yes."

"What do you think he will do when he learns that I have been killed in a duel?"

"He will leave Sullacaro at once to challenge the man who has killed you."

"Just so, and if he is killed in his turn, my mother will be thrice a widow; widowed by the loss of her husband, widowed by the loss of her two sons."

"Ah! I understand. This is fearful!"

"Well, this must be avoided, and that is why I have written this letter. Believing that I have died from brain fever my brother will not seek to avenge me, and my mother will be the more easily consoled, knowing it was the will of God, and that I did not fall by the hand of man. At least—"

"At least what?" I repeated.

"Oh, nothing," replied Louis. "I hope that will not come to pass."

I saw that he was referring to some personal fear, and I did not insist farther.

At this moment the door opened, and the Baron de Giordano entered.

"My dear de Franchi," he said, "I respect your privacy more than anything, but it is past eight, and the meeting is appointed for nine; we have quite a league and a half to drive, and we should start at once."

"I am ready, my dear fellow," said Louis. "I have told my friend here all I had to say to him."

He put his finger on his lips as our eyes met.

"For you, my friend," he continued, turning to the table and taking up a sealed letter, "there is this; if anything should happen to me read this letter, and I pray you to carry out my request contained in it."

"To the very letter," replied the Baron.

"You were to provide the arms," said Louis.

"Yes," I replied, "but just as I was coming away I found that one of the dogs did not bark properly, so we shall be obliged to get a caso of pistols from Devisme.

Louis looked at me, smiled, and held out his hand. He knew quite well that I did not wish to see him killed with my pistols.

"Have you a carriage?" he asked; "if not I will send Joseph for one."

"My coupé is here," said the Baron, "and can carry three at a pinch; besides, my horses will take us more quickly than a *fiacre*."

"Let us go," said Louis.

We went downstairs. Joseph was waiting at the door.

"Shall I accompany you, sir?" he said.

"No, Joseph," replied his master, "I shall not require your services to-day."

Then, stepping back a pace and pressing a roll of gold into the man's hand, he said, "Take this, and if at any time I have appeared brusque to you, pardon my ill-humour."

"Oh, monsieur!" said Joseph, with tears in his eyes, "what is the meaning of this?"

"Chut!" said Louis, and he sprang into the carriage.

"He is a good servant," he murmured, "and if either of you can ever be of use to him I shall be obliged."

"Is he about to leave you?" said the Baron.

"No," said Louis, smiling; "I am leaving him, that is all!"

We stopped at Devismes just long enough to secure a case of pistols, powder and bullets, and then resumed our way at a brisk trot.

XVII

We reached Vincennes at five minutes to nine.

Another carriage, that of Chateau Renaud, arrived at the same time.

We proceeded into the wood by different paths. Our carriages were to await us in the broad avenue. A few minutes later we met at the rendezvous.

"Gentlemen," said Louis, "recollect that no arrangement is possible now."

"Nevertheless—," I said.

"Oh, my dear sir," he replied, "after what I have told you, you should be the last person to think that any reconciliation is possible."

I bowed before this absolute will, which for me was supreme.

We left Louis near the carriages, and advanced towards M. de Boissy and M. de Chateaugrand.

The Baron de Giordano carried the case of pistols. The seconds exchanged salutes.

"Gentlemen," said the Baron, "under these circumstances the shortest compliments are the best, for we may be interrupted any moment. We were requested to provide weapons—here they are. Examine them if you please. We have just procured them from the gunsmith, and we give you our word of honour that M. Louis de Franchi has not even seen them."

"Such an assurance is unnecessary, gentlemen," replied Chateaugrand, "we know with whom we have to deal," and taking one pistol, while M. de Boissy took the other, the seconds examined the bore.

"These are ordinary pistols, and have never been used," said the Baron; "now the question is, how shall the principals fire."

"My advice," said M. de Boissy, "is that they should fire just as they are accustomed to do, together."

"Very well," said the Baron Giordano, "then all chances are equalized."

"Will you advise M. de Franchi, then, and we will tell M. de Chateau Renaud, monsieur."

"Now that is settled, will you have the goodness to load the pistols?"

Each one took a pistol, measured carefully the charges of powder, took two bullets at hazard, and rammed them home.

While the weapons were being loaded, I approached Louis, who received me with a smile.

"You won't forget what I asked you?" he said, "and you will obtain from Giordano a promise that he will say nothing to my mother, or even to my brother. Will you take care, also, that this affair does not get into the papers, or, if it does, that no names are mentioned."

"You are still of opinion, then, this duel will prove fatal to you?" I said.

"I am more than ever convinced of it," he replied, "but you will do me this justice at least, that I met death like a true Corsican."

"My dear de Franchi, your calmness is so astounding that it gives me hopes that you yourself are not convinced on this point."

Louis took out his watch.

"I have but seven minutes to live," he said; "here is my watch, keep it, I beg of you, in remembrance of me." I took the watch, and shook my friend's hand.

"In eight minutes I hope to restore it to you," I said.

"Don't speak of that," he replied. "See, here are the others."

"Gentlemen," said the Viscount de Chateaugrand, "a little distance from here, on the right, is an open space where I had a little practice of my own last year; shall we proceed thither? we shall be less liable to interruption."

"If you will lead the way," said the Baron Giordano, "we will follow."

The Viscount preceded us to the spot indicated. It was about thirty paces distant, at the bottom of a gentle slope surrounded on all sides by a screen of brushwood, and seemed fitted by nature as the theatre of such an event as was about to take place.

"M. Martelli," said the Viscount, "will you measure the distance by me?" The Baron assented, and thus side by side he and M. de Chateaugrand measured twenty ordinary paces.

I was then left for a few seconds alone with M. de Franchi.

"*Apropos*," he said, "you will find my will on the table where I was writing when you came in this morning."

"Good," I replied, "you may rest quite easy on that score."

"When you are ready, gentlemen," said the Viscount de Chateaugrand.

"I am here," replied Louis. "Adieu, dear friend! thank you for all the trouble you have taken for me, without counting all you will have to do for me later on." I pressed his hand. It was cold, but perfectly steady.

"Now," I said, "forget the apparition of last night, and aim your best."

"You remember de Freysckutz?"

"Yes."

"Well, you know, then, that every bullet has its billet. Adieu!"

He met the Baron Giordano, who handed him the pistol; he took it, and, without looking at it, went and placed himself at the spot marked by the handkerchief.

M. de Chateau Renaud had already taken up his position.

There was a moment of mournful silence, during which the young men saluted their seconds, then their adversary's seconds, and finally each other.

M. de Chateau Renaud appeared perfectly accustomed to these affairs, and was smiling like a man sure of success; perhaps, also, he was aware that Louis de Franchi never had fired a pistol in his life.

Louis was calm and collected, his fine head looked almost like a marble bust.

"Well, gentlemen," said Chateau Renaud, "you see we are waiting."

Louis gave me one last glance, and smiling, raised his eyes to heaven.

"Now, gentlemen, make ready," said Chateaugrand. Then, striking his hands one against the other, he cried—

"One! Two! Three!"

The two shots made but one detonation.

An instant afterwards I saw Louis de Franchi turn round twice and then fall upon one knee.

M. de Chateau Renaud remained upright. The lappel of his coat had been shot through.

I rushed towards Louis de Franchi.

"You are wounded?" I said.

He attempted to reply, but in vain. A red froth appeared upon his lips.

At the same moment he let fall his pistol, and pressed his hand against his right side.

On looking closely, we perceived a tiny hole not large enough for the point of a little finger.

I begged the Baron to hasten to the barracks, and bring the surgeon of the regiment.

But de Franchi collected all his strength, and stopping Giordano, signed that all assistance would be useless. This exertion caused him to fall on both knees.

M. de Chateau Renaud kept at a distance, but his seconds now approached the wounded man.

Meanwhile, we had opened his coat and torn away his waistcoat and shirt.

The ball had entered the right side, below the sixth rib, and had come out a little above the left hip.

At each breath the wounded man drew, the blood welled out. It was evident he was mortally hurt.

"M. de Franchi," said the Viscount de Chateaugrand, "we regret extremely the issue of this sad affair. We trust you bear no malice against M. de Chateau Renaud."

"Yes, yes," murmured the wounded man, "I forgive him."

Then turning towards me with an effort he said,

"Remember your promise!"

"I swear to you I will do all you wish."

"And now," he said, smiling, "look at the watch!"

He breathed a long sigh, and fell back. That sigh was his last.

I looked at the watch, it was exactly ten minutes past nine.

I turned to Louis de Franchi—he was dead.

We took back the body to the Rue de Helder, and while the Baron went to make the usual declaration to the Commissary of Police, I went upstairs with Joseph.

The poor lad was weeping bitterly.

As I entered, my eyes unconsciously turned towards the timepiece; it marked ten minutes past nine.

No doubt he had forgotten to wind it, and it had stopped at that hour.

The Baron Giordano returned almost immediately with the officers, who put the seals on the property.

The Baron wished to advise the relatives and friends of the affair, but I begged him, before he did so, to read the letter that Louis had handed to him before we set out that morning.

The letter contained his request that the cause of his death should be concealed from his brother, and that his funeral should be as quiet as possible.

The Baron Giordano charged himself with these details, and I sought MM. de Boissy and de Chateaugrand, to request their silence respecting the unhappy affair, and to induce Chateau Renaud to leave Paris for a time, without mentioning my reason for this last suggestion.

They promised me to do all they could to meet my views, and as I walked to Chateau Renaud's house I posted the letter to Madame de Franchi, informing her that her son had died of brain fever.

XVIII

Contrary to custom, the duel was very little talked about; even the papers were silent on the subject.

A few intimate friends followed the body to Père la Chaise. Chateau Renaud refused to quit Paris, although pressed to do so.

At one time I thought of following Louis' letter to Corsica with one from myself, but although my intentions were good, the misleading statements I should have to make were so repugnant to me that I did not do so. Besides, I was quite convinced that Louis himself had fully weighed before he had decided upon his course of action.

So at the risk of being thought indifferent, or even ungrateful, I kept silence, and I was sure that the Baron Giordano had done as much.

Five days after the duel, at about eleven o'clock in the evening, I was seated by my table in a rather melancholy frame of mind, when my servant entered and shutting the door quickly behind him said, in an agitated whisper, that M. de Franchi desired to speak with me.

I looked at him steadily; he was quite pale.

"Whom did you say, Victor?" I asked.

"Oh, monsieur, in truth I hardly know myself."

"What M. de Franchi wishes to speak to me?"

"Monsieur's friend. The gentleman who was here two or three times."

"You are mad, my good man. Do you not know that I had the misfortune to lose my friend five days ago?"

"Yes, sir; and that is the reason I am so upset. He rang, I was in the ante-chamber, and opened the door, but recoiled at his appearance. However, he entered, and asked if you were at home. I replied that you were, and then he said, 'Go and announce M. de Franchi, who wishes to speak with your master,' and so I came."

"You are stupid, Victor, the ante-chamber is not properly lighted. You were asleep, no doubt, and did not hear correctly. Go, and ask the gentleman his name."

"It would be useless, sir. I swear to you I am not deceived. I heard him, and saw him, distinctly."

"Then go and show him in."

Victor turned tremblingly to the door, opened it, and then standing still in the room, said—

"Will monsieur be kind enough to come in?"

I immediately heard the footsteps of my visitor crossing the ante-chamber, and sure enough, at the door there appeared M. de Franchi.

I confess that I was terrified, and took a step backwards as he approached.

"I trust you will excuse my appearance so late," said my visitor; "I only arrived ten minutes ago, and you will understand that I could not wait till tomorrow without seeing you."

"Oh, my dear Lucien," I exclaimed, advancing quickly, and embracing him. "Then it is realty you." And, in spite of myself, tears really came into my eyes.

"Yes," he said, "it is I."

I made a calculation of the time that had elapsed, and could scarcely imagine that he had received the letter—it could hardly have reached Ajaccio yet.

"Good Heavens! then you do not know what has happened?" I exclaimed.

"I know all," was his reply.

"Victor," I said, turning towards my servant, who was still rather embarrassed, "leave us, and return in a quarter of an hour with some supper. You will have something to eat, and will sleep here of course."

"With great pleasure," he replied. "I have eaten nothing since we left Auxerre. Then, as to lodgings, as nobody knew me in the Rue de Helder, or rather," he added, with a sad smile, "as everybody recognized me there, they declined to let me in, so I left the whole house in a state of alarm."

"In fact, my dear Lucien, your resemblance to Louis is so very striking that even I myself was just now taken aback."

"How," exclaimed Victor, who had not yet ventured to leave us. "Is monsieur the brother—"

"Yes," I replied, "go and get supper."

Victor went out, and we found ourselves alone.

I took Lucien by the hand, and leading him to an easy chair seated myself near him.

"I suppose (I began) you were on your way to Paris when the fatal news met you?"

"No, I was at Sullacaro!"

"Impossible! Why your brother's letter could not have reached you."

"You forget the ballad of *Burger*, my dear Alexander—*the dead travel fast!*"

I shuddered! "I do not understand," I said.

"Have you forgotten what I told you about the apparitions familiar to our family?"

"Do you mean to say that you have *seen* your dead brother?"—"Yes."—"When?"

"On the night of the 16th inst."

"And he told you everything?"—"All!"

"That he was dead?"

"He told me that he had been killed. The dead never lie!"

"And he said in what way?"

"In a duel."

"By whom?"

"By M. de Chateau Renaud."

"Oh no, Lucien, that cannot be," I exclaimed, "you have obtained your information in some other way."

"Do you think I am likely to joke at such a time?"

"I beg your pardon. But truly what you tell me is so strange, and everything that relates to you and your brother so out of ordinary nature, that—"

"That you hesitate to believe it. Well, I can understand the feeling. But wait. My brother was hit here," he continued, as he opened his shirt and showed me the blue mark of the bullet on his flesh, "he was wounded above the sixth rib on the right side—do you believe that?"

"As a matter of fact," I replied, "that is the very spot where he was hit."

"And the bullet went out here," continued Lucien, putting his finger just above his left hip.

"It is miraculous," I exclaimed.

"And now," he went on, "do you wish me to tell you the time he died?"

"Tell me!"

"At ten minutes past nine."

"That will do, Lucien"; I said, "but I lose myself in questions. Give me a connected narrative of the events. I should prefer it."

XIX

Lucien settled himself comfortably in his arm-chair and looking at me fixedly, resumed:—

"It is very simple. The day my brother was killed I was riding very early, and went out to visit the shepherds, when soon after I had looked at my watch and replaced it in my pocket, I received a blow in the side, so violent that I fainted. When I recovered I found myself lying on the ground in the arms of the Orlandini, who was bathing my face with water. My horse was close by.

"'Well,' said Orlandini, 'what has happened?'

"'I know no more about it than you do. Did you not hear a gun fired?'

"'No.'

"'It appears to me that I have received a ball in the side,' and I put my hand upon the place where I felt pain.

"'In the first place,' replied he, 'there has been no shot fired, and besides, there is no mark of a bullet on your clothes.'

"'Then,' I replied, 'it must be my brother who is killed.'

"'Ah, indeed,' he replied, 'that is a different thing.' I opened my coat and I found a mark, only at first it was quite red and not blue as I showed you just now.

"For an instant I was tempted to return to Sullacaro, feeling so upset both mentally and bodily, but I thought of my mother, who did not expect me before supper time, and I should be obliged to give her a reason for my return, and I had no reason to give.

"On the other hand, I did not wish to announce my brother's death to her until I was absolutely certain of it. So I continued my way, and returned home about six o'clock in the evening.

"My poor mother received me as usual. She evidently had no suspicion that anything was wrong.

"Immediately after supper, I went upstairs, and as I passed through the corridor the wind blew my candle out.

"I was going downstairs to get a light when, passing my brother's room, I noticed a gleam within.

"I thought that Griffo had been there and left a lamp burning.

"I pushed open the door; I saw a taper burning near my brother's bed, and on the bed my brother lay extended, naked and bleeding.

"I remained for an instant, I confess, motionless with terror, then I approached.

"I touched the body, he was already dead.

"He had received a ball through the body, which had struck in the same place where I had felt the blow, and some drops of blood were still falling from the wound.

"It was evident to me that my brother had been shot.

"I fell on my knees, and leaning my head against the bed, I prayed fervently.

"When I opened my eyes again the room was in total darkness, the taper had been extinguished, the vision had disappeared.

"I felt all over the bed, it was empty.

"Now I believe I am as brave as most people, but when I tottered out of that room I declare to you my hair was standing on end and the perspiration pouring from my forehead.

"I went downstairs for another candle. My mother noticed me, and uttered a cry of surprise.

"'What is the matter with you,' she said, 'and why are you so pale?'

"'There is nothing the matter,' I replied, as I returned upstairs.

"This time the candle was not extinguished. I looked into my brother's room; it was empty.

"The taper had completely disappeared, nor was there any trace of the body on the bed.

"On the ground was my first candle, which I now relighted.

"Notwithstanding this absence of proof, I had seen enough to be convinced that at ten minutes past nine that morning my brother had been killed. I went to bed in a very agitated frame of mind.

"As you may imagine, I did not sleep very well, but at length fatigue conquered my agitation and I got a little rest.

"Then all the circumstances came before me in the form of a dream. I saw the scene as it had passed. I saw the man who had killed him. I heard his name. He is called M. de Chateau Renaud."

"Alas! that is all too true," I replied; "but what have you come to Paris for?"

"I have come to kill the man who has killed my brother."

"To kill him?"

"Oh, you may rest assured, not in the Corsican fashion from behind a wall or through a hedge, but in the French manner, with white gloves on, a frilled shirt, and white cuffs."

"And does Madame de Franchi know you have come to Paris with this intention?"

"She does."

"And she has let you come?"

"She kissed me, and said, 'Go.' My mother is a true Corsican."

"And so you came."

"Here I am."

"But your brother would not wish to be avenged were he alive."

"Well, then," replied Lucien, smiling bitterly, "he must have changed his mind since he died."

At this moment the valet entered, carrying the supper tray.

Lucien eat like a man without a care in the world.

After supper I showed him to his room. He thanked me, shook me by the hand, and wished me good-night.

Next morning he came into my room as soon as the servant told him I was up.

"Will you accompany me to Vincennes?" he said. "If you are engaged I will go alone."

"Alone!" I replied. "How will you be able to find the spot?"

"Oh, I shall easily recognize it. Do you not remember that I saw it in my dream?"

I was curious to know how far he was correct in this. "Very well," I said, "I will go with you."

"Get ready, then, while I write to Giordano. You will let Victor take the note for me, will you not?"

"He is at your disposal."

"Thank you."

Ten minutes afterwards the letter was despatched. I then sent for a cabriolet and we drove to Vincennes.

When we reached the cross-paths Lucien said, "We are not far off now, I think."

"No; twenty paces further on we shall be at the spot where we entered the forest."

"Here we are," said the young man, as he stopped the carriage.

It was, indeed, the very spot!

Lucien entered the wood without the least hesitation, and as if he had known the place for years. He walked straight to the dell, and when there turned to the eastward, and then advancing he stopped at the place where his brother had fallen: stooping down he perceived the grass wore the red tinge of blood.

"This is the place," he said.

Then he lightly kissed the spot where his brother had lain.

Rising with flashing eyes he paced the dell to the spot whence Chateau Renaud had fired.

"This is where he stood," he said, stamping his foot, "and here he shall lie to-morrow."

"How!" I exclaimed. "To-morrow!"

"Yes, unless he is a coward. For to-morrow he shall give me my revenge."

"But, my dear Lucien," I said, "the custom in France is, as you are aware, that a duel cannot take place without a certain reason. Chateau Benaud called out your brother who had provoked him, but he has had nothing to do with you."

"Ah, really! So Chateau Renaud had the right to quarrel with my brother because he offered his arm to a woman whom Chateau Renaud had scandalously deceived, and according to you he had the right to challenge my brother. M. de Chateau Renaud killed my brother, who had never handled a pistol: he shot him with the same sense of security that a man would shoot a hare; and yet you say I have no right to challenge Chateau Renaud. Nonsense!"

I bowed without speaking.

"Besides," he continued, "you have nothing to do with it. You may be quite easy. I wrote to Giordano this morning, and when we return to Paris all will have been arranged. Do you think that M. de Chateau Renaud will refuse?"

"M. de Chateau Renaud has unfortunately a reputation for courage which may serve to remove any doubt you may entertain on that score."

"All the better," said Lucien. "Let us go to breakfast."

We returned to the road, and entering the cabriolet, I told the man to drive to the Rue Rivoli.

"No," said Lucien, "you shall breakfast with me. Coachman, the *Café de Paris*; is not that the place where my brother usually dined?"

"I believe so," I replied.

"Well, that is where I requested Giordano to meet us."

"To the Café de Paris, then."

In half an hour we were set down at the restaurant.

XX

Lucien's appearance created quite a sensation in consequence of his remarkable likeness to his brother.

The news of Louis' death had gone abroad—not, perhaps, in all its details, but it was known, and Lucien's appearance astonished many.

I requested a private room, saying that we were expecting the Baron Giordano, and we got a room at the end.

Lucien began to read the papers carelessly, as if he were oblivious of everything.

While we were seated at breakfast Giordano arrived.

The two young men had not met for four or five years, nevertheless, a firm clasp of the hand was the only demonstration they permitted themselves.

"Well, everything is settled," he said.

"Then M. de Chateau Renaud has accepted?"

"Yes, on condition, however, that after he has fought you he shall be left in peace."

"Oh, he may be quite easy; I am the last of the de Franchi. Have you seen him, or his seconds?"

"I saw him; he will notify MM. de Boissy and de Chateaugrand. The weapons, the hour and the place will be the same."

"Capital, sit down and have some breakfast."

The Baron seated himself, and we spoke on indifferent topics. After breakfast Lucien begged us to introduce him to the Commissioner of Police, who had sealed up his brother's property, and to the proprietors of the house at which his brother had lived, for he wished to sleep that night, the last night that separated him from his vengeance, in Louis' room.

All these arrangements took up time, so it was not till five o'clock that Lucien entered his brother's apartment. Respecting his grief, we left him there alone.

We had arranged to meet him again next morning at eight o'clock, and he begged me to bring the same pistols, and to buy them if they were for sale.

I went to Devismes and purchased the weapons. Next morning, at eight o'clock I was with Lucien.

When I entered, he was seated writing at the same table, where his brother had sat writing. He smiled when he saw me, but he was very pale.

"Good morning," he said, "I am writing to my mother."

"I hope you will be able to write her a less doleful letter than poor Louis wrote eight days ago."

"I have told her that she may rest happy, for her son is avenged."

"How are you able to speak with such certainty?"

"Did not my brother announce to you his own approaching death? Well, then, I announce to you the death of M. de Chateau Renaud."

He rose as he spoke, and touching me on the temple, said—

"There, that's where I shall put my bullet."

"And yourself."

"I shall not be touched."

"But, at least, wait for the issue of the duel, before you send your letter."

"It would be perfectly useless."

He rang, the servant appeared.

"Joseph," said he, "take this letter to the post."

"But have you seen your dead brother?"

"Yes," he answered.

It is a very strange thing the occurrence of these two duels so close together, and in each of which one of the two combatants was doomed. While we were talking the Baron Giordano arrived. It was eight o'clock, so we started.

Lucien was very anxious to arrive first, so we were on the field ten minutes before the hour.

Our adversaries arrived at nine o'clock punctually. They came on horseback, followed by a groom also on horseback.

M. de Chateau Renaud had his hand in the breast of his coat. I at first thought he was carrying his arm in a sling.

The gentlemen dismounted twenty paces from ns, and gave their bridles to the groom.

Monsieur de Chateau Renaud remained apart, but looked steadfastly at Lucien, and I thought he became paler. He turned aside and amused himself knocking off the little flowers with his riding whip.

"Well, gentlemen, here we are!" said MM. de Chateaugrand and de Boissy, "but you know our conditions. This duel is to be the last, and no matter what the issue may be, M. de Chateau Renaud shall not have to answer to any one for the double result."

"That is understood," we replied. Then Lucien bowed assent.

"You have the weapons, gentlemen?" said the Viscount.

"Here are the same pistols."

"And they are unknown to M. de Franchi?"

"Less known to him than to M. de Chateau Renaud who has already used them once. M. de Franchi has not even seen them."

"That is sufficient, gentlemen. Come, Chateau Renaud!"

We immediately entered the wood, and each one felt, as he revisited the fatal spot, that a tragedy more terrible still was about to be enacted.

We soon arrived in the little dell.

M. de Chateau Renaud, thanks to his great self-command, appeared quite calm, but those who had seen both encounters could appreciate the difference. From time to time he glanced under his lids at Lucien, and his furtive looks denoted a disquietude approaching to fear.

Perhaps it was the great resemblance between the brothers that struck him, and he thought he saw in Lucien the avenging shade of Louis.

While they were loading the pistols I saw him draw his hand from the breast of his coat. The fingers were enveloped in a handkerchief as if to prevent their twitching.

Lucien waited calmly, like a man who was sure of his vengeance.

Without being told, Lucien walked to the place his brother had occupied, which compelled Chateau Renaud to take up his position as before.

Lucien received his weapon with a joyous smile.

When Chateau Renaud took his pistol he became deadly pale. Then he passed his hand between his cravat and his neck as if he were suffocating.

No one can conceive with what feelings of terror I regarded this young man, handsome, rich, and elegant, who but yesterday believed he had many years still before him, and who to-day, with the sweat on his brow and agony at his heart, felt he was condemned.

"Are you ready, gentlemen?" asked M. de Chateaugrand.

"Yes," replied Lucien.

M. de Chateau Renaud made a sign in the affirmative.

As for me I was obliged to turn away, not daring to look upon the scene.

I heard the two successive clappings of the hands, and at the third the simultaneous reports of the pistols. I turned round.

Chateau Renaud was lying on the ground, stark dead; he had not uttered a sound nor made a movement.

I approached the body, impelled by that invincible curiosity which compels one to see the end of a catastrophe.

The bullet had entered the dead man's temple, at the very spot that Lucien had indicated to me previously.

I ran to him, he was calm and motionless, but seeing me coming towards him he let fall the pistol, and threw himself into my arms.

"Ah, my brother, my poor brother!" he cried as he burst into a passion of sobs.

These were the first tears that the young man had shed.

English Steel
and Spanish Passion

Drake Williams and Warren Geiger

THE GODS FROWNED AS EDWARD TERROR AND THE *MAID OF AVON* BEAT
through the Mona Passage off the green land mass that was Hispaniola.
The sea was sparkling blue and the sky was azure as the little Dutch-built
merchantman bowled merrily over the waves. Her hold was fat with spices and cane
and her destination was home, Cardiff, Wales.

"Aye, Duggley, a few more weeks and we'll be back home for good." With
satisfaction in his black eyes and a smile on his tanned face, the master of the Maid of
Avon spoke to his Somersetshire navigator.

"We've all made enough to settle us for life and live like barons, Edward," the
massive, muscular navigator replied. "Although, to be truthful with you, I'm going to
miss the tang of the sea and the good fortune that always seemed to be yours."

"We have been lucky in our voyages and now all that we need is for Lady Luck
to hold with us across the Atlantic and, Duggley, we'll have never a need to press
her again."

At that moment, from a stripe-shirted seaman high in the rigging there came a hail.

"Sail ho, three points off the starboard bow!" The tall, lean figure of Edward
Terror straightened up from its recline against the taffrail. From the side pocket of
his greatcoat, a thing of beauty in silver and blue, he withdrew a glass and mounted
the mizzenmast ratlines. Hand-over-hand, he scrambled up the hemp to the crosstrees
and slapped the eyepiece open. Bearing down upon them under a mighty press of sail
was a large three-master. By her cut, and not by her ensign for she showed none, the
Welshman saw that she was of Spanish build and her open gunports revealed sixteen
cannon to a flank.

"I don't like her looks, Duggley," Edward said as he leaped to the poop deck. His
heavy black brows were knit in thought as he slipped off his coat and flung it to one of
his men. "She flies no flag and her gunports are open. These are pirate waters so let's
clear for action until we can better understand her motive in bearing down upon us so."

In a trice the Maid of Avon was cleared of gear on her upper two decks and her puny armament of ten demi-culverins was run out. Cutlasses and pistols were readied on the quarterdeck and the equipage of the guncrews, rams, powder, balls, buckets, and fuses, was placed by the open ports.

"She's got the weather gauge of us, Edward," the blonde Duggley noted to his captain. "And, by the great bear, I believe she means us foul play."

Edward glanced at the rippling Cross of St. George flying at his own gaff and wondered what manner of foe this stranger on the seas could be. It would do him no good to flee because it was evident that the mighty scarlet stranger was more fleet of sail than his smaller vessel. Bought at Plymouth, the *Maid of Avon* was a captured prize from the great battle at Texel in 1653. She was fine for trade but even the renowned Dutch Admiral De Ruyter could never have made of her a formidable or speedy man-of-war. He must trust to luck and hope for the best.

"There's a flag running up her main-truck," the clear call of the lookout shrilled forth. "She's Spanish!"

There brazenly slapping in the easterly breeze was the red and yellow banner of Castile. At that very moment a cotton-like puff of white blossomed from the Spaniard's bow and later the clap of a cannon shot carried across the rippled skin of the sea as a ball plummeted into the water beneath the Englishman's bowsprit and kicked up a miniature waterspout.

"The dog!"

Knowing her now for what she was, the temper of Edward Terror burnt red hot. He knew that Charles II of Spain felt that the Caribbean was, by Divine Right, the sole property of Spain; he also knew that any lone Englishman was fair bait for the greed of these pompous scavengers of the Main. But why, in God's name, should he, of all men, have to find himself target for these cruel hounds of the sea just when his whole future seemed assured? Blast their parents' passion, he could choose no other course but to fight and that might end eventually in defeat and destruction.

"Bring her more to starboard, Duggley," he shouted above the creak of the rigging and the pounding of the seas. "Lay her as close-hauled as possible on a line with that Spanish dog's bowsprit."

The Maid of Avon heeled around with her port flank deep in the rolling blue waves and with her yardarms almost parallel with her keel line. She bore straight as an arrow for the approaching foe.

"What do you intend, Edward?" the perplexed Duggley asked as he placed twin pistolets in his greatbelt and thrust a vicious looking cutlass into his baldric.

"Nothing more than bravado, old fella. It might serve to confuse their slow witted Castillian minds and give us a fair break to make a run for it if we can weather their first broadside."

When the powerful thirty-two gun foe swung around, as she must eventually do to bring her guns to bear, Edward Terror could then change his course to suit Fortune and, mayhap, break away before the Spaniard could again pick up speed. It was a long dangerous chance—but chance it was.

The foam piled up at the bows of the two approaching vessels and then bubbled and trailed away on their flanks. The white wakes thus formed appeared to the wheeling hurricane birds overhead like unto twin arrows approaching one another. Inexorably the two mountains of sail pounded closer and closer. The masts and white expanse of her sheets grew enormous as the scarlet ship of Spain drew near. Her ratlines and foredeck were crowded with the corseleted figures of a numerous crew and the black snouts of cannon jutted ominously forth from the scroll work on her flanks.

"By the saints, Edward," Duggley exclaimed aghast. "The knave flies the pennant of the Vice-Admiral of the Caribbean Squadron!"

Indeed it was true and served to add fuel to the fires of hate that burned in the hot-tempered Welsh captain's mind. There, at her foremast tip, the sword and dragon of the Spanish West Indian Squadron Vice-Admiral flowed. It was a pennant whose import could well mean war between Spain and England if ever report of this coming action were received in the British Admiralty. It meant too that the Spaniard figured the battle as well as won and the English heretics already put to the sword.

"Duggley, this is as fine a sample of Spanish treachery as you're apt to ever see."

At last the Spaniard heeled around to starboard and the long gleaming line of her cannon revealed themselves yawning hungrily toward the smaller *Maid of Avon*. Then, with a thunderous crash, her flank erupted in orange flame and billowing white clouds of smoke. The *Maid of Avon* shuddered in every timber from the broadside. Ratlines parted, red swathes of destruction swirled across her decks and Edward Terror was dashed against a capstan.

As he arose, his left arm limp and bleeding at his side, he realized that all opportunity for escape was gone. The *Maid of Avon* shuddered to a stop upon the seas that were now turning lavender in the rays of the setting sun. Her mainmast had crashed to the deck and her waist was a mass of broken spars and tangled cordage.

"Fire!"

He heard Duggley's command ring out and then came the answer, a paltry coughing of four demi-culverins. As he stumbled across the mangled bodies of several of his crew and the ripped and scarred boards, a sudden thought occurred to him. The swine of Castile would never board his ship alive. Into the hold he raced, a demonic looking son of battle.

In the powder magazine he planted a long trailing fuse and ran it up to the poop deck hatch combing. There he passed it through and soon came from below himself. His broad brimmed hat had been torn from his black head and his long curling hair flowed in the breeze as, hunched over and with right hand on rapier, he shouted for Duggley.

"I've run a fuse to the powder magazine and mean to blast the Maid of Avon to kingdom come before yonder Hell's children can ever board her."

The grim faced and soot-smeared Somersetshireman was taken aback.

"Aye, Edward, but what of us?"

"We'll take to the longboat—what's left of us—and put our faith in the open sea rather than in the Spaniard's evil heart." He waved his hand toward the red ball of the setting sun. "Night will be upon us in a matter of minutes and, mayhap, we can make an island hereabouts afore the Spaniard can overtake us."

Duggley went to prepare the longboat on the starboard side away from the prying eyes of the foe and the one-sided battle thundered on. The great Spaniard had come up again on a different tack through the dispersing smoke and was presenting her unfired starboard guns for the coup-de-grace. This puny English heretic would get a second dose of Hell for his impudence in not surrendering to the Vice-Admiral of the Caribbean Squadron, Don Alvarez de Perona de Sadista. Then would come the boarding and each and every surviving English dog would feel the cold blade of the sword upon his neck. There should be some valuable cargo and, mayhap, some gold or other treasure aboard.

Night was falling fast as it is wont to do in the Indies when the San Nicolas, for that was the name of the scarlet Spaniard, bore in for another rain of lead. Duggley and Edward Terror could see her rails packed with grinning faces and could hear the vile mouthings and insults of the enemy's crew through the shattered larboard rail and bulwarks. The demi-culverins fired first and it was with glee that the men of the *Maid of Avon* saw a gunport below decks burst into livid flame and death. Then a great rolling roar swallowed every other sound in its enormity and four hundred pounds of lead tore into the shattered Englishman. Both the mizzen and the fore masts came rattling down with a tearing of sails and snapping of ropes. There were screams as more of Edward Terror's men fell to the reddened decks and the rolling clouds of smoke from the enemy's broadside swept and swirled around the stricken vessel.

"Edward, your chest," Duggley coughed through the smoke as he pointed to the Welshman's breast.

A Spanish ball had slashed across his front and left a raw gash six inches wide from nipple to nipple. The navigator hastily bound the bleeding chest with a huge strip of torn sail cloth and helped the begrimed merchant captain to his feet.

"I'll be all right, Duggley," he said as he arose, his face twisted in pain. "If the longboat's ready, let's set the fuse and be away. It's dark enough and those scum will soon be back to board."

The remainder of the crew, eight men, joined Duggley and their captain. Duggley lit the fuse at the poop deck hatch and the ten Englishmen slid down the ropes to the waiting and bobbing longboat. The skies were now black but the flames from the *Maid of Avon*'s fires lighted the sea for many yards around. The powder-begrimed men in their tattered clothing, burdened with bandaged heads, arms and legs, pushed off from the hull of the once proud merchantman.

"Put up the sail, Gallat," the huge, blonde Duggley ordered as Edward Terror, wracked with pain from his torn left arm and bloody chest, lay silently in the sternsheets. "For the present, let's only try to keep the *Maid of Avon* between us and that Spanish hellhound. Once we're away in the night, we'll set our course by the stars for Puerto Rico. There should be some islands in that direction."

Meanwhile, the Spaniard had turned once again and was drawing alongside the shattered and burning hulk. She hove to at a safe distance and launched some cockboats with picked crews to board the vanquished Englishman. Although all was silent from the riddled merchantman but the crackling of her fires, the Spaniards were wary, for these Englishmen might still have strength enough to lay in wait for a bitter boarding fight with cutlass, pistol and pike. As the foe approached in the fire reddened night, aboard the ravaged *Maid of Avon* a slender powder train burned onward creeping slowly and steadily toward the end.

At last the cockboats banged into the sides of the burning vessel and the steel jacketed soldiers of Spain, led by a young captain, scrambled up the sides that were tattered and splintered from their own metal. As they crawled over the railing onto the waist deck they were tense and held their weapons at the ready. All that met their gaze was the ruin and the wreckage of spars and sails, the twisted and contorted bodies of the dead and, by some freak of battle, the shattered gaff standing from amidst the wreckage and ruin with her cocky flag, the red and white Cross of St. George, impudently waving in their faces.

"Virgin Santisima!" the young captain of Castile screamed—but too late.

A great roaring gust of flame leaped skyward and tore the entire stern-works heavenward with it. The very bowels of the ship burst upward and enormous blasts of heat and flame and rubble exploded outward and over the sea. The powder magazine had gone off.

As the great explosion lit the night sky and reflected in shimmering lines from the water in yellow, orange and red streaks, Edward Terror pulled himself up over the gunwales of the Maid of Avon's longboat. With a twisted pain-wracked smile on his blood and sweat-encrusted face, he shook his fist toward the flames and cried forth in hate.

"Carrion of Spain, let that be your first taste of terror. For, by the carnal devils of Stonehedge, I'll make you pay for this night's doings and sink my name into your hearts if I have to trail you to Panama."

The longboat and her crew of survivors escaped into the darkness of the night as the light of the explosion died down and the remains of the *Maid of Avon* slid beneath the waves. Taking his bearings from the stars, Duggley headed due east into a heavy breeze. The little boat heaved and bucked on the running seas and there was not much comfort for any of the men.

With the coming of the dawn the crew was tense for the Spanish man-'o-war might still be in the vicinity; in which case there would be a speedy end to their sufferings, for the Vice-Admiral would not care to have a report of his part in the affair come before the British Admiralty. The golden yellow light of the new day revealed an empty sea and they were alone with the blue-green rollers and the squawking gulls overhead.

"How did the men fare during the dark hours, Duggley?" Edward Terror questioned.

"Well enough," the muscular navigator answered as he attended to the raw reddish gash on his captain's chest. "We've got water and biscuit enough for a few days. With those gulls overhead as an indication, land must be near."

"If the breeze holds, we should sight a landfall before another twenty-four hours."

All through the day the longboat painfully bowled her way over the pitching seas. The sun beat down unmercifully on the men and the sea-spray added its salty sting to their sufferings.

"Land! Land! I can see it faintly in the distance on each rise of the boat." The keen eyes of the young seaman named Gallat at length caught a glimpse of what they all had been waiting for.

"Aye, you're right, lad," the broad face of Duggley beamed as he stood up at his position by the tiller. "Nightfall will find us safe ashore."

It was a small island but, none the less, to them a green jewel of beauty sitting amidst the blue rollers of the Caribbean. As the longboat, her occupants filled with anticipation and exhilaration, piled through the ring of thundering combers and hissing foam-specked breakers, they saw a shimmering golden beach stretching back to a veritable cliff of tropical vegetation.

The longboat grooved her way into the wet sand's edge and the crew leaped out. Edward Terror, his arm limp and swollen and his chest aching miserably, was the last to get out. As the men ran and frolicked on the warm sand like so many London waifs, his voice arose in command.

"Men, we may have to make this our home for many days, so let's be about preparing a shelter afore the chill of another night falls upon us."

As it turned out there were only four cutlasses, five knives, two pistols, and Edward Terror's own jewel-handled rapier among them. Using knives and cutlasses, the men soon had erected a palm frond lean-to well back on the beach. There now arose the problem of supplying food for the men.

"This island is a paradise of game, my hearties," Edward Terror addressed them. "But I'm afraid that we don't have the wherewithal to get any of the fat birds or wild pigs unless some of you are fleet of foot enough to run them through with a cutlass."

The young, eager looking Gallat stepped forth.

"If I might offer a suggestion, Captain Terror why don't we make some longbows? My father's trade is that of bowmaking back in Bridgetown and, methinks, there's both strong wood and hardy vines enough in yonder wood to try his trade right here."

The lad's suggestion was a good one and soon the men of the ill-fated Maid of Avon were handling the roughly fashioned, but nonetheless accurate longbows with growing proficiency. Using stones for arrow heads and gull feathers on their shafts, the castaway archers had soon mastered the technique and were garnering an ample supply of fresh meat and fowl.

As the days stretched into weeks, the new found life of the men proved to be an enjoyable one. Recovered from their wounds and basking in the burning sun and frolicking in the rolling surf, they soon regained their strength and confidence. The island was explored from end to end and a deepwater cove of remarkable shipworthyness was located on the opposite side of the isle.

As one day Captain Terror, Gallat, and Duggley stood on a foliage covered promontory that dropped straight into the deep basin of this cove, Gallat pointed out to sea and exclaimed:

"By the saints, Captain Terror, if my eyes don't mistake me, that's a ship setting her course for this island."

Duggley and the captain squinted in the brilliant daylight and soon they made out the lines of a mighty three-master pursuing a tack that would bring her to the island in a few more hours.

"Your eyes are keen, Gallat, my lad." Captain Terror fingered the hilt of his rapier, and his black eyes, beneath their heavy brows, gleamed as he turned to Duggley. "Stab me, Duggley, but if yonder vessel makes a landing here, she may turn into the weapon of our deliverance."

"What do you mean, Edward? Shouldn't we light a fire to attract her attention?"

"No, my friend, I've had too much experience with unknown ships—and you should have had also—to attract them to us in these pirate-infested waters."

It was certain within another hour that the stranger was indeed heading for the island. As she smoothly sailed closer to the cove her sleek lines proved to be of French design. Under stud sails this French cut vessel was truly slashing a speedy track in the blue waters. She was pierced for thirty-six cannon and was one of the most beautifully designed vessels that Edward Terror had ever seen.

The three castaways dropped into the thick underbrush as the great brown and white vessel slipped majestically into the palm fringed cove. With a great stir of motion, her sails furled and she glided to rest on the tranquil waters as her anchor chain rattled into the clear depths.

"Look at her gaff," the tense grip of Duggley's hand squeezed his captain's arm. "She flies the Jolly Roger!"

Limply drooping in the air hung a black flag with a great skull and crossbones fashioned on its fabric. This beauteous stranger was a pirate vessel!

The trio lay silent in the bush while the curses and shouts of the crew below could be heard about their work of making their ship secure. At length, as the late afternoon sun began to slip toward the western horizon, the yells and murmurings became more raucous. The pirates were in their cups.

"Captain, look there in the stern-works." The voice of Gallat directed Edward Terror's gaze toward the heavily gilded and beautifully wrought stern of the pirate ship.

A jollyboat was trailing from the cabin window out of which a figure was now crawling. Behind him came another and the two of them could be seen lifting between them a mighty seachest. They dropped their cargo into the jolly boat and were soon joined by a third pirate whose figure was clothed in fine style and upon whose head sat a wide brimmed hat with a long trailing green feather.

"How do you like that, Duggley old man?" Captain Terror smiled as he turned to his navigator. "Three of the lads seem to have secret plans afoot. This will bear watching."

Once in their jollyboat, the three pirates headed for shore. The fancily dressed one sat pompously in the sternsheets. The remainder of the crew were evidently well on out of the world if their shouts and curses and bawdy songs were a fair indication of their intoxication.

"Come on, men. Follow me."

Captain Terror arose from his concealment and beckoned to his companions. They slid down the bank from their position of vantage and, at length, found themselves near the spot where the jollyboat should hit the shoreline. Into the bushes they once more slipped as the pirate trio ran their small vessel ashore.

The great bulky figure of their evident leader was first out of the boat and he directed his two mates as they struggled and grunted under the weight of the iron bound chest.

"Get a move on, you scum," the lazy hulking figure hissed in a low coarse voice. "Do you want the rest of those drunken sea rats to discover us gone? If we're smart about it, the fatheads will never realize that we've taken the cream of the treasure when we divide what's left in the morning."

"Aye, Captain Marion," one of the rogues in calico drawers and a dirty red striped cotton shirt replied, "but if LeSandrassa discovers this night's work, he'll have the crew in mutiny in an instant."

"Blast LeSandrassa, you cowardly dog. I intend to run him through before we leave Dragon's Tooth Cove at any rate. He's only a mutinous pig who'll be better for a sticking!"

The trio moved away from the shore into the luxuriant foliage which was now darkening with the approach of nightfall. Captain Terror and his two men followed, making sure to keep in the bushes and well out of sight. The pirates struggled for some distance into the undergrowth until they came to a small clearing. Captain Marion ordered them to stop, pointed out a suitable spot and, within a matter of minutes, his two underlings were digging in the soft sod, the sweat rolling off them in great globules of moisture.

As Captain Terror watched them in the dim light of dusk, his mind turned over the possibility of joining these scavengers of the seas. He knew instinctively, however, that their lawless rough life of piratical deeds was not for him nor his men. There was, nevertheless, the chance that they might— He had time to reflect no longer.

Captain Marion had withdrawn two pistols from his belt and was aiming them at the backs of the men struggling with their spades in the deepening hole.

"No you don't, you—!" Captain Terror exclaimed as he leaped from the concealment of the underbrush and slashed at the pirate chieftain's hands with the slender shank of his drawn rapier.

"Bang!"

The crash of one pistol resounded through the glade and one of the men in the treasure pit crumpled with a great spreading red stain across his back. Captain Terror's slash, nevertheless, had caused the treacherous captain to drop his second weapon as the second pirate in the hole looked up and Duggley and Gallat burst into the clearing.

"Where have you come from, you scum?" His swarthy, evil face contorted, the pirate captain snarled in his rage as he wiped the blood from the back of his hand. "What manner of man are you to dare interfere with Captain Marion?"

"What manner of man are you," said Captain Terror, "a treacherous Judas who pistols his own men in the back without a word?"

The pirate captain snarled another curse and drew his blade as he backed away from the crouching wild-looking half-clad man before him. Duggley and Gallat had seized the other pirate and watched eagerly while the two duelists circled one another warily.

"You stinking woods' rat, I'll have your life's blood for that interference!"

"Actions speak louder than words," the smiling Welshman said as he lunged forward.

The pirate parried the thrust and the woodland began to ring and echo with the clash of steel upon steel as the two antagonists bitterly parried and thrust at one another. Back and forth across the glade they danced and the faint half-light of dusk cast eerie long shadows on the verdant foliage around them. The pirate chieftain was skillful with his weapon and soon he had driven the more agile Edward Terror back toward a half-hidden fallen log.

"Here's for your trouble!" the sweating, panting pirate screamed in derision as his antagonist fell backwards over the unseen obstacle.

His lunge was like lightning, but Edward Terror rolled away in the very nick of time and Captain Marion found his point buried in nothing more than the earth.

"And here's for your trouble." Captain Terror had arisen and he viciously slashed his rapier across the sweating, straining face of the pirate.

"Dog!" screamed the maddened man through the blood streaming down his visage, as he threw himself at the sardonic fiend before him.

Hotter and hotter waxed the fight but Edward Terror could feel his opponent weakening. At length, the pirate dropped his guard too long and, with one smooth lunge, Captain Terror slid his blade into the rogue's chest to the very hilt. He stepped back and the gasping, dying pirate crumbled into the grass.

"Neatly done Edward!" Duggley cried as he moved to his captain's side. When he received a grin in answer, the blonde navigator continued. "That was as pretty a dispatching of a rogue as ever I've seen."

"What'll we do with this one?"

Captain Terror turned at Gallat's question and beheld the frightened figure in the red striped shirt and the calico breeches. Instantly a plan occurred to him. He could use this pirate knave to help the three of them, and the rest of the survivors of the Maid of Avon who were now on the other side of the island, to escape this island prison.

"This man was your leader, wasn't he?" Captain Terror questioned as he prodded the dead pirate from whose chest the rapier protruded.

"Aye, that he was, but LeSandrassa will take over now."

"Who's LeSandrassa?"

"He was Captain Marion's first mate. Ever since we raided Caracas, LeSandrassa has been waiting for a chance to take over. Now you have given it to him."

"Don't be too sure of that, mate," Captain Terror said cryptically and then, laying his finger on the pirate's chest, he continued. "You're free to return to your ship but the treasure stays with us. You can tell this rogue LeSandrassa that, if he wants the treasure, he's to meet me on the spit of sand that forms the northern side of the channel into Dragon's Tooth Cove, tomorrow at dawn. Understand?"

"Aye, but he'll have it anyway even if he has to comb the whole island for you."

"We'll see, my smart friend," Captain Terror grinned. "Now begone with you, else I change my mind and add you to the pile that your two friends will make."

The rogue disappeared along the trail to the cove and Captain Terror withdrew his bloody rapier from the lifeless form of the pirate leader.

"Men, we'll throw this corpse in with the other, bury 'em and move the treasure deeper into the woods."

"What have you got in mind, Edward?" Duggley's brow was wrinkled as he helped.

"I'll tell you the way back to our encampment. If you and the rest agree to my plans, we may well be out of here within a matter of days and on our way to revenge."

More he would not say. They moved the treasure chest and, as night became complete in its blackness, the trio stalked through the underbrush to their encampment. They had a deal of news to spread to their seven other castaway mates.

The long golden fang of the sand spit stretched out into the sea. As the light of the morning sun shimmered across the sea and flashed from the foam tips of the thundering breakers, around from the cove came two boatloads of pirates and buccaneers. The masts of their anchored ship could be seen reaching skyward above the roof of palms as their oars chopped the waters with a regular beat.

In the fore of the lead boat stood a tall hawkish buccaneer with a great scarlet and golden coat covering his thin sinewy body. His oily black hair was held back by a dirty orange bandana and, in his pierced ears, two heavy rings flashed with the light's reflection. As garish a bunch of rogues as the seven seas could sweep up were the two score picaroons and pirates that accompanied him. Clothed in multicolored and dirty calico, cotton and satin finery and rags, the white and black skinned men were armed with every weapon of the times, cutlasses, pistols, pikes, and knives of every variety but of an evil and dangerous looking similarity withall.

The boats pulled through the fresh surf and their crews, jabbering and laughing like a tribe of monkeys, leaped into the backwash and pulled them high and dry on the hot sand. Led by the hawk-like rogue, they ascended the sandy beach and, at length, came to a spot before the fringe of jungle foliage. Here they stopped their trudging through the warm sands for before them stood a lone, almost naked man.

Captain Terror's foot rested on an open seachest which sparkled with the richness of its jeweled and golden content. His hands rested on his slim hips from which dangled a needle thin rapier. His lips, within the parchment brown of his face, were spread in a wide grin and his white teeth flashed in the morning light.

"A good morning to you, my hearties," he greeted the suddenly silent mob.

The greedy eyes of the pirates were upon the sprawling treasure, but the gaze of their leader rested on the muscular suntanned figure who so nonchalantly rested his bare foot on the gleaming wealth.

"So you're the one that did for the captain?" The voice of the tall buccaneer was surly and impudent. "Well, we've come for our treasure."

"Have you now? There's a bit of a deal that we'll settle first before I can let you have it."

At this the surly leader opened his great gash of a mouth and, holding his sides as if they might split from the exertion, he laughed and pointed at Captain Terror in derision.

"Mates, did you hear that? We must deal with him afore we can have our treasure." He stopped his laughter and waved his cutlass before him. "Seize the impudent scum and we'll be away to the ship afore this farce can go any further."

The band of pirates shouted their approval of the hawkish leader's decision and moved ominously forward. Suddenly nine arrows whistled from behind Captain Terror's back and thudded deeply into the sand. They quivered for a moment before the toes of the foremost rogues and brought the garish mob to an instant stop.

"You see, my smart friend, I have the wherewithal to stop you within the trees at my back," smiled Captain Terror as the knaves looked incredulously behind him toward the unseen bowman of the forest. "Now will you deal with me or would you rather have those fuzzy tailed things growing from your chest?"

A look of hate and frustration lit the leader's face and, for an instant, he considered a headlong charge to do for this sardonic woodsman impudently standing before him. He thought better of it and spoke in a voice thick with frustrated rage.

"What's your deal, scum?"

Captain Terror did not answer him immediately but reached instead into the treasure chest and withdrew a leather bag, filled to the brim with gleaming round pearls. Unloosening the leather thong about the bag's neck, he flung it into the midst of the buccaneers.

"There's a sample of what you'll be sharing in a few moments."

Like warfside waifs, the motley band scrambled and fought with one another to obtain part of the flashing cascade of richness that rolled onto the golden sands. The pirate leader stood stolid and tense before him.

"Now for the deal, LeSandrassa—that is your name, is it not?" The hawkish buccaneer nodded his head and Captain Terror continued. "Last night I killed your captain in a fair fight and thus saved for you this treasure. In return for the treasure, which I claim no share of, you will make me your new captain."

There was complete silence for a moment and then, having retrieved all the pearls from the sand and now paying him attention, the pirates spoke up.

"Aye, that's fair enough."

"He did for Captain Marion and, by the rules of the brotherhood, his claim is just."

LeSandrassa turned around in anger and eyed his disloyal crew.

"Shut up, you rats. We'll have the treasure anyway. How do you think this knave could lead you? Remember what I did for you at Caracas, at Blackman's Bluff, and the attack on Pinar del Rio. You need a fighting man, not a landlubberly jack-a-napes." He paused and an evil grin lit his thin face. Winking to his men, he turned and faced the smiling Welshman before him. "Howsomever, I'm a fair and just man. If yonder fop can best me in fair fight, why I'm more than willing to let him take charge."

Now, with their minds whetted for a good fight, the men shouted their approval of LeSandrassa's offer.

"Good enough."

"If the stranger's tough enough to make a good captain, he's hardy enough to beat the Frenchman."

"Let's have the fight."

Captain Terror withdrew his rapier and stepped forward over the glittering treasure.

"All right, my cocky friend. That's fair enough."

"Aye, but discard your pig-stabber," LeSandrassa said with an evil smirk. "My mates have a better liking for knives."

With that he withdrew a long gleaming shaft of steel from his waistband and threw off his coat and kicked off his seaboots. Another pirate, seeing that the half-clad stranger carried no similar weapon, threw a second knife at Captain Terror's feet. Eagerly now the buccaneers crowded around in a semi-circle to watch the bloodletting.

Back amidst the covering foliage Gallat grasped Duggley by the arm. Around about the seven other members of the *Maid of Avon*'s crew stood ready with their longbows and full arrow quivers on their backs.

"This is getting dangerous, Duggley."

"Aye, but we'll wait awhile here. Edward seems to know what he is about. Keep the men ready for instant action."

Captain Terror picked up the knife from the sand and, running his thumb the length of its shaft, found the blade more than sharp enough. The hawkish LeSandrassa had stripped to the waist and his wiry muscles rippled in the warm morning air. The two adversaries circled one another and the Welshman noted that his opponent was lefthanded. This would indeed be a dangerous fight. The crew closed in, shouting for action and blood.

Suddenly the pirate leaped forward and slashed upward at the stomach of the chestnut-brown figure of Captain Terror. The Welshman leaped backward and the deadly blade missed by a hair's breadth. Before he could slash in turn, LeSandrassa had fallen to the ground, rolled over and was on his feet again a half dozen yards away. No wonder he wanted to use knives, thought the half clad woodsman. He was a past master at the deadly game.

Again LeSandrassa lunged, expecting the stranger to leap back. This time, however, Captain Terror, risking all, stepped forward and glided to the right. He felt the pain of a slash as the pirate's turning knife raked his left side but he sunk his own knife deeply into the upper arm of his attacker.

"Aye-e-e-e-e-e—"

The pirates were now screaming madly as the red stain of blood flowed over the antagonists. LeSandrassa was enraged, and his left arm, the one that wielded the bloody blade, was streaming red—Captain Terror knew that its speed had been hindered. He closed with the pirate just as a knee shot into his groin. His body exploded into a white hot bundle of burning nerves with the pain of the unexpected kick and he collapsed onto the sand. In a trice the pirate was upon him, slashing at his stomach. Captain Terror kicked out as the blade dug into his thigh and LeSandrassa fell backward.

Pained and mad with rage himself, the Welshman leaped on the prostrate buccaneer and plunged his dagger into the rogue's heart just as LeSandrassa's knife buried itself inch deep in his shoulder.

Gasping and wracked with pain he rolled off the dead pirate's form as Duggley and his men burst from the woods. He crumbled to the ground senseless as Gallat tenderly removed the knife from his shoulder.

When he finally came to his senses, Duggley was standing over him in an ornate beamed cabin. The beams flickered and wavered in the light reflecting from the water through the open cabin window.

"You're safe aboard your new ship, Edward," the smiling blonde navigator spoke. "You lost a deal of blood but you gained many supporters. Those men of LeSandrassa's have been dividing the treasure on the beach and we've been taking over the ship."

Duggley patched up Captain Terror's many wounds from a medicine chest that he had found in the stern locker as the Welshman looked his new surroundings over. The cabin clothes locker was filled with finery, satins and taffetas, greatcoats and lace shirts and leather boots, periwigs, baldrics, and buckles. Charts of the Caribbean waters lay strewn on a huge oaken table and a fine heavy silverware set lay in its box by an open cabin window.

"By the saints, Duggley," laughed the pale, wounded Welshman, "we're going to live like kings and look like kings even if we do act like pirates.

"Now let us see the contents of this good ship's galley," he continued, "for, faith, my belly touches my backbone from hunger."

"Sure, and you must be near starved," Duggley answered, a solicitous look on his face. "I'll have the cook get you a fine dinner right away."

With this he hurried out, leaving Edward to ruefully contemplate his wounds and his white, haggard face in the cabin mirror.

Soon Duggley returned, carrying a tray laden high with steaming delicacies.

"This Captain Marion believed in keeping a fine table," he grinned as he set the tray down in front of Edward. "There is food below fit for Charles of Spain himself."

Edward fell to with a will under the paternal eye of his brawny navigator. After the sharp edge of his hunger had been dulled somewhat, he said to Duggley:

"My lad, on this bloody ship with its cut-throat crew we will be walking on treacherous ground indeed. I must have men around me whom I can trust. Now, I have in mind yourself for first mate. What think you of young Gallat for second?"

"Aye, Edward," Duggley answered. "He is a fighting-cock if ever I saw one; and, if you lead, he would follow into Hell itself."

"He may have to," laughed Captain Terror, his spirits revived by the hot food and the fine Madeira. "I have been thinking to myself, Tom, of what use is it to pile up wealth by honest toil, only to lose it to the arrogant Dons of Spain? From this day on, I mean to be the hunter instead of the prey."

"Well said, Edward," enthused the usually stolid Somersetshireman. "Once, now, have we been wiped out by the bloody Dons; and fortunate indeed have we been to escape with our lives."

Edward was about to answer, when he was interrupted by the roar of many voices coming from the deck below.

"What is that," he asked intently. "What is the matter with the crew?"

"They have had their spot of grog and I imagine they're having a turn with the dice," Duggley answered. "You know how noisy they can be at times."

"I don't like the sound of it," Edward persisted, "methinks it has a strange ring."

"I'll have a look," Duggley promised, hurrying out. Soon he came back, his face grave. With his eyes cast down he informed slowly:

"They have dragged a wench up from the hold—they mean to have cruel sport with the poor thing."

Captain Terror leaped up, overturning the table with a crash.

"What!" he shouted. "Not on my ship—"

He lurched painfully toward the door. Quickly the mate barred his way.

"No, Captain," he pleaded. "I like it no better than yourself but the men are in an ugly mood and to deprive them of their cruel play would be but to invite mutiny—she is probably only a bawd, the kind you find in every port."

Captain Terror pushed him roughly aside. "She is a woman and defenseless," he proclaimed. "Now, out of my way!"

He flung open the door and stamped out onto the deck, his face like a thundercloud. Duggley followed, with worry etched on his own features.

As quickly as his wounds would permit, Edward led the way down onto the deck. He let out a string of crackling oaths when he saw the tableau spread out before him.

Tied to the mainmast, her hands stretched above her, surrounded by a ring of hooting, blaspheming buccaneers, was a lovely, white-faced Spanish girl.

Her clothes were in tatters and her brown hair hung down over her shoulders in rippling waves. Her eyes were closed and her lips moved regularly as if she were praying.

A huge black bearded ruffian went mincing up to her.

"Don't ye have a little kiss for good old Shark?" he leered.

With this he thrust his hideous face forward and fastened his bearded lips on her mouth. She struggled frantically, twisting her head from side to side and writhing in her bonds, as he pressed his body against hers and held her in his foul embrace.

He laughed as at last he stood back from her shrinking form.

"We'll let all of these handsome lads take turns," he bellowed. "But first we'll show them something to keep them interested."

With this, he put a grimy paw inside her bodice and with a savage tug ripped her dress open.

There was an instant, dreadful silence as the women-starved men stared at the exquisite body so suddenly revealed. Then, there was a vicious roar and the passion-crazed crew began to mill about the terrified girl. One had fastened his hand in her hair and was cutting her bonds with his knife, preparatory to dragging her to the deck, when Edward leaped into action.

Cursing wildly, he stormed through the milling mob of men, tearing a cutlass from one as he went. Belaboring heads and backs as he forced his way through he finally got to the mast.

Shielding the girl with his body he roared:

"Back, you filthy sons-of-dogs!—back, or by Neptune, the fish will feed well this day!"

As the defiant men fell slowly back, nursing their cracked heads and aching backs, Edward turned to the sobbing girl. Her clothes had nearly been torn from her body, and, in spite of his rage, Edward could not resist the instinctive thrill which ran through him.

Her face was lovely and patrician, the skin an ivory white, the eyes a deep blue, the nose finely molded and slightly upturned, the lips full and delicately curved, all crowned by an incredibly long mass of rich brown hair.

As Captain Terror's eyes traveled on along her torn clothing, his heart began to pump strangely. Resolutely forcing his gaze upward, he saw that she was watching him fixedly, the look of a trapped rabbit upon her face.

He quickly drew his knife and sliced the ropes which bound her wrists to the mast. He heard her labored breathing in his ear as he sawed at the ropes about her slim waist. A gust of air blew a silky strand of scented hair across his face and, as he bent down to free her ankles, he discovered that his hands were trembling so that he could barely hold the knife.

The Devil! He swore silently to himself.

As he straightened up, she ineffectually tried to hold the tattered remnants of her dress together. Captain Terror motioned for her to follow him and she took a tentative step forward. Tottering, she almost fell and saved herself only by clutching the mast for support.

"I—I cannot stand," she murmured in a sweet, faintly husky voice. "Those ropes— they were so tight."

Her English was perfect, spoken with a delicious, slurred accent. Once more Captain Terror felt the blood pound in his temples as he put his arm around the waist of the lovely girl. Steadying her, he led the way slowly through the crowd of glowering men.

As they set foot on the poop deck, the muttering of the pirates burst into a roar. The bearded Shark pushed his way from amidst the crew and confronted his new captain. His rugged face was contorted in an expression of mixed frustration and hate.

"What right have you to deprive us of our sport with this Spanish bawd?" he spat. "If her men-folks or the black-robed monks of the Inquisition had ye tied to that mast, they'd have the flesh off your bones in small pieces!"

With a full-arm sweep Captain Terror struck him full in the mouth. Shark went down like a felled tree. After a minute, he arose to one knee, shaking his head slowly.

"Save your passion for the waterfront sluts to whom you are accustomed." Captain Terror said coldly.

"You want her for yourself!" the prostrate buccaneer hissed.

Catlike, Captain Terror leaped across the deck. Drawing his knife he bent down and grasped the surly pirate by his dirty shirt.

"One more word out of you, my Beauty," he said sweetly, "and I'll nail your lying tongue to yonder mast!"

The sullen crew was silent. Duggley and Gallat stood tensely ready before the cowering figure of the Spanish girl. The moment passed and Captain Terror arose, deliberately turned his back upon the hushed crew and joined his two friends and the girl.

"You must run this ship with an iron hand, Edward, if ye expect these devils to follow you," Duggley whispered with a sigh of relief.

"And why do you think I handled yonder knave so abruptly?" Captain Terror answered. "'Twill give the crew something to think about."

As Duggley accompanied his captain and the captive girl to the greatcabin, his eyes watched the dark Welshman with a mixture of silent admiration and wonderment. The change from peaceful merchantman to rugged pirate leader was coming with ease to this amazing man.

Captain Terror followed the girl into the cabin and turned to close the door. It was blocked by Duggley, who was following close upon his heels. Captain Terror put his hand upon Duggley's broad chest and gently pushed him out again.

"I will call you if I need you, friend," he said reprovingly.

As he closed the door, the last thing that he saw was the navigator's grinning face, one eye closed in a broad wink. Swearing softly under his breath, Captain Terror slammed and bolted the door. He turned to his fair hostage who was huddled in the corner on the window seat and was trying vainly to arrange her torn dress so that it would cover the more obvious of her many charms.

"You will be bothered no more, my lady," he said gallantly. "Now tell me how you fell captive to this mangy crew."

He walked over to her, pulled up a stool and sat down. To his amazement she shrank back from him, fear and loathing showing plainly on her pale face. Edward stared at her nonplussed. Then he threw back his head and roared with laughter, showing his even, white teeth.

"No wonder you fear me," he chuckled. "Faith, I must look a sight to receive such a fair visitor. Forgive my appearance for I just arose from a sick bed. At that," he went on, "I should think that you would prefer me to Shark."

She looked at him coldly.

"Prefer any murdering pirate who plunders honest men of the sea to another?" she spoke with disdain. "Indeed, there seems little choice—your men, at least, do not mask their intent behind a lot of pretty phrases."

Edward's face grew grave as the girl continued passionately.

"You shall have short sport of me—I shall throw myself over the side at the first opportunity!"

"Aren't you being ungrateful?" Edward asked her sternly. "If you think that I desire you, or that you are in any way attractive to me, you flatter yourself no end."

The Lord forgive me for that lie, he thought, keeping his face stern.

"Then what do you propose to do with me?"

"First, tell me who you are and where you come from," the Welshman countered.

"My name is Dolores de Vayo. My father is Don Sebastian de Vayo, governor of Panama."

Captain Terror whistled soundlessly as the girl moved closer.

"My father wanted me to marry a much older man," she continued. "A great admiral and nobleman. I refused, but he insisted. So I fled from Porto Bello aboard a small vessel for Jamaica and some English friends of mine. Just two days ago the ship was sunk and I was captured and thrown in your filthy hold—as you well know!"

"But I did not know," Edward told her. "You see, this was not my ship."

He explained to her the recent incidents attendant to his seizure of Captain Marion's pirate frigate. When he had finished, she looked at him with open admiration.

"*Madre de Dios!*" she breathed. "You are a man!"

"I will put you off at the first English possession that we come to," he said. "Until then, I am your servant."

For the first time he saw her smile. She slipped gracefully to her feet and made a low curtsy. The dark-haired girl was indeed breathtaking in her charm.

"Just one thing more, Captain," she smiled. "A tub of hot water, an hour's privacy and some clean clothes."

"They will have to be seaman's clothes, Donna Dolores," Captain Terror replied. "I will bring you the smallest that I can discover."

With that, he arose and left the cabin. He gave instructions to the cook to send up the clothes and a tub of heated water and then he ordered Duggley to pipe the crew on deck.

"Men," Captain Terror addressed the still somewhat sullen pirates, "Duggley, here, is to be your new mate and navigator; Gallat, your second mate. As for the other officers, I'll choose them when I know you better. Now it has been called to my attention that this vessel is in a sad state of repair, her cannon rusty, her 'tween decks filthy, much of her rigging frayed and dangerous, and her bottom foul with barnacles. So, we'll dismantle her in the lagoon, careen her on the beach and make her ship-shape and seaworthy." The men grumbled as Captain Terror paused and then continued coldly. "The first one who molests the Spanish lady by as much as a word will hang from the yardarm— within an hour. Is that clear?"

The savage faces of the buccaneer band reflected the uncertainty that they felt regarding their new captain. The incident of the Spanish girl was still fresh in their minds. But yet not a dissenting word was spoken in the face of the determined Welshman.

At length, after a few moments of lingering silence, Captain Terror turned from the men and addressed his eager young mate.

"Gallat lad, ever since you fashioned your equipage on yonder island and obtained our food for us, I've had it in the back of my mind to have a company of archers aboard deck in action."

"Aye. We could operate from the shrouds and do fearful close-in execution in battle." Gallat's eyes shone with anticipation. "Can I form a company, Captain Terror?"

"That you can, lad. Take any twenty that you want and make yourself captain of the company. Methinks that your archers with their rapid fire will be not only an innovation but a deadly added implement to our fighting power."

Gallat left, scarcely able to contain himself, and Edward strolled on up to his cabin. He paused in front of the door and ran his fingers through his thick, black hair. Taking a deep breath he knocked.

"Come in," the husky voice murmured.

As Edward walked in he saw in the middle of the room what appeared to be a small, waterfront urchin. Her brown hair was tucked under a seaman's cap and she was dressed from head to boot in seaman's garb. The only discordant note to the ensemble was the suspicious swelling of the faded blue shirt-front.

"Do I look enough like one of your men, Captain Terror?" she said, pirouetting about before him.

"Donna Dolores, you could not look like a man if you wore a suit of mail," Edward answered gallantly.

She quickly lowered her eyes.

"How soon can you put me ashore?" she asked, looking up again.

"Perhaps a month, perhaps six weeks."

"Dios! So long!"

"But yes, Donna Dolores. The ship must be repaired and I have a score to settle with a certain Spanish Vice-Admiral." His voice was tinged with bitterness as he paused. "I will leave you here on the island, however, with a guard of trustworthy men—for I have no desire to subject you to the dangers of possible naval action."

"Never!" she interposed hotly. "I will not stay here—I want to come along with you."

"Very well," Captain Terror returned. "I have warned you. Surely you would not care to see a ship of your own Spain destroyed?"

She laughed scornfully.

"I have no love for Charles of Spain," she said heatedly. "Remember, I am an exile because I refused to marry that pig of a de Sadista!"

"De Sadista!" Captain Terror exclaimed. "Not the Vice-Admiral of the Caribbean Squadron?"

"Yes," she said in bewilderment. "Do you know him?"

"Know him?" laughed Captain Terror bitterly. "Let me tell you a story—a long story."

Having previously told her of the events leading from his forced sojourn on the island, he now told the girl of the events leading to his castaway life. When he had finished his tale of the treacherous attack on the Maid of Avon, the Spanish girl surveyed him breathlessly.

"Santa Maria!" she cried, clutching him by the shoulder passionately. "How I will bless you if you send that devil to the bottom!"

Something snapped within Captain Terror. Her beauty and the added incentive of her own hatred for the Spanish Vice-Admiral combined to overwhelm his senses. He reached out and swept her into his arms. Holding her tightly against him, he kissed her surprised mouth.

"Bless me again, Dolores," he said tenderly, "and I would bring you Charles of Spain himself!"

With surprising strength she wrenched away from him.

"How dare you!" she cried, her cheeks scarlet. Her eyes blazed and she balled up her small hands and struck the Welshman on the chest.

Edward looked down from his great height on the dainty creature so busily engaged in pounding on his broad chest. There was a ludicrous expression of surprise on his handsome face and the Spanish girl paused. She looked up at him and her anger passed as suddenly as it had appeared.

"You great hulking fool," she laughed. "If you could only see your silly expression."

Edward flushed.

"I did not realize that I was so amusing," he said stiffly. "It will not happen again."

"Now you are angry," she mocked. "Perhaps I have wounded your pride."

Edward suddenly reached for her again but she quickly pushed a chair between them and skipped nimbly away.

"No, Captain," she protested, backing away. "Please!"

Edward pulled up short, realizing what a fool he was making of himself. He glared at her.

"This cabin is yours," he growled. "I will bunk with the mate. If you need anything, you may call for Duggley!"

He turned and stamped toward the door.

"Captain Terror."

"What do you want?" he tossed over his shoulder.

"I'm sorry I laughed at you—but you did look amusing."

With an oath Edward rushed out and slammed the cabin door behind him. When he had regained his temper, he called Gallat and told him to see to it that the crew commenced the needed repair work—at once.

The crew grumbled at the unaccustomed labor but was, nevertheless, soon at work on the dismantled ship. A camp was made on the golden sand of the beach. A single tent had been pitched for the Spanish girl and Edward resolutely ignored her. Extra spars were cut from the forest growth and before many days had gone by the ship was once again afloat and new rigging was beginning to grow in her upper works.

Gallat formed his company of bowmen who daily increased their skill with the longbow and Captain Terror whipped the remainder of the crew in shape with gunnery drills and sword and pike fighting practice. For already he had in mind many things for this new found crew and ship; the most important of which was the exacting of vengeance from the Spaniard, De Sadista. A hankering for this vengeance seemed to gnaw at his bones like some nauseous disease.

One fine day, Duggley, Gallat and Von Tromp, a Dutch buccaneer who had been a gunner under the great De Ruyter, were standing over the oaken table which stood in the sand on the spit. The table was covered with charts, and Captain Terror was resplendent in black and scarlet taffetas with a curling black periwig falling on his shoulders and his face shielded from the burning sun by a black broad-brimmed hat whose red feather trailed rakishly over his shoulder.

"My lads, it's nigh onto time for some action," the lean Welshman said. "If I only knew what the Spanish squadron was about, I could make up my mind in a trice."

"Pardon, Captain Terror," the gruff, throaty voice of the stubby Von Tromp spoke up. "But this is their usual time for taking their yearly haul of pearls from Rio de la Hache back to Spain."

"Is that so now," said the Captain as his eyes narrowed in thought. "And where do they usually come through, the Windward or the Mona Passage?"

"Always the Mona Passage, Captain, but we dare not attack them. They're six men-of-war, two of which are forty-four gun ships. Even Morgan at his strongest would never have dared that. There are other ways of bleeding the men of Castile."

Captain Terror stood thoughtful for a moment. That Spanish cur must pay for his treachery. What's more, this island itself lay on the eastern edge of the Mona Passage.

"Gentlemen, we slip out with the tide in the morning. We're going to see the Spanish Squadron."

The other three looked at one another aghast. He certainly couldn't be considering the possibility of attacking the most formidable force in the entire Caribbean?

When the others left Von Tromp approached the elegant figure in silver and scarlet.

"Captain, you must reconsider what is in the back of your head."

"You fought with De Ruyter in '73 off the Texel, didn't you?"

"Aye, but—"

"He was a brave admiral and he usually fought against odds."

"I know, Captain Terror, but—"

"But nothing, Von Tromp. You take me for an utter fool before I've proven else. Bide your tongue and time and, mayhap, Fortune will present us with an opening."

The Dutchman shrugged his shoulders and walked off. This mad Englishman was beyond him.

With the ebbing of the tide in the morning, the *Vengeance*, for such was the new name of Captain Terror's great brown and white ship, slipped out of Dragon's Tooth Cove and gayly cleared the sand spit point. It was good to feel the flow of the breeze and be aboard the rocking boards of a fine vessel again, thought the black-browed Welshman. As the *Vengeance* gained steerage and her sheets billowed to the southerly breeze, he knew that underfoot was a vessel of speed and agility. Lacking the sturdiness of the English and Dutch built ships, the *Vengeance*, nonetheless, incorporated all the grace and speed that only a French builder could impart to a sailing vessel.

Within a few days the *Vengeance* had taken up her station off Cape Engano on the western tip of the Mona Passage. At a conference in his cabin over some fine Canary wine, Captain Terror, Duggley, Von Tromp, and Gallat bent over the charts. If they reckoned correctly from the date of his former ill-fated meeting with the *San Nicolas*, the Spanish Squadron should be bearing through the straits within the week, her hulls full of pearls for the coffers of Charles II, King of Spain.

The wind strengthened from the south and chopped the sea up in the straits. If the Spanish Squadron beat through the passage now she would come hell-bent with a strong wind at her stern. Captain Terror had no more of an idea as to what he was going to do in the event of meeting the cursed Spanish foe than he had knowledge of the priesthood, but his Welsh blood gave him a trust in fortune that the others were wont to openly criticize.

"I tell you, my lads, I won't be content until I see this great fearsome fleet that I've heard so much about, even if it ends in our showing them our heels."

The breeze had slackened again but it was still blowing up a bit of lace on the rollers when the lookout sighted some specks on the horizon riding the southerly breeze through the straits. As time gained and distance lessened, it proved to be indeed the fleet of the Spanish Caribbean Admiral. In twin columns the six vessels, under a full press of sail, were wearing through the Mona Passage. Our Blessed Mother and other renderings from the Holy Book decorated the mainsails of the galleons. Bringing up the tail of the closer westernmost column was none other than the *San Nicolas*, with her Vice-Admiral's pennant smartly fluttering at her foremast tip.

"The sight of that pennant burns me like the fires of perdition," exclaimed Captain Terror venomously to Gallat as the two stood in the crosstrees. "But friend Fortune has placed them in our very laps, my hearty. Get your men in the rigging, Gallat, and carry out my bidding for I think that we shall have action."

With that he dropped down the shrouds and ratlines to the waist. He called Duggley and the crotchety Von Tromp to his side.

"Mates, I've got a plan that may cause untold trouble to yonder proud gentlemen of Castile. Listen carefully to what I have to say for there is a mite of danger to be experienced."

There on the deck of his fine ship, Captain Terror told them of his plan of action and also beat off the arguments of that former ace gunner of De Ruyter's, Von Tromp. When he had finished, he glanced toward his cabin and saw the slight figure of the Spanish girl in the doorway.

Quickly he went up to her.

"You must go to the hold below," he told her sharply. "It will not be safe up here— we are about to attack yon fleet."

They were the first words he had spoken to her since the day in the cabin, many days past, when he had kissed her.

"Attack?" She stared at him in wonderment. "Are you mad?"

"Get below," he said, ignoring her remarks, "and hurry."

"I shall stay where I am," she told him, lifting her head proudly and looking him full in the eye. "Whatever our faults, we Spanish are not cowards."

Edward could hardly restrain his admiration as he looked at the beautiful, proud face.

"Very well," he returned briefly. "But keep under cover."

May the Good Lord keep her safe, he thought somberly to himself as he rejoined the men, his ardor for the coming battle somewhat dampened by his concern for her safety.

So it was that Don Berona de Fecento, Admiral of the Caribbean Squadron, saw the approach of a fine looking ship of Spain, with the gold and scarlet emblem of Castile at her main-truck, beating close-hauled into the wind that was at his own stern. This fine ship approached head-on towards his squadron midway between the two columns.

"Shall I run open our ports, Admiral?" his conscientious gunner said as he stood beside him on the forty-four gun *San Felippe*.

"What for, you foolish son of a pig? She's Spanish and she doesn't show her own guns."

"I perceive that, Admiral, but it might be a trick. These are buccaneer waters."

"Tell me, Carlos, do you jump at your own shadow?" The great man was sarcastic. "Do you really believe that a single ship would dare attack the Caribbean Squadron? Why, that foul knave Morgan wouldn't dare it with a fleet. Go back to your post. You need a rest for your nerves."

The brown and white ship had now come closer and many waving men could be discerned lining her yardarms.

"Look, Captain, they are thrilled by the sight of so much Spanish might." The great Admiral beamed as he spoke to the master of the *San Felippe* standing beside him.

"I see, sire, but their impudence in sailing amidst our formation should be reported. I don't like it."

Don Berona de Facento condescended to only a smile at this nervous ship's master. His own egotism was in for quite a shock, however, for aboard the *Vengeance* the guns were loaded, the sparks were lit and the buccaneer guncrews waited tensely behind closed ports.

"Look, Duggley," eagerly Captain Terror spoke to his navigator, "Gallat's company waving in the rigging, our Spanish flag and the closed gunports have completely deceived them. Those poor fools."

Captain Terror stood in the waist and the gunners watched him as the *Vengeance* moved into the hostile center. He waited until the *San Felippe* and the *Infanta*, forty-four guns, were on either side. Then he brought his arm down.

"Pay 'em our compliments, men!"

In a trice the ready gunports snapped open and thirty-six thirty-two pounders lunged forth, eighteen on the starboard side pointing at the *San Felippe* and the port guns pointing at the *Infanta*.

"Crash!"

The two broadsides pounded forth in one terrific blast. At once the guns were run back, swabbed, reloaded, and rammed. As the monstrous clouds of gunsmoke rolled away to her rear, the men on the *Vengeance* let out a scream of derision and joy. The broadsides had caused great damage and consternation to the unsuspecting Spaniards. The mizzenmast of the *Infanta* had come rattling down and great holes and gaps in both shrouds and hulk appeared on the *San Felippe*.

"Crash!"

Once again the twin broadsides let go as the *Vengeance* slid swiftly through the seas to a position between the next two of the Spanish Squadron, both forty gun galleons, the *Santisima Cadiz* and the *Santa Ana*. The dumbfounded men of Castile had no more time than to run out but a few of their guns when the broadsides crashed into them. The *Santisima Cadiz* lost her bowsprit and the *Santa Ana* dropped her foremast. Both received additional damage and casualties in the rigging and among their crews and both looked like shambles.

"Run down that stinking flag of Spain," Captain Terror shouted to one of his hands, "and send aloft the Cross of St. George."

Meanwhile, Vice-Admiral Don Alvarez de Perona de Sadista stood open mouthed in awful amazement on the high poop deck of his scarlet ship, the *San Nicolas*. The affair had come to pass within the brief space of a few minutes and already the two lead ships in the twin columns were wallowing sorely stricken in the blue seas. He crossed himself and screamed at his gunners and first mate. This great blasphemer of his Catholic Majesty's Fleet, the brown and white ship now flying the cursed English ensign, was between his ship and the *Valencia*, last ships in their respective columns.

"Crash!"

A third twin broadside erupted from the flanks of the daring Englishman but this time there was a desultory and hasty return fire. The air eddied with swirling clouds of gunsmoke and the Englishman was hidden in the haze from her guns. Her third twin broadsides had not done the damage of the first two, but yet the *San Nicolas* suffered rents in her rigging and loss of life on her decks while the smaller twenty-two gun *Valencia* showed great gashes in her larboard railing and stern works.

"What did I tell you, Duggley," Captain Terror laughed as he slapped his blonde navigator's broad back. "Smack down the center we bore and blasted each and every one of them, with aught but one stinking ball in our starboard flank for the trouble."

"Aye, Edward, and by the time those heavy lead ships wear around on a fair tack into this head wind, we'll be safely away." The navigator's eyes flashed. "By the great bear, it was brilliant. You've tweaked the beard of the most powerful force on the Main and now we're safe away."

"Not quite, lad," the elegantly clad captain said and pointed over the taffrail.

If the signal system of the Spanish Navy could only have incorporated some of the choice epithets that the Castillian tongue is famed for, the top shrouds of Admiral de Fecento's *San Felippe* would that day have flown them all, such was the rage in which he found himself. As it was, all that he could do was to order the speedier *San Nicolas* and the *Valencia* to turn about and pursue this foul treacherous fiend of England. These two ships had made about and were straining their last ounce of seamanship and skill in the pursuit of the *Vengeance*.

"Shall I pour on more sheet, Edward? Our slick bottom will enable us to outdistance those two bilge drinkers."

"No. Pull in some of the top sheets, Duggley lad. We'll let them chase us for yet awhile and, in time, catch up—but only after we're safe away from interference from their larger sisters."

The pursuit bowled on over the running seas and the remainder of the Spanish Squadron was left behind. Captain Terror had had his crew served with rum and, walking among the garish but well-disciplined pirates, he received their unreserved praise and coarse compliments. Never had any of them served under such a daring and skillful commander.

"You see those two eager hounds that pursue us, my hearties?" He addressed a gathering of buccaneers in the waist. "Well, lads, their holds are bulging with choice pearls that I greatly fear the King of Spain will never fondle. I mean to have them for you." A great roar of approval went up. "Remember it well when the time comes for fighting."

Von Tromp stood beside him at the quarterdeck rail, his sour countenance dismayed at the thought of further unnecessary danger.

"Von Tromp, you Dutch rascal, you've handled the guns with a touch that De Ruyter would have been proud of. I've further tests of your ability shaping up, however."

The stubby Dutch pirate shrugged off his captain's friendly pat and spoke petulantly.

"Captain, these two pursuers outgun us. Your first brilliant success may cause you to tempt Lady Fortune too much. We'd better be out of these waters with all speed."

"Von Tromp, I sometimes wonder what misfortune ever made you take to the pirating trade," said Captain Terror good-naturedly. "Your Dutch reticence and mathematical mind calculate only the risks against an operation. Why, man, you do not think me fool enough to buck them both together, do you? Their own eagerness will be their downfall." With that he pointed over the rail where it was plain to see that the speedier *Valencia* had outdistanced the *San Nicolas* and was coming up at a goodly rate. "Yonder Spaniard thinks that, because we flee for the moment, we do not consider suddenly turning upon him before his consort can come to his aid."

Von Tromp's eyes widened as he understood the captain's plan. Indeed, the Englishman was not the fool that he, Von Tromp, had thought him.

Captain Terror stood beside Duggley on the poop deck and watched his men climb into the rigging. The moment had almost arrived. He would have preferred it if the *Valencia* had outdistanced the Vice-Admiral further—but such was not the case. He issued his orders with a wave of his hand to Gallat in the upper works.

The *Vengeance* suddenly seemed to halt in midstride as the sails furled, the yardarms shifted, and Gallat's men tumbled the wind out of her sheets. The brown and white ship slipped around broadside to the oncoming *Valencia* before the Spaniard knew what was about and her starboard guns roared out a broadside.

"Crash!"

The weight of her load caught the twenty-two gun vessel in the bowsprit, sheared it away with the foremast stays and ratlines and cut swathes of destruction the length of her deck. The *Vengeance*, under the tricky and skillful handling of Gallat's men, swung further around until her unfired port guns came into line. By now the Spaniard had turned to larboard to bring his own guns to bear and the two broadsides crashed out as one.

Von Tromp's skill was not to be denied and the heavier weight of the pirate vessel's metal tore down the main and mizzenmasts, blasted the *Valencia*'s gunports and rails and left her a smoking demi-hulk of ruin.

The smoke of the battle hid the two ships from view as the thirty-two gun *San Nicolas* slid into the battle mist, her eager Spanish gunners waiting tensely to obtain the vengeance that they felt they so richly deserved from this English heretic.

Aboard his vessel Captain Terror had stripped to the waist, thrown off his periwig and donned a red speckled bandana. In his waist sash he had thrust a brace of pistols and the silver needle of his rapier was bared. There would be hand-to-hand fighting ere this day's work were finished. Gallet's bowmen were in the rigging, Von Tromp commanded the guns and Duggley stood by the helmsman. The *Vengeance* had taken some damage as the bloodstained boards attested and hands were busy repairing the parted ratlines, shattered rails, burst cannon, and splintered timbers.

"There are are the topworks of the Vice-Admiral," Duggley pointed to the spars and upper shrouds of the *San Nicolas* ploughing through the hazy fog of smoke roundabout.

"Fire through the smoke, Von Tromp. They're not certain yet as to who's who."

The Spaniard, however, had seen the English ensign at their main-truck, towering through the fast dispelling smoke. She turned and, as the screen of smoke lifted enough for the bucaneers to see her steel studded flank, a blistering broadside ploughed into the *Vengeance*. Von Tromp answered and the battle became a horrible confusion of smoke, flame, screams, and falling spars.

Cooly Captain Terror directed his vessel in closer to the game and bitterly fought *San Nicolas*. The *Valencia* lay now out of the fight, crippled, flaming and licking her many wounds. Through the yellowing haze the *Vengeance* crept with her guns firing continuously. She had taken much damage but, so far, her masts stood intact as did those of the Spaniard.

Gallat and his bowmen, in the ratlines above the thickest of the smoke, could at last pick out targets and soon unexpected shafts were whistling down upon the Spaniard's deck and doing fearful execution. This sudden attack from above their heads unnerved the hard pressed Spaniards as claw-like grappling hooks swung out from the *Vengeance* and the two ships ground together, side-by-side and securely bound. Von Tromp continued his gunnery as did the Spaniard and the execution below decks was frightful at such point blank range.

"Follow me, lads," Captain Terror shouted.

He grabbed a ratline and swung onto the Spaniard's deck with his rapier between his teeth. At his heels swarmed the buccaneer crew, the most deadly and ferocious hand-to-hand shipboard fighters that the world has ever known.

Edward Terror dropped to the deck with a thrill of strange joy racing through his veins. The final accounting with this treacherous sea-wolf for the rape of the *Maid of Avon* was at hand. All the hate and rage that had boiled within him for so many days was now free, and, like a fiend possessed, he slashed and pistoled his way through the struggling mob until, at last, he stood before the final knot of surviving Spaniards in the aft of the waist. A wild savage look was in his black eyes and his blade was bloody when he confronted the red and white pantalooned figure of the Vice-Admiral.

Don Alvarez de Perona de Sadista stood erect in his steel corsolet and helmet. He knew that his end was at hand but, like a true son of Spain, he would die fighting. His sword crossed with that of this wild looking rogue in the red speckled bandana before him. On the blood-slippery deck the two duelists slashed at one another as the end of the fight drew nigh around about them.

Captain Terror knew, in a moment, that he crossed swords with no less than the Vice-Admiral.

"You know me not, Spanish cur, but this is a debt that I'm repaying."

His blade flickered out, twirled and flashed and the Spaniard's sword spun through the air. It is doubtful that Vice-Admiral Don Alvarez de Perona de Sadista ever knew what debt he was atoning for but, in a trice, his body was run through and he lay spread eagled and dead on his wreckage strewn deck.

The battle was over.

Captain Terror wiped the sweat from his brow and, for the first time in many weeks, he felt an inner contentment. It was as if a great overbearing load had been lifted from his shoulders. The hate had been cleansed from his body and soul and vengeance was his.

The joyous crew overran the *San Nicolas* and soon brought forth her chests of pearls. The disabled *Valencia* ran down her flag and Captain Terror led a picked crew aboard her.

Elegantly attired once more, the Welsh pirate preserved the niceties and bowed gallantly to the bloodstained Spanish captain, refusing, however, to speak to him directly.

"The captain says that you need have no further worries for your life, sire," a roguish, Spanish speaking buccaneer translated Captain Terror's word to the thoroughly whipped Spaniard. "All we desire is your pearl cargo and then you may have your ship and begone."

Captain Terror smiled broadly, revealing his flashing teeth as the Spaniard, with a mournful look, surveyed his battered vessel. The pearls were turned over to the lean buccaneer and it was not long thereafter that Captain Terror mounted the accommodation ladder and met the nervous Duggley on deck.

"We had better get out of these waters while we are still able, Edward. The remainder of the squadron may come up at any moment."

"Aye," Captain Terror said, ruefully surveying the damage to his vessel. "Pour on the sheets and we'll be away."

Suddenly his mind reverted to the Spanish girl. Where was she? He hastily searched the tangled aftermath of the battle. She was nowhere to be seen. With a strange feeling of worry, he hurried to his cabin and flung open the door.

The girl was stretched out face down on the window seat, her body shaking with sobs. He paused on the threshold of the cabin and the exhilaration of his vengeance drained from him like bilge water from a tapped hold.

In the heat of the battle he had forgotten her and the effect it must have upon her sensitive being. He had just killed her suitor and had wracked a bloody vengeance from her countrymen. The double realization that he loved this girl and that his rash actions must now have turned her feelings to hatred for him suddenly hurt him. Her previous behavior had only been reaction to a dangerous situation. The reality of his deeds must now make her hate him.

"Dolores," he whispered as he walked over to her prostrate figure and tenderly placed his hand upon her shoulder. "I'm sorry. I know how you feel but it was something I had to do."

Suddenly she raised her tear-stained face and looked at him. A smile appeared as if by magic and she leaped to the floor.

"I was not crying for them," she smiled shyly. "I was afraid for you, Edward. For you see, I love you."

With that she buried her head on his chest and Edward Terror embraced her in his arms.

And thus it was that, at one and the same time, Spain acquired her most relentless enemy and a certain lady of Spain acquired her most devoted lover.

ALAMUT

HAROLD LAMB

I

It was the year of the lion at the very end of the sixteenth century when Khlit guided his horse into Astrakan. No sentries challenged him in the streets of Astrakan, for the Cossacks were masters here and no Cossack would dishonor himself by taking precautions against danger. There were many Mohammedans in the streets of Astrakan, but it was evening and the followers of Allah were repeating the last of their prayers, facing, as was the law, toward the city of Mecca.

Sitting his steppe pony carelessly, Khlit allowed the beast to take its own course. The night, in Midsummer, was warm and his heavy *svitza* was thrown back on his high shoulders. A woolen cap covered one side of his gray head, and his new pair of costly red Morocco boots were smudged with tar to show his contempt for appearances. Under his shaggy mustache a pipe glowed and by his side hung the strangely shaped saber which had earned the Cossack the name of "Khlit of the Curved Saber."

Khlit rode alone, as he had done since he left the Siech, where Cossack leaders had said that he was too old to march with the army of the Ukraine. He paid no attention to the sprawling, drunken figures of Cossacks that his horse stepped over in the street. Clouds of flies from fish houses, odorous along the river front, buzzed around him. Donkeys driven by naked Tatar urchins passed him in the shadows. Occasionally the glow from the open front of an Ispahan rug dealer's shop showed him cloaked Tatars who swaggered and swore at him.

Being weary Khlit paid no heed to these. A dusty armorer's shop under an archway promised a resting-place for the night, and here he dismounted. Pushing aside the rug that served as a door he cursed as he stumbled over the proprietor of the shop, a Syrian who was bowing a yellow face over a purple shawl in prayer.

"*Lailat el kadr*," the Syrian muttered, casting a swift side glance at the tall Cossack.

Khlit did not know the words; but that night thousands of lips were repeating them—*lailat el kadr*, night of power. This was the night which was potent for the followers of the true faith, when the *dhinns* smiled upon Mohammed, and Marduk was hung by his heels in Babylon. It is so written in the book of Abulghazi, called by some Abulfarajii, historian of dynasties.

It was on such a night of power, say the annals of Abulghazi, that Hulagu Khan, nephew of Ghengis Khan and leader of the Golden Horde overcame the citadel of Alamut, the place of strange wickedness, by the river Shahrud, in the province of Rudbar. It was on that night the power of Hagen ben Sabbah was broken.

But the power of Hagen ben Sabbah was evil. Evil, says Abulghazi, is slow to die. The wickedness of Alamut lived, and around it clung the shadow of the power that had belonged to Hagen ben Sabbah—a power not of god or man—who was called by some sheik, by others the Old Man of the Mountain, and by himself the prophet of God.

It was also written in the book of Abulghazi that there was a prophecy that the waters of the Shahrud would be red with blood, and that the evil would be hunted through the hidden places of Alamut. A strange prophecy. And never had Khlit, the Cossack of the Curved Saber, shared in such a hunt. It was not of his own seeking—the hunt that disclosed the secret of Alamut. It was chance that made him a hunter, the chance that brought him to the shop of the Syrian armorer, seeking rest.

So it happened that Khlit saw the prophecy of Abulghazi, who was wise with an ancient wisdom, come to pass—saw the river stair flash with sword blades, and the banquet-place, and the treasure of Alamut under the paradise of the Shadna.

"*Lailat el kadr*," chanted the Syrian, his eye on the curved blade of Khlit, "Allah is mighty and there is no god but he."

"Spawn of Islam," grunted Khlit who disliked prayer, "lift your bones and find for me a place to spend the night. And food."

The Cossack spoke in Tatar, with which language he was on familiar terms. The response was not slow in coming, although from an unexpected quarter. A cloaked figure rose from the shadows behind the one lamp which lighted the shop and con fronted him. The cloak fell to the floor and disclosed a sturdy form clad in a fur-tipped tunic under which gleamed a coat of mail, heavy pantaloons, and a peaked helmet. A pair of slant, bloodshot eyes stared at Khlit from a round face.

Khlit recognized the newcomer as a Tatar warrior of rank, and noted that while the other was short, his shoulders were wide and arms long as his knees. Simultaneously Khlit's curved saber flashed into view, with the Tatar's scimiter.

As quickly, the Syrian merchant darted into a corner. Cossack and Tatar, enemies by instinct and choice, measured each other cautiously. Neither moved, waiting for the other to act. Khlit's pipe fell to the floor and he did not stoop to pick it up.

"Toctamish!"

It was a woman's voice, shrill and angry that broke the silence. Khlit did not shift his gaze. The Tatar scowled sullenly, and growled something beneath his breath.

"Toctamish! Fool watch dog! Is there no end to your quarreling? Do your fingers itch for a sword until you forget my orders?"

The curtains were pushed aside from a recess in the shop, and out of the corner of his eye Khlit saw a slender woman dart forward and seize the Tatar by his squat shoulders. Toctamish tried in vain to throw off the grip that pinned his arms to his side.

"One without understanding," the Tatar growled, "here is a dog of a Cossack who would rather slay than eat. This is the Khlit I told of, the one with the curved sword. Are you a child at play?"

"Nay, you are the child, Toctamish," shrilled the woman, "for you would fight when the Cossack would eat. He means no harm. Allah keep you further from the wine cask! Put up your sword. Have you forgotten you are man and I am mistress?"

To Khlit's amusement Toctamish, who whether by virtue of wine or his natural foolhardiness was eager to match swords, dropped his weapon to his side. Whereupon Khlit lowered his sword and confronted the woman.

Beside the square form of Toctamish, she looked scarcely bigger than a reed of the river. A pale-blue reed, with a flower-face of delicate olive. Above the blue garment which covered her from foot to throat, her black hair hung around a face which arrested Khlit's attention. Too narrow to be a Tatar, yet too dark for a Georgian, her head was poised gracefully on slender shoulders. Her mouth was small, and her cheeks tinted from olive to pink. The eyes were wide and dark. Under Khlit's gaze she scowled. Abruptly she stepped to his side and watched him with frank curiosity.

"Do you leave courtesy outside when you enter a dwelling, Cossack?" she demanded. "You come unbidden, with dirty boots, and you flourish your curved sword in front of Toctamish who would have killed you because he is crafty as a Kurdish *farsang*, and feared you. I do not fear you. You have a soiled coat and you carry a foul stick in your mouth."

Khlit grunted in distaste. He had small liking for women. This one was neither Tatar nor Circassian nor Georgian, yet she spoke fair Tatar.

"Devil take me," he said, "I had not come had I known you were here, oh, loud voiced one. I came for food and a place to sleep."

"You deserve neither," she retorted, following her own thoughts. "Is it true that you are Khlit, who fought with the Tatars of Tal Taulai Khan? Toctamish is the man of Kiragai Khan who follows the banners of Tal Taulai Khan and he has seen you before. It seems he does not like you. Yet you have gray hair.”

The Cossack was not anxious to stay, yet he did not like to go, with Toctamish at his back. While he hesitated, the girl watched him, her lips curved in mockery.

“Is this the Wolf you told me of?” said she to Toctamish. “I do not think he is the one the Tatar fold fear. See, he blinks like an owl in the light. An old, gray owl.”

Toctamish made no reply, eying Khlit sullenly. Khlit was fast recovering from his surprise at the daring of this woman, of a race he had not seen before, and very beautiful, who seemed without fear. The daughter of a chieftain, he meditated; surely she was one brought up among many slaves.

“Aye, daughter,” he responded moodily. “Gray, and therefore forbidden to ride with the free Cossacks, my brothers of the Siech. Wherefore am I alone, and my sword at the service of one who asks it. I am no longer a Cossack of Cossacks but one alone.”

“I have heard tales of you.” The black-eyed woman stared at him boldly, head on one side. “Did you truly enter here in peace, seeking only food?”

“Aye,” said Khlit.

“Wait, then,” said she, “and the nameless one whose house this is will prepare it for you. Meanwhile, sheath the sword you are playing with. I shall not hurt you.”

Motioning Toctamish to her side, the woman of the blue cloak withdrew into a corner of the curtained armorer’s shop. The Cossack, who had keen eyes, noted that the Syrian was bending his black-capped head over a bowl of stew which he was stirring in another corner. No others, he decided, were in the shop.

Toctamish seemed to like his companion’s words little. He muttered angrily, at which the girl retorted sharply. Khlit could not catch their words, but he guessed that an argument was taking place, at which the Tatar was faring ill. The argument seemed to be about himself. Also, he heard the name Berca repeated.

Although Khlit was not of a curious nature, the identity of the girl puzzled him. With the beauty of a high-priced slave, and the manner of a king’s daughter, she went unveiled in a land where women covered their faces from men. Moreover she was young, being scarce eighteen, and of delicate stature.

Khlit bethought him, and it crossed his memory that he had heard of dark-haired and fair-skinned women of unsurpassed beauty whose land was at the far end of the Sea of Khozar, the inland, salt sea. They were Persians, of the province of Rudbar. Yet, fair as they were in the sight of men, none were bought as slaves. Berca, if that were her name, might well be one of these. If that was the case, what was she doing in Astrakan, alone save for one Tatar, who while he was a man of rank and courage, was not her equal?

II

The Cossack's meditation was interrupted by the girl, who motioned to the Syrian to set his stew before Khlit.

"Eat," she cried impatiently, pointing to the steaming bowl. "You are hungry, Father of Battles, and I would speak with you. A man speaks ill on an empty belly, although a woman needs not food nor wine to sharpen her wits. Eh, look at me and say, Father of Battles, is it not true I am beautiful, that men would die for me? It is given to few to look at me so closely."

She stepped near the Cossack, so the edge of her silk garment touched his shaggy face where he crouched over the bowl. Khlit sniffed, and with the odor of lamb stew he smelled, although he knew not its nature, the scent of rose leaves and aloes. He dipped his hand into the bowl and ate.

"Speak, Khlit, Cossack boor," shrilled the woman, shaking his shoulder impatiently, "and say whether it is in your mind I am beautiful. Other men are not slow to say that Berca of Rudbar and Kuhistan is shapely, and tinted as the rose."

Khlit's hand paused midway to his mouth.

"Toctamish has a handsome harlot," he said and swallowed.

The girl stepped back hastily.

"Clown!" she whispered softly. "Nameless one of a dog's breeding. You shall remember that word. It was in my mind to bid you come with me, and be companion to Toctamish—"

"Am I a man for a Tatar's wench?" Khlit was making rapid inroads into the stew.

"Nay, a boor of the steppe. Remember, your speech is not to be forgotten. I am a chief's daughter, with many horsemen."

Berca was watching the Cossack half-angrily, half-anxiously. Toctamish moved his bulk to the bowl, regarding the disappearing contents with regret.

"How can one man be courteous, Berca of Rudbar," he asked gruffly, "when the tribe is without breeding? It were better to cut the throat of this *caphar*, dog without faith, before he ate of our bread and salt."

"Nay, eat also of the food, Toctamish," said Berca, "and let me think."

The Tatar's brown face wrinkled in distaste.

"Am I to share bread with a *caphar*?" he snarled. "Truly, I promised to obey you, but not thus. Bid the Cossack be gone and I will eat. Otherwise he will be brother in arms, and his danger shall be my danger."

Berca stamped her slippered foot impatiently.

"Has Allah given me a donkey to follow me? Eat your share of the stew, Toctamish, and cease your braying. Is it not written in the Koran that the most disagreeable of voices is the voice of asses."

Toctamish remained sullenly silent. He was very hungry. Likewise, Khlit was an enemy of his blood.

"Eat, Flat-Face," chuckled Khlit, who was beginning to enjoy himself, "the stew is rarely made. But the bottom of the bowl is not far off."

The odor of the food tormented the Tatar. And Berca, for reason of her own, allowed him no chance to back away from the bowl. Finally, in desperation, he squatted opposite Khlit and dipped his hand into the stew.

"Remember the law, Flat-Face," guffawed Khlit, as the other ate greedily. "We have shared bread and salt together— I would give a hundred ducats for a mouthful of wine."

"It is not I who will forget, *caphar*," retorted Toctamish with dignity. Tugging at his girdle, he held out a small gourd. "Here is *arak*; drink heartily."

"Aye," said Khlit.

He had tasted the heady mares' milk of the Tatars before and he sucked his mustache appreciatively after the draft. Pulling pipe and tobacco from a pouch he proceeded to smoke.

"Observe," said Toctamish to Berca, to show that he was not softened by what has passed, "that the *caphar* dog is one who must have two weeds to live. He sucks the top of one and drinks the juice of the other."

"Still your tongue," said Berca sharply, "and let me think."

She had seated herself cross-legged by the bowl, and her bird-like glance strayed from Khlit to Toctamish. The Cossack, engrossed in his pipe, ignored her.

"Why did you name me a harlot?" she asked abruptly, a flush deepening the olive of her cheeks.

"Eh, I know not, Sparrow. Devfl take it, a blind man would see you are not kin to Toctamish. He is not of your people. And there is no old woman at hand to keep you out of mischief. You have said you were a chief's daughter. If that is not a lie, then the chief is dead."

The girl's eyes widened, and Toctamish gaped.

"Have you a magician's sight, *caphar*?" she cried. "It is true that the sheik, my father is dead. But I did not tell you."

"Yet you are alone, Berca, across the Sea of Khozar, without attendants. A wise sheik will keep his girl at home, except when she is sent to be married. Is it not true that another sent you out of Rudbar?"

Berca's dark eyes closed and she rested her chin quietly on her folded hands. One hand she thrust into the folds of her cloak at the throat and drew it out clasped around a small object which hung by a chain from her slender neck. Opening her fingers she disclosed a sapphire of splendid size and brilliancy, set in carved gold. The jewel was of value, and appeared to be from the work-shops of skilled jewelers of Tabriz. Khlit eyed it indifferently and waited.

"It is true that another sent me from Rudbar, Khlit," said Berca softly, "and it was to be married. The one who sent me sent also some slaves and an attendant. He swore that a certain chief, a khan of the Kallmarks had asked me for his wife, and I went, not desiring to stay in Rudbar after my father died."

"The Kallmarks?" Khlit frowned. "Why, you are a Persian, and the Kallmark Tatars make war on Persians as did their fathers. A marriage would be strange. Eh, who sent you?"

Berca lowered her voice further and glanced at the Persian armorer who was snoring in his corner.

"One it was who is better not named," she whispered. "He is neither sheik nor khan. Listen, Cossack. This is a jewel of rare value. It has no mate this side of Damascus. Would you like to own it?"

"Aye," said Khlit indifferently, "at what price?"

"Service."

"Do you want another Toctamish? Buy him in the streets of Astrakan. Is a free Cossack to be bought?"

"Nay, Khlit," whispered Berca leaning close to him until her loose curls touched his eyes, "the service is for one who can use his sword. We heard in Tatary how you escaped from Tal Taulai Khan and his myriad horsemen. Men say that you are truly the father of battles. I have work for such a one. Listen! I was sent from Rudbar to Kiragai Khan, up the Sea of Khozar, and across the Jaick River, with one attendant and a box which the attendant said held jewels and gold bars for my dowry. I came to the court of Kiragai Khan—"

"Bah, Sparrow," Khlit yawned sleepily, "you are tiresome. I want sleep, not words. In the morning—"

"We will be gone from Astrakan." Berca held up the sapphire. "You must listen, Cossack. I told Kiragai Khan my mission, for there were no others to speak, and opened the box in the hands of the attendant. The jewels were poor pearls and no gold was in the box. Then Kiragai Khan, before whom I had unveiled my face, laughed and said that he had not sent for me. At first it came to my mind that it was because the jewels were worthless. But it was the truth."

"Aye," said Toctamish suddenly, "it was the truth."

"I went quickly from the country of Kiragai Khan, aided by Toctamish, who pitied me when others tried to sell me a slave—of a race that are not slaves. At Astrakan we learned the whole truth, for here word came to us that the one who sent me in marriage had killed my father. I was sent to be out of the way, for it would not do to sell one of my blood as slave. Such is not the law. He who killed my father heeds no law, yet he is crafty."

"Then," inquired Khlit, "you would slay him? Give Toctamish a dagger and a dark night and it is done."

Berca shook her head scornfully.

"No dagger could come near this man," she said bitterly. "And he is beyond our reach. He has many thousand hidden daggers at his call. His empire is from. Samarkand to Aleppo, and from Tatary to the Indian Sea. He is more feared than Tal Taulai Khan, of the Horde."

"Then he must be a great sheik," yawned Khlit.

"He is not a sheik," protested Berca, and her eyes widened. "And his stronghold is under the ground, not on it. Men say his power lies in his will to break all laws, for he has made his followers free from all law. What he wants, he takes from others. And he is glad when blood is shed. Do you know of him?"

"Aye," said Khlit, grinning, "the steppe fox."

"They call you the Wolf," pleaded Berca, "and I need your counsel and wisdom. This man I am seeking has a name no one makes a jest of—twice. He is called by some the arch prophet, by others the Old Man of the Mountain, and by others the *Shadna* of the Refik folk. He is the head of an empire that lays tribute on every city in Persia, Kurdistan, Khorassan, Syria and Anatolia. If Allah decreed that I should be his death I should be content."

"More likely dead," responded Khlit. "Truly, if these are not lies, your Old Man of the Mountain must be a good fighter and I would cross swords with him. Can you show him to me?"

"Aye, Khlit," said Berca eagerly, "if you come with me. There is the sapphire if you will come to Rudbar with me."

Khlit stretched his tall bulk lazily.

"One way is as good as the other to me, if there is fighting," he muttered sleepily. "Only talk not of rewards, for a Cossack takes his pay from the bodies of enemies. I will kill this Master of the Mountain for you. Let me sleep now, for your voice is shrill."

When Toctamish and Berca had left the shop of the armorer, the former to seek a shed outside, and the Persian girl to sleep in her recess, Khlit's snores matched those of the Syrian shopkeeper in volume. For a while only. Then it happened that the snores of the Syrian ceased.

Without disturbing Khlit who was stretched full length on the floor, the Syrian silently pushed past the hangings over the door. Once outside he broke into a trot, his slippers *pad-padding* the dark street. Nor did he soon slacken his pace.

III

K hlit and Toctamish did not make the best of bed-fellows. Berca, however, was careful to see that no serious quarrel broke out between the two. In a bark that went from Astrakan, the day after their meeting, to the south shore of the Sea of Khozar, the two warriors of different races occupied a small cupboard which adjoined the cabin of the sheik's daughter.

Khlit had embarked not altogether willingly. When the fumes of *arak* had cleared from his head the next morning, he had half-repented of his bargain. Curiosity to see the other side of the salt sea, which he had known as the Caspian, rather than the pleadings of Berca, finally brought him aboard the bark with his horse from which he refused to be separated.

The girl had bought their passage with the last of her pearls, and some gold of Toctamish's, and had remained in her cabin since, to which Toctamish brought food. The Cossack, after a survey of the small vessel which disclosed his fellow-voyagers as some few Syrian silk-merchants, with the Tatar crew, took possession of a nook in the high poop deck, and kept a keen lookout for the islands and other vessels they passed, and for *Bab-al-abuab*, the lofty gate of gates as the ship made its way southward. Toctamish, who had not set foot on a ship before, was very ill, to Khlit's silent satisfaction.

One day, when the wind was too high for comfort on deck, the Cossack sought Toctamish in the cupboard where the latter lay, ill at ease on some skins.

"Hey, Flat-Face," Khlit greeted him, sitting opposite against the side of the dark recess, "you look as if the devil himself was chewing at your entrails. Can you speak as well as you grunt? I have a word for you. Where is the little Berca?"

"In her cabin, oh, dog without breeding," snarled the Tatar, who was less disposed to speak, even, than usual, "looking at silks of a Syrian robber. This sickness of the sea is a great sickness, for I am not accustomed."

"You will not die." Khlit stroked his saber thoughtfully across his boots. "Toctamish, gully-jackal, and dog of an unbelieving race, you have been a fool. Perhaps a greater one than I. How did it happen that you became the follower of the little Berca? Has she bewitched you with her smooth skin and dark eyes?"

"Nay, that is not so," Toctamish growled. "She has told you her story. It is true that Kiragai Khan, my master, did not know of her coming. Her attendant and slaves ran away and she felt great shame. Yet she did not lose courage. When her shame was the greatest she begged me to take her to Astrakan, saying that I should be head of her army. She did not say her army was beyond the Salt Sea. Then she made me promise to take her to her people. As you know, her tongue is golden."

"Aye," said Khlit. "Then you are even a greater fool than I had thought. Have you heard of this emperor she is taking us to?"

Toctamish rolled his eyes, and shook his head vaguely.

"His name is not known in our countries. Mongol Tatars say that their great-grandfathers who followed the banners of Hulagu Khan made war on one calling himself the Old Man of the Mountain and slew many thousands with much booty, beside burning the citadel of Alamut, which was his stronghold. They gave me a dagger which came from Alamut. It is a strange shape."

"If the power of the Old Man of the Mountain was broken in the time of Hulagu Khan," said Khlit idly, "how can it exist now? Have you the dagger?"

The Tatar motioned to his belt with a groan, and Khlit drew from it a long blade with heavy handle. The dagger was of tempered steel, curved like a tongue of fire. On it were inscribed some characters which were meaningless to Khlit. He balanced it curiously in his bony hand.

"I have seen the like, Flat-Face," he meditated idly. "It could strike a good blow. Hey, I remember where I have seen others like it. In the shop of the Syrian armorer, at Astrakan. Who brought you to the shop?"

"We came, dog of a Cossack. The Syrian bade us stay, charging nothing for our beds, only for food."

"Does he understand Tatar language?"

"Nay, Berca spoke with him in her own tongue."

"Aye. Did she speak with you of this Old Man of the Mountain?"

"Once. She said that her people had come under the power of the Old Man of the Mountain. Also that her home was near to Alamut." Toctamish hesitated. "One thing more she said."

"Well, God has given you a tongue to speak."

"She said that your curved sword was useless against him who is called the Old Man of the Mountain."

With this the Tatar rolled over in his skins and kept silence. Wearying of questioning him, Khlit rose and went to the door of Berca's cabin. Toctamish, he meditated, was not one who could invent answers to questions out of his own wit. Either he spoke the truth, or he had been carefully taught what to say. Khlit was half-satisfied that the girl's and the Tatar's story was true in all its details, strange as it seemed. Yet he was wise, with the wisdom of years, and certain things troubled him.

It was not customary for a Tatar of rank to follow the leadership of a woman. Also, it was not clear why Berca should have been so eager for the services of Khlit, the Wolf. Again, she had declared that the Old Man of the Mountain was not to be met with, yet, apparently, she sought him.

Pondering these things, Khlit tapped lightly on the door of the girl's cabin. There was no response and he listened. From within he could hear the quiet breathing of a person in sleep.

He had come to speak with Berca, and he was loath to turn back. Pushing open the door he was about to step inside, when he paused.

Full length on the floor lay Berca, on the blue cloak she always wore. Her black curls flowed over a silk pillow on which her head rested. Her eyes were closed and her face so white that Khlit wondered it had ever been pink.

What drew the Cossack's gaze were two objects on the floor beside her. Khlit saw, so close that some of the dark hairs were caught in them, two daggers sticking upright on either side of the girl's head. The daggers were curved, like a tongue of fire.

Khlit's glance, roaming quickly about the cabin, told him that no one else was there. Berca had not carried two weapons of such size. Another had placed them there. As he noticed the silk cushion, he remembered the Syrian silk-merchant who had been with Berca.

With a muttered curse of surprise, Khlit stepped forward, treading lightly in his heavy boots. Leaning over the girl he scanned her closely. Her breathing was quiet and regular, and her clothing undisturbed. Seeing that she was asleep, the Cossack turned his attention to the weapons.

Drawing the latter softly from the wood, he retreated to the door. Closing this, he climbed to the deck and scanned it for the Syrian merchant. Almost within reach he saw the one he sought, in a group of several ragged traders, squatting by the rail of the ship. No one noticed him, their black sheepskin hats bent together in earnest conversation.

With the daggers under his arm, Khlit swaggered over to the group, the men looking up silently at his approach.

"Hey, infidel dogs," he greeted them, "Here is a pair of good daggers I found lying by the steps. Who owns them? Speak!"

His eye traveled swiftly over the brown faces. None of the group showed interest beyond a curl of the lips at his words. If he had expected the owner to claim his property, he was disappointed. The Syrians resumed their talk together.

"So be it," said Khlit loudly. "They are useless to me. Away with them."

Balancing the weapons, he hurled them along the deck. As he did so, he glanced at the traders. Their conversation was uninterrupted. Yet Khlit saw one of the group look hastily after the flying daggers. It was only a flash of white eyeballs in a lean face, but Khlit stared closer at the fellow, who avoided his eye.

Something in the man's face was familiar to the Cossack. Khlit searched his memory and smiled to himself. The man who had watched the fate of the daggers Khlit had seen in Astrakan. The man had changed his style of garments, but Khlit was reasonably sure that he was no other than the Syrian armorer who had offered his shop to Berca and Toctamish.

Fingering his sword, the Cossack hesitated. It was in his mind to ask at the sword's point what the other had been doing in Berca's cabin. Yet, if the fellow admitted he had left the daggers by the girl, and Khlit did not kill him, the Syrian would be free to work other mischief. And Khlit, careless as he was of life, could see no just reason for killing the Syrian. Better to let the man go, he thought, unaware that he was suspected, and watch.

As an afterthought, Khlit went to where the twisted daggers lay on the deck and threw them over the side.

IV

In the year of the lion, there was a drouth around the Sea of Khozar, and the salt fields of its south shore whitened in the sun. Where the caravan route from Samarkand to Bagdad crossed the salt fields, the watering-places were dry, all save a very few.

The sun was reflected in burning waves from the crusted salt, from which a rock cropped out occasionally, and the wind from the sea did not serve to cool the air. In the annals of Abulghazi, it is written that men and camels of the caravans thirsted in this year, the year in which the waters of Shahrud, by the citadel of Alamut, were to be red with blood.

At one of the few watering-places near the shore, Berca's party of three, with a pack-donkey came to a halt, at the same time that a caravan, coming from the east stopped to refresh the animals.

The Persian girl watched the Kurdish camel-drivers lead their beasts to kneel by the well silently. Khlit, beside her, gazed attentively, although with apparent indifference at the mixed throng of white-and-brown-robed traders with their escort of mounted Kurds. Many looked at Berca, who was heavily veiled, but kept their distance at sight of Khlit.

"It is written, *Abulfetah Harb Issa*, Father of Battles," spoke the girl softly, "that a man must be crafty and wise when peril is 'round his road; else is his labor vain, he follows a luck that flees. Truly there is no luck, for Allah has traced our lives in the divining sands, and we follow our paths as water follows its course. Are you as wise as the masters of evil, oh, Cossack?"

The words were mocking, and Khlit laughed.

"Little Sparrow," he said, "I have seen ever so much evil, and there was none that did not fade when a good sword was waved in front of it. Yet never have I followed a woman."

"You will not follow me much further, Cossack. I will leave you at the foothills to go among my people, the hillmen, where I shall be safe. You and Toctamish will go alone the rest of the way. My face is known to the people of Alamut, who suppose that I am dead or a slave. In time they shall see me, but not yet. Meanwhile it is my wish that you and Toctamish seek the citadel of Alamut, which lies a two-days' journey into the interior."

Khlit shaded his eyes with a lean hand and gazed inland. Above the plain of salt levels he could see a nest of barren foothills which surrounded mountains of great size and height.

"Where lies the path to this Alamut—" he had begun, when Berca shook his arm angrily.

"Not so loud, fool of the steppe! Do you think we are still by the Volga? We are already in the territory of the Old Man of the Mountain. Listen, to what I have already told Toctamish. Two days' travel to the south will bring you to the district of Rudbar. You will find yourself near the River Shahrud which flows from the mountains. There will be hillmen about who do not love the Old Man of the Mountain.

"So do not speak his name, until you come to a bend in the Shahrud where the river doubles on itself, so, like a twisted snake. Across the river will be a mountain of rock which will appear to be a dog kneeling, facing you. Remain there until armed men ride up and question you. Then say you are come to join the ranks of Sheik Halen ibn Shaddah, who is the Old Man of the Mountain."

Khlit shook his head and tapped his sword thoughtfully.

"Nay, little Berca," he said reproachfully, "you have told me lies. You said it was your wish to slay one who had slain your father. And because it was a just quarrel and I was hungry for sight of the world below the Salt Sea, I came to aid you. Are you one, oh, Sparrow, to fight alone against a powerful chief? Where are your men that you told Toctamish of. Devil take me, if I'll put my head in the stronghold of any sheik, as you call him."

Berca bent nearer, rising on tiptoe so her breath was warm in his ear.

"My men are hillmen who will not attack until they see an enemy flee. Also, they have seen men who opposed Halen ibn Shaddah set over a fire, with the skin of their feet torn off. The master of Alamut is all powerful here. Are you afraid, whom they call the Wolf?"

"Nay, little Sparrow, how should I be afraid of women's tales and a mysterious name? Tell me your plan, and I will consider it. How can this sheik be reached?"

"Halen ibn Shaddah is safe from the swords of his enemies. Yet there is a way to reach him, in Alamut. The time will come when you and Toctamish will find yourselves at the head of many swords. How can I tell you, who are a fool in our way of fighting, and know not Alamut, what is in my mind? I swear that soon Halen ibn Shaddah will be attacked. Do you believe my word?"

"Wherefore should I?"

Khlit tugged at his mustache moodily. He was accustomed to settle his quarrels alone, and he liked little to move in the dark. Yet the woman spoke as one having authority, and Toctamish believed in her blindly.

"If this Sheik Halen is powerful and crafty—"

"Still, I am a woman, and wronged by a great wrong. I was sent to offer myself unveiled to a man who had not sought me; and at the same time my father was murdered, so that the hillmen, of whom he was sheik, might come under the shadow of Alamut." The girl's voice was low, but the words trembled with passion and the dark eyes that peered at the Cossack over her veil were dry as with fever, and burning. "Halen ibn Shaddah shall pay for his evil; for he is cursed in the sight of Allah. Wicked—wicked beyond telling is Alamut and therefore cursed."

"Chirp shrilly, little Sparrow," laughed Khlit, "while your white throat is still unslit. This Sheik Halen has no love for you, for one of his men on the bark placed two daggers, one on each side of your black head. Devil take me, if I did not think you would never chirp again. It was the Syrian who took you in for so little pay at Astrakan—"

"Fool! Stupid Cossack!" Berca's eyes suddenly swam with laughter, "did you think I was asleep when you tiptoed in like a bear treading nettles. Or that I did not see the dirty Syrian, who thought to catch me asleep? Look among the men of the caravan, and tell me if you see the Syrian?"

Cautiously, Khlit scanned the groups about the well. Among the Kurdish riders and Tatars who were brown with the dust of the desert trail from Samarkand, he recognized a bent figure in a long gray cloak and black *kollah*. As he watched the figure, it bent still further over a box of goods, and lifted some silks to view. It was the Syrian, without doubt. Khlit felt a thrill, as of one who is hunted and hears the cry of the chase. He stepped forward with an oath, when Berca's grasp tightened on his arm.

"That is a *fedavie* of Alamut," she whispered. "I saw the curved daggers, and they are the weapons of the Refik folk of Halen ibn Shaddah. He must have overheard us in his shop at Astrakan, and has followed to slay, as is the law of Alamut. Probably there are more of the *fedavie* among the men of the caravan."

"Then we must deal with the Syrian before he can speak to them," muttered Khlit, but again Berca tugged him back.

"Did I not say you were a fool among my people, oh, Wolf," she whispered. "Watch. The Syrian shall have his reward. Your folly is very great, yet I need a man who is blunt and brave and knows not my plans. It is written that none knows where his grave is dug, yet the Syrian's grave is here. Watch, and do not move."

Khlit waited. The *fedavie* had stooped over his box. One or two Kurds gathered to look at its contents. Among the group Khlit noticed Toctamish who had come up quietly. The Tatar pushed past the others, heedless of their muttered curses until he stood directly in front of the trader. The Syrian looked up, and, seeing Toctamish, was motionless.

Khlit saw the Kurds stare and draw back as if they sensed trouble. The Syrian, still watching Toctamish, rose with a swift, cat-like movement, his hand hidden in the silks. Toctamish grunted something and spat upon the silks.

"See," whispered Berca softly, "his grave is dug, and the nameless one sees it."

Toctamish thrust his yellow, scarred face near the Syrian's. Around him a crowd pressed, watching with attention. With a cry, the Syrian, who seemed to have found the suspense too much for him, drew a pistol from the silks in which it had been concealed.

Instantly two giant arms were flung 'round him. Toctamish was on him with a speed that baffled him, and the Tatar's huge bulk pressed the Syrian backward to the ground. Writhing impotently, the Syrian saw Toctamish draw a dagger from his girdle. And Khlit grunted as he noted that it was the one he had seen with blade like a curved flame. While he held the smaller man powerless with one arm, Toctamish lifted the dagger and thrust it carefully into his foe's body, into stomach and chest.

Then, rising, he wiped the curved dagger on a handful of the trader's silks. For a moment the arms and legs of the unhappy Syrian stirred on the ground. And Khlit saw a strange thing. For, before life had gone from the body, several men of the caravan, Khirghiz warriors by their dress, pushed through the throng with daggers like that of Toctamish and struck at the Syrian. Not until the body was still did they cease to strike.

Then the Khirghiz men looked around for Toctamish, but the stocky Tatar had disappeared in the throng. Khlit, who had missed nothing of what happened, thought to himself that it was well that the dagger had been in the hand of Toctamish, not of the Syrian. Plainly, he thought, the Khirghiz murderers had been fellows, without knowing, to the Syrian. And he wondered how men of many races came to be banded together, not knowing that he was to wonder soon, and very greatly, at other things.

V

Berca had disappeared; and when Khlit strode through the crowd of the caravan seeking her, his horse at his elbow, he met Toctamish. The Tatar was mounted and leading the pack-mule.

"Mount," he said gruffly, "and follow."

"And what of the girl!" queried Khlit, who was unwilling to take orders from Toctamish.

"She has told us to go on, as you know, *caphar*," snarled the Tatar, who disliked to talk. "Later, she will send word to us. Come."

"We are both fools. You, to be the slave of a painted girl, and I to seek for an empire which is not to be found, to slay a man who is hidden."

Khlit's words were silenced by a sudden uproar in the caravan. Men sprang to their feet and hauled at the camels who had kneeled in weariness. Traders who had been eating gave shouts of lamentation. Laden slaves ran together in confusion.

Toctamish stared at the uproar, until Khlit touched his shoulder.

"Look!" he said.

From the south, over the salt desert a cloud of dust was threading in and out among the rocks. It was advancing swiftly toward them, and the Cossack could see that it was made by mounted men riding very fast. He made out turbans and spear-points in the dust. The horsemen were headed directly toward the caravan.

"Robbers," said Toctamish briefly; "there will be a fight."

"A poor one, it seems," growled Khlit. "The Kurds are leaving us as fast as their horses can take them and your countrymen like the looks of things little—they have not drawn sword or bow."

In truth, the Tatars who were acting as guard, sat their horses stolidly, while the dismayed traders added to the confusion by rushing about frantically, trying to assemble their goods. Khlit turned his attention, in disgust to the oncoming horsemen, and counted a bare two score. In numbers, the caravan was three times as strong; yet no attempt at defense was made.

Instead the traders were anxiously spreading out their bales of goods, so that all were displayed. Camels and donkeys were stripped and their burden placed on the ground. In the meantime the horsemen who had come up were trampling recklessly through the confusion.

A fat Greek merchant held out an armful of rugs to one of the riders who stared at it insolently and pointed to the heavy packs behind the merchant. Other riders jerked out the contents of these packs, and ranged them in nine piles.

Khlit, watching them, saw that they were men of varied race. He guessed at Persian, Kurd, Circassian, Turk and others with whom he was not familiar—dark-skinned, and heavily-cloaked who sat their horses as a swallow rides the wind. Also, the Khirghiz men of the caravan had joined the newcomers.

The first rider flung some words at the Greek who was cowering on the ground and Khlit thought he caught the phrase "Alamut." Then the horsemen picked up three of the nine piles of goods, and flung them over pack-horses. Other riders who had been similarly occupied joined them. All the while the Tatar guardians of the caravan watched without interest, as men who had seen the like before.

It was not until the horsemen were well away over the salt plain that Khlit recovered from his astonishment at the sight of few robbing many.

"Better the mountain-folk than these," he growled, spitting in the direction of the merchants who were putting their goods away amid lamentations.

So it came to pass that a Cossack rode into the foothills of Rudbar where, in the words of the historian Abulghazi, none set foot who held Allah or Christ for their true God, and with him rode a Tatar who, under other circumstances would gladly have slain him.

They rode in silence, as rapidly as the pack animal could move, and by nightfall had gained the edge of the salt deposits that made that part of Persia like a frozen lake.

Each made camp after his fashion. And two fires were lighted instead of one. Khlit produced some barley cakes and wine and made a good meal. Toctamish took some raw meat from under his saddle where he had placed it for seasoning and washed it down with his favorite *arak*. Both kindled pipes and sat in silence in the darkness.

Toctamish's pipe went out first, and Khlit knew that the Tatar had swallowed the smoke until with the burning *arak* he had lost consciousness. The Cossack was soon asleep.

His sleep was unbroken, except that, near dawn, he thought he heard the trampling of many horses' feet, which sounded until the rays of the sun, slipping into his eyes, awoke him. He made out at some distance the track of a cavalcade in the dust, and considered that it might have been a caravan. Yet it was out of the path of caravans. Moreover, he was reasonably sure the track had not been there the night before. Toctamish, when wakened, yawned in bad spirits and told Khlit he was an old woman, of great fear and unmentionable descent.

When they resumed their path, it led upward through the foothills of Rudbar. A few date trees and some thorn bushes lined the way, but for the most part there was little foliage and many rocks. The grass, however, was good, and this was, perhaps, the reason why groups of horses were met with under the care of single, mounted horsemen who watched Khlit and his companion with curiosity.

They rode apart and silently, as before. Khlit's thoughts dwelt on Berca's last words. The girl had spoken as one having authority. She was no ordinary sheik's daughter, living out of sight of men, he thought. She was daring, and he wondered if she came from one of the hill-tribes where the women ride with men.

Berca had told him they were in the land of Halen ibn Shaddah, in the territory of the Refik folk, yet Khlit saw no signs of a town or city. He did see the tracks of multitudes of horses in the mountains where caravans were unknown. And the horses themselves puzzled him. For he could see nothing of their riders.

Toctamish, apparently, wasted no thought on his surroundings. He rode warily, but kept his thoughts to himself and pressed onward rapidly. Thus it was that the two came to a wide, shallow river, and followed the bank along a valley that seemed to sink further into the hills as they advanced.

Until sunset they rode, making detours to avoid waterfalls and fording the river where it curved—for it was very shallow—and then Khlit who was in the lead came to a halt as they rounded a bend.

"By the bones of Satan," he swore, "here is the place Berca told us of. Devil take me, if it does not look like a dog with his front paws in the river."

Like an arched bow the river curved, with the two riders standing at the end of the bow looking inward. Across from them rose a high point of rock, serried and overgrown with bushes, several hundred feet. No trees were on the summit of the rock. Instead, Khlit could make out masses of stones tumbling together and overgrown. A few pillars stood up through the debris.

Around the summit ran the semblance of a wall. So great was the waste of stone that it was hard to see any semblance of order in it, but Khlit judged that a citadel as big as a good sized town had once crowned the dog-promontory. The rock jutted out to make the massive head of the beast, and ridges suggested paws.

"Here is no Alamut, Toctamish," growled Khlit in disgust. "Truly, we are fools— the little sparrow, Berca, has made game of us."

"Wait, *caphar*," retorted Toctamish, dismounting. "She said we would find the dog sitting in the river, thus, and we have found it. We will wait here and see what happens."

"Well, we will wait," laughed Khlit, "and see if the dog will give birth to a tribe."

VI

Little Khlit suspected how true his chance word was to be. The sun had dropped behind the furthest mountain summit, and the night cold of the high elevation had wrapped around the two watchers when they saw a sight that made their blood stir.

The Cossack had stretched on the ground a little distance from Toctamish, who had subsided into snores. He watched the last light melt from the ruins on the summit of the cliff, and as he watched he thought he heard echoes from across the river, as from far off. Straining his ears, he could catch bursts of music and shouting. Remembering his experience with the horses the previous night, he wondered if the mountains were playing tricks with his ears.

The sounds would come in bursts as though a gate had been opened to let them out, followed by silence. Khlit was not at home in the hills, and he did not recognize the peculiar resonance of echoes. What he thought he heard were songs and shouts repeated from mouth to mouth, as by giants, in the heart of the rock opposite him.

Lighting his pipe and cursing himself for a dreaming fool, Khlit sat up and scanned the darkness over the river. As if to mock him, the burst of shouting became clearer. And then the skin moved along Khlit's back of its own accord and his jaw dropped. He shook his head angrily, to make sure he was still awake.

Out of the rock across the river a multitude of lights were flickering. The lights came toward him rapidly, and the shouting grew. There were torches, moving out on the river, and by their glare he could see a mass of moving men armed with spears and bows. Splashing through the water, they were fording the shallow river.

Khlit could see that they were men of varied race, turbaned and cloaked, armed for the most part with bow and arrows, much like those who had robbed the caravan. As the throng came nearer, he shook Toctamish and stood up.

"Loosen your sword, Father of Swine," he grunted, "here are men who are not triflers."

Several of the leaders, who had caught sight of the two, closed around them. The torchlight was thrown in their faces, and for a moment the shouting of the band was silenced as they surveyed Khlit and his companion. One, very lean and dark of face, dressed in a white coat bossed with gold, and wearing a tufted turban of the same colors, spoke in a tongue Khlit did not understand.

"Hey, brothers," swore Khlit genially, laughing, for the presence of danger pleased him, "have you any who speak like Christians? Khlit, called the Wolf, would speak with you."

After some delay, a dirty tribesman was thrust beside the man of white and gold.

"Wherefore are you here?" the tribesman, who seemed to be a Kurd, asked in broken Russian, "and what is your purpose? Be brief, for the *Dais* are impatient to march. Are you a Christian, Cossack?"

"Say that you are not," whispered Toctamish, who had caught what was said, "for none with a god can go into the mountain."

"A dog will give up his faith," snarled Khlit, "but a Cossack does not deny God and the Orthodox Church. Aye," he responded to the Kurd, "I am a Christian. I have come to Rudbar, or to Alamut, whatever you call the place, to seek him who is called the Old Man of the Mountain. What is your name and faith?"

A peculiar look of fear crossed the face of the Kurd.

"Seek you the Master of the Mountain, Sheik Halen ibn Shaddah, Cossack? My name is Iba Kabash, and I was once a Christian. What is your mission with the Lord of Alamut?"

"Tell the unbeliever we have come to join the Refik, where there is no law——" began Toctamish, but Khlit motioned him to silence.

"Take us to Sheik Halen ibn Shaddah, and we will tell him our mission, Iba Kabash," he retorted. "We are not men to parley with slaves."

The man of white and gold had grown impatient, and spoke a few angry words to Iba Kabash, who cringed. Several of the bowmen ranged themselves beside them, and the throng pushed past, leaving a single torch with the Kurd, who motioned to Khlit to follow him. Leaving their horses with an attendant, Khlit and Toctamish made their way after Iba Kabash to the river. The current was not overswift, and the water came barely to their knees.

"It is the wish of the *Dai*, Cossack, that you shall enter Alamut. What is your mission? Tell me and I shall be a true friend. I swear it. Surely you have a strong reason for your coming," the Kurd's greasy head was thrust close to the Cossack's. "Let me hear but a word."

"If the *Dai* named you guide, Iba Kabash, of the mangy beard, lead us, and talk not."

In his heart Khlit distrusted the offered friendship of the Kurd. And he watched closely where they went, across the Shahrud, into the shadows of the further bank. And he saw how it was the *Dai*'s followers had come from the mountain.

Concealed by the shadows, were grottoes, where the water had eaten into the rock, grottoes which ran deep into the mountain. The torch reflected from the dark surface of the water, as they splashed forward, with the river becoming shallower. Presently they stood on dry rock. Here they were in a cave, of which Khlit could not see the top.

Iba Kabash pulled impatiently at his arm and they went forward, and up. Khlit saw that now they were on rock which was the handiwork of man. They were ascending broad steps, each one a pace in width, and so broad that the torch barely showed rows of stone pillars on either side.

Khlit had counted fifty steps when Iba Kabash came to a halt, grinning. Lifting the torch overhead, he pointed to a square stone, set in the rocky roof of the stairs. On this rock were lines of writing strange to Khlit, and blackened with age and the dampness of the place.

"The gateway of Alamut, oh, Cossack," laughed the Kurd. "And the writing of one who was as great as Mohammed, prophet of Allah. And the message:

> "With the help of God
> The ruler of the world
> Loosened the bands of the law,
> Blessed be his name."

Khlit was silent. He had not expected to find himself in a cave in the heart of a mountain. The darkness and damp, rising from the river, chilled him. Glancing ahead, he saw a rocky passage, wide and lofty. The passage had been made by the river, perhaps in a former age, when it had risen to that level. But the hands of men had widened it and smoothed the walls. Toctamish, he saw, was scrutinizing his surroundings, his slant eyes staring from a lined, yellow face.

"Come," said Iba Kabash, who seemed to enjoy the silence of his visitors, "this was not the gateway of Alamut always, in the days of the first Master of the Mountain. And Alamut has changed. It has sunk into the mountain. Men say the old Alamut was destroyed."

"Aye," said Toctamish suddenly, "by Hulagu Khan."

The Kurd stared at him curiously.

"Come," he muttered, and led the way up the winding rock passage.

Khlit followed closely. Other passages joined the one they were in. At times, sounds came down these passages—distant rumblings, and strains of music. Occasionally a figure armed with a spear stepped from them and scanned the group. Always a wind whipped around them, cold, in spite of the heat of the air outside.

After a time, Khlit saw that they were no longer in the passage. The torch did not reveal walls, and the footing was regular, of stone slabs. They had entered a chamber of some kind. Other torches made their appearance suddenly. The sound of voices came to them clearly.

They approached a fire around which lay several armed men. Khlit guessed from their dress that they were Khirghiz men; furthermore, that they appeared drunk.

Only one or two looked up, without interest. Iba Kabash led them past many fires and men until they came to narrow stone stairs which led away from the rock chambers. Here, a giant Turk spoke with Iba Kabash before letting them pass.

"We will speak with Rashideddin," whispered the Kurd, "the astrologer of Halen ibn Shaddah. Tell me now your mission? I can help you."

Toctamish would have spoken, fingering a money pouch at his belt on which the Kurd's gaze fastened greedily, but Khlit shook his head. With a sneer, their guide stepped on the stairway. Khlit climbed after him, and noted that the stairs wound up still further. He guessed that they had ascended several hundred feet since leaving the bed of the river.

Then, leaving the stair, he found himself in a round chamber, hung with tapestries and rugs of great beauty. Several oil lamps, suspended from the ceiling lighted the place. A warm breath of air caused him to look up. A circular opening formed the center of the ceiling, and through this he could see the stars and the velvet vault of the sky.

Two of the dark-faced men, strange to Khlit, like the *Dai* of white and gold, stood by the wall, wearing mail and resting on spears. A small ebony table was loaded with parchments and instruments which the Cossack had never seen before. In the center of the floor was a chess-board, and sitting on either side of the chess-board were two men.

One, Khlit recognized by his tufted turban and brilliant white coat, to be of the kind Iba Kabash had called *Dai*. The other wore a close-fitting skullcap and a gray cloak without a sash. He looked at Khlit and the latter saw a lean face, gray, almost as the cloak, with close-set black eyes, and a loose-lipped mouth, very pale.

"Oh, Rashideddin," said Iba Kabash, "here are the two who have just come, of whom I have sent word. The Cossack is a Christian and insolent. The other is altogether a fool."

VII

Rashideddin is mentioned in the annals of Abulghazi as a savant of the *khali fate* of Bagdad and Damascus. He was a Persian, trained in the arts of astrology and divination, who could recite from memory the works of Jelaleddin Rumi. He was acquainted with many languages including Russian and Tatar. It is believed that he possessed all the works of the Alamut library which escaped the destructive hands of Hulagu Khan.

Inscrutable, and gifted, Rashideddin made a mockery of the Koran. He kept his truly great wisdom to himself, except for certain poems which he sent to princes of Persia and

Arabia, who gained no happiness thereby. So it was not strange that Rashideddin, the savant of dark knowledge came to a place of evil, of strange and very potent evil. So say the annals of Abulghazi.

Rashideddin did not look at his visitors. He lifted a piece with care and replaced it on the chessboard. The *Dai*, who Khlit observed, was drunk, as were the men around the fires, yet very pale, did likewise. Khlit, who had small liking for chess, watched the players rather than the board. Especially did he watch Rashideddin. The pale-lipped astrologer sat with half-closed eyes, intent and motionless. The gray cloak seemed not to move with his breathing. When he spoke, his deep and musical voice startled them.

"Have you a god, Cossack? Is your faith firm in the Christian cross you wear around your neck?"

Startled, Khlit moved his hand to his throat, where hung a small, gold cross. Iba Kabash was making hasty signs to him which he did not see.

"Aye, Rashideddin," said he gravely, "the *batko* has told me about the cross which I carry, and it is a talisman against evil. Hey, it has been good, that cross, because I have killed many and am still living."

"Evil?" said Rashideddin, and moved a jeweled chessman to another square. "The earth is evil. If a saint handles earth it becomes gold. Yet who has seen a saint? Do you seek to bring your cross into Alamut?"

"Not so, Rashideddin," vouchsafed Khlit, crossing his arms. "I bring a sword to Alamut, to Halen ibn Shaddah. The cross is my own. If you can see it through my *svitza* then you must have good eyes. I am outcast from my people of the Ukraine, and men told me there was work for swords with Halen ibn Shaddah."

"And you call yourself Khlit, the Wolf?" queried the astrologer. "How did you find the gate of Alamut?"

Khlit was bewildered at the astrologer's knowledge of his name until he remembered that he had told it to Iba Kabash.

"Aye. There was a caravan by the Sea of Khozar that a band from Alamut robbed. We," Khlit bethought him swiftly, "followed the riders to the mountains and waited by the gate."

Rashideddin considered the chessboard silently.

"You came over the Sea of Khozar," he murmured, "from Astrakan? That must have been the way. There is another way around by land that the caravans take. They are our prey. What the Kallmark Tatars leave the merchants, we share. Did you see a Syrian armorer in Astrakan?"

"Aye, a bearded fellow. We stayed at his house. He told us we might find use for our swords with Halen ibn Shaddah."

With a delicate movement, Rashideddin lifted one of his opponent's pieces from the board.

"And your companion?" he said.

"A Tatar horseman who has quarreled with his kin," spoke up Toctamish bluntly. "I'm tired of laws, noble sir, and I—"

"Laws are too complex, Tatar. If a man has an enemy, slay him. If a man desires a certain thing, take it. Are not these the only laws? In Alamut you are free from all laws except those of the *Refik*. You have an image of Natagai in your girdle, Tatar." Rashideddin had not looked at Toctamish since the first moment. "Take it and throw it on the floor."

Toctamish hesitated. He glanced irresolutely at Khlit; then drew out a small cloth figure, painted like a doll and tossed it on the stones. The Cossack saw that it was ragged and worn by much use. He had not suspected that his companion cherished any holy image.

"Spit on it," directed Rashideddin softly.

With a muttered curse Toctamish did so. His lined face was damp with perspiration, and Khlit saw that his hands were trembling. The shifting eyes of Iba Kabash gleamed mockingly.

"The armorer at Astrakan must have told you that Alamut is no place for one who has a god," went on Rashideddin. "There is one here who is greater than Mohammed. We are his servants. Yet our *akd* says that none go forth who are not of us. Think, Khlit, and decide. Meanwhile—"

The astrologer spoke to Iba Kabash in another tongue and the Kurd went to a corner of the room where a pile of rugs and cloths lay. Selecting a long, white cloth, he laid it in front of Khlit. This done, he stepped back, licking his thick lips softly.

"Tell the Cossack what you have done, Iba Kabash," said Rashideddin.

"This cloth," whispered the Kurd, "is a shroud, Khlit. The astrologer may call his men and lay you in it dead, unless you say you have no god. Do as your friend— remember I have given you good advice. You are in a place where your life is worth no more than a dagger-thrust. Your sword will be useless."

With a beating heart, Khlit glanced around the chamber. The two mailed Tatars were watching him silently. He thought he could see the dim forms of other men in recesses in the wall. And for all Rashideddin's unconcern, he felt that the astrologer was alive to every move he made. He felt as he had once when the Krim Tatars had bound his limbs, leaving him powerless.

"Aye," he said.

Without looking at Rashideddin, he moved to the pile of cloths and selected another shroud. This he brought back and placed beside the other. Iba Kabash watched him with staring eyes. The *Dai* frowned and fingered a dagger at his girdle. Khlit drew his curved sword and stood over the white cloths.

"Tell Rashideddin, Iba Kabash," he said, "what this other shroud is for."

"What—how do you mean?" muttered the Kurd.

"It is for the man who first tries to kill me, dog," snarled Khlit.

The astrologer bent over the chessboard impassively. Apparently he was blind to what passed in the room and to the words of Iba Kabash. The others watched him, and there was silence. Until Rashideddin raised his head suddenly and compressed his pale lips.

"You fool," he smiled, "blunderer of the steppes! This is not Russia. Here there is one law, and punishment; murder! See!"

He pointed a white hand at one of the mailed Tatars. The man started forward, and drew back shivering.

"Kill thyself, fellow," said Rashideddin quietly.

The Tatar stared at him and cast a helpless glance around the room. Khlit saw his right hand go to his girdle and tremble convulsively.

"*Fedavie!*" the astrologer's voice was gentle, "show the Russian our law. By the oath of the *Refik*, kill thyself!"

With a grunt of sheer terror the man dropped his spear. His right hand rose from the girdle, gripping a dagger curved like a flame. Rose, and sank into his throat. With the hilt of the dagger wedged under his chin, the Tatar sagged to the floor, quivered and was still. One bloodstained hand had fallen among the chessmen.

There was silence in the room for a moment, broken by Toctamish. The Tatar stepped to Khlit's side.

"You and I are brothers, Cossack," he growled, "and your danger is my danger."

Rashideddin, who had given a sigh of pleasure at the death of the attendant, studied the disordered chessmen impassively. The *Dai* sprang to his feet with an oath. For several heart-beats no one moved. Iba Kabash stared in fascination at a red pool which had formed under the dead Tatar's head.

VIII

The astrologer, apparently giving up as hopeless the attempt to replace the chessmen, stood up. And Khlit, who was watching, wondered at his figure. The man was bent so that his back was in the form of a bow. His head stuck forward, pale as a fish's belly, topped by the red skullcap. His gray cloak came to the ground. Yet when he moved, it was with a soft quickness.

"You see," he said, as if nothing had happened, "the oath of Alamut—obedience, and—"

He stirred the shroud contemptuously with his foot. Then, as if arriving at a decision, he turned to Iba Kabash.

"Take these clowns to the banquet-place, and give them food. See that they are not harmed."

With that he motioned to the *Dai* and retreated through one of the recesses. Toctamish wiped his brow on which the perspiration had gathered and touched the dead man with his foot.

"The good Rashideddin will not kill you," chanted the Kurd eagerly. "It must be a miracle, for you are both fools. You have me to thank for your safety. I have given good advice, have I not?"

Toctamish eyed him dubiously. He did not feel oversure of safety. Khlit, however, whispered to him. Rashideddin was not the man to play with them if he desired their death. It might be that the astrologer's words were in good faith—Khlit learned later that the latter never troubled to lie—and if so they would gain nothing and lose much by staying where they were.

So it happened that both warriors sheathed their swords with apparent good grace and followed Iba Kabash who led them through empty rooms until they came out on a balcony overlooking the banquetplace of Alamut. And Khlit was little prepared for what he saw now.

The warm wind touched their faces again. Iba Kabash pointed up. In the center of the lofty ceiling of the place a square opening let in the starlight. A crescent moon added to the light which threw a silver sheen over the great floor of the hall. Toctamish grunted in surprise.

At first it seemed as if they were looking on the camp of an army from a hillside. Dozens of fires smoldered on the floor below them, and a hundred oil lamps sprinkled the intervening space. About the lamps men were lying, around small tables on which fruit, wine and dishes massed. A buzz of voices echoed down the hall, and Khlit was reminded of bees stirring about the surface of a hive.

The sound of eating and drinking drowned the noise of voices. Along the stone balcony where they stood other tables were placed with lamps. Numerous dark figures carried food and drink to these and carried away the refuse left at other tables.

"Slaves," said the Kurd, "captives of the *Refik*. Let us find a table and eat. It is a lucky night that I met you, for I shall go into the paradise of Alamut."

Khlit paid little attention to the last phrase. Later, he was to remember it. Being very hungry he sat down with Toctamish at a convenient table and took some of the bread and roasted meat which he found there. Toctamish was less restrained, and gulped down everything with zest.

As he ate Khlit considered his companions, and the banquet-place. All of them, he noticed, seemed drowsy, as if drunk, or very gay. In the lamplight their faces showed white. They lay in heaps about the tables, sometimes one on the other.

To the Cossack drunkenness was no sin, yet there was something about the white faces and limp figures of the men that stirred his blood. And the smell of the place was unpleasant, a damp, musky odor seemed to rise from the hall under them, as of beasts. Piles of fruit lay rotting about the floor.

"It is time," chattered the Kurd, who was sipping at a goblet of wine, "Halen ibn Shaddah showed himself. He comes to the banquet-place every night, and we drink to him. Drink, Khlit—are not Cossacks born with a grape in their mouths? You are lucky to be alive, for Rashideddin is a viper without mercy."

"Who is this Rashideddin?" asked Khlit, setting down the wine, for it was not to his liking.

"Oh, he is the wise man of the archprophet—the master of Alamut. He knows more magic than all the Greeks and dervishes put together. He reads the stars, and tells our master when it is time to send out expeditions. They say he has servants in every city of the world. But I think he learns everything from the magic sands." Iba Kabash's tongue was outstripping his wit. "There is nothing that goes on in Persia and Tartary that he does not see. How did he know you wore a cross?"

"He saw the chain at my neck, fool," retorted Khlit.

He began to feel strangely elated. He had had only a little wine, but his head was whirling and he had a curious languor in his limbs. The trouble extended to his eyes, for as he looked at the banquet-place, it seemed to have grown wider and lighter. He could see that Toctamish was half-unconscious.

Thus it was that Khlit, the Wolf, in the banquet-place of Alamut came under the influence of the strange evil that gripped the place. And came to know of the great wickedness, which set Alamut apart from the world, as with a curse.

Khlit, turning the situation over in his mind, saw that it was best to play the part he had taken on himself. He doubted if it were possible to escape past the guards by the river stairway, even if he could free himself from the guardianship of Iba Kabash. Rashideddin, he felt, had not left his visitors unwatched. Also, he was curious to see further of the strange world of Alamut, which was a riddle of which he had not found the key. He had seen a Tatar kill himself at a word from the astrologer, and Iba Kabash who was a man without honor, speak with awe of the master of Alamut. Who was Halen ibn Shaddah? And what was his power over the men of Alamut?

As it happened, it was not long before Khlit saw the man he was seeking, and whom he was sworn to kill. There came a pause in the murmur of talk and Iba Kabash clutched his shoulder.

"Look!" he whispered. "Here is Sheik Halen ibn Shaddah, who will choose those to go into paradise tonight. You are newcomers in Alamut and he may choose you, whereon I shall follow behind without being seen. Pray that his eye may fall on us, for few go to paradise."

Across the banquet-place, on the stone balcony, Khlit saw a group of torches. The bearers were *Dais*. In the center of the torches stood a tall man, dressed as the *Dais* except that he wore no turban, a cloak covering his head, drawn down so that nothing could be seen of his face. The sheik's shoulders were very broad and the hands that rested on his girdle were heavy.

As Khlit watched, Halen ibn Shaddah moved along the balcony among the eaters. On the banquet floor a murmur grew into a shout—

"Blessed be he that has unmade all laws; who is master of the *akd*; chief of chief, prophet of prophets, sheik of sheiks; who holds the keys of the gate of paradise."

Iba Kabash shouted as if in ecstacy, rising on his knees and beating his palms together, as the group of the sheik came nearer them. Once or twice Khlit saw Halen ibn Shaddah beckon to a man who rose hastily and followed the *Dais*. Iba Kabash, he thought, was drunk, yet not in a fashion known to Cossacks. Khlit himself felt drowsy, although clear in mind. He saw that the noise had wakened Toctamish who was swaying on his haunches and muttering.

Halen ibn Shaddah stood over them, and Khlit thought that one of the *Dais* whispered to him. The Cossack had fastened his gaze greedily on the cloaked face, for he wished to see the face of the master of Alamut. He could make out only a round, dark countenance, and eyes that showed much white. Vaguely he remembered that he had seen others who had faces like that, but he could not think who they were. The sight of Halen ibn Shaddah affected him like the foul smell of the banquet-place and the rat-eyes of Iba Kabash. Halen ibn Shaddah beckoned to him and Toctamish.

Khlit supported his companion to his feet, but found that the wine had taken away all his own strength. Hands, belonging, he suspected to slaves, helped him after the white figures of the *Dais*. They passed from the banquet-place through passages that he could see only dimly. The torchlight vanished, and there came a silence, which was broken by music, very sweet. Khlit's head was swimming strangely, and he felt himself moving forward through darkness. Darkness in which the music echoed, being repeated softly as he had heard the voices repeated when they first came into the passages of Alamut.

IX

If it was a dream, Khlit asked himself, why should he be able to taste the red wine that trinkled down his throat? Yet if it were not a dream, why should a torrent of the red wine issue from a rock? And sunlight burn on the red current, when Khlit was in the passages of Alamut, under the ground?

Truly, it must be a dream, he thought. It seemed that he was lying on his side near the flowing wine, with the sun warm on his face. Whenever he wanted to drink, he did not need to sit up, for he raised his hand and a girl with flowers around her head and breast came, and filled some vessel which she held out to him. Khlit was very thirsty and the wine was good.

The girl, he felt, sat by him, and her finger-nails and the soles of her bare feet were red. He had never seen such a maiden, for her hair also was red, and the sun glinted through it as she drew it across his face. Her hair must be perfumed, he thought, like the harlots of Samarkand, for it smelled very good.

The music came to his ears from time to time, and he snorted, for Khlit was no lover of soft sounds. Neither did he fully relish the wine, which was oversweet. He was well content to be in the sun, and too drowsy to wonder how it happened.

The dream, if it was that, changed, and Khlit was in a boat lying on some rugs. The boat was drifting along a canal. From time to time it would pass under a porcelain *kiosk*, tasselled and inlaid with ivory. From these *kiosks* girls laughed down at him and threw flowers. One of the tinted faces was like Berca's, and Khlit thought then it was surely a dream.

One other thing he remembered. It was in a grove of date trees where young boys ran, shouting, and pelted each other with fruit. In spite of the warmth and pleasantness, Khlit felt very tired. He was in the shade of one of the date trees with his sword across his knees. The music was very faint here, for which he was glad. He seemed very wakeful. The air was clear, and looking up he could see the sky, between jagged walls of stone. He had seen other walls of stone like these. That was when he and Toctamish had stood at the Shahrud looking up at the dog rock that was Alamut.

Even in the dream, Khlit felt ill. He saw the damsel of the red hair and flowers and beckoned to her, for he was thirsty. She ran away, probably at the sight of his sword. Khlit felt angry, for she had given him drink for what seemed many years.

Then he saw the gray-cloaked figure of Rashideddin, the astrologer of Alamut, beside him, and the white face stared at him until Khlit fidgeted. He heard Rashideddin speak, very faintly.

"Where art thou?"

Khlit was too tired to answer at first.

"I know not," he said finally.

"Thou art in paradise, and by favor of Halen ibn Shaddah. Do not forget."

Truly, Khlit had not forgotten. There were other things he remembered. Vistas of blue pools where dark-skinned men bathed, and date groves where bright-colored birds walked, dragging their tails on the ground. He saw girls pass, hand in hand, singing. And the music did not cease.

If it had been a dream, Khlit said to himself, how could the taste of the strange wine stick to his palate? Or the warmth of the sun be still burning on his skin? Nay, surely it must have been a dream. And the waking was disagreeable.

The place where he found himself on waking was dark, wet and smelled strongly of wine dregs. Khlit rose to his knees cautiously and felt about him with his hand. He could feel the outline of something round and moist on all sides except overhead. Also he came upon the body of a man lying by him, which he identified by its fur tunic and peaked helmet as Toctamish. The Tatar was snoring heavily.

"Wake, Flat-Face and son of an unclean animal," he growled, shaking him. "We are no longer in paradise. Devil take me, if it ain't a wine cask."

Toctamish roused at length and sat up reluctantly.

"Is it you, *caphar*?" he asked, stretching himself. "Many times have I been drunk as an ox, but never such as this. May the devil bite me, if there was ever such wine! Let us find some more."

"Then you have been dreaming, also," meditated Khlit. "Did you imagine that you saw Berca?"

"Berca? Nay, but she said that she would visit us here. That was no dream, *caphar*, for there was sunlight, and much feasting. Did Rashideddin tell you it was paradise? I met other Tatars there. They told me what it was."

"Were they also men who dishonored their god at Rashideddin's bidding? What said they concerning this paradise of yours?"

Toctamish snarled in anger, at the memory of the scene by the chessboard.

"You are one without brains, Cossack, and it is well that we are here alive. My companions said this: that all who came to Alamut were admitted to the paradise by Halen ibn Shaddah, if they were worthy. Then, if they were killed in the ranks of the *Refik* their souls returned to the paradise. That was a lie, for how can there be a soul in a man?"

Khlit said nothing. But he thought that he had found the key to the riddle. Halen ibn Shaddah's power lay in the lusts of his men. They looked on him, even so shrewd a man as Iba Kabash, as one who held the secret of paradise. And, although he did not know it, Khlit's thought had come near to the evil of Alamut, which was a plague spot on the face of the world.

X

In the next few days the two warriors, bound together by mutual interest, although cordially hating each other, made frequent explorations of the chambers of Alamut. In the daytime sunlight filtered in at the banquet-place, the round chamber of Rashideddin and other places, but at night the only light was from lamps or torches. The chambers were large enough to hold a hundred men in each and there were many. Khlit, who had keen eyes, learned several things, including the place of the *Refik* treasure.

First, a certain area was guarded against intrusion by picked Tatars and Arabs. Into the guarded chambers he had seen *Dais* and other higher dignitaries called *Dailkebirs* go, and he guessed they were occupied by Halen ibn Shaddah and his court, where was kept the gold that flowed into Alamut as tribute money.

Also, there was no exit from the chambers of Alamut save by way of the stairway and the river, which was guarded. Frequently armed bands went in and out, also messengers of many races, but all were closely watched. Moreover, few except old residents of the place, like Iba Kabash, the Kurd, knew the way to the river stairway.

The slaves, he learned, brought food not from the river stairway, but another source. Also wood for the fires. The warriors of Alamut, *fedavie*, as they were called, lived as they chose, under the eyes of the *Dais*, ornamenting their quarters with spoil taken in raids or from caravans. Each man was richly decked in whatever suited his fancy, of silks or jewels. The *Dais* who commanded them took interest in them only when it was time to take an expedition out of Alamut.

So much Khlit saw, and more he learned from the talkative Iba Kabash, who had won some gold at dice from Toctamish, and was inclined to be friendly. The slaves, he said, brought the food from the side of Alamut away from the river, where they drew it up in baskets to the summit of a wall that barred all egress from the citadel.

Iba Kabash had not been beyond the walls of Alamut since his entry. Yet he had heard much of the empire of the *Refik* that stretched its power from Semarkand to Aleppo and from Astrakan to Basra. The murderers of the *Refik* were feared so greatly, he explained, that tribute was paid by the cities to Alamut. Questioned by Khlit, he admitted that in numbers any of the califates were superior to Alamut. The power of Halen ibn Shaddah lay in the daggers of his men. No enemy escaped assassination once he was marked. And many were marked.

"Then there is no way to leave save by the river stair?" asked Khlit, who had listened attentively.

Iba Kabash stared and shook his head.

"Where is the fool who would escape, Khlit?" he responded. "Thrice lucky are we who are here. There was a calif who marched against us with horsemen from Irak. We rained down stones and baked clay on his men; then sallied forth, and the Shadrud was red with blood."

"Aye," said Toctamish sullenly. "There are no better fighters than those of Irak. Remember Hulaga Khan and his horsemen."

"Nay, I knew them not."

Iba Kabash glanced at the Tatar curiously, and Khlit laughed to distract his mind, for he did not trust the Kurd.

"There was another who opposed us," continued Iba Kabash. "That was a sheik of the hillmen in the mountains around Alamut. Him we killed by tearing out his belly and bowels. He had a daughter, who was a spit-fire. Rashideddin dealt with her."

"How?" asked Khlit carelessly, recognizing the description as Berca.

"Cleverly, very cleverly," chuckled the Kurd, rubbing his hands together. "He had Halen ibn Shaddah order her off to marry some Tatar chief who knew her not. It was when she had gone that we slew the old chief slowly, and scattered his tribe."

"Truly a shrewd trick." Khlit gave Toctamish a warning blow in the ribs that made the stocky warrior grunt. "How fared the chief's daughter at the hands of the Tatar? Your knowledge is greater than that of others, Iba Kabash. Can you tell me that?"

"Nay, that is a hard one," laughed the Kurd. "I have heard, from a slave that the chief's daughter, Berca, was seen in Astrakan. Also that she was taken as a slave by some caravan not far from here. I know not."

"Was the one who told you a slave in Alamut?" demanded Toctamish, who was becoming restive.

"Where else, offspring of a donkey?" muttered Iba Kabash. "I suppose you will also ask how he came to hear of the girl."

"Nay," interrupted Khlit. "Toctamish wondered at the power of Alamut. He is a clown. You and I, Iba Kabash, are men of wisdom."

So it happened that Khlit was not astonished when, as he came from the floor of the banquet-place, one night, his head hazy with the fumes of the strange wine, a girl slave leaned close to him and whispered briefly.

"By the far corner of the balcony," she repeated, "in an hour."

He looked thoughtfully at an object the slave had thrust into his hand. It was the sapphire which Berca had once offered him.

He did not tell Toctamish of the message. And he was at some pains to get rid of Iba Kabash before the time appointed in the message. So he was alone when he went slowly along the stone balcony to a dark corner. The slaves had retired from the banquet-place and the *fedavie* were watching for Halen ibn Shaddah to come from his quarters. Standing so that he could not be seen by those below, Khlit waited. Waited until the torches came, with the *Dais* and the huge figure of Halen ibn Shaddah. He felt a touch on his coat, and turned.

"Follow," whispered the soft voice of the Persian, "and do not tread clumsily."

Khlit found that this was not so easy. Berca carried no light. He could barely see her cloaked form by the reflection of an occasional candle as she passed swiftly through chambers and rock passages. His head was light from the wine, although his mind was clear.

Berca kept to passages where there were few persons, and these Khlit saw to be slaves. She was taking him through the slave quarters where he had not been before. Through corridors that narrowed until he had to turn sideways to pass; by sunken walls which smelled evilly. Through a corridor that led out of the chambers of Alamut into the paradise of Halen ibn Shaddah.

Khlit paused in amazement and felt of his head which was throbbing. A half-moon glimmered down at him, and a cool night wind played in his hair. The branches of date trees stirred lazily. Under his feet he could feel grass, and he saw one of the strange birds that dragged its tail come from the shadow of the date trees.

Berca shook him angrily by the arm.

"One without sense, eater of swine flesh!" she hissed. "Are you a clown to gape at strange things?"

A fountain threw its spray on the wind into Khlit's face, with a scent like the roses of Ispahan. Below the fountain was a canal, which Khlit remembered vaguely, with a boat attached to the shore. In the water he could see the reflection of the moon gleaming at him. And he was dizzy.

"This is the paradise of Halen ibn Shaddah," he muttered unsteadily, "where I came by his favor. So Rashideddin told me."

Berca peered up at him silently. Her cloak fell back and Khlit saw the dark masses of hair which fell on either shoulder, and the white throat under the curved dark mouth that was twisted in scorn.

"A weak fool," she stormed, shaking him. "Toctamish is a better man than you."

"Toctamish is drunk. Nay, little Sparrow, it is my head. It will be better presently. This is no dream. How did you come to Alamut, little Berca?"

For answer the girl drew Khlit, who was fighting the dizziness in his head, to the canal, and into the boat. Pushing it from the shore, she paddled in the water until it floated into the shadows. Not content with this Berca urged the craft along the bank quietly, and Khlit who was flat on his back saw the shadow of a bridge fall over them.

"Nay," he said drowsily, "the stars are good. It is good to see them again. Where are we now? How did you bring me here?"

Berca came and sat by Khlit's head, feeling his hot forehead with a small hand. She wrapped her thin cloak tightly about her and rested her chin on her two hands, gazing at the round moon in the water.

"A man must be crafty and wise," she repeated softly, "yet, lo, it is a weak girl, a creature of the false prophet's paradise, who leads him. They told me you were very shrewd, oh, my Abulfetlah Harb Issa, gray Father of Battles. Soon there will be a great battle and the waters of Shahrud will be red again. Have you ever seen wolves of the steppe tear jackals of the mountains into bits, foam-flecked? Have you ever run with the pack of wolves, oh, one called the Wolf? Nay, they have clipped your fangs."

"That is a lie, Sparrow," growled Khlit surlily, "give me a horse and freedom to swing a sword, and I shall trounce some of these evil *fedavies* for you. Bah, it is a hotbed of sin, a reeking plague-house. Show me the way out of Alamut."

"And your promise," queried Berca, "to cut off the head of Halen ibn Shaddah?"

Khlit was silent. True, he had promised, and was in honor bound to Berca.

"Likewise, Berca," he said moodily, "you said that there was a plan. Why do you keep the plan hidden in your mind, if there is one? Better be in good faith with me. Say how Halen ibn Shaddah can be killed."

"How should I kill so strong a man?" she laughed softly. "The Koran reads that Allah weakens the stratagems of misbelievers. Also that they "who store up evil shall taste what they store up. Such are the words of wisdom, despised by Rashideddin. Nay, destruction shall come upon Alamut like the storm from a cloud, quick as poison from a serpent's fang, and Halen ibn Shaddah—"

"Halen ibn Shaddah," chuckled Khlit, "is not easily to be found."

Abruptly, he gripped the girl's wrist. Beside the round orb of the moon in the water he saw the reflection of a turbaned man. It was a stout man, carrying a sword as broad as a horse's neck, or the reflection lied. Khlit rose on one elbow fingering his saber. At the same time the boat moved backward silently under impulse of the girl's paddling and passed from the bridge along the canal under date trees.

"A *eunuch*, one of the tribe who guard the creatures of the paradise," Berca whispered. "I have seen them often, because I am, also, a celestial houri—while it pleases me. I saw you when you came here a few days ago. Listen—" her voice changed—"for you must serve me, and the time is near."

Khlit nodded. The fresh night air had cleared some of the poison from his brain.

"I shall take you back to the chambers of Alamut, Khlit, by way of the slaves' quarters. We are on the top of Alamut, now, where Halen ibn Shaddah, whom may Allah lay in the dust, has built an evil paradise on the ruins of the old citadel to beguile his men. Verily what they have made—he and Rashideddin—is a magician's trick. The men who come here are drugged with a strange poison that I know not. I have tasted it in the wine—may Allah grant me mercy—and it is evil."

Khlit grunted in assent.

"It is some secret of Rashideddin's," she resumed. "The *fedavie* are foul with it, until they lose fear of death. This drug chains them to Halen ibn Shaddah. That and their lusts. And they have chained others by fear of the *Refik*. Yet their doom is near. It is coming from there—" pointing in the direction which Khlit thought to be north—"and it is swift as the hunting falcon on the wing."

"Another riddle, Berca," muttered Khlit. "Where have you seen a falcon?"

"Where you have seen them, Cossack," she laughed, "and Toctamish has hunted with them. Where swords are sharpened for the cutting down of the *fedavie*. In the land of the Kallmark Tatars, north of the Salt Sea. Oh, the doom of Alamut will be very great, and Munkir and Nakir, the dark angels that flay dead men in their graves will grow big with power."

"Another riddle, little Berca. It is many generations since Tatar horsemen rode into Persia for conquest."

"The answer is under your blind eyes, Father of Battles. Am I not beautiful as the rose garden of Tiflis in Spring? Is not my hair dark as the mantle of Melik, and my skin white as aloes under the dew?" Berca moved her perfumed head close to Khlit, and the Cossack drew away. "Nay, others have eyes; so, Allah has willed that my honor shall be cleared and the doom of Alamut shall come."

"The Tatars are marching on Alamut?" Khlit bit his mustache in glee. "Devil take me, that is good news—"

"Hush, fool." Berca drew in her breath eagerly. "Twenty thousand horsemen are riding along the Salt Sea toward Alamut. They will not stop to plunder or gather spoil. Oh, it will be a good battle. My father shall see it from the footstool of Mohammed. Aye, it will gladden his eyes. I shall open the gate of Alamut to twenty thousand Kallmark horsemen. The gate that leads to the banquet-place, where I bring food every night with the slaves. Here is what you must do, Father of Battles—"

She listened intently for a moment. The paradise of Halen ibn Shaddah was still, and only the birds with long tails moved.

"On the third night, Father of Battles," she whispered, "the *Dai* who is in command at the river stair, will change his sentries at the second watch. Do you and Toctamish get among the sentries of the river gate. I have seen you with Iba Kabash who is one without honor. Pay him and it may be done. Two sentries are as is the custom, in the river, outside the gate. On the third night, those two must be you and Toctamish, none other. That is your task. Then will you have a horse to ride, you and Toctamish. Meanwhile, keep out of sight of Rashideddin—"

"Aye," said Khlit, pondering, "Rashideddin."

XI

It is written in the annals of Abulghazi that as the year of the lion drew to its close, very great riches came to the treasury of Halen ibn Shaddah from the cities which lived in the shadow of fear. Save from the north, by the Salt Sea, where the tithes came not. Nor any riders. And in the north, said Abulghazi, a storm was gathering, swift as wind, rolling up all in its path. Yet no murmur of the storm came to Alamut, to the man who named himself prophet of God, to the banquet-place of the *fedavie*, to the man of wisdom, Rashideddin.

It was the second day after the visit of Berca that Khlit, who had been thinking deeply, sought out Iba Kabash where the Kurd lay sleeping on the floor of the banquet-place and roused him from his stupor.

"I have news for the ear of Halen ibn Shaddah himself," he said, squatting and lighting his pipe, "none other. He will surely reward me."

Iba Kabash ceased yawning and into his lined face came the look of a crafty fox.

"Halen ibn Shaddah will not see you, Khlit. He will see nobody except a few, old fellows of Alamut, of whom I am one. Verily, I have the ear of the master of Alamut. Tell me your message and I will give it, for you are a man of brains. You, Khlit are of the chosen. The others are ones without understanding."

Khlit knew that Iba Kabash lied, for the most part. He considered his pipe gravely and shook his head.

"My news is not to be repeated. Halen ibn Shaddah would pay a good price. How can you get such a good price for it as I?"

"Nay," remonstrated the Kurd, "I shall get a better price. For I know well the value of news. Tell me and we shall both profit, you and I."

Khlit grinned under his mustache. For a while he played, with the skill of one who understood the game well, with the growing inquisitiveness of his companion. Iba Kabash steadily raised the reward he assured Khlit, as he sensed the interest of the Cossack.

"Then," stated Khlit slowly, "you will do this. You will go direct to the master of Alamut and tell him my news. To no other. For here, a man takes what credit he can. And as the price of the good you will get for the telling, you will aid me in the plan I have. The plan concerns a girl that Halen ibn Shaddah would give a finger of his left hand to see brought before him."

"I swear it," said the Kurd readily, "on my *akd*, the oath of a *fedavie*. Now tell me the news, and it shall go to Halen ibn Shaddah as you have said."

Khlit nodded. That much the Kurd would do, he was sure. Whether Iba Kabash would tell the source of his message was dubious. Khlit felt in his heart that if the news was important Iba Kabash would keep the credit for himself. Which was what Khlit wanted.

"Tell Halen ibn Shaddah this," he said slowly, "that Khlit, the Cossack, called the Wolf, has learned that Berca, the Persian girl who was sent from Rudbar by Rashideddin has returned, and is in Alamut. He will be very curious. Say no more, for you and I, Iba Kabash, can find the girl and take her to him. If you help me, it can be managed. That is my message."

Khlit watched the Kurd depart nimbly. Iba Kabash had sensed the importance of the Cossack's words. It would be a rare tale to pour into the ears of the master of Alamut. And, nimbly as the Kurd took his way from the banquet-place, Khlit was as quick to follow, keeping in the shadows of the passages, but well within sight of the other.

So it happened that Iba Kabash did not see Khlit when he turned into the winding stair that led to the room of Rashideddin, but the Cossack saw him and waited by the outer chamber. If Iba Kabash had looked behind, he might not have gone where he did. Yet he did not look behind, and Khlit waited patiently.

Presently one of the Khirghiz men came from the winding stair, walking idly, and Khlit halted him, asking if the Khirghiz had seen aught of a certain Kurd called Iba Kabash.

The man had seen him. Iba Kabash had come to the astrologer's chamber. Of a certainty, he had spoken to Rashideddin. Why else had he come? Was the astrologer one to stare at? They had talked together, and he had not heard what was said, although he listened carefully, for it was in another tongue.

Rashideddin, swore Khlit, was a man to be feared. Doubtless he was the one that spoke most often to Halen ibn Shaddah, the holy prophet. Nay, he surely had the ear of Halen ibn Shaddah, who held the keys to the blessed paradise.

The Khirghiz swore even more fluently. It was a lie that Rashideddin spoke with Halen ibn Shaddah more than others. Rashideddin was favored by the dark powers, for he read books. The Khirghiz knew that, for he was one of the chosen *fedavie* of the astrologer.

Khlit turned, at a step on the stair. Instead of Rashideddin, he saw the stout figure of Iba Kabash who halted in surprise.

"Listen, Cossack," the Kurd whispered, with a glance around the chamber. "I have not yet delivered your message, for Rashideddin stopped me on my way to Halen ibn Shaddah, and ordered me to bring you to him. But do not tell Rashideddin what you know. I shall see that you get a good reward, I swear it. We must try to get the girl. If you know a way tell me, and it shall be done. Remember, say nothing to Rashideddin."

Khlit weighed the words of the Kurd for their gist of truth and found very little. He little liked to face the astrologer, but he ascended the stair at once, swaggering, and stamping his boots.

In the round chamber of the astrologer he halted. It was night and candles were lighted around the tapestried walls. Rashideddin was crouched over rolls of parchment and instruments the like of which Khlit had not seen. In a cleared space on the floor in front of him the wise man of Alamut had ranged a number of images, silver and cleverly wrought, of stars.

The stars formed a circle and in the circle was a bag. Rashideddin sat quietly, arms crossed on knees, staring in front of him. Around the walls of the chamber silk hangings had been placed, on which were woven pictures of scenes which Khlit recognized as belonging to the paradise of Halen ibn Shaddah.

"Seat yourself, Cossack," said Rashideddin, in his slow, deep voice, "in front of me, and watch."

The astrologer's eyes were half-closed. Looking into them, Khlit could see nothing. The room was still and deserted except for the two. Khlit wished that others had been there. He felt ill at ease, and sucked at his pipe loudly.

"In the place of darkness, of the spirit Munkir," said Rashideddin, "there are no stars. Yet when men are alive they can look on the stars. Few can read them. From Alamut I have seen them, and learned many things. Do they read the stars in your country, Cossack?"

"Nay," said Khlit, "we know them not."

Rashideddin contemplated his circle thoughtfully. His hands, yellow and very clean, took up a pair of dividers with which he measured the distance between the silver stars.

"In the heart of Alamut, we have burned the law books of the Persians and the code books of the Medes. They were very old; yet is the dust of age a sacrament? What is there about an old law that makes it graven as on stone in the minds of men? One prophet has said that he who takes a tooth for a tooth is lawful; another has said that he who injures another for his own sake shall suffer greatly. Which is the truth?"

"Nay," answered Khlit, "I know not."

"It was written that when one man kills another the kin of that man shall kill the first. So I have seen many in the world outside Alamut kill each other without cause. Yet in Alamut, we kill only for a reason."

Khlit thought of the dead Tatar who had fallen where Rashideddin sat and was silent.

"Watch," said the astrologer. Putting aside his dividers, he took up the bag. Opening the top of this slightly he held it over the circle in both hands. Tipping it to one side, he allowed a thin stream of sand to fall in the space enclosed by the stars. The sand heaped itself in mounds, which Rashideddin considered carefully, setting down the bag.

"There are laws in the stars, Cossack," he repeated, tracing idly in the sand with his dividers. "And I have read them. Is it not true that when a man has found the sum of wisdom, he has none? The poet has said that no beauty is in the world save that of power over other men. The stars watch the evil and idleness of men. One who reads them learns many things. I shall tell you what I learned of you, Cossack."

"Aye," said Khlit grimly, "tell."

Under the cover of his bushy eyebrows he studied his companion. Rashideddin was a magician, and in Khlit's mind a magician was not to be trusted. Was the astrologer playing with him, using him as a chess-player moves a piece on the board? What had Iba Kabash told Rashideddin? Khlit waited, paying no attention to the stars or the sand, watching only the eyes of the other.

"From the land of Ukraine you came, Khlit," said the astrologer. "Alone, and met Toctamish in Astrakan. When the wolf runs with the jackal over the steppe, the stars have a riddle to solve. Perhaps the wolf is hungry. And the jackal is useful."

"Aye," said Khlit, "Iba Kabash."

Rashideddin's expression did not change as he stirred the sands with his dividers. "At Astrakan there was a *fedavie* who is dead. You and the jackal Toctamish were under his roof. You came with him to a ship. And the *fedavie* was slain. Aye, the wolf was hungered. Much have I learned from the stars. There was a girl with you on the ship. She did not come with you to Alamut."

Khlit made no response, and Rashideddin continued to stir the sands.

"The girl was not one easy to forget. You have not forgotten her. The jackal is drunk. But you have an ear for wisdom. The girl might be found in Alamut. Aye, by one who knows her, in the thousands of slaves."

Khlit shook the ashes from his pipe. Out of the corner of his eye he saw the hangings move behind him. Well he knew the chamber of Rashideddin was pregnant with danger. The pallid astrologer toyed with men's lives as he did with the magic sands. He made no move, waiting for what was to come.

It came in a blinding flash. A burst of flame, and the sands leaped upward. Smoke and a wrenching smell filled Khlit's eyes and throat. The skin of his face burned hotly. Blinking and gasping, he rocked back on his haunches.

"The wolf is wise in the ways of the steppe," purred the astrologer. "Yet he came to Alamut, the vulture's nest. It is a pity. The girl, too, is missing. Perhaps she can be found."

The face of Rashideddin stared at him through thinning clouds of powder smoke, and Khlit wiped the tears of pain from his eyes. Rapidly, he thought. Rashideddin wanted Berca. Halen ibn Shaddah would pay a high price for the girl, who was dangerous, being not as other girls.

"Aye," he muttered, coughing, for the flame had burned his face, "she may be found."

"Tomorrow there will be an audience by Halen ibn Shaddah for the *fedavie*. She will be there. I shall send for you before evening. Fail, and the *fedavie* will break your bones slowly, with stones, or tear the skin from your back."

Khlit rose to his feet without obeisance.

"Have the stars," he asked, "any other message for me?"

For a long moment Rashideddin studied him through narrowed lids. Idly, the dividers traced patterns in the powder ash in the circle of stars. And Khlit cursed himself softly. For in the eyes of the other was the look of one who measures swords. Once too often he had drawn the attention of the astrologer on himself.

Dismissed from the round chamber, Khlit sought out Iba Kabash, and secured the promise of the Kurd that he would be put with Toctamish among the sentries for the next night, for being admitted to the paradise of Alamut this was their privilege. To gain this point, it was necessary to assure the Kurd that Berca could be found. Once more, Iba Kabash swore Khlit would get a good price, whereupon Khlit had the thought that the other was too glib with a promise.

Then he found Toctamish, and told the Tatar enough of what had passed in the garden of Halen ibn Shaddah to keep him sober overnight. This done, Khlit seated himself in a corner of the banquet-place and took out his sword. Placing it across his knees he began to whet it with the stone he always carried. As he did so, men near him stared curiously, for Khlit was singing to himself in a voice without music.

And Rashideddin sat over the circle of silver stars, tracing and retracing patterns in the ashes of powder, with the look of one in whose soul there is no peace.

XII

Came the time of the *divan*, the assembly of the *Refik*, and closed gates that guarded the apartments of Halen ibn Shaddah in the cellars of Alamut swung open. In poured the followers of the *Refik*; *fedavie*, hillmen of Persia, men of the

Khirghiz steppe, *janissaries* of Yussouf, prince of princes. Scattered in the crowd were magicians of Rashideddin in white tunics and red girdles, in company with white and gold *Dais*. Also came Khlit with the Khirghiz chief who had seen fit to keep at his side.

The throng moved in silence, and Khlit waxed curious at this, until he questioned the Khirghiz. For reply, he received a hard blow in the ribs.

"You are surely a fool, Cossack," growled the other, "to bray at what is strange. We are walking through the talking chambers of the *Shadna*, built by Ala-eddin. Harken." He lifted his voice in a shrill syllable. "Aie!"

Instantly the sound was taken up and repeated through the corridors. A hundred echoes caught the word and flung it back. Shrilly, gruffly, it rang further into the caverns. Men near them stared and cursed. Khlit observed that the corridors were lofty and vaulted, with pillars of stone.

"It is said," whispered the Khirghiz, gratified by the effect of his experiment, "that before the time of Rashideddin, when the *Refik* prayed to Allah, these were the chambers of prayer. A man could pray a thousand times with one word."

"And now?"

"We do not pray."

Pushing a way through the crowd recklessly with his elbows, the Khirghiz gained a place where he and Khlit could see the array of the *divan*. In the center of a cleared space in one of the larger chambers stood Halen ibn Shaddah, easily marked by his great height and the cloak that shadowed his face. Around him were grouped certain men in heavy turbans and green embroidered coats. These Khlit recognized as *Daikebirs*, emissaries of the master of Alamut. At his side was the bent figure of Rashideddin.

These were talking in a tongue that Khlit did not know, not loudly, for fear of disturbing the echoes. His eye wandered over the throng. Wandered and halted. A woman's figure stood out from the crowd and he swore under his breath. Arm's length from Rashideddin among the Dais, her blue cloak closely wrapped on her slender form, stood Berca. Her black curls were pushed under a fold of the cloak; her brown eyes, darting from under fringed lashes, swept about the gathered Refik and passed Khlit by in unconcern. Yet he felt that she had seen him.

No other woman was present. Khlit saw that the eyes of many searched her, and he touched the Khirghiz on the shoulder.

"Is there talk about the woman?" he asked softly. "Tell me."

The chief listened, tolerantly, for a space.

"Aye," he said, "there is idle talk. The woman is the daughter of a hill sheik. She was sent to be the wife of Kiragai Khan. That is a good jest, for Kiragai Khan loves not the Refik. She has said that she was sent without a dowry. So, the painted flower has come to one who tramples on flowers, to ask that the dowry be given her."

"And will it be done?"

"Will the tiger give up its slain victim? Nay, you are without understanding, Cossack. Halen ibn Shaddah does not play with such. The sheik's daughter will find a place among the slaves, not otherwise."

"Such is not the law."

"There is no law in Alamut but one—the word of Halen ibn Shaddah. And the law that the curved dagger must avenge a wrong."

Khlit made no reply, considering carefully what had been said. Rashideddin, then, had found Berca as he had declared he would. Was it Berca's purpose to come before Halen ibn Shaddah? Had she forgotten the cunning and cruelty of the man who had dishonored her? Perhaps the girl's pride had impelled her to appeal for justice and a wedding dowry to give the khan to whom she had offered herself. Yet Berca had not forgotten the manner of her father's death, of that Khlit was sure. Wise in the ways of men, the heart of the sheik's daughter was a closed book to him. He looked around for Toctamish. The Tatar was not to be seen.

Meanwhile, Rashideddin had been speaking to the girl.

"What said the astrologer?" asked Khlit.

"The old one is crafty," grunted the Khirghiz. "Aye, he has learned the secrets of magic where Marduk hangs by his heels in the hell of Babylon. He asked why a girl so fair in face and form should bear a gift in offering herself in marriage."

Berca, who seemed to ignore her peril, lifted her dark head and answered quickly in tones that stirred the echoes.

"Hah, the painted flower has a sharp tongue," grunted the chieftain. "She says that her beauty has moved the heart of Kiragai Khan as wind stirs fire. The khan, who desires her, would have taken her for his favorite wife. Yet would she not, being ashamed for reason of the trick Halen ibn Shaddah played her. So she has come back to ask a dowry from the hand of the master of Alamut, who is her lawful ruler now that her father is dead."

The giant form of Halen ibn Shaddah turned on Berca, and a peculiarly shrill voice reached the ears of Khlit. Once more he wondered what kind of man was the master of Alamut, of the giant figure and shrill voice.

"Halen ibn Shaddah says," whispered the other, "that Berca belongs to Alamut. She has returned to Alamut and here she must stay."

Khlit thought of the paradise of the master of evil, and understood why the eyes of the *fedavie* in the throng burned as they stared at the girl's slender figure outlined in the blue cloak.

"She asked for justice—" he began.

"Nay," interrupted the Khirghiz carelessly, "her father was slain by Halen ibn Shaddah. How is she then to be trusted?"

Khlit did not answer. For the gaze of Berca had met his. In it he read anxiety, and a warning. Slowly her glance crept to Rashideddin and back. Again. And Khlit saw the astrologer turn to leave the chamber.

Truly, he considered, the sheik's daughter was daring and proud. And, obeying her look, he followed Rashideddin, slipping away from the Khirghiz.

So it happened that when the astrologer left the *divan*, Khlit did likewise. Rashideddin made his way quickly and alone down one of the corridors without waiting for a light. Khlit followed him, keeping as close as he could without being seen. Presently both halted.

A voice called through the corridor clearly, and seemingly very near.

"A man must be crafty and wise," the voice of Berca came to their ears, "when danger is 'round his path, else is his labor vain."

Khlit crossed himself in astonishment. For a moment he had forgotten the echoes of the corridors of Ala-eddin.

XIII

Rashideddin went straight to the winding stairs that led to his own apartment. At the foot of these stairs Khlit, who had traced the astrologer closely, paused. It would not be easy to go farther without being seen. And this Khlit wanted to avoid. He believed that Rashideddin was having him watched, and that the Khirghiz had attended him to the *divan* under orders. And at all costs he must be free to act that night.

Rashideddin, thought Khlit, sensed something impending. In some way the magician of Alamut kept himself informed of what went on in the citadel. His spies were everywhere. And on the night when Berca planned to admit the enemies of the *Refik*, both were under watch. Where was Toctamish?

Khlit wasted no time by the foot of the winding stair. There were other entrances to the circular chamber where Rashideddin kept his henchmen, and the Cossack cast about until he came to one of these. A passage led upward, unlighted in the direction he sought and this Khlit followed until he came to a curtain which he suspected divided it from the chamber of the astrologer. Beyond the curtain he could hear voices.

Lifting one edge of the hanging, Khlit looked out cautiously. Candle-light in the chamber dazzled him for a moment. He made out a dozen figures, Rashideddin not, among them, dressed in the red and white of the magicians' cult. They were grouped around a man prone on the floor. This man was Toctamish.

The Tatar's coat and shirt had been removed. Two *fedavie* held each of his arms outstretched on the floor. His thick chest was strangely red, and he gasped as if in pain, not once or twice, but long, broken gasps that shook his body.

As Khlit watched, startled, one of the *fedavie*, a gaunt Tatar with a pocked face, placed some brown dust on the chest of the prostrate man. Khlit recognized the dust. It was the same that had singed his face when he sat opposite Rashideddin.

Thrusting aside the hanging, Khlit stepped into the room. The *fedavie* took no notice of him, believing that he was one of Rashideddin's henchmen stationed in the passage. Toctamish, however, lifted his eyes, which gleamed as they fell on the Cossack. Khlit saw that his brow was covered with sweat, and that blood ran from his mouth.

The man of the pitted face lifted some brown powder and sifted it on the chest of his victim. Another pushed a torch into his hand. Khlit realized then how his companion was being tortured. The smell of burning in the air came from singed flesh. And Toctamish was feeling the angry hand of Rashideddin.

Khlit stepped to the side of the *fedavie* with the torch, and peered closely at Toctamish. He saw then what made the Tatar's chest red, of a strange shade. Strips of skin had been torn off over the lungs, and here the powder was laid. Khlit swore and his hand strayed to his sword. And fell to his side. The *fedavie* numbered a full dozen, armed, and able-bodied. To draw his sword would be to bring ten whirling around him.

Khlit had no love for Toctamish. Yet in this room the other had stood with his sword drawn beside him. And they had shared bread and salt. Toctamish was standing the torture with the stark courage which was his creed. The lips of the sufferer moved and Khlit bent closer.

"Kiragai Khan—Khan of the Horde," the cracked lips gasped, "tell him. Blood for blood. We have shared bread—and salt, and *arak*. Tell him."

The Cossack nodded. Toctamish was asking him to report how he had endured torture to Kiragai Khan who was advancing on Alamut at the head of his men, and claiming vengeance. He was weak, and seemed to have no hope of living.

"What said the dog?" muttered the *fedavie* with the torch who had been trying to catch what Toctamish whispered. He spoke in a bastard Tatar with a strange lisping. "He will not speak and Rashideddin has said that he must or we will hang by the heels."

"He is out of his mind," answered Khlit carelessly. "What must he tell?"

"He stuck a dagger into a *fedavie*, a Syrian, on the shore of the Salt Sea. A girl, Berca, the sheik's daughter, was there also. This yellow-faced fool must tell if the girl ordered him to do it. Bah! His skin is tough as oxen hide, and his flesh is senseless as swine."

"And he has not spoken?"

"Nay. Rashideddin was here and questioned him, but the Tatar cursed him."

Khlit scanned the face of Toctamish. The yellow skin was dark and moist with sweat. The eyes were bloodshot and half-closed. The mouth lifted in a snarl, disclosing teeth pointed as an animal's. He felt that Toctamish would not yield to the torture. And great love for the man whose courage was proof against pain rose in the heart of Khlit whose own courage was such that men called him the "Wolf."

"Aye," he growled, "blood for blood. That is the law of Alamut. And Kiragai Khan shall know."

He saw by a quick opening of the eyes that Toctamish caught his words.

"What say you?" queried the *fedavie*. "Kiragai Khan?"

Toctamish's knotted figure writhed under the hands of his captors. He spat, blood and foam combined, at the other.

"Aye," he groaned, "Kiragai Khan—lord of fifty thousand spears—chief of a hundred ensigns—master of Alamut."

"He speaks," interpreted Khlit swiftly, "of one Hulagu Khan who conquered Alamut. Tell Rashideddin. And cease the torture, for the man has nothing to confess."

The *fedavie* stared at Khlit suspiciously.

"Nay," he snarled, "shall we hang by the heels?"

He thrust the torch near the powder. There was a hissing flash, a smell of burning flesh. Toctamish's body quivered spasmodically and sank back. The eyes closed.

Under cover of the flare and smoke Khlit slipped back through the circle and sought the stair. Gaining this he did not pause until he had reached the inner gate of the underground citadel where a *Dai* was assembling his men to guard the outer gate by the river.

When Khlit, who was nursing in his brain the sight he had just left, went down the river stairs to his post in the River Shahrud, he found that his companion was the bearded Khirghiz chieftain.

The outer post of the guard around the citadel of Alamut was in a small nest of rocks several hundred paces from the entrance, and midway in the stream. So shallow was the river that they could wade out to the rocks. The Khirghiz led the way.

It was not yet the middle of the night, and a bright moon lighted the winding ribbon of the Shahrud that twisted between the rocky heights of Rudbar. The mass of Alamut showed dark, giving no sign of the evil world it concealed. A wind from the heights brushed Khlit's face and he breathed it in deeply, for he was nauseated by the stench of the caverns.

"You and I, Cossack," said the Khirghiz, seating himself unsteadily on a ledge of the rocks, for he had been drinking, "will keep the outer post."

"Aye," said Khlit, "you and I."

He stared out into the moonlight haze that hung over the river. Berca had said that he and Toctamish were to hold the outer post. From some quarter the horsemen of Kiragai Khan were nearing the gate of Alamut. Khlit realized that unless the attack came as a surprise the citadel was impregnable. A surprise might carry the Tatar horde into the entrance. Berca had said there was a way. And this was it. Yet, if a surprise was to succeed the Khirghiz must be disposed of. He had bseen drinking, but he was still watchful. No movement of the Cossack escaped him.

Quietly Khlit drew out a small vial. From this he poured a few grains of a white powder into his hand. Lifting his hand he made as if to take the powder into his mouth. The Khirghiz bent forward, and his face lighted with evil desire.

"Have you—" he began.

"Come, Brother," whispered Khlit genially, "we will be comfortable on the rocks. Is not the bread of the *Refik* the vintage of the Shadna to be eaten? Come."

The Khirghiz swore softly and held out his hand. In wine and food, the vintage of the Shadna was often in the hands of the *Refik* men. But not, except on expeditions of the Master of Alamut, or by costly bribery of the *Dais* was the pure powder of *hashish* to be had, the *hashish* that brought bright dreams of paradise and lulled the mind with pleasures, that hardened the souls of the men of Alamut, and steeled their hands to the dagger.

Khlit, who had discovered the secret of the drug through the babblings of Iba Kabash, quietly dropped his portion back into the vial. Later, he knew, the Khirghiz would want more and he had but a little.

XIV

It was not long before Khlit was alone. The Khirghiz lay at his side on the rocks, muttering to himself with enough *hashish* inside him to make an imbecile of an ordinary man. Khlit sat by his side, saber across his knees, and watched the moonlit sides of the heights that frowned down on him. On the slopes he could make out the shadowy outlines of droves of horses, and he wondered if the *Dais* were planning an expedition that night.

Usually, Khlit was not given to forebodings. Yet the black mass of Alamut rising at his back gave him the feeling of approaching danger, and when he scanned the shadows along the river they moved as if filled with the bands of drug-crazed *fedavie*. Especially, Khlit wondered if the spies of Rashideddin were watching him. Rashideddin had learned of the murder of the Syrian, had connected Berca with it, and Toctamish with Berca. Toctamish, at his order, had been tortured with such devilish cruelty that even the Tatar's fortitude might break down.

How much did the astrologer know of Berca's secret? Once the alarm was raised in Alamut a thousand swords would block the stairs at the river gate and the rope hoists of the slaves at the rear would be drawn up. There were no signs of activity that Khlit could see, but few ever saw the movements of the *fedavie*. Accustomed as he was to war on the steppe, he was skeptical of horsemen taking such a stronghold as Alamut.

Once the Tatar horde forced the entrance there would be a battle such as Khlit had never seen before. Himself a Cossack, he cared little whether *Refik* or Khan were the victor—except that he had sworn an oath, a double oath, that the life of the Master of Alamut, Halen ibn Shaddah, would fall to his sword. Wherefore, he waited patiently, eyes searching the road by the river where the invaders might come.

Berca had told him that twenty thousand Tatars were riding through the hills to Alamut. Yet the road was narrow and the way twisted. It would be hard to move quickly. And there were the horse-tenders on the hills who would give the alarm. Khlit had come to grant a grudging admiration to the sheik's daughter who had defied Halen ibn Shaddah. But she was in Rashideddin's hands, and the astrologer was the man Khlit had marked as most dangerous of the *Refik*.

Rising suddenly, Khlit drew in his breath sharply. Outlined against the summit of a hill he saw a horse and rider moving very swiftly. The man was bent low in his saddle and Khlit thought he saw the long cloak of the *fedavie* before the rider came over the brow of the hill. Half-way down the descent the horse stumbled and fell.

Khlit saw a dark object shoot from the rolling horse and lie passive, clear in the moonlight. The messenger, if such it was, of the *fedavie* would not reach his destination. And at the same time Khlit saw something else. Before his eyes as if by magic he beheld Kiragai Khan and thousands of his horsemen.

Then Khlit, surnamed the Wolf, buckled tight his belt and drew on his sheepskin hat firmly. There was to be a battle that would redden the waters of the Shahrud and, among the swords of the *fedavie* Halen ibn Shaddah was to be found.

Apparently there was nothing stirring on the mountain slopes of Rudbar except the shapes of the horse droves that drew down to the river as was their custom, awaiting the bands of the *Dais* which came out for mounts. Tonight there were no men issuing from Alamut. And it was only when one of the herds moved across the face of the moon that Khlit saw the tips of Tatar helmets moving among the horses, and understood why the horses seemed more numerous than before.

Even as Berca had promised, the Tatar horde was approaching the gate of Alamut. One of the herds reached the river's edge and pressed on, in the shadow of the hillside. Khlit could see the faces of men peering at him, and catch the glint of their spears. He gave a hasty glance at his companion. The man was sleeping heavily.

Familiar with the ways of the Tatars, the Cossack could guess how their whirlwind rush into Rudbar had cut off all news being sent to the citadel, and how, after dark, the *Refik* horse-tenders on the pastures had been singled out and cut down. One had broken away with the news that was to carry the doom of Alamut, only to fall by the river.

The foremost warriors had reached him, clinging closely to the sides of their horses. A low voice called out to him cautiously.

"You are the Cossack who will guide us?"

"Aye," said Khlit, "but the moon is bright here and there are others within the caverns. Are you ready to rush forward at once?"

"Lead," said the voice, "and we will follow. Lead us to the gate of Alamut and we will purge the devil's hole of its filth."

Khlit cast a quick glance at the hillsides. Other bodies were moving down. Some were nearly at the river. Thousands were corning over the hillcrest. More were coming by the river road. On the far flanks detachments were moving to the rear of Alamut.

Drawing his sword, he sprang down into the river and splashed toward the shore. Dark forms closed in beside him, and the welcome stench of sweat and leather filled his nose. The river was full of moving forms, and horses that dashed, riderless, to either side. Khlit's heart leaped, and his clasp tightened on his sword. One of the foremost caught him roughly by the arm. Khlit had a quick glimpse of a dark, lined face and flashing eyes.

"I am Kiragai Khan, Cossack. Where is Toctamish? He was to stay by the side of Berca!"

"She sent him to watch with me. Yet, very likely he is dead by now."

The other swore, as they gained the shelter of the caverns.

"Take me to her, then," he snarled.

So it happened that before the light of day touched the date trees on the summit of Alamut, citadel of the *Refik*, and place of plague and evil, the first of the horde that had ridden from the shores of the Salt Sea entered the river gate, overcoming a few guards, forced their way up the stair, and spread through the passages of Alamut, making no sound but silently, as tigers seeking their prey.

XV

In the annals of Abulghazi it is written how, in the year of the lion, came the doom of Alamut. The *Refik* folk were cornered in the cellars of the citadel, and taken by surprise. The swords of the Kallmark Tatars flashed in the passages, and their sharp arrows sped through the corridors. And, as the prophecy said, the waters of the Shadrud were red.

Yet in the book of Abulghazi and the annals of the Persian dynasties there is nothing said of the fate of Halen ibn Shaddah who was the last leader of the *Refik*. The followers of Kiragai Khan sought through Alamut from the wine chambers to the gardens among the ruins on the summit, and they did not find Halen ibn Shaddah.

The battle was not over for many hours. Separate bands of mounted Tatars had surrounded the height on which Alamut stood, and when throngs of slaves, and the eunuchs with the houris of the gardens swept out from hidden tunnels and were lowered over the wall, they were cut down. They were not spared, for that was the word of Kiragai Khan. The *fedavie*, cornered, and led by their *Dais*, rallied and attacked the columns of invaders which were penetrating to the heart of Alamut.

The Tatars without their horses and fighting in the gloom of the caverns were at a disadvantage, which was offset by greater numbers and the leadership of Kiragai Khan. For the *fedavie* had no leader. Messengers who sought through the tapestried apartments of the Shadna for Halen ibn Shaddah found none but panic-struck *Daikebirs*. The tide of battle flung the *fedavie* back to the banquet-place, and to the treasure-house beyond.

If there had been a leader they might have held the dark passages until the Tatars were sickened by the slaughter of their men.

Such was the doom of Alamut. Torches flaring through chambers hung with gold cloth and littered with jeweled statuary from Trebizond, with silk rugs of Ispahan. Swords flashing in dark tunnels, where naught was heard but the gasping of men bitten by steel and the sound of bodies falling to the earth. Wailing and lamentation in the gardens under the date trees which were the evil paradise of Halen ibn Shaddah, and the splash of stricken women in the canals. Dark-faced, squat men in mail and fur cloaks trampling through treasure-rooms where the riches of a thousand caravans and a hundred cities stood.

Never had the followers of Kiragai Khan taken spoil so rich. Pearls from Damascus, golden fish from Che-ting, emeralds and sapphires from Tabriz, urns of gold shekels from the merchants of Samarkand and ornaments from the califate of Bagdad that would grace the court of a Mongol emperor. Slant eyes of the Kallmark horsemen widened, and they urged their dogs into the rivers of wine in the gardens, ripping into shreds rugs and hangings, splintering porcelain *kiosks* with rocks, and trampling on the bodies of the dead. Few lived.

And still the Master of Alamut was not found. Once Iba Kabash, who had attached himself to the winning side, and was spared because he brought Berca safe to Kiragai Khan, paused beside the body of a very large man, cloaked and jeweled. But he spurned it with his foot when he turned it over, for the giant face was that of a black eunuch.

Yet there was one who said he had found Halen ibn Shaddah. Iba Kabash, who was eager to find favor with his new lord, offered, trembling, to take him to the circular chamber of Rashideddin. Berca came with them, for she was not one to leave the side of Kiragai Khan in battle, being the daughter of a hill sheik and not a Tatar woman.

They climbed the winding stairs escorted by the renegade with torch-bearers and armed Kallmarks. In the circular chamber of the astrologer they saw a strange sight. The room had been dark. By the flare of their torches they made out three men, two dead, and the third sitting on the floor. Kiragai Khan paused for a moment by the body of Toctamish, burned and bloody, for the man had been one of his lieutenants, and very brave.

"He died under torture, lord and Celestial Master," gibbered Iba Kabash, pointing. "For he would not tell of the queenly Berca, or the corning of the noble Tatars."

ALAMUT

Kiragai Khan said nothing, passing to the next body, and pressing the hand of
Berca when the girl cried out. This one was Rashideddin, his gray robe stained with
red, and his lean face convulsed. His arms flung wide, and sightless, leering eyes
staring upward through the opening to the stars, the astrologer had died in the grip
of anger. Berca, leaning over him, watched vainly for a breath to stir the gray cloak.
Seated beside Rashideddin she saw Khlit, wiping his sword calmly with a corner of
the dead man's cloak.

"Have you seen Halen ibn Shaddah?" demanded Iba Kabash officiously. "The
noble Kiragai Khan has missed you, since he came into the entrance of Alamut. Was it
you that killed Rashideddin?"

"Aye," answered Khlit, looking up indifferently. "Have the Kallmarks or the *Refik*
the upper hand? I have seen Halen ibn Shaddah."

"The battle is over, Khlit," exclaimed Berca pressing forward, but keeping the
hand of the Tatar leader. Her eyes were shining, and she held her head proudly. "The
doom of Alamut has come, as I swore it would. It was my will that it should, mine
and my lord's. For I came to him without a gift and was ashamed. Yet did he marry
me in spite of that. And I swore to him that if he would avenge my father such a gift
should be his as no other bride could bring. Alamut would be his, with the treasure of
the *Refik*. And now he has seen that the gift is rich. All that Halen ibn Shaddah had."

Khlit's glance sought that of the Tatar leader, and they measured each other
silently.

"The way is long from Tatary," went on Berca, tossing her head, "but I am very
beautiful in the sight of my lord, and he consented to my plan—to come to open the
gate to him—saying only that Toctamish should come. I picked you, Cossack, as
my father of battles. Yet I am grieved. You swore that you would slay for me Halen
ibn Shaddah—"

"Have you seen," broke in Kiragai Khan gruffly, "the one who is called Master of
Alamut?"

"Aye, he was here."

"Which way did he go? Speak."

"He did not go."

The khan looked around the chamber. It was empty except for the two bodies. A
sudden blast of air from the opening overhead made the flame of the torches whirl, and
cast a gleam on the face of Rashideddin as if the dead man had moved. Berca drew back
with a smothered cry.

"The man who was called Halen ibn Shaddah," said Khlit, "was a eunuch of great size. The real Master of Alamut was another. He concealed his identity to avoid the daggers of those who would slay him. Yet is he slain. And I have kept my oath, Berca, princess."

The eyes of the others strayed to the body of Rashideddin, and rested on the red stains that garnished the gray cloak with the red ribbons of death. The blind eyes of Halen ibn Shaddah were fixed on the stars visible through the opening in the ceiling. And Khlit, seeing this, knew that he would be very glad to turn his horse again toward the steppe and away from Alamut.

THE PLOT OF SIGNOR SALVI

MARION POLK ANGELLOTTI

I

There are, to my mind, few things in this world so deeply ingrained in a man as his love of his country. He may owe her no good, may even have to thank her for injury and injustice. It does not matter, the tie remains. For example, long years since I numbered among my acquaintance a certain Frenchman, banished for some misstep in statecraft, hunted like a criminal by his sovereign, driven from court to court so vindictively that he never knew one night where he would lay his head the next.

So bitter had he grown that he was wont to declare his intention of enlisting in a foreign army and one day entering Paris sword in hand. Then came an evening when he and I lay together at a roadside inn. Among the guests was a noted bully who took this occasion to utter, between mouthfuls, some insult leveled against France. And my Frenchman gave him the lie, fought him in a space cleared between the tables, and lost his life in the conflict.

As for me, John Hawkwood, though I have passed two-score years soldiering in Italy and am well enough content to end my days here, this tie of birth is no weaker in me than in another man; and therefore, I held it the greatest of the many honors heaped on me in the latter part of my life when the King of England availed himself of the fact that I was Captain-General of Florence and appointed me his ambassador to that Republic, as well as to the Court of Naples and the Holy See.

Had a serious difference arisen between Florence and England, I would have found myself in no very agreeable imbroglio, considering that I was in the pay of both; but since matters moved along peaceably, all went well, and I took some pride in serving my country and more in serving King Richard, second of his name, who was the son of my old leader, the Black Prince.

To speak frankly, I had never considered myself particularly fitted for diplomacy; but I did my best, and to my surprise and gratification, found that it was possible to accomplish a good deal by sheer resolution and uncompromising grimness of front.

My greatest trial in my new metier proved, as time went on, to be one Walter
Skirlawe, the Dean of St. Martin's, whom it pleased His Majesty to saddle on me as
colleague and fellow-ambassador. An excellent and scholarly gentleman, for whom
I had the highest esteem, he was far more useful in ordinary affairs than I was.
But in any crisis, especially one of personal danger, he lost his head entirely, and
displayed an apparent imbecility that came near to driving me mad.

This being the case, I was by no means overjoyed to hear one evening that he was
awaiting me in my hall, and in a state, so my lackey informed me, of wild alarm and
excitement. In the first place, I was far from being in a humor to listen patiently while
he entertained me with tales of woe. Within the hour, I had reached my villa after
a month's absence at Pisa on the Republic's business; and now, seated at table, with
Lady Hawkwood's dark eyes smiling into mine and our fingers stealing together in the
pauses of our talk, I envied no crowned king, and was certainly not disposed to come
out of my paradise for the purpose of changing words with Walter Skirlawe.

However, I knew enough of the worthy Dean to be quite sure that he would not
desist from his quest until he had succeeded in unbosoming himself and forcing me
to hearten him. So I submitted with a rueful laugh and a shrug of the shoulders.

"We will let him enter here, if you permit," I said to Lady Hawkwood. "Perhaps
if he finds that he cannot see me alone, he will take himself off and leave us to
ourselves—the saints grant it!"

"Amen to that prayer!" she whispered, laughing. "But, listen, he must be in
terror to come at such a pace as this, he who is so stately—"

The door opened on her last word, and the Dean of St. Martin's half dashed, half
stumbled into the room. Until he entered, I had expected nothing more than some
affair of a piece with his ordinary alarms, a molehill made into a mountain by too
much worry; but I confess his appearance gave me a start, for however prone to fears
a man may be, he does not tum white as chalk for nothing, nor do his eyes protrude
from his head and his hands shake as if with palsy over a thing of no consequence.

"Sir John, Sir John! Praise Heaven you are returned!" he panted as he staggered
forward. "The fat is in the fire with a vengeance, and unless you can pull it out, we
must all shrive ourselves and prepare for the end!"

"What fat, pray? If the case is so desperate, we had best lose no time in chatter,"
I said with rising irritation; for, being cool myself in moments of crisis, I find it hard
to keep my patience with those whose wits go wandering just when they are most needed.
"Come to the point, my friend. And do you not see that Lady Hawkwood is with us?"

He saluted her with a muttered apology that had all the sound of a moan, then suddenly dropped into a chair, laid his arms on the table, and dropped his head upon them, overturning with great clatter a gold dish of comfits and one of fruits.

Convinced by this time that there was something serious in the wind, I waved my lackeys out of the room, filled a cup with wine, and forced its rim between Skirlawe's teeth, emptying its contents down his throat.

"Come," I said as encouragingly as I could, while he groaned and straightened, "what is all this pother about, and what do you desire me to do?"

He fell back in his chair.

"Oh, you can do nothing! An angel from Heaven could scarce save us!" he wailed, and I experienced a lively desire to force the truth from him at the dagger's point. "You would hear what has happened? Listen, then! A half-hour ago Peter Whyte was arrested just within the Porta Santa Maria for having stabbed a man near to death!"

For an instant I stared at him blankly, scarce able to believe my ears. Despite myself, I had been sufficiently impressed to expect some startling disclosure, and his revelation left me divided between mirth and anger at his absurdity. This Peter was a member of my White Company, an English knave, thief, and cutthroat, who yet possessed his virtues—astonishing shrewdness, for instance, and courage, and fidelity to me as his Captain, though he was continually in trouble with me by reason of his escapades.

A few months earlier, Skirlawe, who had more than once heard me tell how I had trusted very delicate matters to his quick wits and skill at swordplay, had craved my leave to use him on a private mission, which, as he told me nothing of its aim, was apparently shrouded in mystery; and I had agreed. Since that time I had not troubled my head about Peter, and this was my first news of him.

"Well, man, and what of it?" I demanded when I had recovered the use of my tongue. "Upon my word, one might think you had gone mad! This is not the first time Peter has stabbed a foe, nor is it like to be the last; and if I lay awake o' nights every time such a thing occurred in the White Company. I should get little rest!"

The Dean of St. Martin's waved both hands wildly in the air. "You do not understand, Sir John," he groaned. "He quarreled with a bully in the service of Messer Adriano Salvi of the Signoria, set near the gate to watch for him—"

"Faith, then, I commend Peter's taste," said I with a laugh. "For a scudo, I would follow my rogue's example and draw sword on old Salvi himself, who is forever scheming against me!"

"Scheming? That he is!" cried the Dean. "And now he will be triumphant, and oust you as both ambassador and Captain-General!"

"Heaven grant me patience!" I exclaimed, irritated beyond bearing. "Tell me the kernel of the matter in a word, unless you wish that I should go insane!"

Skirlawe collapsed once more in a woeful heap.

"Can you not see?" he lamented. "They have taken him to the Bargello, to the Capitano di Giustizia, who will have no choice but to order him imprisoned for trial. And since all who are imprisoned are searched, the packet will be discovered, even as Salvi planned."

The packet! Now, indeed, we were coming to the truth.

"Quick, man!" I urged, as he paused to wring his hands.

"I scarce dare tell you, Sir John. You will be angered, and with some cause," he wailed. "The matter concerns the treaty which you made lately between England and Florence, as against Milan. It appears that His Majesty and his ministers, though friendly to Florence, had no wish to quarrel with Milan either. So they planned to arrange a secret treaty with the Milanese Duke, Visconti, that they might stand well with both sides. You see? To be sure, Florence would take this ill if she knew, but why need she know? And why should you know either, since you are—forgive me that I say it—a soldier, and blunt, and little disposed to concealment? So His Majesty confided it only to me, bidding me inform myself of its further progress through Sir Nicholas Dagworth, our envoy to Milan; and I took for messenger this trusty Peter of yours, who has now carried two messages from me to Sir Nicholas and returned with others."

"A curse upon it!" I cried savagely, as the truth burst on me.

"But the matter has come to nothing," he urged propitiatingly, "for the Duke of Milan was minded to ask too much. I do not doubt that the very packet, brought tonight by your Peter, would have told me all was ended, and that we might devote ourselves heart and soul to Florence."

"Aye, she will want our devotion, will she not, when she learns we have leagued behind her back with her worst enemies!" I mocked bitterly. "A rare pass we are come to, with your cursed double-dealing and treachery! If this is diplomacy, then I thank Heaven I am a soldier! Giovanni! Tomaso! My hat and cloak on the instant!"

"Wherefore, Sir John? What is it you intend?" cried the Dean, wildly clutching at my arm.

"What but to get back that packet at whatever cost?" I demanded. "Did you think me likely to sit here feasting while Salvi relates his tale to the Signoria, then?"

"You can do nothing! We are all doomed!" was his cheerful prophecy, as he buried his head in his hands once more.

Lady Hawkwood, who throughout the scene had sat pale and silent, but calm enough to put both the Dean and myself to shame, laid her fingers on my sleeve.

"I will keep him here," she whispered, "lest he betray this elsewhere. Hasten, Sir John. You will succeed, I know it well."

I lingered only to raise her hand to my lips, and then dashed from the room and through my hall into the night.

II

I was panting with exhaustion as I reached the great, looming pile of the Bargello, with its gleaming windows and square-arched tower, and, changing my run for a hasty stride, passed into the colonnaded *loggia*. The distance hither from my house was no small one, and I had traversed it, I verily believe, in less time than ever man did before. Moreover, the thoughts that kept me company had been such that I trust Heaven in its mercy will kill me before visiting me with any repetition of the experience.

Would I be in time? Freely, I acknowledged that it was not likely. Ah, the accursed shrewdness of my foe Salvi's plot! Somehow he had got wind of the fact that Skirlawe was dealing privately between Milan and England; at once he had planned this brawl— an easy thing to accomplish with one of Peter's temper—and the arrest, the search, and the discovery of the packet.

The good Gonfaloniere Francesco de Medici and the members of the Signoria would believe me a traitor, and, worse, believe England treacherous. Perhaps they would hang me before morning; I confessed frankly to myself that I should not blame them a whit if they did. In the name of all the saints, what had inspired the King to such a double-dealing step? Did he not know that a sovereign can hope for good faith in others only when he maintains it himself?

Ah, well, he was little more than a boy, and surrounded by men so steeped in the thing called policy that they could scarce believe any good could come of honest dealing. And firstly and lastly, and above all, he was the son of the Black Prince, my old leader and hero, and it should go hard with me before I would let his indiscretion become known to Salvi of the Signoria and trumpeted over Florence. For the moment, believe it or not, as you choose, I was more concerned for his sake than for myself.

But one hope remained. I must arrive before the interrogation was ended and Peter committed to prison. If I could do that, I might in some way free him, though Heaven alone knew how, for I racked my brain without success for an inspiration. Fervently, I breathed a prayer that Salvi himself would not be present to increase my difficulties; and I was inclined to believe that this much would be granted me, since he would probably not wish to pose as having planned my downfall.

There were two sentinels at the north gate, but they recognized me and drew back with a salute, and I crossed the courtyard and ran up the carved staircase three steps at a time. In the gallery, I found myself confronted by half a dozen obsequiously bowing lackeys.

"Was it your wish, Sir John, to see the Capitano di Giustizia?" one of them asked me. "He is within, and I will announce you on the instant—"

"You may spare yourself the trouble, my friend," I said grimly, "for, truth to tell, I have a fancy to enter unannounced."

And I forced a way through them and entered the great hall of the council. It lay empty; but as I crossed it, I heard from the inner room, where the *capitano* was wont to conduct his examinations, an indignant, strident voice that assuredly belonged to no one but Peter himself.

"A curse on it!" the rogue was vociferating. "If my Captain, Sir John Hawkwood, stood there before us, I think you would use a bit more ceremony with a soldier of the White Company!"

In that instant, a heavy weight of despair seemed to pass from my heart. I was in time; and, better still, Peter's foolish bit of bravado had given me the very idea I needed. Now at last, I knew how to deal with the matter. I straightened, assumed a grimly threatening air and opened the door without the formality of a knock.

In his chair of state sat the Capitano di Giustizia, one Marco Ridolfi, an honest fellow enough, though not too clever; and before him, flushed and disheveled and with a great blood-streak across his face, stood my rogue, Peter. A pair of guards too, were present, a half-dozen members of the watch and an *ecrivain* busily engaged in writing down every word that fell from the culprit's lips.

As they all looked up to see who intruded, I gathered that two, at least, of the party would rather have had me elsewhere; for Ridolfi stared at me with a dropping jaw, and as for Peter, who had a moment earlier been calling so loudly on my name, instead of looking pleased at my advent, he gave back a step in manifest alarm, while his bloody face lost its truculence and assumed a meek look that would have amused me at another time.

The *capitano* was the first to recover himself.

"Why, Sir John, I had not known that you were returned from Pisa! Your presence honors me," he cried.

But judging from his expression rather than his glib tongue, he would have dispensed with the honor and felt small grief.

As for me, I made no pretense of acknowledging his civility, but advanced into the center of the room and favored the company with a black scowl.

"You had not known that I had returned!" I said grimly. "Aye, it is plain enough that! Else I think you would have been more careful how you usurped my rights! Well, I have a way of appearing where I am needed Messer Marco, and I am not one to pass over such interference."

"But, Sir John, indeed, I intend no offense," protested the *capitano*. "Come, consider the matter reasonably. What can I do when the men of the watch bring me a soldier found in the act of stabbing a citizen? But calm yourself, for if you desire a pardon for this fellow, the Republic will certainly deny nothing to one it loves as well as you. I, myself, will back your plea if you wish it!"

"You intend no offense!" I echoed him unrelentingly, ignoring the latter part of his speech. "Then your actions fit your intentions very ill. Go read the signed charter that Florence gave me when she made me Captain-General, and tell me whether it is not plainly written there that I have the right to deal, myself, with the misdemeanors of my men! As for you, Messer Marco, you have no more to do with this fellow and his acts than with the King of England himself, and so I would tell your Gonfaloniere, he who stands for the Republic, if he sought to meddle in what touched me alone!"

For the second time, Ridolfi's jaw dropped; it was not his night to cut a brave figure, this.

"Why, it is true, Sir John," he muttered dazedly, after a somewhat lengthy pause which I made no effort to break. "You have the right, indeed! But you have never claimed it—it had fallen into abeyance. For my part, I vow I had forgotten it utterly."

"Well, it exists, for all that," I retorted, "and if I choose to claim it again, it is nobody's business but my own."

And then I wheeled upon Peter, who backed away from me as if minded to take shelter behind the *ecrivain*. If my bearing had been truculent before, it now became furious, though all the time, could they but have known it, I was shaking in my boots for fear that Salvi would descend upon us, see his prey slipping from him, and inform Ridolfi of the truth.

"I will deal with this affair myself, without the help of the Republic!" I stormed, with every appearance of rage. "It goes too far, this ruffling and dueling, this interference with peaceful citizens of the town that gives us our bread!" Salvi's man had, in the nature of things, probably been anything but peaceful, but this was no time to split straws. "A rare pass, when I cannot turn my back on Florence for a week without some such news as this to greet me on my return! I have ordered a thousand times that these brawls should end, and here we have the result! For a *scudo*, I would disband the entire Company, for I am near maddened by this set of graceless knaves with their plundering and stabbing and rioting!"

And so I thundered on, uttering whatever ideas came into my head, and all the time listening for the sound of Salvi's step. In the midst of my harangue, too, I came near losing all self-control and rocking with laughter at sight of Peter's face.

In his preoccupation over himself and his affairs, he had utterly forgotten the packet he carried, and believed me honestly enraged at his conduct; and since he knew me well, it was plain he would infinitely have preferred to take his chances with the easygoing Florentine Republic, which would not have been too hard on a soldier of the popular White Company. As for the *capitano*, he was in a state of helpless puzzle, and small wonder; for he must have been aware that I was not in the habit of troubling myself greatly over the vagaries of my men.

"Oh, take the fellow, Sir John, in the name of the saints!" he cried, raising his hands despairingly and no doubt feeling as if a tornado had been let loose in his hall of justice. "You are welcome to him, since it is your right."

"To be sure it is, and I will thank you to remember as much another time!" I snapped ungraciously. "Follow me, you!"

And, with Peter trailing meekly at my heels, I strode out of the room as hastily as I might.

III

If I had been inclined to flatter myself on having brought a perilous business to a successful ending, I was doomed to discover my mistake in short order. Peter and I passed unhindered down the stairs and out the gate. Then someone jostled against me in the darkness of the street and passed quickly on; and, looking back over my shoulder, I saw the lights at the Bargello entrance flare full across Salvi's eager face.

Here, indeed, was a pretty state of affairs! He had come to see whether the packet had been discovered, that went without the saying; he would find Peter vanished under my escort. In two minutes, the *capitano* would hear the truth, and in three the alarm would ring out and the street would be thronged with men. However, if I failed now, it should not be my fault.

"Quick, man the packet!" I muttered, seizing Peter's arm.

He stood there, staring stupidly at me, as I divined in spite of the darkness, for so long that it would have given me pleasure to shake him had there been more time at my disposal.

"Your pardon, Sir John?" he stammered.

"The packet!" I hissed again. "You fool, did you think I came here tonight for your sake? Little enough loss you would have been to me had the Republic hanged you, with your cursed stupidity in quarreling with Salvi's man and playing into his hands!"

He understood at last.

"Oh, aye, the packet! An instant, Sir John!" he cried, with, by all the saints, relief in his tone!

In that moment, it was plain, he cared nothing for the honor of England, or for anything else on earth save the one fact that my rage at him had been pretense. With an awkward slowness that made me frantic, he unearthed the cause of all the mischief, and I thrust it into my doublet, breathing a sigh of content as I felt the heavy seal beneath my fingers. At that very instant, I heard a great uproar within the Bargello, many shouting voices, the sound of running feet. Salvi had done his work well.

Once more, I seized Peter's arm.

"Run!" I muttered. "Run as though the devil himself were at your heels! Let them hear you run, too. Lead them a chase over the whole city, and in the end, let them take you and find that you carry nothing! But take heed that they pursue you long enough to let me reach my villa in safety, for if I do not—"

I had no time to finish the threat. Already, the men were at the gate of the Bargello. On the left-side of the street, close at my elbow, was a dark stone gateway, and I slipped through it and flattened myself against the wall within while Peter, entering into his part with a zest I had scarce expected of him, gave a loud terrified cry and clattered off in so uproarious a flight that the deafest of pursuers could not have failed to mark it.

A score of men had dashed out now, bearing torches and weapons, and on marking Peter's departure, they gave utterance to a view-halloo and swept on his track, passing within five feet of where I lay in my hiding place.

So far, so good. I crouched motionless, hearing the sounds of the pursuit grow fainter and fainter, the tread of running feet die on the stones. Complacently, I assured myself that I need feel no further alarm, for Peter was an excellent runner and quite at home in the winding byways of Florence, and would certainly baffle those at his heels for a good half-hour. Meanwhile, I had best get back to my villa. I crept forward cautiously, feeling the wall as I advanced; then suddenly tripped over a loose stone and measured my length on the pavement in a fashion noisy enough to wake the dead.

On the instant, a loud triumphant shout rang out from the Bargello gate, followed closely, as I scrambled to my feet, by a sound that I can truthfully say was less welcome to me than ever sound was before—the noise of hurrying men. Some guard had, it was evident, imagined from the commotion I had made that Peter had eluded pursuit and was lurking in the neighborhood.

Within the moment, they would be upon me—and for John Hawkwood, Captain-General of Florence, to be taken with the treacherous packet on his person would be worse a thousand times than its discovery on my soldier. All things considered, then, I had no choice but to adopt a course which those who know me will bear witness was not my usual mode of meeting difficulties—to take to my heels even as Peter had done. Without a second's hesitation, I sprang from beneath my sheltering gateway and dashed off down the street.

The shout that rang out behind me was ample proof that I had not got away unobserved. After me swept my pursuers, in frantic haste. Truth to tell, the predicament was a desperate one, for I had the briefest of starts; yet, unreasonably enough, my spirits were already rising, for I was more in my element with a score of men after me than lurking perdue in a dark gateway. Let them not exult too soon, these urgent gentlemen, for they did not yet know who it was they followed, and I would lead them a rare chase before surrendering myself and what I carried with me!

I had been, of course, in the Via del Proconsolo when the alarm rang out. Down it I dashed at full speed. Heaven be praised, I was an excellent runner, and fairly safe unless I should find my way blocked by some peasant's cart, or unless my pursuers should head me off by a detour, contingencies upon which, on the whole, I preferred not to dwell.

The entire neighborhood was by now awaking to the fact that something unusual was afoot. Windows were thrown open and heads thrust out; but as Florentines are for the most part prudent folk, with a marked distaste for meddling with what does not nearly touch them, the good citizens made no attempt to stay my flight.

A late moon was rising, faintly lighting the Via del Proconsolo, which is long and broad, and as good a race-course as man could ask. I flattered myself that, as I sped down it, I gained a little. More than once I encountered a wayfarer, and twice I found myself confronted by a small group; but to my fervent relief, they gave back hastily to the side of the street, thus earning themselves, I fancy, heartfelt curses from the *capitano*'s men. So, unchallenged, I sped the entire length of the road, and dashed into the great Piazza del Duomo.

It is a beautiful sight, that cathedral, with its gleaming colored marbles and the strangely sculptured tower of Giotto's building; but if you think I gave it a glance now, you are much mistaken. How was I to give the slip to the knaves at my heels? The question beat itself unceasingly in my ears. Perhaps the best of all my chances was to slip into one of the many streets converging into the Piazza, and so leave them with a lost scent; at any rate, the idea was worth a trial.

Racing across the moonlit space, and running on the balls of my feet lest the noise I made should betray me, I sprang into the Corso degli Adimari, and to my dismay found myself face to face with a fat, comfortable-looking man in a rich mantle, evidently a well-to-do merchant, followed by a servant with a lantern. There was nothing to do save dive on past him, and this I did, praying that he had not recognized me and would refrain from putting my pursuers on my track. The first of my prayers was granted, the second ignored.

As I fled on down the street I could hear him crying in a quavering, excited voice to the *capitano*'s men, who had presumably halted in the Piazza to listen for sounds that might reveal to them where I had vanished.

"Yonder, messers! Down the Corso! He went that way, the man you seek!"

Well, I had no breath to waste in comment, but mentally I bestowed something other than a benediction on him as I heard the pursuit sweep after me once more. Also, though my danger was increasing every moment, I set my teeth and vowed to baffle these bloodhounds yet.

At present I was rushing down a street lined with the great houses of Florentine nobles, and the men-at-arms of these gentry were, alas, proving themselves a good deal more disposed to join the fray than others had been hitherto, as I gathered from the fact that my pursuers were growing continually in numbers. Reassuring myself with the thought that so long as they kept behind me and not before me, there remained hope, I dashed into the narrow Via dei Pittori, passed the stone pile of Or San Michele with its rounded arches, and emerged into the Piazza della Signoria as if I had wings to my feet.

The most perilous part of my adventure was now close upon me, for how could I hope to pass through this great square, blocked solidly with palaces, and neither be recognized nor halted? The bare thought was madness! Yet I darted across at full speed, running close against the Loggia dei Lanzi to avoid, as far as I could, the flickering torches that shone before the Palazzo Vecchio.

A group barred my way. I hurtled through it, sending two men to earth. An alarm rang out, a throng of guards poured from three gates at once, a hundred voices beat in my ears, calling on me to halt. But already, the saints be praised, I was out of the Piazza and in the comparative darkness and security of the Via dei Gondi.

Well, I asked myself as I ran, how much longer was this to continue? I was neither losing nor gaining; so far as I could see, the chase might well endure till dawn and find us still circling about the city. Indeed, unless I altered my course in short order, I would soon find myself passing again between the Bargello and the abbey of the Badia, at the very spot where I had begun my flight. For the life of me I could not but perceive the humor of the situation: that I, Captain-General of Florence, and entitled by virtue of my position to command every man-at-arms in the city, should be fleeing from these fellows like a hare with a pack of dogs in full cry.

Unfortunately, I must confess that I saw a much less diverting side of the matter. It had been many a long day since I had indulged in a run like this, and my breath was coming unpleasantly hard. Wondering what would happen when it failed me altogether, I dashed into the Piazza Sant' Appollinare, and on the instant became aware of something that turned me cold in every limb.

From before me, as well as behind me, came the sound of voices and the clatter of feet! Instantly I understood. The men of the city watch, whom I had hitherto escaped meeting by some miraculous dispensation from above, were approaching from the other direction, and not in any leisurely fashion, either, for they had guessed from the uproar that some fray was afoot, and had promptly experienced a very creditable desire to join in it.

A few instants more, and the Piazza would be seething with men, and I should be taken red-handed. The tumult grew; the *capitano*'s rogues, awaking to the situation, uttered ear-splitting yells of triumph, which found a prompt echo from before me. For a brief moment I halted, panting, my wits working as they had never worked yet.

The voices grew louder still, the light of the advancing torches began to glow faintly in the square, and I wheeled, sprang across to the Church of Sant' Appollinare, and, letting myself through the door, drew it noiselessly shut behind me.

I had followed a desperate impulse, an inspiration, a what you will; and I was perfectly aware that I might find myself a good deal worse off than formerly, if, for example, some penitent chanced to be spending the night at prayer before the altar. However, to my huge relief, the place was empty. I caught a dim vista of sculpted columns, niched saints, frescoed angels gleaming in the dim light of the burning candles; then I stole down the north aisle, slipped into the darkest and smallest of the chapels, and flung myself flat on the floor.

I was panting desperately, and so spent that I thought my pursuers likely, if successful, to find a dead man instead of a live one. Ah well, the game was out of my hands now. I had, so to speak, taken sanctuary. Let the saints lift the rest of the business to their own shoulders, and aid or doom me as they chose.

The Piazza without was now in such a state of tumult that one might have thought the Duke of Milan, the great enemy of Florence, at the city walls. Feet ran desperately hither and thither, fifty voices cried out at once, and on my couch of cold stone I chuckled under my breath as I heard the watch and the *capitano*'s men each accusing the other of having let the quarry slip through their fingers. But my content was fated to be short-lived.

"Come, stir yourselves a bit! All is not lost yet. Who knows but the fellow, whoever he may be, is in one of these houses?" cried the leader of the *capitano*'s force, who would have conceived this clever idea a good deal sooner if he had been a soldier worth his salt.

Instantly there was great confusion; some cried out that they had better search the houses of the Magalotti, which bordered an entire side of the square; others were for invading the doors of Messer Mancini. The servants of these families, as nearly as I could gather from the babel, denied that anyone had entered their gates, and vigorously opposed the invasion, thus causing something like a riot.

At this point, a voice proclaimed over the tumult—one of Mancini's lackeys it was, I fancy, lying to divert the commotion from his master's dwelling—that perhaps the man they sought was in the church; and an instant later, the door of Sant' Appollinare was thrown violently open.

I lay very still, holding my breath. Surely all hope was now gone; and I kept one hand in my breast, clasped about the packet, and the other on my sword; for if the worst came to the worst, I did not mean to leave the church alive.

To my great bewilderment, however, nothing happened. The invaders roamed about a little, making their investigations only near the entrance, and then:

"Oh, let us be gone! You can see for yourselves there is nobody here!" one cried pettishly, quite as if he had expected a desperate fugitive to place himself before the high altar, where he could not fail to be seen.

"To be sure," another sapient member of the party commented, very out of temper. "What man of sense would hide himself in a building sure to be searched? And he is no fool, this rogue, to judge from the chase he has led us!"

Whereupon they went out cursing, and I heard them informing their leader that they had searched the church from end to end, and that there was no one to be found.

"A plague take it!" snapped the *capitano*'s officer. "Where is he, then? For my part, I believe he turned down the Via del Leone just before we entered the Piazza. Indeed, I fancied I saw a form glide that way!" And no doubt he had fancied so; one can imagine anything, and this is especially true in the case of such an imbecile as he was rapidly proving himself.

The suggestion was greeted with acclaim, since all were now weary of the fruitless hunt about the Piazza. To my unbelieving delight, for I vow I would scarce have credited such a happening if foretold to me by one of the saints in person, there was a concerted move toward the Via del Leone. And best of all, with a stupidity quite in keeping with their conduct throughout the whole affair, they refrained from even leaving a small guard to watch the Piazza while they were gone.

For some time I lay at ease on the chapel pavement, listening to the sound of departing feet and voices, chuckling rapturously at my own thoughts. Then, convinced that the square was at peace again, I stole down the aisle and slipped out into the night, and with the leisurely assurance of one respected by the whole Republic, took my way toward my distant villa.

IV

When I at last reached home after a most peaceable transit of Florence, I found the Dean of St. Martin's sitting much as I had left him, with his arms on the table and his head bent over them, and Lady Hawkwood facing him from her seat with perfect calm, though she was pale and her hands were tightly clenched in her lap. As I appeared, she did not speak or stir, but her look met mine in anxious questioning, and my nod had reassured her even before the Dean awoke to the fact of my entrance and leaped wildly to his feet.

"What news, Sir John? Tell me in a word! I can bear this no longer—I am well-nigh mad!" he stammered, his eyes on the point of popping from his head. "Each instant of your absence was a torment to me! Where have you been, then?"

"Where have I not been?" said I, with a last chuckle at thought of my adventures. "But come, man, pluck up heart and rub a bit of color into your cheeks! Here is something that will cheer you," and I thrust my hand into my doublet and pulled out the famous packet, a small, unimposing thing enough, save for the blazoning of its great gold seal!

Walter Skirlawe fell back with a choked cry of relief.

"Sir John, Sir John, I believe there is no miracle you could not work," he babbled, "and I will remember you in my prayers to the end of time!"

"It will be more to the purpose if you refrain from providing any more such miracles for my working," I responded without gratitude, "for you have given me a busier evening than I fancy. And now I think I have earned a peep at this document, even though it was not intended for my eyes."

Being fully occupied in offering up thanks for his deliverance, he made no objection, and I ripped the packet open with my dagger and glanced hastily over the contents, breathing a sigh of relief as I read the last line and noted that the secret treaty with Milan was definitely broken off.

"A good end to all this double-dealing!" I muttered, as I held the parchment to the flame of the candle and watched it crackle and burn to the very edge.

And at that instant, as though we were all acting in a play and the final scene had been reserved for a dramatic moment, one of my lackeys hastened into the room and announced the arrival of three distinguished visitors.

"My lord the Gonfaloniere, Sir John—Messer Salvi of the Signoria—the Capitano di Giustizia. They desire to see you at once on a matter of great urgency. Is it your wish that I should bring them here?"

The Dean of St. Martin's leaped to his feet with a piercing shriek.

"We are lost!" he moaned like a man in the last extremity of torment. "They have come, Sir John! Do you hear, they have come!"

"Let them!" said I, thrusting the ashes of the parchment beneath a dish of fruit. "Little enough I care for their coming now!" Then, catching sight of his face, I added hastily, "But in Heaven's name, do you go through that door and wait within! One look at you would suffice to prove us guilty though angels spoke in our defense! As for you, Giovanni, tell my guests that I beg them to join me here."

As Skirlawe stumbled out of sight and the lackey departed, I turned to Lady Hawkwood; but she shook her head.

"Let me stay. Indeed, I must be with you now," she whispered, and I had but time to nod and cast myself into a seat with every appearance of having lounged there an hour when Giovanni ushered in a *cortège* consisting of the Gonfaloniere of Florence, red-faced and ill at ease and plainly very unhappy over his errand; the good *capitano*, no less embarrassed; and, lastly, Messer Adriano Salvi, glowering at me in anything but friendly fashion.

"Your pardon, Sir John, that we intrude on you and your lady," the Gonfaloniere stammered as he saluted us. He was my good friend, and had come, I was sure, much against his will. "We are here to ask you concerning a matter that is doubtless most simple when explained. Never think, Sir John, we could doubt you after all your services—"

I had risen and was confronting them across the table.

"I am a soldier, my lord, and plain dealing pleases me best," I said grimly. "You have come to accuse me of something. Your manner and Messer Salvi's presence are ample warrant of that. Well, let me hear the latest accusation this foe of mine!"

"Nay, Sir John, nay," protested the Gonfaloniere eagerly, "I swear on my soul I trust you as I trust myself! But since you urge frankness on me, Messer Salvi, here, is so far deceived as to suspect you of intriguing with Milan to our hurt!"

For a moment I stared incredulously at the three men. Then I made them a stern salutation.

"Very good, *signori*," I responded. "In return for my years of service, the battles I have won for Florence, the blood that I have shed that she might know safety, you impute treason to me—the first time, believe me, that such an accusation has fallen on my ears. It is plain that you desire me no more for Captain-General of the Republic. So be it. Tomorrow, I leave your city!"

The Gonfaloniere and the *capitano* started back, no doubt with visions of all Italy thundering at their unprotected gates; and one glance at their horrified faces must have killed Salvi's last hope.

"Sir John! Sir John!" cried the wretched Gonfaloniere. "Such a thought had never passed through my mind. For my part, I would never have come here but for Messer Salvi—"

Looking straight into his eyes, I spoke the plain truth for once that night, and glad enough I was to do it, for, after all, the Florentines were my friends and I would have died sooner than betray their trust.

"My lord," said I, "because of our long alliance, I will be patient. I swear on my honor that never have I dealt with Visconti save sword in hand; and, moreover, I swear that my lord the King of England intends no treaty with Milan and will keep full faith with Florence."

From my good friend, the Gonfaloniere, came an audible sigh of relief, which found prompt echo from the Capitano di Giustizia.

"No need of a word more, Sir John," the former cried with great heartiness. "Why, see you, as we came here I pointed out to Messer Salvi that he was mad to think this English soldier of yours bore a packet from Visconti. For though the *capitano*'s men caught him after chasing him like a hare over half the city—after chasing two rogues, indeed, since it appears one party followed on a false scent and pursued some knave who led them a race for own diversion and gave them the slip at last—when they came to search him, not the ghost of a packet could they find!"

For a moment I stared at him. Then I burst into a shout of laughter that was at great pains to make hearty.

"Now by my golden spurs," I cried, "here is the rarest pother nothing that ever I saw! To be sure, the fellow had a packet; and when I parted with him by the Bargello, after bidding him come settle with tomorrow for this brawl of his, I took the dispatch from him and strolled home most peaceably with it beneath my arm. Had you come to me, instead of chasing Peter all over Florence and filling his head with notions of his own importance, I would have set your minds at rest with a glimpse at this deadly parchment that has kept all Florence awake. Come, read it now, though it will make you look a bit foolish to see for what cause you have lost your sleep!"

So saying, I strode over to a cabinet by the wall, and took from it a packet so like the cause of all the tumult that, had the Dean of St. Martin's been among the company, he would have fainted for sheer terror. But it was, in truth, a harmless document enough, sent me a month earlier by the King and his ministers, and agreeing with apparent heartiness to my treaty with Florence against Milan.

"Read it, see how I plot against you and sell you to your foes!" I jeered as I flung it across the table.

The Gonfaloniere perused it eagerly, Messer Marco and old Salvi in a way that struck me as somewhat informal, reading it one across each of his shoulders; then he came forward and seized both my hands.

"Forgive us, Sir John," he muttered; and I swear there were tears in his eyes. "You are, as always, our best friend!"

"It is not from you I want excuses," I answered meaningly, as, swinging about, I fixed a narrowed gaze on my foe. "It is Messer Salvi, here, I understand, who brought this charge against me. I await what he has to say."

We faced each other for an instant, the old rogue battling with his rage and disappointment. He was clever enough to guess the truth of the matter, but then, what proof had he? With a final effort, he mastered himself and yielded. "I have been at fault, Sir John, through my zeal for Florence," he told me suavely, "and I crave forgiveness most humbly for a mistake which shall not be made again."

His meaning was, I took it, that he would not a second time accuse me till he knew beyond question that he could get the better of me. However, I gave him a curt nod.

"Then let the matter end here," I said. "And now, *signori*, though at another time I will gladly entertain you at my house, this is my homecoming, and I have a fancy to celebrate it alone."

With a renewed murmur of apologies, they took themselves out of the room like children glad to escape a master. The door closed behind them. Lady Hawkwood and I looked at each other and laughed. Then, hand in hand, and quite forgetful of the fact that the Dean of St. Martin's was waiting in an agony to learn the issue of the affair, we turned together toward the door that led out into our moonlit garden.

SCOURGE OF THE MAIN

JAMES PERLEY HUGHES

A nd so you slit the throat of an inoffensive man, just for the fun of it?"
The words were spoken by a young man, whose straight, regular features made him appear almost godlike in that gathering of grotesque characters. His blue eyes were frank and fearless, while his blond hair fell around his collar in careless waves. Only his extraordinary height, Atlantean shoulders and powerful forearm dissipated the impression of frailty a careless glance might give. He had been seen only recently in St. George's town and evidently was a stranger to the Bermudas. Men wondered at his calling, for he had appeared suddenly one afternoon a day or so before, and since then he had been seen frequently about the White Horse Inn.

"And so you murdered a man just for fun?" his level voice questioned.

The sounds of merriment, still rolling through the Inn, stopped as he spoke a second time. Startled eyes flashed toward the speaker and then to Jolly Roger Hawkins, known to his kind as the "Scourge of the Spanish Main." On the other side of Castle Harbor, his ships lay careened in shallow water, which would be pink coral sand when the tide went out. His ship, the *Black Hawk*, had refitted and was ready to take to sea.

Men seated between the two enemies swiftly shoved back their chairs or leaped out of the line of possible pistol fire.

A tenseness gripped that gathering and breaths were held back in that moment of high suspense. The ponderous bulk of Jolly Roger Hawkins heaved up from the chair in which he had sprawled and looked across to where the young man sat, leaning slightly forward as his eye was held upon the face of the killer.

"Ah, we have a gentleman in our midst, a dandy with his hair in a curl," scoffed Hawkins, his voice bellowing through the smoke-filled room, "and he wants to know if I slit the throat of a croaking coward because I thought it funny."

"Yes, did you?"

A grimace crossed the distorted features of Jolly Roger Hawkins and his hand descended to his cutlass.

"And may I ask your distinguished name, before I slit yours?" he asked with mock courtesy.

"Daniel Tucker of Plymouth," was the level response, "and you are going to slit my throat, too?"

"Damn you, yes!"

There was a flash as Hawkins drew his blade, its curved length glittering in the taproom candlelight.

The sharp ring of steel on steel and the swiftly descending blade of the pirate chief was deflected from its course to strike sparks from the flag-paved floor.

A bellow of surprised rage came from Hawkins' hairy throat.

Daniel Tucker slipped from his chair with a sinuous grace that gave small hint of his towering size. As the cutlass of the pirate swept down with a force which would have beaten down most guards, the young man's blade turned the other from its course.

From a near-by table, the pirate chief snatched up a heavy sea-coat and, with a twist, wrapped it about his left arm. Holding this up as a shield, he advanced toward Tucker, his cutlass jabbing awkwardly as he attempted to fence. A quiet smile came to the young man's sober face at this change of tactics. Plainly the pirate knew little of the art of swordsmanship and would depend upon strength rather than skill in the combat to come.

The blade of the pirate chief was flashing down, as he lunged and jabbed with frenzied speed. Although Daniel Tucker continued to hold his ground, he made no attempt to counter-attack, playing with a cool skill which defied his opponent.

"Why don't you spit him, Dan?" a voice called out.

"I'm saving him for the gallows," Tucker called back.

Men whirled around to see who had asked that question, but quickly turned back to watch the combat.

"Gallows, eh!" sneered Jolly Roger Hawkins. "Well, if gallows fruit I am, I'll play the gallows bird. Try this and see if you can save me for the hangman."

The coat-swathed arm dropped to one of the tables and snatched up a pannikin of rum. With a flip, Hawkins sent its contents spraying into Daniel Tucker's face. For an instant the young man was half-blinded and his arm went up to wipe the burning liquor from his eyes.

"Don't—don't—"

Jolly Roger Hawkins' blade was held aloft. He had poised on his toes, ready to cleave the man before him, as a butcher rends the carcass of an ox. The cutlass hesitated as a woman's cry rang through the deathly stillness. At the farther end of the room, peering through a door that was raised from the floor by several steps, was a girl with fear-distended eyes.

"I don't want you to murder him," the girl called, her arms reaching out in supplication. "You say you love me—then do not kill him," she finished with a sob.

The tingling quiet of the room held for an instant. Then a buzz went through the rough assemblage. Phyllis Lightbourn was begging for the life of the blond newcomer. Jolly Roger had claimed her with many a bawling curse and had sworn by the blade he held uplifted that he would cleave the man who dared to hold his eye upon her. Now she was praying for the life of a stranger, who had picked a quarrel with the Scourge of the Main.

"Save your tears, wench," the pirate boomed, "for I shall quarter him."

But as the blade came down, the brawny forearm again felt the sharp sting of an up-driven point and, for an instant, Tucker's cutlass was seen on either side of the dark, hairy flesh of Jolly Roger. A booming oath and Hawkins' weapon rattled to the stone floor. Then his left hand flashed to his waist to snatch a pistol from the colorful sash that girded him.

"Now, damn you!"

Once more the pirate's words ended with the ring of steel. Dan Tucker's point was jerked from the forearm of his foe and flecked away to strike the weapon from the other hand. A murmur of admiration swept the room, although Jolly Roger was their chief.

"A pistol, quick, you dogs, a pistol!"

The baffled giant was raging now, his unwounded hand reaching out to grasp any weapon with which he might kill this smiling enemy. The taproom of the White Horse was in turmoil. As long as the men of the *Black Hawk*'s crew were sure their captain would make short work of this blond-haired stranger, they held back, gazing with cruel smiles at the attack they were sure would end in the young man's slaughter. Now their chieftain's life was in peril and their blades sprang out to strike down the man who had Jolly Roger at his mercy.

"Look out, they're coming!" the scream of the girl stabbed through the room.

They were lunging at the stranger now, their blades vying in an effort to be the first to wet this young upstart's blood. A shot rang out. Then another, but the bullets went wild. The smoke of the heavily loaded pistols made sight almost impossible in that low-ceilinged room, but even in the dim light, Phyllis Lightbourn could see the play of Tucker's blade as he held the pirates back.

He was fighting desperately, staying a dozen attacks .at the same time. Men sank down and writhed upon the floor or dragged their wounded bodies beneath the taproom tables. In the ring of men around him, Tucker saw Jolly Roger leveling a fresh pistol. A heavy chair was hurled in time to strike the weapon down.

Closer drew the ring of slashing blades as the young man retreated toward the door. The voice of the girl, now untouched with terror, directed his feet as he held the pirates off.

"Get out of the way, you curs, if one dancing master is a match for all of you."

With a cutlass in his left hand and a fresh pistol in the right, Jolly Roger Hawkins crashed through the ring of flashing weapons. He was face to face with Tucker now. Behind was the girl, the girl he had claimed as his, in spite of her shrinking in his presence.

"Now, my sweet princeling," the pirate roared, "we shall see who is to be favored by this fair wench, who has rather taken my well-fed fancy. If you live the next two minutes, I shall forget my suit and seek other, redder lips, but—"

The alternative was never spoken. Dan Tucker's swirling blade launched out and the pistol flew across the room. Then—instead of using the keen edge, he dealt a blow on Hawkins' wrist that numbed the left arm to the shoulder.

A roar rose from the men behind the buccaneer, but as they lunged once more with circling blades, the young man dashed up to where Phyllis Lightbourn waited. A crash of a heavy oaken door and then—

"A hundred golden doubloons to the man who brings me the head of that dancing dandy," bellowed the Scourge of the Spanish Main.

Daniel Tucker dodged out the rear door of the White Horse. A whispered warning from Phyllis Lightbourn and he hurried down to the rocky edge of the channel leading to St. George's town. A low whistle and a similar note answered him. Then he disappeared into the shadows and entered a long boat drawn up beneath the overhanging foliage of a giant screw palm. A low command and the rhythmic beat of oars sounded faintly across the water.

From the stone-flagged courtyard of the White Horse came the sound of bellowed curses. Bawling commands rang out as Jolly Roger Hawkins scourged his men to race through the narrow the narrow, winding streets in search of Daniel Tucker. But the shouts died as the long boat veered toward St. David's Isle and were heard no more. An hour of steady pulling and Daniel Tucker glimpsed the wide-spread yards of a trim sailing craft, swinging with the tide. His hand threw the tiller over and they alongside.

In another moment he was scrambling over the bulwarks, to descend a narrow hatchway and knock respectfully upon the door of the master's cabin.

"I've been waiting for an hour!" a bulllike voice bellowed within.

Daniel Tucker opened the door and stepped inside. Arthur Rawlins, commander of the *Air Sprite*, sat before a sea desk upon which a chart was spread. He held dividers in his hand and was evidently plotting a course.

"Hawkins and his crew are in St. George's, sir," the young man began. "They have refitted and are ready to sail at dawn. They are going south and expect to raise the *Alma de Dios* and *Corinto* between here and Nassau."

"*Alma de Dios—Corinto!*" the heavy white brows of the captain were knotted.

"It is evident they have not heard about the war," Tucker added.

A smile crossed the fierce face of the command. England and Spain were at grips once more, but the news had not reached the far-away Bermudas.

"Did they recognize you?"

"I told Hawkins my name, sir. He wanted to know whose throat he was going to slit."

A fierce smile crossed his face and then the keen gray eyes of the master were held upon his mate.

"You didn't kill him, did you?"

"No, sir. You said you wanted to hang him. I told him I was saving him for a yardarm, but did not mention whose."

"All right, all right. Pass the word to pipe to quarters. We'll weigh the hook when the tide turns," and the skipper returned to the chart spread out beneath the rays of a gimballed sea lamp.

A few minutes later the crew of the *Air Sprite* was assembled on the quarterdeck and Captain Arthur Rawlins addressed them from the ladder leading to the poop.

Short, but direct, was the skipper's speech, but his words were received with cheers. Although a man of more than sixty years, one arm cut off between elbow and shoulder, halting in gait, he had all the fierceness of headstrong youth. The *Air Sprite* was to sail for Nassau, hoping to intercept the Spaniard ships, *Alma de Dios* and *Corinto*, on their way north. A fight would follow.

"Each bears gold from Mexico and Peru," the captain told them, "and those who live will have enough for many a lusty measure of rum and nights ashore in Nassau. Share and share—"

Arthur Rawlins stopped as the measured sounds of oars greeted his sea-trained ears. Then a voice, bawling through the darkness, demanded the name of the ship and her business.

"Who seeks to know?" the master of the *Air Sprite* demanded.

"Jolly Roger Hawkins, who the Devil loves," was the reply.

"Bear off, Jolly Roger, or you'll break your fast with your friend in Hell," Rawlins bellowed in return. "I'm keeping a length of Manila hemp with which to swing your worthless weight."

"So, 'tis you that dancing master is spying for," the pirate chief replied. "That is good news, for I'll walk you both from off my plank before this cruise is done."

A laugh, high and shrill, came to the old captain's lips. Then he fired his pistol in the direction from which came the voice of Jolly Roger. There was an answering burst of musketry from a long boat. Then they heard the clink of oars, dying gradually away.

Orders rang out from the *Air Sprite*'s high poop which sent the crew marching around the creaking capstan. Soon the hook came splashing from the sandy bottom and a puff of wind bellied a flapping foresail as the ship swung around.

"Daniel Tucker—" it was a woman's voice.

"What the devil?" Captain Rawlins charged up the hatchway from his cabin.

"Daniel Tucker."

"Ah! Some wench you are leaving behind in St. George's town and now—"

He leaned over the bulwark and shouted into the darkness.

"Boat ahoy!"

"Daniel Tucker, I must see him," it was the voice of Phyllis Lightbourn. "I have important news."

A ship's lantern was put over the side and by its dim rays Tucker could see Phyllis in the stern of a dinghy, a black man at the oars. She had rowed out from St. George's, evading Jolly Roger and his long-boat crew.

A Jacob's ladder was let down and the girl lightly mounted.

"Jolly Roger and his crew have seized the *New Venture*, a faster ship than their *Black Hawk*. They are sailing at dawn and—" She was excited.

"Sailing where?" the captain growled.

"To take the *Alma de Dios* and *Corinto*," she answered breathlessly. "They knew you are after her."

"Over the side, my lass. We have no time to lose," shouted the master. "If Jolly Roger is to race us for the prize, we cannot delay."

"But my boat—it is gone," the girl wailed. "The slave who rowed me out left for Cooper's Island when I came aboard. I cannot go back, for Jolly Roger made my father promise—"

"Keep quiet, hussy. Is this a trick to sail away with my young sprig of a mate?"

"No, sir."

"I have no time to send a boat with you. Neither am I one to make a maid walk the plank when her presence is an annoyance. Get to the galley and brew some tea and tell that greasy swine, the cook, to stand his watch with the other men."

As Phyllis Lightbourn scurried forward, the ringing commands of the master sent the men to the ropes and once mere the *Air Sprite* was slipping through the water, southward bound, racing with Jolly Roger, the Scourge of the Spanish Main, for the rich prizes awaiting them.

Rawlins knew that Hawkins would probably slip through the Reach and thus regain the time the *Air Sprite*'s earlier sailing gave. It would be a contest to see which would first raise the Spanish treasure ships and after that—a fight to keep what the victor won.

Scudding through the seas whose blue deepened as the *Air Sprite* swept on, Captain Rawlins held a course that he was sure would raise the Spanish treasure ships. Hardly had they cleared the reefs south of Sandy's treacherous shoals than the top lookout called a warning of pursuit. Daniel Tucker scrambled aloft to level his glass upon the craft following them. Instead of a single vessel, two of them danced across the waves, each bearing every inch of canvas they could stretch. By the course they were holding, they would be able to hang on or overtake the *Air Sprite*, depending on the speed developed in the brisk northwester before which they were running.

Daniel Tucker recognized the ships. The leader was the *New Venture*, a fast, modern craft, able to give the *Air Sprite* a bitter contest in a race which might last for days. Hawkins had evidently sighted Rawlins and he crowded on staysails, his lee rail half as his ship boiled through the water. After him came the *Black Hawk*, the craft in which he had won his dark fame. Slower than the *Venture*, it was falling behind. Morning would see her over the horizon, if the speed of the day were continued through the night.

"Perhaps it would be better, captain, if we stood at sunrise tomorrow and fought it out," the young man suggested to his chief, when he reported his observations.

"I would, only we might get crippled, and then—" The smoldering light in the old man's eyes blazed up. "Daniel, my boy, you're a lad after my own heart. I don't blame that buxom wench in the galley for following you."

"She's not a wench, sir. Her father was a gentleman until he fell in with Jolly Roger."

"A lady aboard this packet, then!" A shrill cackle came from the skipper's crooked lips. "I did not realize our honor."

With the dawn of the second day, Captain Rawlins began to realize that the *New Venture* would overtake him if the breeze continued to freshen. The *Black Hawk* had dropped behind, but Hawkins' recently captured craft was sailing like a yacht. The *Sprite*, however, was too heavy in the bow to stand further crowding.

Through a long day the two craft raced, the *New Venture* gaining even mere rapidly as the breeze strengthened. New canvas was added to her straining sticks as the afternoon drew on. With the sun nearing the western horizon, Captain Rawlins took his position on the poop. Although he had hesitated to give the pirate battle, it was not fear that stayed his hand. He had fought Jolly Roger before, but no combat had been decisive. Nothing would so please his Spartan soul as to bang Hawkins from his yardarm, but the rich prize of Spanish treasure might be lost if fortune favored the buccaneer.

"Your friend will catch us about sundown," the captain called to Tucker.

"Yes, sir. I'm having the guns swabbed out and double-shotted with grape, sir."

"Without my order!" A scowl replaced the skipper's smile.

"I knew you would give that command when you gauged their speed."

"Then perhaps you'll tell me my next order, young upstart."

The blue eyes of the young man were held upon the fierce face of his commander. He had never quailed before Arthur Rawlins, although mightier men than he had shivered in his presence.

"Yes, sir," Tucker answered. "You would put men in the tops with well-heated tar and pitch. Then, when the *New Venture* comes within cannon shot, you would furl the main and come around with the fore staysail. A broadside fore and aft and then, instead of boarding, sir, you'd order the hot tar and pitch thrown on her decks and canvas and after that a flaming torch."

A rumbling oath as a new light appeared in the skipper's shadowed eyes.

"And then what am I going to do, young know-it-all?" he asked.

"Spread every rag we have, sir, and leave the boarding for another day. Jolly Roger's neck will keep, but the Spaniards may escape while we are fighting."

Captain Rawlins shouted commands that officially confirmed the orders Daniel Tucker had already given. As the *New Venture* drew closer, the old chieftain continued to hold appraising eyes upon his second in command.

"He'll make a man yet," muttered Arthur Rawlins.

The sun was pitching downward toward its evening course as the *New Venture* drew in. On the poop, Captain Rawlins continued to gauge the speed of the enemy but he had given Daniel Tucker orders that caused the young man to buzz with activity from one end of the *Air Sprite* to the other. The brazen throats of the long-necked cannon were filled with freshly broached powder and double-shotted. Cauldrons of pitch and tar were heating on the galley fires and in the forecastle.

As Daniel Tucker quickly leveled his glass on the *Venture*, he noted a new activity aboard the pirate craft. Jolly Roger Hawkins was bellowing orders; the young man could tell by the manner in which the man cupped his hands.

What had caused this?

The answer came, almost before his mind had formed the question.

The pirate had seen Phyllis Lightbourn come from the galley and now and now knew the girl was aboard the *Air Sprite*. Now the attack would be marked by new savagery. For a time Jolly Roger would forget the treasure of gold-bearing galleons and would seek to destroy the *Sprite* and capture this new prize.

Nearer, still nearer, drew the approaching *Venture*. Then a puff of smoke shot from the forward gun. The scream of a solid shot filled the air as it whizzed ahead of the *Air Sprite*'s bow. The battle had begun.

A flash, then a roar came from the second *Venture* gun. Captain Rawlins shouted a series of sharp, quick commands. Men scrambled aloft to the tops and then let down bos'n's seats into which cauldrons of heated pitch and tar were placed. Eager hands hoisted them aloft. At the same time other members of the crew hastened to take in sail.

A yell towards the helmsman and spokes spun madly. Heeling over, the *Air Sprite* turned to starboard, directly in front of the onrushing *Venture*. A yell rose, as Hawkins' men cut ropes and braces to stay the onward course. For an instant, it seemed as though the buccaneer's spit would be thrust into the master's cabin beneath the towering poop.

"Fire!" yelled Tucker.

But as the gunners applied their torches, the *Sprite* heeled from the grazing blow the *Venture* had struck. Those double shots of grape, which would have caused such havoc on the pirate's deck, were hurled impotently into the air. No time to load again. Daniel Tucker snatched up his speaking trumpet and bellowed to the men in the tops.

"Now!" he yelled again fiercely.

A coal-black shower poured down upon the deck and canvas of the *New Venture*.

"The torch!" Dan shouted.

Boiling oaths from above. The fire they had carried aloft had gone out. Until a flame was thrown upon the tarred decks and rigging all of Tucker's strategy would be vain. He could see the buccaneers were forming to board. In another moment their grappling irons would crash down.

"The fire—the fire, you yellow-livered dogs," bellowed the voice of Captain Arthur Rawlins.

Another indistinct reply from the men in the tops. They were trying frantically to start another blaze, but the wind whistling through the upper rigging made their efforts futile.

From the foremast of the *Venture* the grappling irons came clanging down.

Daniel Tucker caught a glimpse of Jolly Roger leading his men in the assault, as they poured over the low bulwarks at the waist.

"Come on, men! Drive them back or throw them into the deep," the young man shouted. "Remember the law of the sea and land is with us."

"Law!" yelled Roger Hawkins, as he heard these words, "what right have you to that?"

His cutlass pointed at the *Air Sprite*'s ensign.

"That you shall know when you stretch my fine Manila rope," barked the voice of the master.

Pikes, cutlasses and pistols, the weapons of the pirate men, clashed and exploded as the crews came to grips. At the head of the boarding party was the massive form of Jolly Roger, while the Atlantean figure of Daniel Tucker led the defense. Lesser men were hurled aside, as the two giants strode through the mêleé to fight, toe to toe.

Then the clangor of steel cut short the words they had hurled at the beginning of battle.

Daniel Tucker found himself attacked not only by Jolly Roger Hawkins, but by two powerful aides armed with long, deadly pikes. As the pirate leader cut back and parried, his men lunged at Tucker with their spear points, seeking to pin him to the mast and allow their captain to butcher at his will.

His cutlass flashing like the play of summer lightning, Daniel Tucker continued to hold back the three. As one of the pikemen plunged in, seeking to score with a short jab, the young man's blade sent the pirate kicking to the deck, no more to rise. The second man fell back as he saw his comrade's fate.

"At him, you dog! Are you afraid of such a dancing master?" howled Jolly Roger Hawkins.

"Are you?" mocked Tucker.

"The Devil, himself, is afraid of me," the buccaneer howled, leaping forward, his cutlass reaching out in a wide sweep that ripped one of the *Air Sprite*'s crew almost in twain.

"He may be, but I am not," Dan shouted to his enemy.

Toe to toe they stood, fighting desperately. So wide was the sweep of their swinging blades that the men on either side edged off, giving them a clear deck on which to battle. Daniel Tucker fought with a well-arranged plan in mind. He promised to save Jolly Roger for Captain Rawlins' yardarm and was sure he could subdue the pirate leader without seriously wounding him. For a while he satisfied himself with purely defensive fighting. Roger's right arm was still bandaged and Tucker knew it would tire soon. Then he could lock his point in the other's cutlass hilt and fling the weapon over the side.

Gradually he backed, seeking to separate Hawkins from his supporters. If he could get him where a quick twist would disarm him, a second's work would bind and hold him prisoner. Slowly, he retreated from the weaving blade before him.

"Dan! Dan!" warned a girlish voice.

For an instant, Tucker took his eyes from the face of his foe. He saw a huge man in pirate garb lunging at him with a pike. Unless he got out of the way, he would be spitted like a fowl. He leaped back as the man plunged on, slashed at the racing form with his swiftly swinging blade. The steel bit home, but at that instant, Daniel Tucker felt himself thrown to the oaken deck. In his backward spring, he had leaped into a pool of blood and his feet had slipped from beneath him.

With a howl, Jolly Roger snatched a poniard from his sash and leaped upon his foe. A scream issued from the galley.

"Now for some throat slitting!"

The poniard flashed aloft, but as its gleaming blow descended, a deluge of smoking black pitch was thrown full in Hawkins' face. A bellowing curse as Jolly Rogers staggered back, pawing at the air.

"Catch that yardarm fruit, we'll hang him now," came the voice of Captain Rawlins from the poop.

"Catch him!" Daniel Tucker yelled, springing to his feet.

A knot of savagely fighting pirates had thrown themselves about their half-blinded chief. Daniel Tucker charged into them, hewing with his slashing blade. Men reeled and fell, kicking weakly as they sprawled upon the deck, but the screaming Hawkins was swept back to the deck of the *New Venture*.

"Board 'em!" ordered the skipper of the *Sprite*.

"Aye, aye, sir," Tucker shouted, placing himself at the head of party of pike and sword men.

Then from the deck of the *New Venture* came a billowing wall of smoke. Fames lanced up into the rigging and the canvas wilted to fall like leaves caught in the swirl of a forest blaze.

"Fire! Fire!" the word rang from one end of the *Air Sprite* to the other.

The men in the tops had finally struck sparks and were hurling their flaming torches into the pitch-saturated decks. The danger was as great for the *Sprite* as the *Venture*.

"Break those grappling irons—veer off—fore and staysail. Look alive now," Captain Rawlins yelled from the poop.

Meantime the crew of the *New Venture* was madly combatting the flames. The canvas had been destroyed, but the woodwork was saved by timely efforts with the pumps. The *Sprite* had broken the grapples and was drifting away. Her sails were catching the breeze. Upon the forecastle of the *Venture* stood Jolly Roger Hawkins. His face was the color of an African slave.

"The cruise is not over, my dandy," he yelled to Daniel Tucker, as the distance between the ships widened.

"When it is, you'll be wriggling on my yardarm," came the answer from the *Sprite*'s master, as he shook the stump of his left arm at his blackened enemy.

Captain Arthur Rawlins was too experienced a sailor not to know that the *New Venture* would have a full set of canvas in the sailmaker's locker, but it would take time to bend it and repair the gear injured by those well-timed flames. Meantime he could race south to meet the treasure-bearing Spaniards. That he would encounter Jolly Roger Hawkins again was assured. Each would hunt the other, as long as they remained upon the western sea.

Racing through the water whose blue deepened with each league that swept beneath their foaming prow, they raised the Spaniards on the morning of the third day. A whiff of shot and the *Alma de Dios* struck he red and golden colors, while the *Corinto* surrendered after a short chase.

Although a stern man, Arthur Rawlins was no Jolly Roger Hawkins. The captain and crews of the two Spanish ships were spared and loaded into the *Corinto* after its store of powder had been taken and its guns well spiked. The Rawlins took possession of the *Alma de Dios* and gave the *Air Sprite* to Tucker's command, halving the crew to take the big prize to port.

With the *Corinto* lost in the haze to the east, the two ships swept west, bearing toward Nassau. The treasure holds of the Spaniards had given up rich loot and the scarred and bearded sailors visioned nights of revelry before they took to sea again. Chests of gold doubloons, boxes of bright, silvery pieces of eight and ingots of both metals had been brought to the skipper's cabin and his methodical mind made inventory before a sail was spread. Into Daniel Tucker's hand was given one-half the treasure, lest the ships become separated and one lost.

"It will make a rich man of you, my lad," Arthur Rawlins told his mate. "Even half would do that, but my share also will be yours if I make a short cruise."

"A short cruise, sir!" astonishment sounded in the young man's voice.

"Aye, my son. Some devil's spawn has whispered in my ear that my head and remaining hand shall follow the left hand before I raise the Hook. If so, all is yours."

In spite of Daniel Tucker's protest, the captain called the bos'n and Phyllis Lightbourn to witness his last testament. Then orders were roared to make sail for the Bahamas. With the transfer of the skipper to the *Alma de Dios*, the girl was ordered to take charge of the galley on the larger ship, while the former cook took up the burden on the *Air Sprite*.

Pacing the *Air Sprite*'s poop, a master before he had a beard, Daniel Tucker held his craft well into the winds as the men followed his orders to many a bawling chantey. The young man, however, was not filled with their vociferous joy. His eyes were held to the north and he ordered the top watches to keep their glasses leveled in that direction. Jolly Roger Hawkins had not fallen over the rim of the world and they could expect him to strike as soon as he raised their sail. The crew of the *Air Sprite* had been divided and, if the two ships were separated by heavy weather, Hawkins would be able to destroy one and then the other. The *Alma de Dios* was a rich prize and he knew Jolly Roger was a pirate who would fight for that fortune until he had not a man to board or fire a gun.

As they made their westing, Tucker noted a decided stiffening of the wind. The season of the West Indian hurricane was upon them and he knew these scourges of the deep might strike at any time. While the *Air Sprite* was built to fight the heaviest weather, the *Alma de Dios* would encounter much trouble in such a tempest. Phyllis Lightbourn was on that high-decked Spaniard and so was Arthur Rawlins, a man who had been a father to him.

Back and forth across the *Air Sprite* poop he strode, his eyes first to the north, seeking to glimpse the first sight of the *New Venture*, and then to the south, watching the clouds driven by the constantly freshening wind. White caps flecked the deep blue of the Gulf Stream and a falling glass told of heavier weather yet to come.

Tucker glanced at the *Alma de Dios*. She was rolling cumbrously already and had ported her helm slightly to keep the strengthening wind from throwing her on her beam ends. The distance between the ships was widening and, with the coming of darkness, contact would be lost. Tucker ordered a shortening of sail to allow the big prize to catch up.

Stiffer, still stiffer, grew the wind. The *Alma de Dios* was laboring now, although the *Air Sprite* held steadily to her task.

Then from the top watch came a call and a man's excited hand pointed to the northward. Daniel Tucker climbed up the shrouds and leveled his glass in that direction. A sail—no, two—and the cut of the canvas on the leader was that of the *New Venture*. Behind her was the *Black Hawk*, now ready to aid the pirate chief. In spite of the strengthening wind, now blowing a howling gale, the buccaneer was bearing down on a wide tack, his spit pointed to the *Alma de Dios*. He had sighted the laboring Spaniard and was making ready to attack. To Jolly Roger Hawkins, it made small difference what flag she flew. He would strike with equal savagery.

Dan Tucker did not hesitate. A swift command sent the men scampering up the ratlines to lower canvas in spite of the wind that grew with every puff. The helm went over and they circled back. The cries of the top watch had told of the pirate's coming and the crew was ready to defend the gold they had won. Part of the store was on the *Alma*.

They sang a warlike chantey as they fought the whipping sails. Then the *Air Sprite* sunk her nose into the boiling water at her prow and leaped toward her laboring companion. A puff of smoke rose from the *New Venture*'s deck. She was attacking. The *Black Hawk*, likewise, was bearing down upon the former Spaniard. Arthur Rawlins had broken out his colors from the main top, but the streaming ensign only brought a new burst of smoke from the pirate craft. Then, from the truck of the leading ship a black ball burst into a sable flag, upon which appeared the skull and bones of piracy. Jolly Roger was flying his colors.

"Double-shot all guns," Tucker ordered, as they raced on.

The *Air Sprite* was racing now, doubling back to the aid of the *Alma*. The *New Venture* had borne down with exceptional speed in the face of that ripping gale, and smoke from the former Spaniard told Tucker that his stern commander was replying with thundering fire to the cannon of his enemy.

Faster, still faster, raced the *Sprite*. The young captain held her to her task, refusing to reef another inch in spite of the rapidly growing wind.

"You'll pull her sticks out, sir," the bos'n shouted above the high shriek of the cordage.

"We may need no sticks in another fifteen minutes," Tucker yelled in return.

The *New Venture* was now alongside the heavily pitching *Alma*. Jolly Roger Hawkins was not a man to allow a gale to keep him from such a prize. His guns were roaring, while the crew swarmed the deck, ready to board when the grappling irons came down.

A word to the helmsman and the *Sprite* turned her tail until she caught the full strength of that howling wind and leaped forward with even greater speed.

Boiling through the water to rescue his commander and Phyllis Lightbourn from the savage arms of Jolly Roger Hawkins, Dan Turner drove the *Sprite* as though it were a living thing. As they bore toward the now bitterly fighting ships, the young man realized that he could not lose a second. With only half the *Sprite*'s crew, the *Alma* would be unable to repel the pirates when they boarded. Faster flew the gallant *Sprite*.

Hawkins was getting his grappling irons in position. In a few minutes he would be in position to drop them. Only the most desperate of seamen would take the chance of locking two vessels with that mounting storm bursting around his ears, but the Spanish Main knew no more savage bravery than that of the swart pirate who led the *Venture*'s crew.

"Starboard guns ready for a broadside," Tucker shouted.

They were cleaving the water at a dizzy speed. A few more cable lengths and they would be ready to fire. The pirates had seen the *Air Sprite* and were doubling their efforts.

"Starboard guns ready, sir." It was the voice of Clancy, the armorer.

The *New Venture* was closing in, her irons ready to fall. The *Black Hawk* had come alongside. Men would soon be matching steel with steel.

The wind had reached a point where it was shrieking through the cordage like some mad banshee of the air. The sea foamed with its lashing. The *Air Sprite* was straining every stay and brace as it lunged on. A bellowing roar of a mighty blast and the air seemed to quiver for an instant before a sudden silence swept down. The raging wind of a moment ago had puffed out like a candle extinguished by a whiff of air. The heeling *Sprite* righted, slid through the water and then began to rock, becalmed a cable length or more out of cannon shot from the attacking pirates.

Daniel Tucker needed no glass to gauge the swiftly moving tragedy ahead. He saw the *Venture* close in with the momentum she had gained and heard the rattle of the falling grapples in the hush that had descended upon the ocean. The yell of the boarders came to his ears and then the sounds of strife. The men from the *Black Hawk* were swarming over the starboard rail, while the *New Venture*'s crew attacked from port. They were crushing the divided company that manned the *Alma* and the ship would be in Jolly Roger's hands before the *Sprite* could hope to fire a shot.

Helpless and distraught, Daniel Tucker watched that awful scene. He could hear the shouts of the buccaneers as they hacked down the weakly defending force on the *Alma*'s deck. The scream of a girl came across the rolling waters.

With only half a crew under him, he dared not send men in long boats to Rawlins' aid. It would only add to the disaster. Then his eyes saw the colorful standard of the *Alma*'s main truck come tumbling down. Jolly Roger had won already. In another moment, the sinister banner, whose name the pirate wore, was floating from the masthead.

A yell from his own fore top and once more the lookout's hand pointed dramatically to the north. A swift glance in that direction. Across the foaming ocean a black cloud was racing with the speed of mighty winds. Daniel Tucker knew what was bearing down upon them. It was the demon of the West Indian ocean that all men feared—the true hurricane. It was plunging at them with a merciless savagery that would make Jolly Roger and his cutthroats seem weak and helpless.

So eager had the pirates been in making their capture that they had noted the swift approach of the enemy all seamen fear worse than any living thing. They would be struck down by that mighty blast unless something could be done immediately.

"Reef every stick—batten all hatches—quick, men, quick!" Tucker shouted.

Came a far-away buzzing, like swarms of angry bees. Its noise swelled to a murmur, then a roar.

A quiver ran through the *Air Sprite*. She was beginning to heel to the first touch of that new wind that soon would toss her, chiplike, towards the pirates when its full force was felt. Daniel Tucker quickly sized up the situation. Perhaps he would be able to strike a blow.

"Gunners make ready," he bellowed, as the storm swept down.

Panic was breaking out on board the laboring *Alma*. Frantic hands were attempting to release the grappling irons. Some of the pirates had leaped back to their own craft. A mighty lurch and the hulking Spaniard crashed into the *Black Hawk*, held only to its towering sides by hand hooks. The splintering of heavy timbers rent the air, a crushing of ribs and decking. Then the shattered remnants of the smaller craft drifted, men plunging from its ruptured decks and swimming for the *Venture*.

As the full force of the storm struck down, the *Sprite* leaped toward the two embattled ships. The *New Venture* was being cast free, at least half its crew gaining its decks as the grappling irons were jerked aloft.

On the high poop of the *Alma*, Daniel Tucker caught a glimpse of the ponderous figure of Jolly Roger Hawkins. Before him, standing in defiant attitude, was Arthur Rawlins, a prisoner, but unbowed.

"Starboard guns ready?" Dan yelled.

"All ready, sir."

"Fire!"

There came a roar as flaming tongues leaped from brazen mouths and blue-white smoke was added to the clouds of spray.

"Port guns ready?"

"Ready, sir."

Daniel Tucker's powerful hands grasped the spokes of the wheel and with the straining helmsman, he labored to bring his ship around.

"Fire!" yelled the young commander.

Another thundering roll was added to the discord of that swiftly mounting storm. The full fury of a West Indian hurricane had swept down upon them. Fifteen minutes ago, they had been becalmed. Now they were lurching through clouds of smoke and spray.

As they raced through the water, Daniel Tucker glimpsed the destruction his two broadsides had wrought. The deck of the *New Venture* was a shambles. Main and mizzen sticks were down. Cordage and splintered spars had gone to port and with the force of the wind, were dragging the pirate craft to its destruction. Should the demoniacal force of that wind last much longer, the *Venture* would be seen no more.

Another bellowing blast from the north. The *Air Sprite* leaped like a startled deer, although her masts were bare. Clinging to the firmly bolted helm, Dan Tucker cast a hurried glance behind. The *Venture* had heeled over with this final smashing blow and her shattered masts had prevented her recovery. He caught a flash of men swarming over the side, seeking to keep above the foaming waters. Then a mountainous sea crashed down and, when its peak had passed, the hulk of the *New Venture* was bare.

The *Venture* and *Black Hawk* had met the fate of those caught unaware by the destructive force of the hurricane, but through the clouds of flying spray he could see the high outline of the *Alma de Dios* racing in the van of the storm.

The *Air Sprite* surged through the seas in pursuit. The tables now were turned and Jolly Roger Hawkins was fleeing, seeking to escape with half the loot, upon which his savage heart was set. Night had come with the racing black clouds. Sheets of rain descended to blot out the fleeing galleon, but Daniel Tucker remained at the helmsman's side, as his ship bounded like an antelope.

Although the greatest fury of the storm died during the night, morning saw a stiff wind still holding, and with the first gray in the east, Daniel Tucker began to sweep the horizon with his glass. Light brightened and an exclamation of joy broke forth as he caught his first sight of the Spanish vessel. The *Sprite* was much the faster craft and he knew he could overtake the galleon.

"Tops'ls, men, tops'ls," he called, as the bos'n piped the crew on deck. "Remember, half the loot is in that Spaniard yet."

"Tops'ls, sir," they answered, as their bare feet carried them aloft.

The *Alma de Dios* answered his maneuver by stretching more canvas to the stiff breeze, but Daniel Tucker only smiled. His large sheets came down to step the *Sprite*'s speeds up until the clumsy galleon could not hope to make a run of it.

Daniel Tucker did not wish to decide the battle with powder and shot. Not a few of the *Sprite*'s crew were held prisoners by the pirate chief and might be wounded. Besides, Arthur Rawlins and Phyllis Lightbourn still lived aboard that fleeing ship.

Closer, still closer, he drew. Hardly a cable-length divided them by noon. One o'clock saw him drawing alongside the laboring Spaniard. Upon the high poop deck, he saw the bulky figure of his enemy. Then once more he glimpsed the white-headed form of his commander. The man's lone arm was piminoned to his side, as Jolly Roger dragged his prisoner to the windward rail.

"Avast there and I'll spare his life," he heard Hawkins bellow through a speaking trumpet. "If he comes nearer, I'll cut his croaking throat."

"Come anyhow, my boy. Don't let this blackleg stay you," came the voice of Arthur Rawlins.

"But, sir—" Dan shouted back.

"It's an order, do you hear?" A fierceness had come into the older man's tone. "Obey me or I'll have you up before the Admiralty when we reach port."

"But, captain—"

"Do as I tell you. This dog has not the nerve—"

"I haven't, huh?" Daniel Tucker could hear Jolly Roger, although he had dropped his speaking trumpet.

Then the eyes of the young man widened as he saw the murderous cutlass raised aloft. A flick, as its blade descended, and he knew that Arthur Rawlins' premonition of coming death had been realized. An oath escaped the young man's lips and he shouted a command that added new canvas to the *Air Sprite*'s straining sticks. Another leap and the smaller craft drew alongside. The crews had begun to fire and the rattle of musketry sounded from the lengths of both ships.

Another bellow from the *Alma*'s poop. Once more Daniel Tucker looked up. This time Jolly Roger had brought the shrinking form of Phyllis Lightbourn to the rail.

"She'll follow him, if you don't bear off," the pirate shouted.

"I'd rather, Dan," the high, clear notes of the girl came across the tumbling waters. "Keep coming—I'm not afraid."

For an instant the young man hesitated. Phyllis would be murdered before his eyes if he closed with the pirates, but—

He gave the wheel another twist that brought the *Sprite* edging toward the heaving galleon. Then he whispered swift instructions into his helmsman's ear. A pause, as he fixed his pistols ready for instant use. His cutlass was drawn from its colorful sheath. Then he kicked off his boots and raced up the mizzen shrouds.

Nearer, still nearer, drew the racing ships. Jolly Roger Hawkins still stood beside the girl, thundering his threats unless the *Air Sprite* drew away.

"I'll cut her throat before your very eyes," he bellowed.

A nod from Daniel Tucker to the upstaring man at the helm, a swift turning of the wheel, and the vessel was warped to port. At the same instant, Tucker grasped a free bight of stout line and leaped to starboard as far as he could swing. Like a pendulum, his body swept back. Now it was almost over the *Alma*'s deck. There was a straining of timbers as the ships came together, but before the grappling hooks could fall, Daniel Tucker dropped lightly to the high poop of the *Alma de Dios*.

"Damn you, I'll kill you!" shrieked Hawkins.

The Scourge of the Spanish Main leaped like a tiger at the young man, who had fallen, almost from the sky. His pistol flashed, but Dan dodged out of harm. His own weapon came out, but as he saw the pirate at the helm reach for a gun, he fired, the bullet dropping the man like a felled ox.

From the forecastle of the galleon came the shouts of men as the *Air Sprite*'s crew boarded. Both ships were sailing with reduced companies and their forces were about equal.

"Here, take this. Keep the others back. I'll take care of him."

Tucker had half circled and he thrust his remaining pistol into Phyllis Lightbourn's hand. Then his cutlass came up to deflect a blow that Hawkins had launched at his unprotected head. They were alone on the towering poop. To one side was the huddled form of murdered Arthur Rawlins. Steel struck on steel and the ring of their blades beat quick tempo.

Jolly Roger was attempting to make quick end of the battle. He knew Tucker's superior skill and suppleness and he sought to break through with ponderous strength to kill with a single, cleaving blow. The younger man, however, fought an entirely different combat. His whole strategy was confined to evading the other's bull-like rushes and awaiting a time when he could disarm his foe.

"Get back, or I'll kill you," came the shrill voice of Phyllis Lightbourn.

No sound of fear was in her tone and Dan could hear the pirates curse mightily, but their footsteps were stayed at the foot of the ladder leading to the poop.

"A fine crowd beneath your Jolly Roger flag," Dan Tucker scoffed. "They let a girl hold them at bay while their brave captain is fighting for his life."

Hawkins' rushes were more furious now, desperation causing him to take every chance in order to break through the lightning play of his cool opponent.

To the Scourge of the Main came the black realization that this supple-wristed youngster had been playing with him. Now the sounds from the forecastle told the fencers that the pirate crew had surrendered and were begging lustily for their lives. Soon Hawkins would have to face a score of foes. He cast one swift glance at the wide yardarm.

A yell and he lunged at the younger man. A half-step to one side and Tucker's weaving point slipped in to engage the crescent guard of Hawkins' cutlass. A flash and the weapon went spinning through the air, disappearing with scarce a splash into the ocean.

"And now, my gallows bird—" the young man began.

The pirate's swart face paled at the sound of Tucker's words. Then with a yell he leaped toward Phyllis Lightbourn, seeking to snatch the pistol from her.

"No!" she cried, leveling the weapon at him, "I'll kill you."

"Come on, men—a rope for the pirate brave," Dan called to his crew.

But his words remained unfinished, as with a wild, despairing cry, Hawkins, the cutthroat, dodged death at another man's hand and hurled himself over the rail. Men leaned over to catch a glimpse of the last of the pirate chief, but the waters closed over him and his head did not reappear.

Gentle trade winds came in the wake of the hurricane. The *Alma de Dios* sailed northward, seeking that speck that is the Bermudas.

"First I shall turn the prize over to the governor," said Daniel Tucker, as he and Phyllis Lightbourn sat together, "and then I'm going back to Plymouth."

"Back to England again?" the girl sighed.

"No, New England," he corrected, "I'm an American, you know."

"But no pirate," she laughed.

"No. You see, I sailed with Captain Rawlins under letters of marque. Since the war with Spain has involved us, as well as Europe, we attack Spanish commerce the same as any naval ship. We knew Jolly Roger Hawkins was hunting the *Alma* and *Corinto*. That is why we anchored off St. George's and that is how I met you."

"I'm glad you're not a pirate," he heard her whisper, "but even if you were, I think all women love the gallants of the Spanish Main."

THE SUBSTITUTE SWORD

ALEXANDER BLADE

SIR MORGAN TALBOT'S HARD CRUEL FACE IDLY SCANNED THE DANCERS AT THE ball. Standing with half a dozen men against the richly brocaded drapes that hung on the wall, he was easily the most commanding figure there with his great height and splendid lace-adorned clothes. And when he spoke others listened with servile respect.

"Indeed Sir Morgan," said one of the men, "there is as likely a bunch of fillies gathered here tonight as one might wish."

"'Tis true," said another. "I haven't seen better in many seasons I have attended these balls."

"Aye," said Sir Morgan drily. "If you say so, then it must indeed be true, for I know no better judge, or one who devotes himself so constantly and assiduously to these petticoat pastimes."

A laugh was raised as the shaft struck home.

"I'm sure, sir," said the smarting dandy, "that the Captain of the King's Guards would do well to yield to me in these matters as I yield to him in the things in which he excels."

Sir Morgan laughed carelessly. "You try me, sir. Perhaps the flat of my sword would improve your manners."

The dandy paled. For a moment it seemed as though he would burst into tears. Then, without a word, he walked quickly away, Sir Morgan's taunting laugh following him.

A white-haired man, apparently in his middle sixties, but carrying his years gracefully approached the group.

"My Lord Greer!" cried Sir Morgan, bowing with a hint of mockery. "I trust your fortunes improve."

Lord Greer surveyed the man calmly. "When a man reaches my time of life, his blood has cooled so that the state of his fortunes seems of little moment. It is you younger men who fight for advancement."

"Fight?" Morgan raised his eyebrows. "What do you mean? I am not sure I like your words."

"They are plain enough," said Greer. "And whether you like them or not matters little to me. I speak of the death of Lord Darney whose position as Captain of the king's guards you now hold."

Morgan scowled darkly. "Old men are like toothless curs. It is common knowledge that I killed Darney in a fairly contested duel." He put his hand menacingly on his sword and looked around. "Is there anyone who dares say otherwise?"

The group of men fell back a little. Only Greer held his ground.

He spoke without fear or hesitation. "There were many strange circumstances. However, that is a matter which will soon be employing younger and more capable hands than mine."

"You speak in riddles, old man," sneered Morgan.

"Then perhaps this will be plainer. Lord Darney's brother, Godfrey, has sailed from Spain and will land here in London tomorrow."

"That young firebrand!" Morgan was openly contemptuous. "He owes his neck to the mercy of a kindly king who sent him to Spain instead of making him answer for his escapades here."

"He has been gone for five years. I think the man who returns will not be the boy who left. And I am sure his brother's death will not go unavenged. Not if he is the Darney I think he is."

Morgan made a careless gesture. "When you see the stripling tell him that I am at his disposal. And you might also tell him," he added, "that I have had six dances this evening with the Lady Eleanor. If my memory serves me, that will be more galling to the young cub than his brother's death."

The two men sat in the quiet room, strongly contrasting pictures of youth and age. The young Lord Godfrey Darney was past middle height, with the suppleness of the trained athlete. He was so blonde his hair seemed almost white against his strongly tanned skin. Greer had lost his habitual calm and was pounding the table.

"By Jupiter, Godfrey," he shouted. "I have been talking to you for an hour and you refuse to understand what I am saying!"

The younger man spoke wearily. "I understand you very well, sir, but we don't seem to agree on what I am to do."

"What are you to do? There is only one thing you *can* do. Your brother, rest his soul, caught that blackguard Morgan cheating at cards, and thrashed him in full view. Naturally Morgan had to challenge him. However he made a very strange stipulation about the duel. It had to be fought in a locked room from which only one living person was to emerge. My boy, I can't tell you how shocked I was when the door opened and Morgan walked out. Inside we found your poor brother, his blade shattered at the hilt lying dead with Morgan's sword run through him."

"My lord, I know you loved my brother as well as I, and I'm deeply grateful to you, but believe me, sir, it's impossible for me to challenge Morgan to a duel."

"And why not?" thundered the old man.

"Because my brother wouldn't want me to. You see, Lord Greer, our family code forbids it. If I were to fight Morgan it would look as though I was taking up my brother's quarrel. As though my brother had summoned help. No, sir, as much as I detest the man, I must allow the matter to end as it stands."

Greer was incredulous. "Good heavens, boy! Don't you realize what that man has done to you and your family? Why the king publicly declared that the crown had been in danger all the time your brother was captain of the guards; and as a reward for slaying your brother he was made captain in his stead. Land grants which your family has enjoyed for generations have been seized by the crown and are even now, perhaps in the process of being turned over to that upstart Morgan."

Godfrey shook his head. "This news distresses me beyond measure, but still I can do nothing."

"People will say you fear him."

"The yapping of curs in the street will not disturb me."

"Then perhaps this will stir your blood, Godfrey. Morgan has been in constant attendance on the Lady Eleanor and there is talk that a marriage is soon to take place."

Godfrey flushed beneath his tan. "I released Eleanor from our betrothal vows when I was sent to Spain. She is free to give her heart where she chooses."

Greer's perplexity was evident. "What happened to the hotheaded youth who went to Spain five years ago? Has a mouse returned in his place?"

"This is fine talk from a man who was constantly chiding me for street brawling," smiled Godfrey.

"Ah, well," replied Greer with some confusion, "you always were an unpredictable lad. Hot when you should have been cold—and now cold when you should be hot." Then suddenly he was angry again. It is well that your father didn't live to see this day. He was a man."

"And so was my brother," said Godfrey sadly.

"The line of men in your family ended there," Greer said acidly.

"Suppose we drop this subject, sir. It is not likely to improve our tempers and my mind is made up."

"Very well, boy, but mark my words, you will find that this course you have decided upon will make you an unpopular figure in town."

The truth of Lord Greer's words was brought painfully home to Godfrey several days later when he chanced upon some old friends on the street. They were curt to the point of rudeness. After a few such incidents, he began to smolder. He resolved to see Lady Eleanor. Remembering the warmth that had existed between them, he was sure he would be well received—especially by her father, who had been an old family friend.

So it was exactly a week after he had arrived in London, that Godfrey found himself in a huge reception hall of the Lady Eleanor's house. A servant had gone upstairs to announce him. He waited below tingling with anticipation. At last he heard a step on the stair. Turning with pleasure, he saw that it was not Eleanor, but her father. Godfrey leaped to his feet and advanced with his face glowing, hand outstretched.

Ignoring the hand, her father spoke grimly. "I am surprised to see you in my house. Has your sense of decency fled along with your courage?"

A hot wave of anger shook Godfrey. "I looked for a warmer welcome from you, sir. However I am here to see Lady Eleanor. Will you please inform her that I await her."

"She is indisposed. She sends her apologies."

"I suppose," said Godfrey sarcastically, "that this indisposition will manifest itself whenever I call upon her."

The other nodded. "I can promise you that."

"I don't believe Eleanor has refused to see me. I have a mind to see her in spite of you!"

"What a stalwart you have suddenly become! Direct your rage to the salvation of your reputation. Your brother's death shrieks for vengeance. What are you doing about it?"

"My brother died as a soldier should; with honor and facing his foe. It was an affair of honor that ended with his death. Everybody is determined that it become my affair. Is there any evidence that Morgan killed my brother by treachery?" Then as the other did not reply, he went on, "As I thought. Still you would have me challenge Morgan for no other reason than that he defeated my brother in a fairly contested duel."

"Fine logic can be spouted when one is seeking to preserve his skin."

It was with a heavy heart that Morgan left the house. He realized the futility of argument. All these people had loved his brother and they refused to understand his position. But Eleanor? He remembered the day he left for Spain when he had released her from all obligation to him, she had declared that no matter how long he was gone she would wait. And now he had returned to a stone wall of hostility. Was Eleanor part of it? Surely she knew he had returned . . . why hadn't she sent him a message? As though in answer to his unspoken thought, the sound of footsteps caused him to turn. It was a young girl whom he recognized as Eleanor's personal maid.

"Oh, sir," she gasped breathlessly, "you do walk so fast!"

"What is it," Godfrey snapped. "Did the Lady Eleanor send you?"

"Cooee," said the girl with fresh young impudence. "You don't think I'd run this far on my own account. I have a message for you."

He hastily unfolded the note and read:

Godfrey, dear, Father would not let me see you although it was my desperate desire. Dearest, I'm so anxious to see you. Can you come tonight to the Green Lacquer Room? I will be there with Father, but perhaps I will be able to slip away for a few moments. Do not fail me if you love me.

Eleanor

His happiness was dizzying. He wanted to sing . . . dance . . . shout.

The girl broke in. "Is there any answer, sir?"

"Yes. Tell your mistress that plague, pestilence or war will not keep me from the Green Lacquer Room tonight."

It didn't bother Godfrey that night when he arrived at the Green Lacquer Room that former friends whom he encountered turned frozen-faced glances upon him. Nothing bothered him. He was going to see Eleanor!

He wandered about the room from table to table where well-dressed men and ladies were gambling large sums of money. But Eleanor was nowhere to be seen. I must have come too early, thought Godfrey. At that moment he saw Sir Morgan. The man was wearing his uniform of Captain of the Guards. It gave Godfrey a pang to see the familiar uniform he had seen so often on his brother being worn by another. Morgan had apparently been drinking for his face was flushed. It also appeared that he was losing heavily as was evidenced by his cursing and the small stack of chips in front of him. A flunkey whispered in Morgan's ear. Morgan turned swiftly to face Godfrey. His dark, malignant face broke into a smile.

"Well, sir," he said, "welcome home. I confess I looked for a visit from you ere this."

"Indeed?" said Godfrey coolly. "And pray why should I visit you? I am not aware that ours is an old friendship."

Morgan laughed delightedly. "If rumor is to be credited, you no longer have any friends. I wonder why?"

People were deserting the tables and forming a ring around the two.

"I see," said Morgan, "that you are admiring my uniform. How do you like it?"

"I have seen it worn by a better man," replied Godfrey.

Morgan flushed even more darkly. The smile became more dangerously wicked. "It is strange that you should say so. I know of a certain quarter where it is greatly admired. A certain young lady whom you know, in fact."

Godfrey's quiet belied the turbulence within him. "I think it would be wiser if you said no more."

"Said no more, by gad!" Morgan bellowed. "Why you young whippersnapper, d'you suppose the Lady Eleanor would even look at you—"

That was as far as he got. The next thing he knew something exploded under his chin, hurling him to the floor. Then he was being helped up by several pairs of hands. The swaying, blurred double image in front of him suddenly resolved itself into a clear picture of Godfrey with clenched hands but perfectly calm.

"You'll give me satisfaction for this, young Darney," Morgan said thickly.

"I'm at your service." Godfrey bowed.

"Here." Morgan waved an imperious hand at a man in the crowd. "You, Stuvey, will you appear as my second?"

"Gladly," said Stuvey, stepping out of the crowd. Then, turning to Godfrey, "And who will appear for you, sir?"

"I don't know." He looked around at the ring of faces. "I don't see anybody who—"

"Look no farther, lad. I'm your man." It was Greer. The old man's face was transformed with happiness. "I knew you didn't mean what you said. You were staking him, eh?"

Godfrey merely smiled at the old man, not bothering to explain what had really happened.

"You have the choice of weapons, Godfrey," said Greer. "What do you choose?"

"It matters not," said Godfrey carelessly. "Arrange all the details to suit yourself."

At that moment, Stuvey, who had been standing to a side whispering with Morgan joined them. "Have you made a choice of weapons, gentlemen?" he asked.

Lord Greer's manner was quite formal. "Yes, sir, we have. It will be swords."

Stuvey bowed. "I trust," he said, "that you will bear with Sir Morgan's whim in the matter of place. He would like the duel to be fought at the Turk's Head Inn in a private room with all barred but the principals."

Lord Greer became volcanic. "That's the way he fought your brother, Godfrey! No, sir! A thousand times no!"

Godfrey laid a restraining hand on the man's arm. His eyes were unnaturally bright. "Not so fast, sir. You may tell Sir Morgan that we accept his terms." Then to the furious Greer. "I should like to see how my brother died," he said softly.

"It's some kind of foul trick," Greer growled.

"That is exactly what I wish to discover for myself."

As had been prearranged, they all met two hours later at the Turk's Head Inn. Lord Greer, grumbling and impatient, insisted on going through the room where the duel was to take place. He explored every corner of the room, poking his stick behind the drapes and into closets. At last he had to admit he was satisfied. He was the last one out of the room, leaving the two opponents facing each other. Godfrey was wearing a silk blouse with the sleeves turned up. Morgan, however, had scorned to remove his scarlet frock coat, declaring that he wouldn't even have acquired a "dew" at the end of the encounter.

"I trust, sir," said Morgan, "that you are prepared for a journey. I propose to send you to join your brother." He advanced with sword raised.

"As to that," replied Godfrey, walking to meet him, "I cannot say for certain, but I'm sure that where you are going *you* will not find him."

They crossed swords. It didn't take long for Godfrey to discover that Morgan was indeed a superb swordsman. They parried thrust for thrust. Both men were catlike as they circled and back-circled, neither able to find a weakness in the other. Morgan's confidence seemed to grow as they fenced. He began taunting Godfrey.

"Why do you leap away? Is this friendly? Come, let me tickle you with my blade."

Godfrey said nothing. Lynx-eyed he watched for an opportunity to make a fatal thrust.

Morgan continued his banter. "Much as I regret it, I'm afraid you will not be here to attend my marriage to Lady Eleanor—"

With unbelievable speed and the full weight of his muscular young body, Godfrey suddenly lunged straight at Morgan's heart. *The blade snapped and Morgan was standing there laughing at him!* Godfrey looked dazedly at his useless blade.

"Now you know my secret," said Morgan. "A finely woven jacket of mail will turn any blade. But you will never live to tell anyone." Menacingly, he began to close in on Godfrey.

Godfrey leaped backward putting the table between him and Morgan. Despairingly he looked around for a weapon. Lying on the table was Lord Greer's walking stick. He snatched it just in time to parry a lunge that would surely have run him through had it not been blocked by the walking stick. Morgan attacked furiously; his darting blade seemed to be everywhere. But although the walking stick was awkward to handle, Godfrey managed somehow to defend himself. Morgan was openly laughing now.

"And now," he said, "the *coup de grace*."

Something was hammering at Godfrey's brain. Some message that was trying to get through . . . Something to do with Lord Greer's walking stick. All at once it came to him. *He remembered that the walking stick was in reality a sword cane!* With one movement he whipped the blade out of the scabbard. Morgan's face dropped.

"Defend yourself," gritted Godfrey. "For now you are surely going to die."

Morgan made a valiant effort, but Godfrey, now thoroughly aroused, was too much for him. A feint, which Morgan saw too late was only a feint, proved his undoing. Godfrey's blade buried itself in his throat cutting to a gurgle what started as a shriek.

Standing over his prostrate form Godfrey said, "That is for my brother's murder. Your armor will be your shroud."

The Gentleman's magazine carried a very fine story of the wedding of Lady Eleanor to Lord Darney, the handsome new Captain of the Guards who had recently been restored in favor with the King and again become the possessor of his hereditary landholdings. The magazine concluded the account with, "extremely perplexing was Lord Darney's delight with the wedding present presented by Lord Greer. The gift was only an ordinary walking stick."

Captain Blood

Rafael Sabatini

I. The Messenger

Peter Blood, bachelor of medicine and several other things besides, smoked a pipe and tended the geraniums boxed on the sill of his window above Water Lane in the town of Bridgewater.

Sternly disapproving eyes considered him from a window opposite, but went disregarded. Mr. Blood's attention was divided between his task and the stream of humanity in the narrow street below; a stream which poured for the second time that day towards Castle Field, where earlier in the afternoon Ferguson, the Duke's chaplain, had preached a sermon containing more treason than divinity.

These straggling, excited groups were mainly composed of men with green boughs in their hats and the most ludicrous of weapons in their hands. Some, it is true, shouldered fowling pieces, and here and there a sword was brandished; but more of them were armed with clubs, and most of them trailed the mammoth pikes fashioned out of scythes, as formidable to the eye as they were clumsy to the hand. There were weavers, brewers, carpenters, smiths, masons, bricklayers, cobblers, and representatives of every other of the trades of peace among these improvised men of war. Bridgewater, like Taunton, had yielded so generously of its manhood to the service of the bastard Duke that for any to abstain whose age and strength admitted of his bearing arms was to brand himself a coward or a papist.

Yet Peter Blood, who was not only able to bear arms, but trained and skilled in their use, who was certainly no coward, and a papist only when it suited him, tended his geraniums and smoked his pipe on that warm July evening as indifferently as if nothing were afoot. One other thing he did. He flung after those war-fevered enthusiasts a line of Horace—a poet for whose work he had early conceived an inordinate affection:

"Quo, quo, scelesti, ruitis?"

And now perhaps you guess why the hot, intrepid blood inherited from the roving sires of his Somersetshire mother remained cool amidst all this frenzied fanatical heat of rebellion; why the turbulent spirit which had forced him once from the sedate academical bonds his father would have imposed upon him, should now remain quiet in the very midst of turbulence. You realize how he regarded these men who were rallying to the banners of liberty—the banners woven by the virgins of Taunton, the girls from the seminaries of Miss Blake and Mrs. Musgrove, who—as the ballad runs—had ripped open their silk petticoats to make colours for King Monmouth's army. That Latin line, contemptuously flung after them as they clattered down the cobbled street, reveals his mind. To him they were fools rushing in wicked frenzy upon their ruin.

You see, he knew too much about this fellow Monmouth and the pretty brown slut who had borne him, to be deceived by the legend of legitimacy, on the strength of which this standard of rebellion had been raised. He had read the absurd proclamation posted at the Cross at Bridgewater—as it had been posted also at Taunton and elsewhere—setting forth that "upon the decease of our Sovereign Lord Charles the Second, the right of succession to the Crown of England, Scotland, France, and Ireland, with the dominions and territories thereunto belonging, did legally descend and devolve upon the most illustrious and high-born Prince James, Duke of Monmouth, son and heir apparent to the said King Charles the Second."

It had moved him to laughter, as had the further announcement that "James Duke of York did first cause the said late King to be poysoned, and immediately thereupon did usurp and invade the Crown."

He knew not which was the greater lie. For Mr. Blood had spent a third of his life in the Netherlands, where this same James Scott—who now proclaimed himself James the Second, by the grace of God, King, et cætera—first saw the light some six-and-thirty years ago, and he was acquainted with the story current there of the fellow's real paternity. Far from being legitimate—by virtue of a pretended secret marriage between Charles Stuart and Lucy Walter—it was possible that this Monmouth who now proclaimed himself King of England was not even the illegitimate child of the late sovereign. What but ruin and disaster could be the end of this grotesque pretension? How could it be hoped that England would ever swallow such a Perkin? And it was on his behalf, to uphold his fantastic claim, that these West Country clods, led by a few armigerous Whigs, had been seduced into rebellion!

"Quo, quo, scelesti, ruitis?"

He laughed and sighed in one; but the laugh dominated the sigh, for Mr. Blood was unsympathetic, as are most self-sufficient men; and he was very self-sufficient; adversity had taught him so to be. A more tender-hearted man, possessing his vision and his knowledge, might have found cause for tears in the contemplation of these ardent, simple, Nonconformist sheep going forth to the shambles—escorted to the rallying ground on Castle Field by wives and daughters, sweethearts and mothers, sustained by the delusion that they were to take the field in defence of Right, of Liberty, and of Religion. For he knew, as all Bridgewater knew and had known now for some hours, that it was Monmouth's intention to deliver battle that same night. The Duke was to lead a surprise attack upon the Royalist army under Feversham that was now encamped on Sedgemoor. Mr. Blood assumed that Lord Feversham would be equally well-informed, and if in this assumption he was wrong, at least he was justified of it. He was not to suppose the Royalist commander so indifferently skilled in the trade he followed.

Mr. Blood knocked the ashes from his pipe, and drew back to close his window. As he did so, his glance travelling straight across the street met at last the glance of those hostile eyes that watched him. There were two pairs, and they belonged to the Misses Pitt, two amiable, sentimental maiden ladies who yielded to none in Bridgewater in their worship of the handsome Monmouth.

Mr. Blood smiled and inclined his head, for he was on friendly terms with these ladies, one of whom, indeed, had been for a little while his patient. But there was no response to his greeting. Instead, the eyes gave him back a stare of cold disdain. The smile on his thin lips grew a little broader, a little less pleasant. He understood the reason of that hostility, which had been daily growing in this past week since Monmouth had come to turn the brains of women of all ages. The Misses Pitt, he apprehended, contemned him that he, a young and vigorous man, of a military training which might now be valuable to the Cause, should stand aloof; that he should placidly smoke his pipe and tend his geraniums on this evening of all evenings, when men of spirit were rallying to the Protestant Champion, offering their blood to place him on the throne where he belonged.

If Mr. Blood had condescended to debate the matter with these ladies, he might have urged that having had his fill of wandering and adventuring, he was now embarked upon the career for which he had been originally intended and for which his studies had equipped him; that he was a man of medicine and not of war; a healer, not a slayer. But they would have answered him, he knew, that in such a cause it behoved every man who deemed himself a man to take up arms. They would have pointed out that their own nephew Jeremiah, who was by trade a sailor, the master of a ship—which by an ill-chance for that young man had come to anchor at this season in Bridgewater Bay— had quitted the helm to snatch up a musket in defence of Right. But Mr. Blood was not of those who argue. As I have said, he was a self-sufficient man.

He closed the window, drew the curtains, and turned to the pleasant, candle-lighted room, and the table on which Mrs. Barlow, his housekeeper, was in the very act of spreading supper. To her, however, he spoke aloud his thought.

"It's out of favour I am with the vinegary virgins over the way."

He had a pleasant, vibrant voice, whose metallic ring was softened and muted by the Irish accent which in all his wanderings he had never lost. It was a voice that could woo seductively and caressingly, or command in such a way as to compel obedience. Indeed, the man's whole nature was in that voice of his. For the rest of him, he was tall and spare, swarthy of tint as a gipsy, with eyes that were startlingly blue in that dark face and under those level black brows. In their glance those eyes, flanking a high-bridged, intrepid nose, were of singular penetration and of a steady haughtiness that went well with his firm lips. Though dressed in black as became his calling, yet it was with an elegance derived from the love of clothes that is peculiar to the adventurer he had been, rather than to the staid medicus he now was. His coat was of fine camlet, and it was laced with silver; there were ruffles of Mechlin at his wrists and a Mechlin cravat encased his throat. His great black periwig was as sedulously curled as any at Whitehall.

Seeing him thus, and perceiving his real nature, which was plain upon him, you might have been tempted to speculate how long such a man would be content to lie by in this little backwater of the world into which chance had swept him some six months ago; how long he would continue to pursue the trade for which he had qualified himself before he had begun to live. Difficult of belief though it may be when you know his history, previous and subsequent, yet it is possible that but for the trick that Fate was about to play him, he might have continued this peaceful existence, settling down completely to the life of a doctor in this Somersetshire haven. It is possible, but not probable.

He was the son of an Irish medicus, by a Somersetshire lady in whose veins ran the rover blood of the Frobishers, which may account for a certain wildness that had early manifested itself in his disposition. This wildness had profoundly alarmed his father, who for an Irishman was of a singularly peace-loving nature. He had early resolved that the boy should follow his own honourable profession, and Peter Blood, being quick to learn and oddly greedy of knowledge, had satisfied his parent by receiving at the age of twenty the degree of baccalaureus medicinæ at Trinity College, Dublin. His father survived that satisfaction by three months only. His mother had then been dead some years already. Thus Peter Blood came into an inheritance of some few hundred pounds, with which he had set out to see the world and give for a season a free rein to that restless spirit by which he was imbued. A set of curious chances led him to take service with the Dutch, then at war with France; and a predilection for the sea made him elect that this service should be upon that element. He had the advantage of a commission under the famous de Ruyter, and fought in the Mediterranean engagement in which that great Dutch admiral lost his life.

After the Peace of Nimeguen his movements are obscure. But we know that he spent two years in a Spanish prison, though we do not know how he contrived to get there. It may be due to this that upon his release he took his sword to France, and saw service with the French in their warring upon the Spanish Netherlands. Having reached, at last, the age of thirty-two, his appetite for adventure surfeited, his health having grown indifferent as the result of a neglected wound, he was suddenly overwhelmed by homesickness. He took ship from Nantes with intent to cross to Ireland. But the vessel being driven by stress of weather into Bridgewater Bay, and Blood's health having grown worse during the voyage, he decided to go ashore there, additionally urged to it by the fact that it was his mother's native soil.

Thus in January of that year 1685 he had come to Bridgewater, possessor of a fortune that was approximately the same as that with which he had originally set out from Dublin eleven years ago.

Because he liked the place, in which his health was rapidly restored to him, and because he conceived that he had passed through adventures enough for a man's lifetime, he determined to settle there, and take up at last the profession of medicine from which he had, with so little profit, broken away.

That is all his story, or so much of it as matters up to that night, six months later, when the battle of Sedgemoor was fought.

Deeming the impending action no affair of his, as indeed it was not, and indifferent to the activity with which Bridgewater was that night agog, Mr. Blood closed his ears to the sounds of it, and went early to bed. He was peacefully asleep long before eleven o'clock, at which hour, as you know, Monmouth rode out with his rebel host along the Bristol Road, circuitously to avoid the marshland that lay directly between himself and the Royal Army. You also know that his numerical advantage—possibly counter-balanced by the greater steadiness of the regular troops on the other side—and the advantages he derived from falling by surprise upon an army that was more or less asleep, were all lost to him by blundering and bad leadership before ever he was at grips with Feversham.

The armies came into collision in the neighbourhood of two o'clock in the morning. Mr. Blood slept undisturbed through the distant boom of cannon. Not until four o'clock, when the sun was rising to dispel the last wisps of mist over that stricken field of battle, did he awaken from his tranquil slumbers.

He sat up in bed, rubbed the sleep from his eyes, and collected himself. Blows were thundering upon the door of his house, and a voice was calling incoherently. This was the noise that had aroused him. Conceiving that he had to do with some urgent obstetrical case, he reached for bedgown and slippers, to go below. On the landing he almost collided with Mrs. Barlow, new-risen and unsightly, in a state of panic. He quieted her cluckings with a word of reassurance, and went himself to open.

There in slanting golden light of the new-risen sun stood a breathless, wild-eyed man and a steaming horse. Smothered in dust and grime, his clothes in disarray, the left sleeve of his doublet hanging in rags, this young man opened his lips to speak, yet for a long moment remained speechless.

In that moment Mr. Blood recognized him for the young shipmaster, Jeremiah Pitt, the nephew of the maiden ladies opposite, one who had been drawn by the general enthusiasm into the vortex of that rebellion. The street was rousing, awakened by the sailor's noisy advent; doors were opening, and lattices were being unlatched for the protrusion of anxious, inquisitive heads.

"Take your time, now," said Mr. Blood. "I never knew speed made by overhaste."

But the wild-eyed lad paid no heed to the admonition. He plunged, headlong, into speech, gasping, breathless.

"It is Lord Gildoy," he panted. "He is sore wounded . . . at Oglethorpe's Farm by the river. I bore him thither . . . and . . . and he sent me for you. Come away! Come away!"

He would have clutched the doctor, and haled him forth by force in bedgown and slippers as he was. But the doctor eluded that too eager hand.

"To be sure, I'll come," said he. He was distressed. Gildoy had been a very friendly, generous patron to him since his settling in these parts. And Mr. Blood was eager enough to do what he now could to discharge the debt, grieved that the occasion should have arisen, and in such a manner—for he knew quite well that the rash young nobleman had been an active agent of the Duke's. "To be sure, I'll come. But first give me leave to get some clothes and other things that I may need."

"There's no time to lose."

"Be easy now. I'll lose none. I tell ye again, ye'll go quickest by going leisurely. Come in . . . take a chair . . ." He threw open the door of a parlour.

Young Pitt waved aside the invitation.

"I'll wait here. Make haste, in God's name."

Mr. Blood went off to dress and to fetch a case of instruments.

Questions concerning the precise nature of Lord Gildoy's hurt could wait until they were on their way. Whilst he pulled on his boots, he gave Mrs. Barlow instructions for the day, which included the matter of a dinner he was not destined to eat.

When at last he went forth again, Mrs. Barlow clucking after him like a disgruntled fowl, he found young Pitt smothered in a crowd of scared, half-dressed townsfolk— mostly women—who had come hastening for news of how the battle had sped. The news he gave them was to be read in the lamentations with which they disturbed the morning air.

At sight of the doctor, dressed and booted, the case of instruments tucked under his arm, the messenger disengaged himself from those who pressed about, shook off his weariness and the two tearful aunts that clung most closely, and seizing the bridle of his horse, he climbed to the saddle.

"Come along, sir," he cried. "Mount behind me."

Mr. Blood, without wasting words, did as he was bidden. Pitt touched the horse with his spur. The little crowd gave way, and thus, upon the crupper of that doubly-laden horse, clinging to the belt of his companion, Peter Blood set out upon his Odyssey. For this Pitt, in whom he beheld no more than the messenger of a wounded rebel gentleman, was indeed the very messenger of Fate.

II. KIRKE'S DRAGOONS

Oglethorpe's farm stood a mile or so to the south of Bridgewater on the right bank of the river. It was a straggling Tudor building showing grey above the ivy that clothed its lower parts. Approaching it now, through the fragrant orchards amid which it seemed to drowse in Arcadian peace beside the waters of the Parrett, sparkling in the morning sunlight, Mr. Blood might have had a difficulty in believing it part of a world tormented by strife and bloodshed.

On the bridge, as they had been riding out of Bridgewater, they had met a vanguard of fugitives from the field of battle, weary, broken men, many of them wounded, all of them terror-stricken, staggering in speedless haste with the last remnants of their strength into the shelter which it was their vain illusion the town would afford them. Eyes glazed with lassitude and fear looked up piteously out of haggard faces at Mr. Blood and his companion as they rode forth; hoarse voices cried a warning that merciless pursuit was not far behind. Undeterred, however, young Pitt rode amain along the dusty road by which these poor fugitives from that swift rout on Sedgemoor came flocking in ever-increasing numbers. Presently he swung aside, and quitting the road took to a pathway that crossed the dewy meadowlands. Even here they met odd groups of these human derelicts, who were scattering in all directions, looking fearfully behind them as they came through the long grass, expecting at every moment to see the red coats of the dragoons.

But as Pitt's direction was a southward one, bringing them ever nearer to Feversham's headquarters, they were presently clear of that human flotsam and jetsam of the battle, and riding through the peaceful orchards heavy with the ripening fruit that was soon to make its annual yield of cider.

At last they alighted on the kidney stones of the courtyard, and Baynes, the master of the homestead, grave of countenance and flustered of manner, gave them welcome.

In the spacious, stone-flagged hall, the doctor found Lord Gildoy—a very tall and dark young gentleman, prominent of chin and nose—stretched on a cane day-bed under one of the tall mullioned windows, in the care of Mrs. Baynes and her comely daughter. His cheeks were leaden-hued, his eyes closed, and from his blue lips came with each laboured breath a faint, moaning noise.

Mr. Blood stood for a moment silently considering his patient. He deplored that a youth with such bright hopes in life as Lord Gildoy's should have risked all, perhaps existence itself, to forward the ambition of a worthless adventurer. Because he had liked and honoured this brave lad he paid his case the tribute of a sigh. Then he knelt to his task, ripped away doublet and underwear to lay bare his lordship's mangled side, and called for water and linen and what else he needed for his work.

He was still intent upon it a half-hour later when the dragoons invaded the homestead. The clatter of hooves and hoarse shouts that heralded their approach disturbed him not at all. For one thing, he was not easily disturbed; for another, his task absorbed him. But his lordship, who had now recovered consciousness, showed considerable alarm, and the battle-stained Jeremy Pitt sped to cover in a clothes-press. Baynes was uneasy, and his wife and daughter trembled. Mr. Blood reassured them.

"Why, what's to fear?" he said. "It's a Christian country, this, and Christian men do not make war upon the wounded, nor upon those who harbour them." He still had, you see, illusions about Christians. He held a glass of cordial, prepared under his directions, to his lordship's lips. "Give your mind peace, my lord. The worst is done."

And then they came rattling and clanking into the stone-flagged hall—a round dozen jack-booted, lobster-coated troopers of the Tangiers Regiment, led by a sturdy, black-browed fellow with a deal of gold lace about the breast of his coat.

Baynes stood his ground, his attitude half-defiant, whilst his wife and daughter shrank away in renewed fear. Mr. Blood, at the head of the day-bed, looked over his shoulder to take stock of the invaders.

The officer barked an order, which brought his men to an attentive halt, then swaggered forward, his gloved hand bearing down the pummel of his sword, his spurs jingling musically as he moved. He announced his authority to the yeoman.

"I am Captain Hobart, of Colonel Kirke's dragoons. What rebels do you harbour?"

The yeoman took alarm at that ferocious truculence. It expressed itself in his trembling voice.

"I . . . I am no harbourer of rebels, sir. This wounded gentleman . . ."

"I can see for myself." The Captain stamped forward to the day-bed, and scowled down upon the grey-faced sufferer.

"No need to ask how he came in this state and by his wounds. A damned rebel, and that's enough for me." He flung a command at his dragoons. "Out with him, my lads."

Mr. Blood got between the day-bed and the troopers.

"In the name of humanity, sir!" said he, on a note of anger. "This is England, not Tangiers. The gentleman is in sore case. He may not be moved without peril to his life."

Captain Hobart was amused.

"Oh, I am to be tender of the lives of these rebels! Odds blood! Do you think it's to benefit his health we're taking him? There's gallows being planted along the road from Weston to Bridgewater, and he'll serve for one of them as well as another. Colonel Kirke'll learn these nonconforming oafs something they'll not forget in generations."

"You're hanging men without trial? Faith, then, it's mistaken I am. We're in Tangiers, after all, it seems, where your regiment belongs."

The Captain considered him with a kindling eye. He looked him over from the soles of his riding-boots to the crown of his periwig. He noted the spare, active frame, the arrogant poise of the head, the air of authority that invested Mr. Blood, and soldier recognized soldier. The Captain's eyes narrowed. Recognition went further.

"Who the hell may you be?" he exploded.

"My name is Blood, sir—Peter Blood, at your service."

"Aye—aye! Codso! That's the name. You were in French service once, were you not?"

If Mr. Blood was surprised, he did not betray it.

"I was."

"Then I remember you—five years ago, or more, you were in Tangiers."

"That is so. I knew your colonel."

"Faith, you may be renewing the acquaintance." The Captain laughed unpleasantly. "What brings you here, sir?"

"This wounded gentleman. I was fetched to attend him. I am a medicus."

"A doctor—you?" Scorn of that lie—as he conceived it—rang in the heavy, hectoring voice.

"Medicinæ baccalaureus," said Mr. Blood.

"Don't fling your French at me, man," snapped Hobart. "Speak English!"

Mr. Blood's smile annoyed him.

"I am a physician practising my calling in the town of Bridgewater."

The Captain sneered. "Which you reached by way of Lyme Regis in the following of your bastard Duke."

It was Mr. Blood's turn to sneer. "If your wit were as big as your voice, my dear, it's the great man you'd be by this."

For a moment the dragoon was speechless. The colour deepened in his face.

"You may find me great enough to hang you."

"Faith, yes. Ye've the look and the manners of a hangman. But if you practise your trade on my patient here, you may be putting a rope round your own neck. He's not the kind you may string up and no questions asked. He has the right to trial, and the right to trial by his peers."

"By his peers?"

The Captain was taken aback by these three words, which Mr. Blood had stressed.

"Sure, now, any but a fool or a savage would have asked his name before ordering him to the gallows. The gentleman is my Lord Gildoy."

And then his lordship spoke for himself, in a weak voice.

"I make no concealment of my association with the Duke of Monmouth. I'll take the consequences. But, if you please, I'll take them after trial—by my peers, as the doctor has said."

The feeble voice ceased, and was followed by a moment's silence. As is common in many blustering men, there was a deal of timidity deep down in Hobart. The announcement of his lordship's rank had touched those depths. A servile upstart, he stood in awe of titles. And he stood in awe of his colonel. Percy Kirke was not lenient with blunderers.

By a gesture he checked his men. He must consider. Mr. Blood, observing his pause, added further matter for his consideration.

"Ye'll be remembering, Captain, that Lord Gildoy will have friends and relatives on the Tory side, who'll have something to say to Colonel Kirke if his lordship should be handled like a common felon. You'll go warily, Captain, or, as I've said, it's a halter for your neck ye'll be weaving this morning."

Captain Hobart swept the warning aside with a bluster of contempt, but he acted upon it none the less. "Take up the day-bed," said he, "and convey him on that to Bridgewater. Lodge him in the gaol until I take order about him."

"He may not survive the journey," Blood remonstrated. "He's in no case to be moved."

"So much the worse for him. My affair is to round up rebels." He confirmed his order by a gesture. Two of his men took up the day-bed, and swung to depart with it.

Gildoy made a feeble effort to put forth a hand towards Mr. Blood. "Sir," he said, "you leave me in your debt. If I live I shall study how to discharge it."

Mr. Blood bowed for answer; then to the men: "Bear him steadily," he commanded. "His life depends on it."

As his lordship was carried out, the Captain became brisk. He turned upon the yeoman.

"What other cursed rebels do you harbour?"

"None other, sir. His lordship . . ."

"We've dealt with his lordship for the present. We'll deal with you in a moment when we've searched your house. And, by God, if you've lied to me . . ." He broke off, snarling, to give an order. Four of his dragoons went out. In a moment they were heard moving noisily in the adjacent room. Meanwhile, the Captain was questing about the hall, sounding the wainscoting with the butt of a pistol.

Mr. Blood saw no profit to himself in lingering.

"By your leave, it's a very good day I'll be wishing you," said he.

"By my leave, you'll remain awhile," the Captain ordered him.

Mr. Blood shrugged, and sat down. "You're tiresome," he said. "I wonder your colonel hasn't discovered it yet."

But the Captain did not heed him. He was stooping to pick up a soiled and dusty hat in which there was pinned a little bunch of oak leaves. It had been lying near the clothes-press in which the unfortunate Pitt had taken refuge. The Captain smiled malevolently.

His eyes raked the room, resting first sardonically on the yeoman, then on the two women in the background, and finally on Mr. Blood, who sat with one leg thrown over the other in an attitude of indifference that was far from reflecting his mind.

Then the Captain stepped to the press, and pulled open one of the wings of its massive oaken door. He took the huddled inmate by the collar of his doublet, and lugged him out into the open.

"And who the devil's this?" quoth he. "Another nobleman?"

Mr. Blood had a vision of those gallows of which Captain Hobart had spoken, and of this unfortunate young shipmaster going to adorn one of them, strung up without trial, in the place of the other victim of whom the Captain had been cheated. On the spot he invented not only a title but a whole family for the young rebel.

"Faith, ye've said it, Captain. This is Viscount Pitt, first cousin to Sir Thomas Vernon, who's married to that slut Moll Kirke, sister to your own colonel, and sometime lady in waiting upon King James's queen."

Both the Captain and his prisoner gasped. But whereas thereafter young Pitt discreetly held his peace, the Captain rapped out a nasty oath. He considered his prisoner again.

"He's lying, is he not?" he demanded, seizing the lad by the shoulder, and glaring into his face. "He's rallying rue, by God!"

"If ye believe that," said Blood, "hang him, and see what happens to you."

The dragoon glared at the doctor and then at his prisoner. "Pah!" He thrust the lad into the hands of his men. "Fetch him along to Bridgewater. And make fast that fellow also," he pointed to Baynes. "We'll show him what it means to harbour and comfort rebels."

There was a moment of confusion. Baynes struggled in the grip of the troopers, protesting vehemently. The terrified women screamed until silenced by a greater terror. The Captain strode across to them. He took the girl by the shoulders. She was a pretty, golden-headed creature, with soft blue eyes that looked up entreatingly, piteously into the face of the dragoon. He leered upon her, his eyes aglow, took her chin in his hand, and set her shuddering by his brutal kiss.

"It's an earnest," he said, smiling grimly. "Let that quiet you, little rebel, till I've done with these rogues."

And he swung away again, leaving her faint and trembling in the arms of her anguished mother. His men stood, grinning, awaiting orders, the two prisoners now fast pinioned.

"Take them away. Let Cornet Drake have charge of them." His smouldering eye again sought the cowering girl. "I'll stay awhile—to search out this place. There may be other rebels hidden here." As an afterthought, he added: "And take this fellow with you." He pointed to Mr. Blood. "Bestir!"

Mr. Blood started out of his musings. He had been considering that in his case of instruments there was a lancet with which he might perform on Captain Hobart a beneficial operation. Beneficial, that is, to humanity. In any case, the dragoon was obviously plethoric and would be the better for a blood-letting. The difficulty lay in making the opportunity. He was beginning to wonder if he could lure the Captain aside with some tale of hidden treasure, when this untimely interruption set a term to that interesting speculation.

He sought to temporize.

"Faith it will suit me very well," said he. "For Bridgewater is my destination, and but that ye detained me I'd have been on my way thither now."

"Your destination there will be the gaol."

"Ah, bah! Ye're surely joking!"

"There's a gallows for you if you prefer it. It's merely a question of now or later."

Rude hands seized Mr. Blood, and that precious lancet was in the case on the table out of reach. He twisted out of the grip of the dragoons, for he was strong and agile, but they closed with him again immediately, and bore him down. Pinning him to the ground, they tied his wrists behind his back, then roughly pulled him to his feet again.

"Take him away," said Hobart shortly, and turned to issue his orders to the other waiting troopers. "Go search the house, from attic to cellar; then report to me here."

The soldiers trailed out by the door leading to the interior. Mr. Blood was thrust by his guards into the courtyard, where Pitt and Baynes already waited. From the threshold of the hall, he looked back at Captain Hobart, and his sapphire eyes were blazing. On his lips trembled a threat of what he would do to Hobart if he should happen to survive this business. Betimes he remembered that to utter it were probably to extinguish his chance of living to execute it. For to-day the King's men were masters in the West, and the West was regarded as enemy country, to be subjected to the worst horror of war by the victorious side. Here a captain of horse was for the moment lord of life and death.

Under the apple-trees in the orchard Mr. Blood and his companions in misfortune were made fast each to a trooper's stirrup leather. Then at the sharp order of the cornet, the little troop started for Bridgewater. As they set out there was the fullest confirmation of Mr. Blood's hideous assumption that to the dragoons this was a conquered enemy country. There were sounds of rending timbers, of furniture smashed and overthrown, the shouts and laughter of brutal men, to announce that this hunt for rebels was no more than a pretext for pillage and destruction. Finally above all other sounds came the piercing screams of a woman in acutest agony.

Baynes checked in his stride, and swung round writhing, his face ashen. As a consequence he was jerked from his feet by the rope that attached him to the stirrup leather, and he was dragged helplessly a yard or two before the trooper reined in, cursing him foully, and striking him with the flat of his sword.

It came to Mr. Blood, as he trudged forward under the laden apple-trees on that fragrant, delicious July morning, that man—as he had long suspected—was the vilest work of God, and that only a fool would set himself up as a healer of a species that was best exterminated.

III. THE LORD CHIEF JUSTICE

It was not until two months later—on the 19th of September, if you must have the actual date—that Peter Blood was brought to trial, upon a charge of high treason. We know that he was not guilty of this; but we need not doubt that he was quite capable of it by the time he was indicted. Those two months of inhuman, unspeakable imprisonment had moved his mind to a cold and deadly hatred of King James and his representatives. It says something for his fortitude that in all the circumstances he should still have had a mind at all. Yet, terrible as was the position of this entirely innocent man, he had cause for thankfulness on two counts. The first of these was that he should have been brought to trial at all; the second, that his trial took place on the date named, and not a day earlier. In the very delay which exacerbated him lay— although he did not realize it—his only chance of avoiding the gallows.

Easily, but for the favour of Fortune, he might have been one of those haled, on the morrow of the battle, more or less haphazard from the overflowing gaol at Bridgewater to be summarily hanged in the market-place by the bloodthirsty Colonel Kirke. There was about the Colonel of the Tangiers Regiment a deadly despatch which might have disposed in like fashion of all those prisoners, numerous as they were, but for the vigorous intervention of Bishop Mews, which put an end to the drumhead courts-martial.

Even so, in that first week after Sedgemoor, Kirke and Feversham contrived between them to put to death over a hundred men after a trial so summary as to be no trial at all. They required human freights for the gibbets with which they were planting the countryside, and they little cared how they procured them or what innocent lives they took. What, after all, was the life of a clod? The executioners were kept busy with rope and chopper and cauldrons of pitch. I spare you the details of that nauseating picture. It is, after all, with the fate of Peter Blood that we are concerned rather than with that of the Monmouth rebels.

He survived to be included in one of those melancholy droves of prisoners who, chained in pairs, were marched from Bridgewater to Taunton. Those who were too sorely wounded to march were conveyed in carts, into which they were brutally crowded, their wounds undressed and festering. Many were fortunate enough to die upon the way. When Blood insisted upon his right to exercise his art so as to relieve some of this suffering, he was accounted importunate and threatened with a flogging. If he had one regret now it was that he had not been out with Monmouth. That, of course, was illogical; but you can hardly expect logic from a man in his position.

His chain companion on that dreadful march was the same Jeremy Pitt who had been the agent of his present misfortunes. The young shipmaster had remained his close companion after their common arrest. Hence, fortuitously, had they been chained together in the crowded prison, where they were almost suffocated by the heat and the stench during those days of July, August, and September.

Scraps of news filtered into the gaol from the outside world. Some may have been deliberately allowed to penetrate. Of these was the tale of Monmouth's execution. It created profoundest dismay amongst those men who were suffering for the Duke and for the religious cause he had professed to champion. Many refused utterly to believe it. A wild story began to circulate that a man resembling Monmouth had offered himself up in the Duke's stead, and that Monmouth survived to come again in glory to deliver Zion and make war upon Babylon.

Mr. Blood heard that tale with the same indifference with which he had received the news of Monmouth's death. But one shameful thing he heard in connection with this which left him not quite so unmoved, and served to nourish the contempt he was forming for King James. His Majesty had consented to see Monmouth. To have done so unless he intended to pardon him was a thing execrable and damnable beyond belief; for the only other object in granting that interview could be the evilly mean satisfaction of spurning the abject penitence of his unfortunate nephew.

Later they heard that Lord Grey, who after the Duke—indeed, perhaps, before him—was the main leader of the rebellion, had purchased his own pardon for forty thousand pounds. Peter Blood found this of a piece with the rest. His contempt for King James blazed out at last.

"Why, here's a filthy mean creature to sit on a throne. If I had known as much of him before as I know to-day, I don't doubt I should have given cause to be where I am now." And then on a sudden thought: "And where will Lord Gildoy be, do you suppose?" he asked.

Young Pitt, whom he addressed, turned towards him a face from which the ruddy tan of the sea had faded almost completely during those months of captivity. His grey eyes were round and questioning. Blood answered him.

"Sure, now, we've never seen his lordship since that day at Oglethorpe's. And where are the other gentry that were taken?—the real leaders of this plaguey rebellion. Grey's case explains their absence, I think. They are wealthy men that can ransom themselves. Here awaiting the gallows are none but the unfortunates who followed; those who had the honour to lead them go free. It's a curious and instructive reversal of the usual way of these things. Faith, it's an uncertain world entirely!"

He laughed, and settled down into that spirit of scorn, wrapped in which he stepped later into the great hall of Taunton Castle to take his trial. With him went Pitt and the yeoman Baynes. The three of them were to be tried together, and their case was to open the proceedings of that ghastly day.

The hall, even to the galleries—thronged with spectators, most of whom were ladies—was hung in scarlet; a pleasant conceit, this, of the Lord Chief Justice's, who naturally enough preferred the colour that should reflect his own bloody mind.

At the upper end, on a raised dais, sat the Lords Commissioners, the five judges in their scarlet robes and heavy dark periwigs, Baron Jeffreys of Wem enthroned in the middle place.

The prisoners filed in under guard. The crier called for silence under pain of imprisonment, and as the hum of voices gradually became hushed, Mr. Blood considered with interest the twelve good men and true that composed the jury. Neither good nor true did they look. They were scared, uneasy, and hangdog as any set of thieves caught with their hands in the pockets of their neighbours. They were twelve shaken men, each of whom stood between the sword of the Lord Chief Justice's recent bloodthirsty charge and the wall of his own conscience.

From them Mr. Blood's calm, deliberate glance passed on to consider the Lords Commissioners, and particularly the presiding Judge, that Lord Jeffreys, whose terrible fame had come ahead of him from Dorchester.

He beheld a tall, slight man on the young side of forty, with an oval face that was delicately beautiful. There were dark stains of suffering or sleeplessness under the low-lidded eyes, heightening their brilliance and their gentle melancholy. The face was very pale, save for the vivid colour of the full lips and the hectic flush on the rather high but inconspicuous cheek-bones. It was something in those lips that marred the perfection of that countenance; a fault, elusive but undeniable, lurked there to belie the fine sensitiveness of those nostrils, the tenderness of those dark, liquid eyes and the noble calm of that pale brow.

The physician in Mr. Blood regarded the man with peculiar interest knowing as he did the agonizing malady from which his lordship suffered, and the amazingly irregular, debauched life that he led in spite of it—perhaps because of it.

"Peter Blood, hold up your hand!"

Abruptly he was recalled to his position by the harsh voice of the clerk of arraigns. His obedience was mechanical, and the clerk droned out the wordy indictment which pronounced Peter Blood a false traitor against the Most Illustrious and Most Excellent Prince, James the Second, by the grace of God, of England, Scotland, France, and Ireland King, his supreme and natural lord. It informed him that, having no fear of God in his heart, but being moved and seduced by the instigation of the Devil, he had failed in the love and true and due natural obedience towards his said lord the King, and had moved to disturb the peace and tranquillity of the kingdom and to stir up war and rebellion to depose his said lord the King from the title, honour, and the regal name of the imperial crown—and much more of the same kind, at the end of all of which he was invited to say whether he was guilty or not guilty. He answered more than was asked.

"It's entirely innocent I am."

A small, sharp-faced man at a table before and to the right of him bounced up. It was Mr. Pollexfen, the Judge-Advocate.

"Are you guilty or not guilty?" snapped this peppery gentleman. "You must take the words."

"Words, is it?" said Peter Blood. "Oh—not guilty." And he went on, addressing himself to the bench. "On this same subject of words, may it please your lordships, I am guilty of nothing to justify any of those words I have heard used to describe me, unless it be of a want of patience at having been closely confined for two months and longer in a fœtid gaol with great peril to my health and even life."

Being started, he would have added a deal more; but at this point the Lord Chief Justice interposed in a gentle, rather plaintive voice.

"Look you, sir: because we must observe the common and usual methods of trial, I must interrupt you now. You are no doubt ignorant of the forms of law?"

"Not only ignorant, my lord, but hitherto most happy in that ignorance. I could gladly have forgone this acquaintance with them."

A pale smile momentarily lightened the wistful countenance.

"I believe you. You shall be fully heard when you come to your defence. But anything you say now is altogether irregular and improper."

Enheartened by that apparent sympathy and consideration, Mr. Blood answered thereafter, as was required of him, that he would be tried by God and his country. Whereupon, having prayed to God to send him a good deliverance, the clerk called upon Andrew Baynes to hold up his hand and plead.

From Baynes, who pleaded not guilty, the clerk passed on to Pitt, who boldly owned his guilt. The Lord Chief Justice stirred at that.

"Come; that's better," quoth he, and his four scarlet brethren nodded. "If all were as obstinate as his two fellow-rebels, there would never be an end."

After that ominous interpolation, delivered with an inhuman iciness that sent a shiver through the court, Mr. Pollexfen got to his feet. With great prolixity he stated the general case against the three men, and the particular case against Peter Blood, whose indictment was to be taken first.

The only witness called for the King was Captain Hobart. He testified briskly to the manner in which he had found and taken the three prisoners, together with Lord Gildoy. Upon the orders of his colonel he would have hanged Pitt out of hand, but was restrained by the lies of the prisoner Blood, who led him to believe that Pitt was a peer of the realm and a person of consideration.

As the Captain's evidence concluded, Lord Jeffreys looked across at Peter Blood.

"Will the prisoner Blood ask the witness any questions?"

"None, my lord. He has correctly related what occurred."

"I am glad to have your admission of that without any of the prevarications that are usual in your kind. And I will say this, that here prevarication would avail you little. For we always have the truth in the end. Be sure of that."

Baynes and Pitt similarly admitted the accuracy of the Captain's evidence, whereupon the scarlet figure of the Lord Chief Justice heaved a sigh of relief.

"This being so, let us get on, in God's name; for we have much to do." There was now no trace of gentleness in his voice. It was brisk and rasping, and the lips through which it passed were curved in scorn. "I take it, Mr. Pollexfen, that the wicked treason of these three rogues being established—indeed, admitted by them—there is no more to be said."

Peter Blood's voice rang out crisply, on a note that almost seemed to contain laughter.

"May it please your lordship, but there's a deal more to be said."

His lordship looked at him, first in blank amazement at his audacity, then gradually with an expression of dull anger. The scarlet lips fell into unpleasant, cruel lines that transfigured the whole countenance.

"How now, rogue? Would you waste our time with idle subterfuge?"

"I would have your lordship and the gentlemen of the jury hear me on my defence, as your lordship promised that I should be heard."

"Why, so you shall, villain; so you shall." His lordship's voice was harsh as a file. He writhed as he spoke, and for an instant his features were distorted. A delicate dead-white hand, on which the veins showed blue, brought forth a handkerchief with which he dabbed his lips and then his brow. Observing him with his physician's eye, Peter Blood judged him a prey to the pain of the disease that was destroying him. "So you shall. But after the admission made, what defence remains?"

"You shall judge, my lord."

"That is the purpose for which I sit here."

"And so shall you, gentlemen." Blood looked from judge to jury. The latter shifted uncomfortably under the confident flash of his blue eyes. Lord Jeffreys's bullying charge had whipped the spirit out of them. Had they, themselves, been prisoners accused of treason, he could not have arraigned them more ferociously.

Peter Blood stood boldly forward, erect, self-possessed, and saturnine. He was freshly shaven, and his periwig, if out of curl, was at least carefully combed and dressed.

"Captain Hobart has testified to what he knows—that he found me at Oglethorpe's Farm on the Monday morning after the battle at Weston. But he has not told you what I did there."

Again the Judge broke in. "Why, what should you have been doing there in the company of rebels, two of whom—Lord Gildoy and your fellow there—have already admitted their guilt?"

"That is what I beg leave to tell your lordship."

"I pray you do, and in God's name be brief, man. For if I am to be troubled with the say of all you traitor dogs, I may sit here until the Spring Assizes."

"I was there, my lord, in my quality as a physician, to dress Lord Gildoy's wounds."

"What's this? Do you tell us that you are a physician?"

"A graduate of Trinity College, Dublin."

"Good God!" cried Lord Jeffreys, his voice suddenly swelling, his eyes upon the jury. "What an impudent rogue is this! You heard the witness say that he had known him in Tangiers some years ago, and that he was then an officer in the French service. You heard the prisoner admit that the witness had spoken the truth?"

"Why, so he had. Yet what I am telling you is also true, so it is. For some years I was a soldier; but before that I was a physician, and I have been one again since January last, established in Bridgewater, as I can bring a hundred witnesses to prove."

"There's not the need to waste our time with that. I will convict you out of your own rascally mouth. I will ask you only this: How came you, who represent yourself as a physician peacefully following your calling in the town of Bridgewater, to be with the army of the Duke of Monmouth?"

"I was never with that army. No witness has sworn to that, and I dare swear that no witness will. I never was attracted to the late rebellion. I regarded the adventure as a wicked madness. I take leave to ask your lordship" (his brogue became more marked than ever) "what should I, who was born and bred a papist, be doing in the army of the Protestant Champion?"

"A papist thou?" The judge gloomed on him a moment. "Art more like a snivelling, canting Jack Presbyter. I tell you, man, I can smell a Presbyterian forty miles."

"Then I'll take leave to marvel that with so keen a nose your lordship can't smell a papist at four paces."

There was a ripple of laughter in the galleries, instantly quelled by the fierce glare of the Judge and the voice of the crier.

Lord Jeffreys leaned farther forward upon his desk. He raised that delicate white hand, still clutching its handkerchief, and sprouting from a froth of lace.

"We'll leave your religion out of account for the moment, friend," said he. "But mark what I say to you." With a minatory forefinger he beat the time of his words. "Know, friend, that there is no religion a man can pretend to can give a countenance to lying. Thou hast a precious immortal soul, and there is nothing in the world equal to it in value. Consider that the great God of Heaven and Earth, before Whose tribunal thou and we and all persons are to stand at the last day, will take vengeance on thee for every falsehood, and justly strike thee into eternal flames, make thee drop into the bottomless pit of fire and brimstone, if thou offer to deviate the least from the truth and nothing but the truth. For I tell thee God is not mocked. On that I charge you to answer truthfully. How came you to be taken with these rebels?"

Peter Blood gaped at him a moment in consternation. The man was incredible, unreal, fantastic, a nightmare judge. Then he collected himself to answer.

"I was summoned that morning to succour Lord Gildoy, and I conceived it to be the duty imposed upon me by my calling to answer that summons."

"Did you so?" The Judge, terrible now of aspect—his face white, his twisted lips red as the blood for which they thirsted—glared upon him in evil mockery. Then he controlled himself as if by an effort. He sighed. He resumed his earlier gentle plaintiveness. "Lord! How you waste our time. But I'll have patience with you. Who summoned you?"

"Master Pitt there, as he will testify."

"Oh! Master Pitt will testify—he that is himself a traitor self-confessed. Is that your witness?"

"There is also Master Baynes here, who can answer to it."

"Good Master Baynes will have to answer for himself; and I doubt not he'll be greatly exercised to save his own neck from a halter. Come, come, sir; are these your only witnesses?"

"I could bring others from Bridgewater, who saw me set out that morning upon the crupper of Master Pitt's horse."

His lordship smiled. "It will not be necessary. For, mark me, I do not intend to waste more time on you. Answer me only this: When Master Pitt, as you pretend, came to summon you, did you know that he had been, as you have heard him confess, of Monmouth's following?"

"I did, my lord."

"You did! Ha!" His lordship looked at the cringing jury and uttered a short, stabbing laugh. "Yet in spite of that you went with him?"

"To succour a wounded man, as was my sacred duty."

"Thy sacred duty, sayest thou?" Fury blazed out of him again. "Good God! What a generation of vipers do we live in! Thy sacred duty, rogue, is to thy King and to God. But let it pass. Did he tell you whom it was that you were desired to succour?"

"Lord Gildoy—yes."

"And you knew that Lord Gildoy had been wounded in the battle, and on what side he fought?"

"I knew."

"And yet, being, as you would have us believe, a true and loyal subject of our Lord the King, you went to succour him?"

Peter Blood lost patience for a moment. "My business, my lord, was with his wounds, not with his politics."

A murmur from the galleries and even from the jury approved him. It served only to drive his terrible judge into a deeper fury.

"Jesus God! Was there ever such an impudent villain in the world as thou?" He swung, white-faced, to the jury. "I hope, gentlemen of the jury, you take notice of the horrible carriage of this traitor rogue, and withal you cannot but observe the spirit of this sort of people, what a villainous and devilish one it is. Out of his own mouth he has said enough to hang him a dozen times. Yet is there more. Answer me this, sir: When you cozened Captain Hobart with your lies concerning the station of this other traitor Pitt, what was your business then?"

"To save him from being hanged without trial, as was threatened."

"What concern was it of yours whether or how the wretch was hanged?"

"Justice is the concern of every loyal subject, for an injustice committed by one who holds the King's commission is in some sense a dishonour to the King's majesty."

It was a shrewd, sharp thrust aimed at the jury, and it reveals, I think, the alertness of the man's mind, his self-possession ever steadiest in moments of dire peril. With any other jury it must have made the impression that he hoped to make. It may even have made its impression upon these poor pusillanimous sheep. But the dread judge was there to efface it.

He gasped aloud, then flung himself violently forward.

"Lord of Heaven!" he stormed. "Was there ever such a canting, impudent rascal? But I have done with you. I see thee, villain, I see thee already with a halter round thy neck."

Having spoken so, gloatingly, evilly, he sank back again, and composed himself. It was as if a curtain fell. All emotion passed again from his pale face. Back to invest it again came that gentle melancholy. Speaking after a moment's pause, his voice was soft, almost tender, yet every word of it carried sharply through that hushed court.

"If I know my own heart it is not in my nature to desire the hurt of anybody, much less to delight in his eternal perdition. It is out of compassion for you that I have used all these words—because I would have you have some regard for your immortal soul, and not ensure its damnation by obdurately persisting in falsehood and prevarication. But I see that all the pains in the world, and all compassion and charity are lost upon you, and therefore I will say no more to you." He turned again to the jury that countenance of wistful beauty. "Gentlemen, I must tell you for law, of which we are the judges, and not you, that if any person be in actual rebellion against the King, and another person—who really and actually was not in rebellion—does knowingly receive, harbour, comfort, or succour him, such a person is as much a traitor as he who indeed bore arms. We are bound by our oaths and consciences to declare to you what is law; and you are bound by your oaths and your consciences to deliver and to declare to us by your verdict the truth of the facts."

Upon that he proceeded to his summing-up, showing how Baynes and Blood were both guilty of treason, the first for having harboured a traitor, the second for having succoured that traitor by dressing his wounds. He interlarded his address by sycophantic allusions to his natural lord and lawful sovereign, the King, whom God had set over them, and with vituperations of Nonconformity and of Monmouth, of whom—in his own words—he dared boldly affirm that the meanest subject within the kingdom that was of legitimate birth had a better title to the crown.

"Jesus God! That ever we should have such a generation of vipers among us," he burst out in rhetorical frenzy. And then he sank back as if exhausted by the violence he had used. A moment he was still, dabbing his lips again; then he moved uneasily; once more his features were twisted by pain, and in a few snarling, almost incoherent words he dismissed the jury to consider the verdict.

Peter Blood had listened to the intemperate, the blasphemous, and almost obscene invective of that tirade with a detachment that afterwards, in retrospect, surprised him. He was so amazed by the man, by the reactions taking place in him between mind and body, and by his methods of bullying and coercing the jury into bloodshed, that he almost forgot that his own life was at stake.

The absence of that dazed jury was a brief one. The verdict found the three prisoners guilty. Peter Blood looked round the scarlet-hung court. For an instant that foam of white faces seemed to heave before him. Then he was himself again, and a voice was asking him what he had to say for himself, why sentence of death should not be passed upon him, being convicted of high treason.

He laughed, and his laugh jarred uncannily upon the deathly stillness of the court. It was all so grotesque, such a mockery of justice administered by that wistful-eyed jack-pudding in scarlet, who was himself a mockery—the venal instrument of a brutally spiteful and vindictive king. His laughter shocked the austerity of that same jack-pudding.

"Do you laugh, sirrah, with the rope about your neck, upon the very threshold of that eternity you are so suddenly to enter into?"

And then Blood took his revenge.

"Faith, it's in better case I am for mirth than your lordship. For I have this to say before you deliver judgment. Your lordship sees me—an innocent man whose only offence is that I practised charity—with a halter round my neck. Your lordship, being the justiciar, speaks with knowledge of what is to come to me. I, being a physician, may speak with knowledge of what is to come to your lordship. And I tell you that I would not now change places with you—that I would not exchange this halter that you fling about my neck for the stone that you carry in your body. The death to which you may doom me is a light pleasantry by contrast with the death to which your lordship has been doomed by that Great Judge with whose name your lordship makes so free."

The Lord Chief Justice sat stiffly upright, his face ashen, his lips twitching, and whilst you might have counted ten there was no sound in that paralyzed court after Peter Blood had finished speaking. All those who knew Lord Jeffreys regarded this as the lull before the storm, and braced themselves for the explosion. But none came. Slowly, faintly, the colour crept back into that ashen face. The scarlet figure lost its rigidity, and bent forward. His lordship began to speak. In a muted voice and briefly— much more briefly than his wont on such occasions and in a manner entirely mechanical, the manner of a man whose thoughts are elsewhere while his lips are speaking—he delivered sentence of death in the prescribed form, and without the least allusion to what Peter Blood had said. Having delivered it, he sank back exhausted, his eyes half-closed, his brow agleam with sweat.

The prisoners filed out.

Mr. Pollexfen—a Whig at heart despite the position of Judge-Advocate which he occupied—was overheard by one of the jurors to mutter in the ear of a brother counsel:

"On my soul, that swarthy rascal has given his lordship a scare. It's a pity he must hang. For a man who can frighten Jeffreys should go far."

IV. HUMAN MERCHANDISE

Mr. Pollexfen was at one and the same time right and wrong—a condition much more common than is generally supposed.

He was right in his indifferently expressed thought that a man whose mien and words could daunt such a lord of terror as Jeffreys, should by the dominance of his nature be able to fashion himself a considerable destiny. He was wrong—though justifiably so—in his assumption that Peter Blood must hang.

I have said that the tribulations with which he was visited as a result of his errand of mercy to Oglethorpe's Farm contained—although as yet he did not perceive it, perhaps—two sources of thankfulness: one that he was tried at all; the other that his trial took place on the 19th of September. Until the 18th, the sentences passed by the court of the Lords Commissioners had been carried out literally and expeditiously. But on the morning of the 19th there arrived at Taunton a courier from Lord Sunderland, the Secretary of State, with a letter for Lord Jeffreys wherein he was informed that His Majesty had been graciously pleased to command that eleven hundred rebels should be furnished for transportation to some of His Majesty's southern plantations, Jamaica, Barbados, or any of the Leeward Islands.

You are not to suppose that this command was dictated by any sense of mercy. Lord Churchill was no more than just when he spoke of the King's heart as being as insensible as marble. It had been realized that in these wholesale hangings there was taking place a reckless waste of valuable material. Slaves were urgently required in the plantations, and a healthy, vigorous man could be reckoned worth at least from ten to fifteen pounds. Then, there were at court many gentlemen who had some claim or other upon His Majesty's bounty. Here was a cheap and ready way to discharge these claims. From amongst the convicted rebels a certain number might be set aside to be bestowed upon those gentlemen, so that they might dispose of them to their own profit.

My Lord Sunderland's letter gives precise details of the royal munificence in human flesh. A thousand prisoners were to be distributed among some eight courtiers and others, whilst a postscriptum to his lordship's letter asked for a further hundred to be held at the disposal of the Queen. These prisoners were to be transported at once to His Majesty's southern plantations, and to be kept there for the space of ten years before being restored to liberty, the parties to whom they were assigned entering into security to see that transportation was immediately effected.

We know from Lord Jeffreys's secretary how the Chief Justice inveighed that night in drunken frenzy against this misplaced clemency to which His Majesty had been persuaded. We know how he attempted by letter to induce the King to reconsider his decision. But James adhered to it. It was—apart from the indirect profit he derived from it—a clemency full worthy of him. He knew that to spare lives in this fashion was to convert them into living deaths. Many must succumb in torment to the horrors of West Indian slavery, and so be the envy of their surviving companions.

Thus it happened that Peter Blood, and with him Jeremy Pitt and Andrew Baynes, instead of being hanged, drawn, and quartered as their sentences directed, were conveyed to Bristol and there shipped with some fifty others aboard the *Jamaica Merchant*. From close confinement under hatches, ill-nourishment and foul water, a sickness broke out amongst them, of which eleven died. Amongst these was the unfortunate yeoman from Oglethorpe's Farm, brutally torn from his quiet homestead amid the fragrant cider orchards for no other sin but that he had practised mercy.

The mortality might have been higher than it was but for Peter Blood. At first the master of the *Jamaica Merchant* had answered with oaths and threats the doctor's expostulations against permitting men to perish in this fashion, and his insistence that he should be made free of the medicine chest and given leave to minister to the sick. But presently Captain Gardner came to see that he might be brought to task for these too heavy losses of human merchandise, and because of this he was belatedly glad to avail himself of the skill of Peter Blood. The doctor went to work zealously and zestfully, and wrought so ably that, by his ministrations and by improving the condition of his fellow-captives, he checked the spread of the disease.

Towards the middle of December the *Jamaica Merchant* dropped anchor in Carlisle Bay, and put ashore the forty-two surviving rebels-convict.

If these unfortunates had imagined—as many of them appear to have done—that they were coming into some wild, savage country, the prospect, of which they had a glimpse before they were hustled over the ship's side into the waiting boats, was enough to correct the impression. They beheld a town of sufficiently imposing proportions composed of houses built upon European notions of architecture, but without any of the huddle usual in European cities. The spire of a church rose dominantly above the red roofs, a fort guarded the entrance of the wide harbour, with guns thrusting their muzzles between the crenels, and the wide façade of Government House revealed itself dominantly placed on a gentle hill above the town. This hill was vividly green as is an English hill in April, and the day was such a day as April gives to England, the season of heavy rains being newly ended.

On a wide cobbled space on the sea front they found a guard of red-coated militia drawn up to receive them, and a crowd—attracted by their arrival—which in dress and manner differed little from a crowd in a seaport at home save that it contained fewer women and a great number of negroes.

To inspect them, drawn up there on the mole, came Governor Steed, a short, stout, red-faced gentleman, in blue taffetas burdened by a prodigious amount of gold lace, who limped a little and leaned heavily upon a stout ebony cane. After him, in the uniform of a colonel of the Barbados Militia, rolled a tall, corpulent man who towered head and shoulders above the Governor, with malevolence plainly written on his enormous yellowish countenance. At his side, and contrasting oddly with his grossness, moving with an easy stripling grace, came a slight young lady in a modish riding-gown. The broad brim of a grey hat with scarlet sweep of ostrich plume shaded an oval face upon which the climate of the Tropic of Cancer had made no impression, so delicately fair was its complexion. Ringlets of red-brown hair hung to her shoulders. Frankness looked out from her hazel eyes which were set wide; commiseration repressed now the mischievousness that normally inhabited her fresh young mouth.

Peter Blood caught himself staring in a sort of amazement at that piquant face, which seemed here so out of place, and finding his stare returned, he shifted uncomfortably. He grew conscious of the sorry figure that he cut. Unwashed, with rank and matted hair and a disfiguring black beard upon his face, and the erstwhile splendid suit of black camlet in which he had been taken prisoner now reduced to rags that would have disgraced a scarecrow, he was in no case for inspection by such dainty eyes as these. Nevertheless, they continued to inspect him with round-eyed, almost childlike wonder and pity. Their owner put forth a hand to touch the scarlet sleeve of her companion, whereupon with an ill-tempered grunt the man swung his great bulk round so that he directly confronted her.

Looking up into his face, she was speaking to him earnestly, but the Colonel plainly gave her no more than the half of his attention. His little beady eyes, closely flanking a fleshly, pendulous nose, had passed from her and were fixed upon fair-haired, sturdy young Pitt, who was standing beside Blood.

The Governor had also come to a halt, and for a moment now that little group of three stood in conversation. What the lady said, Peter could not hear at all, for she lowered her voice; the Colonel's reached him in a confused rumble, but the Governor was neither considerate nor indistinct; he had a high-pitched voice which carried far, and believing himself witty, he desired to be heard by all.

"But, my dear Colonel Bishop, it is for you to take first choice from this dainty nosegay, and at your own price. After that we'll send the rest to auction."

Colonel Bishop nodded his acknowledgment. He raised his voice in answering. "Your excellency is very good. But, faith, they're a weedy lot, not likely to be of much value in the plantation." His beady eyes scanned them again, and his contempt of them deepened the malevolence of his face. It was as if he were annoyed with them for being in no better condition. Then he beckoned forward Captain Gardner, the master of the *Jamaica Merchant*, and for some minutes stood in talk with him over a list which the latter produced at his request.

Presently he waved aside the list and advanced alone towards the rebels-convict, his eyes considering them, his lips pursed. Before the young Somersetshire shipmaster he came to a halt, and stood an instant pondering him. Then he fingered the muscles of the young man's arm, and bade him open his mouth that he might see his teeth. He pursed his coarse lips again and nodded.

He spoke to Gardner over his shoulder.

"Fifteen pounds for this one."

The Captain made a face of dismay. "Fifteen pounds! It isn't half what I meant to ask for him."

"It is double what I had meant to give," grunted the Colonel.

"But he would be cheap at thirty pounds, your honour."

"I can get a negro for that. These white swine don't live. They're not fit for the labour."

Gardner broke into protestations of Pitt's health, youth, and vigour. It was not a man he was discussing; it was a beast of burden. Pitt, a sensitive lad, stood mute and unmoving. Only the ebb and flow of colour in his cheeks showed the inward struggle by which he maintained his self-control.

Peter Blood was nauseated by the loathsome haggle.

In the background, moving slowly away down the line of prisoners, went the lady in conversation with the Governor, who smirked and preened himself as he limped beside her. She was unconscious of the loathly business the Colonel was transacting. Was she, wondered Blood, indifferent to it?

Colonel Bishop swung on his heel to pass on.

"I'll go as far as twenty pounds. Not a penny more, and it's twice as much as you are like to get from Crabston."

Captain Gardner, recognizing the finality of the tone, sighed and yielded. Already Bishop was moving down the line. For Mr. Blood, as for a weedy youth on his left, the Colonel had no more than a glance of contempt. But the next man, a middle-aged Colossus named Wolverstone, who had lost an eye at Sedgemoor, drew his regard, and the haggling was recommenced.

Peter Blood stood there in the brilliant sunshine and inhaled the fragrant air, which was unlike any air that he had ever breathed. It was laden with a strange perfume, blend of logwood flower, pimento, and aromatic cedars. He lost himself in unprofitable speculations born of that singular fragrance. He was in no mood for conversation, nor was Pitt, who stood dumbly at his side, and who was afflicted mainly at the moment by the thought that he was at last about to be separated from this man with whom he had stood shoulder to shoulder throughout all these troublous months, and whom he had come to love and depend upon for guidance and sustenance. A sense of loneliness and misery pervaded him by contrast with which all that he had endured seemed as nothing. To Pitt, this separation was the poignant climax of all his sufferings.

Other buyers came and stared at them, and passed on. Blood did not heed them. And then at the end of the line there was a movement. Gardner was speaking in a loud voice, making an announcement to the general public of buyers that had waited until Colonel Bishop had taken his choice of that human merchandise. As he finished, Blood, looking in his direction, noticed that the girl was speaking to Bishop, and pointing up the line with a silver-hilted riding-whip she carried. Bishop shaded his eyes with his hand to look in the direction in which she was pointing. Then slowly, with his ponderous, rolling gait, he approached again accompanied by Gardner, and followed by the lady and the Governor.

On they came until the Colonel was abreast of Blood. He would have passed on, but that the lady tapped his arm with her whip.

"But this is the man I meant," she said.

"This one?" Contempt rang in the voice. Peter Blood found himself staring into a pair of beady brown eyes sunk into a yellow, fleshly face like currants into a dumpling. He felt the colour creeping into his face under the insult of that contemptuous inspection. "Bah! A bag of bones. What should I do with him?"

He was turning away when Gardner interposed.

"He maybe lean, but he's tough; tough and healthy. When half of them was sick and the other half sickening, this rogue kept his legs and doctored his fellows. But for him there'd ha' been more deaths than there was. Say fifteen pounds for him, Colonel. That's cheap enough. He's tough, I tell your honour—tough and strong, though he be lean. And he's just the man to bear the heat when it comes. The climate'll never kill him."

There came a chuckle from Governor Steed. "You hear, Colonel. Trust your niece. Her sex knows a man when it sees one." And he laughed, well pleased with his wit.

But he laughed alone. A cloud of annoyance swept across the face of the Colonel's niece, whilst the Colonel himself was too absorbed in the consideration of this bargain to heed the Governor's humour. He twisted his lip a little, stroking his chin with his hand the while. Jeremy Pitt had almost ceased to breathe.

"I'll give you ten pounds for him," said the Colonel at last.

Peter Blood prayed that the offer might be rejected. For no reason that he could have given you, he was taken with repugnance at the thought of becoming the property of this gross animal, and in some sort the property of that hazel-eyed young girl. But it would need more than repugnance to save him from his destiny. A slave is a slave, and has no power to shape his fate. Peter Blood was sold to Colonel Bishop—a disdainful buyer—for the ignominious sum of ten pounds.

V. Arabella Bishop

One sunny morning in January, about a month after the arrival of the *Jamaica Merchant* at Bridgetown, Miss Arabella Bishop rode out from her uncle's fine house on the heights to the northwest of the city. She was attended by two negroes who trotted after her at a respectful distance, and her destination was Government House, whither she went to visit the Governor's lady, who had lately been ailing. Reaching the summit of a gentle, grassy slope, she met a tall, lean man dressed in a sober, gentlemanly fashion, who was walking in the opposite direction. He was a stranger to her, and strangers were rare enough in the island. And yet in some vague way he did not seem quite a stranger.

Miss Arabella drew rein, affecting to pause that she might admire the prospect, which was fair enough to warrant it. Yet out of the corner of those hazel eyes she scanned this fellow very attentively as he came nearer. She corrected her first impression of his dress. It was sober enough, but hardly gentlemanly. Coat and breeches were of plain homespun; and if the former sat so well upon him it was more by virtue of his natural grace than by that of tailoring. His stockings were of cotton, harsh and plain, and the broad castor, which he respectfully doffed as he came up with her, was an old one unadorned by band or feather. What had seemed to be a periwig at a little distance was now revealed for the man's own lustrous coiling black hair.

Out of a brown, shaven, saturnine face two eyes that were startlingly blue considered her gravely. The man would have passed on but that she detained him.

"I think I know you, sir," said she.

Her voice was crisp and boyish, and there was something of boyishness in her manner—if one can apply the term to so dainty a lady. It arose perhaps from an ease, a directness, which disdained the artifices of her sex, and set her on good terms with all the world. To this it may be due that Miss Arabella had reached the age of five and twenty not merely unmarried but unwooed. She used with all men a sisterly frankness which in itself contains a quality of aloofness, rendering it difficult for any man to become her lover.

Her negroes had halted at some distance in the rear, and they squatted now upon the short grass until it should be her pleasure to proceed upon her way.

The stranger came to a standstill upon being addressed.

"A lady should know her own property," said he.

"My property?"

"Your uncle's, leastways. Let me present myself. I am called Peter Blood, and I am worth precisely ten pounds. I know it because that is the sum your uncle paid for me. It is not every man has the same opportunities of ascertaining his real value."

She recognized him then. She had not seen him since that day upon the mole a month ago, and that she should not instantly have known him again despite the interest he had then aroused in her is not surprising, considering the change he had wrought in his appearance, which now was hardly that of a slave.

"My God!" said she. "And you can laugh!"

"It's an achievement," he admitted. "But then, I have not fared as ill as I might."

"I have heard of that," said she.

What she had heard was that this rebel-convict had been discovered to be a physician. The thing had come to the ears of Governor Steed, who suffered damnably from the gout, and Governor Steed had borrowed the fellow from his purchaser. Whether by skill or good fortune, Peter Blood had afforded the Governor that relief which his excellency had failed to obtain from the ministrations of either of the two physicians practising in Bridgetown. Then the Governor's lady had desired him to attend her for the megrims. Mr. Blood had found her suffering from nothing worse than peevishness—the result of a natural petulance aggravated by the dulness of life in Barbados to a lady of her social aspirations. But he had prescribed for her none the less, and she had conceived herself the better for his prescription. After that the fame of him had gone through Bridgetown, and Colonel Bishop had found that there was more profit to be made out of this new slave by leaving him to pursue his profession than by setting him to work on the plantations, for which purpose he had been originally acquired.

"It is yourself, madam, I have to thank for my comparatively easy and clean condition," said Mr. Blood, "and I am glad to take this opportunity of doing so."

The gratitude was in his words rather than in his tone. Was he mocking, she wondered, and looked at him with the searching frankness that another might have found disconcerting. He took the glance for a question, and answered it.

"If some other planter had bought me," he explained, "it is odds that the facts of my shining abilities might never have been brought to light, and I should be hewing and hoeing at this moment like the poor wretches who were landed with me."

"And why do you thank me for that? It was my uncle who bought you."

"But he would not have done so had you not urged him. I perceived your interest. At the time I resented it."

"You resented it?" There was a challenge in her boyish voice.

"I have had no lack of experiences of this mortal life; but to be bought and sold was a new one, and I was hardly in the mood to love my purchaser."

"If I urged you upon my uncle, sir, it was that I commiserated you." There was a slight severity in her tone, as if to reprove the mixture of mockery and flippancy in which he seemed to be speaking.

She proceeded to explain herself. "My uncle may appear to you a hard man. No doubt he is. They are all hard men, these planters. It is the life, I suppose. But there are others here who are worse. There is Mr. Crabston, for instance, up at Speightstown. He was there on the mole, waiting to buy my uncle's leavings, and if you had fallen into his hands . . . A dreadful man. That is why."

He was a little bewildered.

"This interest in a stranger . . ." he began. Then changed the direction of his probe. "But there were others as deserving of commiseration."

"You did not seem quite like the others."

"I am not," said he.

"Oh!" She stared at him, bridling a little. "You have a good opinion of yourself."

"On the contrary. The others are all worthy rebels. I am not. That is the difference. I was one who had not the wit to see that England requires purifying. I was content to pursue a doctor's trade in Bridgewater whilst my betters were shedding their blood to drive out an unclean tyrant and his rascally crew."

"Sir!" she checked him. "I think you are talking treason."

"I hope I am not obscure," said he.

"There are those here who would have you flogged if they heard you."

"The Governor would never allow it. He has the gout, and his lady has the megrims."

"Do you depend upon that?" She was frankly scornful.

"You have certainly never had the gout; probably not even the megrims," said he.

She made a little impatient movement with her hand, and looked away from him a moment, out to sea. Quite suddenly she looked at him again; and now her brows were knit.

"But if you are not a rebel, how come you here?"

He saw the thing she apprehended, and he laughed. "Faith, now, it's a long story," said he.

"And one perhaps that you would prefer not to tell?"

Briefly on that he told it her.

"My God! What an infamy!" she cried, when he had done.

"Oh, it's a sweet country England under King James! There's no need to commiserate me further. All things considered I prefer Barbados. Here at least one can believe in God."

He looked first to right, then to left as he spoke, from the distant shadowy bulk of Mount Hillbay to the limitless ocean ruffled by the winds of heaven. Then, as if the fair prospect rendered him conscious of his own littleness and the insignificance of his woes, he fell thoughtful.

"Is that so difficult elsewhere?" she asked him, and she was very grave.

"Men make it so."

"I see." She laughed a little, on a note of sadness, it seemed to him. "I have never deemed Barbados the earthly mirror of heaven," she confessed. "But no doubt you know your world better than I." She touched her horse with her little silver-hilted whip. "I congratulate you on this easing of your misfortunes."

He bowed, and she moved on. Her negroes sprang up, and went trotting after her.

Awhile Peter Blood remained standing there, where she left him, conning the sunlit waters of Carlisle Bay below, and the shipping in that spacious haven about which the gulls were fluttering noisily.

It was a fair enough prospect, he reflected, but it was a prison, and in announcing that he preferred it to England, he had indulged that almost laudable form of boasting which lies in belittling our misadventures.

He turned, and resuming his way, went off in long, swinging strides towards the little huddle of huts built of mud and wattles—a miniature village enclosed in a stockade which the plantation slaves inhabited, and where he, himself, was lodged with them.

Through his mind sang the line of Lovelace:

> Stone walls do not a prison make,
> Nor iron bars a cage.

But he gave it a fresh meaning, the very converse of that which its author had intended. A prison, he reflected, was a prison, though it had neither walls nor bars, however spacious it might be. And as he realized it that morning so he was to realize it increasingly as time sped on. Daily he came to think more of his clipped wings, of his exclusion from the world, and less of the fortuitous liberty he enjoyed. Nor did the contrasting of his comparatively easy lot with that of his unfortunate fellow-convicts bring him the satisfaction a differently constituted mind might have derived from it. Rather did the contemplation of their misery increase the bitterness that was gathering in his soul.

Of the forty-two who had been landed with him from the *Jamaica Merchant*, Colonel Bishop had purchased no less than twenty-five. The remainder had gone to lesser planters, some of them to Speightstown, and others still farther north. What may have been the lot of the latter he could not tell, but amongst Bishop's slaves Peter Blood came and went freely, sleeping in their quarters, and their lot he knew to be a brutalizing misery. They toiled in the sugar plantations from sunrise to sunset, and if their labours flagged, there were the whips of the overseer and his men to quicken them. They went in rags, some almost naked; they dwelt in squalor, and they were ill-nourished on salted meat and maize dumplings—food which to many of them was for a season at least so nauseating that two of them sickened and died before Bishop remembered that their lives had a certain value in labour to him and yielded to Blood's intercessions for a better care of such as fell ill. To curb insubordination, one of them who had rebelled against Kent, the brutal overseer, was lashed to death by negroes under his comrades' eyes, and another who had been so misguided as to run away into the woods was tracked, brought back, flogged, and then branded on the forehead with the letters "F. T.," that all might know him for a fugitive traitor as long as he lived. Fortunately for him the poor fellow died as a consequence of the flogging.

After that a dull, spiritless resignation settled down upon the remainder. The most mutinous were quelled, and accepted their unspeakable lot with the tragic fortitude of despair.

Peter Blood alone, escaping these excessive sufferings, remained outwardly unchanged, whilst inwardly the only change in him was a daily deeper hatred of his kind, a daily deeper longing to escape from this place where man defiled so foully the lovely work of his Creator. It was a longing too vague to amount to a hope. Hope here was inadmissible. And yet he did not yield to despair. He set a mask of laughter on his saturnine countenance and went his way, treating the sick to the profit of Colonel Bishop, and encroaching further and further upon the preserves of the two other men of medicine in Bridgetown.

Immune from the degrading punishments and privations of his fellow-convicts, he was enabled to keep his self-respect, and was treated without harshness even by the soulless planter to whom he had been sold. He owed it all to gout and megrims. He had won the esteem of Governor Steed, and—what is even more important—of Governor Steed's lady, whom he shamelessly and cynically flattered and humoured.

Occasionally he saw Miss Bishop, and they seldom met but that she paused to hold him in conversation for some moments, evincing her interest in him. Himself, he was never disposed to linger. He was not, he told himself, to be deceived by her delicate exterior, her sapling grace, her easy, boyish ways and pleasant, boyish voice. In all his life—and it had been very varied—he had never met a man whom he accounted more beastly than her uncle, and he could not dissociate her from the man. She was his niece, of his own blood, and some of the vices of it, some of the remorseless cruelty of the wealthy planter must, he argued, inhabit that pleasant body of hers. He argued this very often to himself, as if answering and convincing some instinct that pleaded otherwise, and arguing it he avoided her when it was possible, and was frigidly civil when it was not.

Justifiable as his reasoning was, plausible as it may seem, yet he would have done better to have trusted the instinct that was in conflict with it. Though the same blood ran in her veins as in those of Colonel Bishop, yet hers was free of the vices that tainted her uncle's, for these vices were not natural to that blood; they were, in his case, acquired. Her father, Tom Bishop—that same Colonel Bishop's brother—had been a kindly, chivalrous, gentle soul, who, broken-hearted by the early death of a young wife, had abandoned the Old World and sought an anodyne for his grief in the New. He had come out to the Antilles, bringing with him his little daughter, then five years of age, and had given himself up to the life of a planter. He had prospered from the first, as men sometimes will who care nothing for prosperity. Prospering, he had bethought him of his younger brother, a soldier at home reputed somewhat wild. He had advised him to come out to Barbados; and the advice, which at another season William Bishop might have scorned, reached him at a moment when his wildness was beginning to bear such fruit that a change of climate was desirable. William came, and was admitted by his generous brother to a partnership in the prosperous plantation. Some six years later, when Arabella was fifteen, her father died, leaving her in her uncle's guardianship. It was perhaps his one mistake. But the goodness of his own nature coloured his views of other men; moreover, himself, he had conducted the education of his daughter, giving her an independence of character upon which perhaps he counted unduly. As things were, there was little love between uncle and niece. But she was dutiful to him, and he was circumspect in his behaviour before her. All his life, and for all his wildness, he had gone in a certain awe of his brother, whose worth he had the wit to recognize; and now it was almost as if some of that awe was transferred to his brother's child, who was also, in a sense, his partner, although she took no active part in the business of the plantations.

Peter Blood judged her—as we are all too prone to judge—upon insufficient knowledge.

He was very soon to have cause to correct that judgment.

One day towards the end of May, when the heat was beginning to grow oppressive, there crawled into Carlisle Bay a wounded, battered English ship, the *Pride of Devon*, her freeboard scarred and broken, her coach a gaping wreck, her mizzen so shot away that only a jagged stump remained to tell the place where it had stood. She had been in action off Martinique with two Spanish treasure ships, and although her captain swore that the Spaniards had beset him without provocation, it is difficult to avoid a suspicion that the encounter had been brought about quite otherwise. One of the Spaniards had fled from the combat, and if the *Pride of Devon* had not given chase it was probably because she was by then in no case to do so. The other had been sunk, but not before the English ship had transferred to her own hold a good deal of the treasure aboard the Spaniard. It was, in fact, one of those piratical affrays which were a perpetual source of trouble between the courts of St. James's and the Escurial, complaints emanating now from one and now from the other side.

Steed, however, after the fashion of most Colonial governors, was willing enough to dull his wits to the extent of accepting the English seaman's story, disregarding any evidence that might belie it. He shared the hatred so richly deserved by arrogant, overbearing Spain that was common to men of every other nation from the Bahamas to the Main. Therefore he gave the *Pride of Devon* the shelter she sought in his harbour and every facility to careen and carry out repairs.

But before it came to this, they fetched from her hold over a score of English seamen as battered and broken as the ship herself, and together with these some half-dozen Spaniards in like case, the only survivors of a boarding party from the Spanish galleon that had invaded the English ship and found itself unable to retreat. These wounded men were conveyed to a long shed on the wharf, and the medical skill of Bridgetown was summoned to their aid. Peter Blood was ordered to bear a hand in this work, and partly because he spoke Castilian—and he spoke it as fluently as his own native tongue—partly because of his inferior condition as a slave, he was given the Spaniards for his patients.

Now Blood had no cause to love Spaniards. His two years in a Spanish prison and his subsequent campaigning in the Spanish Netherlands had shown him a side of the Spanish character which he had found anything but admirable. Nevertheless he performed his doctor's duties zealously and painstakingly, if emotionlessly, and even with a certain superficial friendliness towards each of his patients. These were so surprised at having their wounds healed instead of being summarily hanged that they manifested a docility very unusual in their kind. They were shunned, however, by all those charitably disposed inhabitants of Bridgetown who flocked to the improvised hospital with gifts of fruit and flowers and delicacies for the injured English seamen. Indeed, had the wishes of some of these inhabitants been regarded, the Spaniards would have been left to die like vermin, and of this Peter Blood had an example almost at the very outset.

With the assistance of one of the negroes sent to the shed for the purpose, he was in the act of setting a broken leg, when a deep, gruff voice, that he had come to know and dislike as he had never disliked the voice of living man, abruptly challenged him.

"What are you doing there?"

Blood did not look up from his task. There was not the need. He knew the voice, as I have said.

"I am setting a broken leg," he answered, without pausing in his labours.

"I can see that, fool." A bulky body interposed between Peter Blood and the window. The half-naked man on the straw rolled his black eyes to stare up fearfully out of a clay-coloured face at this intruder. A knowledge of English was unnecessary to inform him that here came an enemy. The harsh, minatory note of that voice sufficiently expressed the fact. "I can see that, fool; just as I can see what the rascal is. Who gave you leave to set Spanish legs?"

"I am a doctor, Colonel Bishop. The man is wounded. It is not for me to discriminate. I keep to my trade."

"Do you, by God! If you'd done that, you wouldn't now be here."

"On the contrary, it is because I did it that I am here."

"Aye, I know that's your lying tale." The Colonel sneered; and then, observing Blood to continue his work unmoved, he grew really angry. "Will you cease that, and attend to me when I am speaking?"

Peter Blood paused, but only for an instant. "The man is in pain," he said shortly, and resumed his work.

"In pain, is he? I hope he is, the damned piratical dog. But will you heed me, you insubordinate knave?"

The Colonel delivered himself in a roar, infuriated by what he conceived to be defiance, and defiance expressing itself in the most unruffled disregard of himself. His long bamboo cane was raised to strike. Peter Blood's blue eyes caught the flash of it, and he spoke quickly to arrest the blow.

"Not insubordinate, sir, whatever I may be. I am acting upon the express orders of Governor Steed."

The Colonel checked, his great face empurpling. His mouth fell open.

"Governor Steed!" he echoed. Then he lowered his cane, swung round, and without another word to Blood rolled away towards the other end of the shed where the Governor was standing at the moment.

Peter Blood chuckled. But his triumph was dictated less by humanitarian considerations than by the reflection that he had baulked his brutal owner.

The Spaniard, realizing that in this altercation, whatever its nature, the doctor had stood his friend, ventured in a muted voice to ask him what had happened. But the doctor shook his head in silence, and pursued his work. His ears were straining to catch the words now passing between Steed and Bishop. The Colonel was blustering and storming, the great bulk of him towering above the wizened little overdressed figure of the Governor. But the little fop was not to be browbeaten. His excellency was conscious that he had behind him the force of public opinion to support him. Some there might be, but they were not many, who held such ruthless views as Colonel Bishop. His excellency asserted his authority. It was by his orders that Blood had devoted himself to the wounded Spaniards, and his orders were to be carried out. There was no more to be said.

Colonel Bishop was of another opinion. In his view there was a great deal to be said. He said it, with great circumstance, loudly, vehemently, obscenely—for he could be fluently obscene when moved to anger.

"You talk like a Spaniard, Colonel," said the Governor, and thus dealt the Colonel's pride a wound that was to smart resentfully for many a week. At the moment it struck him silent, and sent him stamping out of the shed in a rage for which he could find no words.

It was two days later when the ladies of Bridgetown, the wives and daughters of her planters and merchants, paid their first visit of charity to the wharf, bringing their gifts to the wounded seamen.

Again Peter Blood was there, ministering to the sufferers in his care, moving among those unfortunate Spaniards whom no one heeded. All the charity, all the gifts were for the members of the crew of the *Pride of Devon*. And this Peter Blood accounted natural enough. But rising suddenly from the re-dressing of a wound, a task in which he had been absorbed for some moments, he saw to his surprise that one lady, detached from the general throng, was placing some plantains and a bundle of succulent sugar cane on the cloak that served one of his patients for a coverlet. She was elegantly dressed in lavender silk and was followed by a half-naked negro carrying a basket.

Peter Blood, stripped of his coat, the sleeves of his coarse shirt rolled to the elbow, and holding a bloody rag in his hand, stood at gaze a moment. The lady, turning now to confront him, her lips parting in a smile of recognition, was Arabella Bishop.

"The man's a Spaniard," said he, in the tone of one who corrects a misapprehension, and also tinged never so faintly by something of the derision that was in his soul.

The smile with which she had been greeting him withered on her lips. She frowned and stared at him a moment, with increasing haughtiness.

"So I perceive. But he's a human being none the less," said she.

That answer, and its implied rebuke, took him by surprise.

"Your uncle, the Colonel, is of a different opinion," said he, when he had recovered. "He regards them as vermin to be left to languish and die of their festering wounds."

She caught the irony now more plainly in his voice. She continued to stare at him.

"Why do you tell me this?"

"To warn you that you may be incurring the Colonel's displeasure. If he had had his way, I should never have been allowed to dress their wounds."

"And you thought, of course, that I must be of my uncle's mind?" There was a crispness about her voice, an ominous challenging sparkle in her hazel eyes.

"I'd not willingly be rude to a lady even in my thoughts," said he. "But that you should bestow gifts on them, considering that if your uncle came to hear of it . . ." He paused, leaving the sentence unfinished. "Ah, well—there it is!" he concluded.

But the lady was not satisfied at all.

"First you impute to me inhumanity, and then cowardice. Faith! For a man who would not willingly be rude to a lady even in his thoughts, it's none so bad." Her boyish laugh trilled out, but the note of it jarred his ears this time.

He saw her now, it seemed to him, for the first time, and saw how he had misjudged her.

"Sure, now, how was I to guess that . . . that Colonel Bishop could have an angel for his niece?" said he recklessly, for he was reckless as men often are in sudden penitence.

"You wouldn't, of course. I shouldn't think you often guess aright." Having withered him with that and her glance, she turned to her negro and the basket that he carried. From this she lifted now the fruits and delicacies with which it was laden, and piled them in such heaps upon the beds of the six Spaniards that by the time she had so served the last of them her basket was empty, and there was nothing left for her own fellow-countrymen. These, indeed, stood in no need of her bounty—as she no doubt observed—since they were being plentifully supplied by others.

Having thus emptied her basket, she called her negro, and without another word or so much as another glance at Peter Blood, swept out of the place with her head high and chin thrust forward.

Peter watched her departure. Then he fetched a sigh.

It startled him to discover that the thought that he had incurred her anger gave him concern. It could not have been so yesterday. It became so only since he had been vouchsafed this revelation of her true nature. "Bad cess to it now, it serves me right. It seems I know nothing at all of human nature. But how the devil was I to guess that a family that can breed a devil like Colonel Bishop should also breed a saint like this?"

VI. PLAN OF ESCAPE

After that Arabella Bishop went daily to the shed on the wharf with gifts of fruit, and later of money and of wearing apparel for the Spanish prisoners. But she contrived so to time her visits that Peter Blood never again met her there. Also his own visits were growing shorter in a measure as his patients healed. That they all throve and returned to health under his care, whilst fully one third of the wounded in the care of Whacker and Bronson—the two other surgeons—died of their wounds, served to increase the reputation in which this rebel-convict stood in Bridgetown. It may have been no more than the fortune of war. But the townsfolk did not choose so to regard it. It led to a further dwindling of the practices of his free colleagues and a further increase of his own labours and his owner's profit. Whacker and Bronson laid their heads together to devise a scheme by which this intolerable state of things should be brought to an end. But that is to anticipate.

One day, whether by accident or design, Peter Blood came striding down the wharf a full half-hour earlier than usual, and so met Miss Bishop just issuing from the shed. He doffed his hat and stood aside to give her passage. She took it, chin in the air, and eyes which disdained to look anywhere where the sight of him was possible.

"Miss Arabella," said he, on a coaxing, pleading note.

She grew conscious of his presence, and looked him over with an air that was faintly, mockingly searching.

"La!" said she. "It's the delicate-minded gentleman!"

Peter groaned. "Am I so hopelessly beyond forgiveness? I ask it very humbly."

"What condescension!"

"It is cruel to mock me," said he, and adopted mock-humility. "After all, I am but a slave. And you might be ill one of these days."

"What, then?"

"It would be humiliating to send for me if you treat me like an enemy."

"You are not the only doctor in Bridgetown."

"But I am the least dangerous."

She grew suddenly suspicious of him, aware that he was permitting himself to rally her, and in a measure she had already yielded to it. She stiffened, and looked him over again.

"You make too free, I think," she rebuked him.

"A doctor's privilege."

"I am not your patient. Please to remember it in future." And on that, unquestionably angry, she departed.

"Now is she a vixen or am I a fool, or is it both?" he asked the blue vault of heaven, and then went into the shed.

It was to be a morning of excitements. As he was leaving an hour or so later, Whacker, the younger of the other two physicians, joined him—an unprecedented condescension this, for hitherto neither of them had addressed him beyond an occasional and surly "good-day!"

"If you are for Colonel Bishop's, I'll walk with you a little way, Doctor Blood," said he. He was a short, broad man of five-and-forty with pendulous cheeks and hard blue eyes.

Peter Blood was startled. But he dissembled it.

"I am for Government House," said he.

"Ah! To be sure! The Governor's lady." And he laughed; or perhaps he sneered. Peter Blood was not quite certain. "She encroaches a deal upon your time, I hear. Youth and good looks, Doctor Blood! Youth and good looks! They are inestimable advantages in our profession as in others—particularly where the ladies are concerned."

Peter stared at him. "If you mean what you seem to mean, you had better say it to Governor Steed. It may amuse him."

"You surely misapprehend me."

"I hope so."

"You're so very hot, now!" The doctor linked his arm through Peter's. "I protest I desire to be your friend—to serve you. Now, listen." Instinctively his voice grew lower. "This slavery in which you find yourself must be singularly irksome to a man of parts such as yourself."

"What intuitions!" cried sardonic Mr. Blood. But the doctor took him literally.

"I am no fool, my dear doctor. I know a man when I see one, and often I can tell his thoughts."

"If you can tell me mine, you'll persuade me of it," said Mr. Blood.

Dr. Whacker drew still closer to him as they stepped along the wharf. He lowered his voice to a still more confidential tone. His hard blue eyes peered up into the swart, sardonic face of his companion, who was a head taller than himself.

"How often have I not seen you staring out over the sea, your soul in your eyes! Don't I know what you are thinking? If you could escape from this hell of slavery, you could exercise the profession of which you are an ornament as a free man with pleasure and profit to yourself. The world is large. There are many nations besides England where a man of your parts would be warmly welcomed. There are many colonies besides these English ones." Lower still came the voice until it was no more than a whisper. Yet there was no one within earshot. "It is none so far now to the Dutch settlement of Curaçao. At this time of the year the voyage may safely be undertaken in a light craft. And Curaçao need be no more than a stepping-stone to the great world, which would lie open to you once you were delivered from this bondage."

Dr. Whacker ceased. He was pale and a little out of breath. But his hard eyes continued to study his impassive companion.

"Well?" he said after a pause. "What do you say to that?"

Yet Blood did not immediately answer. His mind was heaving in tumult, and he was striving to calm it that he might take a proper survey of this thing flung into it to create so monstrous a disturbance. He began where another might have ended.

"I have no money. And for that a handsome sum would be necessary."

"Did I not say that I desired to be your friend?"

"Why?" asked Peter Blood at point-blank range.

But he never heeded the answer. Whilst Dr. Whacker was professing that his heart bled for a brother doctor languishing in slavery, denied the opportunity which his gifts entitled him to make for himself, Peter Blood pounced like a hawk upon the obvious truth. Whacker and his colleague desired to be rid of one who threatened to ruin them. Sluggishness of decision was never a fault of Blood's. He leapt where another crawled. And so this thought of evasion never entertained until planted there now by Dr. Whacker sprouted into instant growth.

"I see, I see," he said, whilst his companion was still talking, explaining, and to save Dr. Whacker's face he played the hypocrite. "It is very noble in you—very brotherly, as between men of medicine. It is what I myself should wish to do in like case."

The hard eyes flashed, the husky voice grew tremulous as the other asked almost too eagerly:

"You agree, then? You agree?"

"Agree?" Blood laughed. "If I should be caught and brought back, they'd clip my wings and brand me for life."

"Surely the thing is worth a little risk?" More tremulous than ever was the tempter's voice.

"Surely," Blood agreed. "But it asks more than courage. It asks money. A sloop might be bought for twenty pounds, perhaps."

"It shall be forthcoming. It shall be a loan, which you shall repay us—repay me, when you can."

That betraying "us" so hastily retrieved completed Blood's understanding. The other doctor was also in the business.

They were approaching the peopled part of the mole. Quickly, but eloquently, Blood expressed his thanks, where he knew that no thanks were due.

"We will talk of this again, sir—to-morrow," he concluded. "You have opened for me the gates of hope."

In that at least he tittered no more than the bare truth, and expressed it very baldly. It was, indeed, as if a door had been suddenly flung open to the sunlight for escape from a dark prison in which a man had thought to spend his life.

He was in haste now to be alone, to straighten out his agitated mind and plan coherently what was to be done. Also he must consult another. Already he had hit upon that other. For such a voyage a navigator would be necessary, and a navigator was ready to his hand in Jeremy Pitt. The first thing was to take counsel with the young shipmaster, who must be associated with him in this business if it were to be undertaken. All that day his mind was in turmoil with this new hope, and he was sick with impatience for night and a chance to discuss the matter with his chosen partner. As a result Blood was betimes that evening in the spacious stockade that enclosed the huts of the slaves together with the big white house of the overseer, and he found an opportunity of a few words with Pitt, unobserved by the others.

"To-night when all are asleep, come to my cabin. I have something to say to you."

The young man stared at him, roused by Blood's pregnant tone out of the mental lethargy into which he had of late been lapsing as a result of the dehumanizing life he lived. Then he nodded understanding and assent, and they moved apart.

The six months of plantation life in Barbados had made an almost tragic mark upon the young seaman. His erstwhile bright alertness was all departed. His face was growing vacuous, his eyes were dull and lack-lustre, and he moved in a cringing, furtive manner, like an over-beaten dog. He had survived the ill-nourishment, the excessive work on the sugar plantation under a pitiless sun, the lashes of the overseer's whip when his labours flagged, and the deadly, unrelieved animal life to which he was condemned. But the price he was paying for survival was the usual price. He was in danger of becoming no better than an animal, of sinking to the level of the negroes who sometimes toiled beside him. The man, however, was still there, not yet dormant, but merely torpid from a surfeit of despair; and the man in him promptly shook off that torpidity and awoke at the first words Blood spoke to him that night—awoke and wept.

"Escape?" he panted. "O God!" He took his head in his hands, and fell to sobbing like a child.

"Sh! Steady now! Steady!" Blood admonished him in a whisper, alarmed by the lad's blubbering. He crossed to Pitt's side, and set a restraining hand upon his shoulder. "For God's sake, command yourself. If we're overheard we shall both be flogged for this."

Among the privileges enjoyed by Blood was that of a hut to himself, and they were alone in this. But, after all, it was built of wattles thinly plastered with mud, and its door was composed of bamboos, through which sound passed very easily. Though the stockade was locked for the night, and all within it asleep by now—it was after midnight—yet a prowling overseer was not impossible, and a sound of voices must lead to discovery. Pitt realized this, and controlled his outburst of emotion.

Sitting close thereafter they talked in whispers for an hour or more, and all the while those dulled wits of Pitt's were sharpening themselves anew upon this precious whetstone of hope. They would need to recruit others into their enterprise, a half-dozen at least, a half-score if possible, but no more than that. They must pick the best out of that score of survivors of the Monmouth men that Colonel Bishop had acquired. Men who understood the sea were desirable. But of these there were only two in that unfortunate gang, and their knowledge was none too full. They were Hagthorpe, a gentleman who had served in the Royal Navy, and Nicholas Dyke, who had been a petty officer in the late king's time, and there was another who had been a gunner, a man named Ogle.

It was agreed before they parted that Pitt should begin with these three and then proceed to recruit some six or eight others. He was to move with the utmost caution, sounding his men very carefully before making anything in the nature of a disclosure, and even then avoid rendering that disclosure so full that its betrayal might frustrate the plans which as yet had to be worked out in detail. Labouring with them in the plantations, Pitt would not want for opportunities of broaching the matter to his fellow-slaves.

"Caution above everything," was Blood's last recommendation to him at parting. "Who goes slowly, goes safely, as the Italians have it. And remember that if you betray yourself, you ruin all, for you are the only navigator amongst us, and without you there is no escaping."

Pitt reassured him, and slunk off back to his own hut, and the straw that served him for a bed.

Coming next morning to the wharf, Blood found Dr. Whacker in a generous mood. Having slept on the matter, he was prepared to advance the convict any sum up to thirty pounds that would enable him to acquire a boat capable of taking him away from the settlement. Blood expressed his thanks becomingly, betraying no sign that he saw clearly into the true reason of the other's munificence.

"It's not money I'll require," said he, "but the boat itself. For who will be selling me a boat and incurring the penalties in Governor Steed's proclamation? Ye'll have read it, no doubt?"

Dr. Whacker's heavy face grew overcast. Thoughtfully he rubbed his chin. "I've read it—yes. And I dare not procure the boat for you. It would be discovered. It must be. And the penalty is a fine of two hundred pounds besides imprisonment. It would ruin me. You'll see that?"

The high hopes in Blood's soul began to shrink. And the shadow of his despair overcast his face.

"But then . . ." he faltered. "There is nothing to be done."

"Nay, nay: things are not so desperate." Dr. Whacker smiled a little with tight lips. "I've thought of it. You will see that the man who buys the boat must be one of those who goes with you—so that he is not here to answer questions afterwards."

"But who is to go with me save men in my own case? What I cannot do, they cannot."

"There are others detained on the island besides slaves. There are several who are here for debt, and would be glad enough to spread their wings. There's a fellow Nuttall, now, who follows the trade of a shipwright, whom I happen to know would welcome such a chance as you might afford him."

"But how should a debtor come with money to buy a boat? The question will be asked."

"To be sure it will. But if you contrive shrewdly, you'll all be gone before that happens."

Blood nodded understanding, and the doctor, setting a hand upon his sleeve, unfolded the scheme he had conceived.

"You shall have the money from me at once. Having received it, you'll forget that it was I who supplied it to you. You have friends in England—relatives, perhaps—who sent it out to you through the agency of one of your Bridgetown patients, whose name as a man of honour you will on no account divulge lest you bring trouble upon him. That is your tale if there are questions."

He paused, looking hard at Blood. Blood nodded understanding and assent. Relieved, the doctor continued: "But there should be no questions if you go carefully to work. You concert matters with Nuttall. You enlist him as one of your companions—and a shipwright should be a very useful member of your crew. You engage him to discover a likely sloop whose owner is disposed to sell. Then let your preparations all be made before the purchase is effected, so that your escape may follow instantly upon it before the inevitable questions come to be asked. You take me?"

So well did Blood take him that within an hour he contrived to see Nuttall, and found the fellow as disposed to the business as Dr. Whacker had predicted. When he left the shipwright, it was agreed that Nuttall should seek the boat required, for which Blood would at once produce the money.

The quest took longer than was expected by Blood, who waited impatiently with the doctor's gold concealed about his person. But at the end of some three weeks, Nuttall—whom he was now meeting daily informed him that he had found a serviceable wherry, and that its owner was disposed to sell it for twenty-two pounds. That evening, on the beach, remote from all eyes, Peter Blood handed that sum to his new associate, and Nuttall went off with instructions to complete the purchase late on the following day. He was to bring the boat to the wharf, where under cover of night Blood and his fellow-convicts would join him and make off.

Everything was ready. In the shed, from which all the wounded men had now been removed and which had since remained untenanted, Nuttall had concealed the necessary stores: a hundredweight of bread, a quantity of cheese, a cask of water and some few bottles of Canary, a compass, quadrant, chart, half-hour glass, log and line, a tarpaulin, some carpenter's tools, and a lantern and candles. And in the stockade, all was likewise in readiness. Hagthorpe, Dyke, and Ogle had agreed to join the venture, and eight others had been carefully recruited. In Pitt's hut, which he shared with five other rebels-convict, all of whom were to join in this bid for liberty, a ladder had been constructed in secret during those nights of waiting. With this they were to surmount the stockade and gain the open. The risk of detection, so that they made little noise, was negligible. Beyond locking them all into that stockade at night, there was no great precaution taken. Where, after all, could any so foolish as to attempt escape hope to conceal himself in that island? The chief risk lay in discovery by those of their companions who were to be left behind. It was because of these that they must go cautiously and in silence.

The day that was to have been their last in Barbados was a day of hope and anxiety to the twelve associates in that enterprise, no less than to Nuttall in the town below.

Towards sunset, having seen Nuttall depart to purchase and fetch the sloop to the prearranged moorings at the wharf, Peter Blood came sauntering towards the stockade, just as the slaves were being driven in from the fields. He stood aside at the entrance to let them pass, and beyond the message of hope flashed by his eyes, he held no communication with them.

He entered the stockade in their wake, and as they broke their ranks to seek their various respective huts, he beheld Colonel Bishop in talk with Kent, the overseer. The pair were standing by the stocks, planted in the middle of that green space for the punishment of offending slaves.

As he advanced, Bishop turned to regard him, scowling.

"Where have you been this while?" he bawled, and although a minatory note was normal to the Colonel's voice, yet Blood felt his heart tightening apprehensively.

"I've been at my work in the town," he answered. "Mrs. Patch has a fever and Mr. Dekker has sprained his ankle."

"I sent for you to Dekker's, and you were not there. You are given to idling, my fine fellow. We shall have to quicken you one of these days unless you cease from abusing the liberty you enjoy. D'ye forget that ye're a rebel convict?"

"I am not given the chance," said Blood, who never could learn to curb his tongue.

"By God! Will you be pert with me?"

Remembering all that was at stake, growing suddenly conscious that from the huts surrounding the enclosure anxious ears were listening, he instantly practised an unusual submission.

"Not pert, sir. I . . . I am sorry I should have been sought . . ."

"Aye, and you'll be sorrier yet. There's the Governor with an attack of gout, screaming like a wounded horse, and you nowhere to be found. Be off, man—away with you at speed to Government House! You're awaited, I tell you. Best lend him a horse, Kent, or the lout'll be all night getting there."

They bustled him away, choking almost from a reluctance that he dared not show. The thing was unfortunate; but after all not beyond remedy. The escape was set for midnight, and he should easily be back by then.

He mounted the horse that Kent procured him, intending to make all haste.

"How shall I reenter the stockade, sir?" he enquired at parting.

"You'll not reënter it," said Bishop. "When they've done with you at Government House, they may find a kennel for you there until morning."

Peter Blood's heart sank like a stone through water.

"But . . ." he began.

"Be off, I say. Will you stand there talking until dark? His excellency is waiting for you." And with his cane Colonel Bishop slashed the horse's quarters so brutally that the beast bounded forward all but unseating her rider.

Peter Blood went off in a state of mind bordering on despair. And there was occasion for it. A postponement of the escape at least until to-morrow night was necessary now, and postponement must mean the discovery of Nuttall's transaction and the asking of questions it would be difficult to answer.

It was in his mind to slink back in the night, once his work at Government House were done, and from the outside of the stockade make known to Pitt and the others his presence, and so have them join him that their project might still be carried out. But in this he reckoned without the Governor, whom he found really in the thrall of a severe attack of gout, and almost as severe an attack of temper nourished by Blood's delay.

The doctor was kept in constant attendance upon him until long after midnight, when at last he was able to ease the sufferer a little by a bleeding. Thereupon he would have withdrawn. But Steed would not hear of it. Blood must sleep in his own chamber to be at hand in case of need. It was as if Fate made sport of him. For that night at least the escape must be definitely abandoned.

Not until the early hours of the morning did Peter Blood succeed in making a temporary escape from Government House on the ground that he required certain medicaments which he must, himself, procure from the apothecary.

On that pretext, he made an excursion into the awakening town, and went straight to Nuttall, whom he found in a state of livid panic. The unfortunate debtor, who had sat up waiting through the night, conceived that all was discovered and that his own ruin would be involved. Peter Blood quieted his fears.

"It will be for to-night instead," he said, with more assurance than he felt, "if I have to bleed the Governor to death. Be ready as last night."

"But if there are questions meanwhile?" bleated Nuttall. He was a thin, pale, small-featured man with weak eyes that now blinked desperately.

"Answer as best you can. Use your wits, man. I can stay no longer." And Peter went off to the apothecary for his pretexted drugs.

Within an hour of his going came an officer of the Secretary's to Nuttall's miserable hovel. The seller of the boat had—as by law required since the coming of the rebels-convict—duly reported the sale at the Secretary's office, so that he might obtain the reimbursement of the ten-pound surety into which every keeper of a small boat was compelled to enter. The Secretary's office postponed this reimbursement until it should have obtained confirmation of the transaction.

"We are informed that you have bought a wherry from Mr. Robert Farrell," said the officer.

"That is so," said Nuttall, who conceived that for him this was the end of the world.

"You are in no haste, it seems, to declare the same at the Secretary's office." The emissary had a proper bureaucratic haughtiness.

Nuttall's weak eyes blinked at a redoubled rate.

"To . . . to declare it?"

"Ye know it's the law."

"I . . . I didn't, may it please you."

"But it's in the proclamation published last January."

"I . . . I can't read, sir. I . . . I didn't know."

"Faugh!" The messenger withered him with his disdain. "Well, now you're informed. See to it that you are at the Secretary's office before noon with the ten pounds surety into which you are obliged to enter."

The pompous officer departed, leaving Nuttall in a cold perspiration despite the heat of the morning. He was thankful that the fellow had not asked the question he most dreaded, which was how he, a debtor, should come by the money to buy a wherry. But this he knew was only a respite. The question would presently be asked of a certainty, and then hell would open for him. He cursed the hour in which he had been such a fool as to listen to Peter Blood's chatter of escape. He thought it very likely that the whole plot would be discovered, and that he would probably be hanged, or at least branded and sold into slavery like those other damned rebels-convict, with whom he had been so mad as to associate himself. If only he had the ten pounds for this infernal surety, which until this moment had never entered into their calculations, it was possible that the thing might be done quickly and questions postponed until later. As the Secretary's messenger had overlooked the fact that he was a debtor, so might the others at the Secretary's office, at least for a day or two; and in that time he would, he hoped, be beyond the reach of their questions. But in the meantime what was to be done about this money? And it was to be found before noon!

Nuttall snatched up his hat, and went out in quest of Peter Blood. But where look for him? Wandering aimlessly up the irregular, unpaved street, he ventured to enquire of one or two if they had seen Dr. Blood that morning. He affected to be feeling none so well, and indeed his appearance bore out the deception. None could give him information; and since Blood had never told him of Whacker's share in this business, he walked in his unhappy ignorance past the door of the one man in Barbados who would eagerly have saved him in this extremity.

Finally he determined to go up to Colonel Bishop's plantation. Probably Blood would be there. If he were not, Nuttall would find Pitt, and leave a message with him. He was acquainted with Pitt and knew of Pitt's share in this business. His pretext for seeking Blood must still be that he needed medical assistance.

And at the same time that he set out, insensitive in his anxiety to the broiling heat, to climb the heights to the north of the town, Blood was setting out from Government House at last, having so far eased the Governor's condition as to be permitted to depart. Being mounted, he would, but for an unexpected delay, have reached the stockade ahead of Nuttall, in which case several unhappy events might have been averted. The unexpected delay was occasioned by Miss Arabella Bishop.

They met at the gate of the luxuriant garden of Government House, and Miss Bishop, herself mounted, stared to see Peter Blood on horseback. It happened that he was in good spirits. The fact that the Governor's condition had so far improved as to restore him his freedom of movement had sufficed to remove the depression under which he had been labouring for the past twelve hours and more. In its rebound the mercury of his mood had shot higher far than present circumstances warranted. He was disposed to be optimistic. What had failed last night would certainly not fail again to-night. What was a day, after all? The Secretary's office might be troublesome, but not really troublesome for another twenty-four hours at least; and by then they would be well away.

This joyous confidence of his was his first misfortune. The next was that his good spirits were also shared by Miss Bishop, and that she bore no rancour. The two things conjoined to make the delay that in its consequences was so deplorable.

"Good-morning, sir," she hailed him pleasantly. "It's close upon a month since last I saw you."

"Twenty-one days to the hour," said he. "I've counted them."

"I vow I was beginning to believe you dead."

"I have to thank you for the wreath."

"The wreath?"

"To deck my grave," he explained.

"Must you ever be rallying?" she wondered, and looked at him gravely, remembering that it was his rallying on the last occasion had driven her away in dudgeon.

"A man must sometimes laugh at himself or go mad," said he. "Few realize it. That is why there are so many madmen in the world."

"You may laugh at yourself all you will, sir. But sometimes I think you laugh at me, which is not civil."

"Then, faith, you're wrong. I laugh only at the comic, and you are not comic at all."

"What am I, then?" she asked him, laughing.

A moment he pondered her, so fair and fresh to behold, so entirely maidenly and yet so entirely frank and unabashed.

"You are," he said, "the niece of the man who owns me his slave." But he spoke lightly. So lightly that she was encouraged to insistence.

"Nay, sir, that is an evasion. You shall answer me truthfully this morning."

"Truthfully? To answer you at all is a labour. But to answer truthfully! Oh, well, now, I should say of you that he'll be lucky who counts you his friend." It was in his mind to add more. But he left it there.

"That's mighty civil," said she. "You've a nice taste in compliments, Mr. Blood. Another in your place . . ."

"Faith, now, don't I know what another would have said? Don't I know my fellow-man at all?"

"Sometimes I think you do, and sometimes I think you don't. Anyway, you don't know your fellow-woman. There was that affair of the Spaniards."

"Will ye never forget it?"

"Never."

"Bad cess to your memory. Is there no good in me at all that you could be dwelling on instead?"

"Oh, several things."

"For instance, now?" He was almost eager.

"You speak excellent Spanish."

"Is that all?" He sank back into dismay.

"Where did you learn it? Have you been in Spain?"

"That I have. I was two years in a Spanish prison."

"In prison?" Her tone suggested apprehensions in which he had no desire to leave her.

"As a prisoner of war," he explained. "I was taken fighting with the French—in French service, that is."

"But you're a doctor!" she cried.

"That's merely a diversion, I think. By trade I am a soldier—at least, it's a trade I followed for ten years. It brought me no great gear, but it served me better than medicine, which, as you may observe, has brought me into slavery. I'm thinking it's more pleasing in the sight of Heaven to kill men than to heal them. Sure it must be."

"But how came you to be a soldier, and to serve the French?"

"I am Irish, you see, and I studied medicine. Therefore—since it's a perverse nation we are— . . . Oh, but it's a long story, and the Colonel will be expecting my return."

She was not in that way to be defrauded of her entertainment. If he would wait a moment they would ride back together. She had but come to enquire of the Governor's health at her uncle's request.

So he waited, and so they rode back together to Colonel Bishop's house. They rode very slowly, at a walking pace, and some whom they passed marvelled to see the doctor-slave on such apparently intimate terms with his owner's niece. One or two may have promised themselves that they would drop a hint to the Colonel. But the two rode oblivious of all others in the world that morning. He was telling her the story of his early turbulent days, and at the end of it he dwelt more fully than hitherto upon the manner of his arrest and trial.

The tale was barely done when they drew up at the Colonel's door, and dismounted, Peter Blood surrendering his nag to one of the negro grooms, who informed them that the Colonel was from home at the moment.

Even then they lingered a moment, she detaining him.

"I am sorry, Mr. Blood, that I did not know before," she said, and there was a suspicion of moisture in those clear hazel eyes. With a compelling friendliness she held out her hand to him.

"Why, what difference could it have made?" he asked.

"Some, I think. You have been very hardly used by Fate."

"Och, now . . ." He paused. His keen sapphire eyes considered her steadily a moment from under his level black brows. "It might have been worse," he said, with a significance which brought a tinge of colour to her cheeks and a flutter to her eyelids.

He stooped to kiss her hand before releasing it, and she did not deny him. Then he turned and strode off towards the stockade a half-mile away, and a vision of her face went with him, tinted with a rising blush and a sudden unusual shyness. He forgot in that little moment that he was a rebel-convict with ten years of slavery before him; he forgot that he had planned an escape, which was to be carried into effect that night; forgot even the peril of discovery which as a result of the Governor's gout now overhung him.

VII. Pirates

Mr. James Nuttall made all speed, regardless of the heat, in his journey from Bridgetown to Colonel Bishop's plantation, and if ever man was built for speed in a hot climate that man was Mr. James Nuttall, with his short, thin body, and his long, fleshless legs. So withered was he that it was hard to believe there were any juices left in him, yet juices there must have been, for he was sweating violently by the time he reached the stockade.

At the entrance he almost ran into the overseer Kent, a squat, bow-legged animal with the arms of a Hercules and the jowl of a bulldog.

"I am seeking Doctor Blood," he announced breathlessly.

"You are in a rare haste," growled Kent. "What the devil is it? Twins?"

"Eh? Oh! Nay, nay. I'm not married, sir. It's a cousin of mine, sir."

"What is?"

"He is taken bad, sir," Nuttall lied promptly upon the cue that Kent himself had afforded him. "Is the doctor here?"

"That's his hut yonder." Kent pointed carelessly. "If he's not there, he'll be somewhere else." And he took himself off. He was a surly, ungracious beast at all times, readier with the lash of his whip than with his tongue.

Nuttall watched him go with satisfaction, and even noted the direction that he took. Then he plunged into the enclosure, to verify in mortification that Dr. Blood was not at home. A man of sense might have sat down and waited, judging that to be the quickest and surest way in the end. But Nuttall had no sense. He flung out of the stockade again, hesitated a moment as to which direction he should take, and finally decided to go any way but the way that Kent had gone. He sped across the parched savannah towards the sugar plantation which stood solid as a rampart and gleaming golden in the dazzling June sunshine. Avenues intersected the great blocks of ripening amber cane. In the distance down one of these he espied some slaves at work. Nuttall entered the avenue and advanced upon them. They eyed him dully, as he passed them. Pitt was not of their number, and he dared not ask for him. He continued his search for best part of an hour, up one of those lanes and then down another. Once an overseer challenged him, demanding to know his business. He was looking, he said, for Dr. Blood. His cousin was taken ill. The overseer bade him go to the devil, and get out of the plantation. Blood was not there. If he was anywhere he would be in his hut in the stockade.

Nuttall passed on, upon the understanding that he would go. But he went in the wrong direction; he went on towards the side of the plantation farthest from the stockade, towards the dense woods that fringed it there. The overseer was too contemptuous and perhaps too languid in the stifling heat of approaching noontide to correct his course.

Nuttall blundered to the end of the avenue, and round the corner of it, and there ran into Pitt, alone, toiling with a wooden spade upon an irrigation channel. A pair of cotton drawers, loose and ragged, clothed him from waist to knee; above and below he was naked, save for a broad hat of plaited straw that sheltered his unkempt golden head from the rays of the tropical sun. At sight of him Nuttall returned thanks aloud to his Maker. Pitt stared at him, and the shipwright poured out his dismal news in a dismal tone. The sum of it was that he must have ten pounds from Blood that very morning or they were all undone. And all he got for his pains and his sweat was the condemnation of Jeremy Pitt.

"Damn you for a fool!" said the slave. "If it's Blood you're seeking, why are you wasting your time here?"

"I can't find him," bleated Nuttall. He was indignant at his reception. He forgot the jangled state of the other's nerves after a night of anxious wakefulness ending in a dawn of despair. "I thought that you . . ."

"You thought that I could drop my spade and go and seek him for you? Is that what you thought? My God! that our lives should depend upon such a dummerhead. While you waste your time here, the hours are passing! And if an overseer should catch you talking to me? How'll you explain it?"

For a moment Nuttall was bereft of speech by such ingratitude. Then he exploded.

"I would to Heaven I had never had no hand in this affair. I would so! I wish that . . ."

What else he wished was never known, for at that moment round the block of cane came a big man in biscuit-coloured taffetas followed by two negroes in cotton drawers who were armed with cutlasses. He was not ten yards away, but his approach over the soft, yielding marl had been unheard.

Mr. Nuttall looked wildly this way and that a moment, then bolted like a rabbit for the woods, thus doing the most foolish and betraying thing that in the circumstances it was possible for him to do. Pitt groaned and stood still, leaning upon his spade.

"Hi, there! Stop!" bawled Colonel Bishop after the fugitive, and added horrible threats tricked out with some rhetorical indecencies.

But the fugitive held amain, and never so much as turned his head. It was his only remaining hope that Colonel Bishop might not have seen his face; for the power and influence of Colonel Bishop was quite sufficient to hang any man whom he thought would be better dead.

Not until the runagate had vanished into the scrub did the planter sufficiently recover from his indignant amazement to remember the two negroes who followed at his heels like a brace of hounds. It was a bodyguard without which he never moved in his plantations since a slave had made an attack upon him and all but strangled him a couple of years ago.

"After him, you black swine!" he roared at them. But as they started he checked them. "Wait! Get to heel, damn you!"

It occurred to him that to catch and deal with the fellow there was not the need to go after him, and perhaps spend the day hunting him in that cursed wood. There was Pitt here ready to his hand, and Pitt should tell him the identity of his bashful friend, and also the subject of that close and secret talk he had disturbed. Pitt might, of course, be reluctant. So much the worse for Pitt. The ingenious Colonel Bishop knew a dozen ways—some of them quite diverting—of conquering stubbornness in these convict dogs.

He turned now upon the slave a countenance that was inflamed by heat internal and external, and a pair of beady eyes that were alight with cruel intelligence. He stepped forward swinging his light bamboo cane.

"Who was that runagate?" he asked with terrible suavity.

Leaning over on his spade, Jeremy Pitt hung his head a little, and shifted uncomfortably on his bare feet. Vainly he groped for an answer in a mind that could do nothing but curse the idiocy of Mr. James Nuttall.

The planter's bamboo cane fell on the lad's naked shoulders with stinging force.

"Answer me, you dog! What's his name?"

Jeremy looked at the burly planter out of sullen, almost defiant eyes.

"I don't know," he said, and in his voice there was a faint note at least of the defiance aroused in him by a blow which he dared not, for his life's sake, return. His body had remained unyielding under it, but the spirit within writhed now in torment.

"You don't know? Well, here's to quicken your wits." Again the cane descended. "Have you thought of his name yet?"

"I have not."

"Stubborn, eh?" For a moment the Colonel leered. Then his passion mastered him. "'Swounds! You impudent dog! D'you trifle with me? D'you think I'm to be mocked?"

Pitt shrugged, shifted sideways on his feet again, and settled into dogged silence. Few things are more provocative; and Colonel Bishop's temper was never one that required much provocation. Brute fury now awoke in him. Fiercely now he lashed those defenceless shoulders, accompanying each blow by blasphemy and foul abuse, until, stung beyond endurance, the lingering embers of his manhood fanned into momentary flame, Pitt sprang upon his tormentor.

But as he sprang, so also sprang the watchful blacks. Muscular bronze arms coiled crushingly about the frail white body, and in a moment the unfortunate slave stood powerless, his wrists pinioned behind him in a leathern thong.

Breathing hard, his face mottled, Bishop pondered him a moment. Then: "Fetch him along," he said.

Down the long avenue between those golden walls of cane standing some eight feet high, the wretched Pitt was thrust by his black captors in the Colonel's wake, stared at with fearful eyes by his fellow-slaves at work there. Despair went with him. What torments might immediately await him he cared little, horrible though he knew they would be. The real source of his mental anguish lay in the conviction that the elaborately planned escape from this unutterable hell was frustrated now in the very moment of execution.

They came out upon the green plateau and headed for the stockade and the overseer's white house. Pitt's eyes looked out over Carlisle Bay, of which this plateau commanded a clear view from the fort on one side to the long sheds of the wharf on the other. Along this wharf a few shallow boats were moored, and Pitt caught himself wondering which of these was the wherry in which with a little luck they might have been now at sea. Out over that sea his glance ranged miserably.

In the roads, standing in for the shore before a gentle breeze that scarcely ruffled the sapphire surface of the Caribbean, came a stately red-hulled frigate, flying the English ensign.

Colonel Bishop halted to consider her, shading his eyes with his fleshly hand. Light as was the breeze, the vessel spread no canvas to it beyond that of her foresail. Furled was her every other sail, leaving a clear view of the majestic lines of her hull, from towering stern castle to gilded beakhead that was aflash in the dazzling sunshine.

So leisurely an advance argued a master indifferently acquainted with these waters, who preferred to creep forward cautiously, sounding his way. At her present rate of progress it would be an hour, perhaps, before she came to anchorage within the harbour. And whilst the Colonel viewed her, admiring, perhaps, the gracious beauty of her, Pitt was hurried forward into the stockade, and clapped into the stocks that stood there ready for slaves who required correction.

Colonel Bishop followed him presently, with leisurely, rolling gait.

"A mutinous cur that shows his fangs to his master must learn good manners at the cost of a striped hide," was all he said before setting about his executioner's job.

That with his own hands he should do that which most men of his station would, out of self-respect, have relegated to one of the negroes, gives you the measure of the man's beastliness. It was almost as if with relish, as if gratifying some feral instinct of cruelty, that he now lashed his victim about head and shoulders. Soon his cane was reduced to splinters by his violence. You know, perhaps, the sting of a flexible bamboo cane when it is whole. But do you realize its murderous quality when it has been split into several long lithe blades, each with an edge that is of the keenness of a knife?

When, at last, from very weariness, Colonel Bishop flung away the stump and thongs to which his cane had been reduced, the wretched slave's back was bleeding pulp from neck to waist.

As long as full sensibility remained, Jeremy Pitt had made no sound. But in a measure as from pain his senses were mercifully dulled, he sank forward in the stocks, and hung there now in a huddled heap, faintly moaning.

Colonel Bishop set his foot upon the crossbar, and leaned over his victim, a cruel smile on his full, coarse face.

"Let that teach you a proper submission," said he. "And now touching that shy friend of yours, you shall stay here without meat or drink—without meat or drink, d'ye hear me?—until you please to tell me his name and business." He took his foot from the bar. "When you've had enough of this, send me word, and we'll have the branding-irons to you."

On that he swung on his heel, and strode out of the stockade, his negroes following.

Pitt had heard him, as we hear things in our dreams. At the moment so spent was he by his cruel punishment, and so deep was the despair into which he had fallen, that he no longer cared whether he lived or died.

Soon, however, from the partial stupor which pain had mercifully induced, a new variety of pain aroused him. The stocks stood in the open under the full glare of the tropical sun, and its blistering rays streamed down upon that mangled, bleeding back until he felt as if flames of fire were searing it. And, soon, to this was added a torment still more unspeakable. Flies, the cruel flies of the Antilles, drawn by the scent of blood, descended in a cloud upon him.

Small wonder that the ingenious Colonel Bishop, who so well understood the art of loosening stubborn tongues, had not deemed it necessary to have recourse to other means of torture. Not all his fiendish cruelty could devise a torment more cruel, more unendurable than the torments Nature would here procure a man in Pitt's condition.

The slave writhed in his stocks until he was in danger of breaking his limbs, and writhing, screamed in agony.

Thus was he found by Peter Blood, who seemed to his troubled vision to materialize suddenly before him. Mr. Blood carried a large palmetto leaf. Having whisked away with this the flies that were devouring Jeremy's back, he slung it by a strip of fibre from the lad's neck, so that it protected him from further attacks as well as from the rays of the sun. Next, sitting down beside him, he drew the sufferer's head down on his own shoulder, and bathed his face from a pannikin of cold water. Pitt shuddered and moaned on a long, indrawn breath.

"Drink!" he gasped. "Drink, for the love of Christ!"

The pannikin was held to his quivering lips. He drank greedily, noisily, nor ceased until he had drained the vessel. Cooled and revived by the draught, he attempted to sit up.

"My back!" he screamed.

There was an unusual glint in Mr. Blood's eyes; his lips were compressed. But when he parted them to speak, his voice came cool and steady.

"Be easy, now. One thing at a time. Your back's taking no harm at all for the present, since I've covered it up. I'm wanting to know what's happened to you. D'ye think we can do without a navigator that ye go and provoke that beast Bishop until he all but kills you?"

Pitt sat up and groaned again. But this time his anguish was mental rather than physical.

"I don't think a navigator will be needed this time, Peter."

"What's that?" cried Mr. Blood.

Pitt explained the situation as briefly as he could, in a halting, gasping speech. "I'm to rot here until I tell him the identity of my visitor and his business."

Mr. Blood got up, growling in his throat. "Bad cess to the filthy slaver!" said he. "But it must be contrived, nevertheless. To the devil with Nuttall! Whether he gives surety for the boat or not, whether he explains it or not, the boat remains, and we're going, and you're coming with us."

"You're dreaming, Peter," said the prisoner. "We're not going this time. The magistrates will confiscate the boat since the surety's not paid, even if when they press him Nuttall does not confess the whole plan and get us all branded on the forehead."

Mr. Blood turned away, and with agony in his eyes looked out to sea over the blue water by which he had so fondly hoped soon to be travelling back to freedom.

The great red ship had drawn considerably nearer shore by now. Slowly, majestically, she was entering the bay. Already one or two wherries were putting off from the wharf to board her. From where he stood, Mr. Blood could see the glinting of the brass cannons mounted on the prow above the curving beak-head, and he could make out the figure of a seaman in the forechains on her larboard side, leaning out to heave the lead.

An angry voice aroused him from his unhappy thoughts.

"What the devil are you doing here?"

The returning Colonel Bishop came striding into the stockade, his negroes following ever.

Mr. Blood turned to face him, and over that swarthy countenance—which, indeed, by now was tanned to the golden brown of a half-caste Indian—a mask descended.

"Doing?" said he blandly. "Why, the duties of my office."

The Colonel, striding furiously forward, observed two things. The empty pannikin on the seat beside the prisoner, and the palmetto leaf protecting his back. "Have you dared to do this?" The veins on the planter's forehead stood out like cords.

"Of course I have." Mr. Blood's tone was one of faint surprise.

"I said he was to have neither meat nor drink until I ordered it."

"Sure, now, I never heard ye."

"You never heard me? How should you have heard me when you weren't here?"

"Then how did ye expect me to know what orders ye'd given?" Mr. Blood's tone was positively aggrieved. "All that I knew was that one of your slaves was being murthered by the sun and the flies. And I says to myself, this is one of the Colonel's slaves, and I'm the Colonel's doctor, and sure it's my duty to be looking after the Colonel's property. So I just gave the fellow a spoonful of water and covered his back from the sun. And wasn't I right now?"

"Right?" The Colonel was almost speechless.

"Be easy, now, be easy!" Mr. Blood implored him. "It's an apoplexy ye'll be contracting if ye give way to heat like this."

The planter thrust him aside with an imprecation, and stepping forward tore the palmetto leaf from the prisoner's back.

"In the name of humanity, now . . ." Mr. Blood was beginning.

The Colonel swung upon him furiously. "Out of this!" he commanded. "And don't come near him again until I send for you, unless you want to be served in the same way."

He was terrific in his menace, in his bulk, and in the power of him. But Mr. Blood never flinched. It came to the Colonel, as he found himself steadily regarded by those light-blue eyes that looked so arrestingly odd in that tawny face—like pale sapphires set in copper—that this rogue had for some time now been growing presumptuous. It was a matter that he must presently correct. Meanwhile Mr. Blood was speaking again, his tone quietly insistent.

"In the name of humanity," he repeated, "ye'll allow me to do what I can to ease his sufferings, or I swear to you that I'll forsake at once the duties of a doctor, and that it's devil another patient will I attend in this unhealthy island at all."

For an instant the Colonel was too amazed to speak. Then—

"By God!" he roared. "D'ye dare take that tone with me, you dog? D'ye dare to make terms with me?"

"I do that." The unflinching blue eyes looked squarely into the Colonel's, and there was a devil peeping out of them, the devil of recklessness that is born of despair.

Colonel Bishop considered him for a long moment in silence. "I've been too soft with you," he said at last. "But that's to be mended." And he tightened his lips. "I'll have the rods to you, until there's not an inch of skin left on your dirty back."

"Will ye so? And what would Governor Steed do, then?"

"Ye're not the only doctor on the island."

Mr. Blood actually laughed. "And will ye tell that to his excellency, him with the gout in his foot so bad that he can't stand? Ye know very well it's devil another doctor will he tolerate, being an intelligent man that knows what's good for him."

But the Colonel's brute passion thoroughly aroused was not so easily to be baulked. "If you're alive when my blacks have done with you, perhaps you'll come to your senses."

He swung to his negroes to issue an order. But it was never issued. At that moment a terrific rolling thunderclap drowned his voice and shook the very air. Colonel Bishop jumped, his negroes jumped with him, and so even did the apparently imperturbable Mr. Blood. Then the four of them stared together seawards.

Down in the bay all that could be seen of the great ship, standing now within a cable's-length of the fort, were her topmasts thrusting above a cloud of smoke in which she was enveloped. From the cliffs a flight of startled seabirds had risen to circle in the blue, giving tongue to their alarm, the plaintive curlew noisiest of all.

As those men stared from the eminence on which they stood, not yet understanding what had taken place, they saw the British Jack dip from the main truck and vanish into the rising cloud below. A moment more, and up through that cloud to replace the flag of England soared the gold and crimson banner of Castile. And then they understood.

"Pirates!" roared the Colonel, and again, "Pirates!"

Fear and incredulity were blent in his voice. He had paled under his tan until his face was the colour of clay, and there was a wild fury in his beady eyes. His negroes looked at him, grinning idiotically, all teeth and eyeballs.

VIII. Spaniards

The stately ship that had been allowed to sail so leisurely into Carlisle Bay under her false colours was a Spanish privateer, coming to pay off some of the heavy debt piled up by the predaceous Brethren of the Coast, and the recent defeat by the *Pride of Devon* of two treasure galleons bound for Cadiz. It happened that the galleon which escaped in a more or less crippled condition was commanded by Don Diego de Espinosa y Valdez, who was own brother to the Spanish Admiral Don Miguel de Espinosa, and who was also a very hasty, proud, and hot-tempered gentleman.

Galled by his defeat, and choosing to forget that his own conduct had invited it, he had sworn to teach the English a sharp lesson which they should remember. He would take a leaf out of the book of Morgan and those other robbers of the sea, and make a punitive raid upon an English settlement. Unfortunately for himself and for many others, his brother the Admiral was not at hand to restrain him when for this purpose he fitted out the *Cinco Llagas* at San Juan de Porto Rico. He chose for his objective the island of Barbados, whose natural strength was apt to render her defenders careless. He chose it also because thither had the *Pride of Devon* been tracked by his scouts, and he desired a measure of poetic justice to invest his vengeance. And he chose a moment when there were no ships of war at anchor in Carlisle Bay.

He had succeeded so well in his intentions that he had aroused no suspicion until he saluted the fort at short range with a broadside of twenty guns.

And now the four gaping watchers in the stockade on the headland beheld the great ship creep forward under the rising cloud of smoke, her mainsail unfurled to increase her steering way, and go about close-hauled to bring her larboard guns to bear upon the unready fort.

With the crashing roar of that second broadside, Colonel Bishop awoke from stupefaction to a recollection of where his duty lay. In the town below drums were beating frantically, and a trumpet was bleating, as if the peril needed further advertising. As commander of the Barbados Militia, the place of Colonel Bishop was at the head of his scanty troops, in that fort which the Spanish guns were pounding into rubble.

Remembering it, he went off at the double, despite his bulk and the heat, his negroes trotting after him.

Mr. Blood turned to Jeremy Pitt. He laughed grimly. "Now that," said he, "is what I call a timely interruption. Though what'll come of it," he added as an afterthought, "the devil himself knows."

As a third broadside was thundering forth, he picked up the palmetto leaf and carefully replaced it on the back of his fellow-slave.

And then into the stockade, panting and sweating, came Kent followed by best part of a score of plantation workers, some of whom were black and all of whom were in a state of panic. He led them into the low white house, to bring them forth again, within a moment, as it seemed, armed now with muskets and hangers and some of them equipped with bandoleers.

By this time the rebels-convict were coming in, in twos and threes, having abandoned their work upon finding themselves unguarded and upon scenting the general dismay.

Kent paused a moment, as his hastily armed guard dashed forth, to fling an order to those slaves.

"To the woods!" he bade them. "Take to the woods, and lie close there, until this is over, and we've gutted these Spanish swine."

On that he went off in haste after his men, who were to be added to those massing in the town, so as to oppose and overwhelm the Spanish landing parties.

The slaves would have obeyed him on the instant but for Mr. Blood.

"What need for haste, and in this heat?" quoth he. He was surprisingly cool, they thought. "Maybe there'll be no need to take to the woods at all, and, anyway, it will be time enough to do so when the Spaniards are masters of the town."

And so, joined now by the other stragglers, and numbering in all a round score—rebels-convict all—they stayed to watch from their vantage-ground the fortunes of the furious battle that was being waged below.

The landing was contested by the militia and by every islander capable of bearing arms with the fierce resoluteness of men who knew that no quarter was to be expected in defeat. The ruthlessness of Spanish soldiery was a byword, and not at his worst had Morgan or L'Ollonais ever perpetrated such horrors as those of which these Castilian gentlemen were capable.

But this Spanish commander knew his business, which was more than could truthfully be said for the Barbados Militia. Having gained the advantage of a surprise blow, which had put the fort out of action, he soon showed them that he was master of the situation. His guns turned now upon the open space behind the mole, where the incompetent Bishop had marshalled his men, tore the militia into bloody rags, and covered the landing parties which were making the shore in their own boats and in several of those which had rashly gone out to the great ship before her identity was revealed.

All through the scorching afternoon the battle went on, the rattle and crack of musketry penetrating ever deeper into the town to show that the defenders were being driven steadily back. By sunset two hundred and fifty Spaniards were masters of Bridgetown, the islanders were disarmed, and at Government House, Governor Steed—his gout forgotten in his panic—supported by Colonel Bishop and some lesser officers, was being informed by Don Diego, with an urbanity that was itself a mockery, of the sum that would be required in ransom.

For a hundred thousand pieces of eight and fifty head of cattle, Don Diego would forbear from reducing the place to ashes. And what time that suave and courtly commander was settling these details with the apoplectic British Governor, the Spaniards were smashing and looting, feasting, drinking, and ravaging after the hideous manner of their kind.

Mr. Blood, greatly daring, ventured down at dusk into the town. What he saw there is recorded by Jeremy Pitt—to whom he subsequently related it—in that voluminous log from which the greater part of my narrative is derived. I have no intention of repeating any of it here. It is all too loathsome and nauseating, incredible, indeed, that men however abandoned could ever descend such an abyss of bestial cruelty and lust.

What he saw was fetching him in haste and white-faced out of that hell again, when in a narrow street a girl hurtled into him, wild-eyed, her unbound hair streaming behind her as she ran. After her, laughing and cursing in a breath, came a heavy-booted Spaniard. Almost he was upon her, when suddenly Mr. Blood got in his way. The doctor had taken a sword from a dead man's side some little time before and armed himself with it against an emergency.

As the Spaniard checked in anger and surprise, he caught in the dusk the livid gleam of that sword which Mr. Blood had quickly unsheathed.

"Ah, perro inglés!" he shouted, and flung forward to his death.

"It's hoping I am ye're in a fit state to meet your Maker," said Mr. Blood, and ran him through the body. He did the thing skilfully: with the combined skill of swordsman and surgeon. The man sank in a hideous heap without so much as a groan.

Mr. Blood swung to the girl, who leaned panting and sobbing against a wall. He caught her by the wrist.

"Come!" he said.

But she hung back, resisting him by her weight. "Who are you?" she demanded wildly.

"Will ye wait to see my credentials?" he snapped. Steps were clattering towards them from beyond the corner round which she had fled from that Spanish ruffian. "Come," he urged again. And this time, reassured perhaps by his clear English speech, she went without further questions.

They sped down an alley and then up another, by great good fortune meeting no one, for already they were on the outskirts of the town. They won out of it, and white-faced, physically sick, Mr. Blood dragged her almost at a run up the hill towards Colonel Bishop's house. He told her briefly who and what he was, and thereafter there was no conversation between them until they reached the big white house. It was all in darkness, which at least was reassuring. If the Spaniards had reached it, there would be lights. He knocked, but had to knock again and yet again before he was answered. Then it was by a voice from a window above.

"Who is there?" The voice was Miss Bishop's, a little tremulous, but unmistakably her own.

Mr. Blood almost fainted in relief. He had been imagining the unimaginable. He had pictured her down in that hell out of which he had just come. He had conceived that she might have followed her uncle into Bridgetown, or committed some other imprudence, and he turned cold from head to foot at the mere thought of what might have happened to her.

"It is I—Peter Blood," he gasped.

"What do you want?"

It is doubtful whether she would have come down to open. For at such a time as this it was no more than likely that the wretched plantation slaves might be in revolt and prove as great a danger as the Spaniards. But at the sound of her voice, the girl Mr. Blood had rescued peered up through the gloom.

"Arabella!" she called. "It is I, Mary Traill."

"Mary!" The voice ceased above on that exclamation, the head was withdrawn. After a brief pause the door gaped wide. Beyond it in the wide hall stood Miss Arabella, a slim, virginal figure in white, mysteriously revealed in the gleam of a single candle which she carried.

Mr. Blood strode in followed by his distraught companion, who, falling upon Arabella's slender bosom, surrendered herself to a passion of tears. But he wasted no time.

"Whom have you here with you? What servants?" he demanded sharply.

The only male was James, an old negro groom.

"The very man," said Blood. "Bid him get out horses. Then away with you to Speightstown, or even farther north, where you will be safe. Here you are in danger— in dreadful danger."

"But I thought the fighting was over . . ." she was beginning, pale and startled.

"So it is. But the deviltry's only beginning. Miss Traill will tell you as you go. In God's name, madam, take my word for it, and do as I bid you."

"He . . . he saved me," sobbed Miss Traill.

"Saved you?" Miss Bishop was aghast. "Saved you from what, Mary?"

"Let that wait," snapped Mr. Blood almost angrily. "You've all the night for chattering when you're out of this, and away beyond their reach. Will you please call James, and do as I say—and at once!"

"You are very peremptory . . ."

"Oh, my God! I am peremptory! Speak, Miss Trail!, tell her whether I've cause to be peremptory."

"Yes, yes," the girl cried, shuddering. "Do as he says— Oh, for pity's sake, Arabella."

Miss Bishop went off, leaving Mr. Blood and Miss Traill alone again.

"I . . . I shall never forget what you did, sir," said she, through her diminishing tears. She was a slight wisp of a girl, a child, no more.

"I've done better things in my time. That's why I'm here," said Mr. Blood, whose mood seemed to be snappy.

She didn't pretend to understand him, and she didn't make the attempt.

"Did you . . . did you kill him?" she asked, fearfully.

He stared at her in the flickering candlelight. "I hope so. It is very probable, and it doesn't matter at all," he said. "What matters is that this fellow James should fetch the horses." And he was stamping off to accelerate these preparations for departure, when her voice arrested him.

"Don't leave me! Don't leave me here alone!" she cried in terror.

He paused. He turned and came slowly back. Standing above her he smiled upon her.

"There, there! You've no cause for alarm. It's all over now. You'll be away soon—away to Speightstown, where you'll be quite safe."

The horses came at last—four of them, for in addition to James who was to act as her guide, Miss Bishop had her woman, who was not to be left behind.

Mr. Blood lifted the slight weight of Mary Traill to her horse, then turned to say good-bye to Miss Bishop, who was already mounted. He said it, and seemed to have something to add. But whatever it was, it remained unspoken.

The horses started, and receded into the sapphire starlit night, leaving him standing there before Colonel Bishop's door. The last he heard of them was Mary Traill's childlike voice calling back on a quavering note—

"I shall never forget what you did, Mr. Blood. I shall never forget."

But as it was not the voice he desired to hear, the assurance brought him little satisfaction. He stood there in the dark watching the fireflies amid the rhododendrons, till the hoofbeats had faded. Then he sighed and roused himself. He had much to do. His journey into the town had not been one of idle curiosity to see how the Spaniards conducted themselves in victory. It had been inspired by a very different purpose, and he had gained in the course of it all the information he desired. He had an extremely busy night before him, and must be moving.

He went off briskly in the direction of the stockade, where his fellow-slaves awaited him in deep anxiety and some hope.

IX. THE REBELS-CONVICT

There were, when the purple gloom of the tropical night descended upon the Caribbean, not more than ten men on guard aboard the *Cinco Llagas*, so confident—and with good reason—were the Spaniards of the complete subjection of the islanders. And when I say that there were ten men on guard, I state rather the purpose for which they were left aboard than the duty which they fulfilled. As a matter of fact, whilst the main body of the Spaniards feasted and rioted ashore, the Spanish gunner and his crew—who had so nobly done their duty and ensured the easy victory of the day——were feasting on the gun-deck upon the wine and the fresh meats fetched out to them from shore. Above, two sentinels only kept vigil, at stem and stern. Nor were they as vigilant as they should have been, or else they must have observed the two wherries that under cover of the darkness came gliding from the wharf, with well-greased rowlocks, to bring up in silence under the great ship's quarter.

From the gallery aft still hung the ladder by which Don Diego had descended to the boat that had taken him ashore. The sentry on guard in the stern, coming presently round this gallery, was suddenly confronted by the black shadow of a man standing before him at the head of the ladder.

"Who's there?" he asked, but without alarm, supposing it one of his fellows.

"It is I," softly answered Peter Blood in the fluent Castillan of which he was master.

"Is it you, Pedro?" The Spaniard came a step nearer.

"Peter is my name; but I doubt I'll not be the Peter you're expecting."

"How?" quoth the sentry, checking.

"This way," said Mr. Blood.

The wooden taffrail was a low one, and the Spaniard was taken completely by surprise. Save for the splash he made as he struck the water, narrowly missing one of the crowded boats that waited under the counter, not a sound announced his misadventure. Armed as he was with corselet, cuissarts, and headpiece, he sank to trouble them no more.

"Whist!" hissed Mr. Blood to his waiting rebels-convict. "Come on, now, and without noise."

Within five minutes they had swarmed aboard, the entire twenty of them overflowing from that narrow gallery and crouching on the quarter-deck itself. Lights showed ahead. Under the great lantern in the prow they saw the black figure of the other sentry, pacing on the forecastle. From below sounds reached them of the orgy on the gun-deck: a rich male voice was singing an obscene ballad to which the others chanted in chorus:

"Y estos son los usos de Castilla y de Leon!"

"From what I've seen to-day I can well believe it," said Mr. Blood, and whispered: "Forward——after me."

Crouching low, they glided, noiseless as shadows, to the quarter-deck rail, and thence slipped without sound down into the waist. Two thirds of them were armed with muskets, some of which they had found in the overseer's house, and others supplied from the secret hoard that Mr. Blood had so laboriously assembled against the day of escape. The remainder were equipped with knives and cutlasses.

In the vessel's waist they hung awhile, until Mr. Blood had satisfied himself that no other sentinel showed above decks but that inconvenient fellow in the prow. Their first attention must be for him. Mr. Blood, himself, crept forward with two companions, leaving the others in the charge of that Nathaniel Hagthorpe whose sometime commission in the King's Navy gave him the best title to this office.

Mr. Blood's absence was brief. When he rejoined his comrades there was no watch above the Spaniards' decks.

Meanwhile the revellers below continued to make merry at their ease in the conviction of complete security. The garrison of Barbados was overpowered and disarmed, and their companions were ashore in complete possession of the town, glutting themselves hideously upon the fruits of victory. What, then, was there to fear? Even when their quarters were invaded and they found themselves surrounded by a score of wild, hairy, half-naked men, who—save that they appeared once to have been white—looked like a horde of savages, the Spaniards could not believe their eyes.

Who could have dreamed that a handful of forgotten plantation-slaves would have dared to take so much upon themselves?

The half-drunken Spaniards, their laughter suddenly quenched, the song perishing on their lips, stared, stricken and bewildered at the levelled muskets by which they were checkmated.

And then, from out of this uncouth pack of savages that beset them, stepped a slim, tall fellow with light-blue eyes in a tawny face, eyes in which glinted the light of a wicked humour. He addressed them in the purest Castilian.

"You will save yourselves pain and trouble by regarding yourselves my prisoners, and suffering yourselves to be quietly bestowed out of harm's way."

"Name of God!" swore the gunner, which did no justice at all to an amazement beyond expression.

"If you please," said Mr. Blood, and thereupon those gentlemen of Spain were induced without further trouble beyond a musket prod or two to drop through a scuttle to the deck below.

After that the rebels-convict refreshed themselves with the good things in the consumption of which they had interrupted the Spaniards. To taste palatable Christian food after months of salt fish and maize dumplings was in itself a feast to these unfortunates. But there were no excesses. Mr. Blood saw to that, although it required all the firmness of which he was capable.

Dispositions were to be made without delay against that which must follow before they could abandon themselves fully to the enjoyment of their victory. This, after all, was no more than a preliminary skirmish, although it was one that afforded them the key to the situation. It remained to dispose so that the utmost profit might be drawn from it. Those dispositions occupied some very considerable portion of the night. But, at least, they were complete before the sun peeped over the shoulder of Mount Hillbay to shed his light upon a day of some surprises.

It was soon after sunrise that the rebel-convict who paced the quarter-deck in Spanish corselet and headpiece, a Spanish musket on his shoulder, announced the approach of a boat. It was Don Diego de Espinosa y Valdez coming aboard with four great treasure-chests, containing each twenty-five thousand pieces of eight, the ransom delivered to him at dawn by Governor Steed. He was accompanied by his son, Don Esteban, and by six men who took the oars.

Aboard the frigate all was quiet and orderly as it should be. She rode at anchor, her larboard to the shore, and the main ladder on her starboard side. Round to this came the boat with Don Diego and his treasure. Mr. Blood had disposed effectively. It was not for nothing that he had served under de Ruyter. The swings were waiting, and the windlass manned. Below, a gun-crew held itself in readiness under the command of Ogle, who—as I have said—had been a gunner in the Royal Navy before he went in for politics and followed the fortunes of the Duke of Monmouth. He was a sturdy, resolute fellow who inspired confidence by the very confidence he displayed in himself.

Don Diego mounted the ladder and stepped upon the deck, alone, and entirely unsuspicious. What should the poor man suspect?

Before he could even look round, and survey this guard drawn up to receive him, a tap over the head with a capstan bar efficiently handled by Hagthorpe put him to sleep without the least fuss.

He was carried away to his cabin, whilst the treasure-chests, handled by the men he had left in the boat, were being hauled to the deck. That being satisfactorily accomplished, Don Esteban and the fellows who had manned the boat came up the ladder, one by one, to be handled with the same quiet efficiency. Peter Blood had a genius for these things, and almost, I suspect, an eye for the dramatic. Dramatic, certainly, was the spectacle now offered to the survivors of the raid.

With Colonel Bishop at their head, and gout-ridden Governor Steed sitting on the ruins of a wall beside him, they glumly watched the departure of the eight boats containing the weary Spanish ruffians who had glutted themselves with rapine, murder, and violences unspeakable.

They looked on, between relief at this departure of their remorseless enemies, and despair at the wild ravages which, temporarily at least, had wrecked the prosperity and happiness of that little colony.

The boats pulled away from the shore, with their loads of laughing, jeering Spaniards, who were still flinging taunts across the water at their surviving victims. They had come midway between the wharf and the ship, when suddenly the air was shaken by the boom of a gun.

A round shot struck the water within a fathom of the foremost boat, sending a shower of spray over its occupants. They paused at their oars, astounded into silence for a moment. Then speech burst from them like an explosion. Angrily voluble they anathematized this dangerous carelessness on the part of their gunner, who should know better than to fire a salute from a cannon loaded with shot. They were still cursing him when a second shot, better aimed than the first, came to crumple one of the boats into splinters, flinging its crew, dead and living, into the water.

But if it silenced these, it gave tongue, still more angry, vehement, and bewildered to the crews of the other seven boats. From each the suspended oars stood out poised over the water, whilst on their feet in the excitement the Spaniards screamed oaths at the ship, begging Heaven and Hell to inform them what madman had been let loose among her guns.

Plump into their middle came a third shot, smashing a second boat with fearful execution. Followed again a moment of awful silence, then among those Spanish pirates all was gibbering and jabbering and splashing of oars, as they attempted to pull in every direction at once. Some were for going ashore, others for heading straight to the vessel and there discovering what might be amiss. That something was very gravely amiss there could be no further doubt, particularly as whilst they discussed and fumed and cursed two more shots came over the water to account for yet a third of their boats.

The resolute Ogle was making excellent practice, and fully justifying his claims to know something of gunnery. In their consternation the Spaniards had simplified his task by huddling their boats together.

After the fourth shot, opinion was no longer divided amongst them. As with one accord they went about, or attempted to do so, for before they had accomplished it two more of their boats had been sunk.

The three boats that remained, without concerning themselves with their more unfortunate fellows, who were struggling in the water, headed back for the wharf at speed.

If the Spaniards understood nothing of all this, the forlorn islanders ashore understood still less, until to help their wits they saw the flag of Spain come down from the mainmast of the *Cinco Llagas*, and the flag of England soar to its empty place. Even then some bewilderment persisted, and it was with fearful eyes that they observed the return of their enemies, who might vent upon them the ferocity aroused by these extraordinary events.

Ogle, however, continued to give proof that his knowledge of gunnery was not of yesterday. After the fleeing Spaniards went his shots. The last of their boats flew into splinters as it touched the wharf, and its remains were buried under a shower of loosened masonry.

That was the end of this pirate crew, which not ten minutes ago had been laughingly counting up the pieces of eight that would fall to the portion of each for his share in that act of villainy. Close upon threescore survivors contrived to reach the shore. Whether they had cause for congratulation, I am unable to say in the absence of any records in which their fate may be traced. That lack of records is in itself eloquent. We know that they were made fast as they landed, and considering the offence they had given I am not disposed to doubt that they had every reason to regret the survival.

The mystery of the succour that had come at the eleventh hour to wreak vengeance upon the Spaniards, and to preserve for the island the extortionate ransom of a hundred thousand pieces of eight, remained yet to be probed. That the *Cinco Llagas* was now in friendly hands could no longer be doubted after the proofs it had given. But who, the people of Bridgetown asked one another, were the men in possession of her, and whence had they come? The only possible assumption ran the truth very closely. A resolute party of islanders must have got aboard during the night, and seized the ship. It remained to ascertain the precise identity of these mysterious saviours, and do them fitting honour.

Upon this errand—Governor Steed's condition not permitting him to go in person—went Colonel Bishop as the Governor's deputy, attended by two officers.

As he stepped from the ladder into the vessel's waist, the Colonel beheld there, beside the main hatch, the four treasure-chests, the contents of one of which had been contributed almost entirely by himself. It was a gladsome spectacle, and his eyes sparkled in beholding it.

Ranged on either side, athwart the deck, stood a score of men in two well-ordered files, with breasts and backs of steel, polished Spanish morions on their heads, overshadowing their faces, and muskets ordered at their sides.

Colonel Bishop could not be expected to recognize at a glance in these upright, furbished, soldierly figures the ragged, unkempt scarecrows that but yesterday had been toiling in his plantations. Still less could he be expected to recognize at once the courtly gentleman who advanced to greet him—a lean, graceful gentleman, dressed in the Spanish fashion, all in black with silver lace, a gold-hilted sword dangling beside him from a gold embroidered baldrick, a broad castor with a sweeping plume set above carefully curled ringlets of deepest black.

"Be welcome aboard the *Cinco Llagas*, Colonel, darling," a voice vaguely familiar addressed the planter. "We've made the best of the Spaniards' wardrobe in honour of this visit, though it was scarcely yourself we had dared hope to expect. You find yourself among friends—old friends of yours, all."

The Colonel stared in stupefaction. Mr. Blood tricked out in all this splendour—indulging therein his natural taste—his face carefully shaven, his hair as carefully dressed, seemed transformed into a younger man. The fact is he looked no more than the thirty-three years he counted to his age.

"Peter Blood!" It was an ejaculation of amazement. Satisfaction followed swiftly. "Was it you, then . . . ?"

"Myself it was—myself and these, my good friends and yours." Mr. Blood tossed back the fine lace from his wrist, to wave a hand towards the file of men standing to attention there.

The Colonel looked more closely. "Gad's my life!" he crowed on a note of foolish jubilation. "And it was with these fellows that you took the Spaniard and turned the tables on those dogs! Oddswounds! It was heroic!"

"Heroic, is it? Bedad, it's epic! Ye begin to perceive the breadth and depth of my genius."

Colonel Bishop sat himself down on the hatch-coaming, took off his broad hat, and mopped his brow.

"Y'amaze me!" he gasped. "On my soul, y'amaze me! To have recovered the treasure and to have seized this fine ship and all she'll hold! It will be something to set against the other losses we have suffered. As Gad's my life, you deserve well for this."

"I am entirely of your opinion."

"Damme! You all deserve well, and damme, you shall find me grateful."

"That's as it should be," said Mr. Blood. "The question is how well we deserve, and how grateful shall we find you?"

Colonel Bishop considered him. There was a shadow of surprise in his face.

"Why—his excellency shall write home an account of your exploit, and maybe some portion of your sentences shall be remitted."

"The generosity of King James is well known," sneered Nathaniel Hagthorpe, who was standing by, and amongst the ranged rebels-convict some one ventured to laugh.

Colonel Bishop started up. He was pervaded by the first pang of uneasiness. It occurred to him that all here might not be as friendly as appeared.

"And there's another matter," Mr. Blood resumed. "There's a matter of a flogging that's due to me. Ye're a man of your word in such matters, Colonel—if not perhaps in others—and ye said, I think, that ye'd not leave a square inch of skin on my back."

The planter waved the matter aside. Almost it seemed to offend him.

"Tush! Tush! After this splendid deed of yours, do you suppose I can be thinking of such things?"

"I'm glad ye feel like that about it. But I'm thinking it's mighty lucky for me the Spaniards didn't come to-day instead of yesterday, or it's in the same plight as Jeremy Pitt I'd be this minute. And in that case where was the genius that would have turned the tables on these rascally Spaniards?"

"Why speak of it now?"

"I must, Colonel, darling. Ye've worked a deal of wickedness and cruelty in your time, and I want this to be a lesson to you, a lesson that ye'll remember—for the sake of others who may come after us. There's Jeremy up there in the round-house with a back that's every colour of the rainbow; and the poor lad'll not be himself again for a month. And if it hadn't been for the Spaniards maybe it's dead he'd be by now, and maybe myself with him."

Hagthorpe lounged forward. He was a fairly tall, vigorous man with a clear-cut, attractive face which in itself announced his breeding.

"Why will you be wasting words on the hog?" wondered that sometime officer in the Royal Navy. "Fling him overboard and have done with him."

The Colonel's eyes bulged in his head. "What the devil do you mean?" he blustered.

"It's the lucky man ye are entirely, Colonel, though ye don't guess the source of your good fortune."

And now another intervened—the brawny, one-eyed Wolverstone, less mercifully disposed than his more gentlemanly fellow-convict.

"String him up from the yardarm," he cried, his deep voice harsh and angry, and more than one of the slaves standing to their arms made echo.

Colonel Bishop trembled. Mr. Blood turned. He was quite calm.

"If you please, Wolverstone," said he, "I conduct affairs in my own way. That is the pact. You'll please to remember it." His eyes looked among the ranks, making it plain that he addressed them all. "I desire that Colonel Bishop should have his life. One reason is that I require him as a hostage. If ye insist on hanging him, ye'll have to hang me with him, or in the alternative I'll go ashore."

He paused. There was no answer. But they stood hang-dog and half-mutinous before him, save Hagthorpe, who shrugged and smiled wearily.

Mr. Blood resumed: "Ye'll please to understand that aboard a ship there is one captain. So." He swung again to the startled Colonel. "Though I promise you your life, I must—as you've heard—keep you aboard as a hostage for the good behaviour of Governor Steed and what's left of the fort until we put to sea."

"Until you . . ." Horror prevented Colonel Bishop from echoing the remainder of that incredible speech.

"Just so," said Peter Blood, and he turned to the officers who had accompanied the Colonel. "The boat is waiting, gentlemen. You'll have heard what I said. Convey it with my compliments to his excellency."

"But, sir . . ." one of them began.

"There is no more to be said, gentlemen. My name is Blood—Captain Blood, if you please, of this ship the *Cinco Llagas*, taken as a prize of war from Don Diego de Espinosa y Valdez, who is my prisoner aboard. You are to understand that I have turned the tables on more than the Spaniards. There's the ladder. You'll find it more convenient than being heaved over the side, which is what'll happen if you linger."

They went, though not without some hustling, regardless of the bellowings of Colonel Bishop, whose monstrous rage was fanned by terror at finding himself at the mercy of these men of whose cause to hate him he was very fully conscious.

A half-dozen of them, apart from Jeremy Pitt, who was utterly incapacitated for the present, possessed a superficial knowledge of seamanship. Hagthorpe, although he had been a fighting officer, untrained in navigation, knew how to handle a ship, and under his directions they set about getting under way.

The anchor catted, and the mainsail unfurled, they stood out for the open before a gentle breeze, without interference from the fort.

As they were running close to the headland east of the bay, Peter Blood returned to the Colonel, who, under guard and panic-stricken, had dejectedly resumed his seat on the coamings of the main batch.

"Can ye swim, Colonel?"

Colonel Bishop looked up. His great face was yellow and seemed in that moment of a preternatural flabbiness; his beady eyes were beadier than ever.

"As your doctor, now, I prescribe a swim to cool the excessive heat of your humours." Blood delivered the explanation pleasantly, and, receiving still no answer from the Colonel, continued: "It's a mercy for you I'm not by nature as bloodthirsty as some of my friends here. And it's the devil's own labour I've had to prevail upon them not to be vindictive. I doubt if ye're worth the pains I've taken for you."

He was lying. He had no doubt at all. Had he followed his own wishes and instincts, he would certainly have strung the Colonel up, and accounted it a meritorious deed. It was the thought of Arabella Bishop that had urged him to mercy, and had led him to oppose the natural vindictiveness of his fellow-slaves until he had been in danger of precipitating a mutiny. It was entirely to the fact that the Colonel was her uncle, although he did not even begin to suspect such a cause, that he owed such mercy as was now being shown him.

"You shall have a chance to swim for it," Peter Blood continued. "It's not above a quarter of a mile to the headland yonder, and with ordinary luck ye should manage it. Faith, you're fat enough to float. Come on! Now, don't be hesitating or it's a long voyage ye'll be going with us, and the devil knows what may happen to you. You're not loved any more than you deserve."

Colonel Bishop mastered himself, and rose. A merciless despot, who had never known the need for restraint in all these years, he was doomed by ironic fate to practise restraint in the very moment when his feelings had reached their most violent intensity.

Peter Blood gave an order. A plank was run out over the gunwale, and lashed down.

"If you please, Colonel," said he, with a graceful flourish of invitation.

The Colonel looked at him, and there was hell in his glance. Then, taking his resolve, and putting the best face upon it, since no other could help him here, he kicked off his shoes, peeled off his fine coat of biscuit-coloured taffetas, and climbed upon the plank.

A moment he paused, steadied by a hand that clutched the ratlines, looking down in terror at the green water rushing past some five-and-twenty feet below.

"Just take a little walk, Colonel, darling," said a smooth, mocking voice behind him.

Still clinging, Colonel Bishop looked round in hesitation, and saw the bulwarks lined with swarthy faces—the faces of men that as lately as yesterday would have turned pale under his frown, faces that were now all wickedly agrin.

For a moment rage stamped out his fear. He cursed them aloud venomously and incoherently, then loosed his hold and stepped out upon the plank. Three steps he took before he lost his balance and went tumbling into the green depths below.

When he came to the surface again, gasping for air, the *Cinco Llagas* was already some furlongs to leeward. But the roaring cheer of mocking valediction from the rebels-convict reached him across the water, to drive the iron of impotent rage deeper into his soul.

X. Don Diego

Don Diego de Espinosa y Valdez awoke, and with languid eyes in aching head, he looked round the cabin, which was flooded with sunlight from the square windows astern. Then he uttered a moan, and closed his eyes again, impelled to this by the monstrous ache in his head. Lying thus, he attempted to think, to locate himself in time and space. But between the pain in his head and the confusion in his mind, he found coherent thought impossible.

An indefinite sense of alarm drove him to open his eyes again, and once more to consider his surroundings.

There could be no doubt that he lay in the great cabin of his own ship, the *Cinco Llagas*, so that his vague disquiet must be, surely, ill-founded. And yet, stirrings of memory coming now to the assistance of reflection, compelled him uneasily to insist that here something was not as it should be. The low position of the sun, flooding the cabin with golden light from those square ports astern, suggested to him at first that it was early morning, on the assumption that the vessel was headed westward. Then the alternative occurred to him. They might be sailing eastward, in which case the time of day would be late afternoon. That they were sailing he could feel from the gentle forward heave of the vessel under him. But how did they come to be sailing, and he, the master, not to know whether their course lay east or west, not to be able to recollect whither they were bound?

His mind went back over the adventure of yesterday, if of yesterday it was. He was clear on the matter of the easily successful raid upon the Island of Barbados; every detail stood vividly in his memory up to the moment at which, returning aboard, he had stepped on to his own deck again. There memory abruptly and inexplicably ceased.

He was beginning to torture his mind with conjecture, when the door opened, and to Don Diego's increasing mystification he beheld his best suit of clothes step into the cabin. It was a singularly elegant and characteristically Spanish suit of black taffetas with silver lace that had been made for him a year ago in Cadiz, and he knew each detail of it so well that it was impossible he could now be mistaken.

The suit paused to close the door, then advanced towards the couch on which Don Diego was extended, and inside the suit came a tall, slender gentleman of about Don Diego's own height and shape. Seeing the wide, startled eyes of the Spaniard upon him, the gentleman lengthened his stride.

"Awake, eh?" said he in Spanish.

The recumbent man looked up bewildered into a pair of light-blue eyes that regarded him out of a tawny, sardonic face set in a cluster of black ringlets. But he was too bewildered to make any answer.

The stranger's fingers touched the top of Don Diego's head, whereupon Don Diego winced and cried out in pain.

"Tender, eh?" said the stranger. He took Don Diego's wrist between thumb and second finger. And then, at last, the intrigued Spaniard spoke.

"Are you a doctor?"

"Among other things." The swarthy gentleman continued his study of the patient's pulse. "Firm and regular," he announced at last, and dropped the wrist. "You've taken no great harm."

Don Diego struggled up into a sitting position on the red velvet couch.

"Who the devil are you?" he asked. "And what the devil are you doing in my clothes and aboard my ship?"

The level black eyebrows went up, a faint smile curled the lips of the long mouth.

"You are still delirious, I fear. This is not your ship. This is my ship, and these are my clothes."

"Your ship?" quoth the other, aghast, and still more aghast he added: "Your clothes? But . . . then . . ." Wildly his eyes looked about him. They scanned the cabin once again, scrutinizing each familiar object. "Am I mad?" he asked at last. "Surely this ship is the *Cinco Llagas*?"

"The *Cinco Llagas* it is."

"Then . . ." The Spaniard broke off. His glance grew still more troubled. "Valga me Dios!" he cried out, like a man in anguish. "Will you tell me also that you are Don Diego de Espinosa?"

"Oh, no, my name is Blood—Captain Peter Blood. This ship, like this handsome suit of clothes, is mine by right of conquest. Just as you, Don Diego, are my prisoner."

Startling as was the explanation, yet it proved soothing to Don Diego, being so much less startling than the things he was beginning to imagine.

"But . . . Are you not Spanish, then?"

"You flatter my Castilian accent. I have the honour to be Irish. You were thinking that a miracle had happened. So it has—a miracle wrought by my genius, which is considerable."

Succinctly now Captain Blood dispelled the mystery by a relation of the facts. It was a narrative that painted red and white by turns the Spaniard's countenance. He put a hand to the back of his head, and there discovered, in confirmation of the story, a lump as large as a pigeon's egg. Lastly, he stared wild-eyed at the sardonic Captain Blood.

"And my son? What of my son?" he cried out. "He was in the boat that brought me aboard."

"Your son is safe; he and the boat's crew together with your gunner and his men are snugly in irons under hatches."

Don Diego sank back on the couch, his glittering dark eyes fixed upon the tawny face above him. He composed himself. After all, he possessed the stoicism proper to his desperate trade. The dice had fallen against him in this venture. The tables had been turned upon him in the very moment of success. He accepted the situation with the fortitude of a fatalist.

With the utmost calm he enquired:

"And now, Señor Capitan?"

"And now," said Captain Blood—to give him the title he had assumed—"being a humane man, I am sorry to find that ye're not dead from the tap we gave you. For it means that you'll be put to the trouble of dying all over again."

"Ah!" Don Diego drew a deep breath. "But is that necessary?" he asked, without apparent perturbation.

Captain Blood's blue eyes approved his bearing. "Ask yourself," said he. "Tell me, as an experienced and bloody pirate, what in my place would you do, yourself?"

"Ah, but there is a difference." Don Diego sat up to argue the matter. "It lies in the fact that you boast yourself a humane man."

Captain Blood perched himself on the edge of the long oak table. "But I am not a fool," said he, "and I'll not allow a natural Irish sentimentality to stand in the way of my doing what is necessary and proper. You and your ten surviving scoundrels are a menace on this ship. More than that, she is none so well found in water and provisions. True, we are fortunately a small number, but you and your party inconveniently increase it. So that on every hand, you see, prudence suggests to us that we should deny ourselves the pleasure of your company, and, steeling our soft hearts to the inevitable, invite you to be so obliging as to step over the side."

"I see," said the Spaniard pensively. He swung his legs from the couch, and sat now upon the edge of it, his elbows on his knees. He had taken the measure of his man, and met him with a mock-urbanity and a suave detachment that matched his own. "I confess," he admitted, "that there is much force in what you say."

"You take a load from my mind," said Captain Blood. "I would not appear unnecessarily harsh, especially since I and my friends owe you so very much. For, whatever it may have been to others, to us your raid upon Barbados was most opportune. I am glad, therefore, that you agree the I have no choice."

"But, my friend, I did not agree so much."

"If there is any alternative that you can suggest, I shall be most happy to consider it." Don Diego stroked his pointed black beard.

"Can you give me until morning for reflection? My head aches so damnably that I am incapable of thought. And this, you will admit, is a matter that asks serious thought."

Captain Blood stood up. From a shelf he took a half-hour glass, reversed it so that the bulb containing the red sand was uppermost, and stood it on the table.

"I am sorry to press you in such a matter, Don Diego, but one glass is all that I can give you. If by the time those sands have run out you can propose no acceptable alternative, I shall most reluctantly be driven to ask you to go over the side with your friends."

Captain Blood bowed, went out, and locked the door.

Elbows on his knees and face in his hands, Don Diego sat watching the rusty sands as they filtered from the upper to the lower bulb. And what time he watched, the lines in his lean brown face grew deeper. Punctually as the last grains ran out, the door reopened.

The Spaniard sighed, and sat upright to face the returning Captain Blood with the answer for which he came.

"I have thought of an alternative, sir captain; but it depends upon your charity. It is that you put us ashore on one of the islands of this pestilent archipelago, and leave us to shift for ourselves."

Captain Blood pursed his lips. "It has its difficulties," said he slowly.

"I feared it would be so." Don Diego sighed again, and stood up. "Let us say no more."

The light-blue eyes played over him like points of steel.

"You are not afraid to die, Don Diego?"

The Spaniard threw back his head, a frown between his eyes.

"The question is offensive, sir."

"Then let me put it in another way—perhaps more happily: You do not desire to live?"

"Ah, that I can answer. I do desire to live; and even more do I desire that my son may live. But the desire shall not make a coward of me for your amusement, master mocker." It was the first sign he had shown of the least heat or resentment.

Captain Blood did not directly answer. As before he perched himself on the corner of the table.

"Would you be willing, sir, to earn life and liberty—for yourself, your son, and the other Spaniards who are on board?"

"To earn it?" said Don Diego, and the watchful blue eyes did not miss the quiver that ran through him. "To earn it, do you say? Why, if the service you would propose is one that cannot hurt my honour . . . ."

"Could I be guilty of that?" protested the Captain. "I realize that even a pirate has his honour." And forthwith he propounded his offer. "If you will look from those windows, Don Diego, you will see what appears to be a cloud on the horizon. That is the island of Barbados well astern. All day we have been sailing east before the wind with but one intent—to set as great a distance between Barbados and ourselves as possible. But now, almost out of sight of land, we are in a difficulty. The only man among us schooled in the art of navigation is fevered, delirious, in fact, as a result of certain ill-treatment he received ashore before we carried him away with us. I can handle a ship in action, and there are one or two men aboard who can assist me; but of the higher mysteries of seamanship and of the art of finding a way over the trackless wastes of ocean, we know nothing. To hug the land, and go blundering about what you so aptly call this pestilent archipelago, is for us to court disaster, as you can perhaps conceive. And so it comes to this: We desire to make for the Dutch settlement of Curaçao as straightly as possible. Will you pledge me your honour, if I release you upon parole, that you will navigate us thither? If so, we will release you and your surviving men upon arrival there."

Don Diego bowed his head upon his breast, and strode away in thought to the stern windows. There he stood looking out upon the sunlit sea and the dead water in the great ship's wake—his ship, which these English dogs had wrested from him; his ship, which he was asked to bring safely into a port where she would be completely lost to him and refitted perhaps to make war upon his kin. That was in one scale; in the other were the lives of sixteen men. Fourteen of them mattered little to him, but the remaining two were his own and his son's.

He turned at length, and his back being to the light, the Captain could not see how pale his face had grown.

"I accept," he said.

XI. Filial Piety

By virtue of the pledge he had given, Don Diego de Espinosa enjoyed the freedom of the ship that had been his, and the navigation which he had undertaken was left entirely in his hands. And because those who manned her were new to the seas of the Spanish Main, and because even the things that had happened in Bridgetown were not enough to teach them to regard every Spaniard as a treacherous, cruel dog to be slain at sight, they used him with the civility which his own suave urbanity invited. He took his meals in the great cabin with Blood and the three officers elected to support him: Hagthorpe, Wolverstone, and Dyke.

They found Don Diego an agreeable, even an amusing companion, and their friendly feeling towards him was fostered by his fortitude and brave equanimity in this adversity.

That Don Diego was not playing fair it was impossible to suspect. Moreover, there was no conceivable reason why he should not. And he had been of the utmost frankness with them. He had denounced their mistake in sailing before the wind upon leaving Barbados. They should have left the island to leeward, heading into the Caribbean and away from the archipelago. As it was, they would now be forced to pass through this archipelago again so as to make Curaçao, and this passage was not to be accomplished without some measure of risk to themselves. At any point between the islands they might come upon an equal or superior craft; whether she were Spanish or English would be equally bad for them, and being undermanned they were in no case to fight. To lessen this risk as far as possible, Don Diego directed at first a southerly and then a westerly course; and so, taking a line midway between the islands of Tobago and Grenada, they won safely through the danger-zone and came into the comparative security of the Caribbean Sea.

"If this wind holds," he told them that night at supper, after he had announced to them their position, "we should reach Curaçao inside three days."

For three days the wind held, indeed it freshened a little on the second, and yet when the third night descended upon them they had still made no landfall. The *Cinco Llagas* was ploughing through a sea contained on every side by the blue bowl of heaven. Captain Blood uneasily mentioned it to Don Diego.

"It will be for to-morrow morning," he was answered with calm conviction.

"By all the saints, it is always 'to-morrow morning' with you Spaniards; and to-morrow never comes, my friend."

"But this to-morrow is coming, rest assured. However early you may be astir, you shall see land ahead, Don Pedro."

Captain Blood passed on, content, and went to visit Jerry Pitt, his patient, to whose condition Don Diego owed his chance of life. For twenty-four hours now the fever had left the sufferer, and under Peter Blood's dressings, his lacerated back was beginning to heal satisfactorily. So far, indeed, was he recovered that he complained of his confinement, of the heat in his cabin. To indulge him Captain Blood consented that he should take the air on deck, and so, as the last of the daylight was fading from the sky, Jeremy Pitt came forth upon the Captain's arm.

Seated on the hatch-coamings, the Somersetshire lad gratefully filled his lungs with the cool night air, and professed himself revived thereby. Then with the seaman's instinct his eyes wandered to the darkling vault of heaven, spangled already with a myriad golden points of light. Awhile he scanned it idly, vacantly; then, his attention became sharply fixed. He looked round and up at Captain Blood, who stood beside him.

"D'ye know anything of astronomy, Peter?" quoth he.

"Astronomy, is it? Faith, now, I couldn't tell the Belt of Orion from the Girdle of Venus."

"Ah! And I suppose all the others of this lubberly crew share your ignorance."

"It would be more amiable of you to suppose that they exceed it."

Jeremy pointed ahead to a spot of light in the heavens over the starboard bow. "That is the North Star," said he.

"Is it now? Glory be, I wonder ye can pick it out from the rest."

"And the North Star ahead almost over your starboard bow means that we're steering a course, north, northwest, or maybe north by west, for I doubt if we are standing more than ten degrees westward."

"And why shouldn't we?" wondered Captain Blood.

"You told me—didn't you?—that we came west of the archipelago between Tobago and Grenada, steering for Curaçao. If that were our present course, we should have the North Star abeam, out yonder."

A TREASURY OF SWASHBUCKLING ADVENTURES

On the instant Mr. Blood shed his laziness. He stiffened with apprehension, and was about to speak when a shaft of light clove the gloom above their heads, coming from the door of the poop cabin which had just been opened. It closed again, and presently there was a step on the companion. Don Diego was approaching. Captain Blood's fingers pressed Jerry's shoulder with significance. Then he called the Don, and spoke to him in English as had become his custom when others were present.

"Will ye settle a slight dispute for us, Don Diego?" said he lightly. "We are arguing, Mr. Pitt and I, as to which is the North Star."

"So?" The Spaniard's tone was easy; there was almost a suggestion that laughter lurked behind it, and the reason for this was yielded by his next sentence. "But you tell me Mr. Pitt he is your navigant?"

"For lack of a better," laughed the Captain, good-humouredly contemptuous. "Now I am ready to wager him a hundred pieces of eight that that is the North Star." And he flung out an arm towards a point of light in the heavens straight abeam. He afterwards told Pitt that had Don Diego confirmed him, he would have run him through upon that instant. Far from that, however, the Spaniard freely expressed his scorn.

"You have the assurance that is of ignorance, Don Pedro; and you lose. The North Star is this one." And he indicated it.

"You are sure?"

"But my dear Don Pedro!" The Spaniard's tone was one of amused protest. "But is it possible that I mistake? Besides, is there not the compass? Come to the binnacle and see there what course we make."

His utter frankness, and the easy manner of one who has nothing to conceal resolved at once the doubt that had leapt so suddenly in the mind of Captain Blood. Pitt was satisfied less easily.

"In that case, Don Diego, will you tell me, since Curaçao is our destination, why our course is what it is?"

Again there was no faintest hesitation on Don Diego's part. "You have reason to ask," said he, and sighed. "I had hope' it would not be observe'. I have been careless— oh, of a carelessness very culpable. I neglect observation. Always it is my way. I make too sure. I count too much on dead reckoning. And so to-day I find when at last I take out the quadrant that we do come by a half-degree too much south, so that Curaçao is now almost due north. That is what cause the delay. But we will be there to-morrow."

The explanation, so completely satisfactory, and so readily and candidly forth-coming, left no room for further doubt that Don Diego should have been false to his parole. And when presently Don Diego had withdrawn again, Captain Blood confessed to Pitt that it was absurd to have suspected him. Whatever his antecedents, he had proved his quality when he announced himself ready to die sooner than enter into any undertaking that could hurt his honour or his country.

New to the seas of the Spanish Main and to the ways of the adventurers who sailed it, Captain Blood still entertained illusions. But the next dawn was to shatter them rudely and for ever.

Coming on deck before the sun was up, he saw land ahead, as the Spaniard had promised them last night. Some ten miles ahead it lay, a long coast-line filling the horizon east and west, with a massive headland jutting forward straight before them. Staring at it, he frowned. He had not conceived that Curaçao was of such considerable dimensions. Indeed, this looked less like an island than the main itself.

Beating out aweather, against the gentle landward breeze he beheld a great ship on their starboard bow, that he conceived to be some three or four miles off, and—as well as he could judge her at that distance—of a tonnage equal if not superior to their own. Even as he watched her she altered her course, and going about came heading towards them, closehauled.

A dozen of his fellows were astir on the forecastle, looking eagerly ahead, and the sound of their voices and laughter reached him across the length of the stately *Cinco Llagas.*

"There," said a soft voice behind him in liquid Spanish, "is the Promised Land, Don Pedro."

It was something in that voice, a muffled note of exultation, that awoke suspicion in him, and made whole the half-doubt he had been entertaining. He turned sharply to face Don Diego, so sharply that the sly smile was not effaced from the Spaniard's countenance before Captain Blood's eyes had flashed upon it.

"You find an odd satisfaction in the sight of it—all things considered," said Mr. Blood.

"Of course." The Spaniard rubbed his hands, and Mr. Blood observed that they were unsteady. "The satisfaction of a mariner."

"Or of a traitor—which?" Blood asked him quietly. And as the Spaniard fell back before him with suddenly altered countenance that confirmed his every suspicion, he flung an arm out in the direction of the distant shore. "What land is that?" he demanded. "Will you have the effrontery to tell me that is the coast of Curaçao?"

He advanced upon Don Diego suddenly, and Don Diego, step by step, fell back. "Shall I tell you what land it is? Shall I?" His fierce assumption of knowledge seemed to dazzle and daze the Spaniard. For still Don Diego made no answer. And then Captain Blood drew a bow at a venture—or not quite at a venture. Such a coast-line as that, if not of the main itself, and the main he knew it could not be, must belong to either Cuba or Hispaniola. Now knowing Cuba to lie farther north and west of the two, it followed, he reasoned swiftly, that if Don Diego meant betrayal he would steer for the nearer of these Spanish territories. "That land, you treacherous, forsworn Spanish dog, is the island of Hispaniola."

Having said it, he closely watched the swarthy face now overspread with pallor, to see the truth or falsehood of his guess reflected there. But now the retreating Spaniard had come to the middle of the quarter-deck, where the mizzen sail made a screen to shut them off from the eyes of the Englishmen below. His lips writhed in a snarling smile.

"Ah, perro inglés! You know too much," he said under his breath, and sprang for the Captain's throat.

Tight-locked in each other's arms, they swayed a moment, then together went down upon the deck, the Spaniard's feet jerked from under him by the right leg of Captain Blood. The Spaniard had depended upon his strength, which was considerable. But it proved no match for the steady muscles of the Irishman, tempered of late by the vicissitudes of slavery. He had depended upon choking the life out of Blood, and so gaining the half-hour that might be necessary to bring up that fine ship that was beating towards them—a Spanish ship, perforce, since none other would be so boldly cruising in these Spanish waters off Hispaniola. But all that Don Diego had accomplished was to betray himself completely, and to no purpose. This he realized when he found himself upon his back, pinned down by Blood, who was kneeling on his chest, whilst the men summoned by their Captain's shout came clattering up the companion.

"Will I say a prayer for your dirty soul now, whilst I am in this position?" Captain Blood was furiously mocking him.

But the Spaniard, though defeated, now beyond hope for himself, forced his lips to smile, and gave back mockery for mockery.

"Who will pray for your soul, I wonder, when that galleon comes to lie board and board with you?"

"That galleon!" echoed Captain Blood with sudden and awful realization that already it was too late to avoid the consequences of Don Diego's betrayal of them.

"That galleon," Don Diego repeated, and added with a deepening sneer: "Do you know what ship it is? I will tell you. It is the *Encarnacion*, the flagship of Don Miguel de Espinosa, the Lord Admiral of Castile, and Don Miguel is my brother.

It is a very fortunate encounter. The Almighty, you see, watches over the destinies of Catholic Spain."

There was no trace of humour or urbanity now in Captain Blood. His light eyes blazed: his face was set.

He rose, relinquishing the Spaniard to his men. "Make him fast," he bade them. "Truss him, wrist and heel, but don't hurt him—not so much as a hair of his precious head."

The injunction was very necessary. Frenzied by the thought that they were likely to exchange the slavery from which they had so lately escaped for a slavery still worse, they would have torn the Spaniard limb from limb upon the spot. And if they now obeyed their Captain and refrained, it was only because the sudden steely note in his voice promised for Don Diego Valdez something far more exquisite than death.

"You scum! You dirty pirate! You man of honour!" Captain Blood apostrophized his prisoner.

But Don Diego looked up at him and laughed.

"You underrated me." He spoke English, so that all might hear. "I tell you that I was not fear death, and I show you that I was not fear it. You no understand. You just an English dog."

"Irish, if you please," Captain Blood corrected him. "And your parole, you tyke of Spain?"

"You think I give my parole to leave you sons of filth with this beautiful Spanish ship, to go make war upon other Spaniards! Ha!" Don Diego laughed in his throat. "You fool! You can kill me. Pish! It is very well. I die with my work well done. In less than an hour you will be the prisoners of Spain, and the *Cinco Llagas* will go belong to Spain again."

Captain Blood regarded him steadily out of a face which, if impassive, had paled under its deep tan. About the prisoner, clamant, infuriated, ferocious, the rebels-convict surged, almost literally "athirst for his blood."

"Wait," Captain Blood imperiously commanded, and turning on his heel, he went aside to the rail. As he stood there deep in thought, he was joined by Hagthorpe, Wolverstone, and Ogle the gunner. In silence they stared with him across the water at that other ship. She had veered a point away from the wind, and was running now on a line that must in the end converge with that of the *Cinco Llagas*.

"In less than half-an-hour," said Blood presently, "we shall have her athwart our hawse, sweeping our decks with her guns."

"We can fight," said the one-eyed giant with an oath.

"Fight!" sneered Blood. "Undermanned as we are, mustering a bare twenty men, in what case are we to fight? No, there would be only one way. To persuade her that all is well aboard, that we are Spaniards, so that she may leave us to continue on our course."

"And how is that possible?" Hagthorpe asked.

"It isn't possible," said Blood. "If it were . . ." And then he broke off, and stood musing, his eyes upon the green water. Ogle, with a bent for sarcasm, interposed a suggestion bitterly.

"We might send Don Diego de Espinosa in a boat manned by his Spaniards to assure his brother the Admiral that we are all loyal subjects of his Catholic Majesty."

The Captain swung round, and for an instant looked as if he would have struck the gunner. Then his expression changed: the light of inspiration was in his glance.

"Bedad! ye've said it. He doesn't fear death, this damned pirate; but his son may take a different view. Filial piety's mighty strong in Spain." He swung on his heel abruptly, and strode back to the knot of men about his prisoner. "Here!" he shouted to them. "Bring him below." And he led the way down to the waist, and thence by the booby hatch to the gloom of the 'tween-decks, where the air was rank with the smell of tar and spun yarn. Going aft he threw open the door of the spacious wardroom, and went in followed by a dozen of the hands with the pinioned Spaniard. Every man aboard would have followed him but for his sharp command to some of them to remain on deck with Hagthorpe.

In the ward-room the three stern chasers were in position, loaded, their muzzles thrusting through the open ports, precisely as the Spanish gunners had left them.

"Here, Ogle, is work for you," said Blood, and as the burly gunner came thrusting forward through the little throng of gaping men, Blood pointed to the middle chaser: "Have that gun hauled back," he ordered.

When this was done, Blood beckoned those who held Don Diego.

"Lash him across the mouth of it," he bade them, and whilst, assisted by another two, they made haste to obey, he turned to the others. "To the roundhouse, some of you, and fetch the Spanish prisoners. And you, Dyke, go up and bid them set the flag of Spain aloft."

Don Diego, with his body stretched in an arc across the cannon's mouth, legs and arms lashed to the carriage on either side of it, eyeballs rolling in his head, glared maniacally at Captain Blood. A man may not fear to die, and yet be appalled by the form in which death comes to him.

From frothing lips he hurled blasphemies and insults at his tormentor.

"Foul barbarian! Inhuman savage! Accursed heretic! Will it not content you to kill me in some Christian fashion?"

Captain Blood vouchsafed him a malignant smile, before he turned to meet the fifteen manacled Spanish prisoners, who were thrust into his presence.

Approaching, they had heard Don Diego's outcries; at close quarters now they beheld with horror-stricken eyes his plight. From amongst them a comely, olive-skinned stripling, distinguished in bearing and apparel from his companions, started forward with an anguished cry of "Father!"

Writhing in the arms that made haste to seize and hold him, he called upon heaven and hell to avert this horror, and lastly, addressed to Captain Blood an appeal for mercy that was at once fierce and piteous. Considering him, Captain Blood thought with satisfaction that he displayed the proper degree of filial piety.

He afterwards confessed that for a moment he was in danger of weakening, that for a moment his mind rebelled against the pitiless thing it had planned. But to correct the sentiment he evoked a memory of what these Spaniards had performed in Bridgetown. Again he saw the white face of that child Mary Traill as she fled in horror before the jeering ruffian whom he had slain, and other things even more unspeakable seen on that dreadful evening rose now before the eyes of his memory to stiffen his faltering purpose. The Spaniards had shown themselves without mercy or sentiment or decency of any kind; stuffed with religion, they were without a spark of that Christianity, the Symbol of which was mounted on the mainmast of the approaching ship. A moment ago this cruel, vicious Don Diego had insulted the Almighty by his assumption that He kept a specially benevolent watch over the destinies of Catholic Spain. Don Diego should be taught his error.

Recovering the cynicism in which he had approached his task, the cynicism essential to its proper performance, he commanded Ogle to kindle a match and remove the leaden apron from the touch-hole of the gun that bore Don Diego. Then, as the younger Espinosa broke into fresh intercessions mingled with imprecations, he wheeled upon him sharply.

"Peace!" he snapped. "Peace, and listen! It is no part of my intention to blow your father to hell as he deserves, or indeed to take his life at all."

Having surprised the lad into silence by that promise—a promise surprising enough in all the circumstances—he proceeded to explain his aims in that faultless and elegant Castilian of which he was fortunately master—as fortunately for Don Diego as for himself.

"It is your father's treachery that has brought us into this plight and deliberately into risk of capture and death aboard that ship of Spain. Just as your father recognized his brother's flagship, so will his brother have recognized the *Cinco Llagas*. So far, then, all is well. But presently the *Encarnacion* will be sufficiently close to perceive that here all is not as it should be. Sooner or later, she must guess or discover what is wrong, and then she will open fire or lay us board and board. Now, we are in no case to fight, as your father knew when he ran us into this trap. But fight we will, if we are driven to it. We make no tame surrender to the ferocity of Spain."

He laid his hand on the breech of the gun that bore Don Diego.

"Understand this clearly: to the first shot from the *Encarnacion* this gun will fire the answer. I make myself clear, I hope?"

White-faced and trembling, young Espinosa stared into the pitiless blue eyes that so steadily regarded him.

"If it is clear?" he faltered, breaking the utter silence in which all were standing. "But, name of God, how should it be clear? How should I understand? Can you avert the fight? If you know a way, and if I, or these, can help you to it—if that is what you mean—in Heaven's name let me hear it."

"A fight would be averted if Don Diego de Espinosa were to go aboard his brother's ship, and by his presence and assurances inform the Admiral that all is well with the *Cinco Llagas*, that she is indeed still a ship of Spain as her flag now announces. But of course Don Diego cannot go in person, because he is . . . otherwise engaged. He has a slight touch of fever—shall we say?—that detains him in his cabin. But you, his son, may convey all this and some other matters together with his homage to your uncle. You shall go in a boat manned by six of these Spanish prisoners, and I—a distinguished Spaniard delivered from captivity in Barbados by your recent raid—will accompany you to keep you in countenance. If I return alive, and without accident of any kind to hinder our free sailing hence, Don Diego shall have his life, as shall every one of you. But if there is the least misadventure, be it from treachery or ill-fortune—I care not which—the battle, as I have had the honour to explain, will be opened on our side by this gun, and your father will be the first victim of the conflict."

He paused a moment. There was a hum of approval from his comrades, an anxious stirring among the Spanish prisoners. Young Espinosa stood before him, the colour ebbing and flowing in his cheeks. He waited for some direction from his father. But none came. Don Diego's courage, it seemed, had sadly waned under that rude test. He hung limply in his fearful bonds, and was silent. Evidently he dared not encourage his son to defiance, and presumably was ashamed to urge him to yield. Thus, he left decision entirely with the youth.

"Come," said Blood. "I have been clear enough, I think. What do you say?"

Don Esteban moistened his parched lips, and with the back of his hand mopped the anguish-sweat from his brow. His eyes gazed wildly a moment upon the shoulders of his father, as if beseeching guidance. But his father remained silent. Something like a sob escaped the boy.

"I . . . I accept," he answered at last, and swung to the Spaniards. "And you—you will accept too," he insisted passionately. "For Don Diego's sake and for your own—for all our sakes. If you do not, this man will butcher us all without mercy."

Since he yielded, and their leader himself counselled no resistance, why should they encompass their own destruction by a gesture of futile heroism? They answered without much hesitation that they would do as was required of them.

Blood turned, and advanced to Don Diego.

"I am sorry to inconvenience you in this fashion, but . . ." For a second he checked and frowned as his eyes intently observed the prisoner. Then, after that scarcely perceptible pause, he continued, ". . . But I do not think that you have anything beyond this inconvenience to apprehend, and you may depend upon me to shorten it as far as possible."

Don Diego made him no answer.

Peter Blood waited a moment, observing him; then he bowed and stepped back.

XII. DON PIEDRO SANGRE

The *Cinco Llagas* and the *Encarnacion*, after a proper exchange of signals, lay hove to within a quarter of a mile of each other, and across the intervening space of gently heaving, sunlit waters sped a boat from the former, manned by six Spanish seamen and bearing in her stern sheets Don Esteban de Espinosa and Captain Peter Blood.

She also bore two treasure-chests containing fifty thousand pieces of eight. Gold has at all times been considered the best of testimonies of good faith, and Blood was determined that in all respects appearances should be entirely on his side. His followers had accounted this a supererogation of pretence. But Blood's will in the matter had prevailed. He carried further a bulky package addressed to a grande of Spain, heavily sealed with the arms of Espinosa—another piece of evidence hastily manufactured in the cabin of the *Cinco Llagas*—and he was spending these last moments in completing his instructions to his young companion.

Don Esteban expressed his last lingering uneasiness:

"But if you should betray yourself?" he cried.

"It will be unfortunate for . . . everybody. I advised your father to say a prayer for our success. I depend upon you to help me more materially."

"I will do my best. God knows I will do my best," the boy protested.

Blood nodded thoughtfully, and no more was said until they bumped alongside the towering mass of the *Encarnacion*. Up the ladder went Don Esteban closely followed by Captain Blood. In the waist stood the Admiral himself to receive them, a handsome, self-sufficient man, very tall and stiff, a little older and greyer than Don Diego, whom he closely resembled. He was supported by four officers and a friar in the black and white habit of St. Dominic.

Don Miguel opened his arms to his nephew, whose lingering panic he mistook for pleasurable excitement, and having enfolded him to his bosom turned to greet Don Esteban's companion.

Peter Blood bowed gracefully, entirely at his ease, so far as might be judged from appearances.

"I am," he announced, making a literal translation of his name, "Don Pedro Sangre, an unfortunate gentleman of Leon, lately delivered from captivity by Don Esteban's most gallant father." And in a few words he sketched the imagined conditions of his capture by, and deliverance from, those accursed heretics who held the island of Barbados.

"Benedicamus Domino," said the friar to his tale.

"Ex hoc nunc et usque in seculum," replied Blood, the occasional papist, with lowered eyes.

The Admiral and his attending officers gave him a sympathetic hearing and a cordial welcome. Then came the dreaded question.

"But where is my brother? Why has he not come, himself, to greet me?"

It was young Espinosa who answered this:

"My father is afflicted at denying himself that honour and pleasure. But unfortunately, sir uncle, he is a little indisposed—oh, nothing grave; merely sufficient to make him keep his cabin. It is a little fever, the result of a slight wound taken in the recent raid upon Barbados, which resulted in this gentleman's happy deliverance."

"Nay, nephew, nay," Don Miguel protested with ironic repudiation. "I can have no knowledge of these things. I have the honour to represent upon the seas His Catholic Majesty, who is at peace with the King of England. Already you have told me more than it is good for me to know. I will endeavour to forget it, and I will ask you, sirs," he added, glancing at his officers, "to forget it also." But he winked into the twinkling eyes of Captain Blood; then added matter that at once extinguished that twinkle. "But since Diego cannot come to me, why, I will go across to him."

For a moment Don Esteban's face was a mask of pallid fear. Then Blood was speaking in a lowered, confidential voice that admirably blended suavity, impressiveness, and sly mockery.

"If you please, Don Miguel, but that is the very thing you must not do—the very thing Don Diego does not wish you to do. You must not see him until his wounds are healed. That is his own wish. That is the real reason why he is not here. For the truth is that his wounds are not so grave as to have prevented his coming. It was his consideration of himself and the false position in which you would be placed if you had direct word from him of what has happened. As your excellency has said, there is peace between His Catholic Majesty and the King of England, and your brother Don Diego . . ." He paused a moment. "I am sure that I need say no more. What you hear from us is no more than a mere rumour. Your excellency understands."

His excellency frowned thoughtfully. "I understand . . . in part," said he.

Captain Blood had a moment's uneasiness. Did the Spaniard doubt his bona fides? Yet in dress and speech he knew himself to be impeccably Spanish, and was not Don Esteban there to confirm him? He swept on to afford further confirmation before the Admiral could say another word.

"And we have in the boat below two chests containing fifty thousand pieces of eight, which we are to deliver to your excellency."

His excellency jumped; there was a sudden stir among his officers.

"They are the ransom extracted by Don Diego from the Governor of . . ."

"Not another word, in the name of Heaven!" cried the Admiral in alarm. "My brother wishes me to assume charge of this money, to carry it to Spain for him? Well, that is a family matter between my brother and myself. So, it can be done. But I must not know . . ." He broke off. "Hum! A glass of Malaga in my cabin, if you please," he invited them, "whilst the chests are being hauled aboard."

He gave his orders touching the embarkation of these chests, then led the way to his regally appointed cabin, his four officers and the friar following by particular invitation.

Seated at table there, with the tawny wine before them, and the servant who had poured it withdrawn, Don Miguel laughed and stroked his pointed, grizzled beard.

"Virgen santisima! That brother of mine has a mind that thinks of everything. Left to myself, I might have committed a fine indiscretion by venturing aboard his ship at such a moment. I might have seen things which as Admiral of Spain it would be difficult for me to ignore."

Both Esteban and Blood made haste to agree with him, and then Blood raised his glass, and drank to the glory of Spain and the damnation of the besotted James who occupied the throne of England. The latter part of his toast was at least sincere.

The Admiral laughed.

"Sir, sir, you need my brother here to curb your imprudences. You should remember that His Catholic Majesty and the King of England are very good friends. That is not a toast to propose in this cabin. But since it has been proposed, and by one who has such particular personal cause to hate these English hounds, why, we will honour it—but unofficially."

They laughed, and drank the damnation of King James—quite unofficially, but the more fervently on that account. Then Don Esteban, uneasy on the score of his father, and remembering that the agony of Don Diego was being protracted with every moment that they left him in his dreadful position, rose and announced that they must be returning.

"My father," he explained, "is in haste to reach San Domingo. He desired me to stay no longer than necessary to embrace you. If you will give us leave, then, sir uncle."

In the circumstances "sir uncle" did not insist.

As they returned to the ship's side, Blood's eyes anxiously scanned the line of seamen leaning over the bulwarks in idle talk with the Spaniards in the cock-boat that waited at the ladder's foot. But their manner showed him that there was no ground for his anxiety. The boat's crew had been wisely reticent.

The Admiral took leave of them—of Esteban affectionately, of Blood ceremoniously.

"I regret to lose you so soon, Don Pedro. I wish that you could have made a longer visit to the *Encarnacion*."

"I am indeed unfortunate," said Captain Blood politely.

"But I hope that we may meet again."

"That is to flatter me beyond all that I deserve."

They reached the boat; and she cast off from the great ship. As they were pulling away, the Admiral waving to them from the taffrail, they heard the shrill whistle of the bo'sun piping the hands to their stations, and before they had reached the *Cinco Llagas*, they beheld the *Encarnacion* go about under sail. She dipped her flag to them, and from her poop a gun fired a salute.

Aboard the *Cinco Llagas* some one—it proved afterwards to be Hagthorpe—had the wit to reply in the same fashion. The comedy was ended. Yet there was something else to follow as an epilogue, a thing that added a grim ironic flavour to the whole.

As they stepped into the waist of the *Cinco Llagas*, Hagthorpe advanced to receive them. Blood observed the set, almost scared expression on his face.

"I see that you've found it," he said quietly.

Hagthorpe's eyes looked a question. But his mind dismissed whatever thought it held.

"Don Diego . . ." he was beginning, and then stopped, and looked curiously at Blood.

Noting the pause and the look, Esteban bounded forward, his face livid.

"Have you broken faith, you curs? Has he come to harm?" he cried—and the six Spaniards behind him grew clamorous with furious questionings.

"We do not break faith," said Hagthorpe firmly, so firmly that he quieted them. "And in this case there was not the need. Don Diego died in his bonds before ever you reached the *Encarnacion*."

Peter Blood said nothing.

"Died?" screamed Esteban. "You killed him, you mean. Of what did he die?"

Hagthorpe looked at the boy. "If I am a judge," he said, "Don Diego died of fear."

Don Esteban struck Hagthorpe across the face at that, and Hagthorpe would have struck back, but that Blood got between, whilst his followers seized the lad.

"Let be," said Blood. "You provoked the boy by your insult to his father."

"I was not concerned to insult," said Hagthorpe, nursing his cheek. "It is what has happened. Come and look."

"I have seen," said Blood. "He died before I left the *Cinco Llagas*. He was hanging dead in his bonds when I spoke to him before leaving."

"What are you saying?" cried Esteban.

Blood looked at him gravely. Yet for all his gravity he seemed almost to smile, though without mirth.

"If you had known that, eh?" he asked at last.

For a moment Don Esteban stared at him wide-eyed, incredulous. "I don't believe you," he said at last.

"Yet you may. I am a doctor, and I know death when I see it."

Again there came a pause, whilst conviction sank into the lad's mind.

"If I had known that," he said at last in a thick voice, "you would be hanging from the yardarm of the *Encarnacion* at this moment."

"I know," said Blood. "I am considering it—the profit that a man may find in the ignorance of others."

"But you'll hang there yet," the boy raved.

Captain Blood shrugged, and turned on his heel. But he did not on that account disregard the words, nor did Hagthorpe, nor yet the others who overheard them, as they showed at a council held that night in the cabin.

This council was met to determine what should be done with the Spanish prisoners. Considering that Curaçao now lay beyond their reach, as they were running short of water and provisions, and also that Pitt was hardly yet in case to undertake the navigation of the vessel, it had been decided that, going east of Hispaniola, and then sailing along its northern coast, they should make for Tortuga, that haven of the buccaneers, in which lawless port they had at least no danger of recapture to apprehend. It was now a question whether they should convey the Spaniards thither with them, or turn them off in a boat to make the best of their way to the coast of Hispaniola, which was but ten miles off. This was the course urged by Blood himself.

"There's nothing else to be done," he insisted. "In Tortuga they would be flayed alive."

"Which is less than the swine deserve," growled Wolverstone.

"And you'll remember, Peter," put in Hagthorpe, "that boy's threat to you this morning. If he escapes, and carries word of all this to his uncle, the Admiral, the execution of that threat will become more than possible."

It says much for Peter Blood that the argument should have left him unmoved. It is a little thing, perhaps, but in a narrative in which there is so much that tells against him, I cannot—since my story is in the nature of a brief for the defence—afford to slur a circumstance that is so strongly in his favour, a circumstance revealing that the cynicism attributed to him proceeded from his reason and from a brooding over wrongs rather than from any natural instincts.

"I care nothing for his threats."

"You should," said Wolverstone. "The wise thing'd be to hang him, along o' all the rest."

"It is not human to be wise," said Blood. "It is much more human to err, though perhaps exceptional to err on the side of mercy. We'll be exceptional. Oh, faugh! I've no stomach for cold-blooded killing. At daybreak pack the Spaniards into a boat with a keg of water and a sack of dumplings, and let them go to the devil."

That was his last word on the subject, and it prevailed by virtue of the authority they had vested in him, and of which he had taken so firm a grip. At daybreak Don Esteban and his followers were put off in a boat.

Two days later, the *Cinco Llagas* sailed into the rock-bound bay of Cayona, which Nature seemed to have designed for the stronghold of those who had appropriated it.

XIII. Tortuga

It is time fully to disclose the fact that the survival of the story of Captain Blood's exploits is due entirely to the industry of Jeremy Pitt, the Somersetshire shipmaster. In addition to his ability as a navigator, this amiable young man appears to have wielded an indefatigable pen, and to have been inspired to indulge its fluency by the affection he very obviously bore to Peter Blood.

He kept the log of the forty-gun frigate *Arabella*, on which he served as master, or, as we should say to-day, navigating officer, as no log that I have seen was ever kept. It runs into some twenty-odd volumes of assorted sizes, some of which are missing altogether and others of which are so sadly depleted of leaves as to be of little use. But if at times in the laborious perusal of them—they are preserved in the library of Mr. James Speke of Comerton—I have inveighed against these lacunæ, at others I have been equally troubled by the excessive prolixity of what remains and the difficulty of disintegrating from the confused whole the really essential parts.

I have a suspicion that Esquemeling—though how or where I can make no surmise—must have obtained access to these records, and that he plucked from them the brilliant feathers of several exploits to stick them into the tail of his own hero, Captain Morgan. But that is by the way. I mention it chiefly as a warning, for when presently I come to relate the affair of Maracaybo, those of you who have read Esquemeling may be in danger of supposing that Henry Morgan really performed those things which here are veraciously attributed to Peter Blood. I think, however, that when you come to weigh the motives actuating both Blood and the Spanish Admiral, in that affair, and when you consider how integrally the event is a part of Blood's history—whilst merely a detached incident in Morgan's—you will reach my own conclusion as to which is the real plagiarist.

The first of these logs of Pitt's is taken up almost entirely with a retrospective narrative of the events up to the time of Blood's first coming to Tortuga. This and the Tannatt Collection of State Trials are the chief—though not the only—sources of my history so far.

Pitt lays great stress upon the fact that it was the circumstances upon which I have dwelt, and these alone, that drove Peter Blood to seek an anchorage at Tortuga. He insists at considerable length, and with a vehemence which in itself makes it plain that an opposite opinion was held in some quarters, that it was no part of the design of Blood or of any of his companions in misfortune to join hands with the buccaneers who, under a semi-official French protection, made of Tortuga a lair whence they could sally out to drive their merciless piratical trade chiefly at the expense of Spain.

It was, Pitt tells us, Blood's original intention to make his way to France or Holland. But in the long weeks of waiting for a ship to convey him to one or the other of these countries, his resources dwindled and finally vanished. Also, his chronicler thinks that he detected signs of some secret trouble in his friend, and he attributes to this the abuses of the potent West Indian spirit of which Blood became guilty in those days of inaction, thereby sinking to the level of the wild adventurers with whom ashore he associated.

I do not think that Pitt is guilty in this merely of special pleading, that he is putting forward excuses for his hero. I think that in those days there was a good deal to oppress Peter Blood. There was the thought of Arabella Bishop—and that this thought loomed large in his mind we are not permitted to doubt. He was maddened by the tormenting lure of the unattainable. He desired Arabella, yet knew her beyond his reach irrevocably and for all time. Also, whilst he may have desired to go to France or Holland, he had no clear purpose to accomplish when he reached one or the other of these countries. He was, when all is said, an escaped slave, an outlaw in his own land and a homeless outcast in any other. There remained the sea, which is free to all, and particularly alluring to those who feel themselves at war with humanity. And so, considering the adventurous spirit that once already had sent him a-roving for the sheer love of it, considering that this spirit was heightened now by a recklessness begotten of his outlawry, that his training and skill in militant seamanship clamorously supported the temptations that were put before him, can you wonder, or dare you blame him, that in the end he succumbed? And remember that these temptations proceeded not only from adventurous buccaneering acquaintances in the taverns of that evil haven of Tortuga, but even from M. d'Ogeron, the governor of the island, who levied as his harbour dues a percentage of one tenth of all spoils brought into the bay, and who profited further by commissions upon money which he was desired to convert into bills of exchange upon France.

A trade that might have worn a repellent aspect when urged by greasy, half-drunken adventurers, boucan-hunters, lumbermen, beach-combers, English, French,

vere
that nor
ok obedie
ction. Any t
eader.

itself out, he
he following
er Blood had
There was a
had resulted
raid effected
he Rio de la
here was an
ale of which
crew of the

he following
the fame of
dward Isles,

es's angry
swered that
n the King
d that any
pprobation

is nephew
urer to the
ernational

report of
d him not

he likely,
r what he

d, almost official form of privateering when advocated
ntleman who in representing the French West India
rance herself.

luding Jeremy Pitt himself, in whose blood the call of
ve—those who had escaped with Peter Blood from
, consequently, like himself, knew not whither to
the great Brotherhood of the Coast, as those rovers
theirs to the other voices that were persuading
inue now in the leadership which he had enjoyed
rearing to follow him loyally whithersoever he

my has recorded in the matter, Blood ended by
sure, abandoned himself to the stream of Destiny.
xpression of it.

nk, the thought of Arabella Bishop that restrained
ever to meet again did not weigh at first, or, indeed,
which she would come to hear of his having turned
ct no more than imagined, hurt him as if it were
he conquered this, still the thought of her was ever
conscience that her memory kept so disconcertingly
of her should continue ever before him to help him
might in this desperate trade upon which he was
night entertain no delusive hope of ever winning her
her again, yet the memory of her was to abide in his
influence. The love that is never to be realized will
al.

vent actively to work. Ogeron, most accommodating of
y for the proper equipment of his ship the *Cinco Llagas*,
This after some little hesitation, fearful of thus setting
s Barbados friends accounted it merely an expression of
heir leader dealt.

e already possessed, he added threescore more, picking
rimination—and he was an exceptional judge of men—
s of Tortuga. With them all he entered into the articles
the Coast under which each man was to be paid by a

share in the prizes captured. In other respects, however, the articles

Aboard the *Arabella* there was to be none of the ruffianly indiscipline

prevailed in buccaneering vessels. Those who shipped with him undert

and submission in all things to himself and to the officers appointed by el

whom this clause in the articles was distasteful might follow some other

Towards the end of December, when the hurricane season had blown

put to sea in his well-found, well-manned ship, and before he returned in

May from a protracted and adventurous cruise, the fame of Captain Pe

run like ripples before the breeze across the face of the Caribbean Sea.

fight in the Windward Passage at the outset with a Spanish galleon, which

in the gutting and finally the sinking of the Spaniard. There was a daring

by means of several appropriated piraguas upon a Spanish pearl fleet in

Hacha, from which they had taken a particularly rich haul of pearls. T

overland expedition to the goldfields of Sancta Maria, on the Main, the full

is hardly credible, and there were lesser adventures through all of which th

Arabella came with credit and profit if not entirely unscathed.

And so it happened that before the *Arabella* came homing to Tortuga in t

May to refit and repair—for she was not without scars, as you conceive—

her and of Peter Blood her captain had swept from the Bahamas to the Win

from New Providence to Trinidad.

An echo of it had reached Europe, and at the Court of St. Jam

representations were made by the Ambassador of Spain, to whom it was an

it must not be supposed that this Captain Blood held any commission fro

of England; that he was, in fact, a proscribed rebel, an escaped slave, ar

measures against him by His Catholic Majesty would receive the cordial a

of King James II.

Don Miguel de Espinosa, the Admiral of Spain in the West Indies, and

Don Esteban who sailed with him, did not lack the will to bring the advent

yardarm. With them this business of capturing Blood, which was now an in

affair, was also a family matter.

Spain, through the mouth of Don Miguel, did not spare her threats. Th

them reached Tortuga, and with it the assurance that Don Miguel had behir

only the authority of his own nation, but that of the English King as well.

It was a brutum fulmen that inspired no terrors in Captain Blood. Nor wa:

on account of it, to allow himself to run to rust in the security of Tortuga. F had suffered at the hands of Man he had chosen to make Spain the scapegoat. Thus he accounted that he served a twofold purpose: he took compensation and at the same time served, not indeed the Stuart King, whom he despised, but England and, for that matter, all the rest of civilized mankind which cruel, treacherous, greedy, bigoted Castile sought to exclude from intercourse with the New World.

One day as he sat with Hagthorpe and Wolverstone over a pipe and a bottle of rum in the stifling reek of tar and stale tobacco of a waterside tavern, he was accosted by a splendid ruffian in a gold-laced coat of dark-blue satin with a crimson sash, a foot wide, about the waist.

"C'est vous qu'on appelle Le Sang?" the fellow hailed him.

Captain Blood looked up to consider the questioner before replying. The man was tall and built on lines of agile strength, with a swarthy, aquiline face that was brutally handsome. A diamond of great price flamed on the indifferently clean hand resting on the pummel of his long rapier, and there were gold rings in his ears, half concealed by long ringlets of oily chestnut hair.

Captain Blood took the pipe-stem from between his lips.

"My name," he said, "is Peter Blood. The Spaniards know me for Don Pedro Sangre, and a Frenchman may call me Le Sang if he pleases."

"Good," said the gaudy adventurer in English, and without further invitation he drew up a stool and sat down at that greasy table. "My name," he informed the three men, two of whom at least were eyeing him askance, "it is Levasseur. You may have heard of me."

They had, indeed. He commanded a privateer of twenty guns that had dropped anchor in the bay a week ago, manned by a crew mainly composed of French boucan-hunters from Northern Hispaniola, men who had good cause to hate the Spaniard with an intensity exceeding that of the English. Levasseur had brought them back to Tortuga from an indifferently successful cruise. It would need more, however, than lack of success to abate the fellow's monstrous vanity. A roaring, quarrelsome, hard-drinking, hard-gaming scoundrel, his reputation as a buccaneer stood high among the wild Brethren of the Coast. He enjoyed also a reputation of another sort. There was about his gaudy, swaggering raffishness something that the women found singularly alluring. That he should boast openly of his bonnes fortunes did not seem strange to Captain Blood; what he might have found strange was that there appeared to be some measure of justification for these boasts.

It was current gossip that even Mademoiselle d'Ogeron, the Governor's daughter, had been caught in the snare of his wild attractiveness, and that Levasseur had gone the length of audacity of asking her hand in marriage of her father. M. d'Ogeron had made him the only possible answer. He had shown him the door. Levasseur had departed in a rage, swearing that he would make mademoiselle his wife in the teeth of all the fathers in Christendom, and that M. d'Ogeron should bitterly rue the affront he had put upon him.

This was the man who now thrust himself upon Captain Blood with a proposal of association, offering him not only his sword, but his ship and the men who sailed in her.

A dozen years ago, as a lad of barely twenty, Levasseur had sailed with that monster of cruelty L'Ollonais, and his own subsequent exploits bore witness and did credit to the school in which he had been reared. I doubt if in his day there was a greater scoundrel among the Brethren of the Coast than this Levasseur. And yet, repulsive though he found him, Captain Blood could not deny that the fellow's proposals displayed boldness, imagination, and resource, and he was forced to admit that jointly they could undertake operations of a greater magnitude than was possible singly to either of them. The climax of Levasseur's project was to be a raid upon the wealthy mainland city of Maracaybo; but for this, he admitted, six hundred men at the very least would be required, and six hundred men were not to be conveyed in the two bottoms they now commanded. Preliminary cruises must take place, having for one of their objects the capture of further ships.

Because he disliked the man, Captain Blood would not commit himself at once. But because he liked the proposal he consented to consider it. Being afterwards pressed by both Hagthorpe and Wolverstone, who did not share his own personal dislike of the Frenchman, the end of the matter was that within a week articles were drawn up between Levasseur and Blood, and signed by them and—as was usual—by the chosen representatives of their followers.

These articles contained, inter alia, the common provisions that, should the two vessels separate, a strict account must afterwards be rendered of all prizes severally taken, whilst the vessel taking a prize should retain three fifths of its value, surrendering two fifths to its associate. These shares were subsequently to be subdivided among the crew of each vessel, in accordance with the articles already obtaining between each captain and his own men. For the rest, the articles contained all the clauses that were usual, among which was the clause that any man found guilty of abstracting or concealing any part of a prize, be it of the value of no more than a peso, should be summarily hanged from the yardarm.

All being now settled they made ready for sea, and on the very eve of sailing, Levasseur narrowly escaped being shot in a romantic attempt to scale the wall of the Governor's garden, with the object of taking passionate leave of the infatuated Mademoiselle d'Ogeron. He desisted after having been twice fired upon from a fragrant ambush of pimento trees where the Governor's guards were posted, and he departed vowing to take different and very definite measures on his return.

That night he slept on board his ship, which with characteristic flamboyance he had named *La Foudre*, and there on the following day he received a visit from Captain Blood, whom he greeted half-mockingly as his admiral. The Irishman came to settle certain final details of which all that need concern us is an understanding that, in the event of the two vessels becoming separated by accident or design, they should rejoin each other as soon as might be at Tortuga.

Thereafter Levasseur entertained his admiral to dinner, and jointly they drank success to the expedition, so copiously on the part of Levasseur that when the time came to separate he was as nearly drunk as it seemed possible for him to be and yet retain his understanding.

Finally, towards evening, Captain Blood went over the side and was rowed back to his great ship with her red bulwarks and gilded ports, touched into a lovely thing of flame by the setting sun.

He was a little heavy-hearted. I have said that he was a judge of men, and his judgment of Levasseur filled him with misgivings which were growing heavier in a measure as the hour of departure approached.

He expressed it to Wolverstone, who met him as he stepped aboard the *Arabella*:

"You over persuaded me into those articles, you blackguard; and it'll surprise me if any good comes of this association."

The giant rolled his single bloodthirsty eye, and sneered, thrusting out his heavy jaw. "We'll wring the dog's neck if there's any treachery."

"So we will—if we are there to wring it by then." And on that, dismissing the matter: "We sail in the morning, on the first of the ebb," he announced, and went off to his cabin.

XIV. Levasseur's Heroics

It would be somewhere about ten o'clock on the following morning, a full hour before the time appointed for sailing, when a canoe brought up alongside *La Foudre*, and a half-caste Indian stepped out of her and went up the ladder. He was clad in drawers of hairy, untanned hide, and a red blanket served him for a cloak. He was the bearer of a folded scrap of paper for Captain Levasseur.

The Captain unfolded the letter, sadly soiled and crumpled by contact with the half-caste's person. Its contents may be roughly translated thus:

"*My well-beloved*—I am in the Dutch brig *Jongvrouw*, which is about to sail. Resolved to separate us for ever, my cruel father is sending me to Europe in my brother's charge. I implore you, come to my rescue. Deliver me, my well-beloved hero!—Your desolated Madeleine, who loves you."

The well-beloved hero was moved to the soul of him by that passionate appeal. His scowling glance swept the bay for the Dutch brig, which he knew had been due to sail for Amsterdam with a cargo of hides and tobacco.

She was nowhere to be seen among the shipping in that narrow, rock-bound harbour. He roared out the question in his mind.

In answer the half-caste pointed out beyond the frothing surf that marked the position of the reef constituting one of the stronghold's main defences. Away beyond it, a mile or so distant, a sail was standing out to sea.

"There she go," he said.

"There!" The Frenchman gazed and stared, his face growing white. The man's wicked temper awoke, and turned to vent itself upon the messenger. "And where have you been that you come here only now with this? Answer me!"

The half-caste shrank terrified before his fury. His explanation, if he had one, was paralyzed by fear. Levasseur took him by the throat, shook him twice, snarling the while, then hurled him into the scuppers. The man's head struck the gunwale as he fell, and he lay there, quite still, a trickle of blood issuing from his mouth.

Levasseur dashed one hand against the other, as if dusting them.

"Heave that muck overboard," he ordered some of those who stood idling in the waist. "Then up anchor, and let us after the Dutchman."

"Steady, Captain. What's that?" There was a restraining hand upon his shoulder, and the broad face of his lieutenant Cahusac, a burly, callous Breton scoundrel, was stolidly confronting him.

Levasseur made clear his purpose with a deal of unnecessary obscenity.

Cahusac shook his head. "A Dutch brig!" said he. "Impossible! We should never be allowed."

"And who the devil will deny us?" Levasseur was between amazement and fury.

"For one thing, there's your own crew will be none too willing. For another there's Captain Blood."

"I care nothing for Captain Blood . . ."

"But it is necessary that you should. He has the power, the weight of metal and of men, and if I know him at all he'll sink us before he'll suffer interference with the Dutch. He has his own views of privateering, this Captain Blood, as I warned you."

"Ah!" said Levasseur, showing his teeth. But his eyes, riveted upon that distant sail, were gloomily thoughtful. Not for long. The imagination and resource which Captain Blood had detected in the fellow soon suggested a course.

Cursing in his soul, and even before the anchor was weighed, the association into which he had entered, he was already studying ways of evasion. What Cahusac implied was true: Blood would never suffer violence to be done in his presence to a Dutchman; but it might be done in his absence; and, being done, Blood must perforce condone it, since it would then be too late to protest.

Within the hour the *Arabella* and *La Foudre* were beating out to sea together. Without understanding the change of plan involved, Captain Blood, nevertheless, accepted it, and weighed anchor before the appointed time upon perceiving his associate to do so.

All day the Dutch brig was in sight, though by evening she had dwindled to the merest speck on the northern horizon. The course prescribed for Blood and Levasseur lay eastward along the northern shores of Hispaniola. To that course the *Arabella* continued to hold steadily throughout the night. When day broke again, she was alone. *La Foudre* under cover of the darkness had struck away to the northeast with every rag of canvas on her yards.

Cahusac had attempted yet again to protest against this.

"The devil take you!" Levasseur had answered him. "A ship's a ship, be she Dutch or Spanish, and ships are our present need. That will suffice for the men."

His lieutenant said no more. But from his glimpse of the letter, knowing that a girl and not a ship was his captain's real objective, he gloomily shook his head as he rolled away on his bowed legs to give the necessary orders.

Dawn found *La Foudre* close on the Dutchman's heels, not a mile astern, and the sight of her very evidently flustered the *Jongvrouw*. No doubt mademoiselle's brother recognizing Levasseur's ship would be responsible for the Dutch uneasiness. They saw the *Jongvrouw* crowding canvas in a futile endeavour to outsail them, whereupon they stood off to starboard and raced on until they were in a position whence they could send a warning shot across her bow. The *Jongvrouw* veered, showed them her rudder, and opened fire with her stern chasers. The small shot went whistling through *La Foudre's* shrouds with some slight damage to her canvas. Followed a brief running fight in the course of which the Dutchman let fly a broadside.

Five minutes after that they were board and board, the *Jongvrouw* held tight in the clutches of *La Foudre*'s grapnels, and the buccaneers pouring noisily into her waist.

The Dutchman's master, purple in the face, stood forward to beard the pirate, followed closely by an elegant, pale-faced young gentleman in whom Levasseur recognized his brother-in-law elect.

"Captain Levasseur, this is an outrage for which you shall be made to answer. What do you seek aboard my ship?"

"At first I sought only that which belongs to me, something of which I am being robbed. But since you chose war and opened fire on me with some damage to my ship and loss of life to five of my men, why, war it is, and your ship a prize of war."

From the quarter rail Mademoiselle d'Ogeron looked down with glowing eyes in breathless wonder upon her well-beloved hero. Gloriously heroic he seemed as he stood towering there, masterful, audacious, beautiful. He saw her, and with a glad shout sprang towards her. The Dutch master got in his way with hands upheld to arrest his progress. Levasseur did not stay to argue with him: he was too impatient to reach his mistress. He swung the poleaxe that he carried, and the Dutchman went down in blood with a cloven skull. The eager lover stepped across the body and came on, his countenance joyously alight.

But mademoiselle was shrinking now, in horror. She was a girl upon the threshold of glorious womanhood, of a fine height and nobly moulded, with heavy coils of glossy black hair above and about a face that was of the colour of old ivory. Her countenance was cast in lines of arrogance, stressed by the low lids of her full dark eyes.

In a bound her well-beloved was beside her. Flinging away his bloody poleaxe, he opened wide his arms to enfold her. But she still shrank even within his embrace, which would not be denied; a look of dread had come to temper the normal arrogance of her almost perfect face.

"Mine, mine at last, and in spite of all!" he cried exultantly, theatrically, truly heroic.

But she, endeavouring to thrust him back, her hands against his breast, could only falter: "Why, why did you kill him?"

He laughed, as a hero should; and answered her heroically, with the tolerance of a god for the mortal to whom he condescends: "He stood between us. Let his death be a symbol, a warning. Let all who would stand between us mark it and beware."

It was so splendidly terrific, the gesture of it was so broad and fine and his magnetism so compelling, that she cast her silly tremors and yielded herself freely, intoxicated, to his fond embrace. Thereafter he swung her to his shoulder, and stepping with ease beneath that burden, bore her in a sort of triumph, lustily cheered by his men, to the deck of his own ship. Her inconsiderate brother might have ruined that romantic scene but for the watchful Cahusac, who quietly tripped him up, and then trussed him like a fowl.

Thereafter, what time the Captain languished in his lady's smile within the cabin, Cahusac was dealing with the spoils of war. The Dutch crew was ordered into the longboat, and bidden go to the devil. Fortunately, as they numbered fewer than thirty, the longboat, though perilously overcrowded, could yet contain them. Next, Cahusac having inspected the cargo, put a quartermaster and a score of men aboard the *Jongvrouw*, and left her to follow *La Foudre*, which he now headed south for the Leeward Islands.

Cahusac was disposed to be ill-humoured. The risk they had run in taking the Dutch brig and doing violence to members of the family of the Governor of Tortuga, was out of all proportion to the value of their prize. He said so, sullenly, to Levasseur.

"You'll keep that opinion to yourself," the Captain answered him. "Don't think I am the man to thrust my neck into a noose, without knowing how I am going to take it out again. I shall send an offer of terms to the Governor of Tortuga that he will be forced to accept. Set a course for the Virgen Magra. We'll go ashore, and settle things from there. And tell them to fetch that milksop Ogeron to the cabin."

Levasseur went back to the adoring lady.

Thither, too, the lady's brother was presently conducted. The Captain rose to receive him, bending his stalwart height to avoid striking the cabin roof with his head. Mademoiselle rose too.

"Why this?" she asked Levasseur, pointing to her brother's pinioned wrists—the remains of Cahusac's precautions.

"I deplore it," said he. "I desire it to end. Let M. d'Ogeron give me his parole . . ."

"I give you nothing," flashed the white-faced youth, who did not lack for spirit.

"You see." Levasseur shrugged his deep regret, and mademoiselle turned protesting to her brother.

"Henri, this is foolish! You are not behaving as my friend. You . . ."

"Little fool," her brother answered her—and the "little" was out of place; she was the taller of the twain. "Little fool, do you think I should be acting as your friend to make terms with this blackguard pirate?"

"Steady, my young cockerel!" Levasseur laughed. But his laugh was not nice.

"Don't you perceive your wicked folly in the harm it has brought already? Lives have been lost—men have died—that this monster might overtake you. And don't you yet realize where you stand—in the power of this beast, of this cur born in a kennel and bred in thieving and murder?"

He might have said more but that Levasseur struck him across the mouth. Levasseur, you see, cared as little as another to hear the truth about himself.

Mademoiselle suppressed a scream, as the youth staggered back under the blow. He came to rest against a bulkhead, and leaned there with bleeding lips. But his spirit was unquenched, and there was a ghastly smile on his white face as his eyes sought his sister's.

"You see," he said simply. "He strikes a man whose hands are bound."

The simple words, and, more than the words, their tone of ineffable disdain, aroused the passion that never slumbered deeply in Levasseur.

"And what should you do, puppy, if your hands were unbound?" He took his prisoner by the breast of his doublet and shook him. "Answer me! What should you do? Tchah! You empty windbag! You . . ." And then came a torrent of words unknown to mademoiselle, yet of whose foulness her intuitions made her conscious.

With blanched cheeks she stood by the cabin table, and cried out to Levasseur to stop. To obey her, he opened the door, and flung her brother through it.

"Put that rubbish under hatches until I call for it again," he roared, and shut the door.

Composing himself, he turned to the girl again with a deprecatory smile. But no smile answered him from her set face. She had seen her beloved hero's nature in curl-papers, as it were, and she found the spectacle disgusting and terrifying. It recalled the brutal slaughter of the Dutch captain, and suddenly she realized that what her brother had just said of this man was no more than true. Fear growing to panic was written on her face, as she stood there leaning for support against the table.

"Why, sweetheart, what is this?" Levasseur moved towards her. She recoiled before him. There was a smile on his face, a glitter in his eyes that fetched her heart into her throat.

He caught her, as she reached the uttermost limits of the cabin, seized her in his long arms and pulled her to him.

"No, no!" she panted.

"Yes, yes," he mocked her, and his mockery was the most terrible thing of all. He crushed her to him brutally, deliberately hurtful because she resisted, and kissed her whilst she writhed in his embrace. Then, his passion mounting, he grew angry and stripped off the last rag of hero's mask that still may have hung upon his face. "Little fool, did you not hear your brother say that you are in my power? Remember it, and remember that of your own free will you came. I am not the man with whom a woman can play fast and loose. So get sense, my girl, and accept what you have invited." He kissed her again, almost contemptuously, and flung her off. "No more scowls," he said. "You'll be sorry else."

Some one knocked. Cursing the interruption, Levasseur strode off to open. Cahusac stood before him. The Breton's face was grave. He came to report that they had sprung a leak between wind and water, the consequence of damage sustained from one of the Dutchman's shots. In alarm Levasseur went off with him. The leakage was not serious so long as the weather kept fine; but should a storm overtake them it might speedily become so. A man was slung overboard to make a partial stoppage with a sail-cloth, and the pumps were got to work.

Ahead of them a low cloud showed on the horizon, which Cahusac pronounced one of the northernmost of the Virgin Islands.

"We must run for shelter there, and careen her," said Levasseur. "I do not trust this oppressive heat. A storm may catch us before we make land,"

"A storm or something else," said Cahusac grimly. "Have you noticed that?" He pointed away to starboard.

Levasseur looked, and caught his breath. Two ships that at the distance seemed of considerable burden were heading towards them some five miles away.

"If they follow us what is to happen?" demanded Cahusac.

"We'll fight whether we're in case to do so or not," swore Levasseur.

"Counsels of despair." Cahusac was contemptuous. To mark it he spat upon the deck. "This comes of going to sea with a lovesick madman. Now, keep your temper, Captain, for the hands will be at the end of theirs if we have trouble as a result of this Dutchman business."

For the remainder of that day Levasseur's thoughts were of anything but love. He remained on deck, his eyes now upon the land, now upon those two slowly gaining ships. To run for the open could avail him nothing, and in his leaky condition would provide an additional danger. He must stand at bay and fight. And then, towards evening, when within three miles of shore and when he was about to give the order to strip for battle, he almost fainted from relief to hear a voice from the crow's-nest above announce that the larger of the two ships was the *Arabella*. Her companion was presumably a prize.

But the pessimism of Cahusac abated nothing.

"That is but the lesser evil," he growled. "What will Blood say about this Dutchman?"

"Let him say what he pleases." Levasseur laughed in the immensity of his relief.

"And what about the children of the Governor of Tortuga?"

"He must not know."

"He'll come to know in the end."

"Aye, but by then, morbleu, the matter will be settled. I shall have made my peace with the Governor. I tell you I know the way to compel Ogeron to come to terms."

Presently the four vessels lay to off the northern coast of La Virgen Magra, a narrow little island arid and treeless, some twelve miles by three, uninhabited save by birds and turtles and unproductive of anything but salt, of which there were considerable ponds to the south.

Levasseur put off in a boat accompanied by Cahusac and two other officers, and went to visit Captain Blood aboard the *Arabella*.

"Our brief separation has been mighty profitable," was Captain Blood's greeting. "It's a busy morning we've both had." He was in high good-humour as he led the way to the great cabin for a rendering of accounts.

The tall ship that accompanied the *Arabella* was a Spanish vessel of twenty-six guns, the *Santiago* from Puerto Rico with a hundred and twenty thousand weight of cacao, forty thousand pieces of eight, and the value of ten thousand more in jewels. A rich capture of which two fifths under the articles went to Levasseur and his crew. Of the money and jewels a division was made on the spot. The cacao it was agreed should be taken to Tortuga to be sold.

Then it was the turn of Levasseur, and black grew the brow of Captain Blood as the Frenchman's tale was unfolded. At the end he roundly expressed his disapproval. The Dutch were a friendly people whom it was a folly to alienate, particularly for so paltry a matter as these hides and tobacco, which at most would fetch a bare twenty thousand pieces.

But Levasseur answered him, as he had answered Cahusac, that a ship was a ship, and it was ships they needed against their projected enterprise. Perhaps because things had gone well with him that day, Blood ended by shrugging the matter aside. Thereupon Levasseur proposed that the *Arabella* and her prize should return to Tortuga there to unload the cacao and enlist the further adventurers that could now be shipped. Levasseur meanwhile would effect certain necessary repairs, and then proceeding south, await his admiral at Saltatudos, an island conveniently situated—in the latitude of 11° 11' N.—for their enterprise against Maracaybo.

To Levasseur's relief, Captain Blood not only agreed, but pronounced himself ready to set sail at once.

No sooner had the *Arabella* departed than Levasseur brought his ships into the lagoon, and set his crew to work upon the erection of temporary quarters ashore for himself, his men, and his enforced guests during the careening and repairing of *La Foudre*.

At sunset that evening the wind freshened; it grew to a gale, and from that to such a hurricane that Levasseur was thankful to find himself ashore and his ships in safe shelter. He wondered a little how it might be faring with Captain Blood out there at the mercy of that terrific storm; but he did not permit concern to trouble him unduly.

XV. The Ransom

In the glory of the following morning, sparkling and clear after the storm, with an invigorating, briny tang in the air from the salt-ponds on the south of the island, a curious scene was played on the beach of the Virgen Magra, at the foot of a ridge of bleached dunes, beside the spread of sail from which Levasseur had improvised a tent.

Enthroned upon an empty cask sat the French filibuster to transact important business: the business of making himself safe with the Governor of Tortuga.

A guard of honour of a half-dozen officers hung about him; five of them were rude boucan-hunters, in stained jerkins and leather breeches; the sixth was Cahusac. Before him, guarded by two half-naked negroes, stood young d'Ogeron, in frilled shirt and satin small-clothes and fine shoes of Cordovan leather. He was stripped of doublet, and his hands were tied behind him. The young gentleman's comely face was haggard. Near at hand, and also under guard, but unpinioned, mademoiselle his sister sat hunched upon a hillock of sand. She was very pale, and it was in vain that she sought to veil in a mask of arrogance the fears by which she was assailed.

Levasseur addressed himself to M. d'Ogeron. He spoke at long length. In the end—

"I trust, monsieur," said he, with mock suavity, "that I have made myself quite clear. So that there may be no misunderstandings, I will recapitulate. Your ransom is fixed at twenty thousand pieces of eight, and you shall have liberty on parole to go to Tortuga to collect it. In fact, I shall provide the means to convey you thither, and you shall have a month in which to come and go. Meanwhile, your sister remains with me as a hostage. Your father should not consider such a sum excessive as the price of his son's liberty and to provide a dowry for his daughter. Indeed, if anything, I am too modest, pardi! M. d'Ogeron is reputed a wealthy man."

M. d'Ogeron the younger raised his head and looked the Captain boldly in the face.

"I refuse—utterly and absolutely, do you understand? So do your worst, and be damned for a filthy pirate without decency and without honour."

"But what words!" laughed Levasseur. "What heat and what foolishness! You have not considered the alternative. When you do, you will not persist in your refusal. You will not do that in any case. We have spurs for the reluctant. And I warn you against giving me your parole under stress, and afterwards playing me false. I shall know how to find and punish you. Meanwhile, remember your sister's honour is in pawn to me. Should you forget to return with the dowry, you will not consider it unreasonable that I forget to marry her."

Levasseur's smiling eyes, intent upon the young man's face, saw the horror that crept into his glance. M. d'Ogeron cast a wild glance at mademoiselle, and observed the grey despair that had almost stamped the beauty from her face.

Disgust and fury swept across his countenance.

Then he braced himself and answered resolutely:

"No, you dog! A thousand times, no!"

"You are foolish to persist." Levasseur spoke without anger, with a coldly mocking regret. His fingers had been busy tying knots in a length of whipcord. He held it up. "You know this? It is a rosary of pain that has wrought the conversion of many a stubborn heretic. It is capable of screwing the eyes out of a man's head by way of helping him to see reason. As you please."

He flung the length of knotted cord to one of the negroes, who in an instant made it fast about the prisoner's brows. Then between cord and cranium the black inserted a short length of metal, round and slender as a pipe-stem. That done he rolled his eyes towards Levasseur, awaiting the Captain's signal.

Levasseur considered his victim, and beheld him tense and braced, his haggard face of a leaden hue, beads of perspiration glinting on his pallid brow just beneath the whipcord.

Mademoiselle cried out, and would have risen: but her guards restrained her, and she sank down again, moaning.

"I beg that you will spare yourself and your sister," said the Captain, "by being reasonable. What, after all, is the sum I have named? To your wealthy father a bagatelle. I repeat, I have been too modest. But since I have said twenty thousand pieces of eight, twenty thousand pieces it shall be."

"And for what, if you please, have you said twenty thousand pieces of eight?"

In execrable French, but in a voice that was crisp and pleasant, seeming to echo some of the mockery that had invested Levasseur's, that question floated over their heads.

Startled, Levasseur and his officers looked up and round.

On the crest of the dunes behind them, in sharp silhouette against the deep cobalt of the sky, they beheld a tall, lean figure scrupulously dressed in black with silver lace, a crimson ostrich plume curled about the broad brim of his hat affording the only touch of colour. Under that hat was the tawny face of Captain Blood.

Levasseur gathered himself up with an oath of amazement. He had conceived Captain Blood by now well below the horizon, on his way to Tortuga, assuming him to have been so fortunate as to have weathered last night's storm.

Launching himself upon the yielding sand, into which he sank to the level of the calves of his fine boots of Spanish leather, Captain Blood came sliding erect to the beach. He was followed by Wolverstone, and a dozen others. As he came to a standstill, he doffed his hat, with a flourish, to the lady. Then he turned to Levasseur.

"Good-morning, my Captain," said he, and proceeded to explain his presence. "It was last night's hurricane compelled our return. We had no choice but to ride before it with stripped poles, and it drove us back the way we had gone. Moreover—as the devil would have it!—the *Santiago* sprang her mainmast; and so I was glad to put into a cove on the west of the island a couple of miles away, and we've walked across to stretch our legs, and to give you good-day. But who are these?" And he designated the man and the woman.

Cahusac shrugged his shoulders, and tossed his long arms to heaven.

"Voilà!" said he, pregnantly, to the firmament.

Levasseur gnawed his lip, and changed colour. But he controlled himself to answer civilly:

"As you see, two prisoners."

"Ah! Washed ashore in last night's gale, eh?"

"Not so." Levasseur contained himself with difficulty before that irony. "They were in the Dutch brig."

"I don't remember that you mentioned them before."

"I did not. They are prisoners of my own—a personal matter. They are French."

"French!" Captain Blood's light eyes stabbed at Levasseur, then at the prisoners.

M. d'Ogeron stood tense and braced as before, but the grey horror had left his face. Hope had leapt within him at this interruption, obviously as little expected by his tormentor as by himself. His sister, moved by a similar intuition, was leaning forward with parted lips and gaping eyes.

Captain Blood fingered his lip, and frowned thoughtfully upon Levasseur.

"Yesterday you surprised me by making war upon the friendly Dutch. But now it seems that not even your own countrymen are safe from you."

"Have I not said that these . . . that this is a matter personal to me?"

"Ah! And their names?"

Captain Blood's crisp, authoritative, faintly disdainful manner stirred Levasseur's quick anger. The blood crept slowly back into his blenched face, and his glance grew in insolence, almost in menace. Meanwhile the prisoner answered for him.

"I am Henri d'Ogeron, and this is my sister."

"D'Ogeron?" Captain Blood stared. "Are you related by chance to my good friend the Governor of Tortuga?"

"He is my father."

Levasseur swung aside with an imprecation. In Captain Blood, amazement for the moment quenched every other emotion.

"The saints preserve us now! Are you quite mad, Levasseur? First you molest the Dutch, who are our friends; next you take prisoners two persons that are French, your own countrymen; and now, faith, they're no less than the children of the Governor of Tortuga, which is the one safe place of shelter that we enjoy in these islands . . ."

Levasseur broke in angrily:

"Must I tell you again that it is a matter personal to me? I make myself alone responsible to the Governor of Tortuga."

"And the twenty thousand pieces of eight? Is that also a matter personal to you?"

"It is."

"Now I don't agree with you at all." Captain Blood sat down on the cask that Levasseur had lately occupied, and looked up blandly. "I may inform you, to save time, that I heard the entire proposal that you made to this lady and this gentleman, and I'll also remind you that we sail under articles that admit no ambiguities. You have fixed their ransom at twenty thousand pieces of eight. That sum then belongs to your crews and mine in the proportions by the articles established. You'll hardly wish to dispute it. But what is far more grave is that you have concealed from me this part of the prizes taken on your last cruise, and for such an offence as that the articles provide certain penalties that are something severe in character."

"Ho, ho!" laughed Levasseur unpleasantly. Then added: "If you dislike my conduct we can dissolve the association."

"That is my intention. But we'll dissolve it when and in the manner that I choose, and that will be as soon as you have satisfied the articles under which we sailed upon this cruise."

"What do you mean?"

"I'll be as short as I can," said Captain Blood. "I'll waive for the moment the unseemliness of making war upon the Dutch, of taking French prisoners, and of provoking the anger of the Governor of Tortuga. I'll accept the situation as I find it. Yourself you've fixed the ransom of this couple at twenty thousand pieces, and, as I gather, the lady is to be your perquisite. But why should she be your perquisite more than another's, seeing that she belongs by the articles to all of us, as a prize of war?"

Black as thunder grew the brow of Levasseur.

"However," added Captain Blood, "I'll not dispute her to you if you are prepared to buy her."

"Buy her?"

"At the price you have set upon her."

Levasseur contained his rage, that he might reason with the Irishman. "That is the ransom of the man. It is to be paid for him by the Governor of Tortuga."

"No, no. Ye've parcelled the twain together—very oddly, I confess. Ye've set their value at twenty thousand pieces, and for that sum you may have them, since you desire it; but you'll pay for them the twenty thousand pieces that are ultimately to come to you as the ransom of one and the dowry of the other; and that sum shall be divided among our crews. So that you do that, it is conceivable that our followers may take a lenient view of your breach of the articles we jointly signed."

Levasseur laughed savagely. "Ah ça! Crédieu! The good jest!"

"I quite agree with you," said Captain Blood.

To Levasseur the jest lay in that Captain Blood, with no more than a dozen followers, should come there attempting to hector him who had a hundred men within easy call. But it seemed that he had left out of his reckoning something which his opponent had counted in. For as, laughing still, Levasseur swung to his officers, he saw that which choked the laughter in his throat. Captain Blood had shrewdly played upon the cupidity that was the paramount inspiration of those adventurers. And Levasseur now read clearly on their faces how completely they adopted Captain Blood's suggestion that all must participate in the ransom which their leader had thought to appropriate to himself.

It gave the gaudy ruffian pause, and whilst in his heart he cursed those followers of his, who could be faithful only to their greed, he perceived—and only just in time—that he had best tread warily.

"You misunderstand," he said, swallowing his rage. "The ransom is for division, when it comes. The girl, meanwhile, is mine on that understanding."

"Good!" grunted Cahusac. "On that understanding all arranges itself."

"You think so?" said Captain Blood. "But if M. d'Ogeron should refuse to pay the ransom? What then?" He laughed, and got lazily to his feet. "No, no. If Captain Levasseur is meanwhile to keep the girl, as he proposes, then let him pay this ransom, and be his the risk if it should afterwards not be forthcoming."

"That's it!" cried one of Levasseur's officers. And Cahusac added: "It's reasonable, that! Captain Blood is right. It is in the articles."

"What is in the articles, you fools?" Levasseur was in danger of losing his head. "Sacré Dieu! Where do you suppose that I have twenty thousand pieces? My whole share of the prizes of this cruise does not come to half that sum. I'll be your debtor until I've earned it. Will that content you?"

All things considered, there is not a doubt that it would have done so had not Captain Blood intended otherwise.

"And if you should die before you have earned it? Ours is a calling fraught with risks, my Captain."

"Damn you!" Levasseur flung upon him livid with fury. "Will nothing satisfy you?"

"Oh, but yes. Twenty thousand pieces of eight for immediate division."

"I haven't got it."

"Then let some one buy the prisoners who has."

"And who do you suppose has it if I have not?"

"I have," said Captain Blood.

"You have!" Levasseur's mouth fell open. "You . . . you want the girl?"

"Why not? And I exceed you in gallantry in that I will make sacrifices to obtain her, and in honesty in that I am ready to pay for what I want."

Levasseur stared at him foolishly agape. Behind him pressed his officers, gaping also.

Captain Blood sat down again on the cask, and drew from an inner pocket of his doublet a little leather bag. "I am glad to be able to resolve a difficulty that at one moment seemed insoluble." And under the bulging eyes of Levasseur and his officers, he untied the mouth of the bag and rolled into his left palm four or five pearls each of the size of a sparrow's egg. There were twenty such in the bag, the very pick of those taken in that raid upon the pearl fleet. "You boast a knowledge of pearls, Cahusac. At what do you value this?"

The Breton took between coarse finger and thumb the proffered lustrous, delicately iridescent sphere, his shrewd eyes appraising it.

"A thousand pieces," he answered shortly.

"It will fetch rather more in Tortuga or Jamaica," said Captain Blood, "and twice as much in Europe. But I'll accept your valuation. They are almost of a size, as you can see. Here are twelve, representing twelve thousand pieces of eight, which is *La Foudre*'s share of three fifths of the prize, as provided by the articles. For the eight thousand pieces that go to the *Arabella*, I make myself responsible to my own men. And now, Wolverstone, if you please, will you take my property aboard the *Arabella*?" He stood up again, indicating the prisoners.

"Ah, no!" Levasseur threw wide the floodgates of his fury. "Ah, that, no, by example! You shall not take her . . ." He would have sprung upon Captain Blood, who stood aloof, alert, tight-lipped, and watchful.

But it was one of Levasseur's own officers who hindered him.

"Nom de Dieu, my Captain! What will you do? It is settled; honourably settled with satisfaction to all."

"To all?" blazed Levasseur. "Ah ça! To all of you, you animals! But what of me?"

Cahusac, with the pearls clutched in his capacious hand, stepped up to him on the other side. "Don't be a fool, Captain. Do you want to provoke trouble between the crews? His men outnumber us by nearly two to one. What's a girl more or less? In Heaven's name, let her go. He's paid handsomely for her, and dealt fairly with us."

"Dealt fairly?" roared the infuriated Captain. "You . . ." In all his foul vocabulary he could find no epithet to describe his lieutenant. He caught him a blow that almost sent him sprawling. The pearls were scattered in the sand.

Cahusac dived after them, his fellows with him. Vengeance must wait. For some moments they groped there on hands and knees, oblivious of all else. And yet in those moments vital things were happening.

Levasseur, his hand on his sword, his face a white mask of rage, was confronting Captain Blood to hinder his departure.

"You do not take her while I live!" he cried.

"Then I'll take her when you're dead," said Captain Blood, and his own blade flashed in the sunlight. "The articles provide that any man of whatever rank concealing any part of a prize, be it of the value of no more than a peso, shall be hanged at the yardarm. It's what I intended for you in the end. But since ye prefer it this way, ye muckrake, faith, I'll be humouring you."

He waved away the men who would have interfered, and the blades rang together.

M. d'Ogeron looked on, a man bemused, unable to surmise what the issue either way could mean for him. Meanwhile, two of Blood's men who had taken the place of the Frenchman's negro guards, had removed the crown of whipcord from his brow.

As for mademoiselle, she had risen, and was leaning forward, a hand pressed tightly to her heaving breast, her face deathly pale, a wild terror in her eyes.

It was soon over. The brute strength, upon which Levasseur so confidently counted, could avail nothing against the Irishman's practised skill. When, with both lungs transfixed, he lay prone on the white sand, coughing out his rascally life, Captain Blood looked calmly at Cahusac across the body.

"I think that cancels the articles between us," he said.

With soulless, cynical eyes Cahusac considered the twitching body of his recent leader. Had Levasseur been a man of different temper, the affair might have ended in a very different manner. But, then, it is certain that Captain Blood would have adopted in dealing with him different tactics. As it was, Levasseur commanded neither love nor loyalty. The men who followed him were the very dregs of that vile trade, and cupidity was their only inspiration. Upon that cupidity Captain Blood had deftly played, until he had brought them to find Levasseur guilty of the one offence they deemed unpardonable, the crime of appropriating to himself something which might be converted into gold and shared amongst them all.

Thus now the threatening mob of buccaneers that came hastening to the theatre of that swift tragi-comedy were appeased by a dozen words of Cahusac's.

Whilst still they hesitated, Blood added something to quicken their decision.

"If you will come to our anchorage, you shall receive at once your share of the booty of the *Santiago*, that you may dispose of it as you please."

They crossed the island, the two prisoners accompanying them, and later that day, the division made, they would have parted company but that Cahusac, at the instances of the men who had elected him Levasseur's successor, offered Captain Blood anew the services of that French contingent.

"If you will sail with me again," the Captain answered him, "you may do so on the condition that you make your peace with the Dutch, and restore the brig and her cargo."

The condition was accepted, and Captain Blood went off to find his guests, the children of the Governor of Tortuga.

Mademoiselle d'Ogeron and her brother—the latter now relieved of his bonds— sat in the great cabin of the *Arabella*, whither they had been conducted.

Wine and food had been placed upon the table by Benjamin, Captain Blood's negro steward and cook, who had intimated to them that it was for their entertainment. But it had remained untouched. Brother and sister sat there in agonized bewilderment, conceiving that their escape was but from frying-pan to fire. At length, overwrought by the suspense, mademoiselle flung herself upon her knees before her brother to implore his pardon for all the evil brought upon them by her wicked folly.

M. d'Ogeron was not in a forgiving mood.

"I am glad that at least you realize what you have done. And now this other filibuster has bought you, and you belong to him. You realize that, too, I hope."

He might have said more, but he checked upon perceiving that the door was opening. Captain Blood, coming from settling matters with the followers of Levasseur, stood on the threshold. M. d'Ogeron had not troubled to restrain his high-pitched voice, and the Captain had overheard the Frenchman's last two sentences. Therefore he perfectly understood why mademoiselle should bound up at sight of him, and shrink back in fear.

He doffed his feathered hat, and came forward to the table.

"Mademoiselle," said he in his vile but fluent French, "I beg you to dismiss your fears. Aboard this ship you shall be treated with all honour. So soon as we are in case to put to sea again, we steer a course for Tortuga to take you home to your father. And pray do not consider that I have bought you, as your brother has just said. All that I have done has been to provide the ransom necessary to bribe a gang of scoundrels to depart from obedience to the arch-scoundrel who commanded them, and so deliver you from all peril. Count it, if you please, a friendly loan to be repaid entirely at your convenience."

Mademoiselle stared at him in unbelief. M. d'Ogeron rose to his feet.

"Monsieur, is it possible that you are serious?"

"I am. It may not happen often nowadays. I may be a pirate. But my ways are not the ways of Levasseur, who should have stayed in Europe, and practised purse-cutting. I have a sort of honour—shall we say, some rags of honour?—remaining me from better days." Then on a brisker note he added: "We dine in an hour, and I trust that you will honour my table with your company. Meanwhile, Benjamin will see, monsieur, that you are more suitably provided in the matter of wardrobe."

He bowed to them, and turned to depart again, but mademoiselle detained him.

"Monsieur!" she cried sharply.

He checked and turned, whilst slowly she approached him, regarding him between dread and wonder.

"Oh, you are noble!"

"I shouldn't put it as high as that myself," said he.

"You are, you are! And it is but right that you should know all."

"Madelon!" her brother cried out, to restrain her.

But she would not be restrained. Her surcharged heart must overflow in confidence.

"Monsieur, for what befell I am greatly at fault. This man—this Levasseur . . ."

He stared, incredulous in his turn. "My God! Is it possible? That animal!"

Abruptly she fell on her knees, caught his hand and kissed it before he could wrench it from her.

"What do you do?" he cried.

"An amende. In my mind I dishonoured you by deeming you his like, by conceiving your fight with Levasseur a combat between jackals. On my knees, monsieur, I implore you to forgive me."

Captain Blood looked down upon her, and a smile broke on his lips, irradiating the blue eyes that looked so oddly light in that tawny face.

"Why, child," said he, "I might find it hard to forgive you the stupidity of having thought otherwise."

As he handed her to her feet again, he assured himself that he had behaved rather well in the affair. Then he sighed. That dubious fame of his that had spread so quickly across the Caribbean would by now have reached the ears of Arabella Bishop. That she would despise him, he could not doubt, deeming him no better than all the other scoundrels who drove this villainous buccaneering trade. Therefore he hoped that some echo of this deed might reach her also, and be set by her against some of that contempt. For the whole truth, which he withheld from Mademoiselle d'Ogeron, was that in venturing his life to save her, he had been driven by the thought that the deed must be pleasing in the eyes of Miss Bishop could she but witness it.

XVI. The Trap

That affair of Mademoiselle d'Ogeron bore as its natural fruit an improvement in the already cordial relations between Captain Blood and the Governor of Tortuga. At the fine stone house, with its green-jalousied windows, which M. d'Ogeron had built himself in a spacious and luxuriant garden to the east of Cayona, the Captain became a very welcome guest. M. d'Ogeron was in the Captain's debt for more than the twenty thousand pieces of eight which he had provided for mademoiselle's ransom; and shrewd, hard bargain-driver though he might be, the Frenchman could be generous and understood the sentiment of gratitude. This he now proved in every possible way, and under his powerful protection the credit of Captain Blood among the buccaneers very rapidly reached its zenith.

So when it came to fitting out his fleet for that enterprise against Maracaybo, which had originally been Levasseur's project, he did not want for either ships or men to follow him. He recruited five hundred adventurers in all, and he might have had as many thousands if he could have offered them accommodation. Similarly without difficulty he might have increased his fleet to twice its strength of ships but that he preferred to keep it what it was. The three vessels to which he confined it were the *Arabella*, the *La Foudre*, which Cahusac now commanded with a contingent of some sixscore Frenchmen, and the *Santiago*, which had been refitted and rechristened the *Elizabeth*, after that Queen of England whose seamen had humbled Spain as Captain Blood now hoped to humble it again. Hagthorpe, in virtue of his service in the navy, was appointed by Blood to command her, and the appointment was confirmed by the men.

It was some months after the rescue of Mademoiselle d'Ogeron—in August of that year 1687—that this little fleet, after some minor adventures which I pass over in silence, sailed into the great lake of Maracaybo and effected its raid upon that opulent city of the Main.

The affair did not proceed exactly as was hoped, and Blood's force came to find itself in a precarious position. This is best explained in the words employed by Cahusac— which Pitt has carefully recorded—in the course of an altercation that broke out on the steps of the Church of Nuestra Señora del Carmen, which Captain Blood had impiously appropriated for the purpose of a corps-de-garde. I have said already that he was a papist only when it suited him.

The dispute was being conducted by Hagthorpe, Wolverstone, and Pitt on the one side, and Cahusac, out of whose uneasiness it all arose, on the other. Behind them in the sun-scorched, dusty square, sparsely fringed by palms, whose fronds drooped listlessly in the quivering heat, surged a couple of hundred wild fellows belonging to both parties, their own excitement momentarily quelled so that they might listen to what passed among their leaders.

Cahusac appeared to be having it all his own way, and he raised his harsh, querulous voice so that all might hear his truculent denunciation. He spoke, Pitt tells us, a dreadful kind of English, which the shipmaster, however, makes little attempt to reproduce. His dress was as discordant as his speech. It was of a kind to advertise his trade, and ludicrously in contrast with the sober garb of Hagthorpe and the almost foppish daintiness of Jeremy Pitt. His soiled and blood-stained shirt of blue cotton was open in front, to cool his hairy breast, and the girdle about the waist of his leather breeches carried an arsenal of pistols and a knife, whilst a cutlass hung from a leather baldrick loosely slung about his body; above his countenance, broad and flat as a Mongolian's, a red scarf was swathed, turban-wise, about his head.

"Is it that I have not warned you from the beginning that all was too easy?" he demanded between plaintiveness and fury. "I am no fool, my friends. I have eyes, me. And I see. I see an abandoned fort at the entrance of the lake, and nobody there to fire a gun at us when we came in. Then I suspect the trap. Who would not that had eyes and brain? Bah! we come on. What do we find? A city, abandoned like the fort; a city out of which the people have taken all things of value. Again I warn Captain Blood. It is a trap, I say. We are to come on; always to come on, without opposition, until we find that it is too late to go to sea again, that we cannot go back at all. But no one will listen to me. You all know so much more. Name of God! Captain Blood, he will go on, and we go on. We go to Gibraltar. True that at last, after long time, we catch the Deputy-Governor; true, we make him pay big ransom for Gibraltar; true between that ransom and the loot we return here with some two thousand pieces of eight. But what is it, in reality, will you tell me? Or shall I tell you? It is a piece of cheese—a piece of cheese in a mousetrap, and we are the little mice. Goddam! And the cats—oh, the cats they wait for us! The cats are those four Spanish ships of war that have come meantime. And they wait for us outside the bottle-neck of this lagoon. Mort de Dieu! That is what comes of the damned obstinacy of your fine Captain Blood."

Wolverstone laughed. Cahusac exploded in fury.

"Ah, sangdieu! Tu ris, animal? You laugh! Tell me this: How do we get out again unless we accept the terms of Monsieur the Admiral of Spain?"

From the buccaneers at the foot of the steps came an angry rumble of approval. The single eye of the gigantic Wolverstone rolled terribly, and he clenched his great fists as if to strike the Frenchman, who was exposing them to mutiny. But Cahusac was not daunted. The mood of the men enheartened him.

"You think, perhaps, this your Captain Blood is the good God. That he can make miracles, eh? He is ridiculous, you know, this Captain Blood; with his grand air and his . . ."

He checked. Out of the church at that moment, grand air and all, sauntered Peter Blood. With him came a tough, long-legged French sea-wolf named Yberville, who, though still young, had already won fame as a privateer commander before the loss of his own ship had driven him to take service under Blood. The Captain advanced towards that disputing group, leaning lightly upon his long ebony cane, his face shaded by a broad-plumed hat. There was in his appearance nothing of the buccaneer. He had much more the air of a lounger in the Mall or the Alameda—the latter rather, since his elegant suit of violet taffetas with gold-embroidered button-holes was in the Spanish fashion. But the long, stout, serviceable rapier, thrust up behind by the left hand resting lightly on the pummel, corrected the impression. That and those steely eyes of his announced the adventurer.

"You find me ridiculous, eh, Cahusac?" said he, as he came to a halt before the Breton, whose anger seemed already to have gone out of him. "What, then, must I find you?" He spoke quietly, almost wearily. "You will be telling them that we have delayed, and that it is the delay that has brought about our danger. But whose is the fault of that delay? We have been a month in doing what should have been done, and what but for your blundering would have been done, inside of a week."

"Ah ça! Nom de Dieu! Was it my fault that . . ."

"Was it any one else's fault that you ran your ship *La Foudre* aground on the shoal in the middle of the lake? You would not be piloted. You knew your way. You took no soundings even. The result was that we lost three precious days in getting canoes to bring off your men and your gear. Those three days gave the folk at Gibraltar not only time to hear of our coming, but time in which to get away. After that, and because of it, we had to follow the Governor to his infernal island fortress, and a fortnight and best part of a hundred lives were lost in reducing it. That's how we come to have delayed until this Spanish fleet is fetched round from La Guayra by a guarda-costa; and if ye hadn't lost *La Foudre*, and so reduced our fleet from three ships to two, we should even now be able to fight our way through with a reasonable hope of succeeding. Yet you think it is for you to come hectoring here, upbraiding us for a situation that is just the result of your own ineptitude."

He spoke with a restraint which I trust you will agree was admirable when I tell you that the Spanish fleet guarding the bottle-neck exit of the great Lake of Maracaybo, and awaiting there the coming forth of Captain Blood with a calm confidence based upon its overwhelming strength, was commanded by his implacable enemy, Don Miguel de Espinosa y Valdez, the Admiral of Spain. In addition to his duty to his country, the Admiral had, as you know, a further personal incentive arising out of that business aboard the *Encarnacion* a year ago, and the death of his brother Don Diego; and with him sailed his nephew Esteban, whose vindictive zeal exceeded the Admiral's own.

Yet, knowing all this, Captain Blood could preserve his calm in reproving the cowardly frenzy of one for whom the situation had not half the peril with which it was fraught for himself. He turned from Cahusac to address the mob of buccaneers, who had surged nearer to hear him, for he had not troubled to raise his voice. "I hope that will correct some of the misapprehension that appears to have been disturbing you," said he.

"There's no good can come of talking of what's past and done," cried Cahusac, more sullen now than truculent. Whereupon Wolverstone laughed, a laugh that was like the neighing of a horse. "The question is: what are we to do now?"

"Sure, now, there's no question at all," said Captain Blood.

"Indeed, but there is," Cahusac insisted. "Don Miguel, the Spanish Admiral, have offer' us safe passage to sea if we will depart at once, do no damage to the town, release our prisoners, and surrender all that we took at Gibraltar."

Captain Blood smiled quietly, knowing precisely how much Don Miguel's word was worth. It was Yberville who replied, in manifest scorn of his compatriot:

"Which argues that, even at this disadvantage as he has us, the Spanish Admiral is still afraid of us."

"That can be only because he not know our real weakness," was the fierce retort. "And, anyway, we must accept these terms. We have no choice. That is my opinion."

"Well, it's not mine, now," said Captain Blood. "So, I've refused them."

"Refuse'!" Cahusac's broad face grew purple. A muttering from the men behind enheartened him. "You have refuse'? You have refuse' already—and without consulting me?"

"Your disagreement could have altered nothing. You'd have been outvoted, for Hagthorpe here was entirely of my own mind. Still," he went on, "if you and your own French followers wish to avail yourselves of the Spaniard's terms, we shall not hinder you. Send one of your prisoners to announce it to the Admiral. Don Miguel will welcome your decision, you may be sure."

Cahusac glowered at him in silence for a moment. Then, having controlled himself, he asked in a concentrated voice:

"Precisely what answer have you make to the Admiral?"

A smile irradiated the face and eyes of Captain Blood.

"I have answered him that unless within four-and-twenty hours we have his parole to stand out to sea, ceasing to dispute our passage or hinder our departure, and a ransom of fifty thousand pieces of eight for Maracaybo, we shall reduce this beautiful city to ashes, and thereafter go out and destroy his fleet."

The impudence of it left Cahusac speechless. But among the English buccaneers in the square there were many who savoured the audacious humour of the trapped dictating terms to the trappers. Laughter broke from them. It spread into a roar of acclamation; for bluff is a weapon dear to every adventurer. Presently, when they understood it, even Cahusac's French followers were carried off their feet by that wave of jocular enthusiasm, until in his truculent obstinacy Cahusac remained the only dissentient. He withdrew in mortification. Nor was he to be mollified until the following day brought him his revenge. This came in the shape of a messenger from Don Miguel with a letter in which the Spanish Admiral solemnly vowed to God that, since the pirates had refused his magnanimous offer to permit them to surrender with the honours of war, he would now await them at the mouth of the lake there to destroy them on their coming forth. He added that should they delay their departure, he would so soon as he was reënforced by a fifth ship, the *Santo Niño*, on its way to join him from La Guayra, himself come inside to seek them at Maracaybo.

This time Captain Blood was put out of temper.

"Trouble me no more," he snapped at Cahusac, who came growling to him again. "Send word to Don Miguel that you have seceded from me. He'll give you safe conduct, devil a doubt. Then take one of the sloops, order your men aboard and put to sea, and the devil go with you."

Cahusac would certainly have adopted that course if only his men had been unanimous in the matter. They, however, were torn between greed and apprehension. If they went they must abandon their share of the plunder, which was considerable, as well as the slaves and other prisoners they had taken. If they did this, and Captain Blood should afterwards contrive to get away unscathed—and from their knowledge of his resourcefulness, the thing, however unlikely, need not be impossible—he must profit by that which they now relinquished. This was a contingency too bitter for contemplation. And so, in the end, despite all that Cahusac could say, the surrender was not to Don Miguel, but to Peter Blood. They had come into the venture with him, they asserted, and they would go out of it with him or not at all. That was the message he received from them that same evening by the sullen mouth of Cahusac himself.

He welcomed it, and invited the Breton to sit down and join the council which was even then deliberating upon the means to be employed. This council occupied the spacious patio of the Governor's house—which Captain Blood had appropriated to his own uses—a cloistered stone quadrangle in the middle of which a fountain played coolly under a trellis of vine. Orange-trees grew on two sides of it, and the still, evening air was heavy with the scent of them. It was one of those pleasant exterior-interiors which Moorish architects had introduced to Spain and the Spaniards had carried with them to the New World.

Here that council of war, composed of six men in all, deliberated until late that night upon the plan of action which Captain Blood put forward.

The great freshwater lake of Maracaybo, nourished by a score of rivers from the snow-capped ranges that surround it on two sides, is some hundred and twenty miles in length and almost the same distance across at its widest. It is—as has been indicated—in the shape of a great bottle having its neck towards the sea at Maracaybo.

Beyond this neck it widens again, and then the two long, narrow strips of land known as the islands of Vigilias and Palomas block the channel, standing lengthwise across it. The only passage out to sea for vessels of any draught lies in the narrow strait between these islands. Palomas, which is some ten miles in length, is unapproachable for half a mile on either side by any but the shallowest craft save at its eastern end, where, completely commanding the narrow passage out to sea, stands the massive fort which the buccaneers had found deserted upon their coming. In the broader water between this passage and the bar, the four Spanish ships were at anchor in mid-channel. The Admiral's *Encarnacion*, which we already know, was a mighty galleon of forty-eight great guns and eight small. Next in importance was the *Salvador* with thirty-six guns; the other two, the *Infanta* and the *San Felipe*, though smaller vessels, were still formidable enough with their twenty guns and a hundred and fifty men apiece.

Such was the fleet of which the gauntlet was to be run by Captain Blood with his own *Arabella* of forty guns, the *Elizabeth* of twenty-six, and two sloops captured at Gibraltar, which they had indifferently armed with four culverins each. In men they had a bare four hundred survivors of the five hundred-odd that had left Tortuga, to oppose to fully a thousand Spaniards manning the galleons.

The plan of action submitted by Captain Blood to that council was a desperate one, as Cahusac uncompromisingly pronounced it.

"Why, so it is," said the Captain. "But I've done things more desperate." Complacently he pulled at a pipe that was loaded with that fragrant Sacerdotes tobacco for which Gibraltar was famous, and of which they had brought away some hogsheads. "And what is more, they've succeeded. Audaces fortuna juvat. Bedad, they knew their world, the old Romans."

He breathed into his companions and even into Cahusac some of his own spirit of confidence, and in confidence all went busily to work. For three days from sunrise to sunset, the buccaneers laboured and sweated to complete the preparations for the action that was to procure them their deliverance. Time pressed. They must strike before Don Miguel de Espinosa received the reënforcement of that fifth galleon, the *Santo Niño*, which was coming to join him from La Guayra.

Their principal operations were on the larger of the two sloops captured at Gibraltar; to which vessel was assigned the leading part in Captain Blood's scheme. They began by tearing down all bulkheads, until they had reduced her to the merest shell, and in her sides they broke open so many ports that her gunwale was converted into the semblance of a grating. Next they increased by a half-dozen the scuttles in her deck, whilst into her hull they packed all the tar and pitch and brimstone that they could find in the town, to which they added six barrels of gunpowder, placed on end like guns at the open ports on her larboard side.

On the evening of the fourth day, everything being now in readiness, all were got aboard, and the empty, pleasant city of Maracaybo was at last abandoned. But they did not weigh anchor until some two hours after midnight. Then, at last, on the first of the ebb, they drifted silently down towards the bar with all canvas furled save only their spritsails, which, so as to give them steering way, were spread to the faint breeze that stirred through the purple darkness of the tropical night.

The order of their going was as follows: Ahead went the improvised fire-ship in charge of Wolverstone, with a crew of six volunteers, each of whom was to have a hundred pieces of eight over and above his share of plunder as a special reward. Next came the *Arabella*. She was followed at a distance by the *Elizabeth*, commanded by Hagthorpe, with whom was the now shipless Cahusac and the bulk of his French followers. The rear was brought up by the second sloop and some eight canoes, aboard of which had been shipped the prisoners, the slaves, and most of the captured merchandise. The prisoners were all pinioned, and guarded by four buccaneers with musketoons who manned these boats in addition to the two fellows who were to sail them. Their place was to be in the rear and they were to take no part whatever in the coming fight.

As the first glimmerings of opalescent dawn dissolved the darkness, the straining eyes of the buccaneers were able to make out the tall rigging of the Spanish vessels, riding at anchor less than a quarter of a mile ahead. Entirely without suspicion as the Spaniards were, and rendered confident by their own overwhelming strength, it is unlikely that they used a vigilance keener than their careless habit. Certain it is that they did not sight Blood's fleet in that dim light until some time after Blood's fleet had sighted them. By the time that they had actively roused themselves, Wolverstone's sloop was almost upon them, speeding under canvas which had been crowded to her yards the moment the galleons had loomed into view.

Straight for the Admiral's great ship, the *Encarnacion*, did Wolverstone head the sloop; then, lashing down the helm, he kindled from a match that hung ready lighted beside him a great torch of thickly plaited straw that had been steeped in bitumen. First it glowed, then as he swung it round his head, it burst into flame, just as the slight vessel went crashing and bumping and scraping against the side of the flagship, whilst rigging became tangled with rigging, to the straining of yards and snapping of spars overhead. His six men stood at their posts on the larboard side, stark naked, each armed with a grapnel, four of them on the gunwale, two of them aloft. At the moment of impact these grapnels were slung to bind the Spaniard to them, those aloft being intended to complete and preserve the entanglement of the rigging.

Aboard the rudely awakened galleon all was confused hurrying, scurrying, trumpeting, and shouting. At first there had been a desperately hurried attempt to get up the anchor; but this was abandoned as being already too late; and conceiving themselves on the point of being boarded, the Spaniards stood to arms to ward off the onslaught. Its slowness in coming intrigued them, being so different from the usual tactics of the buccaneers. Further intrigued were they by the sight of the gigantic Wolverstone speeding naked along his deck with a great flaming torch held high. Not until he had completed his work did they begin to suspect the truth—that he was lighting slow-matches—and then one of their officers rendered reckless by panic ordered a boarding-party on to the shop.

The order came too late. Wolverstone had seen his six fellows drop overboard after the grapnels were fixed, and then had sped, himself, to the starboard gunwale. Thence he flung his flaming torch down the nearest gaping scuttle into the hold, and thereupon dived overboard in his turn, to be picked up presently by the longboat from the *Arabella*. But before that happened the sloop was a thing of fire, from which explosions were hurling blazing combustibles aboard the *Encarnacion*, and long tongues of flame were licking out to consume the galleon, beating back those daring Spaniards who, too late, strove desperately to cut her adrift.

And whilst the most formidable vessel of the Spanish fleet was thus being put out of action at the outset, Blood had sailed in to open fire upon the *Salvador*. First athwart her hawse he had loosed a broadside that had swept her decks with terrific effect, then going on and about, he had put a second broadside into her hull at short range. Leaving her thus half-crippled, temporarily, at least, and keeping to his course, he had bewildered the crew of the *Infanta* by a couple of shots from the chasers on his beakhead, then crashed alongside to grapple and board her, whilst Hagthorpe was doing the like by the *San Felipe*.

And in all this time not a single shot had the Spaniards contrived to fire, so completely had they been taken by surprise, and so swift and paralyzing had been Blood's stroke.

Boarded now and faced by the cold steel of the buccaneers, neither the *San Felipe* nor the *Infanta* offered much resistance. The sight of their admiral in flames, and the *Salvador* drifting crippled from the action, had so utterly disheartened them that they accounted themselves vanquished, and laid down their arms.

If by a resolute stand the *Salvador* had encouraged the other two undamaged vessels to resistance, the Spaniards might well have retrieved the fortunes of the day. But it happened that the *Salvador* was handicapped in true Spanish fashion by being the treasure-ship of the fleet, with plate on board to the value of some fifty thousand pieces. Intent above all upon saving this from falling into the hands of the pirates, Don Miguel, who, with a remnant of his crew, had meanwhile transferred himself aboard her, headed her down towards Palomas and the fort that guarded the passage. This fort the Admiral, in those days of waiting, had taken the precaution secretly to garrison and rearm. For the purpose he had stripped the fort of Cojero, farther out on the gulf, of its entire armament, which included some cannon-royal of more than ordinary range and power.

With no suspicion of this, Captain Blood gave chase, accompanied by the *Infanta*, which was manned now by a prize-crew under the command of Yberville. The stern chasers of the *Salvador* desultorily returned the punishing fire of the pursuers; but such was the damage she, herself, sustained, that presently, coming under the guns of the fort, she began to sink, and finally settled down in the shallows with part of her hull above water. Thence, some in boats and some by swimming, the Admiral got his crew ashore on Palomas as best he could.

And then, just as Captain Blood accounted the victory won, and that his way out of that trap to the open sea beyond lay clear, the fort suddenly revealed its formidable and utterly unsuspected strength. With a roar the cannons-royal proclaimed themselves, and the *Arabella* staggered under a blow that smashed her bulwarks at the waist and scattered death and confusion among the seamen gathered there.

Had not Pitt, her master, himself seized the whipstaff and put the helm hard over to swing her sharply off to starboard, she must have suffered still worse from the second volley that followed fast upon the first.

Meanwhile it had fared even worse with the frailer *Infanta*. Although hit by one shot only, this had crushed her larboard timbers on the waterline, starting a leak that must presently have filled her, but for the prompt action of the experienced Yberville in ordering her larboard guns to be flung overboard. Thus lightened, and listing now to starboard, he fetched her about, and went staggering after the retreating *Arabella*, followed by the fire of the fort, which did them, however, little further damage.

Out of range, at last, they lay to, joined by the *Elizabeth* and the *San Felipe*, to consider their position.

XVII. The Dupes

It was a crestfallen Captain Blood who presided over that hastily summoned council held on the poop-deck of the *Arabella* in the brilliant morning sunshine. It was, he declared afterwards, one of the bitterest moments in his career. He was compelled to digest the fact that having conducted the engagement with a skill of which he might justly be proud, having destroyed a force so superior in ships and guns and men that Don Miguel de Espinosa had justifiably deemed it overwhelming, his victory was rendered barren by three lucky shots from an unsuspected battery by which they had been surprised. And barren must their victory remain until they could reduce the fort that still remained to defend the passage.

At first Captain Blood was for putting his ships in order and making the attempt there and then. But the others dissuaded him from betraying an impetuosity usually foreign to him, and born entirely of chagrin and mortification, emotions which will render unreasonable the most reasonable of men. With returning calm, he surveyed the situation. The *Arabella* was no longer in case to put to sea; the *Infanta* was merely kept afloat by artifice, and the *San Felipe* was almost as sorely damaged by the fire she had sustained from the buccaneers before surrendering.

Clearly, then, he was compelled to admit in the end that nothing remained but to return to Maracaybo, there to refit the ships before attempting to force the passage.

And so, back to Maracaybo came those defeated victors of that short, terrible fight. And if anything had been wanting further to exasperate their leader, he had it in the pessimism of which Cahusac did not economize expressions. Transported at first to heights of dizzy satisfaction by the swift and easy victory of their inferior force that morning, the Frenchman was now plunged back and more deeply than ever into the abyss of hopelessness. And his mood infected at least the main body of his own followers.

"It is the end," he told Captain Blood. "This time we are checkmated."

"I'll take the liberty of reminding you that you said the same before," Captain Blood answered him as patiently as he could. "Yet you've seen what you've seen, and you'll not deny that in ships and guns we are returning stronger than we went. Look at our present fleet, man."

no quarter from us, and that I shall begin by leaving a heap of ashes where this pleasant city of Maracaybo now stands."

The letter written, he bade them bring him from among the prisoners the Deputy-Governor of Maracaybo, who had been taken at Gibraltar. Disclosing its contents to him, he despatched him with it to Don Miguel.

His choice of a messenger was shrewd. The Deputy-Governor was of all men the most anxious for the deliverance of his city, the one man who on his own account would plead most fervently for its preservation at all costs from the fate with which Captain Blood was threatening it.

And as he reckoned so it befell. The Deputy-Governor added his own passionate pleading to the proposals of the letter.

But Don Miguel was of stouter heart. True, his fleet had been partly destroyed and partly captured. But then, he argued, he had been taken utterly by surprise. That should not happen again. There should be no surprising the fort. Let Captain Blood do his worst at Maracaybo, there should be a bitter reckoning for him when eventually he decided—as, sooner or later, decide he must—to come forth.

The Deputy-Governor was flung into panic. He lost his temper, and said some hard things to the Admiral. But they were not as hard as the thing the Admiral said to him in answer.

"Had you been as loyal to your King in hindering the entrance of these cursed pirates as I shall be in hindering their going forth again, we should not now find ourselves in our present straits. So weary me no more with your coward counsels. I make no terms with Captain Blood. I know my duty to my King, and I intend to perform it. I also know my duty to myself. I have a private score with this rascal, and I intend to settle it. Take you that message back."

So back to Maracaybo, back to his own handsome house in which Captain Blood had established his quarters, came the Deputy-Governor with the Admiral's answer. And because he had been shamed into a show of spirit by the Admiral's own stout courage in adversity, he delivered it as truculently as the Admiral could have desired.

"And is it like that?" said Captain Blood with a quiet smile, though the heart of him sank at this failure of his bluster. "Well, well, it's a pity now that the Admiral's so headstrong. It was that way he lost his fleet, which was his own to lose. This pleasant city of Maracaybo isn't. So no doubt he'll lose it with fewer misgivings. I am sorry. Waste, like bloodshed, is a thing abhorrent to me. But there ye are! I'll have the

"I am looking at it," said Cahusac.

"Pish! Ye're a white-livered cur when all is said."

"You call me a coward?"

"I'll take that liberty."

The Breton glared at him, breathing hard. But he had no mind to ask sat
for the insult. He knew too well the kind of satisfaction that Captain Blood w
to afford him. He remembered the fate of Levasseur. So he confined himself t
"It is too much! You go too far!" he complained bitterly.

"Look you, Cahusac: it's sick and tired I am of your perpetual whir
complaining when things are not as smooth as a convent dining-table. If ye
things smooth and easy, ye shouldn't have taken to the sea, and ye should r
sailed with me, for with me things are never smooth and easy. And that, I thin
have to say to you this morning."

Cahusac flung away cursing, and went to take the feeling of his men.

Captain Blood went off to give his surgeon's skill to the wounded, among
remained engaged until late afternoon. Then, at last, he went ashore, his mi
up, and returned to the house of the Governor, to indite a truculent but very s
letter in purest Castilian to Don Miguel.

"I have shown your excellency this morning of what I am capable," h
"Although outnumbered by more than two to one in men, in ships, and in gun
sunk or captured the vessels of the great fleet with which you were to come to Ma
to destroy us. So that you are no longer in case to carry out your boast, even wl
reënforcements on the *Santo Niño*, reach you from La Guayra. From what has o
you may judge of what must occur. I should not trouble your excellency with t
but that I am a humane man, abhorring bloodshed. Therefore before proceedin
with your fort, which you may deem invincible, as I have dealt already with yo
which you deemed invincible, I make you, purely out of humanitarian consid
this last offer of terms. I will spare this city of Maracaybo and forthwith eva
leaving behind me the forty prisoners I have taken, in consideration of your pa
the sum of fifty thousand pieces of eight and one hundred head of cattle as a
thereafter granting me unmolested passage of the bar. My prisoners, most of w
persons of consideration, I will retain as hostages until after my departure, sendi
back in the canoes which we shall take with us for that purpose. If your ex
should be so ill-advised as to refuse these terms, and thereby impose upor
necessity of reducing your fort at the cost of some lives, I warn you that you ma

faggots to the place in the morning, and maybe when he sees the blaze to-morrow night he'll begin to believe that Peter Blood is a man of his word. Ye may go, Don Francisco."

The Deputy-Governor went out with dragging feet, followed by guards, his momentary truculence utterly spent.

But no sooner had he departed than up leapt Cahusac, who had been of the council assembled to receive the Admiral's answer. His face was white and his hands shook as he held them out in protest.

"Death of my life, what have you to say now?" he cried, his voice husky. And without waiting to hear what it might be, he raved on: "I knew you not frighten the Admiral so easy. He hold us entrap', and he knows it; yet you dream that he will yield himself to your impudent message. Your fool letter it have seal' the doom of us all."

"Have ye done?" quoth Blood quietly, as the Frenchman paused for breath.

"No, I have not."

"Then spare me the rest. It'll be of the same quality, devil a doubt, and it doesn't help us to solve the riddle that's before us."

"But what are you going to do? Is it that you will tell me?" It was not a question, it was a demand.

"How the devil do I know? I was hoping you'd have some ideas yourself. But since ye're so desperately concerned to save your skin, you and those that think like you are welcome to leave us. I've no doubt at all the Spanish Admiral will welcome the abatement of our numbers even at this late date. Ye shall have the sloop as a parting gift from us, and ye can join Don Miguel in the fort for all I care, or for all the good ye're likely to be to us in this present pass."

"It is to my men to decide," Cahusac retorted, swallowing his fury, and on that stalked out to talk to them, leaving the others to deliberate in peace.

Next morning early he sought Captain Blood again. He found him alone in the patio, pacing to and fro, his head sunk on his breast. Cahusac mistook consideration for dejection. Each of us carries in himself a standard by which to measure his neighbour.

"We have take' you at your word, Captain," he announced, between sullenness and defiance. Captain Blood paused, shoulders hunched, hands behind his back, and mildly regarded the buccaneer in silence. Cahusac explained himself. "Last night I send one of my men to the Spanish Admiral with a letter. I make him offer to capitulate if he will accord us passage with the honours of war. This morning I receive his answer. He accord us this on the understanding that we carry nothing away with us. My men they are embarking them on the sloop. We sail at once."

"Bon voyage," said Captain Blood, and with a nod he turned on his heel again to resume his interrupted mediation.

"Is that all that you have to say to me?" cried Cahusac.

"There are other things," said Blood over his shoulder. "But I know ye wouldn't like them."

"Ha! Then it's adieu, my Captain." Venomously he added: "It is my belief that we shall not meet again."

"Your belief is my hope," said Captain Blood.

Cahusac flung away, obscenely vituperative. Before noon he was under way with his followers, some sixty dejected men who had allowed themselves to be persuaded by him into that empty-handed departure—in spite even of all that Yberville could do to prevent it. The Admiral kept faith with him, and allowed him free passage out to sea, which, from his knowledge of Spaniards, was more than Captain Blood had expected.

Meanwhile, no sooner had the deserters weighed anchor than Captain Blood received word that the Deputy-Governor begged to be allowed to see him again. Admitted, Don Francisco at once displayed the fact that a night's reflection had quickened his apprehensions for the city of Maracaybo and his condemnation of the Admiral's intransigence.

Captain Blood received him pleasantly.

"Good-morning to you, Don Francisco. I have postponed the bonfire until nightfall. It will make a better show in the dark."

Don Francisco, a slight, nervous, elderly man of high lineage and low vitality, came straight to business.

"I am here to tell you, Don Pedro, that if you will hold your hand for three days, I will undertake to raise the ransom you demand, which Don Miguel de Espinosa refuses."

Captain Blood confronted him, a frown contracting the dark brows above his light eyes:

"And where will you be raising it?" quoth he, faintly betraying his surprise.

Don Francisco shook his head. "That must remain my affair," he answered. "I know where it is to be found, and my compatriots must contribute. Give me leave for three days on parole, and I will see you fully satisfied. Meanwhile my son remains in your hands as a hostage for my return." And upon that he fell to pleading. But in this he was crisply interrupted.

"By the Saints! Ye're a bold man, Don Francisco, to come to me with such a tale—to tell me that ye know where the ransom's to be raised, and yet to refuse to say. D'ye think now that with a match between your fingers ye'd grow more communicative?"

If Don Francisco grew a shade paler, yet again he shook his head.

"That was the way of Morgan and L'Ollonais and other pirates. But it is not the way of Captain Blood. If I had doubted that I should not have disclosed so much."

The Captain laughed. "You old rogue," said he. "Ye play upon my vanity, do you?"

"Upon your honour, Captain."

"The honour of a pirate? Ye're surely crazed!"

"The honour of Captain Blood," Don Francisco insisted. "You have the repute of making war like a gentleman."

Captain Blood laughed again, on a bitter, sneering note that made Don Francisco fear the worst. He was not to guess that it was himself the Captain mocked.

"That's merely because it's more remunerative in the end. And that is why you are accorded the three days you ask for. So about it, Don Francisco. You shall have what mules you need. I'll see to it."

Away went Don Francisco on his errand, leaving Captain Blood to reflect, between bitterness and satisfaction, that a reputation for as much chivalry as is consistent with piracy is not without its uses.

Punctually on the third day the Deputy-Governor was back in Maracaybo with his mules laden with plate and money to the value demanded and a herd of a hundred head of cattle driven in by negro slaves.

These bullocks were handed over to those of the company who ordinarily were boucan-hunters, and therefore skilled in the curing of meats, and for best part of a week thereafter they were busy at the waterside with the quartering and salting of carcases.

While this was doing on the one hand and the ships were being refitted for sea on the other, Captain Blood was pondering the riddle on the solution of which his own fate depended. Indian spies whom he employed brought him word that the Spaniards, working at low tide, had salved the thirty guns of the *Salvador*, and thus had added yet another battery to their already overwhelming strength. In the end, and hoping for inspiration on the spot, Captain Blood made a reconnaissance in person. At the risk of his life, accompanied by two friendly Indians, he crossed to the island in a canoe under cover of dark. They concealed themselves and the canoe in the short thick scrub with which that side of the island was densely covered, and lay there until daybreak. Then Blood went forward alone, and with infinite precaution, to make his survey. He went to verify a suspicion that he had formed, and approached the fort as nearly as he dared and a deal nearer than was safe.

On all fours he crawled to the summit of an eminence a mile or so away, whence he found himself commanding a view of the interior dispositions of the stronghold. By the aid of a telescope with which he had equipped himself he was able to verify that, as he had suspected and hoped, the fort's artillery was all mounted on the seaward side.

Satisfied, he returned to Maracaybo, and laid before the six who composed his council—Pitt, Hagthorpe, Yberville, Wolverstone, Dyke, and Ogle—a proposal to storm the fort from the landward side. Crossing to the island under cover of night, they would take the Spaniards by surprise and attempt to overpower them before they could shift their guns to meet the onslaught.

With the exception of Wolverstone, who was by temperament the kind of man who favours desperate chances, those officers received the proposal coldly. Hagthorpe incontinently opposed it.

"It's a harebrained scheme, Peter," he said gravely, shaking his handsome head. "Consider now that we cannot depend upon approaching unperceived to a distance whence we might storm the fort before the cannon could be moved. But even if we could, we can take no cannon ourselves; we must depend entirely upon our small arms, and how shall we, a bare three hundred" (for this was the number to which Cahusac's defection had reduced them), "cross the open to attack more than twice that number under cover?"

The others—Dyke, Ogle, Yberville, and even Pitt, whom loyalty to Blood may have made reluctant—loudly approved him. When they had done, "I have considered all," said Captain Blood. "I have weighed the risks and studied how to lessen them. In these desperate straits . . ."

He broke off abruptly. A moment he frowned, deep in thought; then his face was suddenly alight with inspiration. Slowly he drooped his head, and sat there considering, weighing, chin on breast. Then he nodded, muttering, "Yes," and again, "Yes." He looked up, to face them. "Listen," he cried. "You may be right. The risks may be too heavy. Whether or not, I have thought of a better way. That which should have been the real attack shall be no more than a feint. Here, then, is the plan I now propose."

He talked swiftly and clearly, and as he talked one by one his officers' faces became alight with eagerness. When he had done, they cried as with one voice that he had saved them.

"That is yet to be proved in action," said he.

Since for the last twenty-four hours all had been in readiness for departure, there was nothing now to delay them, and it was decided to move next morning.

Such was Captain Blood's assurance of success that he immediately freed the prisoners held as hostages, and even the negro slaves, who were regarded by the others as legitimate plunder. His only precaution against those released prisoners was to order them into the church and there lock them up, to await deliverance at the hands of those who should presently be coming into the city.

Then, all being aboard the three ships, with the treasure safely stowed in their holds and the slaves under hatches, the buccaneers weighed anchor and stood out for the bar, each vessel towing three piraguas astern.

The Admiral, beholding their stately advance in the full light of noon, their sails gleaming white in the glare of the sunlight, rubbed his long, lean hands in satisfaction, and laughed through his teeth.

"At last!" he cried. "God delivers him into my hands!" He turned to the group of staring officers behind him. "Sooner or later it had to be," he said. "Say now, gentlemen, whether I am justified of my patience. Here end to-day the troubles caused to the subjects of the Catholic King by this infamous Don Pedro Sangre, as he once called himself to me."

He turned to issue orders, and the fort became lively as a hive. The guns were manned, the gunners already kindling fuses, when the buccaneer fleet, whilst still heading for Palomas, was observed to bear away to the west. The Spaniards watched them, intrigued.

Within a mile and a half to westward of the fort, and within a half-mile of the shore— that is to say, on the very edge of the shoal water that makes Palomas unapproachable on either side by any but vessels of the shallowest draught—the four ships cast anchor well within the Spaniards' view, but just out of range of their heaviest cannon.

Sneeringly the Admiral laughed.

"Aha! They hesitate, these English dogs! Por Dios, and well they may."

"They will be waiting for night," suggested his nephew, who stood at his elbow quivering with excitement.

Don Miguel looked at him, smiling. "And what shall the night avail them in this narrow passage, under the very muzzles of my guns? Be sure, Esteban, that to-night your father will be paid for."

He raised his telescope to continue his observation of the buccaneers. He saw that the piraguas towed by each vessel were being warped alongside, and he wondered a little what this manœuver might portend. Awhile those piraguas were hidden from view behind the hulls. Then one by one they reappeared, rowing round and away from the ships, and each boat, he observed, was crowded with armed men. Thus laden, they were headed for the shore, at a point where it was densely wooded to the water's edge. The eyes of the wondering Admiral followed them until the foliage screened them from his view.

Then he lowered his telescope and looked at his officers.

"What the devil does it mean?" he asked.

None answered him, all being as puzzled as he was himself.

After a little while, Esteban, who kept his eyes on the water, plucked at his uncle's sleeve. "There they go!" he cried, and pointed.

And there, indeed, went the piraguas on their way back to the ships. But now it was observed that they were empty, save for the men who rowed them. Their armed cargo had been left ashore.

Back to the ships they pulled, to return again presently with a fresh load of armed men, which similarly they conveyed to Palomas. And at last one of the Spanish officers ventured an explanation:

"They are going to attack us by land—to attempt to storm the fort."

"Of course." The Admiral smiled. "I had guessed it. Whom the gods would destroy they first make mad."

"Shall we make a sally?" urged Esteban, in his excitement.

"A sally? Through that scrub? That would be to play into their hands. No, no, we will wait here to receive this attack. Whenever it comes, it is themselves will be destroyed, and utterly. Have no doubt of that."

But by evening the Admiral's equanimity was not quite so perfect. By then the piraguas had made a half-dozen journeys with their loads of men, and they had landed also—as Don Miguel had clearly observed through his telescope—at least a dozen guns.

His countenance no longer smiled; it was a little wrathful and a little troubled now as he turned again to his officers.

"Who was the fool who told me that they number but three hundred men in all? They have put at least twice that number ashore already."

Amazed as he was, his amazement would have been deeper had he been told the truth: that there was not a single buccaneer or a single gun ashore on Palomas. The deception had been complete. Don Miguel could not guess that the men he had beheld in those piraguas were always the same; that on the journeys to the shore they sat and stood upright in full view; and that on the journeys back to the ships, they lay invisible at the bottom of the boats, which were thus made to appear empty.

The growing fears of the Spanish soldiery at the prospect of a night attack from the landward side by the entire buccaneer force—and a force twice as strong as they had suspected the pestilent Blood to command—began to be communicated to the Admiral.

In the last hours of fading daylight, the Spaniards did precisely what Captain Blood so confidently counted that they would do—precisely what they must do to meet the attack, preparations for which had been so thoroughly simulated. They set themselves to labour like the damned at those ponderous guns emplaced to command the narrow passage out to sea.

Groaning and sweating, urged on by the curses and even the whips of their officers, they toiled in a frenzy of panic-stricken haste to shift the greater number and the more powerful of their guns across to the landward side, there to emplace them anew, so that they might be ready to receive the attack which at any moment now might burst upon them from the woods not half a mile away.

Thus, when night fell, although in mortal anxiety of the onslaught of those wild devils whose reckless courage was a byword on the seas of the Main, at least the Spaniards were tolerably prepared for it. Waiting, they stood to their guns.

And whilst they waited thus, under cover of the darkness and as the tide began to ebb, Captain Blood's fleet weighed anchor quietly; and, as once before, with no more canvas spread than that which their sprits could carry, so as to give them steering way—and even these having been painted black—the four vessels, without a light showing, groped their way by soundings to the channel which led to that narrow passage out to sea.

The *Elizabeth* and the *Infanta*, leading side by side, were almost abreast of the fort before their shadowy bulks and the soft gurgle of water at their prows were detected by the Spaniards, whose attention until that moment had been all on the other side. And now there arose on the night air such a sound of human baffled fury as may have resounded about Babel at the confusion of tongues. To heighten that confusion, and to scatter disorder among the Spanish soldiery, the *Elizabeth* emptied her larboard guns into the fort as she was swept past on the swift ebb.

At once realizing—though not yet how—he had been duped, and that his prey was in the very act of escaping after all, the Admiral frantically ordered the guns that had been so laboriously moved to be dragged back to their former emplacements, and commanded his gunners meanwhile to the slender batteries that of all his powerful, but now unavailable, armament still remained trained upon the channel. With these, after the loss of some precious moments, the fort at last made fire.

It was answered by a terrific broadside from the *Arabella*, which had now drawn abreast, and was crowding canvas to her yards. The enraged and gibbering Spaniards had a brief vision of her as the line of flame spurted from her red flank, and the thunder of her broadside drowned the noise of the creaking halyards. After that they saw her no more. Assimilated by the friendly darkness which the lesser Spanish guns were speculatively stabbing, the escaping ships fired never another shot that might assist their baffled and bewildered enemies to locate them.

Some slight damage was sustained by Blood's fleet. But by the time the Spaniards had resolved their confusion into some order of dangerous offence, that fleet, well served by a southerly breeze, was through the narrows and standing out to sea.

Thus was Don Miguel de Espinosa left to chew the bitter cud of a lost opportunity, and to consider in what terms he would acquaint the Supreme Council of the Catholic King that Peter Blood had got away from Maracaybo, taking with him two twenty-gun frigates that were lately the property of Spain, to say nothing of two hundred and fifty thousand pieces of eight and other plunder. And all this in spite of Don Miguel's four galleons and his heavily armed fort that at one time had held the pirates so securely trapped.

Heavy, indeed, grew the account of Peter Blood, which Don Miguel swore passionately to Heaven should at all costs to himself be paid in full.

Nor were the losses already detailed the full total of those suffered on this occasion by the King of Spain. For on the following evening, off the coast of Oruba, at the mouth of the Gulf of Venezuela, Captain Blood's fleet came upon the belated *Santo Niño*, speeding under full sail to reenforce Don Miguel at Maracaybo.

At first the Spaniard had conceived that she was meeting the victorious fleet of Don Miguel, returning from the destruction of the pirates. When at comparatively close quarters the pennon of St. George soared to the *Arabella*'s masthead to disillusion her, the *Santo Niño* chose the better part of valour, and struck her flag.

Captain Blood ordered her crew to take to the boats, and land themselves at Oruba or wherever else they pleased. So considerate was he that to assist them he presented them with several of the piraguas which he still had in tow.

"You will find," said he to her captain, "that Don Miguel is in an extremely bad temper. Commend me to him, and say that I venture to remind him that he must blame himself for all the ills that have befallen him. The evil has recoiled upon him which he loosed when he sent his brother unofficially to make a raid upon the island of Barbados. Bid him think twice before he lets his devils loose upon an English settlement again."

With that he dismissed the Captain, who went over the side of the *Santo Niño*, and Captain Blood proceeded to investigate the value of this further prize. When her hatches were removed, a human cargo was disclosed in her hold.

"Slaves," said Wolverstone, and persisted in that belief, cursing Spanish devilry until Cahusac crawled up out of the dark bowels of the ship, and stood blinking in the sunlight.

There was more than sunlight to make the Breton pirate blink. And those that crawled out after him—the remnants of his crew—cursed him horribly for the pusillanimity which had brought them into the ignominy of owing their deliverance to those whom they had deserted as lost beyond hope.

Their sloop had encountered and had been sunk three days ago by the *Santo Niño*, and Cahusac had narrowly escaped hanging merely that for some time he might be a mock among the Brethren of the Coast.

For many a month thereafter he was to hear in Tortuga the jeering taunt:

"Where do you spend the gold that you brought back from Maracaybo?"

XVIII. The Milagrosa

The affair at Maracaybo is to be considered as Captain Blood's buccaneering masterpiece. Although there is scarcely one of the many actions that he fought— recorded in such particular detail by Jeremy Pitt—which does not afford some instance of his genius for naval tactics, yet in none is this more shiningly displayed than in those two engagements by which he won out of the trap which Don Miguel de Espinosa had sprung upon him.

The fame which he had enjoyed before this, great as it already was, is dwarfed into insignificance by the fame that followed. It was a fame such as no buccaneer—not even Morgan—has ever boasted, before or since.

In Tortuga, during the months he spent there refitting the three ships he had captured from the fleet that had gone out to destroy him, he found himself almost an object of worship in the eyes of the wild Brethren of the Coast, all of whom now clamoured for the honour of serving under him. It placed him in the rare position of being able to pick and choose the crews for his augmented fleet, and he chose fastidiously. When next he sailed away it was with a fleet of five fine ships in which went something over a thousand men. Thus you behold him not merely famous, but really formidable. The three captured Spanish vessels he had renamed with a certain scholarly humour the *Clotho*, *Lachesis*, and *Atropos*, a grimly jocular manner of conveying to the world that he made them the arbiters of the fate of any Spaniards he should henceforth encounter upon the seas.

In Europe the news of this fleet, following upon the news of the Spanish Admiral's defeat at Maracaybo, produced something of a sensation. Spain and England were variously and unpleasantly exercised, and if you care to turn up the diplomatic correspondence exchanged on the subject, you will find that it is considerable and not always amiable.

And meanwhile in the Caribbean, the Spanish Admiral Don Miguel de Espinosa might be said—to use a term not yet invented in his day—to have run amok. The disgrace into which he had fallen as a result of the disasters suffered at the hands of Captain Blood had driven the Admiral all but mad. It is impossible, if we dispose our minds impartially, to withhold a certain sympathy from Don Miguel. Hate was now this unfortunate man's daily bread, and the hope of vengeance an obsession to his mind. As a madman he went raging up and down the Caribbean seeking his enemy, and in the meantime, as an hors d'œuvre to his vindictive appetite, he fell upon any ship of England or of France that loomed above his horizon.

I need say no more to convey the fact that this illustrious sea-captain and great gentleman of Castile had lost his head, and was become a pirate in his turn. The Supreme Council of Castile might anon condemn him for his practices. But how should that matter to one who already was condemned beyond redemption? On the contrary, if he should live to lay the audacious and ineffable Blood by the heels, it was possible that Spain might view his present irregularities and earlier losses with a more lenient eye.

And so, reckless of the fact that Captain Blood was now in vastly superior strength, the Spaniard sought him up and down the trackless seas. But for a whole year he sought him vainly. The circumstances in which eventually they met are very curious.

An intelligent observation of the facts of human existence will reveal to shallow-minded folk who sneer at the use of coincidence in the arts of fiction and drama that life itself is little more than a series of coincidences. Open the history of the past at whatsoever page you will, and there you shall find coincidence at work bringing about events that the merest chance might have averted. Indeed, coincidence may be defined as the very tool used by Fate to shape the destinies of men and nations.

Observe it now at work in the affairs of Captain Blood and of some others.

On the 15th September of the year 1688—a memorable year in the annals of England—three ships were afloat upon the Caribbean, which in their coming conjunctions were to work out the fortunes of several persons.

The first of these was Captain Blood's flagship the *Arabella*, which had been separated from the buccaneer fleet in a hurricane off the Lesser Antilles. In somewhere about 17° N. Lat., and 74° Long., she was beating up for the Windward Passage, before the intermittent southeasterly breezes of that stifling season, homing for Tortuga, the natural rendezvous of the dispersed vessels.

The second ship was the great Spanish galleon, the *Milagrosa*, which, accompanied by the smaller frigate *Hidalga*, lurked off the Caymites, to the north of the long peninsula that thrusts out from the southwest corner of Hispaniola. Aboard the *Milagrosa* sailed the vindictive Don Miguel.

The third and last of these ships with which we are at present concerned was an English man-of-war, which on the date I have given was at anchor in the French port of St. Nicholas on the northwest coast of Hispaniola. She was on her way from Plymouth to Jamaica, and carried on board a very distinguished passenger in the person of Lord Julian Wade, who came charged by his kinsman, my Lord Sunderland, with a mission of some consequence and delicacy, directly arising out of that vexatious correspondence between England and Spain.

The French Government, like the English, excessively annoyed by the depredations of the buccaneers, and the constant straining of relations with Spain that ensued, had sought in vain to put them down by enjoining the utmost severity against them upon her various overseas governors. But these, either— like the Governor of Tortuga—throve out of a scarcely tacit partnership with the filibusters, or—like the Governor of French Hispaniola—felt that they were to be encouraged as a check upon the power and greed of Spain, which might otherwise be exerted to the disadvantage of the colonies of other nations. They looked, indeed, with apprehension upon recourse to any vigorous measures which must result in driving many of the buccaneers to seek new hunting-grounds in the South Sea.

To satisfy King James's anxiety to conciliate Spain, and in response to the Spanish Ambassador's constant and grievous expostulations, my Lord Sunderland, the Secretary of State, had appointed a strong man to the deputy-governorship of Jamaica. This strong man was that Colonel Bishop who for some years now had been the most influential planter in Barbados.

Colonel Bishop had accepted the post, and departed from the plantations in which his great wealth was being amassed with an eagerness that had its roots in a desire to pay off a score of his own with Peter Blood.

From his first coming to Jamaica, Colonel Bishop had made himself felt by the buccaneers. But do what he might, the one buccaneer whom he made his particular quarry—that Peter Blood who once had been his slave—eluded him ever, and continued undeterred and in great force to harass the Spaniards upon sea and land, and to keep the relations between England and Spain in a state of perpetual ferment, particularly dangerous in those days when the peace of Europe was precariously maintained.

Exasperated not only by his own accumulated chagrin, but also by the reproaches for his failure which reached him from London, Colonel Bishop actually went so far as to consider hunting his quarry in Tortuga itself and making an attempt to clear the island of the buccaneers it sheltered. Fortunately for himself, he abandoned the notion of so insane an enterprise, deterred not only by the enormous natural strength of the place, but also by the reflection that a raid upon what was, nominally at least, a French settlement, must be attended by grave offence to France. Yet short of some such measure, it appeared to Colonel Bishop that he was baffled. He confessed as much in a letter to the Secretary of State.

This letter and the state of things which it disclosed made my Lord Sunderland despair of solving this vexatious problem by ordinary means. He turned to the consideration of extraordinary ones, and bethought him of the plan adopted with Morgan, who had been enlisted into the King's service under Charles II. It occurred to him that a similar course might be similarly effective with Captain Blood. His lordship did not omit the consideration that Blood's present outlawry might well have been undertaken not from inclination, but under stress of sheer necessity; that he had been forced into it by the circumstances of his transportation, and that he would welcome the opportunity of emerging from it.

Acting upon this conclusion, Sunderland sent out his kinsman, Lord Julian Wade, with some commissions made out in blank, and full directions as to the course which the Secretary considered it desirable to pursue and yet full discretion in the matter of pursuing them. The crafty Sunderland, master of all labyrinths of intrigue, advised his kinsman that in the event of his finding Blood intractable, or judging for other reasons that it was not desirable to enlist him in the King's service, he should turn his attention to the officers serving under him, and by seducing them away from him leave him so weakened that he must fall an easy victim to Colonel Bishop's fleet.

The *Royal Mary*—the vessel bearing that ingenious, tolerably accomplished, mildly dissolute, entirely elegant envoy of my Lord Sunderland's—made a good passage to St. Nicholas, her last port of call before Jamaica. It was understood that as a preliminary Lord Julian should report himself to the Deputy-Governor at Port Royal, whence at need he might have himself conveyed to Tortuga. Now it happened that the Deputy-Governor's niece had come to St. Nicholas some months earlier on a visit to some relatives, and so that she might escape the insufferable heat of Jamaica in that season. The time for her return being now at hand, a passage was sought for her aboard the *Royal Mary*, and in view of her uncle's rank and position promptly accorded.

Lord Julian hailed her advent with satisfaction. It gave a voyage that had been full of interest for him just the spice that it required to achieve perfection as an experience. His lordship was one of your gallants to whom existence that is not graced by womankind is more or less of a stagnation.

Miss Arabella Bishop—this straight up and down slip of a girl with her rather boyish voice and her almost boyish ease of movement—was not perhaps a lady who in England would have commanded much notice in my lord's discerning eyes. His very sophisticated, carefully educated tastes in such matters inclined him towards the plump, the languishing, and the quite helplessly feminine. Miss Bishop's charms were undeniable. But they were such that it would take a delicate-minded man to appreciate them; and my Lord Julian, whilst of a mind that was very far from gross, did not possess the necessary degree of delicacy. I must not by this be understood to imply anything against him.

It remained, however, that Miss Bishop was a young woman and a lady; and in the latitude into which Lord Julian had strayed this was a phenomenon sufficiently rare to command attention. On his side, with his title and position, his personal grace and the charm of a practised courtier, he bore about him the atmosphere of the great world in which normally he had his being—a world that was little more than a name to her, who had spent most of her life in the Antilles. It is not therefore wonderful that they should have been attracted to each other before the *Royal Mary* was warped out of St. Nicholas. Each could tell the other much upon which the other desired information. He could regale her imagination with stories of St. James's—in many of which he assigned himself a heroic, or at least a distinguished part—and she could enrich his mind with information concerning this new world to which he had come.

Before they were out of sight of St. Nicholas they were good friends, and his lordship was beginning to correct his first impressions of her and to discover the charm of that frank, straightforward attitude of comradeship which made her treat every man as a brother. Considering how his mind was obsessed with the business of his mission, it is not wonderful that he should have come to talk to her of Captain Blood. Indeed, there was a circumstance that directly led to it.

"I wonder now," he said, as they were sauntering on the poop, "if you ever saw this fellow Blood, who was at one time on your uncle's plantations as a slave."

Miss Bishop halted. She leaned upon the taffrail, looking out towards the receding land, and it was a moment before she answered in a steady, level voice:

"I saw him often. I knew him very well."

"Ye don't say!" His lordship was slightly moved out of an imperturbability that he had studiously cultivated. He was a young man of perhaps eight-and-twenty, well above the middle height in stature and appearing taller by virtue of his exceeding leanness. He had a thin, pale, rather pleasing hatchet-face, framed in the curls of a golden periwig, a sensitive mouth and pale blue eyes that lent his countenance a dreamy expression, a rather melancholy pensiveness. But they were alert, observant eyes notwithstanding, although they failed on this occasion to observe the slight change of colour which his question had brought to Miss Bishop's cheeks or the suspiciously excessive composure of her answer.

"Ye don't say!" he repeated, and came to lean beside her. "And what manner of man did you find him?"

"In those days I esteemed him for an unfortunate gentleman."

"You were acquainted with his story?"

"He told it me. That is why I esteemed him—for the calm fortitude with which he bore adversity. Since then, considering what he has done, I have almost come to doubt if what he told me of himself was true."

"If you mean of the wrongs he suffered at the hands of the Royal Commission that tried the Monmouth rebels, there's little doubt that it would be true enough. He was never out with Monmouth; that is certain. He was convicted on a point of law of which he may well have been ignorant when he committed what was construed into treason. But, faith, he's had his revenge, after a fashion."

"That," she said in a small voice, "is the unforgivable thing. It has destroyed him—deservedly."

"Destroyed him?" His lordship laughed a little. "Be none so sure of that. He has grown rich, I hear. He has translated, so it is said, his Spanish spoils into French gold, which is being treasured up for him in France. His future father-in-law, M. d'Ogeron, has seen to that."

"His future father-in-law?" said she, and stared at him round-eyed, with parted lips. Then added: "M. d'Ogeron? The Governor of Tortuga?"

"The same. You see the fellow's well protected. It's a piece of news I gathered in St. Nicholas. I am not sure that I welcome it, for I am not sure that it makes any easier a task upon which my kinsman, Lord Sunderland, has sent me hither. But there it is. You didn't know?"

She shook her head without replying. She had averted her face, and her eyes were staring down at the gently heaving water. After a moment she spoke, her voice steady and perfectly controlled.

"But surely, if this were true, there would have been an end to his piracy by now. If he . . . if he loved a woman and was betrothed, and was also rich as you say, surely he would have abandoned this desperate life, and . . ."

"Why, so I thought," his lordship interrupted, "until I had the explanation. D'Ogeron is avaricious for himself and for his child. And as for the girl, I'm told she's a wild piece, fit mate for such a man as Blood. Almost I marvel that he doesn't marry her and take her a-roving with him. It would be no new experience for her. And I marvel, too, at Blood's patience. He killed a man to win her."

"He killed a man for her, do you say?" There was horror now in her voice.

"Yes—a French buccaneer named Levasseur. He was the girl's lover and Blood's associate on a venture. Blood coveted the girl, and killed Levasseur to win her. Pah! It's an unsavoury tale, I own. But men live by different codes out in these parts . . ."

She had turned to face him. She was pale to the lips, and her hazel eyes were blazing, as she cut into his apologies for Blood.

"They must, indeed, if his other associates allowed him to live after that."

"Oh, the thing was done in fair fight, I am told."

"Who told you?"

"A man who sailed with them, a Frenchman named Cahusac, whom I found in a waterside tavern in St. Nicholas. He was Levasseur's lieutenant, and he was present on the island where the thing happened, and when Levasseur was killed."

"And the girl? Did he say the girl was present, too?"

"Yes. She was a witness of the encounter. Blood carried her off when he had disposed of his brother-buccaneer."

"And the dead man's followers allowed it?" He caught the note of incredulity in her voice, but missed the note of relief with which it was blent. "Oh, I don't believe the tale. I won't believe it!"

"I honour you for that, Miss Bishop. It strained my own belief that men should be so callous, until this Cahusac afforded me the explanation."

"What?" She checked her unbelief, an unbelief that had uplifted her from an inexplicable dismay. Clutching the rail, she swung round to face his lordship with that question. Later he was to remember and perceive in her present behaviour a certain oddness which went disregarded now.

"Blood purchased their consent, and his right to carry the girl off. He paid them in pearls that were worth more than twenty thousand pieces of eight." His lordship laughed again with a touch of contempt. "A handsome price! Faith, they're scoundrels all—just thieving, venal curs. And faith, it's a pretty tale this for a lady's ear."

She looked away from him again, and found that her sight was blurred. After a moment in a voice less steady than before she asked him:

"Why should this Frenchman have told you such a tale? Did he hate this Captain Blood?"

"I did not gather that," said his lordship slowly. "He related it . . . oh, just as a commonplace, an instance of buccaneering ways."

"A commonplace!" said she. "My God! A commonplace!"

"I dare say that we are all savages under the cloak that civilization fashions for us," said his lordship. "But this Blood, now, was a man of considerable parts, from what else this Cahusac told me. He was a bachelor of medicine . . ."

"That is true, to my own knowledge."

"And he has seen much foreign service on sea and land. Cahusac said—though this I hardly credit—that he had fought under de Ruyter."

"That also is true," said she. She sighed heavily. "Your Cahusac seems to have been accurate enough. Alas!"

"You are sorry, then?"

She looked at him. She was very pale, he noticed.

"As we are sorry to hear of the death of one we have esteemed. Once I held him in regard for an unfortunate but worthy gentleman. Now . . ."

She checked, and smiled a little crooked smile. "Such a man is best forgotten."

And upon that she passed at once to speak of other things.

The friendship, which it was her great gift to command in all she met, grew steadily between those two in the little time remaining, until the event befell that marred what was promising to be the pleasantest stage of his lordship's voyage.

The marplot was the mad-dog Spanish Admiral, whom they encountered on the second day out, when halfway across the Gulf of Gonaves. The Captain of the *Royal Mary* was not disposed to be intimidated even when Don Miguel opened fire on him. Observing the Spaniard's plentiful seaboard towering high above the water and offering him so splendid a mark, the Englishman was moved to scorn. If this Don who flew the banner of Castile wanted a fight, the *Royal Mary* was just the ship to oblige him. It may be that he was justified of his gallant confidence, and that he would that day have put an end to the wild career of Don Miguel de Espinosa, but that a lucky shot from the *Milagrosa* got among some powder stored in his forecastle, and blew up half his ship almost before the fight had started. How the powder came there will never now be known, and the gallant Captain himself did not survive to enquire into it.

Before the men of the *Royal Mary* had recovered from their consternation, their captain killed and a third of their number destroyed with him, the ship yawing and rocking helplessly in a crippled state, the Spaniards boarded her.

In the Captain's cabin under the poop, to which Miss Bishop had been conducted for safety, Lord Julian was seeking to comfort and encourage her, with assurances that all would yet be well, at the very moment when Don Miguel was stepping aboard. Lord Julian himself was none so steady, and his face was undoubtedly pale. Not that he was by any means a coward. But this cooped-up fighting on an unknown element in a thing of wood that might at any moment founder under his feet into the depths of ocean was disturbing to one who could be brave enough ashore. Fortunately Miss Bishop did not appear to be in desperate need of the poor comfort he was in case to offer. Certainly she, too, was pale, and her hazel eyes may have looked a little larger than usual. But she had herself well in hand. Half sitting, half leaning on the Captain's table, she preserved her courage sufficiently to seek to calm the octoroon waiting-woman who was grovelling at her feet in a state of terror.

And then the cabin-door flew open, and Don Miguel himself, tall, sunburned, and aquiline of face, strode in. Lord Julian span round, to face him, and clapped a hand to his sword.

The Spaniard was brisk and to the point.

"Don't be a fool," he said in his own tongue, "or you'll come by a fool's end. Your ship is sinking."

There were three or four men in morions behind Don Miguel, and Lord Julian realized the position. He released his hilt, and a couple of feet or so of steel slid softly back into the scabbard. But Don Miguel smiled, with a flash of white teeth behind his grizzled beard, and held out his hand.

"If you please," he said.

Lord Julian hesitated. His eyes strayed to Miss Bishop's.

"I think you had better," said that composed young lady, whereupon with a shrug his lordship made the required surrender.

"Come you—all of you—aboard my ship," Don Miguel invited them, and strode out.

They went, of course. For one thing the Spaniard had force to compel them; for another a ship which he announced to be sinking offered them little inducement to remain. They stayed no longer than was necessary to enable Miss Bishop to collect some spare articles of dress and my lord to snatch up his valise.

As for the survivors in that ghastly shambles that had been the *Royal Mary*, they were abandoned by the Spaniards to their own resources. Let them take to the boats, and if those did not suffice them, let them swim or drown. If Lord Julian and Miss Bishop were retained, it was because Don Miguel perceived their obvious value. He received them in his cabin with great urbanity. Urbanely he desired to have the honour of being acquainted with their names.

Lord Julian, sick with horror of the spectacle he had just witnessed, commanded himself with difficulty to supply them. Then haughtily he demanded to know in his turn the name of their aggressor. He was in an exceedingly ill temper. He realized that if he had done nothing positively discreditable in the unusual and difficult position into which Fate had thrust him, at least he had done nothing creditable. This might have mattered less but that the spectator of his indifferent performance was a lady. He was determined if possible to do better now.

"I am Don Miguel de Espinosa," he was answered. "Admiral of the Navies of the Catholic King."

Lord Julian gasped. If Spain made such a hubbub about the depredations of a runagate adventurer like Captain Blood, what could not England answer now?

"Will you tell me, then, why you behave like a damned pirate?" he asked. And added: "I hope you realize what will be the consequences, and the strict account to which you shall be brought for this day's work, for the blood you have murderously shed, and for your violence to this lady and to myself."

"I offer you no violence," said the Admiral, smiling, as only the man who holds the trumps can smile. "On the contrary, I have saved your lives . . ."

"Saved our lives!" Lord Julian was momentarily speechless before such callous impudence. "And what of the lives you have destroyed in wanton butchery? By God, man, they shall cost you dear."

Don Miguel's smile persisted. "It is possible. All things are possible. Meantime it is your own lives that will cost you dear. Colonel Bishop is a rich man; and you, milord, are no doubt also rich. I will consider and fix your ransom."

"So that you're just the damned murderous pirate I was supposing you," stormed his lordship. "And you have the impudence to call yourself the Admiral of the Navies of the Catholic King? We shall see what your Catholic King will have to say to it."

The Admiral ceased to smile. He revealed something of the rage that had eaten into his brain. "You do not understand," he said. "It is that I treat you English heretic dogs just as you English heretic dogs have treated Spaniards upon the seas—you robbers and thieves out of hell! I have the honesty to do it in my own name—but you, you perfidious beasts, you send your Captain Bloods, your Hagthorpes, and your Morgans against us and disclaim responsibility for what they do. Like Pilate, you wash your hands." He laughed savagely. "Let Spain play the part of Pilate. Let her disclaim responsibility for me, when your ambassador at the Escurial shall go whining to the Supreme Council of this act of piracy by Don Miguel de Espinosa."

"Captain Blood and the rest are not admirals of England!" cried Lord Julian.

"Are they not? How do I know? How does Spain know? Are you not liars all, you English heretics?"

"Sir!" Lord Julian's voice was harsh as a rasp, his eyes flashed. Instinctively he swung a hand to the place where his sword habitually hung. Then he shrugged and sneered: "Of course," said he, "it sorts with all I have heard of Spanish honour and all that I have seen of yours that you should insult a man who is unarmed and your prisoner."

The Admiral's face flamed scarlet. He half raised his hand to strike. And then, restrained, perhaps, by the very words that had cloaked the retorting insult, he turned on his heel abruptly and went out without answering.

XIX. The Meeting

As the door slammed after the departing Admiral, Lord Julian turned to Arabella, and actually smiled. He felt that he was doing better, and gathered from it an almost childish satisfaction—childish in all the circumstances. "Decidedly I think I had the last word there," he said, with a toss of his golden ringlets.

Miss Bishop, seated at the cabin-table, looked at him steadily, without returning his smile. "Does it matter, then, so much, having the last word? I am thinking of those poor fellows on the *Royal Mary*. Many of them have had their last word, indeed. And for what? A fine ship sunk, a score of lives lost, thrice that number now in jeopardy, and all for what?"

"You are overwrought, ma'am. I . . ."

"Overwrought!" She uttered a single sharp note of laughter. "I assure you I am calm. I am asking you a question, Lord Julian. Why has this Spaniard done all this? To what purpose?"

"You heard him." Lord Julian shrugged angrily. "Blood-lust," he explained shortly.

"Blood-lust?" she asked. She was amazed. "Does such a thing exist, then? It is insane, monstrous."

"Fiendish," his lordship agreed. "Devil's work."

"I don't understand. At Bridgetown three years ago there was a Spanish raid, and things were done that should have been impossible to men, horrible, revolting things which strain belief, which seem, when I think of them now, like the illusions of some evil dream. Are men just beasts?"

"Men?" said Lord Julian, staring. "Say Spaniards, and I'll agree." He was an Englishman speaking of hereditary foes. And yet there was a measure of truth in what he said. "This is the Spanish way in the New World. Faith, almost it justifies such men as Blood of what they do."

She shivered, as if cold, and setting her elbows on the table, she took her chin in her hands, and sat staring before her.

Observing her, his lordship noticed how drawn and white her face had grown. There was reason enough for that, and for worse. Not any other woman of his acquaintance would have preserved her self-control in such an ordeal; and of fear, at least, at no time had Miss Bishop shown any sign. It is impossible that he did not find her admirable.

A Spanish steward entered bearing a silver chocolate service and a box of Peruvian candies, which he placed on the table before the lady.

"With the Admiral's homage," he said, then bowed, and withdrew.

Miss Bishop took no heed of him or his offering, but continued to stare before her, lost in thought. Lord Julian took a turn in the long low cabin, which was lighted by a skylight above and great square windows astern. It was luxuriously appointed: there were rich Eastern rugs on the floor, well-filled bookcases stood against the bulkheads, and there was a carved walnut sideboard laden with silverware. On a long, low chest standing under the middle stern port lay a guitar that was gay with ribbons. Lord Julian picked it up, twanged the strings once as if moved by nervous irritation, and put it down.

He turned again to face Miss Bishop.

"I came out here," he said, "to put down piracy. But—blister me!—I begin to think that the French are right in desiring piracy to continue as a curb upon these Spanish scoundrels."

He was to be strongly confirmed in that opinion before many hours were past. Meanwhile their treatment at the hands of Don Miguel was considerate and courteous. It confirmed the opinion, contemptuously expressed to his lordship by Miss Bishop, that since they were to be held to ransom they need not fear any violence or hurt. A cabin was placed at the disposal of the lady and her terrified woman, and another at Lord Julian's. They were given the freedom of the ship, and bidden to dine at the Admiral's table; nor were his further intentions regarding them mentioned, nor yet his immediate destination.

The *Milagrosa*, with her consort the *Hidalga* rolling after her, steered a south by westerly course, then veered to the southeast round Cape Tiburon, and thereafter, standing well out to sea, with the land no more than a cloudy outline to larboard, she headed directly east, and so ran straight into the arms of Captain Blood, who was making for the Windward Passage, as we know. That happened early on the following morning. After having systematically hunted his enemy in vain for a year, Don Miguel chanced upon him in this unexpected and entirely fortuitous fashion. But that is the ironic way of Fortune. It was also the way of Fortune that Don Miguel should thus come upon the *Arabella* at a time when, separated from the rest of the fleet, she was alone and at a disadvantage. It looked to Don Miguel as if the luck which so long had been on Blood's side had at last veered in his own favour.

Miss Bishop, newly risen, had come out to take the air on the quarter-deck with his lordship in attendance—as you would expect of so gallant a gentleman—when she beheld the big red ship that had once been the *Cinco Llagas* out of Cadiz. The vessel was bearing down upon them, her mountains of snowy canvas bellying forward, the long pennon with the cross of St. George fluttering from her main truck in the morning breeze, the gilded portholes in her red hull, and the gilded beak-head aflash in the morning sun.

Miss Bishop was not to recognize this for that same *Cinco Llagas* which she had seen once before—on a tragic day in Barbados three years ago. To her it was just a great ship that was heading resolutely, majestically, towards them, and an Englishman to judge by the pennon she was flying. The sight thrilled her curiously; it awoke in her an uplifting sense of pride that took no account of the danger to herself in the encounter that must now be inevitable.

Beside her on the poop, whither they had climbed to obtain a better view, and equally arrested and at gaze, stood Lord Julian. But he shared none of her exultation. He had been in his first sea-fight yesterday, and he felt that the experience would suffice him for a very considerable time. This, I insist, is no reflection upon his courage.

"Look," said Miss Bishop, pointing; and to his infinite amazement he observed that her eyes were sparkling. Did she realize, he wondered, what was afoot? Her next sentence resolved his doubt. "She is English, and she comes resolutely on. She means to fight."

"God help her, then," said his lordship gloomily. "Her captain must be mad. What can he hope to do against two such heavy hulks as these? If they could so easily blow the *Royal Mary* out of the water, what will they do to this vessel? Look at that devil Don Miguel. He's utterly disgusting in his glee."

From the quarter-deck, where he moved amid the frenzy of preparation, the Admiral had turned to flash a backward glance at his prisoners. His eyes were alight, his face transfigured. He flung out an arm to point to the advancing ship, and bawled something in Spanish that was lost to them in the noise of the labouring crew.

They advanced to the poop-rail, and watched the bustle. Telescope in hand on the quarter-deck, Don Miguel was issuing his orders. Already the gunners were kindling their matches; sailors were aloft, taking in sail; others were spreading a stout rope net above the waist, as a protection against falling spars. And meanwhile Don Miguel had been signalling to his consort, in response to which the *Hidalga* had drawn steadily forward until she was now abeam of the *Milagrosa*, half cable's length to starboard, and from the height of the tall poop my lord and Miss Bishop could see her own bustle of preparation. And they could discern signs of it now aboard the advancing English ship as well. She was furling tops and mainsail, stripping in fact to mizzen and sprit for the coming action. Thus, almost silently without challenge or exchange of signals, had action been mutually determined.

Of necessity now, under diminished sail, the advance of the *Arabella* was slower; but it was none the less steady. She was already within saker shot, and they could make out the figures stirring on her forecastle and the brass guns gleaming on her prow. The gunners of the *Milagrosa* raised their linstocks and blew upon their smouldering matches, looking up impatiently at the Admiral.

But the Admiral solemnly shook his head.

"Patience," he exhorted them. "Save your fire until we have him. He is coming straight to his doom—straight to the yardarm and the rope that have been so long waiting for him."

"Stab me!" said his lordship. "This Englishman may be gallant enough to accept battle against such odds. But there are times when discretion is a better quality than gallantry in a commander."

"Gallantry will often win through, even against overwhelming strength," said Miss Bishop. He looked at her, and noted in her bearing only excitement. Of fear he could still discern no trace. His lordship was past amazement. She was not by any means the kind of woman to which life had accustomed him.

"Presently," he said, "you will suffer me to place you under cover."

"I can see best from here," she answered him. And added quietly: "I am praying for this Englishman. He must be very brave."

Under his breath Lord Julian damned the fellow's bravery.

The *Arabella* was advancing now along a course which, if continued, must carry her straight between the two Spanish ships. My lord pointed it out. "He's crazy surely!" he cried. "He's driving straight into a death-trap. He'll be crushed to splinters between the two. No wonder that black-faced Don is holding his fire. In his place, I should do the same."

But even at that moment the Admiral raised his hand; in the waist, below him, a trumpet blared, and immediately the gunner on the prow touched off his guns. As the thunder of them rolled out, his lordship saw ahead beyond the English ship and to larboard of her two heavy splashes. Almost at once two successive spurts of flame leapt from the brass cannon on the *Arabella*'s beak-head, and scarcely had the watchers on the poop seen the shower of spray, where one of the shots struck the water near them, then with a rending crash and a shiver that shook the *Milagrosa* from stem to stern, the other came to lodge in her forecastle. To avenge that blow, the *Hidalga* blazed at the Englishman with both her forward guns. But even at that short range—between two and three hundred yards—neither shot took effect.

At a hundred yards the *Arabella*'s forward guns, which had meanwhile been reloaded, fired again at the *Milagrosa*, and this time smashed her bowsprit into splinters; so that for a moment she yawed wildly to port. Don Miguel swore profanely, and then, as the helm was put over to swing her back to her course, his own prow replied. But the aim was too high, and whilst one of the shots tore through the *Arabella*'s shrouds and scarred her mainmast, the other again went wide. And when the smoke of that discharge had lifted, the English ship was found almost between the Spaniards, her bows in line with theirs and coming steadily on into what his lordship deemed a death-trap.

Lord Julian held his breath, and Miss Bishop gasped, clutching the rail before her. She had a glimpse of the wickedly grinning face of Don Miguel, and the grinning faces of the men at the guns in the waist.

At last the *Arabella* was right between the Spanish ships prow to poop and poop to prow. Don Miguel spoke to the trumpeter, who had mounted the quarter-deck and stood now at the Admiral's elbow. The man raised the silver bugle that was to give the signal for the broadsides of both ships. But even as he placed it to his lips, the Admiral seized his arm, to arrest him. Only then had he perceived what was so obvious—or should have been to an experienced sea-fighter: he had delayed too long and Captain Blood had outmanœuvred him. In attempting to fire now upon the Englishman, the *Milagrosa* and her consort would also be firing into each other. Too late he ordered his helmsman to put the tiller hard over and swing the ship to larboard, as a preliminary to manœuvring for a less impossible position of attack. At that very moment the *Arabella* seemed to explode as she swept by. Eighteen guns from each of her flanks emptied themselves at that point-blank range into the hulls of the two Spanish vessels.

Half stunned by that reverberating thunder, and thrown off her balance by the sudden lurch of the ship under her feet, Miss Bishop hurtled violently against Lord Julian, who kept his feet only by clutching the rail on which he had been leaning. Billowing clouds of smoke to starboard blotted out everything, and its acrid odour, taking them presently in the throat, set them gasping and coughing.

From the grim confusion and turmoil in the waist below arose a clamour of fierce Spanish blasphemies and the screams of maimed men. The *Milagrosa* staggered slowly ahead, a gaping rent in her bulwarks; her foremast was shattered, fragments of the yards hanging in the netting spread below. Her beak-head was in splinters, and a shot had smashed through into the great cabin, reducing it to wreckage.

Don Miguel was bawling orders wildly, and peering ever and anon through the curtain of smoke that was drifting slowly astern, in his anxiety to ascertain how it might have fared with the *Hidalga*.

Suddenly, and ghostly at first through that lifting haze, loomed the outline of a ship; gradually the lines of her red hull became more and more sharply defined as she swept nearer with poles all bare save for the spread of canvas on her sprit.

Instead of holding to her course as Don Miguel had expected she would, the *Arabella* had gone about under cover of the smoke, and sailing now in the same direction as the *Milagrosa*, was converging sharply upon her across the wind, so sharply that almost before the frenzied Don Miguel had realized the situation, his vessel staggered under the rending impact with which the other came hurtling alongside. There was a rattle and clank of metal as a dozen grapnels fell, and tore and caught in the timbers of the *Milagrosa*, and the Spaniard was firmly gripped in the tentacles of the English ship.

Beyond her and now well astern the veil of smoke was rent at last and the *Hidalga* was revealed in desperate case. She was bilging fast, with an ominous list to larboard, and it could be no more than a question of moments before she settled down. The attention of her hands was being entirely given to a desperate endeavour to launch the boats in time.

Of this Don Miguel's anguished eyes had no more than a fleeting but comprehensive glimpse before his own decks were invaded by a wild, yelling swarm of boarders from the grappling ship. Never was confidence so quickly changed into despair, never was hunter more swiftly converted into helpless prey. For helpless the Spaniards were. The swiftly executed boarding manœuvre had caught them almost unawares in the moment of confusion following the punishing broadside they had sustained at such short range. For a moment there was a valiant effort by some of Don Miguel's officers to rally the men for a stand against these invaders. But the Spaniards, never at their best in close-quarter fighting, were here demoralized by knowledge of the enemies with whom they had to deal. Their hastily formed ranks were smashed before they could be steadied; driven across the waist to the break of the poop on the one side, and up to the forecastle bulkheads on the other, the fighting resolved itself into a series of skirmishes between groups. And whilst this was doing above, another horde of buccaneers swarmed through the hatch to the main deck below to overpower the gun-crews at their stations there.

On the quarter deck, towards which an overwhelming wave of buccaneers was sweeping, led by a one-eyed giant, who was naked to the waist, stood Don Miguel, numbed by despair and rage. Above and behind him on the poop, Lord Julian and Miss Bishop looked on, his lordship aghast at the fury of this cooped-up fighting, the lady's brave calm conquered at last by horror so that she reeled there sick and faint.

Soon, however, the rage of that brief fight was spent. They saw the banner of Castile come fluttering down from the masthead. A buccaneer had slashed the halyard with his cutlass. The boarders were in possession, and on the upper deck groups of disarmed Spaniards stood huddled now like herded sheep.

Suddenly Miss Bishop recovered from her nausea, to lean forward staring wild-eyed, whilst if possible her cheeks turned yet a deadlier hue than they had been already.

Picking his way daintily through that shambles in the waist came a tall man with a deeply tanned face that was shaded by a Spanish headpiece. He was armed in back-and-breast of black steel beautifully damascened with golden arabesques. Over this, like a stole, he wore a sling of scarlet silk, from each end of which hung a silver-mounted pistol. Up the broad companion to the quarter-deck he came, moving with easy assurance, until he stood before the Spanish Admiral. Then he bowed stiff and formally. A crisp, metallic voice, speaking perfect Spanish, reached those two spectators on the poop, and increased the admiring wonder in which Lord Julian had observed the man's approach.

"We meet again at last, Don Miguel," it said. "I hope you are satisfied. Although the meeting may not be exactly as you pictured it, at least it has been very ardently sought and desired by you."

Speechless, livid of face, his mouth distorted and his breathing laboured, Don Miguel de Espinosa received the irony of that man to whom he attributed his ruin and more beside. Then he uttered an inarticulate cry of rage, and his hand swept to his sword. But even as his fingers closed upon the hilt, the other's closed upon his wrist to arrest the action.

"Calm, Don Miguel!" he was quietly but firmly enjoined. "Do not recklessly invite the ugly extremes such as you would, yourself, have practised had the situation been reversed."

A moment they stood looking into each other's eyes.

"What do you intend by me?" the Spaniard enquired at last, his voice hoarse.

Captain Blood shrugged. The firm lips smiled a little. "All that I intend has been already accomplished. And lest it increase your rancour, I beg you to observe that you have brought it entirely upon yourself. You would have it so." He turned and pointed to the boats, which his men were heaving from the boom amidships. "Your boats are being launched. You are at liberty to embark in them with your men before we scuttle this ship. Yonder are the shores of Hispaniola. You should make them safely. And if you'll take my advice, sir, you'll not hunt me again. I think I am unlucky to you. Get you home to Spain, Don Miguel, and to concerns that you understand better than this trade of the sea."

For a long moment the defeated Admiral continued to stare his hatred in silence, then, still without speaking, he went down the companion, staggering like a drunken man, his useless rapier clattering behind him. His conqueror, who had not even troubled to disarm him, watched him go, then turned and faced those two immediately above him on the poop. Lord Julian might have observed, had he been less taken up with other things, that the fellow seemed suddenly to stiffen, and that he turned pale under his deep tan. A moment he stood at gaze; then suddenly and swiftly he came up the steps. Lord Julian stood forward to meet him.

"Ye don't mean, sir, that you'll let that Spanish scoundrel go free?" he cried.

The gentleman in the black corselet appeared to become aware of his lordship for the first time.

"And who the devil may you be?" he asked, with a marked Irish accent. "And what business may it be of yours, at all?"

His lordship conceived that the fellow's truculence and utter lack of proper deference must be corrected. "I am Lord Julian Wade," he announced, with that object.

Apparently the announcement made no impression.

"Are you, indeed! Then perhaps ye'll explain what the plague you're doing aboard this ship?"

Lord Julian controlled himself to afford the desired explanation. He did so shortly and impatiently.

"He took you prisoner, did he—along with Miss Bishop there?"

"You are acquainted with Miss Bishop?" cried his lordship, passing from surprise to surprise.

But this mannerless fellow had stepped past him, and was making a leg to the lady, who on her side remained unresponsive and forbidding to the point of scorn. Observing this, he turned to answer Lord Julian's question.

"I had that honour once," said he. "But it seems that Miss Bishop has a shorter memory."

His lips were twisted into a wry smile, and there was pain in the blue eyes that gleamed so vividly under his black brows, pain blending with the mockery of his voice. But of all this it was the mockery alone that was perceived by Miss Bishop; she resented it.

"I do not number thieves and pirates among my acquaintance, Captain Blood," said she; whereupon his lordship exploded in excitement.

"Captain Blood!" he cried. "Are you Captain Blood?"

"What else were ye supposing?"

Blood asked the question wearily, his mind on other things. "I do not number thieves and pirates among my acquaintance." The cruel phrase filled his brain, reëchoing and reverberating there.

But Lord Julian would not be denied. He caught him by the sleeve with one hand, whilst with the other he pointed after the retreating, dejected figure of Don Miguel.

"Do I understand that ye're not going to hang that Spanish scoundrel?"

"What for should I be hanging him?"

"Because he's just a damned pirate, as I can prove, as I have proved already."

"Ah!" said Blood, and Lord Julian marvelled at the sudden haggardness of a countenance that had been so devil-may-care but a few moments since. "I am a damned pirate, myself; and so I am merciful with my kind. Don Miguel goes free."

Lord Julian gasped. "After what I've told you that he has done? After his sinking of the *Royal Mary?* After his treatment of me—of us?" Lord Julian protested indignantly.

"I am not in the service of England, or of any nation, sir. And I am not concerned with any wrongs her flag may suffer."

His lordship recoiled before the furious glance that blazed at him out of Blood's haggard face. But the passion faded as swiftly as it had arisen. It was in a level voice that the Captain added:

"If you'll escort Miss Bishop aboard my ship, I shall be obliged to you. I beg that you'll make haste. We are about to scuttle this hulk."

He turned slowly to depart. But again Lord Julian interposed. Containing his indignant amazement, his lordship delivered himself coldly. "Captain Blood, you disappoint me. I had hopes of great things for you."

"Go to the devil," said Captain Blood, turning on his heel, and so departed.

XX. THIEF AND PIRATE

Captain Blood paced the poop of his ship alone in the tepid dusk, and the growing golden radiance of the great poop lantern in which a seaman had just lighted the three lamps. About him all was peace. The signs of the day's battle had been effaced, the decks had been swabbed, and order was restored above and below. A group of men squatting about the main hatch were drowsily chanting, their hardened natures softened, perhaps, by the calm and beauty of the night. They were the men of the larboard watch, waiting for eight bells which was imminent.

Captain Blood did not hear them; he did not hear anything save the echo of those cruel words which had dubbed him thief and pirate.

Thief and pirate!

It is an odd fact of human nature that a man may for years possess the knowledge that a certain thing must be of a certain fashion, and yet be shocked to discover through his own senses that the fact is in perfect harmony with his beliefs. When first, three years ago, at Tortuga he had been urged upon the adventurer's course which he had followed ever since, he had known in what opinion Arabella Bishop must hold him if he succumbed. Only the conviction that already she was for ever lost to him, by introducing a certain desperate recklessness into his soul had supplied the final impulse to drive him upon his rover's course.

That he should ever meet her again had not entered his calculations, had found no place in his dreams. They were, he conceived, irrevocably and for ever parted. Yet, in spite of this, in spite even of the persuasion that to her this reflection that was his torment could bring no regrets, he had kept the thought of her ever before him in all those wild years of filibustering. He had used it as a curb not only upon himself, but also upon those who followed him. Never had buccaneers been so rigidly held in hand, never had they been so firmly restrained, never so debarred from the excesses of rapine and lust that were usual in their kind as those who sailed with Captain Blood. It was, you will remember, stipulated in their articles that in these as in other matters they must submit to the commands of their leader. And because of the singular good fortune which had attended his leadership, he had been able to impose that stern condition of a discipline unknown before among buccaneers. How would not these men laugh at him now if he were to tell them that this he had done out of respect for a slip of a girl of whom he had fallen romantically enamoured? How would not that laughter swell if he added that this girl had that day informed him that she did not number thieves and pirates among her acquaintance.

Thief and pirate!

How the words clung, how they stung and burnt his brain!

It did not occur to him, being no psychologist, nor learned in the tortuous workings of the feminine mind, that the fact that she should bestow upon him those epithets in the very moment and circumstance of their meeting was in itself curious. He did not perceive the problem thus presented; therefore he could not probe it. Else he might have concluded that if in a moment in which by delivering her from captivity he deserved her gratitude, yet she expressed herself in bitterness, it must be because that bitterness was anterior to the gratitude and deep-seated. She had been moved to it by hearing of the course he had taken. Why? It was what he did not ask himself, or some ray of light might have come to brighten his dark, his utterly evil despondency. Surely she would never have been so moved had she not cared—had she not felt that in what he did there was a personal wrong to herself. Surely, he might have reasoned, nothing short of this could have moved her to such a degree of bitterness and scorn as that which she had displayed.

That is how you will reason. Not so, however, reasoned Captain Blood. Indeed, that night he reasoned not at all. His soul was given up to conflict between the almost sacred love he had borne her in all these years and the evil passion which she had now awakened in him. Extremes touch, and in touching may for a space become confused, indistinguishable. And the extremes of love and hate were to-night so confused in the soul of Captain Blood that in their fusion they made up a monstrous passion.

Thief and pirate!

Pitt answered readily. There was no reason why he should not, though he began to find the catechism intriguing.

"Captain Blood killed him."

"Why?"

Pitt hesitated. It was not a tale for a maid's ears.

"They quarrelled," he said shortly.

"Was it about a . . . a lady?" Miss Bishop relentlessly pursued him.

"You might put it that way."

"What was the lady's name?"

Pitt's eyebrows went up; still he answered.

"Miss d'Ogeron. She was the daughter of the Governor of Tortuga. She had gone off with this fellow Levasseur, and . . . and Peter delivered her out of his dirty clutches. He was a black-hearted scoundrel, and deserved what Peter gave him."

"I see. And . . . and yet Captain Blood has not married her?"

"Not yet," laughed Pitt, who knew the utter groundlessness of the common gossip in Tortuga which pronounced Mdlle. d'Ogeron the Captain's future wife.

Miss Bishop nodded in silence, and Jeremy Pitt turned to depart, relieved that the catechism was ended. He paused in the doorway to impart a piece of information.

"Maybe it'll comfort you to know that the Captain has altered our course for your benefit. It's his intention to put you both ashore on the coast of Jamaica, as near Port Royal as we dare venture. We've gone about, and if this wind holds ye'll soon be home again, mistress."

"Vastly obliging of him," drawled his lordship, seeing that Miss Bishop made no shift to answer. Sombre-eyed she sat, staring into vacancy.

"Indeed, ye may say so," Pitt agreed. "He's taking risks that few would take in his place. But that's always been his way."

He went out, leaving his lordship pensive, those dreamy blue eyes of his intently studying Miss Bishop's face for all their dreaminess; his mind increasingly uneasy. At length Miss Bishop looked at him, and spoke.

"Your Cahusac told you no more than the truth, it seems."

"I perceived that you were testing it," said his lordship. "I am wondering precisely why."

Receiving no answer, he continued to observe her silently, his long, tapering fingers toying with a ringlet of the golden periwig in which his long face was set.

Miss Bishop sat bemused, her brows knit, her brooding glance seeming to study the fine Spanish point that edged the tablecloth. At last his lordship broke the silence.

"He amazes me, this man," said he, in his slow, languid voice that never seemed to change its level. "That he should alter his course for us is in itself matter for wonder; but that he should take a risk on our behalf—that he should venture into Jamaica waters . . . It amazes me, as I have said."

Miss Bishop raised her eyes, and looked at him. She appeared to be very thoughtful. Then her lip flickered curiously, almost scornfully, it seemed to him. Her slender fingers drummed the table.

"What is still more amazing is that he does not hold us to ransom," said she at last.

"It's what you deserve."

"Oh, and why, if you please?"

"For speaking to him as you did."

"I usually call things by their names."

"Do you? Stab me! I shouldn't boast of it. It argues either extreme youth or extreme foolishness." His lordship, you see, belonged to my Lord Sunderland's school of philosophy. He added after a moment: "So does the display of ingratitude."

A faint colour stirred in her cheeks. "Your lordship is evidently aggrieved with me. I am disconsolate. I hope your lordship's grievance is sounder than your views of life. It is news to me that ingratitude is a fault only to be found in the young and the foolish."

"I didn't say so, ma'am." There was a tartness in his tone evoked by the tartness she had used. "If you would do me the honour to listen, you would not misapprehend me. For if unlike you I do not always say precisely what I think, at least I say precisely what I wish to convey. To be ungrateful may be human; but to display it is childish."

"I . . . I don't think I understand." Her brows were knit. "How have I been ungrateful and to whom?"

"To whom? To Captain Blood. Didn't he come to our rescue?"

"Did he?" Her manner was frigid. "I wasn't aware that he knew of our presence aboard the *Milagrosa*."

His lordship permitted himself the slightest gesture of impatience.

"You are probably aware that he delivered us," said he. "And living as you have done in these savage places of the world, you can hardly fail to be aware of what is known even in England: that this fellow Blood strictly confines himself to making war upon the Spaniards. So that to call him thief and pirate as you did was to overstate the case against him at a time when it would have been more prudent to have understated it."

"Prudence?" Her voice was scornful. "What have I to do with prudence?"

"Nothing—as I perceive. But, at least, study generosity. I tell you frankly, ma'am, that in Blood's place I should never have been so nice. Sink me! When you consider what he has suffered at the hands of his fellow-countrymen, you may marvel with me that he should trouble to discriminate between Spanish and English. To be sold into slavery! Ugh!" His lordship shuddered. "And to a damned colonial planter!" He checked abruptly. "I beg your pardon, Miss Bishop. For the moment . . ."

"You were carried away by your heat in defence of this . . . sea-robber." Miss Bishop's scorn was almost fierce.

His lordship stared at her again. Then he half-closed his large, pale eyes, and tilted his head a little. "I wonder why you hate him so," he said softly.

He saw the sudden scarlet flame upon her cheeks, the heavy frown that descended upon her brow. He had made her very angry, he judged. But there was no explosion. She recovered.

"Hate him? Lord! What a thought! I don't regard the fellow at all."

"Then ye should, ma'am." His lordship spoke his thought frankly. "He's worth regarding. He'd be an acquisition to the King's navy—a man that can do the things he did this morning. His service under de Ruyter wasn't wasted on him. That was a great seaman, and—blister me!—the pupil's worthy the master if I am a judge of anything. I doubt if the Royal Navy can show his equal. To thrust himself deliberately between those two, at point-blank range, and so turn the tables on them! It asks courage, resource, and invention. And we land-lubbers were not the only ones he tricked by his manœuvre. That Spanish Admiral never guessed the intent until it was too late and Blood held him in check. A great man, Miss Bishop. A man worth regarding."

Miss Bishop was moved to sarcasm.

"You should use your influence with my Lord Sunderland to have the King offer him a commission."

His lordship laughed softly. "Faith, it's done already. I have his commission in my pocket." And he increased her amazement by a brief exposition of the circumstances. In that amazement he left her, and went in quest of Blood. But he was still intrigued. If she were a little less uncompromising in her attitude towards Blood, his lordship would have been happier.

He found the Captain pacing the quarter-deck, a man mentally exhausted from wrestling with the Devil, although of this particular occupation his lordship could have no possible suspicion. With the amiable familiarity he used, Lord Julian slipped an arm through one of the Captain's, and fell into step beside him.

"What's this?" snapped Blood, whose mood was fierce and raw. His lordship was not disturbed.

"I desire, sir, that we be friends," said he suavely.

"That's mighty condescending of you!"

Lord Julian ignored the obvious sarcasm.

"It's an odd coincidence that we should have been brought together in this fashion, considering that I came out to the Indies especially to seek you."

"Ye're not by any means the first to do that," the other scoffed. "But they've mainly been Spaniards, and they hadn't your luck."

"You misapprehend me completely," said Lord Julian. And on that he proceeded to explain himself and his mission.

When he had done, Captain Blood, who until that moment had stood still under the spell of his astonishment, disengaged his arm from his lordship's, and stood squarely before him.

"Ye're my guest aboard this ship," said he, "and I still have some notion of decent behaviour left me from other days, thief and pirate though I may be. So I'll not be telling you what I think of you for daring to bring me this offer, or of my Lord Sunderland— since he's your kinsman—for having the impudence to send it. But it does not surprise me at all that one who is a minister of James Stuart's should conceive that every man is to be seduced by bribes into betraying those who trust him." He flung out an arm in the direction of the waist, whence came the half-melancholy chant of the lounging buccaneers.

"Again you misapprehend me," cried Lord Julian, between concern and indignation. "That is not intended. Your followers will be included in your commission."

"And d'ye think they'll go with me to hunt their brethren—the Brethren of the Coast? On my soul, Lord Julian, it is yourself does the misapprehending. Are there not even notions of honour left in England? Oh, and there's more to it than that, even. D'ye think I could take a commission of King James's? I tell you I wouldn't be soiling my hands with it—thief and pirate's hands though they be. Thief and pirate is what you heard Miss Bishop call me to-day—a thing of scorn, an outcast. And who made me that? Who made me thief and pirate?"

"If you were a rebel . . . ?" his lordship was beginning.

"Ye must know that I was no such thing—no rebel at all. It wasn't even pretended. If it were, I could forgive them. But not even that cloak could they cast upon their foulness. Oh, no; there was no mistake. I was convicted for what I did, neither more nor less. That bloody vampire Jeffreys—bad cess to him!—sentenced me to death, and his worthy master James Stuart afterwards sent me into slavery, because I had performed an act of mercy; because compassionately and without thought for creed or politics I had sought to relieve the sufferings of a fellow-creature; because I had dressed the wounds of a man who was convicted of treason. That was all my offence. You'll find it in the records. And for that I was sold into slavery: because by the law of England, as administered by James Stuart in violation of the laws of God, who harbours or comforts a rebel is himself adjudged guilty of rebellion. D'ye dream, man, what it is to be a slave?"

He checked suddenly at the very height of his passion. A moment he paused, then cast it from him as if it had been a cloak. His voice sank again. He uttered a little laugh of weariness and contempt.

"But there! I grow hot for nothing at all. I explain myself, I think, and God knows, it is not my custom. I am grateful to you, Lord Julian, for your kindly intentions. I am so. But ye'll understand, perhaps. Ye look as if ye might."

Lord Julian stood still. He was deeply stricken by the other's words, the passionate, eloquent outburst that in a few sharp, clear-cut strokes had so convincingly presented the man's bitter case against humanity, his complete apologia and justification for all that could be laid to his charge. His lordship looked at that keen, intrepid face gleaming lividly in the light of the great poop lantern, and his own eyes were troubled. He was abashed.

He fetched a heavy sigh. "A pity," he said slowly. "Oh, blister me—a cursed pity!" He held out his hand, moved to it on a sudden generous impulse. "But no offence between us, Captain Blood!"

"Oh, no offence. But . . . I'm a thief and a pirate." He laughed without mirth, and, disregarding the proffered hand, swung on his heel.

Lord Julian stood a moment, watching the tall figure as it moved away towards the taffrail. Then letting his arms fall helplessly to his sides in dejection, he departed.

Just within the doorway of the alley leading to the cabin, he ran into Miss Bishop. Yet she had not been coming out, for her back was towards him, and she was moving in the same direction. He followed her, his mind too full of Captain Blood to be concerned just then with her movements.

In the cabin he flung into a chair, and exploded, with a violence altogether foreign to his nature.

"Damme if ever I met a man I liked better, or even a man I liked as well. Yet there's nothing to be done with him."

"So I heard," she admitted in a small voice. She was very white, and she kept her eyes upon her folded hands.

He looked up in surprise, and then sat conning her with brooding glance. "I wonder, now," he said presently, "if the mischief is of your working. Your words have rankled with him. He threw them at me again and again. He wouldn't take the King's commission; he wouldn't take my hand even. What's to be done with a fellow like that? He'll end on a yardarm for all his luck. And the quixotic fool is running into danger at the present moment on our behalf."

"How?" she asked him with a sudden startled interest.

"How? Have you forgotten that he's sailing to Jamaica, and that Jamaica is the headquarters of the English fleet? True, your uncle commands it . . ."

She leaned across the table to interrupt him, and he observed that her breathing had grown labored, that her eyes were dilating in alarm.

"But there is no hope for him in that!" she cried. "Oh, don't imagine it! He has no bitterer enemy in the world! My uncle is a hard, unforgiving man. I believe that it was nothing but the hope of taking and hanging Captain Blood that made my uncle leave his Barbados plantations to accept the deputy-governorship of Jamaica. Captain Blood doesn't know that, of course . . ." She paused with a little gesture of helplessness.

"I can't think that it would make the least difference if he did," said his lordship gravely. "A man who can forgive such an enemy as Don Miguel and take up this uncompromising attitude with me isn't to be judged by ordinary rules. He's chivalrous to the point of idiocy."

"And yet he has been what he has been and done what he has done in these last three years," said she, but she said it sorrowfully now, without any of her earlier scorn.

Lord Julian was sententious, as I gather that he often was. "Life can be infernally complex," he sighed.

XXI. THE SECRET SERVICE OF KING JAMES

Miss Arabella Bishop was aroused very early on the following morning by the brazen voice of a bugle and the insistent clanging of a bell in the ship's belfry. As she lay awake, idly watching the rippled green water that appeared to be streaming past the heavily glazed porthole, she became gradually aware of the sounds of swift, laboured bustle—the clatter of many feet, the shouts of hoarse voices, and the persistent trundlings of heavy bodies in the ward-room immediately below the deck of the cabin. Conceiving these sounds to portend a more than normal activity, she sat up, pervaded by a vague alarm, and roused her still slumbering woman.

In his cabin on the starboard side Lord Julian, disturbed by the same sounds, was already astir and hurriedly dressing. When presently he emerged under the break of the poop, he found himself staring up into a mountain of canvas. Every foot of sail that she could carry had been crowded to the *Arabella*'s yards, to catch the morning breeze. Ahead and on either side stretched the limitless expanse of ocean, sparkling golden in the sun, as yet no more than a half-disc of flame upon the horizon straight ahead.

About him in the waist, where all last night had been so peaceful, there was a frenziedly active bustle of some threescore men. By the rail, immediately above and behind Lord Julian, stood Captain Blood in altercation with a one-eyed giant, whose head was swathed in a red cotton kerchief, whose blue shirt hung open at the waist. As his lordship, moving forward, revealed himself, their voices ceased, and Blood turned to greet him.

"Good-morning to you," he said, and added: "I've blundered badly, so I have. I should have known better than to come so close to Jamaica by night. But I was in haste to land you. Come up here. I have something to show you."

Wondering, Lord Julian mounted the companion as he was bidden. Standing beside Captain Blood, he looked astern, following the indication of the Captain's hand, and cried out in his amazement. There, not more than three miles away, was land—an uneven wall of vivid green that filled the western horizon. And a couple of miles this side of it, bearing after them, came speeding three great white ships.

"They fly no colours, but they're part of the Jamaica fleet." Blood spoke without excitement, almost with a certain listlessness. "When dawn broke we found ourselves running to meet them. We went about, and it's been a race ever since. But the *Arabella*'s been at sea these four months, and her bottom's too foul for the speed we're needing."

Wolverstone hooked his thumbs into his broad leather belt, and from his great height looked down sardonically upon Lord Julian, tall man though his lordship was. "So that you're like to be in yet another sea-fight afore ye've done wi' ships, my lord."

"That's a point we were just arguing," said Blood. "For I hold that we're in no case to fight against such odds."

"The odds be damned!" Wolverstone thrust out his heavy jowl. "We're used to odds. The odds was heavier at Maracaybo; yet we won out, and took three ships. They was heavier yesterday when we engaged Don Miguel."

"Aye—but those were Spaniards."

"And what better are these?—Are ye afeard of a lubberly Barbados planter? Whatever ails you, Peter? I've never known ye scared afore."

A gun boomed out behind them.

"That'll be the signal to lie to," said Blood, in the same listless voice; and he fetched a sigh.

Wolverstone squared himself defiantly before his captain.

"I'll see Colonel Bishop in hell or ever I lies to for him." And he spat, presumably for purposes of emphasis.

His lordship intervened.

"Oh, but—by your leave—surely there is nothing to be apprehended from Colonel Bishop. Considering the service you have rendered to his niece and to me . . ."

Wolverstone's horse-laugh interrupted him. "Hark to the gentleman!" he mocked. "Ye don't know Colonel Bishop, that's clear. Not for his niece, not for his daughter, not for his own mother, would he forgo the blood what he thinks due to him. A drinker of blood, he is. A nasty beast. We knows, the Cap'n and me. We been his slaves."

"But there is myself," said Lord Julian, with great dignity.

Wolverstone laughed again, whereat his lordship flushed. He was moved to raise his voice above its usual languid level.

"I assure you that my word counts for something in England."

"Oh, aye—in England. But this ain't England, damme."

Came the roar of a second gun, and a round shot splashed the water less than half a cable's-length astern. Blood leaned over the rail to speak to the fair young man immediately below him by the helmsman at the whipstaff.

"Bid them take in sail, Jeremy," he said quietly. "We lie to."

But Wolverstone interposed again.

"Hold there a moment, Jeremy!" he roared. "Wait!" He swung back to face the Captain, who had placed a hand on is shoulder and was smiling, a trifle wistfully.

"Steady, Old Wolf! Steady!" Captain Blood admonished him.

"Steady, yourself, Peter. Ye've gone mad! Will ye doom us all to hell out of tenderness for that cold slip of a girl?"

"Stop!" cried Blood in sudden fury.

But Wolverstone would not stop. "It's the truth, you fool. It's that cursed petticoat's making a coward of you. It's for her that ye're afeard—and she, Colonel Bishop's niece! My God, man, ye'll have a mutiny aboard, and I'll lead it myself sooner than surrender to be hanged in Port Royal."

Their glances met, sullen defiance braving dull anger, surprise, and pain.

"There is no question," said Blood, "of surrender for any man aboard save only myself. If Bishop can report to England that I am taken and hanged, he will magnify himself and at the same time gratify his personal rancour against me. That should satisfy him. I'll send him a message offering to surrender aboard his ship, taking Miss Bishop and Lord Julian with me, but only on condition that the *Arabella* is allowed to proceed unharmed. It's a bargain that he'll accept, if I know him at all."

"It's a bargain he'll never be offered," retorted Wolverstone, and his earlier vehemence was as nothing to his vehemence now. "Ye're surely daft even to think of it, Peter!"

"Not so daft as you when you talk of fighting that." He flung out an arm as he spoke to indicate the pursuing ships, which were slowly but surely creeping nearer. "Before we've run another half-mile we shall be within range."

Wolverstone swore elaborately, then suddenly checked. Out of the tail of his single eye he had espied a trim figure in grey silk that was ascending the companion. So engrossed had they been that they had not seen Miss Bishop come from the door of the passage leading to the cabin. And there was something else that those three men on the poop, and Pitt immediately below them, had failed to observe. Some moments ago Ogle, followed by the main body of his gun-deck crew, had emerged from the booby hatch, to fall into muttered, angrily vehement talk with those who, abandoning the gun-tackles upon which they were labouring, had come to crowd about him.

Even now Blood had no eyes for that. He turned to look at Miss Bishop, marvelling a little, after the manner in which yesterday she had avoided him, that she should now venture upon the quarter-deck. Her presence at this moment, and considering the nature of his altercation with Wolverstone, was embarrassing.

Very sweet and dainty she stood before him in her gown of shimmering grey, a faint excitement tinting her fair cheeks and sparkling in her clear, hazel eyes, that looked so frank and honest. She wore no hat, and the ringlets of her gold-brown hair fluttered distractingly in the morning breeze.

Captain Blood bared his head and bowed silently in a greeting which she returned composedly and formally.

"What is happening, Lord Julian?" she enquired.

As if to answer her a third gun spoke from the ships towards which she was looking intent and wonderingly. A frown rumpled her brow. She looked from one to the other of the men who stood there so glum and obviously ill at ease.

"They are ships of the Jamaica fleet," his lordship answered her.

It should in any case have been a sufficient explanation. But before more could be added, their attention was drawn at last to Ogle, who came bounding up the broad ladder, and to the men lounging aft in his wake, in all of which, instinctively, they apprehended a vague menace.

At the head of the companion, Ogle found his progress barred by Blood, who confronted him, a sudden sternness in his face and in every line of him.

"What's this?" the Captain demanded sharply. "Your station is on the gun-deck. Why have you left it?"

Thus challenged, the obvious truculence faded out of Ogle's bearing, quenched by the old habit of obedience and the natural dominance that was the secret of the Captain's rule over his wild followers. But it gave no pause to the gunner's intention. If anything it increased his excitement.

"Captain," he said, and as he spoke he pointed to the pursuing ships, "Colonel Bishop holds us. We're in no case either to run or fight."

Blood's height seemed to increase, as did his sternness.

"Ogle," said he, in a voice cold and sharp as steel, "your station is on the gun-deck. You'll return to it at once, and take your crew with you, or else . . ."

But Ogle, violent of mien and gesture, interrupted him.

"Threats will not serve, Captain."

"Will they not?"

It was the first time in his buccaneering career that an order of his had been disregarded, or that a man had failed in the obedience to which he pledged all those who joined him. That this insubordination should proceed from one of those whom he most trusted, one of his old Barbados associates, was in itself a bitterness, and made him reluctant to that which instinct told him must be done. His hand closed over the butt of one of the pistols slung before him.

"Nor will that serve you," Ogle warned him, still more fiercely. "The men are of my thinking, and they'll have their way."

"And what way may that be?"

"The way to make us safe. We'll neither sink nor hang whiles we can help it."

From the three or four score men massed below in the waist came a rumble of approval. Captain Blood's glance raked the ranks of those resolute, fierce-eyed fellows, then it came to rest again on Ogle. There was here quite plainly a vague threat, a mutinous spirit he could not understand.

"You come to give advice, then, do you?" quoth he, relenting nothing of his sternness.

"That's it, Captain; advice. That girl, there." He flung out a bare arm to point to her. "Bishop's girl; the Governor of Jamaica's niece . . . We want her as a hostage for our safety."

"Aye!" roared in chorus the buccaneers below, and one or two of them elaborated that affirmation.

In a flash Captain Blood saw what was in their minds. And for all that he lost nothing of his outward stern composure, fear invaded his heart.

"And how," he asked, "do you imagine that Miss Bishop will prove such a hostage?"

"It's a providence having her aboard; a providence. Heave to, Captain, and signal them to send a boat, and assure themselves that Miss is here. Then let them know that if they attempt to hinder our sailing hence, we'll hang the doxy first and fight for it after. That'll cool Colonel Bishop's heat, maybe."

"And maybe it won't." Slow and mocking came Wolverstone's voice to answer the other's confident excitement, and as he spoke he advanced to Blood's side, an unexpected ally. "Some o' them dawcocks may believe that tale." He jerked a contemptuous thumb towards the men in the waist, whose ranks were steadily being increased by the advent of others from the forecastle. "Although even some o' they should know better, for there's still a few was on Barbados with us, and are acquainted like me and you with Colonel Bishop. If ye're counting on pulling Bishop's heartstrings, ye're a bigger fool, Ogle, than I've always thought you was with anything but guns. There's no heaving to for such a matter as that unless you wants to make quite sure of our being sunk. Though we had a cargo of Bishop's nieces it wouldn't make him hold his hand. Why, as I was just telling his lordship here, who thought like you that having Miss Bishop aboard would make us safe, not for his mother would that filthy slaver forgo what's due to him. And if ye' weren't a fool, Ogle, you wouldn't need me to tell you this. We've got to fight, my lads . . ."

"How can we fight, man?" Ogle stormed at him, furiously battling the conviction which Wolverstone's argument was imposing upon his listeners. "You may be right, and you may be wrong. We've got to chance it. It's our only chance . . ."

The rest of his words were drowned in the shouts of the hands insisting that the girl be given up to be held as a hostage. And then louder than before roared a gun away to leeward, and away on their starboard beam they saw the spray flung up by the shot, which had gone wide.

"They are within range," cried Ogle. And leaning from the rail, "Put down the helm," he commanded.

Pitt, at his post beside the helmsman, turned intrepidly to face the excited gunner.

"Since when have you commanded on the main deck, Ogle? I take my orders from the Captain."

"You'll take this order from me, or, by God, you'll . . ."

"Wait!" Blood bade him, interrupting, and he set a restraining hand upon the gunner's arm. "There is, I think, a better way."

He looked over his shoulder, aft, at the advancing ships, the foremost of which was now a bare quarter of a mile away. His glance swept in passing over Miss Bishop and Lord Julian standing side by side some paces behind him. He observed her pale and tense, with parted lips and startled eyes that were fixed upon him, an anxious witness of this deciding of her fate. He was thinking swiftly, reckoning the chances if by pistolling Ogle he were to provoke a mutiny. That some of the men would rally to him, he was sure. But he was no less sure that the main body would oppose him, and prevail in spite of all that he could do, taking the chance that holding Miss Bishop to ransom seemed to afford them. And if they did that, one way or the other, Miss Bishop would be lost. For even if Bishop yielded to their demand, they would retain her as a hostage.

Meanwhile Ogle was growing impatient. His arm still gripped by Blood, he thrust his face into the Captain's.

"What better way?" he demanded. "There is none better. I'll not be bubbled by what Wolverstone has said. He may be right, and he may be wrong. We'll test it. It's our only chance, I've said, and we must take it."

The better way that was in Captain Blood's mind was the way that already he had proposed to Wolverstone. Whether the men in the panic Ogle had aroused among them would take a different view from Wolverstone's he did not know. But he saw quite clearly now that if they consented, they would not on that account depart from their intention in the matter of Miss Bishop; they would make of Blood's own surrender merely an additional card in this game against the Governor of Jamaica.

"It's through her that we're in this trap," Ogle stormed on. "Through her and through you. It was to bring her to Jamaica that you risked all our lives, and we're not going to lose our lives as long as there's a chance to make ourselves safe through her."

He was turning again to the helmsman below, when Blood's grip tightened on his arm. Ogle wrenched it free, with an oath. But Blood's mind was now made up. He had found the only way, and repellent though it might be to him, he must take it.

"That is a desperate chance," he cried. "Mine is the safe and easy way. Wait!" He leaned over the rail. "Put the helm down," he bade Pitt. "Heave her to, and signal to them to send a boat."

A silence of astonishment fell upon the ship—of astonishment and suspicion at this sudden yielding. But Pitt, although he shared it, was prompt to obey. His voice rang out, giving the necessary orders, and after an instant's pause, a score of hands sprang to execute them. Came the creak of blocks and the rattle of slatting sails as they swung aweather, and Captain Blood turned and beckoned Lord Julian forward. His lordship, after a moment's hesitation, advanced in surprise and mistrust—a mistrust shared by Miss Bishop, who, like his lordship and all else aboard, though in a different way, had been taken aback by Blood's sudden submission to the demand to lie to.

Standing now at the rail, with Lord Julian beside him, Captain Blood explained himself.

Briefly and clearly he announced to all the object of Lord Julian's voyage to the Caribbean, and he informed them of the offer which yesterday Lord Julian had made to him.

"That offer I rejected, as his lordship will tell you, deeming myself affronted by it. Those of you who have suffered under the rule of King James will understand me. But now in the desperate case in which we find ourselves—outsailed, and likely to be outfought, as Ogle has said—I am ready to take the way of Morgan: to accept the King's commission and shelter us all behind it."

It was a thunderbolt that for a moment left them all dazed. Then Babel was reënacted. The main body of them welcomed the announcement as only men who have been preparing to die can welcome a new lease of life. But many could not resolve one way or the other until they were satisfied upon several questions, and chiefly upon one which was voiced by Ogle.

"Will Bishop respect the commission when you hold it?"

It was Lord Julian who answered:

"It will go very hard with him if he attempts to flout the King's authority. And though he should dare attempt it, be sure that his own officers will not dare to do other than oppose him."

"Aye," said Ogle, "that is true."

But there were some who were still in open and frank revolt against the course. Of these was Wolverstone, who at once proclaimed his hostility.

"I'll rot in hell or ever I serves the King," he bawled in a great rage.

But Blood quieted him and those who thought as he did.

"No man need follow me into the King's service who is reluctant. That is not in the bargain. What is in the bargain is that I accept this service with such of you as may choose to follow me. Don't think I accept it willingly. For myself, I am entirely of Wolverstone's opinion. I accept it as the only way to save us all from the certain destruction into which my own act may have brought us. And even those of you who do not choose to follow me shall share the immunity of all, and shall afterwards be free to depart. Those are the terms upon which I sell myself to the King. Let Lord Julian, the representative of the Secretary of State, say whether he agrees to them."

Prompt, eager, and clear came his lordship's agreement. And that was practically the end of the matter. Lord Julian, the butt now of good-humouredly ribald jests and half-derisive acclamations, plunged away to his cabin for the commission, secretly rejoicing at a turn of events which enabled him so creditably to discharge the business on which he had been sent.

Meanwhile the bo'sun signalled to the Jamaica ships to send a boat, and the men in the waist broke their ranks and went noisily flocking to line the bulwarks and view the great stately vessels that were racing down towards them.

As Ogle left the quarter-deck, Blood turned, and came face to face with Miss Bishop. She had been observing him with shining eyes, but at sight of his dejected countenance, and the deep frown that scarred his brow, her own expression changed. She approached him with a hesitation entirely unusual to her. She set a hand lightly upon his arm.

"You have chosen wisely, sir," she commended him, "however much against your inclinations."

He looked with gloomy eyes upon her for whom he had made this sacrifice.

"I owed it to you—or thought I did," he said.

She did not understand. "Your resolve delivered me from a horrible danger," she admitted. And she shivered at the memory of it. "But I do not understand why you should have hesitated when first it was proposed to you. It is an honourable service."

"King James's?" he sneered.

"England's," she corrected him in reproof. "The country is all, sir; the sovereign naught. King James will pass; others will come and pass; England remains, to be honourably served by her sons, whatever rancour they may hold against the man who rules her in their time."

He showed some surprise. Then he smiled a little. "Shrewd advocacy," he approved it. "You should have spoken to the crew."

And then, the note of irony deepening in his voice: "Do you suppose now that this honourable service might redeem one who was a pirate and a thief?"

Her glance fell away. Her voice faltered a little in replying. "If he . . . needs redeeming. Perhaps . . . perhaps he has been judged too harshly."

The blue eyes flashed, and the firm lips relaxed their grim set.

"Why . . . if ye think that," he said, considering her, an odd hunger in his glance, "life might have its uses, after all, and even the service of King James might become tolerable."

Looking beyond her, across the water, he observed a boat putting off from one of the great ships, which, hove to now, were rocking gently some three hundred yards away. Abruptly his manner changed. He was like one recovering, taking himself in hand again. "If you will go below, and get your gear and your woman, you shall presently be sent aboard one of the ships of the fleet." He pointed to the boat as he spoke.

She left him, and thereafter with Wolverstone, leaning upon the rail, he watched the approach of that boat, manned by a dozen sailors, and commanded by a scarlet figure seated stiffly in the stern sheets. He levelled his telescope upon that figure.

"It'll not be Bishop himself," said Wolverstone, between question and assertion.

"No." Blood closed his telescope. "I don't know who it is."

"Ha!" Wolverstone vented an ejaculation of sneering mirth. "For all his eagerness, Bishop'd be none so willing to come, hisself. He's been aboard this hulk afore, and we made him swim for it that time. He'll have his memories. So he sends a deputy."

This deputy proved to be an officer named Calverley, a vigorous, self-sufficient fellow, comparatively fresh from England, whose manner made it clear that he came fully instructed by Colonel Bishop upon the matter of how to handle the pirates.

His air, as he stepped into the waist of the *Arabella*, was haughty, truculent, and disdainful.

Blood, the King's commission now in his pocket, and Lord Julian standing beside him, waited to receive him, and Captain Calverley was a little taken aback at finding himself confronted by two men so very different outwardly from anything that he had expected. But he lost none of his haughty poise, and scarcely deigned a glance at the swarm of fierce, half-naked fellows lounging in a semicircle to form a background.

"Good-day to you, sir," Blood hailed him pleasantly. "I have the honour to give you welcome aboard the *Arabella*. My name is Blood—Captain Blood, at your service. You may have heard of me."

Captain Calverley stared hard. The airy manner of this redoubtable buccaneer was hardly what he had looked for in a desperate fellow, compelled to ignominious surrender. A thin, sour smile broke on the officer's haughty lips.

"You'll ruffle it to the gallows, no doubt," he said contemptuously. "I suppose that is after the fashion of your kind. Meanwhile it's your surrender I require, my man, not your impudence."

Captain Blood appeared surprised, pained. He turned in appeal to Lord Julian.

"D'ye hear that now? And did ye ever hear the like? But what did I tell ye? Ye see, the young gentleman's under a misapprehension entirely. Perhaps it'll save broken bones if your lordship explains just who and what I am."

Lord Julian advanced a step and bowed perfunctorily and rather disdainfully to that very disdainful but now dumbfounded officer. Pitt, who watched the scene from the quarter-deck rail, tells us that his lordship was as grave as a parson at a hanging. But I suspect this gravity for a mask under which Lord Julian was secretly amused.

"I have the honour to inform you, sir," he said stiffly, "that Captain Blood holds a commission in the King's service under the seal of my Lord Sunderland, His Majesty's Secretary of State."

Captain Calverley's face empurpled; his eyes bulged. The buccaneers in the background chuckled and crowed and swore among themselves in their relish of this comedy. For a long moment Calverley stared in silence at his lordship, observing the costly elegance of his dress, his air of calm assurance, and his cold, fastidious speech, all of which savoured distinctly of the great world to which he belonged.

"And who the devil may you be?" he exploded at last.

Colder still and more distant than ever grew his lordship's voice.

"You're not very civil, sir, as I have already noticed. My name is Wade—Lord Julian Wade. I am His Majesty's envoy to these barbarous parts, and my Lord Sunderland's near kinsman. Colonel Bishop has been notified of my coming."

The sudden change in Calverley's manner at Lord Julian's mention of his name showed that the notification had been received, and that he had knowledge of it.

"I . . . I believe that he has," said Calverley, between doubt and suspicion. "That is: that he has been notified of the coming of Lord Julian Wade. But . . . but . . . aboard this ship . . . ?" The officer made a gesture of helplessness, and, surrendering to his bewilderment, fell abruptly silent.

"I was coming out on the *Royal Mary* . . ."

"That is what we were advised."

"But the *Royal Mary* fell a victim to a Spanish privateer, and I might never have arrived at all but for the gallantry of Captain Blood, who rescued me."

Light broke upon the darkness of Calverley's mind. "I see. I understand."

"I will take leave to doubt it." His lordship's tone abated nothing of its asperity. "But that can wait. If Captain Blood will show you his commission, perhaps that will set all doubts at rest, and we may proceed. I shall be glad to reach Port Royal."

Captain Blood thrust a parchment under Calverley's bulging eyes. The officer scanned it, particularly the seals and signature. He stepped back, a baffled, impotent man. He bowed helplessly.

"I must return to Colonel Bishop for my orders," he informed them.

At that moment a lane was opened in the ranks of the men, and through this came Miss Bishop followed by her octoroon woman. Over his shoulder Captain Blood observed her approach.

"Perhaps, since Colonel Bishop is with you, you will convey his niece to him. Miss Bishop was aboard the *Royal Mary* also, and I rescued her together with his lordship. She will be able to acquaint her uncle with the details of that and of the present state of affairs."

Swept thus from surprise to surprise, Captain Calverley could do no more than bow again.

"As for me," said Lord Julian, with intent to make Miss Bishop's departure free from all interference on the part of the buccaneers, "I shall remain aboard the *Arabella* until we reach Port Royal. My compliments to Colonel Bishop. Say that I look forward to making his acquaintance there."

XXII. HOSTILITIES

In the great harbour of Port Royal, spacious enough to have given moorings to all the ships of all the navies of the world, the *Arabella* rode at anchor. Almost she had the air of a prisoner, for a quarter of a mile ahead, to starboard, rose the lofty, massive single round tower of the fort, whilst a couple of cables'-length astern, and to larboard, rode the six men-of-war that composed the Jamaica squadron.

Abeam with the *Arabella*, across the harbour, were the flat-fronted white buildings of that imposing city that came down to the very water's edge. Behind these the red roofs rose like terraces, marking the gentle slope upon which the city was built, dominated here by a turret, there by a spire, and behind these again a range of green hills with for ultimate background a sky that was like a dome of polished steel.

On a cane day-bed that had been set for him on the quarter-deck, sheltered from the dazzling, blistering sunshine by an improvised awning of brown sailcloth, lounged Peter Blood, a calf-bound, well-thumbed copy of Horace's Odes neglected in his hands.

From immediately below him came the swish of mops and the gurgle of water in the scuppers, for it was still early morning, and under the directions of Hayton, the bo'sun, the swabbers were at work in the waist and forecastle. Despite the heat and the stagnant air, one of the toilers found breath to croak a ribald buccaneering ditty:

> "For we laid her board and board,
> And we put her to the sword,
> And we sank her in the deep blue sea.
> So it's heigh-ho, and heave-a-ho!
> Who'll sail for the Main with me?"

Blood fetched a sigh, and the ghost of a smile played over his keen, lean, sun-tanned face. Then the black brows came together above the vivid blue eyes, and thought swiftly closed the door upon his immediate surroundings.

Things had not sped at all well with him in the past fortnight since his acceptance of the King's commission. There had been trouble with Bishop from the moment of landing. As Blood and Lord Julian had stepped ashore together, they had been met by a man who took no pains to dissemble his chagrin at the turn of events and his determination to change it. He awaited them on the mole, supported by a group of officers.

"You are Lord Julian Wade, I understand," was his truculent greeting. For Blood at the moment he had nothing beyond a malignant glance.

Lord Julian bowed. "I take it I have the honour to address Colonel Bishop, Deputy-Governor of Jamaica." It was almost as if his lordship were giving the Colonel a lesson in deportment. The Colonel accepted it, and belatedly bowed, removing his broad hat. Then he plunged on.

"You have granted, I am told, the King's commission to this man." His very tone betrayed the bitterness of his rancour. "Your motives were no doubt worthy . . . your gratitude to him for delivering you from the Spaniards. But the thing itself is unthinkable, my lord. The commission must be cancelled."

"I don't think I understand," said Lord Julian distantly.

"To be sure you don't, or you'd never ha' done it. The fellow's bubbled you. Why, he's first a rebel, then an escaped slave, and lastly a bloody pirate. I've been hunting him this year past."

"I assure you, sir, that I was fully informed of all. I do not grant the King's commission lightly."

"Don't you, by God! And what else do you call this? But as His Majesty's Deputy-Governor of Jamaica, I'll take leave to correct your mistake in my own way."

"Ah! And what way may that be?"

"There's a gallows waiting for this rascal in Port Royal."

Blood would have intervened at that, but Lord Julian forestalled him.

"I see, sir, that you do not yet quite apprehend the circumstances. If it is a mistake to grant Captain Blood a commission, the mistake is not mine. I am acting upon the instructions of my Lord Sunderland; and with a full knowledge of all the facts, his lordship expressly designated Captain Blood for this commission if Captain Blood could be persuaded to accept it."

Colonel Bishop's mouth fell open in surprise and dismay.

"Lord Sunderland designated him?" he asked, amazed.

"Expressly."

His lordship waited a moment for a reply. None coming from the speechless Deputy-Governor, he asked a question: "Would you still venture to describe the matter as a mistake, sir? And dare you take the risk of correcting it?"

"I . . . I had not dreamed . . ."

"I understand, sir. Let me present Captain Blood."

Perforce Bishop must put on the best face he could command. But that it was no more than a mask for his fury and his venom was plain to all.

From that unpromising beginning matters had not improved; rather had they grown worse.

Blood's thoughts were upon this and other things as he lounged there on the day-bed. He had been a fortnight in Port Royal, his ship virtually a unit now in the Jamaica squadron. And when the news of it reached Tortuga and the buccaneers who awaited his return, the name of Captain Blood, which had stood so high among the Brethren of the Coast, would become a byword, a thing of execration, and before all was done his life might pay forfeit for what would be accounted a treacherous defection. And for what had he placed himself in this position? For the sake of a girl who avoided him so persistently and intentionally that he must assume that she still regarded him with aversion. He had scarcely been vouchsafed a glimpse of her in all this fortnight, although with that in view for his main object he had daily haunted her uncle's residence, and daily braved the unmasked hostility and baffled rancour in which Colonel Bishop held him. Nor was that the worst of it. He was allowed plainly to perceive that it was the graceful, elegant young trifler from St. James's, Lord Julian Wade, to whom her every moment was devoted. And what chance had he, a desperate adventurer with a record of outlawry, against such a rival as that, a man of parts, moreover, as he was bound to admit?

You conceive the bitterness of his soul. He beheld himself to be as the dog in the fable that had dropped the substance to snatch at a delusive shadow.

He sought comfort in a line on the open page before him:

levius fit patientia quicquid corrigere est nefas.

Sought it, but hardly found it.

A boat that had approached unnoticed from the shore came scraping and bumping against the great red hull of the *Arabella*, and a raucous voice sent up a hailing shout. From the ship's belfry two silvery notes rang clear and sharp, and a moment or two later the bo'sun's whistle shrilled a long wail.

The sounds disturbed Captain Blood from his disgruntled musings. He rose, tall, active, and arrestingly elegant in a scarlet, gold-laced coat that advertised his new position, and slipping the slender volume into his pocket, advanced to the carved rail of the quarter-deck, just as Jeremy Pitt was setting foot upon the companion.

"A note for you from the Deputy-Governor," said the master shortly, as he proffered a folded sheet.

Blood broke the seal, and read. Pitt, loosely clad in shirt and breeches, leaned against the rail the while and watched him, unmistakable concern imprinted on his fair, frank countenance.

Blood uttered a short laugh, and curled his lip. "It is a very peremptory summons," he said, and passed the note to his friend.

The young master's grey eyes skimmed it. Thoughtfully he stroked his golden beard.

"You'll not go?" he said, between question and assertion.

"Why not? Haven't I been a daily visitor at the fort . . . ?"

"But it'll be about the Old Wolf that he wants to see you. It gives him a grievance at last. You know, Peter, that it is Lord Julian alone has stood between Bishop and his hate of you. If now he can show that . . ."

"What if he can?" Blood interrupted carelessly. "Shall I be in greater danger ashore than aboard, now that we've but fifty men left, and they lukewarm rogues who would as soon serve the King as me? Jeremy, dear lad, the *Arabella*'s a prisoner here, bedad, 'twixt the fort there and the fleet yonder. Don't be forgetting that."

Jeremy clenched his hands. "Why did ye let Wolverstone and the others go?" he cried, with a touch of bitterness. "You should have seen the danger."

"How could I in honesty have detained them? It was in the bargain. Besides, how could their staying have helped me?" And as Pitt did not answer him: "Ye see?" he said, and shrugged. "I'll be getting my hat and cane and sword, and go ashore in the cock-boat. See it manned for me."

"Ye're going to deliver yourself into Bishop's hands," Pitt warned him.

"Well, well, maybe he'll not find me quite so easy to grasp as he imagines. There's a thorn or two left on me." And with a laugh Blood departed to his cabin.

Jeremy Pitt answered the laugh with an oath. A moment he stood irresolute where Blood had left him. Then slowly, reluctance dragging at his feet, he went down the companion to give the order for the cock-boat.

"If anything should happen to you, Peter," he said, as Blood was going over the side, "Colonel Bishop had better look to himself. These fifty lads may be lukewarm at present, as you say, but—sink me!—they'll be anything but lukewarm if there's a breach of faith."

"And what should be happening to me, Jeremy? Sure, now, I'll be back for dinner, so I will."

Blood climbed down into the waiting boat. But laugh though he might, he knew as well as Pitt that in going ashore that morning he carried his life in his hands. Because of this, it may have been that when he stepped on to the narrow mole, in the shadow of the shallow outer wall of the fort through whose crenels were thrust the black noses of its heavy guns, he gave order that the boat should stay for him at that spot. He realized that he might have to retreat in a hurry.

Walking leisurely, he skirted the embattled wall, and passed through the great gates into the courtyard. Half-a-dozen soldiers lounged there, and in the shadow cast by the wall, Major Mallard, the Commandant, was slowly pacing. He stopped short at sight of Captain Blood, and saluted him, as was his due, but the smile that lifted the officer's stiff mostachios was grimly sardonic. Peter Blood's attention, however, was elsewhere.

On his right stretched a spacious garden, beyond which rose the white house that was the residence of the Deputy-Governor. In that garden's main avenue, that was fringed with palm and sandalwood, he had caught sight of Miss Bishop alone. He crossed the courtyard with suddenly lengthened stride.

"Good-morning to ye, ma'am," was his greeting as he overtook her; and hat in hand now, he added on a note of protest: "Sure, it's nothing less than uncharitable to make me run in this heat."

"Why do you run, then?" she asked him coolly, standing slim and straight before him, all in white and very maidenly save in her unnatural composure. "I am pressed," she informed him. "So you will forgive me if I do not stay."

"You were none so pressed until I came," he protested, and if his thin lips smiled, his blue eyes were oddly hard.

"Since you perceive it, sir, I wonder that you trouble to be so insistent."

That crossed the swords between them, and it was against Blood's instincts to avoid an engagement.

"Faith, you explain yourself after a fashion," said he. "But since it was more or less in your service that I donned the King's coat, you should suffer it to cover the thief and pirate."

She shrugged and turned aside, in some resentment and some regret. Fearing to betray the latter, she took refuge in the former. "I do my best," said she.

"So that ye can be charitable in some ways!" He laughed softly. "Glory be, now, I should be thankful for so much. Maybe I'm presumptuous. But I can't forget that when I was no better than a slave in your uncle's household in Barbados, ye used me with a certain kindness."

"Why not? In those days you had some claim upon my kindness. You were just an unfortunate gentleman then."

"And what else would you be calling me now?"

"Hardly unfortunate. We have heard of your good fortune on the seas—how your luck has passed into a byword. And we have heard other things: of your good fortune in other directions."

She spoke hastily, the thought of Mademoiselle d'Ogeron in her mind. And instantly would have recalled the words had she been able. But Peter Blood swept them lightly aside, reading into them none of her meaning, as she feared he would.

"Aye—a deal of lies, devil a doubt, as I could prove to you."

"I cannot think why you should trouble to put yourself on your defence," she discouraged him.

"So that ye may think less badly of me than you do."

"What I think of you can be a very little matter to you, sir."

This was a disarming stroke. He abandoned combat for expostulation.

"Can ye say that now? Can ye say that, beholding me in this livery of a service I despise? Didn't ye tell me that I might redeem the past? It's little enough I am concerned to redeem the past save only in your eyes. In my own I've done nothing at all that I am ashamed of, considering the provocation I received."

Her glance faltered, and fell away before his own that was so intent.

"I . . . I can't think why you should speak to me like this," she said, with less than her earlier assurance.

"Ah, now, can't ye, indeed?" he cried. "Sure, then, I'll be telling ye."

"Oh, please." There was real alarm in her voice. "I realize fully what you did, and I realize that partly, at least, you may have been urged by consideration for myself. Believe me, I am very grateful. I shall always be grateful."

"But if it's also your intention always to think of me as a thief and a pirate, faith, ye may keep your gratitude for all the good it's like to do me."

A livelier colour crept into her cheeks. There was a perceptible heave of the slight breast that faintly swelled the flimsy bodice of white silk. But if she resented his tone and his words, she stifled her resentment. She realized that perhaps she had, herself, provoked his anger. She honestly desired to make amends.

"You are mistaken," she began. "It isn't that."

But they were fated to misunderstand each other. Jealousy, that troubler of reason, had been over-busy with his wits as it had with hers.

"What is it, then?" quoth he, and added the question: "Lord Julian?"

She started, and stared at him blankly indignant now.

"Och, be frank with me," he urged her, unpardonably. "'Twill be a kindness, so it will."

For a moment she stood before him with quickened breathing, the colour ebbing and flowing in her cheeks. Then she looked past him, and tilted her chin forward.

"You . . . you are quite insufferable," she said. "I beg that you will let me pass."

He stepped aside, and with the broad feathered hat which he still held in his hand, he waved her on towards the house.

"I'll not be detaining you any longer, ma'am. After all, the cursed thing I did for nothing can be undone. Ye'll remember afterwards that it was your hardness drove me."

She moved to depart, then checked, and faced him again. It was she now who was on her defence, her voice quivering with indignation.

"You take that tone! You dare to take that tone!" she cried, astounding him by her sudden vehemence. "You have the effrontery to upbraid me because I will not take your hands when I know how they are stained; when I know you for a murderer and worse?"

He stared at her open-mouthed.

"A murderer—I?" he said at last.

"Must I name your victims? Did you not murder Levasseur?"

"Levasseur?" He smiled a little. "So they've told you about that!"

"Do you deny it?"

"I killed him, it is true. I can remember killing another man in circumstances that were very similar. That was in Bridgetown on the night of the Spanish raid. Mary Traill would tell you of it. She was present."

He clapped his hat on his head with a certain abrupt fierceness, and strode angrily away, before she could answer or even grasp the full significance of what he had said.

XXIII. Hostages

Peter Blood stood in the pillared portico of Government House, and with unseeing eyes that were laden with pain and anger, stared out across the great harbour of Port Royal to the green hills rising from the farther shore and the ridge of the Blue Mountains beyond, showing hazily through the quivering heat.

He was aroused by the return of the negro who had gone to announce him, and following now this slave, he made his way through the house to the wide piazza behind it, in whose shade Colonel Bishop and my Lord Julian Wade took what little air there was.

"So ye've come," the Deputy-Governor hailed him, and followed the greeting by a series of grunts of vague but apparently ill-humoured import.

He did not trouble to rise, not even when Lord Julian, obeying the instincts of finer breeding, set him the example. From under scowling brows the wealthy Barbados planter considered his sometime slave, who, hat in hand, leaning lightly upon his long beribboned cane, revealed nothing in his countenance of the anger which was being steadily nourished by this cavalier reception.

At last, with scowling brow and in self-sufficient tones, Colonel Bishop delivered himself.

"I have sent for you, Captain Blood, because of certain news that has just reached me. I am informed that yesterday evening a frigate left the harbour having on board your associate Wolverstone and a hundred men of the hundred and fifty that were serving under you. His lordship and I shall be glad to have your explanation of how you came to permit that departure."

"Permit?" quoth Blood. "I ordered it."

The answer left Bishop speechless for a moment. Then:

"You ordered it?" he said in accents of unbelief, whilst Lord Julian raised his eyebrows. "'Swounds! Perhaps you'll explain yourself? Whither has Wolverstone gone?"

"To Tortuga. He's gone with a message to the officers commanding the other four ships of the fleet that is awaiting me there, telling them what's happened and why they are no longer to expect me."

Bishop's great face seemed to swell and its high colour to deepen. He swung to Lord Julian.

"You hear that, my lord? Deliberately he has let Wolverstone loose upon the seas again—Wolverstone, the worst of all that gang of pirates after himself. I hope your lordship begins at last to perceive the folly of granting the King's commission to such a man as this against all my counsels. Why, this thing is . . . it's just mutiny . . . treason! By God! It's matter for a court-martial."

"Will you cease your blather of mutiny and treason and courts-martial?" Blood put on his hat, and sat down unbidden. "I have sent Wolverstone to inform Hagthorpe and Christian and Yberville and the rest of my lads that they've one clear month in which to follow my example, quit piracy, and get back to their boucans or their logwood, or else sail out of the Caribbean Sea. That's what I've done."

"But the men?" his lordship interposed in his level, cultured voice. "This hundred men that Wolverstone has taken with him?"

"They are those of my crew who have no taste for King James's service, and have preferred to seek work of other kinds. It was in our compact, my lord, that there should be no constraining of my men."

"I don't remember it," said his lordship, with sincerity.

Blood looked at him in surprise. Then he shrugged. "Faith, I'm not to blame for your lordship's poor memory. I say that it was so; and I don't lie. I've never found it necessary. In any case ye couldn't have supposed that I should consent to anything different."

And then the Deputy-Governor exploded.

"You have given those damned rascals in Tortuga this warning so that they may escape! That is what you have done. That is how you abuse the commission that has saved your own neck!"

Peter Blood considered him steadily, his face impassive.

"I will remind you," he said at last, very quietly, "that the object in view was—leaving out of account your own appetites which, as every one knows, are just those of a hangman—to rid the Caribbean of buccaneers. Now, I've taken the most effective way of accomplishing that object. The knowledge that I've entered the King's service should in itself go far towards disbanding the fleet of which I was until lately the admiral."

"I see!" sneered the Deputy-Governor malevolently. "And if it does not?"

"It will be time enough then to consider what else is to be done."

Lord Julian forestalled a fresh outburst on the part of Bishop.

"It is possible," he said, "that my Lord Sunderland will be satisfied, provided that the solution is such as you promise."

It was a courteous, conciliatory speech. Urged by friendliness towards Blood and understanding of the difficult position in which the buccaneer found himself, his lordship was disposed to take his stand upon the letter of his instructions. Therefore he now held out a friendly hand to help him over the latest and most difficult obstacle which Blood himself had enabled Bishop to place in the way of his redemption. Unfortunately the last person from whom Peter Blood desired assistance at that moment was this young nobleman, whom he regarded with the jaundiced eyes of jealousy.

"Anyway," he answered, with a suggestion of defiance and more than a suggestion of a sneer, "it's the most ye should expect from me, and certainly it's the most ye'll get."

His lordship frowned, and dabbed his lips with a handkerchief.

"I don't think that I quite like the way you put it. Indeed, upon reflection, Captain Blood, I am sure that I do not."

"I am sorry for that, so I am," said Blood impudently. "But there it is. I'm not on that account concerned to modify it."

His lordship's pale eyes opened a little wider. Languidly he raised his eyebrows.

"Ah!" he said. "You're a prodigiously uncivil fellow. You disappoint me, sir. I had formed the notion that you might be a gentleman."

"And that's not your lordship's only mistake," Bishop cut in. "You made a worse when you gave him the King's commission, and so sheltered the rascal from the gallows I had prepared for him in Port Royal."

"Aye—but the worst mistake of all in this matter of commissions," said Blood to his lordship, "was the one that made this greasy slaver Deputy-Governor of Jamaica instead of its hangman, which is the office for which he's by nature fitted."

"Captain Blood!" said his lordship sharply in reproof. "Upon my soul and honour, sir, you go much too far. You are . . ."

But here Bishop interrupted him. He had heaved himself to his feet, at last, and was venting his fury in unprintable abuse. Captain Blood, who had also risen, stood apparently impassive, for the storm to spend itself. When at last this happened, he addressed himself quietly to Lord Julian, as if Colonel Bishop had not spoken.

"Your lordship was about to say?" he asked, with challenging smoothness.

But his lordship had by now recovered his habitual composure, and was again disposed to be conciliatory. He laughed and shrugged.

"Faith! here's a deal of unnecessary heat," said he. "And God knows this plaguey climate provides enough of that. Perhaps, Colonel Bishop, you are a little uncompromising; and you, sir, are certainly a deal too peppery. I have said, speaking on behalf of my Lord Sunderland, that I am content to await the result of your experiment."

But Bishop's fury had by now reached a stage in which it was not to be restrained.

"Are you, indeed?" he roared. "Well, then, I am not. This is a matter in which your lordship must allow me to be the better judge. And, anyhow, I'll take the risk of acting on my own responsibility."

Lord Julian abandoned the struggle. He smiled wearily, shrugged, and waved a hand in implied resignation. The Deputy-Governor stormed on.

"Since my lord here has given you a commission, I can't regularly deal with you out of hand for piracy as you deserve. But you shall answer before a court-martial for your action in the matter of Wolverstone, and take the consequences."

"I see," said Blood. "Now we come to it. And it's yourself as Deputy-Governor will preside over that same court-martial. So that ye can wipe off old scores by hanging me, it's little ye care how ye do it!" He laughed, and added: "Præmonitus, præmunitus."

"What shall that mean?" quoth Lord Julian sharply.

"I had imagined that your lordship would have had some education."

He was at pains, you see, to be provocative.

"It's not the literal meaning I am asking, sir," said Lord Julian, with frosty dignity. "I want to know what you desire me to understand?"

"I'll leave your lordship guessing," said Blood. "And I'll be wishing ye both a very good day." He swept off his feathered hat, and made them a leg very elegantly.

"Before you go," said Bishop, "and to save you from any idle rashness, I'll tell you that the Harbour-Master and the Commandant have their orders. You don't leave Port Royal, my fine gallows bird. Damme, I mean to provide you with permanent moorings here, in Execution Dock."

Peter Blood stiffened, and his vivid blue eyes stabbed the bloated face of his enemy. He passed his long cane into his left hand, and with his right thrust negligently into the breast of his doublet, he swung to Lord Julian, who was thoughtfully frowning.

"Your lordship, I think, promised me immunity from this."

"What I may have promised," said his lordship, "your own conduct makes it difficult to perform." He rose. "You did me a service, Captain Blood, and I had hoped that we might be friends. But since you prefer to have it otherwise . . ." He shrugged, and waved a hand towards the Deputy-Governor.

Blood completed the sentence in his own way:

"Ye mean that ye haven't the strength of character to resist the urgings of a bully." He was apparently at his ease, and actually smiling. "Well, well—as I said before—præmonitus, præmunitus. I'm afraid that ye're no scholar, Bishop, or ye'd know that I means forewarned, forearmed."

"Forewarned? Ha!" Bishop almost snarled. "The warning comes a little late. You do not leave this house." He took a step in the direction of the doorway, and raised his voice. "Ho there . . ." he was beginning to call.

Then with a sudden audible catch in his breath, he stopped short. Captain Blood's right hand had reëmerged from the breast of his doublet, bringing with it a long pistol with silver mountings richly chased, which he levelled within a foot of the Deputy-Governor's head.

"And forearmed," said he. "Don't stir from where you are, my lord, or there may be an accident."

And my lord, who had been moving to Bishop's assistance, stood instantly arrested. Chap-fallen, with much of his high colour suddenly departed, the Deputy-Governor was swaying on unsteady legs. Peter Blood considered him with a grimness that increased his panic.

"I marvel that I don't pistol you without more ado, ye fat blackguard. If I don't, it's for the same reason that once before I gave ye your life when it was forfeit. Ye're not aware of the reason, to be sure; but it may comfort ye to know that it exists. At the same time I'll warn ye not to put too heavy a strain on my generosity, which resides at the moment in my trigger-finger. Ye mean to hang me, and since that's the worst that can happen to me anyway, you'll realize that I'll not boggle at increasing the account by spilling your nasty blood." He cast his cane from him, thus disengaging his left hand. "Be good enough to give me your arm, Colonel Bishop. Come, come, man, your arm."

Under the compulsion of that sharp tone, those resolute eyes, and that gleaming pistol, Bishop obeyed without demur. His recent foul volubility was stemmed. He could not trust himself to speak. Captain Blood tucked his left arm through the Deputy-Governor's proffered right. Then he thrust his own right hand with its pistol back into the breast of his doublet.

"Though invisible, it's aiming at ye none the less, and I give you my word of honour that I'll shoot ye dead upon the very least provocation, whether that provocation is yours or another's. Ye'll bear that in mind, Lord Julian. And now, ye greasy hangman, step out as brisk and lively as ye can, and behave as naturally as ye may, or it's the black stream of Cocytus ye'll be contemplating." Arm in arm they passed through the house, and down the garden, where Arabella lingered, awaiting Peter Blood's return.

Consideration of his parting words had brought her first turmoil of mind, then a clear perception of what might be indeed the truth of the death of Levasseur. She perceived that the particular inference drawn from it might similarly have been drawn from Blood's deliverance of Mary Traill. When a man so risks his life for a woman, the rest is easily assumed. For the men who will take such risks without hope of personal gain are few. Blood was of those few, as he had proved in the case of Mary Traill.

It needed no further assurances of his to convince her that she had done him a monstrous injustice. She remembered words he had used—words overheard aboard his ship (which he had named the *Arabella*) on the night of her deliverance from the Spanish admiral; words he had uttered when she had approved his acceptance of the King's commission; the words he had spoken to her that very morning, which had but served to move her indignation. All these assumed a fresh meaning in her mind, delivered now from its unwarranted preconceptions.

Therefore she lingered there in the garden, awaiting his return that she might make amends; that she might set a term to all misunderstanding. In impatience she awaited him. Yet her patience, it seemed, was to be tested further. For when at last he came, it was in company—unusually close and intimate company—with her uncle. In vexation she realized that explanations must be postponed. Could she have guessed the extent of that postponement, vexation would have been changed into despair.

He passed, with his companion, from that fragrant garden into the courtyard of the fort. Here the Commandant, who had been instructed to hold himself in readiness with the necessary men against the need to effect the arrest of Captain Blood, was amazed by the curious spectacle of the Deputy-Governor of Jamaica strolling forth arm in arm and apparently on the friendliest terms with the intended prisoner. For as they went, Blood was chatting and laughing briskly.

They passed out of the gates unchallenged, and so came to the mole where the cock-boat from the *Arabella* was waiting. They took their places side by side in the stern sheets, and were pulled away together, always very close and friendly, to the great red ship where Jeremy Pitt so anxiously awaited news.

You conceive the master's amazement to see the Deputy-Governor come toiling up the entrance ladder, with Blood following very close behind him.

"Sure, I walked into a trap, as ye feared, Jeremy," Blood hailed him. "But I walked out again, and fetched the trapper with me. He loves his life, does this fat rascal."

Colonel Bishop stood in the waist, his great face blenched to the colour of clay, his mouth loose, almost afraid to look at the sturdy ruffians who lounged about the shot-rack on the main hatch.

Blood shouted an order to the bo'sun, who was leaning against the forecastle bulkhead.

"Throw me a rope with a running noose over the yardarm there, against the need of it. Now, don't be alarming yourself, Colonel, darling. It's no more than a provision against your being unreasonable, which I am sure ye'll not be. We'll talk the matter over whiles we are dining, for I trust ye'll not refuse to honour my table by your company."

He led away the will-less, cowed bully to the great cabin. Benjamin, the negro steward, in white drawers and cotton shirt, made haste by his command to serve dinner.

Colonel Bishop collapsed on the locker under the stern ports, and spoke now for the first time.

"May I ask wha . . . what are your intentions?" he quavered.

"Why, nothing sinister, Colonel. Although ye deserve nothing less than that same rope and yardarm, I assure you that it's to be employed only as a last resource. Ye've said his lordship made a mistake when he handed me the commission which the Secretary of State did me the honour to design for me. I'm disposed to agree with you; so I'll take to the sea again. Cras ingens iterabimus æquor. It's the fine Latin scholar ye'll be when I've done with ye. I'll be getting back to Tortuga and my buccaneers, who at least are honest, decent fellows. So I've fetched ye aboard as a hostage."

"My God!" groaned the Deputy-Governor. "Ye . . . ye never mean that ye'll carry me to Tortuga!"

Blood laughed outright. "Oh, I'd never serve ye such a bad turn as that. No, no. All I want is that ye ensure my safe departure from Port Royal. And, if ye're reasonable,

I'll not even trouble you to swim for it this time. Ye've given certain orders to your Harbour-Master, and others to the Commandant of your plaguey fort. Ye'll be so good as to send for them both aboard here, and inform them in my presence that the *Arabella* is leaving this afternoon on the King's service and is to pass out unmolested. And so as to make quite sure of their obedience, they shall go a little voyage with us, themselves. Here's what you require. Now write—unless you prefer the yardarm."

Colonel Bishop heaved himself up in a pet. "You constrain me with violence . . ." he was beginning.

Blood smoothly interrupted him.

"Sure, now, I am not constraining you at all. I'm giving you a perfectly free choice between the pen and the rope. It's a matter for yourself entirely."

Bishop glared at him; then shrugging heavily, he took up the pen and sat down at the table. In an unsteady hand he wrote that summons to his officers. Blood despatched it ashore; and then bade his unwilling guest to table.

"I trust, Colonel, your appetite is as stout as usual."

The wretched Bishop took the seat to which he was commanded. As for eating, however, that was not easy to a man in his position; nor did Blood press him. The Captain, himself, fell to with a good appetite. But before he was midway through the meal came Hayton to inform him that Lord Julian Wade had just come aboard, and was asking to see him instantly.

"I was expecting him," said Blood. "Fetch him in."

Lord Julian came. He was very stern and dignified. His eyes took in the situation at a glance, as Captain Blood rose to greet him.

"It's mighty friendly of you to have joined us, my lord."

"Captain Blood," said his lordship with asperity, "I find your humour a little forced. I don't know what may be your intentions; but I wonder do you realize the risks you are running."

"And I wonder does your lordship realize the risk to yourself in following us aboard as I had counted that you would."

"What shall that mean, sir?"

Blood signalled to Benjamin, who was standing behind Bishop.

"Set a chair for his lordship. Hayton, send his lordship's boat ashore. Tell them he'll not be returning yet awhile."

"What's that?" cried his lordship. "Blister me! D'ye mean to detain me? Are ye mad?"

"Better wait, Hayton, in case his lordship should turn violent," said Blood. "You, Benjamin, you heard the message. Deliver it."

"Will you tell me what you intend, sir?" demanded his lordship, quivering with anger.

"Just to make myself and my lads here safe from Colonel Bishop's gallows. I've said that I trusted to your gallantry not to leave him in the lurch, but to follow him hither, and there's a note from his hand gone ashore to summon the Harbour-Master and the Commandant of the fort. Once they are aboard, I shall have all the hostages I need for our safety."

"You scoundrel!" said his lordship through his teeth.

"Sure, now, that's entirely a matter of the point of view," said Blood. "Ordinarily it isn't the kind of name I could suffer any man to apply to me. Still, considering that ye willingly did me a service once, and that ye're likely unwillingly to do me another now, I'll overlook your discourtesy, so I will."

His lordship laughed. "You fool," he said. "Do you dream that I came aboard your pirate ship without taking my measures? I informed the Commandant of exactly how you had compelled Colonel Bishop to accompany you. Judge now whether he or the Harbour-Master will obey the summons, or whether you will be allowed to depart as you imagine."

Blood's face became grave. "I'm sorry for that," said he.

"I thought you would be," answered his lordship.

"Oh, but not on my own account. It's the Deputy-Governor there I'm sorry for. D'ye know what ye've done? Sure, now, ye've very likely hanged him."

"My God!" cried Bishop in a sudden increase of panic.

"If they so much as put a shot across my bows, up goes their Deputy-Governor to the yardarm. Your only hope, Colonel, lies in the fact that I shall send them word of that intention. And so that you may mend as far as you can the harm you have done, it's yourself shall bear them the message, my lord."

"I'll see you damned before I do," fumed his lordship.

"Why, that's unreasonable and unreasoning. But if ye insist, why, another messenger will do as well, and another hostage aboard—as I had originally intended—will make my hand the stronger."

Lord Julian stared at him, realizing exactly what he had refused.

"You'll think better of it now that ye understand?" quoth Blood.

"Aye, in God's name, go, my lord," spluttered Bishop, "and make yourself obeyed. This damned pirate has me by the throat."

His lordship surveyed him with an eye that was not by any means admiring. "Why, if that is your wish . . ." he began. Then he shrugged, and turned again to Blood.

"I suppose I can trust you that no harm will come to Colonel Bishop if you are allowed to sail?"

"You have my word for it," said Blood. "And also that I shall put him safely ashore again without delay."

Lord Julian bowed stiffly to the cowering Deputy-Governor. "You understand, sir, that I do as you desire," he said coldly.

"Aye, man, aye!" Bishop assented hastily.

"Very well." Lord Julian bowed again and took his departure. Blood escorted him to the entrance ladder at the foot of which still swung the *Arabella*'s own cock-boat.

"It's good-bye, my lord," said Blood. "And there's another thing." He proffered a parchment that he had drawn from his pocket. "It's the commission. Bishop was right when he said it was a mistake."

Lord Julian considered him, and considering him his expression softened.

"I am sorry," he said sincerely.

"In other circumstances . . ." began Blood. "Oh, but there! Ye'll understand. The boat's waiting."

Yet with his foot on the first rung of the ladder, Lord Julian hesitated.

"I still do not perceive—blister me if I do!—why you should not have found some one else to carry your message to the Commandant, and kept me aboard as an added hostage for his obedience to your wishes."

Blood's vivid eyes looked into the other's that were clear and honest, and he smiled, a little wistfully. A moment he seemed to hesitate. Then he explained himself quite fully.

"Why shouldn't I tell you? It's the same reason that's been urging me to pick a quarrel with you so that I might have the satisfaction of slipping a couple of feet of steel into your vitals. When I accepted your commission, I was moved to think it might redeem me in the eyes of Miss Bishop—for whose sake, as you may have guessed, I took it. But I have discovered that such a thing is beyond accomplishment. I should have known it for a sick man's dream. I have discovered also that if she's choosing you, as I believe she is, she's choosing wisely between us, and that's why I'll not have your life risked by keeping you aboard whilst the message goes by another who might bungle it. And now perhaps ye'll understand."

Lord Julian stared at him bewildered. His long, aristocratic face was very pale.

"My God!" he said. "And you tell me this?"

"I tell you because . . . Oh, plague on it!—so that ye may tell her; so that she may be made to realize that there's something of the unfortunate gentleman left under the thief and pirate she accounts me, and that her own good is my supreme desire. Knowing that, she may . . . faith, she may remember me more kindly—if it's only in her prayers. That's all, my lord."

Lord Julian continued to look at the buccaneer in silence. In silence, at last, he held out his hand; and in silence Blood took it.

"I wonder whether you are right," said his lordship, "and whether you are not the better man."

"Where she is concerned see that you make sure that I am right. Good-bye to you."

Lord Julian wrung his hand in silence, went down the ladder, and was pulled ashore. From the distance he waved to Blood, who stood leaning on the bulwarks watching the receding cock-boat.

The *Arabella* sailed within the hour, moving lazily before a sluggish breeze. The fort remained silent and there was no movement from the fleet to hinder her departure. Lord Julian had carried the message effectively, and had added to it his own personal commands.

XXIV. WAR

Five miles out at sea from Port Royal, whence the details of the coast of Jamaica were losing their sharpness, the *Arabella* hove to, and the sloop she had been towing was warped alongside.

Captain Blood escorted his compulsory guest to the head of the ladder. Colonel Bishop, who for two hours and more had been in a state of mortal anxiety, breathed freely at last; and as the tide of his fears receded, so that of his deep-rooted hate of this audacious buccaneer resumed its normal flow. But he practised circumspection. If in his heart he vowed that once back in Port Royal there was no effort he would spare, no nerve he would not strain, to bring Peter Blood to final moorings in Execution Dock, at least he kept that vow strictly to himself.

Peter Blood had no illusions. He was not, and never would be, the complete pirate. There was not another buccaneer in all the Caribbean who would have denied himself the pleasure of stringing Colonel Bishop from the yardarm, and by thus finally stifling the vindictive planter's hatred have increased his own security. But Blood was not of these. Moreover, in the case of Colonel Bishop there was a particular reason for restraint. Because he was Arabella Bishop's uncle, his life must remain sacred to Captain Blood.

And so the Captain smiled into the sallow, bloated face and the little eyes that fixed him with a malevolence not to be dissembled.

"A safe voyage home to you, Colonel, darling," said he in valediction, and from his easy, smiling manner you would never have dreamt of the pain he carried in his breast. "It's the second time ye've served me for a hostage. Ye'll be well advised to avoid a third. I'm not lucky to you, Colonel, as you should be perceiving."

Jeremy Pitt, the master, lounging at Blood's elbow, looked darkly upon the departure of the Deputy-Governor. Behind them a little mob of grim, stalwart, sun-tanned buccaneers were restrained from cracking Bishop like a flea only by their submission to the dominant will of their leader. They had learnt from Pitt while yet in Port Royal of their Captain's danger, and whilst as ready as he to throw over the King's service which had been thrust upon them, yet they resented the manner in which this had been rendered necessary, and they marvelled now at Blood's restraint where Bishop was concerned. The Deputy-Governor looked round and met the lowering hostile glances of those fierce eyes. Instinct warned him that his life at that moment was held precariously, that an injudicious word might precipitate an explosion of hatred from which no human power could save him. Therefore he said nothing. He inclined his head in silence to the Captain, and went blundering and stumbling in his haste down that ladder to the sloop and its waiting negro crew.

They pushed off the craft from the red hull of the *Arabella*, bent to their sweeps, then, hoisting sail, headed back for Port Royal, intent upon reaching it before darkness should come down upon them. And Bishop, the great bulk of him huddled in the stern sheets, sat silent, his black brows knitted, his coarse lips pursed, malevolence and vindictiveness so whelming now his recent panic that he forgot his near escape of the yardarm and the running noose.

On the mole at Port Royal, under the low, embattled wall of the fort, Major Mallard and Lord Julian waited to receive him, and it was with infinite relief that they assisted him from the sloop.

Major Mallard was disposed to be apologetic.

"Glad to see you safe, sir," said he. "I'd have sunk Blood's ship in spite of your excellency's being aboard but for your own orders by Lord Julian, and his lordship's assurance that he had Blood's word for it that no harm should come to you so that no harm came to him. I'll confess I thought it rash of his lordship to accept the word of a damned pirate . . ."

"I have found it as good as another's," said his lordship, cropping the Major's too eager eloquence. He spoke with an unusual degree of that frosty dignity he could assume upon occasion. The fact is that his lordship was in an exceedingly bad humour. Having written jubilantly home to the Secretary of State that his mission had succeeded, he was now faced with the necessity of writing again to confess that this success had been ephemeral. And because Major Mallard's crisp mostachios were lifted by a sneer at the notion of a buccaneer's word being acceptable, he added still more sharply: "My justification is here in the person of Colonel Bishop safely returned. As against that, sir, your opinion does not weigh for very much. You should realize it."

"Oh, as your lordship says." Major Mallard's manner was tinged with irony. "To be sure, here is the Colonel safe and sound. And out yonder is Captain Blood, also safe and sound, to begin his piratical ravages all over again."

"I do not propose to discuss the reasons with you, Major Mallard."

"And, anyway, it's not for long," growled the Colonel, finding speech at last. "No, by . . ." He emphasized the assurance by an unprintable oath. "If I spend the last shilling of my fortune and the last ship of the Jamaica fleet, I'll have that rascal in a hempen necktie before I rest. And I'll not be long about it." He had empurpled in his angry vehemence, and the veins of his forehead stood out like whipcord. Then he checked.

"You did well to follow Lord Julian's instructions," he commended the Major. With that he turned from him, and took his lordship by the arm. "Come, my lord. We must take order about this, you and I."

They went off together, skirting the redoubt, and so through courtyard and garden to the house where Arabella waited anxiously. The sight of her uncle brought her infinite relief, not only on his own account, but on account also of Captain Blood.

"You took a great risk, sir," she gravely told Lord Julian after the ordinary greetings had been exchanged.

But Lord Julian answered her as he had answered Major Mallard. "There was no risk, ma'am."

She looked at him in some astonishment. His long, aristocratic face wore a more melancholy, pensive air than usual. He answered the enquiry in her glance:

"So that Blood's ship were allowed to pass the fort, no harm could come to Colonel Bishop. Blood pledged me his word for that."

A faint smile broke the set of her lips, which hitherto had been wistful, and a little colour tinged her cheeks. She would have pursued the subject, but the Deputy-

Governor's mood did not permit it. He sneered and snorted at the notion of Blood's word being good for anything, forgetting that he owed to it his own preservation at that moment.

At supper, and for long thereafter he talked of nothing but Blood—of how he would lay him by the heels, and what hideous things he would perform upon his body. And as he drank heavily the while, his speech became increasingly gross and his threats increasingly horrible; until in the end Arabella withdrew, white-faced and almost on the verge of tears. It was not often that Bishop revealed himself to his niece. Oddly enough, this coarse, overbearing planter went in a certain awe of that slim girl. It was as if she had inherited from her father the respect in which he had always been held by his brother.

Lord Julian, who began to find Bishop disgusting beyond endurance, excused himself soon after, and went in quest of the lady. He had yet to deliver the message from Captain Blood, and this, he thought, would be his opportunity. But Miss Bishop had retired for the night, and Lord Julian must curb his impatience—it amounted by now to nothing less—until the morrow.

Very early next morning, before the heat of the day came to render the open intolerable to his lordship, he espied her from his window moving amid the azaleas in the garden. It was a fitting setting for one who was still as much a delightful novelty to him in womanhood as was the azalea among flowers. He hurried forth to join her, and when, aroused from her pensiveness, she had given him a good-morrow, smiling and frank, he explained himself by the announcement that he bore her a message from Captain Blood.

He observed her little start and the slight quiver of her lips, and observed thereafter not only her pallor and the shadowy rings about her eyes, but also that unusually wistful air which last night had escaped his notice.

They moved out of the open to one of the terraces, where a pergola of orange-trees provided a shaded sauntering space that was at once cool and fragrant. As they went, he considered her admiringly, and marvelled at himself that it should have taken him so long fully to realize her slim, unusual grace, and to find her, as he now did, so entirely desirable, a woman whose charm must irradiate all the life of a man, and touch its commonplaces into magic.

He noted the sheen of her red-brown hair, and how gracefully one of its heavy ringlets coiled upon her slender, milk-white neck. She wore a gown of shimmering grey silk, and a scarlet rose, fresh-gathered, was pinned at her breast like a splash of blood.

Always thereafter when he thought of her it was as he saw her at that moment, as never, I think, until that moment had he seen her.

In silence they paced on a little way into the green shade. Then she paused and faced him.

"You said something of a message, sir," she reminded him, thus betraying some of her impatience.

He fingered the ringlets of his periwig, a little embarrassed how to deliver himself, considering how he should begin.

"He desired me," he said at last, "to give you a message that should prove to you that there is still something left in him of the unfortunate gentleman that . . . that . . . for which once you knew him."

"That is not now necessary," said she very gravely.

He misunderstood her, of course, knowing nothing of the enlightenment that yesterday had come to her.

"I think . . . nay, I know that you do him an injustice," said he.

Her hazel eyes continued to regard him.

"If you will deliver the message, it may enable me to judge."

To him, this was confusing. He did not immediately answer. He found that he had not sufficiently considered the terms he should employ, and the matter, after all, was of an exceeding delicacy, demanding delicate handling. It was not so much that he was concerned to deliver a message as to render it a vehicle by which to plead his own cause. Lord Julian, well versed in the lore of womankind and usually at his ease with ladies of the beau-monde, found himself oddly constrained before this frank and unsophisticated niece of a colonial planter.

They moved on in silence and as if by common consent towards the brilliant sunshine where the pergola was intersected by the avenue leading upwards to the house. Across this patch of light fluttered a gorgeous butterfly, that was like black and scarlet velvet and large as a man's hand. His lordship's brooding eyes followed it out of sight before he answered.

"It is not easy. Stab me, it is not. He was a man who deserved well. And amongst us we have marred his chances: your uncle, because he could not forget his rancour; you, because . . . because having told him that in the King's service he would find his redemption of what was past, you would not afterwards admit to him that he was so redeemed. And this, although concern to rescue you was the chief motive of his embracing that same service."

She had turned her shoulder to him so that he should not see her face.

"I know. I know now," she said softly. Then after a pause she added the question: "And you? What part has your lordship had in this—that you should incriminate yourself with us?"

"My part?" Again he hesitated, then plunged recklessly on, as men do when determined to perform a thing they fear. "If I understood him aright, if he understood aright, himself, my part, though entirely passive, was none the less effective. I implore you to observe that I but report his own words. I say nothing for myself." His lordship's unusual nervousness was steadily increasing. "He thought, then—so he told me—that my presence here had contributed to his inability to redeem himself in your sight; and unless he were so redeemed, then was redemption nothing."

She faced him fully, a frown of perplexity bringing her brows together above her troubled eyes.

"He thought that you had contributed?" she echoed. It was clear she asked for enlightenment. He plunged on to afford it her, his glance a little scared, his cheeks flushing.

"Aye, and he said so in terms which told me something that I hope above all things, and yet dare not believe, for, God knows, I am no coxcomb, Arabella. He said . . . But first let me tell you how I was placed. I had gone aboard his ship to demand the instant surrender of your uncle whom he held captive. He laughed at me. Colonel Bishop should be a hostage for his safety. By rashly venturing aboard his ship, I afforded him in my own person yet another hostage as valuable at least as Colonel Bishop. Yet he bade me depart; not from the fear of consequences, for he is above fear, nor from any personal esteem for me whom he confessed that he had come to find detestable; and this for the very reason that made him concerned for my safety."

"I do not understand," she said, as he paused. "Is not that a contradiction in itself?"

"It seems so only. The fact is, Arabella, this unfortunate man has the . . . the temerity to love you."

She cried out at that, and clutched her breast whose calm was suddenly disturbed. Her eyes dilated as she stared at him.

"I . . . I've startled you," said he, with concern. "I feared I should. But it was necessary so that you may understand."

"Go on," she bade him.

"Well, then: he saw in me one who made it impossible that he should win you—so he said. Therefore he could with satisfaction have killed me. But because my death might cause you pain, because your happiness was the thing that above all things he desired, he surrendered that part of his guarantee of safety which my person afforded him. If his departure should be hindered, and I should lose my life in what might follow, there was the risk that . . . that you might mourn me. That risk he would not take. Him you deemed a thief and a pirate, he said, and added that—I am giving you his own words always—if in choosing between us two, your choice, as he believed, would fall on me, then were you in his opinion choosing wisely. Because of that he bade me leave his ship, and had me put ashore."

She looked at him with eyes that were aswim with tears. He took a step towards her, a catch in his breath, his hand held out.

"Was he right, Arabella? My life's happiness hangs upon your answer."

But she continued silently to regard him with those tear-laden eyes, without speaking, and until she spoke he dared not advance farther.

A doubt, a tormenting doubt beset him. When presently she spoke, he saw how true had been the instinct of which that doubt was born, for her words revealed the fact that of all that he had said the only thing that had touched her consciousness and absorbed it from all other considerations was Blood's conduct as it regarded herself.

"He said that!" she cried. "He did that! Oh!" She turned away, and through the slender, clustering trunks of the bordering orange-trees she looked out across the glittering waters of the great harbour to the distant hills. Thus for a little while, my lord standing stiffly, fearfully, waiting for fuller revelation of her mind. At last it came, slowly, deliberately, in a voice that at moments was half suffocated. "Last night when my uncle displayed his rancour and his evil rage, it began to be borne in upon me that such vindictiveness can belong only to those who have wronged. It is the frenzy into which men whip themselves to justify an evil passion. I must have known then, if I had not already learnt it, that I had been too credulous of all the unspeakable things attributed to Peter Blood. Yesterday I had his own explanation of that tale of Levasseur that you heard in St. Nicholas. And now this . . . this but gives me confirmation of his truth and worth. To a scoundrel such as I was too readily brought to believe him, the act of which you have just told me would have been impossible."

"That is my own opinion," said his lordship gently.

"It must be. But even if it were not, that would now weigh for nothing. What weighs—oh, so heavily and bitterly—is the thought that but for the words in which yesterday I repelled him, he might have been saved. If only I could have spoken to him again before he went! I waited for him; but my uncle was with him, and I had no suspicion that he was going away again. And now he is lost—back at his outlawry and piracy, in which ultimately he will be taken and destroyed. And the fault is mine—mine!"

"What are you saying? The only agents were your uncle's hostility and his own obstinacy which would not study compromise. You must not blame yourself for anything."

She swung to him with some impatience, her eyes aswim in tears. "You can say that, and in spite of his message, which in itself tells how much I was to blame! It was my treatment of him, the epithets I cast at him that drove him. So much he has told you. I know it to be true."

"You have no cause for shame," said he. "As for your sorrow—why, if it will afford you solace—you may still count on me to do what man can to rescue him from this position."

She caught her breath.

"You will do that!" she cried with sudden eager hopefulness. "You promise?" She held out her hand to him impulsively. He took it in both his own.

"I promise," he answered her. And then, retaining still the hand she had surrendered to him—"Arabella," he said very gently, "there is still this other matter upon which you have not answered me."

"This other matter?" Was he mad, she wondered. Could any other matter signify in such a moment.

"This matter that concerns myself; and all my future, oh, so very closely. This thing that Blood believed, that prompted him . . . that . . . that you are not indifferent to me." He saw the fair face change colour and grow troubled once more.

"Indifferent to you?" said she. "Why, no. We have been good friends; we shall continue so, I hope, my lord."

"Friends! Good friends?" He was between dismay and bitterness. "It is not your friendship only that I ask, Arabella. You heard what I said, what I reported. You will not say that Peter Blood was wrong?"

Gently she sought to disengage her hand, the trouble in her face increasing. A moment he resisted; then, realizing what he did, he set her free.

"Arabella!" he cried on a note of sudden pain.

"I have friendship for you, my lord. But only friendship."

His castle of hopes came clattering down about him, leaving him a little stunned. As he had said, he was no coxcomb. Yet there was something that he did not understand.

She confessed to friendship, and it was in his power to offer her a great position, one to which she, a colonial planter's niece, however wealthy, could never have aspired even in her dreams. This she rejected, yet spoke of friendship. Peter Blood had been mistaken, then. How far had he been mistaken? Had he been as mistaken in her feelings towards himself as he obviously was in her feelings towards his lordship? In that case . . . His reflections broke short. To speculate was to wound himself in vain. He must know. Therefore he asked her with grim frankness:

"Is it Peter Blood?"

"Peter Blood?" she echoed. At first she did not understand the purport of his question. When understanding came, a flush suffused her face.

"I do not know," she said, faltering a little.

This was hardly a truthful answer. For, as if an obscuring veil had suddenly been rent that morning, she was permitted at last to see Peter Blood in his true relations to other men, and that sight, vouchsafed her twenty-four hours too late, filled her with pity and regret and yearning.

Lord Julian knew enough of women to be left in no further doubt. He bowed his head so that she might not see the anger in his eyes, for as a man of honour he took shame in that anger which as a human being he could not repress.

And because Nature in him was stronger—as it is in most of us—than training, Lord Julian from that moment began, almost in spite of himself, to practise something that was akin to villainy. I regret to chronicle it of one for whom— if I have done him any sort of justice—you should have been conceiving some esteem. But the truth is that the lingering remains of the regard in which he had held Peter Blood were choked by the desire to supplant and destroy a rival. He had passed his word to Arabella that he would use his powerful influence on Blood's behalf. I deplore to set it down that not only did he forget his pledge, but secretly set himself to aid and abet Arabella's uncle in the plans he laid for the trapping and undoing of the buccaneer. He might reasonably have urged—had he been taxed with it—that he conducted himself precisely as his duty demanded. But to that he might have been answered that duty with him was but the slave of jealousy in this.

When the Jamaica fleet put to sea some few days later, Lord Julian sailed with Colonel Bishop in Vice-Admiral Craufurd's flagship. Not only was there no need for either of them to go, but the Deputy-Governor's duties actually demanded that he should remain ashore, whilst Lord Julian, as we know, was a useless man aboard a ship. Yet both set out to hunt Captain Blood, each making of his duty a pretext for the satisfaction of personal aims; and that common purpose became a link between them, binding them in a sort of friendship that must otherwise have been impossible between men so dissimilar in breeding and in aspirations.

The hunt was up. They cruised awhile off Hispaniola, watching the Windward Passage, and suffering the discomforts of the rainy season which had now set in. But they cruised in vain, and after a month of it, returned empty-handed to Port Royal, there to find awaiting them the most disquieting news from the Old World.

The megalomania of Louis XIV had set Europe in a blaze of war. The French legionaries were ravaging the Rhine provinces, and Spain had joined the nations leagued to defend themselves from the wild ambitions of the King of France. And there was worse than this: there were rumours of civil war in England, where the people had grown weary of the bigoted tyranny of King James. It was reported that William of Orange had been invited to come over.

Weeks passed, and every ship from home brought additional news. William had crossed to England, and in March of that year 1689 they learnt in Jamaica that he had accepted the crown and that James had thrown himself into the arms of France for rehabilitation.

To a kinsman of Sunderland's this was disquieting news, indeed. It was followed by letters from King William's Secretary of State informing Colonel Bishop that there was war with France, and that in view of its effect upon the Colonies a Governor-General was coming out to the West Indies in the person of Lord Willoughby, and that with him came a squadron under the command of Admiral van der Kuylen to reënforce the Jamaica fleet against eventualities.

Bishop realized that this must mean the end of his supreme authority, even though he should continue in Port Royal as Deputy-Governor. Lord Julian, in the lack of direct news to himself, did not know what it might mean to him. But he had been very close and confidential with Colonel Bishop regarding his hopes of Arabella, and Colonel Bishop more than ever, now that political events put him in danger of being retired, was anxious to enjoy the advantages of having a man of Lord Julian's eminence for his relative.

They came to a complete understanding in the matter, and Lord Julian disclosed all that he knew.

"There is one obstacle in our path," said he. "Captain Blood. The girl is in love with him."

"Ye're surely mad!" cried Bishop, when he had recovered speech.

"You are justified of the assumption," said his lordship dolefully. "But I happen to be sane, and to speak with knowledge."

"With knowledge?"

"Arabella herself has confessed it to me."

"The brazen baggage! By God, I'll bring her to her senses." It was the slave-driver speaking, the man who governed with a whip.

"Don't be a fool, Bishop." His lordship's contempt did more than any argument to calm the Colonel. "That's not the way with a girl of Arabella's spirit. Unless you want to wreck my chances for all time, you'll hold your tongue, and not interfere at all."

"Not interfere? My God, what, then?"

"Listen, man. She has a constant mind. I don't think you know your niece. As long as Blood lives, she will wait for him."

"Then with Blood dead, perhaps she will come to her silly senses."

"Now you begin to show intelligence," Lord Julian commended him. "That is the first essential step."

"And here is our chance to take it." Bishop warmed to a sort of enthusiasm. "This war with France removes all restrictions in the matter of Tortuga. We are free to invest it in the service of the Crown. A victory there and we establish ourselves in the favour of this new government."

"Ah!" said Lord Julian, and he pulled thoughtfully at his lip.

"I see that you understand," Bishop laughed coarsely. "Two birds with one stone, eh? We'll hunt this rascal in his lair, right under the beard of the King of France, and we'll take him this time, if we reduce Tortuga to a heap of ashes."

On that expedition they sailed two days later—which would be some three months after Blood's departure—taking every ship of the fleet, and several lesser vessels as auxiliaries. To Arabella and the world in general it was given out that they were going to raid French Hispaniola, which was really the only expedition that could have afforded Colonel Bishop any sort of justification for leaving Jamaica at all at such a time. His sense of duty, indeed, should have kept him fast in Port Royal; but his sense of duty was smothered in hatred—that most fruitless and corruptive of all the emotions. In the great cabin of Vice-Admiral Craufurd's flagship, the *Imperator*, the Deputy-Governor got drunk that night to celebrate his conviction that the sands of Captain Blood's career were running out.

XXV. The Service of King Louis

Meanwhile, some three months before Colonel Bishop set out to reduce Tortuga, Captain Blood, bearing hell in his soul, had blown into its rockbound harbour ahead of the winter gales, and two days ahead of the frigate in which Wolverstone had sailed from Port Royal a day before him.

In that snug anchorage he found his fleet awaiting him—the four ships which had been separated in that gale off the Lesser Antilles, and some seven hundred men composing their crews. Because they had been beginning to grow anxious on his behalf, they gave him the greater welcome. Guns were fired in his honour and the ships made themselves gay with bunting. The town, aroused by all this noise in the harbour, emptied itself upon the jetty, and a vast crowd of men and women of all creeds and nationalities collected there to be present at the coming ashore of the great buccaneer.

Ashore he went, probably for no other reason than to obey the general expectation. His mood was taciturn; his face grim and sneering. Let Wolverstone arrive, as presently he would, and all this hero-worship would turn to execration.

His captains, Hagthorpe, Christian, and Yberville, were on the jetty to receive him, and with them were some hundreds of his buccaneers. He cut short their greetings, and when they plagued him with questions of where he had tarried, he bade them await the coming of Wolverstone, who would satisfy their curiosity to a surfeit. On that he shook them off, and shouldered his way through that heterogeneous throng that was composed of bustling traders of several nations—English, French, and Dutch—of planters and of seamen of various degrees, of buccaneers who were legitimate boucan-hunters from Hispaniola and buccaneers who were frankly pirates, of lumbermen and Indians, of fruit-selling half-castes, negro slaves, some doll-tearsheets and dunghill-queans from the Old World, and all the other types of the human family that converted the quays of Cayona into a disreputable image of Babel.

Winning clear at last, and after difficulties, Captain Blood took his way alone to the fine house of M. d'Ogeron, there to pay his respects to his friends, the Governor and the Governor's family.

At first the buccaneers jumped to the conclusion that Wolverstone was following with some rare prize of war, but gradually from the reduced crew of the *Arabella* a very different tale leaked out to stem their satisfaction and convert it into perplexity. Partly out of loyalty to their captain, partly because they perceived that if he was guilty of defection they were guilty with him, and partly because being simple, sturdy men of their hands, they were themselves in the main a little confused as to what really had happened, the crew of the *Arabella* practised reticence with their brethren in Tortuga during those two days before Wolverstone's arrival. But they were not reticent enough to prevent the circulation of certain uneasy rumours and extravagant stories of discreditable adventures—discreditable, that is, from the buccaneering point of view—of which Captain Blood had been guilty.

But that Wolverstone came when he did, it is possible that there would have been an explosion. When, however, the Old Wolf cast anchor in the bay two days later, it was to him all turned for the explanation they were about to demand of Blood.

Now Wolverstone had only one eye; but he saw a deal more with that one eye than do most men with two; and despite his grizzled head—so picturesquely swathed in a green and scarlet turban—he had the sound heart of a boy, and in that heart much love for Peter Blood.

The sight of the *Arabella* at anchor in the bay had at first amazed him as he sailed round the rocky headland that bore the fort. He rubbed his single eye clear of any deceiving film and looked again. Still he could not believe what it saw. And then a voice at his elbow—the voice of Dyke, who had elected to sail with him—assured him that he was not singular in his bewilderment.

"In the name of Heaven, is that the *Arabella* or is it the ghost of her?"

The Old Wolf rolled his single eye over Dyke, and opened his mouth to speak. Then he closed it again without having spoken; closed it tightly. He had a great gift of caution, especially in matters that he did not understand. That this was the *Arabella* he could no longer doubt. That being so, he must think before he spoke. What the devil should the *Arabella* be doing here, when he had left her in Jamaica? And was Captain Blood aboard and in command, or had the remainder of her hands made off with her, leaving the Captain in Port Royal?

Dyke repeated his question. This time Wolverstone answered him.

"Ye've two eyes to see with, and ye ask me, who's only got one, what it is ye see!"

"But I see the *Arabella*."

"Of course, since there she rides. What else was you expecting?"

"Expecting?" Dyke stared at him, open-mouthed. "Was you expecting to find the *Arabella* here?"

Wolverstone looked him over in contempt, then laughed and spoke loud enough to be heard by all around him.

"Of course. What else?" And he laughed again, a laugh that seemed to Dyke to be calling him a fool. On that Wolverstone turned to give his attention to the operation of anchoring.

Anon when ashore he was beset by questioning buccaneers, it was from their very questions that he gathered exactly how matters stood, and perceived that either from lack of courage or other motive Blood, himself, had refused to render any account of his doings since the *Arabella* had separated from her sister ships. Wolverstone congratulated himself upon the discretion he had used with Dyke.

"The Captain was ever a modest man," he explained to Hagthorpe and those others who came crowding round him. "It's not his way to be sounding his own praises. Why, it was like this. We fell in with old Don Miguel, and when we'd scuttled him we took aboard a London pimp sent out by the Secretary of State to offer the Captain the King's commission if so be him'd quit piracy and be o' good behaviour. The Captain damned his soul to hell for answer. And then we fell in wi' the Jamaica fleet and that grey old devil Bishop in command, and there was a sure end to Captain Blood and to every mother's son of us all. So I goes to him, and 'accept this poxy commission,' says I; 'turn King's man and save your neck and ours.' He took me at my word, and the London pimp gave him the King's commission on the spot, and Bishop all but choked hisself with rage when he was told of it. But happened it had, and he was forced to swallow it. We were King's men all, and so into Port Royal we sailed along o' Bishop. But Bishop didn't trust us. He knew too much. But for his lordship, the fellow from London, he'd ha' hanged the Captain, King's commission and all. Blood would ha' slipped out o' Port Royal again that same night. But that hound Bishop had passed the word, and the fort kept a sharp lookout. In the end, though it took a fortnight, Blood bubbled him. He sent me and most o' the men off in a frigate that I bought for the voyage. His game—as he'd secretly told me—was to follow and give chase. Whether that's the game he played or not I can't tell ye; but here he is afore me as I'd expected he would be."

There was a great historian lost in Wolverstone. He had the right imagination that knows just how far it is safe to stray from the truth and just how far to colour it so as to change its shape for his own purposes.

Having delivered himself of his decoction of fact and falsehood, and thereby added one more to the exploits of Peter Blood, he enquired where the Captain might be found. Being informed that he kept his ship, Wolverstone stepped into a boat and went aboard, to report himself, as he put it.

In the great cabin of the *Arabella* he found Peter Blood alone and very far gone in drink—a condition in which no man ever before remembered to have seen him. As Wolverstone came in, the Captain raised bloodshot eyes to consider him. A moment they sharpened in their gaze as he brought his visitor into focus. Then he laughed, a loose, idiot laugh, that yet somehow was half a sneer.

"Ah! The Old Wolf!" said he. "Got here at last, eh? And whatcher gonnerdo wi' me, eh?" He hiccoughed resoundingly, and sagged back loosely in his chair.

Old Wolverstone stared at him in sombre silence. He had looked with untroubled eye upon many a hell of devilment in his time, but the sight of Captain Blood in this condition filled him with sudden grief. To express it he loosed an oath. It was his only expression for emotion of all kinds. Then he rolled forward, and dropped into a chair at the table, facing the Captain.

"My God, Peter, what's this?"

"Rum," said Peter. "Rum, from Jamaica." He pushed bottle and glass towards Wolverstone.

Wolverstone disregarded them.

"I'm asking you what ails you?" he bawled.

"Rum," said Captain Blood again, and smiled. "Jus' rum. I answer all your queshons. Why donjerr answer mine? Whatcher gonerdo wi' me?"

"I've done it," said Wolverstone. "Thank God, ye had the sense to hold your tongue till I came. Are ye sober enough to understand me?"

"Drunk or sober, allus 'derstand you."

"Then listen." And out came the tale that Wolverstone had told. The Captain steadied himself to grasp it.

"It'll do as well asertruth," said he when Wolverstone had finished. "And . . . oh, no marrer! Much obliged to ye, Old Wolf—faithful Old Wolf! But was it worthertrouble? I'm norrer pirate now; never a pirate again. 'S finished!" He banged the table, his eyes suddenly fierce.

"I'll come and talk to you again when there's less rum in your wits," said Wolverstone, rising. "Meanwhile ye'll please to remember the tale I've told, and say nothing that'll make me out a liar. They all believes me, even the men as sailed wi' me from Port Royal. I've made 'em. If they thought as how you'd taken the King's commission in earnest, and for the purpose o' doing as Morgan did, ye guess what would follow."

"Hell would follow," said the Captain. "An' tha's all I'm fit for."

"Ye're maudlin," Wolverstone growled. "We'll talk again to-morrow."

They did; but to little purpose, either that day or on any day thereafter while the rains—which set in that night—endured. Soon the shrewd Wolverstone discovered that rum was not what ailed Blood. Rum was in itself an effect, and not by any means the cause of the Captain's listless apathy. There was a canker eating at his heart, and the Old Wolf knew enough to make a shrewd guess of its nature. He cursed all things that daggled petticoats, and, knowing his world, waited for the sickness to pass.

But it did not pass. When Blood was not dicing or drinking in the taverns of Tortuga, keeping company that in his saner days he had loathed, he was shut up in his cabin aboard the *Arabella*, alone and uncommunicative. His friends at Government House, bewildered at this change in him, sought to reclaim him. Mademoiselle d'Ogeron, particularly distressed, sent him almost daily invitations, to few of which he responded.

Later, as the rainy season approached its end, he was sought by his captains with proposals of remunerative raids on Spanish settlements. But to all he manifested an indifference which, as the weeks passed and the weather became settled, begot first impatience and then exasperation.

Christian, who commanded the *Clotho*, came storming to him one day, upbraiding him for his inaction, and demanding that he should take order about what was to do.

"Go to the devil!" Blood said, when he had heard him out.

Christian departed fuming, and on the morrow the *Clotho* weighed anchor and sailed away, setting an example of desertion from which the loyalty of Blood's other captains would soon be unable to restrain their men.

Sometimes Blood asked himself why had he come back to Tortuga at all. Held fast in bondage by the thought of Arabella and her scorn of him for a thief and a pirate, he had sworn that he had done with buccaneering. Why, then, was he here? That question he would answer with another: Where else was he to go? Neither backward nor forward could he move, it seemed.

He was degenerating visibly, under the eyes of all. He had entirely lost the almost foppish concern for his appearance, and was grown careless and slovenly in his dress. He allowed a black beard to grow on cheeks that had ever been so carefully shaven; and the long, thick black hair, once so sedulously curled, hung now in a lank, untidy mane about a face that was changing from its vigorous swarthiness to an unhealthy sallow, whilst the blue eyes, that had been so vivid and compelling, were now dull and lacklustre.

Wolverstone, the only one who held the clue to this degeneration, ventured once— and once only—to beard him frankly about it.

"Lord, Peter! Is there never to be no end to this?" the giant had growled. "Will you spend your days moping and swilling 'cause a white-faced ninny in Port Royal'll have none o' ye? 'Sblood and 'Ounds! If ye wants the wench, why the plague doesn't ye go and fetch her?"

The blue eyes glared at him from under the jet-black eyebrows, and something of their old fire began to kindle in them. But Wolverstone went on heedlessly.

"I'll be nice wi' a wench as long as niceness be the key to her favour. But sink me now if I'd rot myself in rum on account of anything that wears a petticoat. That's not the Old Wolf's way. If there's no other expedition'll tempt you, why not Port Royal? What a plague do it matter if it is an English settlement? It's commanded by Colonel Bishop, and there's no lack of rascals in your company'd follow you to hell if it meant getting Colonel Bishop by the throat. It could be done, I tell you. We've but to spy the chance when the Jamaica fleet is away. There's enough plunder in the town to tempt the lads, and there's the wench for you. Shall I sound them on 't?"

Blood was on his feet, his eyes blazing, his livid face distorted. "Ye'll leave my cabin this minute, so ye will, or, by Heaven, it's your corpse'll be carried out of it. Ye mangy hound, d'ye dare come to me with such proposals?"

He fell to cursing his faithful officer with a virulence the like of which he had never yet been known to use. And Wolverstone, in terror before that fury, went out without another word. The subject was not raised again, and Captain Blood was left to his idle abstraction.

But at last, as his buccaneers were growing desperate, something happened, brought about by the Captain's friend M. d'Ogeron. One sunny morning the Governor of Tortuga came aboard the *Arabella*, accompanied by a chubby little gentleman, amiable of countenance, amiable and self-sufficient of manner.

"My Captain," M. d'Ogeron delivered himself, "I bring you M. de Cussy, the Governor of French Hispaniola, who desires a word with you."

Out of consideration for his friend, Captain Blood pulled the pipe from his mouth, shook some of the rum out of his wits, and rose and made a leg to M. de Cussy.

"Serviteur!" said he.

M. de Cussy returned the bow and accepted a seat on the locker under the stern windows.

"You have a good force here under your command, my Captain," said he.

"Some eight hundred men."

"And I understand they grow restive in idleness."

"They may go to the devil when they please."

M. de Cussy took snuff delicately. "I have something better than that to propose," said he.

"Propose it, then," said Blood, without interest.

M. de Cussy looked at M. d'Ogeron, and raised his eyebrows a little. He did not find Captain Blood encouraging. But M. d'Ogeron nodded vigorously with pursed lips, and the Governor of Hispaniola propounded his business.

"News has reached us from France that there is war with Spain."

"That is news, is it?" growled Blood.

"I am speaking officially, my Captain. I am not alluding to unofficial skirmishes, and unofficial predatory measures which we have condoned out here. There is war—formally war—between France and Spain in Europe. It is the intention of France that this war shall be carried into the New World. A fleet is coming out from Brest under the command of M. le Baron de Rivarol for that purpose. I have letters from him desiring me to equip a supplementary squadron and raise a body of not less than a thousand men to reënforce him on his arrival. What I have come to propose to you, my Captain, at the suggestion of our good friend M. d'Ogeron, is, in brief, that you enrol your ships and your force under M. de Rivarol's flag."

Blood looked at him with a faint kindling of interest. "You are offering to take us into the French service?" he asked. "On what terms, monsieur?"

"With the rank of Capitaine de Vaisseau for yourself, and suitable ranks for the officers serving under you. You will enjoy the pay of that rank, and you will be entitled, together with your men, to one-tenth share in all prizes taken."

"My men will hardly account it generous. They will tell you that they can sail out of here to-morrow, disembowel a Spanish settlement, and keep the whole of the plunder."

"Ah, yes, but with the risks attaching to acts of piracy. With us your position will be regular and official, and considering the powerful fleet by which M. de Rivarol is backed, the enterprises to be undertaken will be on a much vaster scale than anything you could attempt on your own account. So that the one tenth in this case may be equal to more than the whole in the other."

Captain Blood considered. This, after all, was not piracy that was being proposed. It was honourable employment in the service of the King of France.

"I will consult my officers," he said; and he sent for them.

They came and the matter was laid before them by M. de Cussy himself. Hagthorpe announced at once that the proposal was opportune. The men were grumbling at their protracted inaction, and would no doubt be ready to accept the service which M. de Cussy offered on behalf of France. Hagthorpe looked at Blood as he spoke. Blood nodded gloomy agreement. Emboldened by this, they went on to discuss the terms. Yberville, the young French filibuster, had the honour to point out to M. de Cussy that the share offered was too small. For one fifth of the prizes, the officers would answer for their men; not for less.

M. de Cussy was distressed. He had his instructions. It was taking a deal upon himself to exceed them. The buccaneers were firm. Unless M. de Cussy could make it one fifth there was no more to be said. M. de Cussy finally consenting to exceed his instructions, the articles were drawn up and signed that very day. The buccaneers were to be at Petit Goave by the end of January, when M. de Rivarol had announced that he might be expected.

After that followed days of activity in Tortuga, refitting the ships, boucanning meat, laying in stores. In these matters which once would have engaged all Captain Blood's attention, he now took no part. He continued listless and aloof. If he had given his consent to the undertaking, or, rather, allowed himself to be swept into it by the wishes of his officers—it was only because the service offered was of a regular and honourable kind, nowise connected with piracy, with which he swore in his heart that he had done for ever. But his consent remained passive. The service entered awoke no zeal in him. He was perfectly indifferent—as he told Hagthorpe, who ventured once to offer a remonstrance—whether they went to Petit Goave or to Hades, and whether they entered the service of Louis XIV or of Satan.

XXVI. M. DE RIVAROL

Captain Blood was still in that disgruntled mood when he sailed from Tortuga, and still in that mood when he came to his moorings in the bay of Petit Goave. In that same mood he greeted M. le Baron de Rivarol when this nobleman with his fleet of five men-of-war at last dropped anchor alongside the buccaneer ships, in the middle of February. The Frenchman had been six weeks on the voyage, he announced, delayed by unfavourable weather.

Summoned to wait on him, Captain Blood repaired to the Castle of Petit Goave, where the interview was to take place. The Baron, a tall, hawk-faced man of forty, very cold and distant of manner, measured Captain Blood with an eye of obvious disapproval. Of Hagthorpe, Yberville, and Wolverstone who stood ranged behind their captain, he took no heed whatever. M. de Cussy offered Captain Blood a chair.

"A moment, M. de Cussy. I do not think M. le Baron has observed that I am not alone. Let me present to you, sir, my companions: Captain Hagthorpe of the *Elizabeth*, Captain Wolverstone of the *Atropos*, and Captain Yberville of the *Lachesis*."

The Baron stared hard and haughtily at Captain Blood, then very distantly and barely perceptibly inclined his head to each of the other three. His manner implied plainly that he despised them and that he desired them at once to understand it. It had a curious effect upon Captain Blood. It awoke the devil in him, and it awoke at the same time his self-respect which of late had been slumbering. A sudden shame of his disordered, ill-kempt appearance made him perhaps the more defiant. There was almost a significance in the way he hitched his sword-belt round, so that the wrought hilt of his very serviceable rapier was brought into fuller view. He waved his captains to the chairs that stood about.

"Draw up to the table, lads. We are keeping the Baron waiting."

They obeyed him, Wolverstone with a grin that was full of understanding. Haughtier grew the stare of M. de Rivarol. To sit at table with these bandits placed him upon what he accounted a dishonouring equality. It had been his notion that—with the possible exception of Captain Blood—they should take his instructions standing, as became men of their quality in the presence of a man of his. He did the only thing remaining to mark a distinction between himself and them. He put on his hat.

"Ye're very wise now," said Blood amiably. "I feel the draught myself." And he covered himself with his plumed castor.

M. de Rivarol changed colour. He quivered visibly with anger, and was a moment controlling himself before venturing to speak. M. de Cussy was obviously very ill at ease.

"Sir," said the Baron frostily, "you compel me to remind you that the rank you hold is that of Capitaine de Vaisseau, and that you are in the presence of the General of the Armies of France by Sea and Land in America. You compel me to remind you further that there is a deference due from your rank to mine."

"I am happy to assure you," said Captain Blood, "that the reminder is unnecessary. I am by way of accounting myself a gentleman, little though I may look like one at present; and I should not account myself that were I capable of anything but deference to those whom nature or fortune may have placed above me, or to those who being placed beneath me in rank may labour under a disability to resent my lack of it." It was a neatly intangible rebuke. M. de Rivarol bit his lip. Captain Blood swept on without giving him time to reply: "Thus much being clear, shall we come to business?"

M. de Rivarol's hard eyes considered him a moment. "Perhaps it will be best," said he. He took up a paper. "I have here a copy of the articles into which you entered with

M. de Cussy. Before going further, I have to observe that M. de Cussy has exceeded his instructions in admitting you to one fifth of the prizes taken. His authority did not warrant his going beyond one tenth."

"That is a matter between yourself and M. de Cussy, my General."

"Oh, no. It is a matter between myself and you."

"Your pardon, my General. The articles are signed. So far as we are concerned, the matter is closed. Also out of regard for M. de Cussy, we should not desire to be witnesses of the rebukes you may consider that he deserves."

"What I may have to say to M. de Cussy is no concern of yours."

"That is what I am telling you, my General."

"But—nom de Dieu!—it is your concern, I suppose, that we cannot award you more than one tenth share." M. de Rivarol smote the table in exasperation. This pirate was too infernally skilful a fencer.

"You are quite certain of that, M. le Baron—that you cannot?"

"I am quite certain that I will not."

Captain Blood shrugged, and looked down his nose. "In that case," said he, "it but remains for me to present my little account for our disbursement, and to fix the sum at which we should be compensated for our loss of time and derangement in coming hither. That settled, we can part friends, M. le Baron. No harm has been done."

"What the devil do you mean?" The Baron was on his feet, leaning forward across the table.

"Is it possible that I am obscure? My French, perhaps, is not of the purest, but . . ."

"Oh, your French is fluent enough; too fluent at moments, if I may permit myself the observation. Now, look you here, M. le filibustier, I am not a man with whom it is safe to play the fool, as you may very soon discover. You have accepted service of the King of France—you and your men; you hold the rank and draw the pay of a Capitaine de Vaisseau, and these your officers hold the rank of lieutenants. These ranks carry obligations which you would do well to study, and penalties for failing to discharge them which you might study at the same time. They are something severe. The first obligation of an officer is obedience. I commend it to your attention. You are not to conceive yourselves, as you appear to be doing, my allies in the enterprises I have in view, but my subordinates. In me you behold a commander to lead you, not a companion or an equal. You understand me, I hope."

"Oh, be sure that I understand," Captain Blood laughed. He was recovering his normal self amazingly under the inspiring stimulus of conflict. The only thing that marred his enjoyment was the reflection that he had not shaved. "I forget nothing, I assure you, my General. I do not forget, for instance, as you appear to be doing, that the articles we signed are the condition of our service; and the articles provide that we receive one-fifth share. Refuse us that, and you cancel the articles; cancel the articles, and you cancel our services with them. From that moment we cease to have the honour to hold rank in the navies of the King of France."

There was more than a murmur of approval from his three captains.

Rivarol glared at them, checkmated.

"In effect . . ." M. de Cussy was beginning timidly.

"In effect, monsieur, this is your doing," the Baron flashed on him, glad to have some one upon whom he could fasten the sharp fangs of his irritation. "You should be broke for it. You bring the King's service into disrepute; you force me, His Majesty's representative, into an impossible position."

"Is it impossible to award us the one-fifth share?" quoth Captain Blood silkily. "In that case, there is no need for heat or for injuries to M. de Cussy. M. de Cussy knows that we would not have come for less. We depart again upon your assurance that you cannot award us more. And things are as they would have been if M. de Cussy had adhered rigidly to his instructions. I have proved, I hope, to your satisfaction, M. le Baron, that if you repudiate the articles you can neither claim our services nor hinder our departure—not in honour."

"Not in honour, sir? To the devil with your insolence! Do you imply that any course that were not in honour would be possible to me?"

"I do not imply it, because it would not be possible," said Captain Blood. "We should see to that. It is, my General, for you to say whether the articles are repudiated."

The Baron sat down. "I will consider the matter," he said sullenly. "You shall be advised of my resolve."

Captain Blood rose, his officers rose with him. Captain Blood bowed.

"M. le Baron!" said he.

Then he and his buccaneers removed themselves from the august and irate presence of the General of the King's Armies by Land and Sea in America.

You conceive that there followed for M. de Cussy an extremely bad quarter of an hour. M. de Cussy, in fact, deserves your sympathy. His self-sufficiency was blown from him by the haughty M. de Rivarol, as down from a thistle by the winds of autumn. The General of the King's Armies abused him—this man who was Governor of Hispaniola—as if he were a lackey. M. de Cussy defended himself by urging the thing that Captain Blood had so admirably urged already on his behalf—that if the terms he had made with the buccaneers were not confirmed there was no harm done. M. de Rivarol bullied and browbeat him into silence.

Having exhausted abuse, the Baron proceeded to indignities. Since he accounted that M. de Cussy had proved himself unworthy of the post he held, M. de Rivarol took over the responsibilities of that post for as long as he might remain in Hispaniola, and to give effect to this he began by bringing soldiers from his ships, and setting his own guard in M. de Cussy's castle.

Out of this, trouble followed quickly. Wolverstone coming ashore next morning in the picturesque garb that he affected, his head swathed in a coloured handkerchief, was jeered at by an officer of the newly landed French troops. Not accustomed to derision, Wolverstone replied in kind and with interest. The officer passed to insult, and Wolverstone struck him a blow that felled him, and left him only the half of his poor senses. Within the hour the matter was reported to M. de Rivarol, and before noon, by M. de Rivarol's orders, Wolverstone was under arrest in the castle.

The Baron had just sat down to dinner with M. de Cussy when the negro who waited on them announced Captain Blood. Peevishly M. de Rivarol bade him be admitted, and there entered now into his presence a spruce and modish gentleman, dressed with care and sombre richness in black and silver, his swarthy, clear-cut face scrupulously shaven, his long black hair in ringlets that fell to a collar of fine point. In his right hand the gentleman carried a broad black hat with a scarlet ostrich-plume, in his left hand an ebony cane. His stockings were of silk, a bunch of ribbons masked his garters, and the black rosettes on his shoes were finely edged with gold.

For a moment M. de Rivarol did not recognize him. For Blood looked younger by ten years than yesterday. But the vivid blue eyes under their level black brows were not to be forgotten, and they proclaimed him for the man announced even before he had spoken. His resurrected pride had demanded that he should put himself on an equality with the baron and advertise that equality by his exterior.

"I come inopportunely," he courteously excused himself. "My apologies. My business could not wait. It concerns, M. de Cussy, Captain Wolverstone of the *Lachesis*, whom you have placed under arrest."

"It was I who placed him under arrest," said M. de Rivarol.

"Indeed! But I thought that M. de Cussy was Governor of Hispaniola."

"Whilst I am here, monsieur, I am the supreme authority. It is as well that you should understand it."

"Perfectly. But it is not possible that you are aware of the mistake that has been made."

"Mistake, do you say?"

"I say mistake. On the whole, it is polite of me to use that word. Also it is expedient. It will save discussions. Your people have arrested the wrong man, M. de Rivarol. Instead of the French officer, who used the grossest provocation, they have arrested Captain Wolverstone. It is a matter which I beg you to reverse without delay."

M. de Rivarol's hawk-face flamed scarlet. His dark eyes bulged.

"Sir, you . . . you are insolent! But of an insolence that is intolerable!" Normally a man of the utmost self-possession, he was so rudely shaken now that he actually stammered.

"M. le Baron, you waste words. This is the New World. It is not merely new; it is novel to one reared amid the superstitions of the Old. That novelty you have not yet had time, perhaps, to realize; therefore I overlook the offensive epithet you have used. But justice is justice in the New World as in the Old, and injustice as intolerable here as there. Now justice demands the enlargement of my officer and the arrest and punishment of yours. That justice I invite you, with submission, to administer."

"With submission?" snorted the Baron in furious scorn.

"With the utmost submission, monsieur. But at the same time I will remind M. le Baron that my buccaneers number eight hundred; your troops five hundred; and M. de Cussy will inform you of the interesting fact that any one buccaneer is equal in action to at least three soldiers of the line. I am perfectly frank with you, monsieur, to save time and hard words. Either Captain Wolverstone is instantly set at liberty, or we must take measures to set him at liberty ourselves. The consequences may be appalling. But it is as you please, M. le Baron. You are the supreme authority. It is for you to say."

M. de Rivarol was white to the lips. In all his life he had never been so bearded and defied. But he controlled himself.

"You will do me the favour to wait in the ante-room, M. le Capitaine. I desire a word with M. de Cussy. You shall presently be informed of my decision."

When the door had closed, the baron loosed his fury upon the head of M. de Cussy.

"So, these are the men you have enlisted in the King's service, the men who are to serve under me—men who do not serve, but dictate, and this before the enterprise that has brought me from France is even under way! What explanations do you offer me, M. de Cussy? I warn you that I am not pleased with you. I am, in fact, as you may perceive, exceedingly angry."

The Governor seemed to shed his chubbiness. He drew himself stiffly erect.

"Your rank, monsieur, does not give you the right to rebuke me; nor do the facts. I have enlisted for you the men that you desired me to enlist. It is not my fault if you do not know how to handle them better. As Captain Blood has told you, this is the New World."

"So, so!" M. de Rivarol smiled malignantly. "Not only do you offer no explanation, but you venture to put me in the wrong. Almost I admire your temerity. But there!" he waved the matter aside. He was supremely sardonic. "It is, you tell me, the New World, and—new worlds, new manners, I suppose. In time I may conform my ideas to this new world, or I may conform this new world to my ideas." He was menacing on that. "For the moment I must accept what I find. It remains for you, monsieur, who have experience of these savage by-ways, to advise me out of that experience how to act."

"M. le Baron, it was a folly to have arrested the buccaneer captain. It would be madness to persist. We have not the forces to meet force."

"In that case, monsieur, perhaps you will tell me what we are to do with regard to the future. Am I to submit at every turn to the dictates of this man Blood? Is the enterprise upon which we are embarked to be conducted as he decrees? Am I, in short, the King's representative in America, to be at the mercy of these rascals?"

"Oh, by no means. I am enrolling volunteers here in Hispaniola, and I am raising a corps of negroes. I compute that when this is done we shall have a force of a thousand men, the buccaneers apart."

"But in that case why not dispense with them?"

"Because they will always remain the sharp edge of any weapon that we forge. In the class of warfare that lies before us they are so skilled that what Captain Blood has just said is not an overstatement. A buccaneer is equal to three soldiers of the line. At the same time we shall have a sufficient force to keep them in control. For the rest, monsieur, they have certain notions of honour. They will stand by their articles, and so that we deal justly with them, they will deal justly with us, and give no trouble. I have experience of them, and I pledge you my word for that."

M. de Rivarol condescended to be mollified. It was necessary that he should save his face, and in a degree the Governor afforded him the means to do so, as well as a certain guarantee for the future in the further force he was raising.

"Very well," he said. "Be so good as to recall this Captain Blood."

The Captain came in, assured and very dignified. M. de Rivarol found him detestable; but dissembled it.

"M. le Capitaine, I have taken counsel with M. le Gouverneur. From what he tells me, it is possible that a mistake has been committed. Justice, you may be sure, shall be done. To ensure it, I shall myself preside over a council to be composed of two of my senior officers, yourself and an officer of yours. This council shall hold at once an impartial investigation into the affair, and the offender, the man guilty of having given provocation, shall be punished."

Captain Blood bowed. It was not his wish to be extreme.

"Perfectly, M. le Baron. And now, sir, you have had the night for reflection in this matter of the articles. Am I to understand that you confirm or that you repudiate them?"

M. de Rivarol's eyes narrowed. His mind was full of what M. de Cussy had said—that these buccaneers must prove the sharp edge of any weapon he might forge. He could not dispense with them. He perceived that he had blundered tactically in attempting to reduce the agreed share. Withdrawal from a position of that kind is ever fraught with loss of dignity. But there were those volunteers that M. de Cussy was enrolling to strengthen the hand of the King's General. Their presence might admit anon of the reopening of this question. Meanwhile he must retire in the best order possible.

"I have considered that, too," he announced. "And whilst my opinion remains unaltered, I must confess that since M. de Cussy has pledged us, it is for us to fulfil the pledges. The articles are confirmed, sir."

Captain Blood bowed again. In vain M. de Rivarol looked searchingly for the least trace of a smile of triumph on those firm lips. The buccaneer's face remained of the utmost gravity.

Wolverstone was set at liberty that afternoon, and his assailant sentenced to two months' detention. Thus harmony was restored. But it had been an unpromising beginning, and there was more to follow shortly of a similar discordant kind.

Blood and his officers were summoned a week later to a council which sat to determine their operations against Spain. M. de Rivarol laid before them a project for a raid upon the wealthy Spanish town of Cartagena. Captain Blood professed astonishment. Sourly invited by M. de Rivarol to state his grounds for it, he did so with the utmost frankness.

"Were I General of the King's Armies in America," said he, "I should have no doubt or hesitation as to the best way in which to serve my royal master and the French nation. That which I think will be obvious to M. de Cussy, as it is to me, is that we should at once invade Spanish Hispaniola and reduce the whole of this fruitful and splendid island into the possession of the King of France."

"That may follow," said M. de Rivarol. "It is my wish that we begin with Cartagena."

"You mean, sir, that we are to sail across the Caribbean on an adventurous expedition, neglecting that which lies here at our very door. In our absence, a Spanish invasion of French Hispaniola is possible. If we begin by reducing the Spaniards here, that possibility will be removed. We shall have added to the Crown of France the most coveted possession in the West Indies. The enterprise offers no particular difficulty; it may be speedily accomplished, and once accomplished, it would be time to look farther afield. That would seem the logical order in which this campaign should proceed."

He ceased, and there was silence. M. de Rivarol sat back in his chair, the feathered end of a quill between his teeth. Presently he cleared his throat and asked a question.

"Is there anybody else who shares Captain Blood's opinion?"

None answered him. His own officers were overawed by him; Blood's followers naturally preferred Cartagena, because offering the greater chance of loot. Loyalty to their leader kept them silent.

"You seem to be alone in your opinion," said the Baron with his vinegary smile.

Captain Blood laughed outright. He had suddenly read the Baron's mind. His airs and graces and haughtiness had so imposed upon Blood that it was only now that at last he saw through them, into the fellow's peddling spirit. Therefore he laughed; there was really nothing else to do. But his laughter was charged with more anger even than contempt. He had been deluding himself that he had done with piracy. The conviction that this French service was free of any taint of that was the only consideration that had induced him to accept it. Yet here was this haughty, supercilious gentleman, who dubbed himself General of the Armies of France, proposing a plundering, thieving raid which, when stripped of its mean, transparent mask of legitimate warfare, was revealed as piracy of the most flagrant.

M. de Rivarol, intrigued by his mirth, scowled upon him disapprovingly.

"Why do you laugh, monsieur?"

"Because I discover here an irony that is supremely droll. You, M. le Baron, General of the King's Armies by Land and Sea in America, propose an enterprise of a purely buccaneering character; whilst I, the buccaneer, am urging one that is more concerned with upholding the honour of France. You perceive how droll it is."

M. de Rivarol perceived nothing of the kind. M. de Rivarol in fact was extremely angry. He bounded to his feet, and every man in the room rose with him—save only M. de Cussy, who sat on with a grim smile on his lips. He, too, now read the Baron like an open book, and reading him despised him.

"M. le filibustier," cried Rivarol in a thick voice, "it seems that I must again remind you that I am your superior officer."

"My superior officer! You! Lord of the World! Why, you are just a common pirate! But you shall hear the truth for once, and that before all these gentlemen who have the honour to serve the King of France. It is for me, a buccaneer, a sea-robber, to stand here and tell you what is in the interest of French honour and the French Crown. Whilst you, the French King's appointed General, neglecting this, are for spending the King's resources against an outlying settlement of no account, shedding French blood in seizing a place that cannot be held, only because it has been reported to you that there is much gold in Cartagena, and that the plunder of it will enrich you. It is worthy of the huckster who sought to haggle with us about our share, and to beat us down after the articles pledging you were already signed. If I am wrong—let M. de Cussy say so. If I am wrong, let me be proven wrong, and I will beg your pardon. Meanwhile, monsieur, I withdraw from this council. I will have no further part in your deliberations. I accepted the service of the King of France with intent to honour that service. I cannot honour that service by lending countenance to a waste of life and resources in raids upon unimportant settlements, with plunder for their only object. The responsibility for such decisions must rest with you, and with you alone. I desire M. de Cussy to report me to the Ministers of France. For the rest, monsieur, it merely remains for you to give me your orders. I await them aboard my ship—and anything else, of a personal nature, that you may feel I have provoked by the terms I have felt compelled to use in this council. M. le Baron, I have the honour to wish you good-day."

He stalked out, and his three captains—although they thought him mad—rolled after him in loyal silence.

M. de Rivarol was gasping like a landed fish. The stark truth had robbed him of speech. When he recovered, it was to thank Heaven vigorously that the council was relieved by Captain Blood's own act of that gentleman's further participation in its deliberations. Inwardly M. de Rivarol burned with shame and rage. The mask had been plucked from him, and he had been held up to scorn—he, the General of the King's Armies by Sea and Land in America.

Nevertheless, it was to Cartagena that they sailed in the middle of March. Volunteers and negroes had brought up the forces directly under M. de Rivarol to twelve hundred men. With these he thought he could keep the buccaneer contingent in order and submissive.

They made up an imposing fleet, led by M. de Rivarol's flagship, the *Victorieuse*, a mighty vessel of eighty guns. Each of the four other French ships was at least as powerful as Blood's *Arabella*, which was of forty guns. Followed the lesser buccaneer vessels, the *Elizabeth*, *Lachesis*, and *Atropos*, and a dozen frigates laden with stores, besides canoes and small craft in tow.

Narrowly they missed the Jamaica fleet with Colonel Bishop, which sailed north for Tortuga two days after the Baron de Rivarol's southward passage.

XXVII. Cartagena

Having crossed the Caribbean in the teeth of contrary winds, it was not until the early days of April that the French fleet hove in sight of Cartagena, and M. de Rivarol summoned a council aboard his flagship to determine the method of assault.

"It is of importance, messieurs," he told them, "that we take the city by surprise, not only before it can put itself into a state of defence; but before it can remove its treasures inland. I propose to land a force sufficient to achieve this to the north of the city to-night after dark." And he explained in detail the scheme upon which his wits had laboured.

He was heard respectfully and approvingly by his officers, scornfully by Captain Blood, and indifferently by the other buccaneer captains present. For it must be understood that Blood's refusal to attend councils had related only to those concerned with determining the nature of the enterprise to be undertaken.

Captain Blood was the only one amongst them who knew exactly what lay ahead. Two years ago he had himself considered a raid upon the place, and he had actually made a survey of it in circumstances which he was presently to disclose.

The Baron's proposal was one to be expected from a commander whose knowledge of Cartagena was only such as might be derived from maps.

Geographically and strategically considered, it is a curious place. It stands almost four-square, screened east and north by hills, and it may be said to face south upon the inner of two harbours by which it is normally approached. The entrance to the outer harbour, which is in reality a lagoon some three miles across, lies through a neck known as the Boca Chica—or Little Mouth—and defended by a fort. A long strip of densely wooded land to westward acts here as a natural breakwater, and as the inner harbour is approached, another strip of land thrusts across at right angles from the first, towards the mainland on the east. Just short of this it ceases, leaving a deep but very narrow channel, a veritable gateway, into the secure and sheltered inner harbour. Another fort defends this second passage. East and north of Cartagena lies the mainland, which may be left out of account. But to the west and northwest this city, so well guarded on every other side, lies directly open to the sea. It stands back beyond a half-mile of beach, and besides this and the stout walls which fortify it, would appear to have no other defences. But those appearances are deceptive, and they had utterly deceived M. de Rivarol, when he devised his plan.

It remained for Captain Blood to explain the difficulties when M. de Rivarol informed him that the honour of opening the assault in the manner which he prescribed was to be accorded to the buccaneers.

Captain Blood smiled sardonic appreciation of the honour reserved for his men. It was precisely what he would have expected. For the buccaneers the dangers; for M. de Rivarol the honour, glory and profit of the enterprise.

"It is an honour which I must decline," said he quite coldly.

Wolverstone grunted approval and Hagthorpe nodded. Yberville, who as much as any of them resented the superciliousness of his noble compatriot, never wavered in loyalty to Captain Blood. The French officers—there were six of them present—stared their haughty surprise at the buccaneer leader, whilst the Baron challengingly fired a question at him.

"How? You decline it, sir? You decline to obey orders, do you say?"

"I understood, M. le Baron, that you summoned us to deliberate upon the means to be adopted."

"Then you understood amiss, M. le Capitaine. You are here to receive my commands. I have already deliberated, and I have decided. I hope you understand."

"Oh, I understand," laughed Blood. "But, I ask myself, do you?" And without giving the Baron time to set the angry question that was bubbling to his lips, he swept on: "You have deliberated, you say, and you have decided. But unless your decision rests upon a wish to destroy my buccaneers, you will alter it when I tell you something of which I have knowledge. This city of Cartagena looks very vulnerable on the northern side, all open to the sea as it apparently stands. Ask yourself, M. le Baron, how came the Spaniards who built it where it is to have been at such trouble to fortify it to the south, if from the north it is so easily assailable."

That gave M. de Rivarol pause.

"The Spaniards," Blood pursued, "are not quite the fools you are supposing them. Let me tell you, messieurs, that two years ago I made a survey of Cartagena as a preliminary to raiding it. I came hither with some friendly trading Indians, myself disguised as an Indian, and in that guise I spent a week in the city and studied carefully

ance on the forts of this settlement, the loss of some treasure should

r much."

bit his lip in chagrin. His gloomy eye smouldered as it considered the

uccaneer.

ommand you to go—to make the attempt?" he asked. "Answer me,

us know once for all where we stand, and who commands this expedition."

ely, I find you tiresome," said Captain Blood, and he swung to M. de Cussy,

ere gnawing his lip, intensely uncomfortable. "I appeal to you, monsieur, to

to the General."

e Cussy started out of his gloomy abstraction. He cleared his throat. He was

ely nervous.

n view of what Captain Blood has submitted . . ."

Oh, to the devil with that!" snapped Rivarol. "It seems that I am followed by

troons. Look you, M. le Capitaine, since you are afraid to undertake this thing,

will myself undertake it. The weather is calm, and I count upon making good my

anding. If I do so, I shall have proved you wrong, and I shall have a word to say to you

to-morrow which you may not like. I am being very generous with you, sir." He waved

his hand regally. "You have leave to go."

It was sheer obstinacy and empty pride that drove him, and he received the lesson
he deserved. The fleet stood in during the afternoon to within a mile of the coast, and
under cover of darkness three hundred men, of whom two hundred were negroes—the
whole of the negro contingent having been pressed into the undertaking —were pulled
away for the shore in the canoes, piraguas, and ships' boats. Rivarol's pride compelled
him, however much he may have disliked the venture, to lead them in person.

The first six boats were caught in the surf, and pounded into fragments before their
occupants could extricate themselves. The thunder of the breakers and the cries of the
shipwrecked warned those who followed, and thereby saved them from sharing the
same fate. By the Baron's urgent orders they pulled away again out of danger, and
stood about to pick up such survivors as contrived to battle towards them. Close upon
fifty lives were lost in the adventure, together with half-a-dozen boats stored with
ammunition and light guns.

The Baron went back to his flagship an infuriated, but by no means a wiser man.
Wisdom—not even the pungent wisdom experience thrusts upon us—is not for such
as M. de Rivarol. His anger embraced all things, but focussed chiefly upon Captain
Blood. In some warped process of reasoning he held the buccaneer chiefly responsible

all its approaches. On the side of the s~

there is shoal water for over half ~

that no ship shall come within bomb.

land than three quarters of a mile."

"But our landing will be effected in ca~

officer impatiently.

"In the calmest season of the year, the surf w~

will also bear in mind that if landing were possible ~

could not be covered by the ships' guns. In fact, it is ~

danger from their own artillery."

"If the attack is made by night, as I propose, covering~

should be ashore in force before the Spaniards are aware of the~

"You are assuming that Cartagena is a city of the blind, that~

they are not conning our sails and asking themselves who we are and~

"But if they feel themselves secure from the north, as you suggest," ~

impatiently, "that very security will lull them."

"Perhaps. But, then, they are secure. Any attempt to land on this side is de~

failure at the hands of Nature."

"Nevertheless, we make the attempt," said the obstinate Baron, whose haughtin~

would not allow him to yield before his officers.

"If you still choose to do so after what I have said, you are, of course, the person to

decide. But I do not lead my men into fruitless danger."

"If I command you . . ." the Baron was beginning. But Blood unceremoniously

interrupted him.

"M. le Baron, when M. de Cussy engaged us on your behalf, it was as much on

account of our knowledge and experience of this class of warfare as on account of

our strength. I have placed my own knowledge and experience in this particular

matter at your disposal. I will add that I abandoned my own project of raiding

Cartagena, not being in sufficient strength at the time to force the entrance of the

harbour, which is the only way into the city. The strength which you now command

is ample for that purpose."

"But whilst we are doing that, the Spaniards will have time to remove great part of

the wealth this city holds. We must take them by surprise."

Captain Blood shrugged. "If this is a mere pirating raid, that, of course, is a prime

consideration. It was with me. But if you are concerned to abate the pride of Spain and

plant the Lilies of F~

not really weigh f~

M. de Rivaro~

self-contained ~

"But if I ~

monsieur, le~

"Positiv~

who sat th~

justify m~

M. ~

extrem~

for this misadventure. He went to bed considering furiously what he should say to Captain Blood upon the morrow.

He was awakened at dawn by the rolling thunder of guns. Emerging upon the poop in nightcap and slippers, he beheld a sight that increased his unreasonable and unreasoning fury. The four buccaneer ships under canvas were going through extraordinary manœuvres half a mile off the Boca Chica and little more than half a mile away from the remainder of the fleet, and from their flanks flame and smoke were belching each time they swung broadside to the great round fort that guarded that narrow entrance. The fort was returning the fire vigorously and viciously. But the buccaneers timed their broadsides with extraordinary judgment to catch the defending ordnance reloading; then as they drew the Spaniards' fire, they swung away again, not only taking care to be ever moving targets, but, further, to present no more than bow or stern to the fort, their masts in line, when the heaviest cannonades were to be expected.

Gibbering and cursing, M. de Rivarol stood there and watched this action, so presumptuously undertaken by Blood on his own responsibility. The officers of the *Victorieuse* crowded round him, but it was not until M. de Cussy came to join the group that he opened the sluices of his rage. And M. de Cussy himself invited the deluge that now caught him. He had come up rubbing his hands and taking a proper satisfaction in the energy of the men whom he had enlisted.

"Aha, M. de Rivarol!" he laughed. "He understands his business, eh, this Captain Blood. He'll plant the Lilies of France on that fort before breakfast."

The Baron swung upon him snarling. "He understands his business, eh? His business, let me tell you, M. de Cussy, is to obey my orders, and I have not ordered this. Par la Mordieu! When this is over I'll deal with him for his damned insubordination."

"Surely, M. le Baron, he will have justified it if he succeeds."

"Justified it! Ah, parbleu! Can a soldier ever justify acting without orders?" He raved on furiously, his officers supporting him out of their detestation of Captain Blood.

Meanwhile the fight went merrily on. The fort was suffering badly. Yet for all their manœuvring the buccaneers were not escaping punishment. The starboard gunwale of the *Atropos* had been hammered into splinters, and a shot had caught her astern in the coach. The *Elizabeth* was badly battered about the forecastle, and the *Arabella's* maintop had been shot away, whilst towards the end of that engagement the *Lachesis* came reeling out of the fight with a shattered rudder, steering herself by sweeps.

The absurd Baron's fierce eyes positively gleamed with satisfaction.

"I pray Heaven they may sink all his infernal ships!" he cried in his frenzy.

But Heaven didn't hear him. Scarcely had he spoken than there was a terrific explosion, and half the fort went up in fragments. A lucky shot from the buccaneers had found the powder magazine.

It may have been a couple of hours later, when Captain Blood, as spruce and cool as if he had just come from a levee, stepped upon the quarter-deck of the *Victorieuse*, to confront M. de Rivarol, still in bedgown and nightcap.

"I have to report, M. le Baron, that we are in possession of the fort on Boca Chica. The standard of France is flying from what remains of its tower, and the way into the outer harbour is open to your fleet."

M. de Rivarol was compelled to swallow his fury, though it choked him. The jubilation among his officers had been such that he could not continue as he had begun. Yet his eyes were malevolent, his face pale with anger.

"You are fortunate, M. Blood, that you succeeded," he said. "It would have gone very ill with you had you failed. Another time be so good as to await my orders, lest you should afterwards lack the justification which your good fortune has procured you this morning."

Blood smiled with a flash of white teeth, and bowed.

"I shall be glad of your orders now, General, for pursuing our advantage. You realize that speed in striking is the first essential."

Rivarol was left gaping a moment. Absorbed in his ridiculous anger, he had considered nothing. But he made a quick recovery. "To my cabin, if you please," he commanded peremptorily, and was turning to lead the way, when Blood arrested him.

"With submission, my General, we shall be better here. You behold there the scene of our coming action. It is spread before you like a map." He waved his hand towards the lagoon, the country flanking it and the considerable city standing back from the beach. "If it is not a presumption in me to offer a suggestion . . ." He paused. M. de Rivarol looked at him sharply, suspecting irony. But the swarthy face was bland, the keen eyes steady.

"Let us hear your suggestion," he consented.

Blood pointed out the fort at the mouth of the inner harbour, which was just barely visible above the waving palms on the intervening tongue of land. He announced that its armament was less formidable than that of the outer fort, which they had reduced; but on the other hand, the passage was very much narrower than the Boca Chica, and before they could attempt to make it in any case, they must dispose of those defences. He proposed that the French ships should enter the outer harbour, and proceed at once to bombardment. Meanwhile, he would land three hundred buccaneers and some artillery on the eastern side of the lagoon, beyond the fragrant garden islands dense with richly bearing fruit-trees, and proceed simultaneously to storm the fort in the rear. Thus beset on both sides at once, and demoralized by the fate of the much stronger outer fort, he did not think the Spaniards would offer a very long resistance. Then it would be for M. de Rivarol to garrison the fort, whilst Captain Blood would sweep on with his men, and seize the Church of Nuestra Señora de la Poupa, plainly visible on its hill immediately eastward of the town. Not only did that eminence afford them a valuable and obvious strategic advantage, but it commanded the only road that led from Cartagena to the interior, and once it were held there would be no further question of the Spaniards attempting to remove the wealth of the city.

That to M. de Rivarol was—as Captain Blood had judged that it would be—the crowning argument. Supercilious until that moment, and disposed for his own pride's sake to treat the buccaneer's suggestions with cavalier criticism, M. de Rivarol's manner suddenly changed. He became alert and brisk, went so far as tolerantly to commend Captain Blood's plan, and issued orders that action might be taken upon it at once.

It is not necessary to follow that action step by step. Blunders on the part of the French marred its smooth execution, and the indifferent handling of their ships led to the sinking of two of them in the course of the afternoon by the fort's gunfire. But by evening, owing largely to the irresistible fury with which the buccaneers stormed the place from the landward side, the fort had surrendered, and before dusk Blood and his men with some ordnance hauled thither by mules dominated the city from the heights of Nuestra Señora de la Poupa.

At noon on the morrow, shorn of defences and threatened with bombardment, Cartagena sent offers of surrender to M. de Rivarol.

Swollen with pride by a victory for which he took the entire credit to himself, the Baron dictated his terms. He demanded that all public effects and office accounts be delivered up; that the merchants surrender all moneys and goods held by them for their correspondents; the inhabitants could choose whether they would remain in the city or depart; but those who went must first deliver up all their property, and those who elected to remain must surrender half, and become the subjects of France; religious houses and churches should be spared, but they must render accounts of all moneys and valuables in their possession.

Cartagena agreed, having no choice in the matter, and on the next day, which was the 5th of April, M. de Rivarol entered the city and proclaimed it now a French colony, appointing M. de Cussy its Governor. Thereafter he proceeded to the Cathedral, where very properly a Te Deum was sung in honour of the conquest. This by way of grace, whereafter M. de Rivarol proceeded to devour the city. The only detail in which the French conquest of Cartagena differed from an ordinary buccaneering raid was that under the severest penalties no soldier was to enter the house of any inhabitant. But this apparent respect for the persons and property of the conquered was based in reality upon M. de Rivarol's anxiety lest a doubloon should be abstracted from all the wealth that was pouring into the treasury opened by the Baron in the name of the King of France. Once the golden stream had ceased, he removed all restrictions and left the city in prey to his men, who proceeded further to pillage it of that part of their property which the inhabitants who became French subjects had been assured should remain inviolate. The plunder was enormous. In the course of four days over a hundred mules laden with gold went out of the city and down to the boats waiting at the beach to convey the treasure aboard the ships.

XXVIII. The Honour of M. de Rivarol

During the capitulation and for some time after, Captain Blood and the greater portion of his buccaneers had been at their post on the heights of Nuestra Señora de la Poupa, utterly in ignorance of what was taking place. Blood, although the man chiefly, if not solely, responsible for the swift reduction of the city, which was proving a veritable treasure-house, was not even shown the consideration of being called to the council of officers which with M. de Rivarol determined the terms of the capitulation.

This was a slight that at another time Captain Blood would not have borne for a moment. But at present, in his odd frame of mind, and its divorcement from piracy, he was content to smile his utter contempt of the French General. Not so, however, his captains, and still less his men. Resentment smouldered amongst them for a while, to flame out violently at the end of that week in Cartagena. It was only by undertaking to voice their grievance to the Baron that their captain was able for the moment to pacify them. That done, he went at once in quest of M. de Rivarol.

He found him in the offices which the Baron had set up in the town, with a staff of clerks to register the treasure brought in and to cast up the surrendered account-books, with a view to ascertaining precisely what were the sums yet to be delivered up. The Baron sat there scrutinizing ledgers, like a city merchant, and checking figures to make sure that all was correct to the last peso. A choice occupation this for the General of the King's Armies by Sea and Land. He looked up irritated by the interruption which Captain Blood's advent occasioned.

"M. le Baron," the latter greeted him. "I must speak frankly; and you must suffer it. My men are on the point of mutiny."

M. de Rivarol considered him with a faint lift of the eyebrows.

"Captain Blood, I, too, will speak frankly; and you, too, must suffer it. If there is a mutiny, you and your captains shall be held personally responsible. The mistake you make is in assuming with me the tone of an ally, whereas I have given you clearly to understand from the first that you are simply in the position of having accepted service under me. Your proper apprehension of that fact will save the waste of a deal of words."

Blood contained himself with difficulty. One of these fine days, he felt, that for the sake of humanity he must slit the comb of this supercilious, arrogant cockerel.

"You may define our positions as you please," said he. "But I'll remind you that the nature of a thing is not changed by the name you give it. I am concerned with facts; chiefly with the fact that we entered into definite articles with you. Those articles provide for a certain distribution of the spoil. My men demand it. They are not satisfied."

"Of what are they not satisfied?" demanded the Baron.

"Of your honesty, M. de Rivarol."

A blow in the face could scarcely have taken the Frenchman more aback. He stiffened, and drew himself up, his eyes blazing, his face of a deathly pallor. The clerks at the tables laid down their pens, and awaited the explosion in a sort of terror.

For a long moment there was silence. Then the great gentleman delivered himself in a voice of concentrated anger. "Do you really dare so much, you and the dirty thieves that follow you? God's Blood! You shall answer to me for that word, though it entail a yet worse dishonour to meet you. Faugh!"

"I will remind you," said Blood, "that I am speaking not for myself, but for my men. It is they who are not satisfied, they who threaten that unless satisfaction is afforded them, and promptly, they will take it."

"Take it?" said Rivarol, trembling in his rage. "Let them attempt it, and . . ."

"Now don't be rash. My men are within their rights, as you are aware. They demand to know when this sharing of the spoil is to take place, and when they are to receive the fifth for which their articles provide."

"God give me patience! How can we share the spoil before it has been completely gathered?"

"My men have reason to believe that it is gathered; and, anyway, they view with mistrust that it should all be housed aboard your ships, and remain in your possession. They say that hereafter there will be no ascertaining what the spoil really amounts to."

"But—name of Heaven!—I have kept books. They are there for all to see."

"They do not wish to see account-books. Few of them can read. They want to view the treasure itself. They know—you compel me to be blunt—that the accounts have been falsified. Your books show the spoil of Cartagena to amount to some ten million livres. The men know—and they are very skilled in these computations—that it exceeds the enormous total of forty millions. They insist that the treasure itself be produced and weighed in their presence, as is the custom among the Brethren of the Coast."

"I know nothing of filibuster customs." The gentleman was disdainful.

"But you are learning quickly."

"What do you mean, you rogue? I am a leader of armies, not of plundering thieves."

"Oh, but of course!" Blood's irony laughed in his eyes. "Yet, whatever you may be, I warn you that unless you yield to a demand that I consider just and therefore uphold, you may look for trouble, and it would not surprise me if you never leave Cartagena at all, nor convey a single gold piece home to France."

"Ah, pardieu! Am I to understand that you are threatening me?"

"Come, come, M. le Baron! I warn you of the trouble that a little prudence may avert. You do not know on what a volcano you are sitting. You do not know the ways of buccaneers. If you persist, Cartagena will be drenched in blood, and whatever the outcome the King of France will not have been well served."

That shifted the basis of the argument to less hostile ground. Awhile yet it continued, to be concluded at last by an ungracious undertaking from M. de Rivarol to submit to the demands of the buccaneers. He gave it with an extreme ill-grace, and only because Blood made him realize at last that to withhold it longer would be dangerous. In an engagement, he might conceivably defeat Blood's followers. But conceivably he might not. And even if he succeeded, the effort would be so costly to him in men that he might not thereafter find himself in sufficient strength to maintain his hold of what he had seized.

The end of it all was that he gave a promise at once to make the necessary preparations, and if Captain Blood and his officers would wait upon him on board the *Victorieuse* to-morrow morning, the treasure should be produced, weighed in their presence, and their fifth share surrendered there and then into their own keeping.

Among the buccaneers that night there was hilarity over the sudden abatement of M. de Rivarol's monstrous pride. But when the next dawn broke over Cartagena, they had the explanation of it. The only ships to be seen in the harbour were the *Arabella* and the *Elizabeth* riding at anchor, and the *Atropos* and the *Lachesis* careened on the beach for repair of the damage sustained in the bombardment. The French ships were gone. They had been quietly and secretly warped out of the harbour under cover of night, and three sails, faint and small, on the horizon to westward was all that remained to be seen of them. The absconding M. de Rivarol had gone off with the treasure, taking with him the troops and mariners he had brought from France. He had left behind him at Cartagena not only the empty-handed buccaneers, whom he had swindled, but also M. de Cussy and the volunteers and negroes from Hispaniola, whom he had swindled no less.

The two parties were fused into one by their common fury, and before the exhibition of it the inhabitants of that ill-fated town were stricken with deeper terror than they had yet known since the coming of this expedition.

Captain Blood alone kept his head, setting a curb upon his deep chagrin. He had promised himself that before parting from M. de Rivarol he would present a reckoning for all the petty affronts and insults to which that unspeakable fellow—now proved a scoundrel—had subjected him.

"We must follow," he declared. "Follow and punish."

At first that was the general cry. Then came the consideration that only two of the buccaneer ships were seaworthy—and these could not accommodate the whole force, particularly being at the moment indifferently victualled for a long voyage. The crews of the *Lachesis* and *Atropos* and with them their captains, Wolverstone and Yberville, renounced the intention. After all, there would be a deal of treasure still hidden in Cartagena. They would remain behind to extort it whilst fitting their ships for sea. Let Blood and Hagthorpe and those who sailed with them do as they pleased.

Then only did Blood realize the rashness of his proposal, and in attempting to draw back he almost precipitated a battle between the two parties into which that same proposal had now divided the buccaneers. And meanwhile those French sails on the horizon were growing less and less. Blood was reduced to despair. If he went off now, Heaven knew what would happen to the town, the temper of those whom he was leaving being what it was. Yet if he remained, it would simply mean that his own and Hagthorpe's crews would join in the saturnalia and increase the hideousness of events now inevitable. Unable to reach a decision, his own men and Hagthorpe's took the matter off his hands, eager to give chase to Rivarol. Not only was a dastardly cheat to be punished, but an enormous treasure to be won by treating as an enemy this French commander who, himself, had so villainously broken the alliance.

When Blood, torn as he was between conflicting considerations, still hesitated, they bore him almost by main force aboard the *Arabella*.

Within an hour, the water-casks at least replenished and stowed aboard, the *Arabella* and the *Elizabeth* put to sea upon that angry chase.

"When we were well at sea, and the *Arabella*'s course was laid," writes Pitt, in his log, "I went to seek the Captain, knowing him to be in great trouble of mind over these events. I found him sitting alone in his cabin, his head in his hands, torment in the eyes that stared straight before him, seeing nothing."

"What now, Peter?" cried the young Somerset mariner. "Lord, man, what is there here to fret you? Surely 't isn't the thought of Rivarol!"

"No," said Blood thickly. And for once he was communicative. It may well be that he must vent the thing that oppressed him or be driven mad by it. And Pitt, after all, was his friend and loved him, and, so, a proper man for confidences. "But if she knew! If she knew! O God! I had thought to have done with piracy; thought to have done with it for ever. Yet here have I been committed by this scoundrel to the worst piracy that ever I was guilty of. Think of Cartagena! Think of the hell those devils will be making of it now! And I must have that on my soul!"

"Nay, Peter—'t isn't on your soul; but on Rivarol's. It is that dirty thief who has brought all this about. What could you have done to prevent it?"

"I would have stayed if it could have availed."

"It could not, and you know it. So why repine?"

"There is more than that to it," groaned Blood. "What now? What remains? Loyal service with the English was made impossible for me. Loyal service with France has led to this; and that is equally impossible hereafter. What remains, then? Piracy? I have done with it. Egad, if I am to live clean, I believe the only thing is to go and offer my sword to the King of Spain."

But something remained—the last thing that he could have expected—something towards which they were rapidly sailing over the tropical, sunlit sea. All this against which he now inveighed so bitterly was but a necessary stage in the shaping of his odd destiny.

Setting a course for Hispaniola, since they judged that thither must Rivarol go to refit before attempting to cross to France, the *Arabella* and the *Elizabeth* ploughed briskly northward with a moderately favourable wind for two days and nights without ever catching a glimpse of their quarry. The third dawn brought with it a haze which circumscribed their range of vision to something between two and three miles, and deepened their growing vexation and their apprehension that M. de Rivarol might escape them altogether.

Their position then—according to Pitt's log—was approximately 75° 30' W. Long. by 17° 45' N. Lat., so that they had Jamaica on their larboard beam some thirty miles to westward, and, indeed, away to the northwest, faintly visible as a bank of clouds, appeared the great ridge of the Blue Mountains whose peaks were thrust into the clear upper air above the low-lying haze. The wind, to which they were sailing very close, was westerly, and it bore to their ears a booming sound which in less experienced ears might have passed for the breaking of surf upon a lee shore.

"Guns!" said Pitt, who stood with Blood upon the quarter-deck. Blood nodded, listening.

"Ten miles away, perhaps fifteen—somewhere off Port Royal, I should judge," Pitt added. Then he looked at his captain. "Does it concern us?" he asked.

"Guns off Port Royal . . . that should argue Colonel Bishop at work. And against whom should he be in action but against friends of ours? I think it may concern us. Anyway, we'll stand in to investigate. Bid them put the helm over."

Close-hauled they tacked aweather, guided by the sound of combat, which grew in volume and definition as they approached it. Thus for an hour, perhaps. Then, as, telescope to his eye, Blood raked the haze, expecting at any moment to behold the battling ships, the guns abruptly ceased.

They held to their course, nevertheless, with all hands on deck, eagerly, anxiously scanning the sea ahead. And presently an object loomed into view, which soon defined itself for a great ship on fire. As the *Arabella* with the *Elizabeth* following closely raced nearer on their northwesterly tack, the outlines of the blazing vessel grew clearer. Presently her masts stood out sharp and black above the smoke and flames, and through his telescope Blood made out plainly the pennon of St. George fluttering from her maintop.

"An English ship!" he cried.

He scanned the seas for the conqueror in the battle of which this grim evidence was added to that of the sounds they had heard, and when at last, as they drew closer to the doomed vessel, they made out the shadowy outlines of three tall ships, some three or four miles away, standing in toward Port Royal, the first and natural assumption was that these ships must belong to the Jamaica fleet, and that the burning vessel was a defeated buccaneer, and because of this they sped on to pick up the three boats that were standing away from the blazing hulk. But Pitt, who through the telescope was examining the receding squadron, observed things apparent only to the eye of the trained mariner, and made the incredible announcement that the largest of these three vessels was Rivarol's *Victorieuse*.

They took in sail and hove to as they came up with the drifting boats, laden to capacity with survivors. And there were others adrift on some of the spars and wreckage with which the sea was strewn, who must be rescued.

XXIX. The Service of King William

One of the boats bumped alongside the *Arabella*, and up the entrance ladder came first a slight, spruce little gentleman in a coat of mulberry satin laced with gold, whose wizened, yellow, rather peevish face was framed in a heavy black periwig. His modish and costly apparel had nowise suffered by the adventure through which he had passed, and he carried himself with the easy assurance of a man of rank. Here, quite clearly, was no buccaneer. He was closely followed by one who in every particular, save that of age, was his physical opposite, corpulent in a brawny, vigorous way, with a full, round, weather-beaten face whose mouth was humourous and whose eyes were blue and twinkling. He was well dressed without fripperies, and bore with him an air of vigorous authority.

As the little man stepped from the ladder into the waist, whither Captain Blood had gone to receive him, his sharp, ferrety dark eyes swept the uncouth ranks of the assembled crew of the *Arabella*.

"And where the devil may I be now?" he demanded irritably. "Are you English, or what the devil are you?"

"Myself, I have the honour to be Irish, sir. My name is Blood—Captain Peter Blood, and this is my ship the *Arabella*, all very much at your service."

"Blood!" shrilled the little man. "O 'Sblood! A pirate!" He swung to the Colossus who followed him—"A damned pirate, van der Kuylen. Rend my vitals, but we're come from Scylla to Charybdis."

"So?" said the other gutturally, and again, "So?" Then the humour of it took him, and he yielded to it.

"Damme! What's to laugh at, you porpoise?" spluttered mulberry-coat. "A fine tale this'll make at home! Admiral van der Kuylen first loses his fleet in the night, then has his flagship fired under him by a French squadron, and ends all by being captured by a pirate. I'm glad you find it matter for laughter. Since for my sins I happen to be with you, I'm damned if I do."

"There's a misapprehension, if I may make so bold as to point it out," put in Blood quietly. "You are not captured, gentlemen; you are rescued. When you realize it, perhaps it will occur to you to acknowledge the hospitality I am offering you. It may be poor, but it is the best at my disposal."

The fierce little gentleman stared at him. "Damme! Do you permit yourself to be ironical?" he disapproved him, and possibly with a view to correcting any such tendency, proceeded to introduce himself. "I am Lord Willoughby, King William's Governor-General of the West Indies, and this is Admiral van der Kuylen, commander of His Majesty's West Indian fleet, at present mislaid somewhere in this damned Caribbean Sea."

"King William?" quoth Blood, and he was conscious that Pitt and Dyke, who were behind him, now came edging nearer, sharing his own wonder. "And who may be King William, and of what may he be King?"

"What's that?" In a wonder greater than his own, Lord Willoughby stared back at him. At last: "I am alluding to His Majesty King William III—William of Orange—who, with Queen Mary, has been ruling England for two months and more."

There was a moment's silence, until Blood realized what he was being told.

"D'ye mean, sir, that they've roused themselves at home, and kicked out that scoundrel James and his gang of ruffians?"

Admiral van der Kuylen nudged his lordship, a humourous twinkle in his blue eyes.

"His bolitics are fery sound, I dink," he growled.

His lordship's smile brought lines like gashes into his leathery cheeks. "'Slife! Hadn't you heard? Where the devil have you been at all?"

"Out of touch with the world for the last three months," said Blood.

"Stab me! You must have been. And in that three months the world has undergone some changes." Briefly he added an account of them. King James was fled to France, and living under the protection of King Louis, wherefore, and for other reasons, England had joined the league against her, and was now at war with France. That was how it happened that the Dutch Admiral's flagship had been attacked by M. de Rivarol's fleet that morning, from which it clearly followed that in his voyage from Cartagena, the Frenchman must have spoken some ship that gave him the news.

After that, with renewed assurances that aboard his ship they should be honourably entreated, Captain Blood led the Governor-General and the Admiral to his cabin, what time the work of rescue went on. The news he had received had set Blood's mind in a turmoil. If King James was dethroned and banished, there was an end to his own outlawry for his alleged share in an earlier attempt to drive out that tyrant. It became possible for him to return home and take up his life again at the point where it was so unfortunately interrupted four years ago. He was dazzled by the prospect so abruptly opened out to him. The thing so filled his mind, moved him so deeply, that he must afford it expression. In doing so, he revealed of himself more than he knew or intended to the astute little gentleman who watched him so keenly the while.

"Go home, if you will," said his lordship, when Blood paused. "You may be sure that none will harass you on the score of your piracy, considering what it was that drove you to it. But why be in haste? We have heard of you, to be sure, and we know of what you are capable upon the seas. Here is a great chance for you, since you declare yourself sick of piracy. Should you choose to serve King William out here during this war, your knowledge of the West Indies should render you a very valuable servant to His Majesty's Government, which you would not find ungrateful. You should consider it. Damme, sir, I repeat: it is a great chance you are given."

"That your lordship gives me," Blood amended, "I am very grateful. But at the moment, I confess, I can consider nothing but this great news. It alters the shape of the world. I must accustom myself to view it as it now is, before I can determine my own place in it."

Pitt came in to report that the work of rescue was at an end, and the men picked up—some forty-five in all—safe aboard the two buccaneer ships. He asked for orders. Blood rose.

"I am negligent of your lordship's concerns in my consideration of my own. You'll be wishing me to land you at Port Royal."

"At Port Royal?" The little man squirmed wrathfully on his seat. Wrathfully and at length he informed Blood that they had put into Port Royal last evening to find its Deputy-Governor absent. "He had gone on some wild-goose chase to Tortuga after buccaneers, taking the whole of the fleet with him."

Blood stared in surprise a moment; then yielded to laughter.

"He went, I suppose, before news reached him of the change of government at home, and the war with France?"

"He did not," snapped Willoughby. "He was informed of both, and also of my coming before he set out."

"Oh, impossible!"

"So I should have thought. But I have the information from a Major Mallard whom I found in Port Royal, apparently governing in this fool's absence."

"But is he mad, to leave his post at such a time?" Blood was amazed.

"Taking the whole fleet with him, pray remember, and leaving the place open to French attack. That is the sort of Deputy-Governor that the late Government thought fit to appoint: an epitome of its misrule, damme! He leaves Port Royal unguarded save by a ramshackle fort that can be reduced to rubble in an hour. Stab me! It's unbelievable!"

The lingering smile faded from Blood's face. "Is Rivarol aware of this?" he cried sharply.

It was the Dutch Admiral who answered him. "Vould he go dere if he were not? M. de Rivarol he take some of our men prisoners. Berhabs dey dell him. Berhabs he make dem tell. Id is a great obbordunidy."

His lordship snarled like a mountain-cat. "That rascal Bishop shall answer for it with his head if there's any mischief done through this desertion of his post. What if it were deliberate, eh? What if he is more knave than fool? What if this is his way of serving King James, from whom he held his office?"

Captain Blood was generous. "Hardly so much. It was just vindictiveness that urged him. It's myself he's hunting at Tortuga, my lord. But, I'm thinking that while he's about it, I'd best be looking after Jamaica for King William." He laughed, with more mirth than he had used in the last two months.

"Set a course for Port Royal, Jeremy, and make all speed. We'll be level yet with M. de Rivarol, and wipe off some other scores at the same time."

Both Lord Willoughby and the Admiral were on their feet.

"But you are not equal to it, damme!" cried his lordship. "Any one of the Frenchman's three ships is a match for both yours, my man."

"In guns—aye," said Blood, and he smiled. "But there's more than guns that matter in these affairs. If your lordship would like to see an action fought at sea as an action should be fought, this is your opportunity."

Both stared at him. "But the odds!" his lordship insisted.

"Id is imbossible," said van der Kuylen, shaking his great head. "Seamanship is imbordand. Bud guns is guns."

"If I can't defeat him, I can sink my own ships in the channel, and block him in until Bishop gets back from his wild-goose chase with his squadron, or until your own fleet turns up."

"And what good will that be, pray?" demanded Willoughby.

"I'll be after telling you. Rivarol is a fool to take this chance, considering what he's got aboard. He carried in his hold the treasure plundered from Cartagena, amounting to forty million livres." They jumped at the mention of that colossal sum. "He has gone into Port Royal with it. Whether he defeats me or not, he doesn't come out of Port Royal with it again, and sooner or later that treasure shall find its way into King William's coffers, after, say, one fifth share shall have been paid to my buccaneers. Is that agreed, Lord Willoughby?"

His lordship stood up, and shaking back the cloud of lace from his wrist, held out a delicate white hand.

"Captain Blood, I discover greatness in you," said he.

"Sure it's your lordship has the fine sight to perceive it," laughed the Captain.

"Yes, yes! Bud how vill you do id?" growled van der Kuylen.

"Come on deck, and it's a demonstration I'll be giving you before the day's much older."

XXX. THE LAST FIGHT OF THE ARABELLA

"Vhy do you vait, my friend?" growled van der Kuylen.

"Aye—in God's name!" snapped Willoughby.

It was the afternoon of that same day, and the two buccaneer ships rocked gently with idly flapping sails under the lee of the long spit of land forming the great natural harbour of Port Royal, and less than a mile from the straits leading into it, which the fort commanded. It was two hours and more since they had brought up thereabouts, having crept thither unobserved by the city and by M. de Rivarol's ships, and all the time the air had been aquiver with the roar of guns from sea and land, announcing that battle was joined between the French and the defenders of Port Royal. That long, inactive waiting was straining the nerves of both Lord Willoughby and van der Kuylen.

"You said you vould show us zome vine dings. Vhere are dese vine dings?"

Blood faced them, smiling confidently. He was arrayed for battle, in back-and-breast of black steel. "I'll not be trying your patience much longer. Indeed, I notice already a slackening in the fire. But it's this way, now: there's nothing at all to be gained by precipitancy, and a deal to be gained by delaying, as I shall show you, I hope."

Lord Willoughby eyed him suspiciously. "Ye think that in the meantime Bishop may come back or Admiral van der Kuylen's fleet appear?"

"Sure, now, I'm thinking nothing of the kind. What I'm thinking is that in this engagement with the fort M. de Rivarol, who's a lubberly fellow, as I've reason to know, will be taking some damage that may make the odds a trifle more even. Sure, it'll be time enough to go forward when the fort has shot its bolt."

"Aye, aye!" The sharp approval came like a cough from the little Governor-General. "I perceive your object, and I believe ye're entirely right. Ye have the qualities of a great commander, Captain Blood. I beg your pardon for having misunderstood you."

"And that's very handsome of your lordship. Ye see, I have some experience of this kind of action, and whilst I'll take any risk that I must, I'll take none that I needn't. But . . ." He broke off to listen. "Aye, I was right. The fire's slackening. It'll mean the end of Mallard's resistance in the fort. Ho there, Jeremy!"

He leaned on the carved rail and issued orders crisply. The bo'sun's pipe shrilled out, and in a moment the ship that had seemed to slumber there, awoke to life. Came the padding of feet along the decks, the creaking of blocks and the hoisting of sail. The helm was put over hard, and in a moment they were moving, the Elizabeth following, ever in obedience to the signals from the *Arabella*, whilst Ogle the gunner, whom he had summoned, was receiving Blood's final instructions before plunging down to his station on the main deck.

Within a quarter of an hour they had rounded the head, and stood in to the harbour mouth, within saker shot of Rivarol's three ships, to which they now abruptly disclosed themselves.

Where the fort had stood they now beheld a smoking rubbish heap, and the victorious Frenchman with the lily standard trailing from his mastheads was sweeping forward to snatch the rich prize whose defences he had shattered.

Blood scanned the French ships, and chuckled. The *Victorieuse* and the *Medusa* appeared to have taken no more than a few scars; but the third ship, the *Baleine*, listing heavily to larboard so as to keep the great gash in her starboard well above water, was out of account.

"You see!" he cried to van der Kuylen, and without waiting for the Dutchman's approving grunt, he shouted an order: "Helm, hard-a-port!"

The sight of that great red ship with her gilt beak-head and open ports swinging broadside on must have given check to Rivarol's soaring exultation. Yet before he could move to give an order, before he could well resolve what order to give, a volcano of fire and metal burst upon him from the buccaneers, and his decks were swept by the murderous scythe of the broadside. The *Arabella* held to her course, giving place to the *Elizabeth*, which, following closely, executed the same manœuver. And then whilst still the Frenchmen were confused, panic-stricken by an attack that took them so utterly by surprise, the *Arabella* had gone about, and was returning in her tracks, presenting now her larboard guns, and loosing her second broadside in the wake of the first. Came yet another broadside from the *Elizabeth* and then the *Arabella*'s trumpeter sent a call across the water, which Hagthorpe perfectly understood.

"On, now, Jeremy!" cried Blood. "Straight into them before they recover their wits. Stand by, there! Prepare to board! Hayton . . . the grapnels! And pass the word to the gunner in the prow to fire as fast as he can load."

He discarded his feathered hat, and covered himself with a steel head-piece, which a negro lad brought him. He meant to lead this boarding-party in person. Briskly he explained himself to his two guests. "Boarding is our only chance here. We are too heavily outgunned."

Of this the fullest demonstration followed quickly. The Frenchmen having recovered their wits at last, both ships swung broadside on, and concentrating upon the *Arabella* as the nearer and heavier and therefore more immediately dangerous of their two opponents, volleyed upon her jointly at almost the same moment.

Unlike the buccaneers, who had fired high to cripple their enemies above decks, the French fired low to smash the hull of their assailant. The *Arabella* rocked and staggered under that terrific hammering, although Pitt kept her headed towards the French so that she should offer the narrowest target. For a moment she seemed to hesitate, then she plunged forward again, her beak-head in splinters, her forecastle smashed, and a gaping hole forward, that was only just above the water-line. Indeed, to make her safe from bilging, Blood ordered a prompt jettisoning of the forward guns, anchors, and water-casks and whatever else was moveable.

Meanwhile, the Frenchmen going about, gave the like reception to the *Elizabeth*. The *Arabella*, indifferently served by the wind, pressed forward to come to grips. But before she could accomplish her object, the *Victorieuse* had loaded her starboard guns again, and pounded her advancing enemy with a second broadside at close quarters. Amid the thunder of cannon, the rending of timbers, and the screams of maimed men, the half-necked *Arabella* plunged and reeled into the cloud of smoke that concealed her prey, and then from Hayton went up the cry that she was going down by the head.

Blood's heart stood still. And then in that very moment of his despair, the blue and gold flank of the *Victorieuse* loomed through the smoke. But even as he caught that enheartening glimpse he perceived, too, how sluggish now was their advance, and how with every second it grew more sluggish. They must sink before they reached her.

Thus, with an oath, opined the Dutch Admiral, and from Lord Willoughby there was a word of blame for Blood's seamanship in having risked all upon this gambler's throw of boarding.

"There was no other chance!" cried Blood, in broken-hearted frenzy. "If ye say it was desperate and foolhardy, why, so it was; but the occasion and the means demanded nothing less. I fail within an ace of victory."

But they had not yet completely failed. Hayton himself, and a score of sturdy rogues whom his whistle had summoned, were crouching for shelter amid the wreckage of the forecastle with grapnels ready. Within seven or eight yards of the *Victorieuse*, when their way seemed spent, and their forward deck already awash under the eyes of the jeering, cheering Frenchmen, those men leapt up and forward, and hurled their grapnels across the chasm. Of the four they flung, two reached the Frenchman's decks, and fastened there. Swift as thought itself, was then the action of those sturdy, experienced buccaneers. Unhesitatingly all threw themselves upon the chain of one of those grapnels, neglecting the other, and heaved upon it with all their might to warp the ships together. Blood, watching from his own quarter-deck, sent out his voice in a clarion call:

"Musketeers to the prow!"

The musketeers, at their station at the waist, obeyed him with the speed of men who know that in obedience is the only hope of life. Fifty of them dashed forward instantly, and from the ruins of the forecastle they blazed over the heads of Hayton's men, mowing down the French soldiers who, unable to dislodge the irons, firmly held where they had deeply bitten into the timbers of the *Victorieuse*, were themselves preparing to fire upon the grapnel crew.

Starboard to starboard the two ships swung against each other with a jarring thud. By then Blood was down in the waist, judging and acting with the hurricane speed the occasion demanded. Sail had been lowered by slashing away the ropes that held the yards. The advance guard of boarders, a hundred strong, was ordered to the poop, and his grapnel-men were posted, and prompt to obey his command at the very moment of impact. As a result, the foundering *Arabella* was literally kept afloat by the half-dozen grapnels that in an instant moored her firmly to the *Victorieuse*.

Willoughby and van der Kuylen on the poop had watched in breathless amazement the speed and precision with which Blood and his desperate crew had gone to work. And now he came racing up, his bugler sounding the charge, the main host of the buccaneers following him, whilst the vanguard, led by the gunner Ogle, who had been driven from his guns by water in the gun-deck, leapt shouting to the prow of the

Victorieuse, to whose level the high poop of the water-logged *Arabella* had sunk. Led now by Blood himself, they launched themselves upon the French like hounds upon the stag they have brought to bay. After them went others, until all had gone, and none but Willoughby and the Dutchman were left to watch the fight from the quarter-deck of the abandoned *Arabella*.

For fully half-an-hour that battle raged aboard the Frenchman. Beginning in the prow, it surged through the forecastle to the waist, where it reached a climax of fury. The French resisted stubbornly, and they had the advantage of numbers to encourage them. But for all their stubborn valour, they ended by being pressed back and back across the decks that were dangerously canted to starboard by the pull of the water-logged *Arabella*. The buccaneers fought with the desperate fury of men who know that retreat is impossible, for there was no ship to which they could retreat, and here they must prevail and make the *Victorieuse* their own, or perish.

And their own they made her in the end, and at a cost of nearly half their numbers. Driven to the quarter-deck, the surviving defenders, urged on by the infuriated Rivarol, maintained awhile their desperate resistance. But in the end, Rivarol went down with a bullet in his head, and the French remnant, numbering scarcely a score of whole men, called for quarter.

Even then the labours of Blood's men were not at an end. The *Elizabeth* and the *Medusa* were tight-locked, and Hagthorpe's followers were being driven back aboard their own ship for the second time. Prompt measures were demanded. Whilst Pitt and his seamen bore their part with the sails, and Ogle went below with a gun-crew, Blood ordered the grapnels to be loosed at once. Lord Willoughby and the Admiral were already aboard the *Victorieuse*. As they swung off to the rescue of Hagthorpe, Blood, from the quarter-deck of the conquered vessel, looked his last upon the ship that had served him so well, the ship that had become to him almost as a part of himself. A moment she rocked after her release, then slowly and gradually settled down, the water gurgling and eddying about her topmasts, all that remained visible to mark the spot where she had met her death.

As he stood there, above the ghastly shambles in the waist of the *Victorieuse*, some one spoke behind him. "I think, Captain Blood, that it is necessary I should beg your pardon for the second time. Never before have I seen the impossible made possible by resource and valour, or victory so gallantly snatched from defeat."

He turned, and presented to Lord Willoughby a formidable front. His head-piece was gone, his breastplate dinted, his right sleeve a rag hanging from his shoulder about a naked arm. He was splashed from head to foot with blood, and there was blood from a scalp-wound that he had taken matting his hair and mixing with the grime of powder on his face to render him unrecognizable.

But from that horrible mask two vivid eyes looked out preternaturally bright, and from those eyes two tears had ploughed each a furrow through the filth of his cheeks.

XXXI. HIS EXCELLENCY THE GOVERNOR

When the cost of that victory came to be counted, it was found that of three hundred and twenty buccaneers who had left Cartagena with Captain Blood, a bare hundred remained sound and whole. The *Elizabeth* had suffered so seriously that it was doubtful if she could ever again be rendered seaworthy, and Hagthorpe, who had so gallantly commanded her in that last action, was dead. Against this, on the other side of the account, stood the facts that, with a far inferior force and by sheer skill and desperate valour, Blood's buccaneers had saved Jamaica from bombardment and pillage, and they had captured the fleet of M. de Rivarol, and seized for the benefit of King William the splendid treasure which she carried.

It was not until the evening of the following day that van der Kuylen's truant fleet of nine ships came to anchor in the harbour of Port Royal, and its officers, Dutch and English, were made acquainted with their Admiral's true opinion of their worth.

Six ships of that fleet were instantly refitted for sea. There were other West Indian settlements demanding the visit of inspection of the new Governor-General, and Lord Willoughby was in haste to sail for the Antilles.

"And meanwhile," he complained to his Admiral, "I am detained here by the absence of this fool of a Deputy-Governor."

"So?" said van der Kuylen. "But vhy should dad dedam you?"

"That I may break the dog as he deserves, and appoint his successor in some man gifted with a sense of where his duty lies, and with the ability to perform it."

"Aha! But id is not necessary you remain for dat. And meandime de Vrench vill haf deir eye on Barbados, vhich is nod vell defended. You haf here chust de man you vant. He vill require no insdrucshons, dis one. He vill know how to make Port Royal safe, bedder nor you or me."

"You mean Blood?"

"Of gourse. Could any man be bedder? You haf seen vhad he can do."

"You think so, too, eh? Egad! I had thought of it; and, rip me, why not? He's a better man than Morgan, and Morgan was made Governor."

Blood was sent for. He came, spruce and debonair once more, having exploited the resources of Port Royal so to render himself. He was a trifle dazzled by the honour proposed to him, when Lord Willoughby made it known. It was so far beyond anything that he had dreamed, and he was assailed by doubts of his capacity to undertake so onerous a charge.

"Damme!" snapped Willoughby, "Should I offer it unless I were satisfied of your capacity? If that's your only objection . . ."

"It is not, my lord. I had counted upon going home, so I had. I am hungry for the green lanes of England." He sighed. "There will be apple-blossoms in the orchards of Somerset."

"Apple-blossoms!" His lordship's voice shot up like a rocket, and cracked on the word. "What the devil . . .? Apple-blossoms!" He looked at van der Kuylen.

The Admiral raised his brows and pursed his heavy lips. His eyes twinkled humourously in his great face.

"So!" he said. "Fery boedical!"

My lord wheeled fiercely upon Captain Blood. "You've a past score to wipe out, my man!" he admonished him. "You've done something towards it, I confess; and you've shown your quality in doing it. That's why I offer you the governorship of Jamaica in His Majesty's name—because I account you the fittest man for the office that I have seen."

Blood bowed low. "Your lordship is very good. But . . ."

"Tchah! There's no 'but' to it. If you want your past forgotten, and your future assured, this is your chance. And you are not to treat it lightly on account of apple-blossoms or any other damned sentimental nonsense. Your duty lies here, at least for as long as the war lasts. When the war's over, you may get back to Somerset and cider or your native Ireland and its potheen; but until then you'll make the best of Jamaica and rum."

Van der Kuylen exploded into laughter. But from Blood the pleasantry elicited no smile. He remained solemn to the point of glumness. His thoughts were on Miss Bishop, who was somewhere here in this very house in which they stood, but whom he had not seen since his arrival. Had she but shown him some compassion . . .

And then the rasping voice of Willoughby cut in again, upbraiding him for his hesitation, pointing out to him his incredible stupidity in trifling with such a golden opportunity as this. He stiffened and bowed.

"My lord, you are in the right. I am a fool. But don't be accounting me an ingrate as well. If I have hesitated, it is because there are considerations with which I will not trouble your lordship."

"Apple-blossoms, I suppose?" sniffed his lordship.

This time Blood laughed, but there was still a lingering wistfulness in his eyes.

"It shall be as you wish—and very gratefully, let me assure your lordship. I shall know how to earn His Majesty's approbation. You may depend upon my loyal service."

"If I didn't, I shouldn't offer you this governorship."

Thus it was settled. Blood's commission was made out and sealed in the presence of Mallard, the Commandant, and the other officers of the garrison, who looked on in round-eyed astonishment, but kept their thoughts to themselves.

"Now ve can aboud our business go," said van der Kuylen.

"We sail to-morrow morning," his lordship announced.

Blood was startled.

"And Colonel Bishop?" he asked.

"He becomes your affair. You are now the Governor. You will deal with him as you think proper on his return. Hang him from his own yardarm. He deserves it."

"Isn't the task a trifle invidious?" wondered Blood.

"Very well. I'll leave a letter for him. I hope he'll like it."

Captain Blood took up his duties at once. There was much to be done to place Port Royal in a proper state of defence, after what had happened there. He made an inspection of the ruined fort, and issued instructions for the work upon it, which was to be started immediately. Next he ordered the careening of the three French vessels that they might be rendered seaworthy once more. Finally, with the sanction of Lord Willoughby, he marshalled his buccaneers and surrendered to them one fifth of the captured treasure, leaving it to their choice thereafter either to depart or to enrol themselves in the service of King William.

A score of them elected to remain, and amongst these were Jeremy Pitt, Ogle, and Dyke, whose outlawry, like Blood's, had come to an end with the downfall of King James. They were—saving old Wolverstone, who had been left behind at Cartagena—the only survivors of that band of rebels-convict who had left Barbados over three years ago in the *Cinco Llagas*.

On the following morning, whilst van der Kuylen's fleet was making finally ready for sea, Blood sat in the spacious whitewashed room that was the Governor's office, when Major Mallard brought him word that Bishop's homing squadron was in sight.

"That is very well," said Blood. "I am glad he comes before Lord Willoughby's departure. The orders, Major, are that you place him under arrest the moment he steps ashore. Then bring him here to me. A moment." He wrote a hurried note. "That to Lord Willoughby aboard Admiral van der Kuylen's flagship."

Major Mallard saluted and departed. Peter Blood sat back in his chair and stared at the ceiling, frowning. Time moved on. Came a tap at the door, and an elderly negro slave presented himself. Would his excellency receive Miss Bishop?

His excellency changed colour. He sat quite still, staring at the negro a moment, conscious that his pulses were drumming in a manner wholly unusual to them. Then quietly he assented.

He rose when she entered, and if he was not as pale as she was, it was because his tan dissembled it. For a moment there was silence between them, as they stood looking each at the other. Then she moved forward, and began at last to speak, haltingly, in an unsteady voice, amazing in one usually so calm and deliberate.

"I . . . I . . . Major Mallard has just told me . . ."

"Major Mallard exceeded his duty," said Blood, and because of the effort he made to steady his voice it sounded harsh and unduly loud.

He saw her start, and stop, and instantly made amends. "You alarm yourself without reason, Miss Bishop. Whatever may lie between me and your uncle, you may be sure that I shall not follow the example he has set me. I shall not abuse my position to prosecute a private vengeance. On the contrary, I shall abuse it to protect him. Lord Willoughby's recommendation to me is that I shall treat him without mercy. My own intention is to send him back to his plantation in Barbados."

She came slowly forward now. "I . . . I am glad that you will do that. Glad, above all, for your own sake." She held out her hand to him.

He considered it critically. Then he bowed over it. "I'll not presume to take it in the hand of a thief and a pirate," said he bitterly.

"You are no longer that," she said, and strove to smile.

"Yet I owe no thanks to you that I am not," he answered. "I think there's no more to be said, unless it be to add the assurance that Lord Julian Wade has also nothing to apprehend from me. That, no doubt, will be the assurance that your peace of mind requires?"

"For your own sake—yes. But for your own sake only. I would not have you do anything mean or dishonouring."

"Thief and pirate though I be?"

She clenched her hand, and made a little gesture of despair and impatience.

"Will you never forgive me those words?"

"I'm finding it a trifle hard, I confess. But what does it matter, when all is said?"

Her clear hazel eyes considered him a moment wistfully. Then she put out her hand again.

"I am going, Captain Blood. Since you are so generous to my uncle, I shall be returning to Barbados with him. We are not like to meet again—ever. Is it impossible that we should part friends? Once I wronged you, I know. And I have said that I am sorry. Won't you . . . won't you say 'good-bye'?"

He seemed to rouse himself, to shake off a mantle of deliberate harshness. He took the hand she proffered. Retaining it, he spoke, his eyes sombrely, wistfully considering her.

"You are returning to Barbados?" he said slowly. "Will Lord Julian be going with you?"

"Why do you ask me that?" she confronted him quite fearlessly.

"Sure, now, didn't he give you my message, or did he bungle it?"

"No. He didn't bungle it. He gave it me in your own words. It touched me very deeply. It made me see clearly my error and my injustice. I owe it to you that I should say this by way of amend. I judged too harshly where it was a presumption to judge at all."

He was still holding her hand. "And Lord Julian, then?" he asked, his eyes watching her, bright as sapphires in that copper-coloured face.

"Lord Julian will no doubt be going home to England. There is nothing more for him to do out here."

"But didn't he ask you to go with him?"

"He did. I forgive you the impertinence."

A wild hope leapt to life within him.

"And you? Glory be, ye'll not be telling me ye refused to become my lady, when . . ."

"Oh! You are insufferable!" She tore her hand free and backed away from him. "I should not have come . . . Good-bye!" She was speeding to the door.

He sprang after her, and caught her. Her face flamed, and her eyes stabbed him like daggers. "These are pirate's ways, I think! Release me!"

"Arabella!" he cried on a note of pleading. "Are ye meaning it? Must I release ye? Must I let ye go and never set eyes on ye again? Or will ye stay and make this exile endurable until we can go home together? Och, ye're crying now! What have I said to make ye cry, my dear?"

"I . . . I thought you'd never say it," she mocked him through her tears.

"Well, now, ye see there was Lord Julian, a fine figure of a . . ."

"There was never, never anybody but you, Peter."

They had, of course, a deal to say thereafter, so much, indeed, that they sat down to say it, whilst time sped on, and Governor Blood forgot the duties of his office. He had reached home at last. His odyssey was ended.

And meanwhile Colonel Bishop's fleet had come to anchor, and the Colonel had landed on the mole, a disgruntled man to be disgruntled further yet. He was accompanied ashore by Lord Julian Wade.

A corporal's guard was drawn up to receive him, and in advance of this stood Major Mallard and two others who were unknown to the Deputy-Governor: one slight and elegant, the other big and brawny.

Major Mallard advanced. "Colonel Bishop, I have orders to arrest you. Your sword, sir!"

Bishop stared, empurpling. "What the devil . . . ? Arrest me, d'ye say? Arrest me?"

"By order of the Governor of Jamaica," said the elegant little man behind Major Mallard. Bishop swung to him.

"The Governor? Ye're mad!" He looked from one to the other. "I am the Governor."

"You were," said the little man dryly. "But we've changed that in your absence. You're broke for abandoning your post without due cause, and thereby imperilling the settlement over which you had charge. It's a serious matter, Colonel Bishop, as you may find. Considering that you held your office from the Government of King James, it is even possible that a charge of treason might lie against you. It rests with your successor entirely whether ye're hanged or not."

Bishop rapped out an oath, and then, shaken by a sudden fear: "Who the devil may you be?" he asked.

"I am Lord Willoughby, Governor-General of His Majesty's colonies in the West Indies. You were informed, I think, of my coming."

The remains of Bishop's anger fell from him like a cloak. He broke into a sweat of fear. Behind him Lord Julian looked on, his handsome face suddenly white and drawn.

"But, my lord . . ." began the Colonel.

"Sir, I am not concerned to hear your reasons," his lordship interrupted him harshly. "I am on the point of sailing and I have not the time. The Governor will hear you, and no doubt deal justly by you." He waved to Major Mallard, and Bishop, a crumpled, broken man, allowed himself to be led away.

To Lord Julian, who went with him, since none deterred him, Bishop expressed himself when presently he had sufficiently recovered.

"This is one more item to the account of that scoundrel Blood," he said, through his teeth. "My God, what a reckoning there will be when we meet!"

Major Mallard turned away his face that he might conceal his smile, and without further words led him a prisoner to the Governor's house, the house that so long had been Colonel Bishop's own residence. He was left to wait under guard in the hall, whilst Major Mallard went ahead to announce him.

Miss Bishop was still with Peter Blood when Major Mallard entered. His announcement startled them back to realities.

"You will be merciful with him. You will spare him all you can for my sake, Peter," she pleaded.

"To be sure I will," said Blood. "But I'm afraid the circumstances won't."

She effaced herself, escaping into the garden, and Major Mallard fetched the Colonel.

"His excellency the Governor will see you now," said he, and threw wide the door. Colonel Bishop staggered in, and stood waiting.

At the table sat a man of whom nothing was visible but the top of a carefully curled black head. Then this head was raised, and a pair of blue eyes solemnly regarded the prisoner. Colonel Bishop made a noise in his throat, and, paralyzed by amazement, stared into the face of his excellency the Deputy-Governor of Jamaica, which was the face of the man he had been hunting in Tortuga to his present undoing.

The situation was best expressed to Lord Willoughby by van der Kuylen as the pair stepped aboard the Admiral's flagship.

"Id is fery boedigal!" he said, his blue eyes twinkling. "Cabdain Blood is fond of boedry—you remember de abble-blossoms. So? Ha, ha!"

ORIGINAL SOURCES

Angellotti, Marion Polk. "The Plot of Signor Salvi," *Adventure*, June 1912.

Blade, Alexander. "The Substitute Sword," *Mammoth Adventure*, May 1947.

Bloundelle-Burton, John. "The Adventures of a Night." *Yule-Tide Yarns*, edited by G. A. Henty. London: Longmans, Green, and Co., 1899.

Doyle, Arthur Conan. "How the Brigadier Bore Himself at Waterloo." *Adventures of Gerard*. London: George Newnes, 1903.

Dumas, Alexandre. *The Corsican Brothers*. London: George Routledge and Sons, 1880.

Hope, Anthony. *The Prizoner of Zenda*. London: J. W. Arrowsmith, 1894.

Hughes, James Perley. "Scourge of the Main," *Pirate Stories*, November 1934.

Lamb, Harold. "Alamut," *Adventure*, August 1, 1918.

Levett-Yeats, Sidney. "The Captain Moratti's Last Affair." *The Heart of Denise and Other Tales*. London: Longmans, Green, and Co., 1899.

Orczy, Baroness. "How Jean-Pierre Met the Scarlet Pimpernel." *The League of the Scarlet Pimpernel*. London: Cassell and Company, Ltd., 1919

Rostand, Edmond and Anne O'Hagan. *The Story of Cyrano de Bergerac*. New York: J. S. Ogilvie Publishing Company, 1898.

Sabatini, Rafael. *Captain Blood*. New York: Houghton Mifflin Company, 1922.

Weyman, Stanley J. "Crillon's Stake." *In King's Byways*. London: Smith, Elder & Co., 1902.

Williams, Drake and Warren Geiger. "English Steel and Spanish Passion," *Mammoth Adventure*, July 1947.